The Land
Beyond the Sea

ALSO BY SHARON KAY PENMAN

The Land
Beyond the Sea

Sharon Kay Penman

G. P. PUTNAM'S SONS
New York

PUTNAM
— EST. 1838 —
G. P. PUTNAM'S SONS
Publishers Since 1838
An imprint of Penguin Random House LLC
penguinrandomhouse.com

First U.S. edition published in 2020 by G. P. Putnam's Sons, an imprint of Penguin Random House (LLC).

Library of Congress Cataloging-in-Publication Data
Names: Penman, Sharon Kay, author.
Title: The land beyond the sea / Sharon Kay Penman.
Description: First U.S. edition. | New York: G. P. Putnam's Sons, 2020.
Identifiers: LCCN 2019009998 | ISBN 9780399165283 (hardcover) | ISBN 9781101621752 (epub)
Subjects: LCSH: Baudouin IV, King of Jerusalem, 1160–1185—Fiction. |
Jerusalem—History—Latin Kingdom, 1099–1244—Fiction. |
GSAFD: Historical fiction | Biographical fiction.
Classification: LCC PS3566.E474 L36 2020 | DDC 813/.54—dc23
LC record available at https://lccn.loc.gov/2019009998
p.   cm.

Printed in the United States of America
1   3   5   7   9   10   8   6   4   2

Book design by Laura K. Corless
Map by John Burgoyne

To
Enda Junkins and Paula Mildenhall

CAST OF CHARACTERS AS OF 1172

Royal House of Kingdom of Jerusalem, Aka Outremer

Baldwin III, King of Jerusalem, deceased 1163; uncle of Henry II, King of England

Amalric, King of Jerusalem; Baldwin's brother

Maria Comnena, Queen of Jerusalem; great-niece of Manuel Comnenus, the Greek emperor of what is today known as Byzantium

Sybilla, daughter of Amalric and Agnes de Courtenay, b. 1159

Baldwin, son of Amalric and Agnes de Courtenay, b. 1161

Isabella, daughter of Amalric and Maria Comnena, b. 1172

Nobility of Kingdom of Jerusalem

Baudouin d'Ibelin, Lord of Ramlah and Mirabel

Richilda, Baudouin's wife

Esquiva and Etiennette, their daughters

Balian d'Ibelin, Lord of Ibelin; Baudouin's younger brother

Hugh d'Ibelin, their elder brother, deceased 1169

Renaud (Denys) de Grenier, Lord of Sidon

Agnes de Courtenay, his wife; mother of Baldwin and Sybilla; daughter of the Count of Edessa, who died in a Saracen dungeon

Joscelin de Courtenay, brother to Agnes; son of the Count of Edessa

Humphrey de Toron, constable of the kingdom

Philippa, a princess of Antioch; Humphrey's wife

Humphrey de Toron, the constable's son, recently deceased

Stephanie de Milly, widow of the constable's son; heiress to Outrejourdain

Humphrey de Toron, their young son

Eschiva, Princess of Galilee
Hugues, her eldest son and heir
William, Odo, and Raoul, his younger brothers

Miles de Plancy, seneschal of the kingdom
Guyon, Lord of Caesarea; cousin to Lord of Sidon
Gautier, Guyon's brother and heir
Walter de Brisebarre, Lord of Blanchegarde
Guidon de Brisebarre, Walter's brother
Mary de Brisebarre, their sister
Amaury de Lusignan, French lord newly arrived in Outremer

Churchmen of Kingdom of Jerusalem

Emeric de Nesle, the patriarch
Lethard, Archbishop of Nazareth
Joscius, Bishop of Acre
William, Archdeacon of Tyre
Eraclius, Archdeacon of Jerusalem

Military Orders

Odo de St. Amand, grand master of the Poor Fellow-Soldiers of Christ and of the
    Temple of Solomon, better known as the Knights Templar
Jobert, grand master of Knights of the Hospital of St. John of Jerusalem, better
    known as the Knights Hospitaller
Jakelin de Mailly, Templar knight

Principality of Antioch

Bohemond, Prince of Antioch; cousin to King Amalric and the Count of Tripoli
Mary, Bohemond's sister; wed to Manuel Comnenus, emperor of the Greeks

Reynald de Chatillon; wed to Bohemond's mother, Princess Constance, now
   deceased

County of Tripoli

Raymond de St. Gilles, Count of Tripoli; cousin to King Amalric and Prince
   Bohemond

Saracens

Nūr al-Dīn Maḥmūd b. Zangī, ruler of Egypt and Syria
al-Sāliḥ Ismail b. Nūr al-Dīn, Nūr al-Dīn's young son and heir
al-Malik al-Nāsir Salāh al-Dīn Abū al-Muzaffar Yūsuf b. Ayyūb, Nūr al-Dīn's
   vizier in Egypt, known to history as Salāh al-Dīn or Saladin, called Yūsuf by
   family
al-Malik al-ʿĀdil, Saif al-Dīn Abū Bakr Aḥmad b. Ayyūb, Saladin's younger
   brother, best known as al-ʿĀdil, called Ahmad by family
Taqī al-Dīn, al-Malik al-Muzaffar ʿUmar b. Shāhanshāh b. Ayyūb, nephew to
   Saladin and al-ʿĀdil, called ʿUmar by family
Farrukh-Shāh, ʿIzz al-Dīn Daʾud b. Shāhanshāh b. Ayyūb, Taqī al-Dīn's younger
   brother, called Daʾud by family

European Rulers

Henry II, King of England
Eleanor of Aquitaine, his queen
Louis Capet, King of France
William, King of Sicily
Frederick, Holy Roman Emperor
Philip, Count of Flanders

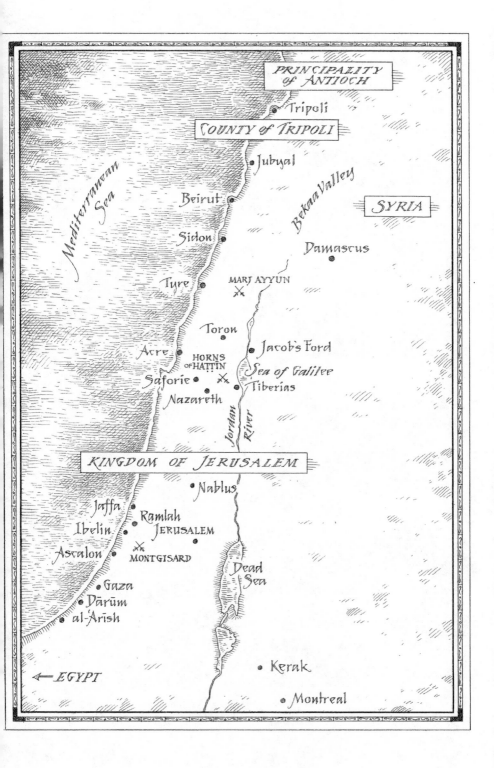

The Land
Beyond the Sea

PROLOGUE

February 1163
City of Jerusalem, Outremer

Agnes de Courtenay knew that most people would say she'd been blessed, for she was both beautiful and highborn, the daughter of the Count of Edessa, cousin to the rulers of Antioch and Jerusalem. None would have believed her had she confessed her secret fear—that she was accursed. But how else explain why her family had suffered so many sorrows?

Their litany of woes had begun with the loss of Edessa. Agnes was ten when the city fell to the Saracens. She'd known that the young Christian realms of Antioch, Tripoli, Edessa, and Outremer were viewed as infidel intruders by their Muslim neighbors in the Levant, saplings surrounded by enemy oaks. But she'd not realized how vulnerable they were, not until Edessa was captured and its citizens slaughtered.

Her father had clung to power for a few more years and when Agnes was thirteen, he'd wed her to Reinald, the Lord of Marash. Her new husband had treated her kindly and Agnes had been happy as his wife, envisioning a tranquil future as the Lady of Marash.

It was not to be. She'd been wed less than a year when the Prince of Antioch was defeated by a large Saracen army. Among the dead was the prince himself and Reinald, Lord of Marash. The stunned young widow returned home to her family, where worse was to come. Agnes knew her father was a flawed man, caring more for his own pleasures than the welfare of his subjects. But she still loved him and grieved when he was captured by the Saracen amir, Nūr al-Dīn. Refusing to ransom him, Nūr al-Dīn had him blinded, condemning him to die in an Aleppo dungeon. It was then that Agnes understood—God had cursed the de Courtenays.

Her mother, Beatrice, had done her best, securing a pension from the emperor of the Greeks, Manuel Comnenus, for herself and her children, Agnes and Joscelin. They'd moved to Antioch, having enough to live upon but not enough to provide a proper marriage portion for Agnes, and she soon discovered that beauty alone would not tempt a highborn husband.

The years that followed had not been happy ones for the de Courtenays. Then, in early 1157, Hugh d'Ibelin came to Antioch and was smitten with Agnes. Hugh was just eighteen, more than three years her junior, but he was the heir to his mother's wealthy fief of Ramlah in the Kingdom of Jerusalem and his father was dead, so there were none to protest his willingness to wed Agnes without a marriage portion. He was a handsome lad, too, and Agnes gladly agreed to marry him, grateful that the Almighty had restored her family to His favor.

That summer, Agnes, Joscelin, and their mother had traveled to Outremer, where Hugh awaited them. But upon their arrival at Jaffa, Agnes learned of yet another battlefield defeat, this one on June 19, when a force led by King Baldwin was ambushed by Nūr al-Dīn. While Baldwin had escaped, among the men taken prisoner was Hugh d'Ibelin.

Agnes had despaired, for how could Hugh raise his ransom? His brothers, Baudouin and Balian, were too young to help, and his mother was dying. Only King Baldwin could rescue Hugh, and so she sought out the Count of Jaffa, the king's brother, Amalric. She'd heard that Amalric was unlike Baldwin, who was renowned for his generosity. Amalric was said to lust after money even more than he lusted after women. She did not see why he'd object to spending his brother's money, though, and was hopeful he'd agree to approach Baldwin on her behalf.

Her meeting with Amalric did not go as planned. He was obviously impressed by her beauty and she was willing to flirt with him if that would win his cooperation. But within moments, she found herself fending off a mauling that went well beyond flirtation. She managed to free herself and flee. She'd heard the gossip that he was no respecter of marital vows. She'd not expected to be treated like a whore, though, for she was Amalric's cousin. She'd not realized that with Hugh and her father both held prisoner in Aleppo, Amalric might well see her as fair game, vulnerable as only a woman without male protectors could be.

This sudden understanding of her peril—a guest in his castle, his city—had impelled her to confide in her mother and brother. Joscelin had been angry at this affront to his sister's honor but was wary of antagonizing so powerful a man as the king's brother. Their mother had more steel in her spine, and she went to confront Amalric, warning him that Agnes was no peasant wench to be swived at his pleasure, reminding him that she was his kinswoman, the betrothed of one of the king's most loyal vassals. Agnes could only hope that would be enough to shame Amalric to his senses.

But when her mother finally returned, it was with stunning news. Six years later, Agnes could remember that scene as vividly as if it were yesterday.

"Well, it seems we misread the count's intentions. Amalric swears he would not have raped you. He wants to marry you."

Agnes gasped, shocked into silence. But when Joscelin let out a whoop of joy, she glared at him. She opened her mouth to say that she did not want to marry Amalric, catching herself in time. Marriages were not based upon personal whims, after all. "Count Amalric seems to have forgotten that I am plight trothed to Hugh d'Ibelin and in the eyes of Holy Church, that is a binding commitment. Moreover, we are fourth cousins and thus forbidden to marry."

Joscelin insisted plight troths could be broken, dispensations issued for cousins to wed. Agnes ignored him. "Mother? Do you want me to wed this man?"

"It is a far better match than the one with Hugh d'Ibelin. You would be the Countess of Jaffa and Ascalon, your rank second only to Baldwin's queen once he weds. Our family's fortunes would be mended, restoring us to the prominence we enjoyed ere your father lost Edessa—"

"And Amalric is the king's heir," Joscelin interrupted. "If Baldwin dies ere he marries and sires a son, Amalric will be king. You could be the queen one day, Sister!"

While Agnes was fond of her younger brother, she'd never taken him all that seriously. "Jos, leave us alone for a time," she snapped and, as unhappy as he was to be banished from this crucial family conclave, he obeyed; she'd always been the stronger of the two. Once he'd gone, Agnes crossed to Beatrice's side. "I will be honest with you, Mother. I do not deny this is an opportunity none of us could have expected. But I would rather wed Hugh d'Ibelin. As Lady of Ramlah, I would be respected, and I am sure Hugh would do his best for you and Joscelin. Whilst he may not have the power that Amalric wields, he has a more generous nature."

Beatrice seemed to sigh. "There is something you need to know, Agnes. I had a long and forthright conversation with Amalric. When he said he wanted to marry you, he seemed as surprised as I was to hear those words coming from his mouth. I think it was only then that he realized he wanted more from you than a quick tumble in bed. It appears you've bewitched him as you did Hugh. With one difference. Amalric is a young man accustomed to getting what he wants. Now that he has decided he wants you, he means to have you. He is indifferent to the plight troth, to your lack of a marriage portion, or that you are cousins. And he would be just as indifferent to your refusal should you tell him nay."

"You are saying that he'd force me to wed him?" Agnes tried to sound indignant, but what was the point? The Church said a marriage was not valid without consent. Yet in the world beyond the Holy See, it was not so unusual for an heiress to be abducted and wed against her will. If it could almost happen to Queen Eleanor of England, who would care if it happened to the penniless daughter of a man rotting away in an Aleppo dungeon?

"We do what we must, Agnes. Even if this marriage is not entirely to your liking, there is much to commend it. You'll have a privileged life with the king's brother, and you'll have power. That is not a draught you've ever tasted, but I think it is one you will learn to savor."

"And Hugh?"

"You can get Amalric to pay his ransom."

Others might have found that answer cold, uncaring. Agnes did not. Her mother was simply recognizing the reality confronting them, as women had been compelled to do down through the ages.

There had been opposition to the marriage. The Patriarch of Jerusalem had objected, raising the issues of consanguinity and Agnes's plight troth to Hugh d'Ibelin. But Amalric paid him no heed. If it was not a happy marriage, it had been a successful one. Even after the novelty wore off, Amalric continued to desire her, while Agnes fulfilled a wife's primary duty, giving him a daughter and then a son. She did not find the pleasure in his bed that she'd have found in Hugh's, for she was not attracted to him. Her mother had been right, though. The taste of power was intoxicating.

"My lady? Do you think your lord husband will be back soon?"

Agnes blinked as her past receded and her present came into focus again. "I expect so, Mabilla." She knew her ladies assumed she was daydreaming of her golden future, and why not? She was finally to be rewarded for all the sacrifices she'd made, for all she'd lost. King Baldwin had suddenly sickened and his doctors could not save him. He'd died five days ago, leaving behind a grieving young widow but no children. The heir to the throne was his brother, Amalric. It was true that the crown was elective, not strictly hereditary, yet Agnes saw that as a formality. Amalric was meeting now with the High Court, composed of the barons of the realm. By week's end, he would be crowned and she would be Queen of Jerusalem.

Sitting on a coffer, Agnes relaxed as Mabilla unpinned her hair. It reached to her waist in a swirl of pale gold. Amalric often said it was a pity that women could not venture out in public with their hair uncovered; he was proud of having such a desirable wife and enjoyed the envy he saw in the eyes of other men. Agnes decided she would wear it loose at her coronation, as only queens and virgin brides could do, and for a moment, she envisioned her long, flowing hair graced with a jeweled crown—the ultimate accessory, she thought with a smile.

Amalric returned as the city's church bells were chiming for Vespers. He strode into the chamber, glanced at the women, and said, "Out." As they fled, Agnes's eyebrows rose. Even for Amalric, who was taciturn on his best days, that was unusually rude.

Agnes got to her feet, studying him with a puzzled frown. For a man who'd just been given a crown, he did not look very happy. "How did the High Court session go? Is it settled?"

"Yes, it is settled." He moved restlessly around the chamber, like a man in unfamiliar surroundings, and he'd yet to meet her gaze. "It did not go as I expected."

Agnes had rarely seen him so tense. "Surely they chose you as the next king?"

"They agreed to recognize my claim to the crown." He paused and then raised his head, looking her in the face for the first time since entering the chamber. "But they would only do so if I end our marriage, for they will not accept you as queen."

Agnes stared at him in disbelief. "You . . . you are not serious?"

Amalric had been seething since his confrontation with the High Court, and it was a relief now to have a target for that rage. "You think I would jest about this? The patriarch insisted our marriage is invalid because we are related within the forbidden fourth degree. He even raised your plight troth with d'Ibelin again. And the barons backed him up. I could tell the whoresons were enjoying it, too, getting to play kingmaker!"

Agnes was desperately trying to make sense of this. "The Church often gives dispensations for consanguinity. Why could the papal legate not issue one for us?"

"You think I did not point that out? The legate refused to consider it. He agreed with the patriarch that we'd been living in sin and I could not be crowned until I put you aside."

Agnes's body was reacting as if she'd taken a physical blow, her breath quickening, her knees going weak. But her brain was still numbed, still struggling to comprehend. "Why?"

Amalric shook his head impatiently. "They all acted as if their motives were as pure as newly fallen snow, that they cared only to make right this grievous wrong. But I know better. Our bishops were punishing me for defying the patriarch by marrying you. And the barons wanted to assert their authority over me, to show me that I owed my kingship to them." He gave Agnes a look that was oddly accusatory, as if their predicament were somehow her fault. "Baudouin d'Ibelin was amongst the most vocal; clearly he still bears a grudge against me for claiming his brother's bride. Christ Jesus, that was nigh on six years ago!"

"And . . . and you agreed, Amalric?" She sounded so stunned that he flushed, his hands clenching into fists. She'd later realize that much of his anger was defensive, that he was ashamed of yielding to the High Court's demands. Now she was aware only of her own anger, her own pain, and her searing sense of betrayal. "How could you? By denying the legality of our marriage, you made your own children bastards!"

"No," he said sharply, "I would never let that happen. I insisted upon a papal dispensation, recognizing their legitimacy even if the marriage itself is invalid."

"I see. You found the backbone to defend your son and daughter, but not your wife!"

"I had no choice. They told me that if I did not agree to their terms, they would offer the crown to my cousin Raymond, the Count of Tripoli."

"You owed me better than this, Amalric!"

He gave a shrug and then the brutal truth. "You are not worth a crown, Agnes." She flinched and then said, very low, "God will punish you for this."

He shrugged again. "You can continue to call yourself the Countess of Jaffa."

"How generous," she jeered. "Are you going to give me Jaffa as my dower?"

"Of course not."

"That is not unreasonable," she said, gritting her teeth to keep from shrieking. "Your brother's widow was given Acre as her dower."

"She is a Greek princess."

His matter-of-fact tone was the ultimate insult. She felt so much hatred that she feared she might choke on it. "Will it not shame you, my lord king, to have your former wife begging for her bread by the side of the road?"

He was stung by her sarcasm. "The children will remain with me, of course."

"No!"

"Surely you'd have expected that. Sons are never left in their mothers' care for long."

"They are until age seven. Baldwin is not yet two!" When he did not bother to argue, she realized there was no hope. "And Sybilla? You cannot take them both away from me!"

"Do not play the bereft mother, Agnes. I am willing for you to see the children."

If you cooperate, if you do as you're told. The threat was an unspoken one, for it did not need to be put into words. Agnes had begun to tremble. She sank down on the edge of the bed, her face blanched. She looked so devastated that Amalric found himself wanting to tell her that he was sorry, that this was not his fault. He said nothing, for if she knew he felt guilty, she'd use that knowledge to coax him into letting her have Sybilla. It was not a risk he was willing to take; he feared she'd pour poison into the little girl's ear, turning her against him.

"I have also asked the papal legate for a dispensation absolving you of any moral blame for entering into an invalid marriage," he said at last, and Agnes raised her head to stare at him.

"How magnanimous of you, Amalric! And what a short memory you have. Have you truly forgotten that you coerced my consent?"

"That is nonsense! You were as eager as I for the match, for you saw that I could offer you much more than d'Ibelin." No longer feeling pity for her plight, he started for the door.

Seeing that he was about to walk out of their bedchamber, out of her life, Agnes panicked. "For the love of God, how can you abandon me like this? What am I supposed to do?"

He halted, his hand on the door latch. "Hugh d'Ibelin did not marry after paying his ransom and regaining his freedom. Mayhap he'll take you back."

Agnes would later be thankful she'd had no weapon close at hand, for she did not doubt she'd have used it. She wanted to claw him till he bled, to kick and bite and scratch, to curse him and the patriarch and the papal legate and the High Court and God, to make them all pay for doing this to her. But Amalric had not waited for her response and the door was already closing.

Lurching to her feet, she reached for the table to steady herself. It was set for a private celebration of Amalric's kingship. There were two goblets of the red glass for which Acre was famed, a flagon of his favorite wine, a plate laden with wafers, and a silver bowl of almonds and dried fruit. She cleared the table with a wild sweep of her arm. Her gaze fell then on his new tunic, hanging on a wall pole.

Snatching up the fruit knife, she slashed at it until the garment hung in tatters. A book of his was the next to feel her wrath, flung into the smoldering hearth.

She was panting by now. She still held the knife and she stumbled toward the bed she'd shared with Amalric. After shredding the coverlet, she turned to the pillows, stabbing so fiercely that she was inhaling a cloud of escaping feathers as she plunged the blade into the mattress.

"My lady!"

Agnes paused, knife upraised, to see two of her ladies in the doorway. They had yet to move, staring at her in horror. If they were so distraught over the wreckage of her bedchamber, how would they react to the wreckage of her life? At that, she began to laugh, laughter so shrill and brittle that, even to her own ears, it sounded like the laughter of a madwoman.

CHAPTER 1

April 1172
Jerusalem, Outremer

I t was a great destiny to be a queen, but it was not an easy one. Maria Comnena had been only thirteen when she was wed to the King of Jerusalem, a man almost twenty years older than she, a man who spoke not a word of her Greek while she spoke not a word of his native French. Even religion had not been a bond between them, for he followed the Latin Church of Rome and she had been raised in the Greek Orthodox faith. And she soon discovered that her husband's past was inextricably entwined with her present, for Amalric had two young children and a former wife, a woman very beautiful and very bitter.

Her new kingdom was not a welcoming one. Known as Outremer, French for "the land beyond the sea," it was a country cursed with pestilent fevers and the constant shadow of war. Nor were her husband's subjects enthusiastic about the marriage; she'd soon discovered that the Franks scorned Greeks as untrustworthy and effeminate and were suspicious of this new alliance with the Greek empire. It was, in every respect, an alien world to her, and she'd been desperately homesick, missing her family and the familiar splendor of Constantinople, which made Jerusalem and Acre and Tyre seem like paltry villages. Looking back now, Maria was embarrassed to remember how often she'd cried herself to sleep in those first weeks of her marriage.

But she was a Greek princess, great-niece to the Emperor Manuel Comnenus, and she was determined not to bring shame upon the Greek Royal House. She set about learning French. She spent hours memorizing the names of the bishops and barons of Outremer. She hid her shock at the sight of clean-shaven lords; beards were a cherished symbol of masculinity in her old life. She adopted the Frankish fashions, wearing her hair in two long braids and not always veiling her face when she ventured out in public, as highborn ladies of the Greek empire did.

And she did her best to please her new husband. Her mother had warned her that Amalric would not be the easiest of men to live with. He was courageous, strong-willed, and intelligent, and men believed him to be a good king. He inspired respect, not affection, for there was a coldness about him that kept others at arm's length. He was reserved and often aloof, a man of few words who was sensitive about his slight stammer. But Maria had not expected to find love in marriage, or even companionship, asking only that her husband show her the honor due her rank. She'd learned at an early age that theirs was a world in which men set the rules and women had to play by them—even queens.

In her infrequent letters back home, she'd assured her parents that Amalric treated her well, and that was not a lie. While he was unfaithful, he did not flaunt his concubines at court. He'd not consummated their marriage until she was fourteen, and at first, she'd been worried that he found her unattractive, for Greek brides of twelve were deemed old enough to share their husbands' beds. But it seemed that was not the custom among the Franks, who believed pregnancies to be dangerous for half-grown girls. When Amalric did claim his marital rights, Maria did not enjoy it and she sensed he did not enjoy it much, either, merely doing his duty to get her with child. He'd not reproached her, though, for failing to get pregnant straightaway and she'd been grateful for that. In public, he was unfailingly courteous, in private, preoccupied and distant. They never quarreled, rarely spoke at all. The truth was that even after more than four years of marriage, they were still two strangers who sometimes shared a bed.

Easter was the most sacred of holy days for both the Latin and the Greek Orthodox Churches. It was also a social occasion and Amalric's lords and their ladies had already begun to arrive in Jerusalem, not wanting to miss the lavish festivities of the king's Easter court. For Maria, these royal revelries were a mixed blessing. She enjoyed the feasting and entertainment, but not the inevitable appearances of Amalric's onetime wife.

She'd not expected that Agnes de Courtenay would continue to play a role in their lives. Fairly or not, scandal attached itself to a repudiated wife and she'd assumed that Agnes must have withdrawn to a nunnery as such women usually did. Instead, Agnes had promptly remarried, taking as her new husband Hugh d'Ibelin, who'd once been her betrothed, and as Hugh's wife, she had to be made welcome at court, however little Amalric or Maria liked it. When Hugh died unexpectedly on a pilgrimage to Santiago de Compostela three years ago, Maria had naïvely hoped that Agnes would retreat into the sequestered shadow world of widowhood.

To the contrary, she'd soon found another highborn husband, the Lord of Sidon, and continued to haunt the royal court with her prickly presence, reminding one and all without saying a word of her checkered history with Maria's husband.

As always, there was a stir as Agnes entered the great hall, heads turning in her direction. She paused dramatically in the doorway—to make sure that she was the center of attention, Maria thought sourly. Amalric avoided Agnes whenever he could and he'd put in a perfunctory appearance earlier, then disappeared. In his absence, Maria knew she'd be the other woman's quarry, and she was not surprised when Agnes began to move in her direction, as nonchalantly as a lioness stalking a herd of grazing deer. At first, she'd wondered why Agnes hated her so much, finally realizing it was because she had what Agnes so desperately wanted—not the gold band on her finger, but the jeweled crown that had been placed upon Maria's head on the day of her coronation.

She watched Agnes approach. Maria was not yet eighteen and Agnes must be nigh on twenty years older, her youth long gone, but Maria knew she would never be the beauty that Agnes once was. Agnes could make her feel awkward and inadequate merely by arching a delicately plucked brow. No matter how often Maria had reminded herself that she was the Queen of Jerusalem, she'd been acutely uncomfortable in the older woman's presence, tensing whenever that cool sapphire-blue gaze took her measure, knowing she'd been judged and found wanting.

But she was no longer intimidated by this worldly, elegant enemy. Turning to one of her attendants, she said, "Let me hold her," and as soon as the baby was lifted from her cradle and placed in her arms, she felt it again—a surge of such happiness that it was as if God Himself were smiling over her shoulder, sharing her joy. When the midwife had declared that she'd birthed a girl, she'd felt a stab of guilt, fearing that she'd failed Amalric by not giving him a son. Yet once she held her daughter for the first time, all else was forgotten. She'd not known she was capable of a love so intense, so overwhelming; she spent hours watching the baby sleep, listening to her breathing, marveling at the softness of her skin, the silky feel of her hair. That past week, Isabella had smiled for the first time and Maria did not doubt that this was a memory she'd cherish till the end of her days. Why had no one told her that motherhood was so life changing?

But it was only after Isabella's birth that she fully comprehended how much Agnes de Courtenay had taken from her. When Amalric told her that his two children with Agnes would come before any child of hers in the line of succession, it had seemed a remote concern to a thirteen-year-old girl with more immediate worries of her own. Now, though, as she looked down lovingly into the small, petal face upturned to hers, she felt a resentful rage that her beautiful daughter would never be a queen, cheated of her rightful destiny because Amalric had been foolish enough to wed that hateful, unworthy woman.

Agnes's curtsy was so grudgingly given that those watching smothered smiles and edged closer; interactions between the two women were morbidly entertaining to many. Their exchange of greetings was edged in ice, followed by silence as Maria waited for the customary congratulations due a new mother. When she saw it was not coming, she made an effort at courtesy, acutely aware of their audience. "Your lord husband is not with you?"

"Oh, he is around somewhere," Agnes said with a graceful wave of her hand. "I see your husband is missing, too. Mayhap we should send out lymer hounds to track them down."

Isabella began to squirm then, and Maria lowered her head to brush a kiss against that smooth little cheek. To some, it might have been a touching tableau of young motherhood; to Agnes, it was an intolerable reminder of all she'd lost—her crown and her children.

"I'd heard that you gave birth to a daughter. I hope you and Amalric were not too disappointed?"

Maria's head came up sharply. "I am young. God willing, we will be blessed with many sons in the years to come."

Agnes's smile faded. "May I see her?" she asked, poisonously polite, and before Maria could respond, she leaned over to study the child.

"Oh, my," she murmured, sounding surprised. "She does not look at all like Amalric, does she? Dark as a Saracen, she is." Her smile came back then, for as soon as she saw Maria's face, she knew she'd drawn blood. "But a sweet child, I am sure," she added dismissively, and turned away, sure that she'd gotten the last word.

Hours later, Maria was still seething. The words, innocuous in themselves, had been infused with such venom that they'd left her speechless, and thank God Almighty for that; if not, she might have caused a scene that the court would be talking about for years to come. It was not even the malicious insinuation about Isabella's paternity that had so enraged her, for that was too outrageous to be taken seriously. It was that Agnes saw Isabella—saw her daughter—as a legitimate target in this ugly vendetta of hers. She would come to regret it, to regret it dearly. Maria swore a silent, holy vow to make it so, but even that did not assuage her fury. She needed to give voice to her wrath, needed a sympathetic audience.

Amalric would not want to be dragged into what he'd see as a female feud; he preferred to deal with Agnes by ignoring her. And friendship was a luxury denied to those in power. Maria had been taught that the highborn dared not let down their guard. Servants could be bribed or threatened, handmaidens suborned, and spies were everywhere. But she was luckier than most queens, for she did have a friend, one whom she trusted implicitly.

It was language that had brought them together initially, for Master William was a linguist, fluent in four languages, one of which was Greek. Maria had been thankful to be able to converse with someone in her native tongue, and she'd been grateful, too, that William approved of her marriage, believing an alliance with the Greek empire to be in the best interests of his kingdom. He'd engaged a tutor to teach her French and began to instruct her in the intricacies of Outremer politics. Having grown up at the highly political royal court in Constantinople, Maria was fascinated by statecraft and power. When she'd tried to discuss such matters with Amalric, she'd been politely rebuffed, but William found her to be an apt pupil; as their friendship deepened, Maria no longer felt so utterly alone.

Such a relationship would have been frowned upon in Constantinople, where women led more segregated lives, with few opportunities to mingle with men not of their family. But William was a man of God, now the Archdeacon of Tyre, and that helped to dampen any hint of scandal. So, too, did Amalric's approval. He admired William greatly, commissioning him to write histories of their kingdom and their Saracen foes. Two years ago, he'd even entrusted his son, Baldwin, into William's keeping, making him responsible for the young prince's education. He had no problems with his queen spending time with William, provided that they were chaperoned.

While William and Baldwin were often in the coastal city of Tyre, they were back for the king's Easter court, with quarters here in the palace. So, when her inner turmoil did not abate, Maria knew what she must do. Summoning two of her ladies and her chief eunuch, Michael, she announced that she was going to visit Master William.

William's lodgings showed how high he stood in the king's favor. Space was at a premium at court, even in the new royal palace, yet William been given two rooms. The antechamber was comfortably furnished with a table, desk, and chairs, for it was here that he did his writing and met with guests. Double doors opened onto a small balcony, and a closed door led to his bedchamber, which she knew would be austere and simple. Unlike many churchmen, William had no taste for luxury; whatever money he had, he spent on books. He was holding one in his hand now as he opened the door, his face breaking into a smile at the sight of Maria.

Even in her agitation, she'd not entirely forgotten her manners. "Forgive me for bursting in like this, Master William, but I had such a need to talk with you. Agnes de Courtenay is surely the greatest bitch in all of Christendom! You'll not believe what that woman dared to say about my daughter. She—"

She got no further, for it was only then that she saw the shadow cast by the man standing on the balcony. She clapped her hand to her mouth, dismayed that she'd uttered such intemperate words for a stranger to hear. But worse was to come. As he moved into the chamber, she gave a horrified gasp, for she knew him. Balian d'Ibelin, the youngest of the Ibelin brothers, Agnes de Courtenay's former brother-in-law.

For a moment, they stared at each other. She shuddered at the thought of him repeating what he'd overheard. How Agnes would laugh to learn how hurtful her words had been. Dare she ask him to keep silent? But why would he? "I . . . I fear I have been indiscreet. . . ."

"My lady queen," he said with flawless courtesy and reached for her hand, his lips barely grazing her clenched fingers. And then he smiled. "It is not indiscreet to speak the truth. I know Agnes well enough to assure you that if there are any in Outremer who do *not* think she is a bitch, they have not yet met her."

Maria's eyes widened and then she surprised them both by laughing. Balian had never heard her laugh before; whenever he'd seen her in public at Amalric's side, she'd been serious, even somber, with a gravity that seemed sad to him in one so young. He liked this Maria better, he decided, and with a gallant bow he ushered her toward a chair, as if he and not William were her host, asking if he could fetch her wine.

"No, I'll not stay. I do not want to interrupt your visit with Master William." When Balian claimed he'd just been about to leave, Maria shook her head, insisting he remain. William did not argue, for he sensed that she was still embarrassed. Maria was not comfortable with the unexpected, and what could be more unexpected than sympathy from Agnes's brother-in-law?

Michael and her women did not speak French, so they looked puzzled when their mistress told them that she was leaving. She smiled at William and then at Balian. While she felt as if he had given her a gift, she was not about to unburden her heart to him. "Master William, I shall speak with you later. Lord Balian, I bid you a good morrow," she added politely, retreating into the formality that served as her shield. And before the men could react, she had gone, leaving behind only the faintest hint of perfume and the memory of a moment in which she'd shown them a glimpse of the girl hidden away behind the turrets and towers of queenship.

William sat down again. "That was very chivalrous of you, lad, easing her discomfort the way you did. I know you have that unaccountable liking for Agnes, so—"

"What makes you say that, William?"

"Well, I've heard you defend her in the past, so I assumed . . . ?"

Balian was shaking his head. "The little queen is right. Agnes is a bitch. I understand, though, why she became such a bitch, so I suppose I judge her less harshly than others." He grinned then, saying with mock regret, "Truly, it is a curse—seeing both sides of every issue. It has gotten me into trouble more times than I can count."

"I daresay it has," William agreed, with a grin of his own. "Even those who are ignorant of Scriptures seem to know that verse from Matthew: 'He that is not with me is against me.' I confess I am glad to hear that you are not fond of your former sister by marriage," he said, for he was very protective of his young charge and considered Agnes de Courtenay to be a detrimental influence upon her son. But he seized this opportunity to indulge his curiosity. "Was your brother happy with Agnes?"

He was not surprised when Balian paused to consider the question, for as young as he was—in his twenty-second year—he was deliberate in all that he did, utterly unlike his elder brothers, Hugh of blessed memory and the impulsive, hot-tempered Baudouin. "I think he was, William, at least at first. Hugh was besotted with her. It well-nigh broke his heart when Amalric married her whilst he was languishing in that Saracen gaol. So, when she came to him after her divorce and offered herself, he was eager to take her as his wife. But it is no easy thing to live with a woman so filled with rage. I suspect it wore him down. . . ."

Not wanting to talk about his brother, whose untimely death still had the power to bring tears to his eyes, Balian nudged the conversation in another direction. "What's this I hear about young Baldwin's latest adventure? Is it true that he tried to ride the king's roan destrier?"

"Sadly, it is. The lad is a fine rider, but he's too young to ride a fiery beast like Caesar. Yet that is exactly what he would have done had he not been caught by one of the grooms."

"It is a wonder the lad was not trampled as soon as he ventured into that stall," Balian said, for Caesar's ill temper was known to all who'd ridden to war with King Amalric.

"Baldwin is too clever by half. He confessed he'd been sneaking into the stable with treats for the stallion. At least I got him to promise he'd not do it again, and he keeps his word. But I am sure he'll think of another scheme just as daft."

Balian knew William had not expected to become so fond of the boy. But watching them together now was almost like watching a father and son, for William gave Baldwin the affection and attention he did not get from Amalric, who was not one for displaying his emotions even with his only son and heir. For that matter, Balian realized, there was something paternal, too, in William's friendship with the young queen. Looking over at the older man, he startled and pleased William by saying, "The day that Amalric chose you to tutor his son was a lucky day for Baldwin . . . and for the kingdom. With your guidance, he is sure to grow into a good king one day." Balian was not often so serious and he could not resist teasing, "Assuming, of course, that you can keep the lad from breaking that spirited neck of his."

William laughed and began to tell Balian about some of Baldwin's other escapades, never imagining that he would later look back upon that moment with such bittersweet regret, recognizing it for what it was—the last afternoon of utter innocence for him, for his young charge, and for the kingdom Baldwin was destined one day to rule.

Later that evening, William entered Baldwin's bedchamber to make sure he was settled in. That was not one of his duties, but Baldwin had a friend staying the night and William wanted to be sure that they got to bed at a reasonable hour; Baldwin was too good at charming servants into bending the rules for him.

As he expected, they were doing anything but sleeping. Feathers floating on the air gave evidence of a recent pillow fight. Baldwin's wolfhound was helping himself to the remains of their bedtime snack. The boys' bath had apparently turned into a splashing contest, for towels had been spread around the tub to soak up the overflow. The boys themselves were sprawled on the bed as they took turns carving a thick tallow candle. William got only a glimpse of their handiwork, for they hid it under the sheets as soon as they realized they were no longer alone. It looked to him as if they'd been trying to whittle a woman's torso from the soft wax, and his initial disapproval gave way at once to resignation. Baldwin would be eleven in June, so it was only to be expected that he'd have begun to show curiosity about the female body.

"We were going to bed," Hubert insisted, for he was very much in awe of their tutor.

Baldwin was made of sterner stuff. "Eventually," he said with a grin that William found hard to resist. He did, though, saying calmly that eventually was now. Baldwin raised no protests, seeing no point in fighting a war he was sure to lose. Under William's watchful eye, the boys stripped off their shirts and braies and slid under the sheets of Baldwin's huge bed. William reached out to stop the wolf-hound from joining them but forgot the dog when he noticed Baldwin's bruises.

"What happened to your arm? Did you fall?" The boys exchanged glances and Baldwin nodded, but when William moved closer, he saw that the bruises were spaced at intervals, as if deliberately done. Giving Baldwin what they privately called "the look," he waited for the truth.

"We were playing dare," Baldwin admitted, and Hubert nervously explained that dare was a challenge game in which boys pinched one another, the winner being the one who held out the longest without showing signs of pain.

"We were playing it yesterday with Arnulf, Gerald, and Adam," Hubert continued, naming three of the boys who attended classes with them. "Baldwin won. He always wins, and that vexes them no end. They think he somehow cheats!"

Both boys laughed, but William was looking at a deep scratch on Baldwin's wrist. When Hubert got up to use the privy chamber, he called the scratch to Baldwin's attention. "The other boys did this, too?" Frowning when Baldwin nodded. "That was foolish, lad. Pinching is one thing, but a scratch like this could easily become infected. I thought you knew better than that."

Baldwin could have made light of a lecture, but not the disappointment in William's voice. "I will not play the game anymore," he promised. "I did not know Arnulf had scratched me like that, for I did not feel it." Glancing around to make sure Hubert was still in the privy chamber, he lowered his voice. "I do not feel pain in my hand or arm. That is how I always win. Do not tell Hubert, though."

"You feel no pain? How long has that been true, Baldwin?" The boy shrugged, saying it was not long. William said nothing more, but he could not take his eyes from those mottled bruises, a memory long forgotten beginning to fight its way to the surface, one that sent a chill rippling up his spine.

William was seated on a bench in the courtyard, staring up at the window of Baldwin's palace bedchamber. Despite the lateness of the hour, he'd gone at once to Amalric, who ordered a medical examination on the morrow for his son. He'd reacted to William's news with his usual sangfroid, but William knew he was concerned. William was waiting now for the results, squinting as the sun rose

higher in the sky while doing his best to allay his own anxiety, reminding himself
that he'd been trained in the liberal arts, theology, and the law, not medicine.

He leaped to his feet when the doctor finally emerged, hastening to intercept
him. Unlike many of his countrymen, he did not approve of consulting Saracen
doctors, but he did have some confidence in Abū Sulayman Dāwūd, who was well
educated and a Syrian Christian. He knew better than to ask, for the physician
would deliver his report first to the king. He intended to be there for that, and after
an exchange of greetings, he fell in step beside the other man. The doctor was
uncommonly tall, his height accentuated by his bright yellow turban, and William,
who was of moderate stature, had to hurry to match his longer strides. He was out
of breath by the time they reached Amalric's private quarters and his heart was
racing, although he did not know if that was due to the physical exertion or his
lingering unease.

Amalric was dictating to a scribe; even his critics acknowledged he was not one
to shirk his royal responsibilities. He dismissed the scribe and the others in the
chamber as soon as William and the doctor were announced. "Well? Did you find
out what ails my son?"

"No, my lord king. It was impossible to make a diagnosis of the young prince.
I can tell you only what might be afflicting him. To be certain, we must wait to see
if he develops other symptoms."

Amalric scowled. "Forget certainty, then. Tell me what you think is causing his
numbness."

"It is probably the result of an injury. Lord Baldwin insists he suffered no falls,
yet even a minor mishap can cause nerve damage." Knowing that Amalric's medical knowledge was confined to the treatment of battle wounds, the doctor offered
a brief explanation, one a layman could understand. "Nerves are hollow ducts that
originate in the brain and control movement and sensation. So, if they are injured,
the result can be a lack of feeling such as your son is experiencing."

"Can this nerve injury be treated?"

"Yes, my king. Poultices often help. So does rubbing the afflicted limb with
warm olive oil. And there are herbs, of course: wormwood, foxglove, and red net-
tle to name just a few—"

"But you cannot promise these remedies will work?"

"No, my liege," the other man said calmly. "We are all in the Almighty's hands.
Your son is young, though, and otherwise healthy. He ought to respond well to
these treatments." Seeing that Amalric still looked unsatisfied, he said, "And we
can rule out a far more serious malady than an injury, God be praised. When I was

first told of the young lord's symptoms, I feared it might be a deadly ailment called diabetes, but that is diagnosed by frequent and excessive urination and your son assures me that he has no great need to pass water."

Amalric glared at the physician, thinking that leeches always told men more than they wanted to know. Why even mention this diabetes disease if Baldwin did not have it? "Start treating him straightaway," he ordered, and the doctor inclined his head. But despite being dismissed, he did not move.

"There is something you need to know, my liege. I am not saying it will happen, but because your son is the heir to the kingdom, you must be prepared for all eventualities. If the lad does not respond to treatment, it is possible that his condition could worsen . . . that in time he could lose the use of that hand and arm."

"Christ Jesus!" Amalric stared at the doctor in horror. "A king must lead men into battle. How could Baldwin fight with a crippled arm?"

William was so relieved that the doctor had not spoken of what he most feared that he took the risk of paralysis in stride. "Baldwin is young enough to learn to wield a sword with his left hand. It might even give him an advantage, for men expect their foes to be right-handed."

Amalric continued to pace and curse, and William was not sure his words had registered with the other man. But Amalric had a practical nature, utterly lacking in sentimentality, and he never wasted time or energy in denying a truth merely because he did not want to accept it. If there was a chance, however slight, that his son might be crippled, better to face it now. "How could Baldwin control a destrier if he were unable to grip the reins?"

William had the answer to that, too. Abū Sulaymān Dāwūd was quicker, though. "My brother has served as your son's horse master since he was old enough to get his feet into the stirrups. He tells me the boy is a natural-born rider, that he is utterly fearless on horseback. He could be taught to control a horse by the pressure of his knees. It is not so difficult to learn, either for men or stallions. Look at the Saracen archers if you need proof of that."

Amalric considered that for a long moment and then nodded. The Franks had never learned to shoot from horseback as their enemies did, but if the Saracens could guide their mounts without the need of reins, then Baldwin could, too, by God. And it might never come to that. "Send your brother to me," he instructed the doctor. "And nothing that was said here is to leave this chamber. Is that understood?"

The doctor obviously resented this warning, as needless as it was insulting. Bowing stiffly, he backed toward the door. There he paused, his hand on the latch.

"There is another malady that can cause a loss of feeling or paralysis. I am not saying I fear the young lord has been afflicted with it, for there is no evidence of that. Yet I would be remiss in my duties as a physician if I did not mention it to you, my liege. I do not believe you need—"

"By the rood, man, spit it out! What is this ailment?"

The doctor met Amalric's gaze steadily. "Leprosy."

William sank down abruptly on a nearby coffer chest. The blood had drained from Amalric's face; he opened his mouth, but no words emerged. And then he lunged across the chamber, grabbing the doctor and shoving him against the door. "If I ever hear you say that my son could be a leper, I'll cut your tongue out myself!"

The other man looked more offended than alarmed. "My first responsibility is to my patient. I would never break a sickbed confidence, would never speak of Lord Baldwin's ailment to anyone but you. If you do not trust me to honor my vow, it might be better for you to seek another doctor for the young prince."

Amalric was the first to look away. Stepping back, he released his hold on the doctor's arm. "I trust you," he said, his voice thick and scratchy, and Abū Sulayman Dāwūd yielded, knowing this was as close as the king could come to an apology.

As soon as the doctor departed, Amalric strode over to a side table and poured himself wine with a shaking hand. Emptying it in several swallows, he splashed more wine into the cup and brought it to his mouth. But he did not drink, instead flung the cup to the floor. A swipe of his arm sent the flagon after it, soaking the carpet. He stared down for a moment at the pooling wine, as red as newly spilled blood, and then crossed the chamber, slumping into a chair beside William.

"You were not surprised," he said after a long silence; there was no accusation in his voice, though, nothing but exhaustion. "Why would you ever have suspected that?"

"I would not say I suspected, my liege; that is too strong a word. It is rather that I was remembering. When I was a boy in Jerusalem, a neighbor's son was diagnosed with that vile malady." He did not elaborate, not wanting to tell Amalric that the boy's first symptom had been a lack of feeling in one of his hands, not wanting to say anything that would connect their blessed young prince with that doomed child.

Amalric leaned back in his seat and closed his eyes. "Christ on the cross," he muttered, and another oppressive silence fell. "I do not believe it," he said abruptly. "Not any of it. I do not believe Baldwin will not heal or that he'll be crippled. As for the other . . ." His mouth twisted, as if he'd tasted something unspeakably foul.

"There is no way that my son could be stricken with that accursed disease. God would never let that happen—never."

William studied the other man and then slowly nodded. "I do not believe God would let that happen, either, my lord king."

The rest of the day passed in a blur for William. He delighted Baldwin and the other boys by canceling their classes, and sought to occupy himself with his writing. Despite spending hours on his task, he was unhappy with what he'd written and ended up scraping the parchment clean, erasing all his afternoon's efforts. It was the eve of Maundy Thursday and the service that night was the hauntingly beautiful and tragic ceremony of Tenebrae, one of his favorites. But even as the candles were symbolically quenched, one by one, until the church of the Holy Sepulchre was plunged into darkness, he remained distracted and restless, unable to meditate upon the Savior's suffering. He retired early to his own chambers. When he realized he'd been sitting for an hour with a book open in his lap, not a page turned, he put it aside and, picking up an oil lamp, made his way into the stairwell toward Baldwin's chambers.

The boy was already in bed. His attendants greeted William by putting fingers to their lips. He indicated he'd not wake the young prince, detouring around the wolfhound stretched out on the carpet by Baldwin's bed. He stood for several moments, gazing down at the sleeping child. A lock of sunlit hair had fallen across his forehead and William resisted the urge to smooth it back into place. It was then that the boy's lashes flickered and he looked up drowsily.

"Are you here to scold me for what I did today?"

"No . . . what did you do?"

"It was just in fun. . . ." Baldwin yawned. "You do not know? Well, I'd be foolish to tell you, then," he murmured with a sleepy smile. "You might not find out. . . ."

"I always do," William reminded him. "It does not involve Queen Maria, does it? You promised me that you'd play no more tricks upon her after that last bit of mischief."

"She has no sense of humor at all."

"Baldwin, you let a bat loose in her bedchamber!"

The corner of the boy's mouth twitched in amusement. "My mother would have laughed."

William doubted that, but he usually tried to hold his peace where Agnes de

Courtenay was concerned, not feeling it proper to share his disapproval of the woman with her young son. In truth, the boy did not really know his mother, for once Amalric realized how bitter she was about their divorce, he saw to it that her visits with Baldwin were infrequent and always supervised.

"You did keep your word about the queen?" William persisted, relieved when the boy nodded. He was sorry, although not truly surprised, that there was so little affection between Maria and Baldwin. Baldwin had been six at the time of her marriage to his father and he'd not been pleased, seeing her as an intruder into their lives. And what thirteen-year-old girl was equipped to be a stepmother to a youngster who was resentful, strong-willed, and somewhat spoiled? It did not help, either, he thought with a sigh, that Baldwin was such a tease and Maria so protective of her dignity. Just a few days ago, William had been worried about their failure to forge any sort of bond, realizing that their rivalry was likely to get worse now that Maria had a child of her own. Tonight, it no longer seemed to matter.

"Go back to sleep, Baldwin," he said softly. "I did not mean to awaken you."

"Master William?"

"Yes, lad?"

"My arm . . . it will get better?"

"Yes, I am sure it will. Have you been worried about it, Baldwin?"

"No . . . not until I saw that you and my father were worried."

"Well, now that you've seen the doctor, none of us need worry." William looked into the boy's candid blue eyes and summoned up a smile. "May God and His holy angels keep you safe, lad." It was a blessing he'd often bestowed upon Baldwin and the words came to his lips of their own bidding. But as he spoke them tonight, there was a catch in his throat.

CHAPTER 2

December 1173
Jerusalem, Outremer

W illiam had been keeping a protective eye upon the young queen, for this was Maria's first public appearance since the death of her second daughter two months ago. He did not need the evidence of her pallor, the shadows smudged under her eyes, and the fingers clenching and unclenching in her lap to show him what an emotional toll it was taking on her. Most of the kingdom's lords and their ladies had not seen her in those two months and so their greetings were then followed by condolences, which meant that Maria was being forced to acknowledge her child's death in virtually every conversation. That would have been painful for any mourning mother, but William knew Maria's grieving was darkened by guilt.

Born more than a month before her due date, the baby had been named after Amalric's late mother, yet from her first day on God's earth, Melisende had seemed too frail and tiny to bear the weight of a queen's name, and only Maria had clung to hope. Melisende lingered barely a fortnight and Maria had soon confided tearfully to William what she could not say to Amalric, that she blamed herself. Surely there must have been something she could have done to prevent the premature birth that had doomed her daughter? William's superb education did not include the female subjects of pregnancy and the birthing chamber, but he pointed out gently that all that happened was God's will, so there had to be a reason why the Almighty had called Melisende home after such a heartbreakingly brief stay. He doubted, though, that his words had given Maria much comfort.

As soon as there was a pause in the stream of people approaching the dais, William suggested that Maria take a brief respite from her queenly duties. A walk in the gardens would do her good, he insisted, and she glanced wistfully toward the window but then shook her head, pointing out that someone had to be there to greet their guests in Amalric's absence.

"Where is the king?" he asked, irked with Amalric for not giving his vulnerable wife more support. He thought he'd phrased the question neutrally but Maria knew him well enough to catch the implied criticism and she shook her head again.

"It is not his fault," she said softly. "That wretched woman ambushed us as we left the chapel, demanding that she have some moments alone with him. Naturally he refused, yet she persisted, saying it concerned their son. She made such a scene that granting her a private audience was the lesser of evils, and Amalric grudgingly agreed to talk with her."

Maria stopped speaking then, for Humphrey de Toron was approaching. He scorned the clean-shaven fashion of younger lords, his beard grizzled and thicker than the receding hair on his head. He was well into his sixth decade, yet still sturdy and robust. Constable of the kingdom for the past ten years, he had earned a well-deserved reputation for battlefield valor and was respected for his cool head in a crisis. He looked pleased when Maria rose and took several steps toward him, a deft recognition of his status as one of the most important barons of the realm. Feeling like a proud tutor with a clever pupil, William smiled approvingly as she made the constable welcome and then greeted his daughter-in-law, Stephanie de Milly.

Like Maria, the de Toron family was in mourning, for Humphrey's son and namesake had died after a brief illness earlier that year. Stephanie was a great heiress, though, so William doubted she'd remain a widow for long. He saw now that she was accompanied by her seven-year-old son, yet another Humphrey. He was a startlingly handsome child, with perfectly sculpted features, long-lashed dark eyes, and hair the color of burnished chestnut, but there was something about his beauty—for there was no other word for it—that seemed delicate to William, almost effeminate. Certain, though, that the lad could have no better role model than his grandfather, William smiled at young Humphrey, who smiled shyly back.

Leaving Maria in conversation with the constable and his daughter-in-law, William began to search the hall for Baldwin, disappointed when the lad was nowhere to be found. His frown disappeared, though, as his gaze lit upon the girl in a window alcove, flirting openly with one of Amalric's household knights. Sybilla was so obviously excited to be at the Christmas court that William felt a twinge of pity. She'd been four when Amalric had sent her off to the nunnery at Bethany to be raised by the elderly abbess, his aunt, and the ten years since then must have been lonely ones for her, judging by how happy she always was to attend her father's Easter and Christmas courts. He'd tried in vain to persuade Amalric to have her educated in the royal household. He had fond memories of sharing his

Jerusalem childhood with his brother and it seemed sad that Baldwin should grow up not knowing his own sister.

When he said "Lady Sybilla," she rose from the seat, winked at the knight, and moved to meet him. Like Baldwin, she had inherited the fair coloring of their parents. She would never have the stunning beauty that had been her mother's, but she had the appeal of youth and when she smiled, her resemblance to Agnes was suddenly so pronounced that William wondered if that was why Amalric had kept her secluded at the Bethany convent.

"How good to see you again, Master William!" she exclaimed, showing she had some of Baldwin's charm. He did not know if she also had her brother's sharp intelligence, but she appeared to have the same strong will, for she kept begging Amalric to bring her back to court, not at all discouraged by his inevitable refusals. When William explained the favor he sought, she seemed delighted. "You want me to greet guests on my father's behalf? Of course I will!"

She danced toward the dais with a light step, so eager to be the center of attention that William felt another flicker of sympathy; how suffocating she must find life behind those nunnery walls. By the time William caught up with her, she and her stepmother had already exchanged places. There was not the same tension between them as there was between Maria and Baldwin, yet they were still strangers with little to say to each other; he doubted that Maria had seen Sybilla more than a dozen times in the entire six years of her marriage. He knew Sybilla found it odd to have a stepmother only five years her senior, for he'd heard her say so. He suspected that Maria felt the same way, but she'd learned to be circumspect while growing up at the Greek royal court.

As he moved away with Maria, William glanced over his shoulder at Sybilla, happily holding court on the dais, and it occurred to him that a sequestered convent childhood was not the best education for a girl who stood so close to the throne. The thought was so troubling that he stopped abruptly, causing Maria to look at him in surprise. It was the first time that he'd viewed Sybilla as a possible queen and he felt a pang of remorse, for it seemed disloyal to Baldwin even to consider it, a secret admission that if the boy's health deteriorated, he might not be capable of ruling.

It was an unusually mild day for December and the royal gardens were dappled in sunlight. There were no flowers in bloom at that time of year and the fruit trees were bare, but palms and olive trees knew no seasons and their fronds and silvery-green leaves rustled in the breeze as Maria and William strolled along the walkway, followed by her women and the ever-present Michael. William was pleased to see that the color was returning to her cheeks and she paused when they heard a sweet twittering coming from a blackthorn bush, smiling as she caught a glimpse of the small bird perched on a twig. It soon took flight, black and yellow wings glinting in the sun. William identified it for Maria as a goldfinch, also called the thistle finch, explaining it was a symbol of the Resurrection, the thistle being associated with the Savior's crown of thorns.

William had a penchant for sometimes oversharing, but Maria did not mind; his digressions were usually interesting and it was a relief to talk about an innocuous subject like the goldfinch. He was telling her about a legend that the thistle finch had plucked a thorn from the Lord Christ's bleeding brow, when a sudden shout turned their heads toward the far end of the garden.

"So that is where Baldwin disappeared to," William said, pointing toward the raucous game of quoits being played by his young charge and several of his friends. They'd attracted an audience, for everything the king's son did was of interest to the men and women he would one day rule. The spectators were prudently keeping their distance, though, as the boys were flinging the horseshoes about with wild abandon. Had he been alone, William would have gone over to watch, too. But Maria looked tired and so he led her toward a nearby bench.

They did not speak for a time, for they'd long ago reached that stage in their friendship where they were comfortable with silence. Maria's ladies settled onto another bench, while Michael stayed on his feet, leaning against the gnarled trunk of an olive tree. Maria's gaze had shifted back to her stepson's game. "Amalric says Baldwin's injury is healing," she said, switching from French to Greek once she'd assured herself that her attendants were not within earshot. "But I notice that he is using his left hand to throw the horseshoes at the hob."

William had noticed it, too. Glancing at the queen from the corner of his eye, he wished he could confide in her. Impossible, of course, for the question of Baldwin's health was shrouded in secrecy. When word had slowly trickled out of the palace that the young prince was learning to wield a sword with his left hand, Amalric had tersely explained it as the result of a shoulder injury. That had not stopped people from gossiping or rumors from spreading. Fortunately, whenever Baldwin appeared in public, he showed no signs of sickness and seemed to be a normal, lively lad of twelve, and William thought that reduced speculation to occasional tavern talk.

He wondered if Amalric truly believed that his son was on the mend. It had been twenty months since he'd first noticed those damnable bruises, and he saw no indication that Baldwin's arm was healing. William feared that the boy was losing the ability to use his afflicted hand, just as Abū Sulaymān Dāwūd had warned. But Baldwin was subjected to frequent physical examinations by the doctor and no other symptoms had manifested themselves. William took great comfort from that, even though an insidious inner voice occasionally whispered that such comfort was ephemeral.

Maria was sorry she'd brought the subject up, for it was obvious he did not want to discuss Baldwin's injury. His reluctance made her uneasy. Amalric acted as if his son's impairment was a minor matter, temporary at best. She hoped that was so. She would never have admitted it to anyone, but she did not like Baldwin. She'd assured herself that it was his fault, not hers, for he'd rejected her early overtures and soon she'd stopped trying. There were moments, however, when she acknowledged that it had been up to her to win him over and she'd taken the easy way out. She was relieved that Baldwin lived with William and not with Amalric, even though she was vaguely ashamed that she felt that way. It took her by surprise, therefore, that the possibility that Baldwin might have a serious health problem troubled her so much.

She studied William's profile, finding it on the tip of her tongue to ask him if he'd tell her if there was reason to worry about Baldwin's injury. She bit the words back, realizing how unfair that would be. Another silence fell between them, this one not as comfortable.

The quiet of the gardens was suddenly shattered by the intrusion of boisterous male voices. The Lord of Ramlah, Baudouin d'Ibelin, was striding along the pathway, bantering with a newcomer to Outremer, Amaury de Lusignan. Baudouin's wife, Richilde, trailed behind them, while his younger brother, Balian, ambled along in the rear.

Maria did not know what to make of the older d'Ibelin brother. Baudouin could be rather overwhelming; her private name for him was Sirokos, the Greek term for a powerful, gusting wind that originated in the African desert and swept all before it. He was loud, exuberant, and utterly lacking in subtlety, qualities that were not admired at the Greek court. But his swagger was well-earned, for he was renowned for his battlefield prowess, and she came to see that, while he might be brash and alarmingly blunt, he was not malicious, nor was he mean-spirited.

Catching sight of the queen and the archdeacon, Baudouin veered in their direction. "William, you sly dog! Leave it to you to lay claim to the prettiest woman at the court!"

Maria knew by now that his heavy-handed flirting was harmless; she still wondered how his wife felt about it. William did not appreciate Baudouin's humor, either, for there was no way to respond to it without sounding like a fool. Yet as much as he disapproved of Baudouin's behavior at times, he found it impossible to dislike the other man, and he rose to greet the new arrivals with a smile.

Maria and William had already met Amaury de Lusignan, a member of a noble French family that was notorious for their feuding with the English king, Henry FitzEmpress, who was also their liege lord because of his marriage to Eleanor, Duchess of Aquitaine. Amaury had a reputation as a good soldier and so they hoped he would extend his stay in Outremer. Too many who took the cross were eager to return home once they'd visited the holy sites in Jerusalem. The kingdom was always seriously short of manpower, dangerously outnumbered by their Saracen enemies.

Richilde greeted them listlessly. Maria did not take it personally, for she had never seen the older woman animated. She'd been wed to Baudouin for nigh on twenty years, had given him two daughters but no sons, and rumor had it that their marriage was not a happy one. Maria, who'd now failed twice to produce a son for Amalric, felt some sympathy for Richilde, for Baudouin was outspoken in his disappointment at not having a male heir.

She smiled at Balian as he kissed her hand, for she'd not forgotten his kindness on the day that she'd burst into William's chambers and blurted out her hatred of Agnes de Courtenay. The d'Ibelins had earlier expressed their condolences and Amaury de Lusignan was likely ignorant of her loss, so she hoped she'd be spared having to discuss her daughter's death yet again.

Her hopes were justified, for Baudouin was interested only in talking about the troubles that had befallen the English king. Word had recently reached Outremer that Henry's sons had risen up in rebellion against him. That was not so shocking; royal fathers and unruly sons had been known since the days of King David and Absalom. What people found so incredible was that Eleanor was said to have joined in their rebellion, for no one could think of a case in which a queen had turned upon her husband. The rebellion was of great interest to all at Amalric's court; the English king was his nephew and he'd recently promised to take the cross, pledging desperately needed funds for the defense of the Holy Land.

After they exhausted the subject of the royal rebellion, they began discussing the other topic that was never far from their minds: the danger posed by their Saracen neighbors. The man who ruled Syria and Egypt, Nūr al-Dīn, was said to be ailing, and the men began to speculate about his successor should his illness prove fatal. As usual, Baudouin was dominating the conversation and William, noticing that Balian had drawn away from the others, moved to join him, saying, "They are wasting their time worrying about Nūr al-Dīn's son. He's just a lad and he'll not hold power for long if his father dies whilst he's still a minor."

Balian knew the man that William most feared was one who served Nūr al-Dīn, the current vizier of Egypt, Salāh al-Dīn, known to the Franks as Saladin. "You think Saladin will be the force to the reckoned with once Nūr al-Dīn dies?"

"I am sure of it." William was about to elaborate upon why he thought Saladin to be such a threat when he saw that Balian was no longer listening, gazing over his shoulder with the expression of one watching an approaching storm.

"Trouble," he said softly and succinctly, and William turned to see Agnes de Courtenay entering the gardens. Looking back at his brother, Balian confided, "Baudouin and Agnes are like flint and tinder whenever they get together. He truly loathes the woman, blaming her for abandoning Hugh to wed Amalric. She swore to Hugh that she'd been given no say in the matter, and Hugh must have believed her, for he married her. But Baudouin still insists she'd seen the Count of Jaffa as a greater prize than the Lord of Ramlah. And she detests Baudouin in equal measure, for he spoke out forcefully against allowing her to become queen."

Agnes was alone, unusual in itself, and she was close enough now for them to see the hot color burning in her cheeks and the taut set of her mouth; clearly her private talk with Amalric had not gone well. William did not care if she and Baudouin raged at each other like ravening wolves, but he was not going to let her take out her frustration upon Maria and he tensed as she glanced their way, then swerved toward them.

She did not even look at Maria or Baudouin, though, heading directly for William. "I want to speak with you—privately," she said abruptly, ignoring Balian's wry "Good to see you, too, Agnes."

"I cannot do that, madame, William said just as tersely, thinking he'd sooner wear a hair shirt for the rest of his born days than spend any time alone with Agnes de Courtenay.

"Yes," she said, hissing the word through clenched teeth. "You can and you will, for if anyone knows what is wrong with my son, it is you!"

"If you have questions about the young prince's health, my lady countess, you should ask them of the king."

"I did!" Her voice rose, and others in the garden began to glance in her direction. "He lied to me, insisting Baldwin is fine. Fine? He cannot even use his right hand!"

William's discomfort was giving way to anger. Mayhap she truly was concerned for the lad. Yet that did not give her the right to make a scene like this, to put her needs before Baldwin's. When word of this got around, people would say that the boy's own mother thought he was ailing, unfit to be king.

"I have nothing to say to you," he said coldly.

She stared at him and then slapped him across the face.

William's head jerked back and he tasted blood in his mouth, having bitten his lip. There were gasps from those watching, for by now they'd begun to draw a crowd. Before he could react, Maria was at his side, dark eyes blazing.

"How dare you strike Master William! He is devoted to your son, would give his life for Baldwin if need be."

"He is Amalric's puppet, willing to sell his soul for a king's favor whilst my son suffers!"

"Baldwin injured his shoulder. You know that because my lord husband told you so. He told you, too, that Baldwin is getting better—"

"And are you going to assure me of that, too? As if you care about Baldwin's welfare!"

"Of course I do!"

"You are such a hypocrite. You'd thank God fasting if my children died, for whilst they live, your brat will never become queen!"

Maria went ashen. Fighting back tears, she swung away from Agnes, began to walk blindly up the path as her attendants scrambled to catch up with her. William gave Agnes a look of utter outrage, then hastened after Maria. Balian was shaking his head in disbelief, but it was Baudouin who drew all eyes, rising to his feet and slowly beginning to clap.

"Well done, sister-in-law. Most people know better than to mention rope in the house of a man who'd been hanged. But no one except you would think to speak of dead children to a woman who'd just buried her own child."

Agnes drew a sharp breath. She was given no chance to retort, though, for it was then that Balian's hand clamped down on her wrist. She tried to pull free, but his grip was too tight and she found herself being forced off the path, away from the others. He did not halt until he was sure they were out of hearing of their audience.

"No—do not say a word," he warned. "For once you are going to listen. If you choose to make a fool of yourself, so be it. But your son is in the far end of the gardens. Do you truly want him to see you like this?"

"Baldwin . . . he's here?"

"Down by the fish pond, playing quoits with his friends."

She glanced in that direction, then back at Balian. "You cannot imagine what it's like, knowing that something is wrong with my son, whilst Amalric keeps shutting me out, lying to me."

"You have to stop lashing out like this, Agnes, if not for your own sake, for Baldwin's. Even if the worst happens and he does lose the use of his hand, he can still do what a king must, still command men and lead them into battle. But if you keep carrying on like this, he'll start to doubt that, to doubt himself."

"You do not understand, Balian," she said very low, and he was taken aback by what he saw in her eyes—real fear.

She straightened her shoulders then, raising her chin, and turned away. She'd only taken a few steps before she stopped. "I'd forgotten that the Greek's daughter had died." Not waiting for his response, she began to walk toward the far end of the gardens.

Balian watched her go, thinking that at least she was still capable of shame. But he could not keep from wondering why a shoulder injury had her so frightened.

When Balian returned to the great hall later that afternoon, he was relieved to see that all seemed tranquil after the morning's turmoil. Amalric was seated upon the dais, with Maria at his side, welcoming new arrivals to the Christmas court. Trestle tables would soon be set up for the evening meal; for now, a harpist played for the guests and the men and their wives were showing off their finery, greeting friends, gossiping, and laughing. There was a swirl of brilliant colors and the rustle of silk, satin, sarcenet, and damask, for despite the kingdom's precarious position, its people enjoyed greater comforts and luxuries than their Christian brethren in France and England. Balian was a Poulain, the term for those born in Outremer, originally one of disdain but proudly adopted by the Poulains as their own. Unlike Master William, who'd spent twenty years studying in Paris and Bologna, Balian had never left Outremer, nor had he any wish to do so. The Holy Land was not a pilgrimage destination for the Poulains. It was home.

As he moved closer to the dais, he noticed that Amalric would occasionally glance across the hall. Following his gaze, Balian soon saw what was attracting his attention. His daughter Sybilla was sitting in a window seat with her mother, the girl chattering away vivaciously, laughing frequently, while Agnes listened with a smile. Watching them, it occurred to Balian that if Amalric had wanted to limit his former wife's influence upon their children, he'd gone about it the wrong way.

By trying to keep Agnes at a distance, he'd only succeeded in making her a figure of glamour and mystery to Baldwin and Sybilla. The appeal of forbidden fruit, he thought, and then started when he heard his name said, close at hand. He spun around to find himself facing Agnes's fourth and current husband, Renaud de Grenier, Lord of Sidon.

Balian greeted the other man warmly, but not as Renaud, for although that was his baptismal name, his friends and family all knew him as Denys. As an infant, he'd been near death with a high fever until his desperate mother had prayed to St. Denys, whose feast day it was. When he recovered, she'd begun calling him Denys and the name stuck.

Denys's surprise marriage to Agnes had stirred up gossip and speculation, as well as some cruel jokes about the beauty and the beast, for Denys was as ill-favored as she was comely. Balian was not amused by these jests, finding the older man to be very likable and extremely intelligent, with a strong streak of irony and a droll sense of humor. He did think Denys and Agnes were an odd pairing but kept that to himself.

"I owe you a debt of gratitude for your intercession in the gardens this morning," Denys said with a faint smile.

"If only horses could travel as fast as gossip," Balian said, with a smile of his own, "I'd be able to ride to Acre and back in the course of a day. What did you hear?"

"That Agnes slapped the archdeacon of Tyre and mortally offended the queen. God forbid there was more?"

"No, that covers it. You owe me no thanks, though, Denys. When I see a fire, my instinct is to pour water on the flames."

Denys was following Amalric's example, keeping his gaze upon Agnes and Sybilla. "I am not defending her behavior," he said quietly, "but she is very worried about Baldwin."

"Why?"

Denys glanced around to make sure no others were within hearing. "Because Amalric is very worried. He has sent for Saracen physicians from Cairo to examine the lad, keeps Abū Sulayman Dāwūd close at hand, and he does not sleep well at nights, often rising to pace and brood."

"How does Agnes know that?" Denys did not reply, regarding him with a cynical smile, and Balian wondered how he could have been so naïve. Hugh's death had made Agnes a wealthy woman, entitled to one half of the revenues of the lordship of Ramlah, yet another reason why Baudouin resented her so much. She could afford to pay and pay well for information. "She has spies in Amalric's own household, then?"

Denys nodded. "She'd probably have planted spies in the queen's household, too, but Maria surrounds herself with attendants who speak only Greek."

"Why are you telling me this?"

"Because I want you to understand why she is so distraught, so lacking in control. She has few friends at court, Balian. But whatever others say of her, Agnes loves her son dearly."

There was a sudden stir in the crowd, and both men turned to watch as Baldwin entered the hall and made his way toward the dais. The boy was so handsome, so spirited, so vibrant, that Balian found it impossible to believe that he could be seriously ill. "I think Amalric could well be grieving for the lad's injury, coming to terms with the realization that it is not going to heal, that he'll be crippled."

"I thought of that, too, but Agnes insists that a mother's intuition tells her otherwise." Denys sighed, and Balian thought that life with Agnes must be challenging at times. He realized that the other man wanted to enlist him in a conspiracy to protect Agnes from herself, and he hoped that Denys would not ask him outright. Feeling pity for Agnes did not make him like her any better.

Denys did not push it further, apparently satisfied that he'd planted a seed. "Even if Agnes's fears prove to be valid, at least we need not fear for the future of the kingdom. Amalric is thirty-seven and his queen just nineteen, so there is no reason to doubt that she'll give him sons. God willing, Amalric will reign for years to come. We shall desperately need a strong king like Amalric once Nūr al-Dīn dies."

"You mean Saladin?"

Denys nodded grimly. "Yes," he said, "Saladin."

CHAPTER 3

July 1174
Jerusalem, Outremer

I s the king dying?"

Maria had her answer in the silence and averted eyes of the doctors. She wanted to argue with them, to deny that her husband was doomed; she could not. The truth was writ in Amalric's face, in the occasional groans that escaped his blistered lips. His eyes were sunken, his skin dry and shriveled. Although he was burning with fever, he could not perspire, and when he was able to urinate at all, it was a dark, cloudy yellow. Despite being sparing in what he ate and drank, he'd always been corpulent, but he'd lost so much weight in the past week that his double chin was utterly gone. When she'd put her fingers to his wrist, she could barely find a pulse. She felt as if she were gazing down at a stranger, and that only contributed to the unreality of the scene.

How could this be happening? The Christians of Outremer had been so hopeful when they'd gotten word of the May death of Nūr al-Dīn in Damascus, leaving as his heir an eleven-year-old boy. Amalric had moved at once to take advantage of his Saracen enemy's demise, leading a force to recapture the city of Bāniās. After meeting stiff resistance, he'd agreed to lift the siege in return for a large sum of money offered by Nūr al-Dīn's widow. But by the time Amalric reached Tiberias, he was ailing, suffering from the malady called dysentery or the bloody flux.

He had stubbornly rejected a litter, continuing on to Jerusalem by horseback, where doctors were immediately summoned. They'd managed to get his bowels under control; then he was stricken by a high fever. When he'd not responded to treatment, he demanded that he be given a purgative. While Abū Sulayman Dāwūd refused, saying he was too weak, the Frankish doctors agreed to administer it. The Syrian physician's concern proved to be justified, and as Amalric's strength ebbed away, so, too, did any hope that he'd survive.

Resuming her vigil at her husband's bedside, Maria leaned over to place her hand upon his forehead and winced, for his fever continued to rage. How could this be God's will? Amalric's death would leave his kingdom at the mercy of their Saracen foes. How could an untried boy fend off Saladin? And what would befall her little girl? No longer the cherished daughter of a powerful king, with only her mother to speak up for her rights as that vile de Courtenay woman whispered her poison in Baldwin's inexperienced ear. Shutting her eyes tightly, Maria shivered despite the summer heat infiltrating the chamber.

As she reached over to take Amalric's hand, his lashes flickered. Her fingers felt cool and smooth against his feverish skin. Whenever he'd awakened, she'd been there, forsaking sleep to stay at his side. Even if it was duty and not devotion, he was glad for her presence. Dying was lonely. He'd seen his chaplain, had confessed and been shriven of his sins. A pity a man could not be as easily absolved of his regrets. His fear had always been for his son, not for his kingdom. He'd not doubted that Maria would give him other sons, so even if his greatest dread had indeed been realized, the succession would have been safe. Like most of God's fools, he'd assumed his earthly time was infinite. He'd never imagined he'd be dying at thirty-eight, leaving a twenty-year-old widow, two defenseless daughters, and a young son who could be accursed with the very worst of scourges.

"Maria . . ." It was not easy to talk, for his mouth was as dry as the Negev Desert. "Fetch my children," he whispered. He must have dozed off after that, for when he opened his eyes again, Maria was sitting by the bed, holding Isabella in her lap, with Sybilla and Baldwin standing awkwardly behind her.

Amalric found himself suddenly remembering the bitter prophesy Agnes had flung at him during one of their quarrels about Baldwin's health. "When you die," she'd spat, "no one will weep for you." As his gaze moved from his queen to his children, he did indeed see no tears. Maria's eyes were dry, filled with fear. Isabella was, at two, too young to understand. It pleased him that she showed signs of growing into a beauty, with wide-set dark eyes and her mother's black hair. She was a sweet-natured child, eager to please, but also an observant one. She was both curious and cautious, qualities he could appreciate for they were his character traits, too. Very unlike his older daughter; at Isabella's age, Sybilla had already been a handful.

Sybilla was subdued now, her lashes veiling her eyes, her hands clasped nervously behind her back. He did not blame her for not grieving for him; hellfire, she barely knew him. His gaze moved past her to his son. The lad looked overwhelmed, as well he might. He was clever enough to understand that a kingship at thirteen was more of a burden than a blessing.

Amalric's throat tightened. How could God be so cruel? He'd shocked poor William once by asking if he truly believed that souls were raised from the dead. Imagine how horrified the archdeacon would be if he confided what he was thinking now—that mayhap God was a Muslim. How else explain their kingdom's plight? He wished he had words of wisdom for his son, words that would comfort and guide him in years to come. But he knew there were none, not if what he so dreaded came to pass. "I am proud of you, lad," he said hoarsely, and the boy swallowed, blinking rapidly. *See, Agnes, there is one to weep for me, after all.*

He found himself drifting away again, but he could not let the tide take him, not yet. "Maria . . . I must speak with you in private. William, too. And the patriarch."

She rose, handed Isabella to her nurse, and signaled for Baldwin and Sybilla to withdraw, which they quickly did, ill at ease and frightened that their father might die while they watched. Amalric glanced toward the bedside table, and William reached for the wine cup, holding it to his parched lips. No matter how much he drank, he could not ease this great thirst. "Maria . . . fetch Agnes, too."

Her head whipped around. "Amalric, are you . . . sure?"

He nodded and after she'd departed to send word to the patriarch and his former wife, he met William's eyes, saying softly, "I suppose I owe Agnes this much." He saw that William understood, although he did not look any happier about it than Maria. But the High Court had to know. He could not go to his grave without speaking up, for there was too much at stake. He must betray his son or betray his kingdom. Had any man ever faced a choice like that?

"I lied to you, William," he confessed once they were alone.

"My liege?"

"When . . . when I told you that I did not believe God would curse Baldwin with leprosy."

William's eyes filled with tears. "I know, sire. I lied, too."

Baudouin and Balian d'Ibelin were sitting on the steps of the great hall, gazing toward the north tower, where the king's bedchamber was located. The city had come to a standstill, large, somber crowds gathering out on the Street of the Armenians. Those able to gain access to the palace were congregating in the great hall or the courtyard—some of the soldier-monks of the Knights Templar and the Knights Hospitaller, clerics, members of the royal household, and lords of the realm. Across the courtyard, Denys de Grenier was striding back and forth; he had acknowledged Baudouin and Balian with a brief wave but had not come over to talk, keeping his eyes on the north tower entrance. He was trailed by his cousin, Guyon de Grenier, who'd recently inherited the lordship of Caesarea, paying Guyon no more mind than he had the d'Ibelins. He was the object of considerable curiosity, for his presence there confirmed the wild rumor that the dying king had sent for Agnes.

Until he'd seen Denys, Baudouin had been skeptical of that rumor, saying that no man in his right senses would want to spend his last hours of life with a hellcat like Agnes. "By putting himself through this earthly ordeal, do you think Amalric will get some time taken off his stay in Purgatory?"

Balian shrugged, too preoccupied to heed his brother's jesting.

Baudouin was still nursing a cup of wine he'd brought from the great hall. "Who'd have guessed that a coldhearted bastard like Amalric would be mourned like this? I suppose the Devil we know is always preferable to the one we do not."

He'd often been one for belaboring the obvious and Balian waited now for him to quote from Scriptures. "'Woe unto thee, O land, when thy king is a child.'" Baudouin surprised him, though. "It is not that I fear Baldwin will be a bad king. He's a good lad, dealt with that shoulder injury better than many grown men would have done. No whining or self-pity; he just set about learning how to wield a sword with his left hand. And he's one of the best riders I've ever seen. But he'll not reach his majority for another two years, two years in which Agnes will do all in her power to entangle him in her web."

Baudouin frowned, genuinely alarmed at the prospect of Agnes exercising her baneful influence upon young Baldwin. "Thank God her brother has been languishing in a Saracen dungeon these ten years past," he said, draining his wine cup and setting it down upon the steps with a thud.

Balian was taken aback. "That is rather harsh," he said, for they all dreaded the fate that had befallen Agnes's brother. In yet another downturn of Fortune's wheel for the de Courtenays, the year after Amalric had divorced Agnes, the Franks had suffered a major defeat at the hands of Nūr al-Dīn. Among the highborn prisoners taken at the battle of Hārim had been Raymond, the Count of Tripoli; Bohemond, the Prince of Antioch; and Joscelin de Courtenay. The Greek emperor had been able to ransom Bohemond of Antioch, but Nūr al-Dīn refused to ransom the others, and they'd been held captive in Aleppo for almost a decade. Treatment of prisoners could vary widely, from the brutality accorded Agnes and Joscelin's father to reasonably comfortable confinement, yet even for the lucky ones not thrown into an underground dungeon, imprisonment had to scar a man's soul.

"I am not saying I do not feel some pity for Joscelin," Baudouin protested. "But tell me the truth, Little Brother. Do you want to see Baldwin turned into a de Courtenay puppet, with Agnes and Joscelin both getting to pull his strings? No, better for the kingdom's sake that Joscelin stays in his Aleppo gaol."

Balian did not want to see Joscelin as one of Baldwin's advisers either, but he sympathized with any man shut away from the sun, denied wine and women and all worldly joys. He wondered how a man kept his wits intact as the years dragged by and was thankful that their brother Hugh had been ransomed after less than a year of captivity. He sat up straight then, for Baudouin had just elbowed him sharply in the ribs.

"Look, they're coming out!"

The first to emerge from the tower stairwell was the Patriarch of Jerusalem. An elderly man, he looked as if he'd added a decade or two to his years during the time he'd spent in Amalric's bedchamber. Leaning heavily upon his cane, he tottered across the courtyard toward his waiting attendants and departed in such haste that the bystanders began to murmur uneasily among themselves. Maria was the next to appear, and she, too, seemed dazed. Balian was on his feet by now and offered a polite greeting as she passed, but he doubted that she'd even heard him. *Holy Mother Mary, what did Amalric tell them?*

He was staring after Maria when Baudouin poked him in the ribs again. "I do not believe it," he gasped, and Balian turned around to see what had so astounded his brother. Agnes de Courtenay was standing in the tower entranceway, leaning against the door frame as if she had need of physical support. Her head was bowed, her shoulders shaking, and there was a moment of shocked silence as the spectators realized she was weeping. Her husband shoved his way toward her and as soon as Denys put his arm around her, she collapsed against his chest and began to sob.

"I'd sooner have expected to see a crocodile shed tears than that woman," Baudouin admitted, and then, "Ah, there's Master William. You're a friend of his, Balian. Go and see if you can get him to tell us what went on up there."

Balian knew better. To stop Baudouin from hectoring him, though, he crossed the courtyard toward the archdeacon, just now stepping from the shadows of the stairwell into the light. William looked exhausted, showing every one of his forty-four years at that moment, his shoulders slumped, perspiration beading his forehead and upper lip. He glanced up dully as Balian approached, with Baudouin right on his heels. They were both very tall men and towered over him in the best of times, but now he seemed to have shrunk, as if his very bones had somehow contracted. Balian's greeting died in his throat, and even Baudouin could not bring himself to cross-examine a man so careworn.

William wanted only to retreat to his own chambers. But he paused long enough to say in a low, strained voice, "I cannot tell you anything, not yet. You'll know soon enough."

Balian patted the older man's shoulder, all he could think to do. Baudouin had less self-restraint. "When?" he demanded. "When will we know?"

William paused again. "After the king dies. When the High Court meets."

Amalric died on July 11, 1174, after reigning for eleven years and five months. He was given a royal funeral and buried beside his brother in the Church of the Holy Sepulchre. The next day, the High Court convened to elect his successor.

The *Haute Cour*, or High Court, was composed of the vassals of the king and its duties were varied. It had the power to levy taxes, to vote on military missions, to try civil and criminal cases, yet its most cherished prerogative was the right to select a king. Although six hundred or so men were eligible to vote, in practice the court was run by a much smaller group, one that consisted of the greatest lords of the realm. They normally met in the great hall of the massive stronghold known as David's Tower, but on the morning after Amalric's funeral, they were gathering in the upper-story solar of the citadel keep, which provided better security from eavesdroppers.

By sunrise, people had begun to congregate out on David Street and the castle bailey was already crowded with spectators. They nodded and pointed as the king's young widow was escorted toward the tower keep by the Archdeacon of Tyre. Maria looked pale and tense, oblivious that she was being watched by unfriendly eyes as well as curious ones. Agnes was outraged that Maria would be permitted to attend the High Court session, and as soon as she caught sight of the constable, she hastened across the bailey to intercept Humphrey de Toron.

He anticipated her, saying before she could speak, "Nothing has changed, my lady countess. As I told you yesterday, you cannot participate in the succession debate."

"I just saw that Greek woman enter."

"Queen Maria is the king's widow and the mother of his daughter."

"But she is not Baldwin's mother, I am!"

"I am sure your lord husband will tell you what happened during the session," he said brusquely and turned away before she could argue further.

Agnes could only fume in silence as others followed Humphrey into the tower keep. Just two bishops had permanent seats on the High Court; however, all of the kingdom's prelates and abbots would take part in the election of a new king, and she watched as a parade of churchmen passed by. The lords of Caesarea and Bethsan and Arsuf came next, and then the grand masters of the Knights Templar and the Knights Hospitaller. She bristled when she saw Walter de Brisebarre and his brother Guidon. Walter had once held the important fief of Beirut. But when his wife inherited the even larger and richer fief of Outrejourdain, Amalric had objected to a vassal having such power and compelled Walter to relinquish Beirut for the much less significant lordship of Blanchegarde. Although Walter subsequently lost any claim to Outrejourdain when his wife died, Amalric had not restored Beirut, which remained part of the royal demesne. Agnes was resentful that despite his paltry holdings, Walter was still a member of the High Court while she was shut out and ignored.

Nor was her temper improved any when she noticed Balian d'Ibelin strolling across the bailey; did the man ever hurry? The d'Ibelins had become one of the most influential families of Outremer after Barisan d'Ibelin had gained the king's favor and was rewarded with marriage to the heiress of Ramlah. When their mother had died, her sons Hugh and then Baudouin had inherited the important lordships of Ramlah and Mirabel, but Balian's holdings were much more modest. Once Baudouin succeeded Hugh as Lord of Ramlah, he'd generously bestowed the family fief of Ibelin upon his youngest brother. Ibelin was a small lordship, though. Yet like Walter de Brisebarre, Balian would have a say in whether her son became Outremer's next king, these lesser lords given the vote that Agnes was denied.

Agnes reminded herself that unlike his lout of a brother, Balian was not deaf to the voice of reason; he even seemed to have a sense of fair play. Calling out his name, she hurried to overtake him and, grasping his arm, steered him toward a corner of the bailey where they could speak more privately. "I want you to promise me," she said, "that you will speak up for Baldwin. He is the rightful king. Do not let them forget that, Balian."

Balian was mildly surprised by her urgency. "Baldwin has your husband to speak up for him and the others are more likely to be swayed by the Lord of Sidon than by me."

She was unable to explain that her son would need all the champions he could get. If only Joscelin were here. But she'd been left to fight her battles alone yet again. This time she was fighting for her son, and never had the stakes been higher. She'd wept all night. By morning, though, she was dry-eyed and resolute. She was not going to let Baldwin be cheated of his kingship by suspicions and conjecture. Even if the harrowing specter of leprosy proved to be real and not just Amalric's deathbed delusion, that was a war to be fought later, if at all. What mattered now was getting him the crown that was his birthright.

"I have to go, Agnes. I am not important enough for them to wait for me," Balian said with a smile, gently prying her fingers from his sleeve when she did not move. "I can assure you that I know of no reason not to elect Baldwin as our next king."

You will hear one soon enough, she thought, tasting the bitterness in her mouth like wormwood and gall.

The solar was a spacious chamber, but with more than forty men to accommodate, it was crowded and already unpleasantly warm. Chairs had been provided for Queen Maria and Emeric de Nesle, the patriarch. The others were sitting on wooden benches. Balian was heading for the back of the room when his brother called out, "I saved you a seat," and beckoned him toward the front row. Even though he felt out of place in the midst of the most powerful lords of the realm, Balian hastened over and slid onto the bench beside Baudouin.

Normally it would have been for the patriarch to do the invocation. Emeric seemed lost in his own thoughts and Baudouin was not the only one to think he might actually be dozing, although he was the only one to say so, in a sotto voce aside to Balian. Emeric had never had a forceful personality, and he'd become more ineffectual as he dealt with the twin crosses of age and illness, but even for him, such passive behavior was unusual. Balian found himself wondering again just what Amalric had confided to the patriarch and the women in his last hours.

The invocation was finally offered by Lethard, the Archbishop of Nazareth, who had a permanent seat on the court. The seneschal had fidgeted impatiently as Lethard prayed for the repose of Amalric's soul and the weal of the kingdom, and as soon as the archbishop paused for breath, Miles de Plancy was on his feet, thanking Lethard even though it was obvious he was not done.

Miles was one of the most influential men on the court. A member of Amalric's inner circle, he'd held the powerful post of seneschal for the past five years, and in March, he'd been lavishly rewarded for his unwavering loyalty to the king when

Amalric arranged his marriage to Stephanie de Milly, Humphrey de Toron's widowed daughter-in-law, heiress to the great fief of Outrejourdain. Miles was not well liked by the other barons, in part because he was not one of them, not a Poulain, and there were always tensions between the native-born barons and newcomers to Outremer. Some of them also resented his good fortune and rapid ascent. But Miles made it very easy for others to dislike him. He was hot-tempered and autocratic, often clashing with the kingdom's other officers, with both grand masters, and with several of the bishops, none of whom looked pleased to see him take command of the court now, even though it was his right as seneschal in the absence of the king.

Miles wasted no time with formalities. "It is barely past the third hour and already it is hotter than Hades in here. Fortunately, there is no need for prolonged debate. We know what we must do—choose young Baldwin as our king. The only other candidate is his sister and who in his right mind would want a lass raised as a nun—"

He was interrupted at that, first by Maria, who reminded him that King Amalric had another child, her daughter, Isabella, and then by Archbishop Frederick of Tyre, who pointed out that Sybilla had been sent to the nunnery to be educated, not to take holy vows.

"I did not forget your daughter, madame," Miles assured Maria, with a condescending smile that set her teeth on edge. "Yet surely a child of her tender years could only be given serious consideration if there were no other heirs. As for Sybilla, my lord archbishop, whilst she may not have taken vows, the road from the cloisters to a queenship would be a very rocky one. Thankfully, we need not concern ourselves with female claims to the throne, for King Amalric sired a son, one who has the makings of a fine king. Yes, he injured his shoulder, but that has not slowed him down. I've watched him practice at swordplay and I can assure you that once he's of an age to lead men into battle, he'll acquit himself well. And as young as he is, he is already a superb horseman; I'd wager the lad could ride a lion if we put a saddle on it!"

Miles chuckled at his own joke. "I propose that we vote now to confirm Baldwin as our next king. We'll also need to appoint a regent until he reaches his majority in two years. It was King Amalric's dying wish that I serve as regent until his son comes of age, and I swore to him that I would serve Baldwin as faithfully as I served him."

That did not go down well with most of the men, few of whom were willing to turn the reins of government over to Miles. Humphrey de Toron spoke for many of them when he said skeptically, "Any witnesses to this deathbed declaration by the king?"

Miles scowled, for he'd long viewed Humphrey as a dangerous rival. Despite the authority Miles wielded as seneschal, controlling the crown's finances and castles, he had no say about military matters, that power vesting solely in the constable. "Are you doubting my word?"

"If he is not, I am," Odo de St. Amand interjected and there were muted expressions of alarm, for even those who detested Miles did not want to see the court session disintegrate into a brawl between the seneschal and the grand master of the Templars.

Before the enraged Miles could lash back, William got hastily to his feet. "It is premature to consider a regency," he said loudly enough to drown out any murmurings from the audience. "Ere we vote to select our next ruler, it was the king's command that the patriarch address the court. Patriarch Emeric has delegated me to speak in his stead."

As William waited to be sure he had their attention, Balian stiffened, for he'd caught that, the use of "ruler" rather than "king," and he knew William never chose words carelessly.

"It is well known that Baldwin suffered a shoulder injury that limited his use of his right hand. He has learned to compensate for that, and, as the seneschal said, he continues to excel at his lessons in swordplay and horsemanship. What you do not know is that the story of the shoulder injury is false. Two years ago, I discovered that Baldwin no longer could feel sensations in his right hand and arm. But his doctors have been unable to determine the cause of his impairment."

There were muffled exclamations at that. William swallowed with difficulty, for his mouth was going dry. "Many of you are familiar with Baldwin's doctor, Abū Sulayman Dāwūd, if only by reputation as a skilled physician. When I am done speaking, he will be available to answer your questions about the young prince's health. It is his belief that Baldwin's condition is the result of a nerve injury. This was his initial diagnosis and he says he has seen no evidence since then that would change his mind. In other words, for more than two years Baldwin has shown no other symptoms than this numbness."

William paused to draw a deep, bracing breath, feeling as if he were about to fling a torch into a field of sun-dried hay. "Because so much is at stake, King Amalric decided that you need to know there is another malady that can cause a loss of feeling—even though we do not believe Baldwin is afflicted with it. That ailment is leprosy."

He'd expected his revelation to result in pandemonium, imagining the chamber erupting into chaos, benches overturned as men leaped to their feet, all shouting at once in their urgency to be heard. Instead, there was only stunned silence.

The two days that followed were among the worst of William's life. Once the shock had worn off, the members of the court had begun to debate with a vengeance. William and Abū Sulaymān Dāwūd and even Maria were subjected to intense interrogation about the state of Baldwin's health. It soon became apparent that there was no consensus. Miles continued to argue on Baldwin's behalf and he probably had the most support. But the names of other candidates soon found their way into the deliberations—Baldwin's two closest male kin, Bohemond, the Prince of Antioch, and Raymond, the Count of Tripoli. Sybilla began to attract attention, too. Only Isabella did not find backers, ruled out of contention because of her extreme youth.

By the second day, the debate had grown argumentative. To William's dismay, factions began to develop and old animosities to surface. At one point, Miles and Odo de St. Amand had to be separated by others. Walter de Brisebarre emerged as an impassioned partisan of Raymond, the Count of Tripoli, but William suspected his motivation was really to thwart Miles, whose marriage to Stephanie de Milly had made him the Lord of Outrejourdain, the vast fief that had once been Walter's. And William suspected, too, that self-interest was behind much of the enthusiastic support for Sybilla. She would need a husband to rule with her if she were chosen, which put visions of crowns into the heads of some. He reluctantly included Baudouin in this category, for he'd ended his marriage to Richilde earlier that year and was on the lookout for another wife; one who brought the kingdom as her marriage portion would be irresistible.

As the arguments dragged on, they'd even resorted to polling all those present, but that exercise merely emphasized how bogged down they'd become. By the third day, William had begun to despair that they could ever reach a decision, so foreboding a shadow did leprosy cast over the proceedings.

He was no longer bothering to listen to the debates, for by now they were offering more heat than light or clarity. Instead, he crossed the chamber and slumped down in a window seat next to Balian. "Saladin must be blessing his good fortune by now," he muttered, "whilst laughing at us for our inability to identify the true enemy in our midst."

Balian had begun to bring food in to get through the marathon sessions, and he offered William a choice of figs or dates. "Does Baldwin think it odd that they are taking so long to confirm his kingship?"

"I told him that lengthy deliberations were normal in such cases." William's mouth tightened. "As if there were anything even remotely normal about this!"

He was reaching for Balian's wineskin when a sudden demand for silence brought the ongoing din to a halt. Humphrey de Toron had stalked to the front of the solar. He was accustomed to shouting commands on the battlefield and was not a man to be easily defied, so the chamber slowly quieted.

"Enough of this," he said angrily. "I am ashamed that we've allowed such solemn deliberations to degenerate into petty and selfish squabbling. We have become a dog chasing its tail and I say it stops now."

He glared at his audience. "No more wasting time. There are four possible candidates for the crown." Glancing over at Maria, he said bluntly, "That does not include your daughter, my lady, for we'd have to be desperate indeed to anoint a two-year-old girl as our queen." He waited to see if she would protest. When she did not, he acknowledged her pragmatism with an approving nod, thankful that the Greeks were such a practical people.

"We can also dismiss Baldwin's cousin Bohemond, the Prince of Antioch, for he cannot rule both Antioch and Outremer and he is not about to abdicate in order to become our king. That leaves Baldwin, his sister Sybilla, and his other cousin Raymond, the Count of Tripoli.

"Sybilla has her supporters, many of you quite vocal. But the fact is that she is a fifteen-year-old girl with no experience whatsoever in the world beyond the convent walls at Bethany. She is an innocent and we cannot afford an innocent at this time in our history."

Humphrey paused again, as if daring anyone to object. "Unlike Bohemond and Sybilla, Count Raymond of Tripoli is a serious candidate. He is a grown man of thirty-four, one with experience in ruling, and he has proven his worth on the battlefield. But he has only recently been freed after being held prisoner in Aleppo for more than nine years. Men can be changed by such an ordeal. As most of you know, he was ransomed for the vast sum of eighty thousand bezants, and he had to provide hostages as pledges that he'd pay the balance due of sixty thousand bezants. I am not impugning his integrity, for I believe him to be a man of honor. Nonetheless, we must consider if we'd want our king to be so deeply in debt to our Saracen foes."

Humphrey again raked the chamber with challenging eyes, heartened that they were listening so attentively. "Count Raymond's greatest handicap is that he is a stranger to so many. Whilst I knew him ere he was captured by Nūr al-Dīn, many of the men here cannot say as much. I am guessing that few of you would be comfortable crowning a man about whom you know so little, and I think that uncertainty is enough to eliminate him."

He waited for that to sink in and then asked if anyone had wine, saying wryly that preaching was thirsty work. Balian rose and sent his wineskin flying through the air. Humphrey caught it deftly with one hand, then drank deeply before resuming.

"That brings us back to where we began—to King Amalric's son, Baldwin. There are only two reasons to balk at voting for the lad—that he *is* a lad, not yet of age. And then there is the specter of leprosy."

He drank again, as if the very mention of leprosy left a bad taste in his mouth. "Whilst we would rather Baldwin be older, he could be guided by wiser counsel until he reaches his majority. So, his age does not present insurmountable difficulties.

"What of leprosy, then? It is obvious to all that we cannot anoint a leper as our king. But will Baldwin become a leper? No one can answer that question. You've heard his doctor testify that he has no other symptoms of that accursed ailment. When each man was asked to express his opinions yesterday, I was struck by something that Balian d'Ibelin said. He asked if we could deny Baldwin his birthright merely on the basis of suspicion or fear."

As a younger son, Balian was not accustomed to being the center of attention and he flushed when all eyes turned in his direction, both pleased and startled by the constable's praise.

"If Baldwin were not a king's son, if he were the heir to a lordship like Jaffa or Sidon, he could not be denied his inheritance unless and until he was formally diagnosed as a leper." Before Humphrey could continue, he was finally interrupted, the Templar grand master rising to his feet and pointing out that once a lord was declared a leper, he had to become a leper knight, entering the Order of St. Lazarus.

"That is true," Humphrey agreed. "But he would not forfeit his fief, continuing to hold it for the rest of his life. Leprosy does not make a mockery of the laws of inheritance."

This time it was the turn of Jobert, the grand master of the Hospitallers, to speak out. Less confrontational than the fiery Odo de St. Amand, he framed his question politely, but nevertheless went to the heart of the matter. "It is true that once a lord joins the knights of St. Lazarus, he is not stripped of his fief. Yet he does have to arrange for it to be ruled by another. What would happen if we elect Baldwin as our king and he then develops leprosy?"

Humphrey had given that a great deal of thought, too. "A fair question," he admitted. "Let us assume the very worst, then, that Baldwin does carry the seeds of his own destruction, although that is by no means certain. He will not come of age for two more years. We would have that time to find a husband for his sister, Sybilla, one capable of ruling in Baldwin's stead if he becomes too incapacitated to fulfill his duties as king."

Walter de Brisebarre started to protest again, angrily aware that if Baldwin were crowned, it would be difficult to deny Miles the regency. But Baudouin cut him off. "Any man who weds Sybilla will do so now knowing that she could become queen if Baldwin's health fails. Not only would we have no trouble finding suitors for her, we'd have men begging for the privilege!"

And you'd be one of them, Humphrey thought. He genuinely liked Baudouin but did not see him as an ideal husband for Sybilla. He believed none of the Poulains were, for the kingdom would be better served by an alliance with a foreign prince. There was no need to discuss this yet, so he merely smiled, welcoming Baudouin as his ally in his quest to get Baldwin crowned.

That turned out to be easier than he'd hoped, for his speech carried the day, and when a vote was called for, Amalric's son was elected as Outremer's next king. The boy's backers did not have long to celebrate their victory, though, for a question posed by Joscius, the young Bishop of Acre, brought home to them how complicated life was about to get for them all. Joscius had made a sensible suggestion—that each man should swear upon holy relics that he would say nothing of what had transpired during the court session. His advice was quickly seconded by Humphrey, for while he knew word would eventually get out about the leprosy threat to the young king, he was in favor of doing whatever they could to keep it secret as long as possible. But it was then that Joscius brought them up short with his next query.

"What of Baldwin? Should he be told?"

The men had been so caught up in choosing a king that few of them had acknowledged there was more at stake than a crown—that a thirteen-year-old boy could be facing a horror beyond imagining. They instinctively shrank from that awareness, and it was William who answered, saying in a horrified voice, "Good God, no! You cannot tell him!"

To William's great relief, Joscius indicated he was in full agreement with that, and other men were nodding, too. William sat down on the closest bench, suddenly so exhausted that he was not sure his legs would support his weight. At least it was over now. And then Miles came forward to demand that he be appointed as regent for the underage king.

At once the solar was in turmoil again, with Miles's friends being outshouted by his more numerous enemies. Some of the men looked imploringly toward the constable, hoping he would be able to resolve this dilemma, too. But Humphrey kept silent, for as little as he wanted to see Miles in a position of such power, he could muster up no arguments against it, not after the patriarch had bestirred himself to reveal Amalric had told him, too, that he wanted Miles as regent.

This time it was Denys de Grenier who came to the rescue. Arguing that the regency ought to go to Baldwin's nearest male relative, he alarmed Miles and his supporters, who assumed he was referring to Count Raymond of Tripoli. But then he explained that he meant the English king, for Henry was Amalric's nephew, his father and Amalric being half brothers, therefore making him and Baldwin first cousins. Denys argued further that Henry had taken the cross and would therefore be coming to the Holy Land to fulfill his vow, yet in any event, he was owed the courtesy of the right of first refusal. And until he responded, Miles could be the acting regent. It was a clever compromise, offering Miles just enough to blunt his opposition to it and reassuring his adversaries that his position would not be an official one, sanctioned by the High Court. And with that, the longest and most tumultuous session in the history of Outremer's High Court finally came to an end.

Coronations were usually performed on Sundays in the Holy Land, but Baldwin was crowned the next day, a Monday, in a solemn ceremony in the Church of the Holy Sepulchre, becoming the sixth Latin king of Jerusalem at age thirteen. Most of his new subjects thought it was an auspicious beginning of his reign, for it was the seventy-fifth anniversary of the fall of the Holy City to the men of the First Crusade.

CHAPTER 4

September 1174
City of Acre, Outremer

Amalric and the King of Sicily had been planning a summer attack upon Saladin's power base in Egypt; their ambitious plans were sabotaged by Amalric's sudden death. Worse was to follow, for the Franks were warned that Saladin intended to move on Damascus, still under the control of Nūr al-Dīn's young heir. This news sent shivers of alarm across Outremer. In the past, they'd occasionally made temporary alliances with the Egyptian caliphs or the amirs of Damascus. But if Saladin could gain control of both Egypt and Syria, the Poulains would have no leverage, facing a united enemy for the first time since the birth of their kingdom. And so, once Baldwin was crowned, his barons and vassals hastened to muster men in response to the royal summons, with the urgent intent to block Saladin from marching on Damascus.

Balian had hastened south to his fief at Ibelin and summoned his ten knights. Before they could depart for the agreed-upon rendezvous at the great stronghold of Kerak, which guarded the Cairo–Damascus road, a terse message arrived from the constable: the campaign had been called off. Balian was troubled by this unexpected turn of events; why had this decision been made? After learning that Baldwin had left Jerusalem and was currently holding court at Acre, he set out along the coastal road and on a hot morning in September three days later, he and his men finally saw the soaring walls of Acre rising against the sky.

❧

"Is that Acre, my lord?"

Rolf sounded so breathless that Balian glanced back at the boy with a smile. Rolf had never ventured far from his village before Balian had taken him on as a squire a month ago, and he'd been very excited on their journey north, never having seen cities as large as Jaffa and Caesarea and Haifa, each with a population of more than four thousand. He'd never even been to a public bathhouse until Balian and his knights had gone to one in Caesarea and he'd been astonished by the sweating chamber heated with earthenware pipes from an outside furnace and by the hot and cold pools. He claimed to be fourteen, but his innocence made him seem younger to Balian, who could only marvel that they were now ruled by a king even younger than Rolf.

Balian's knights had been amused by Rolf's naïveté and spun stories for him about the lions in the north and the fearsome beasts called crocodiles, said to lurk in a river near Caesarea. As they approached Acre, they filled his ears with tales of the scandalous seaport, notorious for its brawling, its bawdy houses, and its endless opportunities for sinning. Rolf's eyes got even wider as he listened, and he was both eager and uneasy as Acre came into view, never imaging he'd get to see a city as wicked as Sodom or Gomorrah.

"It has a double harbor!" he cried, dazzled by what looked to be a floating forest of masts, flying the flags of lands he'd never see. Balian explained that Acre was the kingdom's chief port for both pilgrims and merchants. When the boy asked how many people dwelled within its massive stone walls, Balian paused to consider it.

"Archdeacon William once told me that Acre, Tyre, and Jerusalem each have a population of over thirty thousand."

Rolf gasped. He took his lord's most casual words as gospel, yet he wondered now if Balian was jesting with him, for he could not envision a city almost ten times the size of Jaffa or Caesarea. But by then, they were caught up in the throng of travelers seeking to pass through the Patriarch's Gate, the stone tower that was the southeast entrance into Acre.

Rolf gasped again as they rode in, for never had he seen such a wave of humanity, flowing into every crevice, every space as far as his eye could see—sailors, peddlers, Templar and Hospitaller knights, priests, pilgrims, beggars, drovers whipping their mules as they tried to force a path for their swaying carts, respectably clad matrons, other women who looked like walking sin, street urchins, merchants. Some were astride horses, most afoot, dodging stray dogs and the gutter running down the center of the street, elbowing their way toward the shops, taverns, and churches, all thriving on the sheer chaos of life in the kingdom's chief seaport.

Rolf found the noise level physically painful. Balian had told him Acre had nigh on forty churches, and the boy thought that all of them must be tolling their bells. A man shouted above the din that his master had opened a new keg of wine at his tavern on St. Anne Street. Sailors already half-drunk squabbled with one another, whistling at the sight of pretty girls. Rolf suddenly remembered the story their village priest had told them of the Tower of Babel in Scriptures, for Acre seemed like that to him. So many languages were assailing his ears—French, Greek, the Syriac and Arabic spoken by the native Christians, German, English, Armenian, Italian dialects, and tongues utterly foreign to him.

But then he gagged, his face contorting. "What is that stink?"

Balian and his knights laughed. "That is the perfumed air of Acre, lad. It takes getting used to, but you will. In truth, I think the townsfolk take a perverse pride in it, for I've heard them boasting that their city stench is ripe enough to sicken a pig."

To take the lad's mind off the onslaught of so many foul odors, Balian began to describe the sights likely to interest his squire, pointing out the banner of the Templars flying above their commandery in the southwest corner of the city. The Hospitallers' quarters and hospital were to the north, he said, as was the royal palace. The Genoese, Venetian, and now the Pisan merchants all had their own quarters, too.

"Down the Street of Chains is the customhouse," he continued, "where foreign and Saracen merchants go to have their goods inspected and a toll levied upon them." He smiled then, thinking of the shock of European newcomers to Outremer when they discovered that trade between the Franks and the Saracens continued even during war. Rolf was a Poulain, so he'd understand that their kingdom's survival often depended as much upon compromise and conciliation as it did upon the steel of their swords.

Balian was telling Rolf about the fortified sea tower known as the Tower of the Flies that protected the harbor's approach, when he heard his name called out, loudly enough to rise above the clamor of street traffic.

Turning toward the sound, Balian grinned at the sight of Jakelin de Mailly and guided his palfrey across the crowded street. Swinging from the saddle, Balian handed the reins to Rolf, instructing his knights to continue on to his brother's town house. Seeing Rolf's dismay at being left on his own, he said, "You need not fret, lad. They know where it is, on Provençal Street, not far from St. Mary's church. I'll not be needing any of you for the rest of the day, so you can amuse yourselves as you like. Just try not to get arrested by the city's viscount."

They laughed, delighted by the prospect of a free afternoon, and rode on, Rolf stealing an occasional glance back over his shoulder. Balian watched them go, then smiled at Jakelin. "I often bless Baudouin for buying a town house here, sparing us a stay in one of Acre's flea-ridden inns. It is not as if you could take us in, after all."

"True," Jakelin acknowledged, with a smile of his own. "Our grand master sets high standards when approving Temple guests. Luckily for you, Lord Baudouin is less particular."

Balian still found the sight of Jakelin in the white mantle and red cross of the Templars startling, though it had been two years since his friend had declared his wish to join the order. Balian had tried to talk him out of it, fearing this was another of Jakelin's spur-of-the-moment whims, one he'd soon come to regret. Despite Balian's admiration for the Templars, the best fighters in the kingdom, he did not understand what had motivated Jakelin. A Templar's life was not an easy one. They courted danger the way other men courted women, and had to swear oaths of obedience, poverty, and chastity—all of which would have presented an enormous challenge to Balian. Nor had Jakelin been able to explain satisfactorily to Balian why he'd made such a drastic decision. But he had to admit that Jakelin seemed content with his choice and he supposed that was what mattered, even if he did miss visiting the Acre bordels with Jakelin.

He and Jakelin de Mailly were such opposites that Baudouin had jokingly dubbed them Salt and Pepper. Balian was tall and lean, clean-shaven, with olive skin deeply tanned by the sun, and dark hair and eyes. Jakelin had blue eyes, hair so blond it looked white in the sun, a neatly trimmed Templar beard, a fair complexion that burned easily during the hot Outremer summers, and he was only of average height, but as powerfully built as a blacksmith. He was also as impulsive as Balian was deliberate and as idealistic as Balian was pragmatic. Yet their friendship had taken root at their first meeting four years ago when the young Frenchman had arrived in the Holy Land, eager to fulfill his crusader's vow and perhaps to make his fortune, being a younger son with limited prospects back in Lorraine.

"Let's get a drink so we can catch up," Balian said, looking around for the closest tavern. That did not take long, for Acre had taverns beyond counting. Glad to be out of the burning sun, they ducked under the sagging sign, peeling paint turning its half-moon into something unrecognizable, and found a table.

Balian knew that Templars were permitted to drink wine, but he thought it was not made easy for them; Jakelin had explained that it could not be drunk between dinner and Vespers, nor could it be drunk in a tavern or house that was less than a league from a Templar commandery. So, when a morose serving maid with tired eyes finally shuffled over to them, he ordered wine for himself and water for Jakelin, apologizing as she turned away. "We'd never find fruit juice or almond milk in a hellhole like this."

Jakelin merely smiled and shrugged, as if what he drank was a matter of indifference, and Balian supposed that was true; a man who craved the luxuries of life was not likely to have joined the Order of the Temple. Settling back on the bench, he wasted no time. "Do you know why the campaign was called off, Jake?"

"Of course. Our grand master confides in me daily, never making a move without my counsel." Jakelin leaned across the table then, lowering his voice. "I can hazard a guess, though. Master Odo is peacock proud and Miles de Plancy commanded him to join the army at Kerak. He did it in public, too, the fool."

Balian was both surprised and puzzled, for the Templars and Hospitallers were not subject to the king's authority, being independent orders answerable only to the Pope. "Miles ought to have known better than that. It is not as if he is a newcomer to the Holy Land."

"Men say that holding the regency has gone to his head. I hear he has been denying others access to the young king."

"At times I think there must be something in the Outremer water that scrambles men's wits. How else explain why they think we have the luxury of ignoring the Saracens whilst we feud with our own? I assume the king is at the palace?"

"Yes, but you'll not find him there. They are holding races this afternoon. If you hurry, you'll be in time to put down a few wagers ere they start. Although you'd do better to abstain, given your rotten luck in picking winners."

"That was only when I heeded your advice," Balian countered, using the past tense since gambling was forbidden to Templars. Before Jakelin could retort, another serving maid approached their table and set two chipped cups before them. This one was sultry, not sullen, with flashing black eyes and golden skin that proclaimed some Saracen blood, although she wore a small wooden cross at her throat. When she asked if there was anything else they wanted, she made that innocuous sentence sound like an invitation to engage in mortal sin, and it was an offer Balian found very tempting. He resisted her appeal, though, shaking his head with a smile.

"If you change your mind, my lord, you need only ask for Salma," she said with a provocative pout, and sauntered away.

Balian watched those swaying hips and sighed. No man with a few coins in his scrip would have trouble finding a bedmate in Acre, where bawdy houses sprang up like weeds, resourceful young women used taverns for hunting grounds, and whores who could do no better for themselves lurked in doorways after dark. But Salma's exotic good looks and spirited self-confidence had stirred the desire that never fully slept in a man of Balian's age, and he felt a real regret when she moved off to flirt with other customers.

"Jesu, Balian, call her back! You're all but drooling."

Balian blinked in surprise, for he'd been trying to spare Jakelin's feelings. "I did not think it was good manners to accept her offer whilst you looked on," he protested. "I would not boast of having enjoyed a five-course meal to a man who was starving."

Jakelin burst out laughing. "I am touched by your concern for my well-being. But do you truly think I am so weak that I'd violate my vows because you futtered a whore?"

Rather than matching Jakelin's bantering tone, Balian seized this opportunity to admit he was both awed and baffled by his friend's resolve. "I do not know how you do it, Jake," he confessed. "You've given up so much and you make it sound so . . . so easy."

"Easy?" Jakelin gave a hoot of disbelief. "Whoever said it was easy? It is a constant struggle, with my body always at war with my will. But that is as it ought to be. If it were too easy to honor these vows, then anyone could become a Templar. Even the likes of you," he added with a grin, rising to his feet and slapping Balian on the back. "I have to go, for we are patrolling this afternoon. I assume you'll be in Acre for a while? Stop by the commandery when you can find some free time."

With a wave, he headed for the door, pausing to thank Balian for "that costly swallow of pure spring water." Balian laughed, for even when they did drink wine together, he always paid, as Jakelin claimed the rules of their order forbade him to carry money. Skeptical at first, he'd been surprised to learn that this was indeed a serious sin, one that could cause a Templar's expulsion. Taking another sip of the wretched wine, he thought that he'd never understand how Jakelin could embrace such an austere life when there were other ways to serve God.

The voluptuous serving maid was glancing in his direction again and he beckoned her over. As he expected, the tavern keeper allowed her to rent a small room abovestairs, and they soon agreed upon a price acceptable to them both. He'd be back by Vespers, he assured her, for the sweet sins she offered would have to wait. First, he must seek out the young king and try to learn why they were letting Damascus fall into Saladin's clutches like a ripe plum.

Races and tournaments were held out on the plain east of Acre, not far from the mouth of the Belus River. Balian was not surprised to find a large crowd had gathered, for racing was a popular sport with the Poulains. Dismounting, he tethered his horse to a railing provided for that purpose and tossed a coin to a youngster to watch over the palfrey. Looking around for the stands set up for those of noble rank, he headed in that direction.

Agnes de Courtenay had been given the seat of honor under a canvas awning protecting them from the sun, and Balian had to admit that she looked quite elegant in a gown of scarlet silk. Beside her, Sybilla appeared suddenly grown-up in green brocade. Miles de Plancy was seated on Agnes's other side, carrying on an animated conversation with her, while his new wife, Stephanie de Milly, scolded her young son, Humphrey, for some minor misdeed. Balian thought the lad was the best-behaved child he'd ever met, but his mother set standards so high that not even an archangel could have met them.

A wide space separated Agnes's party from those gathered around the constable. Humphrey de Toron was looking bored; a man of action, he found any inactivity to be tedious. His wife was attracting the most stares, for she was highborn, beautiful, and had been involved in a great scandal. Philippa was the sister of the current Prince of Antioch, Bohemond, and she'd shocked their society by embarking upon a blatant affair with a Greek nobleman, Andronicus Comnenus, a kinsman of the Greek emperor. He was a man of undeniable charm, but one who seemed better suited for the lawless life of a pirate, as he soon proved. He and Philippa had lived openly together in Antioch until Andronicus paid a visit to Outremer. While there, he caused an even greater scandal by seducing a queen, Theodora, widow of Amalric's late brother, Baldwin, and eloping with her to Nūr al-Dīn's court in Damascus. Humiliated, her reputation in tatters, Philippa had agreed to marry the much older widower Humphrey de Toron, knowing he'd face down the scandal with the same fierce defiance he displayed upon the battlefield.

Seated with the de Torons was a woman who looked vaguely familiar to Balian; after a moment, he recognized the Lady Eschiva, the very rich and recently widowed Princess of Galilee. She had none of the alluring blond beauty that God had bestowed upon Agnes and Philippa. She did have a serene demeanor and wry humor that both Agnes and Philippa lacked, and Balian found her quite likable. Eschiva had four young sons and word had it that she was a devoted mother, very involved in her offspring's lives, so it was no surprise to see them beside her, jostling, squirming, and joking under her tolerant eye.

On the other side of Humphrey de Toron was the Templar grand master, glowering from time to time in Miles de Plancy's direction. As he glanced between these two groups, Balian realized that he was looking at a court breaking up into factions, so antagonistic that they could not even keep up public appearances and mingle on social occasions. His brother was back at Ramlah, but had Baudouin been here, Balian knew he'd be seated with the constable and the grand master. Had Denys de Grenier not returned to Sidon after Baldwin's coronation, Balian assumed his loyalty to his wife would have kept him at Agnes's side even though he was good friends with Humphrey and distrusted Miles. The more Balian regarded these warring camps, the more unsettled he became. How could a thirteen-year-old boy be expected to mend rifts as deep and dangerous as these?

And where was Baldwin? Balian had been stunned by the secret that William had revealed to the High Court. It was not just that a sickly king would put Outremer at great risk. He was horrified to think Baldwin might be afflicted with leprosy. He'd done his best to convince himself that the Almighty would not curse Baldwin or their kingdom like that. But when he noticed Baldwin's absence, he felt a sudden pang, his first thought that the boy must be ailing. He realized almost at once that if Baldwin were ill, Agnes would not have left his side. Unlike his brother and William and many others, Balian did not doubt that Agnes loved her son.

Deciding not to approach the stands now that choosing a seat had become a public declaration of loyalty to the regent or the constable, he went looking for William and soon spotted the archdeacon on the edge of the crowd. William was pleased to see him and quickly assuaged the last of his lingering concern about Baldwin. "The lad is around somewhere," William said nonchalantly. "You know him and horses. He wanted to see the racers up close."

Balian had noted another conspicuous absentee. "Where is Queen Maria?"

William's face shadowed. "Gone."

"Gone? Where?"

"She has taken her daughter and retreated to her dower fief at Nablus. Thankfully, Amalric provided generously for her in the event of his death, for that overweening, spiteful woman made it abundantly clear that Maria is not welcome at court now that Baldwin is king."

Balian was sorry to hear that, though not surprised. "Agnes wasted no time, did she?" Glancing back toward the stands, he said, "She looks downright regal—the queen without a crown. How much influence do you think she truly wields over Baldwin?"

"Unfortunately, the lad is quite taken with her. It is not his fault, though. Such young shoulders were not meant to bear such heavy burdens. All eyes are looking to him, and people he's known for years seem like strangers of a sudden. Already he is learning a king's hardest lesson—that everyone wants something from him. I doubt that his sister has ever had a thought she left unexpressed. Baldwin is not like her, keeps much to himself. But I know he must be lonely, missing his father's guidance, even feeling overwhelmed at times."

Balian had never known his own father, who'd died in the year of his birth; his mother had quickly remarried, giving birth to two daughters, and dying when he was just eight. But he'd always had security, for he'd always had his older brothers to stand between him and the unknown. How much more vulnerable Baldwin was, called upon to be a king ere he was even old enough to shave. "And at such times, Agnes is there for him."

William nodded glumly. "She is cunning, too, more so than I realized. Had she sought to smother him or coddle him, he'd have rebelled straightaway. Instead, she listens and laughs and does what women have always done well—makes him feel as if he is truly special. He is, of course, and he knows it. It must still be comforting to him that she thinks so, too."

They'd drawn away from the crowd so they could speak without fear of being overheard. But they still had a clear view of the stands and the split on such public display for all to see, including Salāh al-Dīn's spies. "I came to Acre to find out why we are not trying to stop Saladin from laying claim to Damascus," Balian said quietly. "I fear the answer can be found over there. Has it truly come to this, William? Our leaders would rather settle old grudges than defend the realm?"

William nodded again. "I fear so, Balian. Whilst Miles has always been obstinate and prideful, Amalric was quick to tell him if he overstepped. Now there is no one to rein Miles in. He and Odo de St. Amand are not even on speaking terms anymore. Miles has also alienated the grand master of the Hospitallers and Jobert is no firebrand like Odo. The latter must bear his share of the blame for the breach with Miles. Not Jobert, though. He is amenable to reason, yet Miles so offended him that he flatly refused to take part in the campaign."

"And Humphrey?"

"He was not about to lead an army against Saladin without the support of the Templars and Hospitallers, especially since he was not sure how many lords he could rely upon. He told me that he'd heard there were some who were loath to see Miles triumph, fearing that would firmly entrench his hold upon the regency." William saw Balian frown and felt a dart of sympathy for his young friend, for Baudouin was rumored to be one of those reluctant barons. He would never confide that to Balian, of course, and so he began to talk instead about a bitter altercation between Miles and Walter de Brisebarre, the disgruntled lord of Blanchegarde.

"Walter has never gotten over losing Beirut to Amalric and then losing Outrejourdain when his wife died and it passed to her sister, Stephanie. I think most men feel he got an unfair deal, so he had some support when he asked Miles to return Beirut to him or, failing that, to arrange a marriage for him with the next available heiress. Miles refused both requests. Whilst I am not often in agreement with the man, Miles was right about Beirut. It is part of the royal domain now and it is his responsibility as regent to protect Baldwin's interests. He erred, though, in not throwing Walter a bone. Had he promised an heiress, at least that would have salvaged Walter's pride. Instead, he mocked Walter and with others looking on. Coming from the man who now holds Outrejourdain, that was too much for Walter to accept. He made a fool of himself, raging and cursing and screaming out threats. One more drop of poison into an already toxic brew."

Balian could only shake his head in disgust. "This is madness, William. Amalric would have dragged himself from his deathbed to keep Saladin from taking over Damascus. How can so many be so blind? What of Baldwin? Is he aware that his is a house divided?"

"I've not talked to him about it, but he is a bright lad. I am sure he knows that Miles is hated. He also knows that his father wanted Miles as regent. He has a mind of his own, though, always has," William said with his first real smile of the day, one of almost paternal pride.

"Miles may forge ahead like a stampeding bull, yet he was shrewd enough to ingratiate himself with Baldwin's mother, and for now Agnes is on his side. I saw proof of that less than a fortnight ago when I overheard Miles and Agnes trying to convince Baldwin that he ought to replace Humphrey de Toron as constable. Whilst the lad heard them out, he was obviously not swayed by their arguments, and so Agnes made a personal appeal, saying that she did not trust Humphrey. Baldwin effectively silenced her then by saying calmly, 'Well, I do, Mother.' She had the sense to back off after that, but I do not doubt she and Miles are still plotting to get Humphrey dismissed, and God help the realm if that ever happens."

A sudden blare of trumpets signaled that the first race was about to begin. The riders and horses had entered the track and there was a loud roar of approval when the spectators recognized the youth on a chestnut stallion. "Baldwin is riding?" Balian swung toward William, but the older man was just as surprised. Looking toward the stands, Balian saw that Agnes had not expected this, either, for she half rose, then sank back in her seat. As the riders paraded past the crowd on their way to the start, Baldwin acknowledged the cheers with a jaunty wave, doffing his cap playfully when he caught sight of William and Balian. By then, though, Balian had eyes only for the young king's mount, for he knew horses. This one was smaller and lighter than the usual Frankish stallion, with a finely chiseled head, deep chest, graceful arching neck, and a tail carried high. "That is an Arabian! Where did Baldwin get him?"

William had the typical cleric's lack of interest in horses. "He was a gift from Agnes, I think. I take it an Arabian is something out of the ordinary?"

"You could say that," Balian said dryly, thinking he'd have pledged the surety of his soul to have one of those magnificent stallions. "No wonder Baldwin has fallen under his mother's spell! Clever lady. You can rest assured that he'll be well mounted in the race, for Arabians are cat-quick, agile, and highly intelligent, whilst not as hard to handle as our destriers."

"I pray you're right," William said, trying to fend off frightening visions of Baldwin being thrown and slammed into the dirt in a welter of flying legs and down-plunging hooves. And then he caught his breath, for the flag was dropped and the horses and riders were off in a cloud of dust.

Now that Baldwin was doing this mad thing, William wanted the boy to win and he felt a throb of disappointment to see that the chestnut was blocked as they thundered past the stands. But Baldwin bided his time and began to weave his way between horses as they hit midstretch, finding holes where William was sure there were none. He was fourth with a quarter mile to go and then, in the blink of an eye, it was over. Like a golden streak of light, the Arabian overtook the leaders and then he was in front, pulling away from the others with every stride. By the time he crossed the finish line in solitary splendor, the crowd was cheering wildly, even those who'd wagered against him, and Baldwin was laughing. William suddenly found himself on the verge of tears, almost as if he knew he'd just been given a precious gift, a memory of the young king at a perfect moment in his life, one that held no shadows or dread, only bright promise.

Balian declined William's invitation to dine with him that evening, explaining he'd already made plans, and if the archdeacon suspected those plans would require Balian to seek out a priest, confess, and do penance, he politely gave no indication of it. The next day, Balian arrived at the palace to discover that Baldwin was still flying high after his triumph at the races. He'd always liked Balian, who was young enough to joke with, and they passed an enjoyable quarter hour discussing Baldwin's new stallion, which he'd named Asad, Arabic for "lion," both because of his tawny coat and his lion-like courage. He'd just invited Balian to accompany him to the stables so he could see Asad's majesty for himself when Agnes reminded him that he'd agreed to hear petitions that morning. Baldwin was not happy about it, but he did not attempt to evade his royal responsibilities and promised Balian they'd visit the stables later. Balian was amused by what he did next, showing he did indeed have a mind of his own, as William claimed. Instead of staying in the stifling hall, he declared, he'd hold court up on the rooftop garden.

He was soon sitting on a marble bench, shielded from the sun by a striped canvas canopy, with Agnes on one side and Miles on the other, as men were ushered forward to kneel and state their grievances. Watching with William from another bench, Balian was impressed by the boy's conduct. He listened attentively and if the complaint involved a point of law, he said it would be taken under deliberation and told the petitioner to return in a few days for his decision. If he occasionally glanced wistfully toward the turquoise sea and the ships sailing for the horizon, Balian thought no one could blame him.

William shared with Balian now the nonmilitary news, revealing that the Archbishop of Tyre was very ill; he'd accompanied Maria to Nablus, only to be stricken with a stomach ailment. And word had reached Outremer of the latest chapter in the English king's ongoing struggles with his own queen and sons. The lads were still in rebellion, having fled to the French court, but Eleanor had not been so fortunate; she'd been captured by a royal patrol and taken off to confinement in one of Henry's castles. William disapproved strongly of the English queen, and he began quoting from Scriptures to bolster his argument that a wife who was not obedient to her husband violated the condition of nature and the divine will of the Almighty.

"William . . . forgive the interruption, but Humphrey de Toron has just arrived." Balian was intrigued by the expression on the constable's face. "Smug" was not a word he'd normally apply to Humphrey, yet he thought the other man definitely had the look of a cat that had gotten into the cream. He was intrigued, too, by the stranger at Humphrey's side. He appeared to be in his thirties, of medium height and slender build, with a swarthy complexion and straight, dark brown hair. His posture was very erect, his head held high, and his deportment that of one accustomed to privilege and power. "That man with Humphrey . . . do you know him, William?"

William shook his head, no less curious than Balian, and they rose to follow as Humphrey and his companion strode toward the king and seneschal. Miles had risen abruptly, the expression on his face indicating he did know the identity of this newcomer. The stranger made a deep obeisance to Baldwin, kissed Agnes's hand, and acknowledged Miles with courtesy that was utterly correct and yet somehow seemed like an afterthought. Balian and William got within hearing range just in time to hear Miles say, with a smile that was almost a sneer, "You are a long way from home, my lord count. I would think you'd be loath to leave Tripoli after such a prolonged stay in the prisons of Aleppo."

Balian and William exchanged quick glances. So, this was Raymond de St. Gilles, Count of Tripoli, the young king's cousin, the man Humphrey had described as a "serious candidate" for the crown of Jerusalem. They smiled at each other, the same thought in both their minds: that things were about to get interesting.

Miles was very good at provoking other men to bad behavior. His barb went astray now, for Raymond ignored it, as if the implied insult—like the man himself—was not worthy of notice. Addressing himself to Baldwin, he said, "My king, I would offer my condolences for the death of your father, may God assoil him. I held him in great esteem and I believe that he thought equally well of me. He ruled Tripoli for me during those years that I was held prisoner by Nūr al-Dīn and it was my wish that Tripoli pass to him if I died during my captivity."

"You are most welcome at my court, Cousin Raymond," Baldwin said politely but cautiously, for he did not give his trust easily to men he did not know. Agnes was regarding the count warily, and it was clear that her trust would have to be earned, too. Many in their audience were looking suddenly hopeful, however, seeing Raymond de St. Gilles as a formidable rival to the detested Miles.

"I am here," the count continued, "because I am your closest male kin, and so I am the one who ought to serve as regent until you reach your majority. I base my claim upon the laws of your kingdom, our shared blood, and the bond that existed between your lord father and me."

"You have not heard, then?" Miles queried with heavy sarcasm. "That position has been filled. I was named regent by the High Court, in accordance with the dying wishes of King Amalric."

"I heard. But the High Court chose you as acting regent, no more than that. I was not present to argue my own claim. Now I am."

"You are not the king's only male kin," Miles snapped. "The Prince of Antioch is his cousin, too!"

"But *you* are not," Raymond responded coolly. "I will right gladly debate the merits of my claim against those of my cousin in Antioch, if that be the wish of the king and High Court. You will be free, or course, my lord seneschal, to argue your own claim—such as it is."

Many of those listening were grinning widely, for they knew this was a new experience for the imperious Miles—discovering how deadly a weapon icy indifference could be. Miles was looking baneful. Baldwin seemed uncertain and, seeing that, Agnes leaned over to whisper in his ear.

Giving his mother a grateful smile, Baldwin raised his hand in time to keep Miles from launching a verbal assault upon the count. "None would deny you deserve to be considered for the regency, Cousin Raymond. But this is a decision for the High Court, and, alas, we do not have enough lords in Acre for a quorum. We will have to summon them to a session in Jerusalem."

If Raymond was vexed by the delaying tactic, it did not show in his face. "Of course," he said. "I welcome the opportunity to be heard before the High Court." He made another respectful obeisance to the young king before adding, "I trust that will be soon."

William was delighted by the Count of Tripoli's challenge to Miles. Once he and Balian had a chance to talk in private, he sounded more optimistic than he had since Amalric's death, telling Balian that all he'd heard of the count was to his credit. He'd fought bravely on the battlefield before his capture; he was well educated and was said to have learned Arabic during his captivity; he was of high birth and a Poulain, not an outsider like Miles. Balian agreed that Raymond de St. Gilles was an impressive figure and his credentials were impeccable. He wished, though, that the count was not as reserved or aloof; not once had he smiled. Balian hoped he was wrong, but he wondered if Raymond would be able to win over the members of the High Court, for despite the strength of his claim, he was a stranger to most of Outremer.

CHAPTER 5

Balian had intended to leave Acre by week's end, wanting to inform Baudouin about the arrival at court of the Count of Tripoli, news his brother would welcome. Miles had other ideas and ordered him and his knights to escort a supply caravan to the Hospitallers' frontier stronghold at Belvoir. Balian knew Baudouin would be highly indignant when he heard, for it was questionable whether this duty fell within the scope of those owed by vassals to the Crown. But Balian had learned at an early age to pick his battles and he decided it did not make sense to turn a vindictive man like Miles into a personal enemy by refusing.

The roads were always dangerous, for pilgrims and merchants were tempting targets for bandits, both Franks and Saracens. The journey to Belvoir had proved uneventful, though, and Balian was glad to accept the castellan's offer of hospitality. He and his men were made so welcome that by the time he departed, he was no longer vexed with Miles for disrupting his plans.

It was now October and they kept an eye on the cloud-mottled sky, although heavy rains did not usually begin until November. They were traveling the watershed road, a major route to Jerusalem, but when Balian saw a milestone indicating they were approaching Nablus, he decided to stop there and see how Queen Maria was faring in her new home.

The seigneury of Nablus was one of the larger lordships, covering almost six hundred square miles and ninety villages, a center for sugarcane production and the manufacture of soap, so Balian thought Maria ought to have enough income to live comfortably. The town was an ancient one, and although it had no bishop, the canons of the Church of the Holy Sepulchre had property there, as did the Hospitallers. Nablus was not a backwater like Balian's Ibelin, but he thought it must still be quite a change for a woman who'd grown up amid the cosmopolitan grandeur of Constantinople and passed her married life in Jerusalem and Acre.

A half mile from Nablus was Jacob's Well, where the Lord Christ had met the Samaritan woman, and Balian and his men stopped to say a prayer and leave a donation at the church. All around them was proof of the prosperity of Maria's dower fief: orchards, vineyards, and olive groves. But what struck Balian most forcefully was the absence of town walls. Villages like Ibelin had no walls, either, its inhabitants depending upon the small castle for protection. In light of its size, Nablus's lack of fortifications was notable. On past visits, Balian had never given it much thought. Now he frowned, not happy that Maria and her daughter should be living in a town so vulnerable to Saracen attack.

When traveling, Franks of Balian's rank rarely stayed at inns, preferring to accept the hospitality of local lords. So his men were surprised when he instructed them to take lodgings at one of the inns, but he did not want Maria to think him presumptuous, arriving unannounced and then expecting her to feed and house his men for the night. Saying he'd join them after paying his respects to the queen, he agreed to let Rolf accompany him, and they rode down the dusty main street toward the palace.

Leaving his squire to watch their horses, Balian was escorted into the great hall. He could see that Maria had attempted to make the palace seem more like a home; woven hangings that had once hung in her Jerusalem chambers now adorned the whitewashed walls of the hall, and bright embroidered rugs provided splashes of color. A cupboard held her silver plate, and the elaborately carved coffers were obviously part of her past life, too. He admired her for her determination to put up a brave front, but he felt anger stirring that Agnes was set upon making things as difficult as possible for a young widow in a country not her own.

He rarely acted on impulse; nor was he one for second-guessing his choices. His decision to seek Maria out was undeniably an impulsive one, though, and now he began to regret it, suddenly not sure what reception to expect from her. While she'd always been gracious to him at the royal court, his sudden appearance at Nablus might not be as welcome. He'd begun to pace as he awaited her entrance, gradually becoming aware that he was being watched. Turning, he found himself under scrutiny by a small child.

He knew at once that this was Maria's daughter, for she had her mother's dark coloring and the gown she wore was of the finest cotton, her hair braided with ribbons of silk. She tilted her head so far back that she seemed in danger of losing her balance, saying, "You're tall."

Balian squatted down so they were closer to eye level. "Are you sure? It may be that you are just short."

She gave that some serious thought before deciding, "No . . . you are tall." When Balian grinned, she grinned back at him, and that was how Maria found them. He rose quickly to his feet, but what he'd meant to say was forgotten, for there was no mistaking the expression on her face, one of pleasure.

"Lord Balian, how glad I am to see you," she exclaimed, and it was only then that he realized how much this woman's good opinion had come to mean to him.

The day's warmth had not yet begun to ebb away, and Maria invited Balian to join her in the courtyard, ordering wine and wafers and fruit for her guest. Once they'd been seated and served, she answered his polite query about the health of the Archbishop of Tyre with a sad shake of her head, saying his doctors had no hope for his recovery. Isabella held out her arms and Maria lifted the child onto her lap, unconcerned that the little girl's shoes were getting dirt on her dress. Balian liked her for that, watching with a smile as she peeled an orange for her daughter.

Once Isabella was sucking contentedly upon an orange segment, Maria glanced over at Balian, her dark eyes speculative. "We've not had many visitors since moving to Nablus. I suppose there are few who want to risk offending the new queen bee. I remember, though, that you've never been in thrall to the Lady Agnes, have you?"

He was surprised by her candor, until he realized that no longer being the king's wife had given her the liberty to speak her mind, probably for the first time in her life. "I am sorry that Agnes has been so spiteful," he said with such sincerity that she smiled. "I never understood why she bears you such a grudge. Once, when I was young and foolish—about seventeen or so—she was raving and ranting to Hugh about the 'Greek foreigner' that Amalric had married, making it sound as if he'd taken a female demon into his bed. I finally spoke up, pointing out that you had naught to do with the end of her marriage, being all of nine years old and residing in far-off Constantinople when the High Court decided she could not be queen."

Shaking his head at the memory, he said ruefully, "She did not speak to me again for fully two months after that."

Maria sipped her wine to hide another smile. As tempting as it was to trade stories with Balian about Agnes's bad behavior, she knew she could not match his light tone, for by now she'd learned to hate Amalric's former wife with a loathing that had seeped into every corner of her soul, all the more intense because she feared Agnes, too, knowing that she saw Isabella as a threat to her own children.

"So . . . ," she said, "what brings you to Nablus, Lord Balian? I assume you are on your way to somewhere else. Visitors to Nablus always are."

"True enough, my lady. I am returning to Ibelin from Belvoir."

"The Hospitaller castle? Why were you there?" she asked curiously, for Belvoir was one of the most strategic strongholds in the kingdom, yet one of the most isolated, too.

"It was not my idea," he admitted, explaining how Miles had conscripted him for caravan duty. "I have not been able to decide if this was a belated effort by Miles to curry favor with the Hospitallers, showing them that he was concerned for the safety of their supplies, or if he was simply amusing himself by moving my men and me hither and yon as if we were pieces on his chessboard. Whatever his reasons, I—" He stopped in midsentence then, for Maria was looking at him oddly.

"You do not know? You've not heard about Miles?"

"No . . . what happened? Is it too much to hope that he's been removed from the regency?"

"In a manner of speaking, yes. He was murdered last week in Acre."

Balian set his cup down so abruptly that wine splashed onto the sleeve of his tunic. "God's wrath! How did it happen? Was his killer caught?"

"He was attacked by two men as he returned to his house on Cyprus Street. It happened so quickly that he had no chance to defend himself. They stabbed him repeatedly, left him dying in a pool of his own blood. It occurred as dusk was falling and the few witnesses that could be found said only that the killers wore Saracen clothing, including the kaffiyeh headdress with the cloth pulled up to hide their faces."

"Were they Assassins?" Balian asked, for that renegade Shia sect had struck down men of power before; murder was their political weapon of choice. Their victims were usually their fellow Muslims, who considered them heretics, but the Count of Tripoli's father had been slain by Assassins when Raymond was only twelve.

"No one thinks the Assassins did it, for they want people to know of their killings and always claim credit for them. It is believed that these killers used the Saracen garb as a disguise, for one witness said he heard them speaking in French."

Balian leaned back in his seat, trying to take in the magnitude of her news. "Usually when a man is slain, it is asked who'd want to kill him. With Miles, the better question is who would not. He had more enemies than Rome has priests. There have been no arrests, then?"

He'd wondered how she'd heard so quickly, and had his answer when she said,

"William wrote that suspicion has fallen upon the de Brisebarre brothers, Walter and Guidon. But there is no evidence to connect them to the crime, and they cannot be charged without proof."

Balian doubted that Acre's viscount would greatly exert himself to find that proof. Miles's death was welcome to so many that few would be motivated to hunt for his killers. He could see how the de Brisebarres would be the obvious suspects, but he wondered if others had been involved, too. He remembered a Latin phrase William once taught him—*Cui bono?* To whose benefit? Here the question might better be who would *not* benefit. One who certainly did was Raymond of Tripoli, for he was now likely to be named as regent. Yet Balian could not envision him engaging in a sordid murder plot like this. It would seem wildly out of character, to say the least. Curious if others shared his view of the count, he said, "Miles's death ought to clear the road for Count Raymond to become regent. None suspect him of having a hand in this, do they?"

Maria looked startled. "Good Lord, no! From what Amalric told me about the count, he values his honor above all else. William believes he has a strong sense of duty and is convinced he is the one best able to protect Amalric's son. It is not as if Raymond needs the regency, either. Not only does he rule Tripoli, he is going to wed the greatest heiress in all Outremer."

"You are marrying Count Raymond, madame?"

Her eyes widened and then she smiled. "That is a deft compliment, Lord Balian, one I did not even see coming. But, no, I am not the woman Raymond wants to wed. His bride-to-be is far richer than me—the Lady Eschiva, the Princess of Galilee."

Balian gave a low, approving whistle. "That is a good match for them both. She is quite a marital prize and he is a wise choice for her, too, as she'll need a husband strong enough to protect her and her sons' inheritance." The marriage would probably stir up some jealousy, though, among the lords of Outremer. It was a sad truth, one he'd long ago recognized, that too many of the highborn Poulains begrudged the good fortune of their fellow barons.

Isabella asked suddenly for a sip of her mother's wine, but Maria was able to satisfy her with another orange section. Watching them, Balian found himself marveling that it had only been three months since Maria was widowed, since Baldwin became king, since the world as they knew it had been turned upside down. "I've wondered sometimes," he said, "if we are blessed or cursed in not knowing what lies ahead. If I were given the choice, I think I'd want to know."

"So would I," Maria said with a sigh, and he realized that she was speaking of her own future, not just the fate of their kingdom.

The High Court convened at Jerusalem in late October to consider Count Raymond's claim to the regency. Even though he was supported by Humphrey de Toron, the d'Ibelin brothers, Denys de Grenier, and most of the bishops, not all the men were keen to hand over the reins of government to a stranger, and the debate dragged on for two days. Then what so many had been dreading came to pass. Word reached the Holy City that Salāh al-Dīn had been welcomed into Damascus on October 28. The boy amir had been dwelling in Aleppo and Salāh al-Dīn declared that he was acting to protect the youngster's interests from evil advisers. But all knew what his occupation of Damascus really meant and the members of Outremer's High Court belatedly united against this new threat and recognized the Count of Tripoli as regent for their young king.

William was impressed by Count Raymond's conduct since being named as regent, for he did what Miles had refused to do—he consulted with the other lords, making no arbitrary decisions on his own. It was true he did not have an easy way with others, and William regretted that, knowing humor would have helped the count to establish a good relationship with Baldwin. But he saw no indication that there was any tension between the regent and the boy king, and he was content with that.

The summons from Raymond had come on a December evening not long after the city's church bells had pealed for Compline. The Poulain lords were unlike their counterparts in England and France, who lived out in the countryside in their fortified castles and manors. In Outremer, the noble class was utterly urban, and all who could afford it had residences in Jerusalem and Acre or Tyre, visiting their rural holdings only when necessary. While Raymond's new wife had a town house near Zion's Gate, he put in such long hours that he'd requested a chamber in the palace for working and it was there that William found him. He'd been poring over documents with his scribe, but he dismissed the man and invited William to take a seat at the table.

"I am trying to become better acquainted with those whom the king trusts," he said, with one of his rare smiles. "I understand that you are writing two histories, Master William, one of Outremer and one of the Muslim princes. If you would not take it amiss, I would be most interested in reading some of your work."

"I would be honored, my lord count."

"Excellent." Raymond glanced around the chamber, saw that he had no wine to offer his guest, and shrugged. "I have spoken with Baldwin's physician about the state of his health and I was encouraged by what I heard. Whilst I have never been one for secrets, preferring to speak out plainly about what is on my mind, I think it was a wise decision to keep any talk of leprosy from the lad. Regrettably, there will always be fools who gossip and delight in spreading rumors. But as long as the members of the High Court keep faith and keep quiet about what they've heard, these rumors will do no harm, for they'll be based only on speculation, curiosity, and conjecture. Nor is any of this sort of loose tavern talk likely to reach Baldwin's ears."

"I agree, my lord," William said, reassured that Raymond seemed to be genuinely concerned about the lad himself, seeing the thirteen-year-old boy in the king.

"Now . . . on to why I've asked you here tonight. As you know, the post of chancellor has been vacant since the death of the Bishop of Bethlehem. I want you to serve as the next chancellor of the realm."

William stared at him. "Nothing would give me greater pleasure!" After the bishop's death, he had briefly entertained the hope that he might be considered for the chancellorship, a post that always went to a cleric. But he'd soon realized that neither Agnes nor Miles would ever let that happen. Even after Miles's murder, he'd not expected to be chosen, knowing how much Agnes disliked him. Striving now for a more dignified response, William declared that he would serve the king and kingdom to the best of his abilities, all the while wondering how the count had managed to circumvent Agnes's objections.

Almost as if reading his mind, Raymond said, "You have eloquent friends on the High Court, Master William. The d'Ibelin brothers and Denys de Grenier all spoke out on your behalf. And, of course, you had an even more persuasive advocate in our king. Baldwin made it quite clear to me that he wanted you and only you as his chancellor."

William found himself momentarily at a loss for words. "Nothing means more to me than the young king's trust and I will do all in my power to prove worthy of it."

Despite the hour, William headed for Baldwin's private chambers, knowing the boy had always been one for delaying his bedtime as long as possible. As he expected, he found Baldwin still up. He was not as pleased to find Agnes in the bedchamber, too, playing chess with her son, but he greeted her with all the civility he could muster.

"I want to thank you for your faith in me," he told Baldwin. "I promise you will never regret it."

Baldwin had been quick to abandon the chess game, for he was losing. "I know you will sweep all the cobwebs out of the chancellery," he said with a smile. "I imagine, though, that now you'll be too busy to continue our lessons."

"That was the first thought to cross my mind," William assured him gravely. "Your lessons will indeed have to end—in June of God's year 1176, once you come of age."

Baldwin struggled to keep a straight face and failed. "It is very disappointing to discover you are not susceptible to bribes, William," he said, and as their eyes met, they both burst out laughing. Agnes did not share their amusement, for the archdeacon's easy intimacy with her son never failed to irritate her. She did feign a smile when Baldwin looked in her direction and she offered William her congratulations, though she did not even attempt to sound as if she meant it.

"Shall we finish the game tomorrow, Mother?" Baldwin turned back to his new chancellor, suddenly remembering he had something to show William. "Come take a look at this. I'll be shaving soon, for I've begun growing whiskers!"

William dutifully peered at the boy's chin, but in vain. Seeing that Baldwin was let down by his response, he explained that his eyesight was no longer as sharp as he aged.

"But they are there," Baldwin insisted. "Look again!" His blond hair was shoulder length, as that was the fashion for the men of Outremer, and he tossed his head now so William could see better. As he did, William froze.

"What . . . what is that on your throat?"

"Just a bruise. Come over to the light so you can see the whiskers."

William could not take his eyes from the boy's neck, now covered again by his hair. "Let me see that bruise, lad."

Baldwin scowled. "It is nothing, William. If you must know, I was thrown when practicing at the quintain yesterday. My lance did not hit the target dead-on and the sandbag swung around and unhorsed me." He hated to admit it, for learning to handle a lance with his left hand was proving to be more of a challenge than swordplay. He was determined to master the skill, though, and was vexed with William for making so much of a minor spill.

He did not know that behind him, his mother had come to her feet so quickly that her chair rocked. Her face whitening, she clapped a hand to her mouth as William pleaded, "Humor me, Baldwin. Let me see that bruise." The first time she'd heard the archdeacon call her son by his given name, she'd bristled, reminding

William that Baldwin was his king, only to have Baldwin say he'd asked William to ignore his title in private. Now she never even heard his words, for there was nothing in her world but sudden, surging fear.

Baldwin rolled his eyes. "I also bruised my shoulder in the fall. Shall I strip for you?" But he grudgingly swept his hair back, revealing his throat.

William stared at the bruise, shaped like a crescent, as purple as a plum, not yet starting to yellow. His throat had gone too dry for speech, and he had to struggle to say hoarsely, "That is quite a spectacular contusion, Baldwin. In a day or so, it will hold all the colors of a rainbow."

Baldwin's initial annoyance had faded and he was regarding William with genuine puzzlement. "I told you it was just a bruise," he said mildly.

"And you were right." William looked at Agnes over the boy's head and nodded almost imperceptibly, to assure her he was speaking the truth. She swayed slightly and sat down abruptly in her chair, her shoulders slumping.

Baldwin was still studying him and he made haste to distract the boy from his strange behavior, furious with himself for losing control like that. "You know," he said, "now that the light is better, I do see a few golden whiskers along your jawline."

"Yes!" Baldwin pumped his fist in the air. "I was beginning to think the both of you were blind," he teased, glancing back at his mother with a grin. "I told you they were there."

"Yes, you did, dearest," she acknowledged, and as her eyes met William's again, he could only marvel that for the first time in their contentious relationship, they'd actually shared a moment of wordless understanding, experiencing the same acute emotion—sheer terror followed by relief sweeter than any nectar could be. He doubted it would ever happen again. But he knew now that in this, he'd wronged her. He could no longer deny that she loved her son.

CHAPTER 6

William was not happy to find himself cornered by Eraclius, the new Archbishop of Caesarea. He had never liked Eraclius, considering the other cleric to be pompous, luxury loving, and far too worldly for one now a prince of the Church. It was especially aggravating to have to listen as Eraclius criticized Raymond de St. Gilles, for he thought there was some truth in the complaints.

William's feelings for the regent had become complicated, even conflicted, in recent months. He knew he owed his chancellorship to Raymond as much as to Baldwin, and was grateful for the count's backing. He still believed Raymond was performing his duties as regent admirably—when it concerned matters within the kingdom itself. Raymond continued to include the other barons in his decision-making, and he'd not attempted to deny access to the young king as Miles had done. He'd even shared royal patronage with the king's mother; Eraclius had been Agnes's choice for the archbishopric of Caesarea. And unlike Miles, he'd established good relations with Grand Master Jobert of the Knights Hospitaller and the far more prickly grand master of the Templars, Odo de St. Amand. But his diplomacy was giving William cause for concern.

Raymond had immediately abandoned their alliance with the Greek emperor Manuel, which had been the cornerstone of Amalric's foreign policy. Instead, he'd turned for aid to the Holy Roman Emperor Frederick Barbarossa, seeking his advice in finding a suitable husband for Sybilla and putting Outremer firmly in the German emperor's camp. William agreed that Frederick enjoyed great prestige throughout Christendom, having proven himself to be a strong ruler and a courageous warrior. But in reaching out to Frederick, Raymond was denying their kingdom any further assistance from Emperor Manuel or the Sicilian king, both of whom loathed the German emperor and had what he lacked—formidable naval fleets.

William knew that Baldwin was uneasy about Raymond's decision to cut the ties his father had labored so hard to forge. Not surprisingly, Maria was quite upset by this sudden diplomatic shift from Constantinople to Germany. But the Greeks had never been popular in Outremer and many of the barons of the High Court welcomed this rupture with Emperor Manuel. William could only hope that they'd have no reason to regret it.

William was even more troubled by Raymond's dealings with Saladin. After assuming power in Damascus, the sultan had turned his attention to Aleppo, ruled in the name of Nūr al-Dīn's young son, and Mosul, whose amir was the boy's uncle. In January, Raymond had mustered the kingdom's army and marched north into Syria, determined to keep Saladin from capturing Aleppo. The amirs in Aleppo and Mosul had hastily requested aid from the Franks. While newcomers to Outremer were always shocked to learn of these opportunistic alliances between enemies, the Poulains and Saracens were far more pragmatic, willing to embrace the axiom that "the enemy of my enemy is my friend." Raymond set a high price for his help: the release of a large number of Christian hostages, sixty of whom were his own, pledges for his payment of the balance of his ransom. The Aleppo amirs agreed, but the deal fell through and Raymond angrily withdrew from the field.

What happened next had given William some uneasy nights. Saladin had seized the Aleppine castle holding the Frankish hostages and he offered to release all of them without any ransom in return for a truce. Raymond had accepted, and once Saladin no longer needed to fear an attack by Raymond's army, he marched on Aleppo. Its amirs had been desperate enough to reach out to the outlaw sect, the Assassins, who sent men into Saladin's siege camp at Aleppo. But they failed to kill him, and in April, he fought a pitched battle with the combined forces of Aleppo and Mosul, winning a decisive victory. The defeated amirs had been compelled to accept his terms, and although Aleppo and Mosul retained some degree of independence, they'd been seriously weakened while Saladin's power and prestige had been greatly strengthened.

The Frankish army had disbanded then, after four months in the field, and William thought they had little to show for it. While he approved of forming pacts with Saracens, he believed it should only be done to encourage disunity and rivalries among them. Supporting the rebellious rulers of Aleppo and Mosul made sense; a truce with Saladin did not, for he'd profited far more from it than the Franks did.

William was still loath to hear the Archbishop of Caesarea give voice to his own misgivings, and he felt compelled by gratitude and loyalty to defend Raymond's decision, saying coolly, "You seem to have overlooked the fact that nigh on a hundred of our Christian brethren gained their freedom because of Count Raymond."

Eraclius's response was a sardonic smile. "And how convenient for the count that sixty of them were his own hostages, so now he need not worry about paying the rest of his ransom."

"I am sure the count will fulfill the terms of his agreement with the amir of Aleppo, for he is a man of honor," William said, thinking sheepishly that he was beginning to sound as pompous as Eraclius. He was relieved, then, when Balian joined them and provided him with an excuse to end this disagreeable conversation by declaring that the king and Count Raymond wished to see him.

As William hastened across the palace courtyard, Balian fell in step beside him. He'd been mildly irked by Eraclius's patronizing greeting, calling him "Young d'Ibelin" as if he were still a green stripling, not the twenty-five-year-old lord of his own fief. "That man can vex me merely by opening his mouth," he confided, and William smiled wryly.

"He vexes me just by breathing. Does the king truly want to see me or were you kindly throwing me a lifeline?" When Balian confirmed the summons was real, William quickened his pace and they parted upon reaching the great hall. There, Balian sauntered toward his brother and the d'Ibelins' newest family member, Amaury de Lusignan, who had recently wed Baudouin's eldest daughter, Esquiva. Baudouin had celebrated his own wedding less than a fortnight ago, marrying Elizabeth, the widow of the Lord of Caesarea, for he'd finally acknowledged that no baron of Outremer would be chosen as Sybilla's husband. Smiling as Balian approached, Baudouin slid over to make room in the window seat before resuming their discussion. Amaury had heard that Saladin was very skilled at a game called mall, and wanted to know more about it. It was not a sport of the Poulains, however. While Baudouin had heard of it, he did not know how it was played, although that did not keep him from hazarding some guesses.

Balian waited until Baudouin paused for breath and then said nonchalantly, "Mall is played on horseback, with two teams trying to score against each other by swinging long-handled mallets to drive a ball toward designated goal lines. It is a very fast game and quite dangerous even for expert riders, so it says much for Saladin's horsemanship if he excels at it."

He grinned at Baudouin's look of astonishment, for no one ever fully outgrew sibling rivalry, and younger brothers would always enjoy outshining their older ones. Baudouin demanded to know how he was so well-informed about mall, but

Balian had no intention of revealing his source—that the subject had once come up in a casual conversation with Queen Maria, whose father had played the game in Constantinople, where it was called *tzykanion*.

"Let's just hope that our young king does not become curious about mall," Balian said, "for if he learns that it is a challenging game even for the best of riders, nothing will keep him from trying it."

Baudouin grinned, too, for all of Baldwin's vassals were proud of his horsemanship, one of the most admired skills in their world. "He would, indeed! If not for that weak arm of his, he might even have learned to shoot a bow on horseback, the way the Saracen archers do."

Soon after that, Amaury produced a pair of dice and they began to play hazard. Balian excused himself after the second game, for a stir at the end of the hall heralded the entrance of the king, flanked by his chancellor and regent. They clearly had good news to share, for Baldwin and William were beaming and Raymond was almost smiling. Catching sight of Balian, Baldwin waved him over.

"It is my pleasure," he announced, "to introduce the new Archbishop of Tyre."

Balian made William a playful bow, then offered his heartfelt congratulations. He was delighted for his friend, knowing how much William had wanted the archbishopric and how much he'd feared Agnes would sabotage his hopes.

"As soon as he is elected," Baldwin said, "we will celebrate his consecration with a great feast." Adding, with a mischievous, sidelong glance toward William, "One that will strike envy into the Archbishop of Caesarea's heart."

William flushed, for he'd not realized that Baldwin had noticed his rivalry with Eraclius. Now that he was to be an archbishop, he would have to learn how to keep his face from being the mirror of his soul, he vowed, for that was a skill that had so far evaded him.

Baldwin had just invited Balian to accompany him on a visit to the stables, saying one of their best broodmares had foaled a colt, sired by his father's favorite destrier, Caesar. Grateful that he'd not been included, William was looking around to see if Raymond was still in the hall when Baldwin suddenly turned back and retraced his steps.

"I forgot to tell you," he said, "that I shall be inviting Maria to your feast." Smiling at the look of surprise on William's face, he lowered his voice. "I'll not deny that I like that lady not. But I know you'd be pleased to have her there, so consider this a gift, my lord archbishop." Shrugging off William's thanks, he said, "I've thought about it and I want Isabella to feel welcome at my court. I'll admit I never found her very interesting, yet her company is bound to have improved now that she's learned to talk," he joked, before saying revealingly, "I do not want my sister to grow up a stranger to me."

William felt a pang at that, for Baldwin had just confirmed his suspicions, that Sybilla *was* a stranger to him, for all that the same blood ran in their veins. Apparently, it was too late for affection to take root in a garden so long neglected. He was proud of Baldwin for being willing to include Isabella in his life, even knowing how greatly that would displease his mother. And if he could not resist smiling at that thought, William did not see that as such a sin, not for the man who'd just been elevated to the highest ranks of Holy Church, such an unlikely destiny for a merchant's son born in Jerusalem forty-five years ago.

William was sure that he'd never have a week as happy as this past week in June. Baldwin's fourteenth birthday had been celebrated in grand style, and William's heart had swelled with pride at the fine young man he was becoming. He'd even managed to keep his fears at bay, for every day that passed without Baldwin showing any symptoms of leprosy was a day that edged them farther away from the cliff's edge. William's consecration as Archbishop of Tyre in the sacred Church of the Holy Sepulchre, presided over by the patriarch himself, was a deeply emotional experience, for never had he felt so close to God, and the festivities that followed had given him memories to cherish for the rest of his life.

"My lord archbishop?"

William blinked, once more back in the present, back in his comfortable new quarters in the royal palace. His servant was standing before him, patiently holding out a cup of watered-down red wine. Accepting it with a smile, William carried it over to his writing desk; he was indulging himself for a few hours, putting aside his duties as chancellor and archbishop to work upon his history of the kingdom. He was about to dip his quill pen in his inkpot when the door banged open with a loud thud and Baldwin stormed into the chamber.

He was obviously furious, his fair skin scorched with hot color. But he seemed so distraught that William was alarmed. Anger alone could not explain his agitation, for Baldwin had never had a temper that would kindle at the slightest spark.

"You'll not believe what I was told, William!" In recent months, Baldwin's voice had begun to deepen, but it cracked now, making him sound more like the boy he still was.

Getting hastily to his feet, William signaled for his servants to leave, and as soon as they were gone, he urged Baldwin to sit down and take several deep breaths to calm himself before continuing.

Baldwin did not seem to hear. He'd begun to pace the chamber, too upset to keep still. "Arnulf's older brother has returned from his studies in Italy," he said, and William was so disquieted himself by now that it took him a moment to remember that Arnulf was one of Baldwin's former schoolmates.

"Arnulf brought him to the palace to meet me, and when I learned he'd been studying at the medical school in Salerno, I decided to talk with him. Salerno doctors are said to be the best in Christendom and I thought he might know a way to restore feeling to my arm." Baldwin gave William a quick, almost apologetic glance. "It is not that I've lost faith in my doctors. But sometimes it seems to me that they are not telling me all they know."

He'd not meant that as an accusation. William still flushed; they had indeed been keeping much from Baldwin. "Take this," he entreated, holding out his own wine cup with a hand no longer steady, for he already knew what was coming.

Baldwin accepted the cup and took a deep swallow of wine. "So, I told Arnulf that I wanted to speak with his brother—Eustace, his name is—in private, and once we were alone, I confided in him about my injury and how it has not gotten any better despite all the poultices and ointments. I was beginning to regret asking him, for he kept interrupting with questions. But when I explained that I could not feel anything in my arm or hand, not pain nor heat nor cold, he . . . he went whiter than chalk and looked at me as if . . ."

Baldwin did not want to relive that chilling moment and let his words trail off. Taking another gulp of wine, he braced himself to tell William the rest. "I demanded to know what he thought was wrong with me. He did not want to say, stammering and no longer meeting my eyes. I insisted, though, and finally he . . . he blurted out that a loss of sensation was a symptom of leprosy.

"Leprosy," Baldwin repeated incredulously. "Leprosy! I lost my temper and said he did not know what he was talking about, that I'd have been told if this were so." Surprised to find that he'd already finished the wine, he looked around, then set the cup on a coffer. "I do not want this man practicing medicine in my kingdom, William. He is either incompetent or a fraud, for who knows if he really did study in Salerno."

Baldwin began to pace again, welcoming the anger surging through his body, almost hot enough to melt that small, icy prickle of fear. But then he turned back toward William and saw the stricken look on his face.

"Oh, God . . . it is true? I have leprosy?"

"No, lad, no! We do not know that is so!"

"But it could be so? I could be a leper?" They stared at each other, and for a moment it seemed as if time itself had stopped. When William reached out, the boy jerked away and his hand just brushed Baldwin's sleeve. "How could you keep this from me?"

"We . . . we did not want to burden you with such fear, for it might never come to pass."

"'We,'" Baldwin echoed, his voice cracking again. "Who else knows? My mother? Count Raymond?"

William nodded miserably, for although he'd been sure they were acting for the best, he saw now that their silence had inflicted yet another wound, one almost as shattering to Baldwin as Eustace's shocking diagnosis. "And the High Court," he admitted. "Your father felt they had to know ere they elected you king."

"My father, too? You all knew? You all knew but me?"

William would be haunted by the memory of this moment until he drew his final breath. "Sit and let's talk," he pleaded. "I promise to answer all your questions, lad, will hold nothing back, I swear it."

Baldwin's mouth contorted. "Why should I believe anything you have to say?" Not waiting for William to respond, he whirled then and fled the chamber.

"Baldwin, wait!" William hastened after him, but he did not have the speed of youth and when he finally emerged, panting, from the stairwell into the courtyard, Baldwin was nowhere in sight.

It had not been a very hot day, but William had to keep blotting sweat from his brow with his sleeve. Slumping down upon a bench in the gardens, he gazed up at the sky. Dusk was still an hour or so away. If he could not find Baldwin by dark, he'd have to let others know the king was missing. He did not want to do that, for surely the last thing the boy needed was to be thrust into such a maelstrom of concern and curiosity. Yet he did not know where else to look.

Even though he'd not expected to find him there, he'd gone first to Baldwin's private chambers. He'd sent his servants to make discreet queries of Agnes's servants, casually asking if the king was with her. He'd tried Count Raymond next, again with no results. It had occurred to him then that Baldwin might want to pray; that would have been his own first impulse. But that frail hope soon died, for the chapel was empty. He'd already questioned the palace guards himself, receiving assurances that the young king had not gone out through any of the gates. Now he was utterly at a loss, not knowing where to search next.

Ignoring the curious glances of passersby, he rubbed his eyes wearily. The longer that Baldwin was missing, the more guilt ridden William became, devastated to realize that Baldwin had believed there was no one to turn to in his hour of greatest need. That he'd sought out neither his mother nor his chaplain told William that he felt betrayed both by his family and by God.

He glanced up again at the sky, watching as the sun began its slide toward the western hills. If only he had more time, he could send for Balian. He was young enough to remember what it was like to be fourteen; mayhap he'd have been able to discover Baldwin's hiding place. Thoughts of Balian reminded him of Baldwin's birthday, for Balian had suggested he give the lad an ornate saddle, and it had been an inspired idea; Baldwin could quite happily ride from dawn till dusk. . . . William sat up straight then, suddenly sure where the boy had gone.

The stable grooms looked relieved to see the archbishop, for they'd slowly begun to realize that something was wrong but did not know what to do about it. Yes, they confirmed eagerly, the king had appeared without warning several hours ago and had gone into the stall of his stallion, Asad.

"I offered to saddle Asad, my lord," the chief groom volunteered, "for I assumed the king meant to go for a ride. He said no, though. He often comes here to see Asad, and at first I thought nothing of it. Time passed and so I decided I ought to make sure he did not need anything. When I asked, he told me right sharply to go away, saying he was not to be disturbed. He . . . he did not sound like himself, my lord. . . ."

William picked up a lantern hanging from a hook, for while there were rushlights on the wall, they'd be quenched when the grooms departed for the night. "If the king does not want to be disturbed, he is to be obeyed," he said tersely, and then began to walk slowly toward the back of the stable. Asad had a stall even more spacious than Caesar's. It was deep in shadows, but William could still see that the stallion was not tethered. Peering over the door, he was able to discern the motionless figure sitting cross-legged in the straw, and he gasped to see Baldwin so close to the horse's hooves.

"Baldwin," he said quietly, "it is William." When the boy did not respond, keeping his head turned away, William had no choice and cautiously opened the door, watching the stallion nervously all the while. Asad snorted and he was sure the horse could sense his fear. Knowing that he'd already be dead if this were the fiery Caesar, William could only pray that Balian was right and an Arabian was not as temperamental as the Frankish destriers.

Edging cautiously around the Arabian, he sank down in the straw beside Baldwin. The boy still did not look at him, but he snapped, "No lantern!" William hastily extinguished it. The closest rushlight cast just enough illumination to give him a glimpse of Baldwin's swollen, reddened eyes, and William's own eyes burned with tears. The silence was smothering. He waited, though, for Baldwin, and eventually the boy said in a hard voice, a stranger's voice, "Have you come to make excuses, to argue that you were right to keep this from me?"

"No. I have come to beg your forgiveness. What we did, we did from love, but it was still wrong. We should have told you."

Baldwin did not reply, but William thought he heard a soft sigh, like a breath being expelled. Another silence fell, broken only by the nickering of nearby horses, the occasional thump of hooves hitting wood. Each time that happened, William twitched, looking uneasily at Asad, who looked back at him calmly, glowing dark eyes utterly inscrutable.

"He'll not hurt you, William," Baldwin finally said, "not unless you give him cause."

Even at such a moment, William was embarrassed that his fear was so obvious to the boy. But he was heartened that Baldwin had spoken at all, and held his breath, waiting. "Is it certain that . . . that I have leprosy?" Baldwin said at last, so softly that William barely heard him.

"Ah, no, Baldwin! It is a possibility, not a certainty, for your arm's numbness is a symptom, not a diagnosis. And the longer you go without displaying any other signs of leprosy, the less likely it is that you've been afflicted with it."

William knew most youngsters—and most men—would have snatched at that hope, using it as a shield against the terrifying threat of leprosy. He knew, too, that Baldwin would not. He was a clever lad, already showing flashes of a strategic sense that might one day have made him a brilliant battle commander. William was not surprised, therefore, by Baldwin's next question, for he would need to know exactly what he could be facing.

"If . . . it happened, William, would I have to become a knight of St. Lazarus?"

"I do not know, Baldwin. If you were a lord, yes. I am not sure if the rules would apply to a king, though."

The boy shifted in the straw, turning toward William for the first time. "I want you to tell me what the symptoms are," he said, managing to keep his voice almost steady.

William opened his mouth, shut it again. How could he tell the lad what horrors might lie ahead? In the past three years, he'd read everything he could find about leprosy, and the more he'd learned, the more appalled he'd been. The disease was usually slow moving, yet relentless. A leper could become dreadfully disfigured, horribly maimed, losing the use of his hands and feet. He could even go blind. William had sworn to Baldwin that there would be no more lies between them. But how could he plant such terrible fears in the boy's brain?

"I need to know, William. If I do not, how can I tell if a bruise is just a bruise?" Baldwin said, and William knew he was remembering that December night in his bedchamber six months ago, innocently assuring them that his minor mishap at the quintain was no cause for concern.

Realizing that Baldwin was not asking him to describe the dark path that lepers were doomed to follow, William slumped back against the wall, so great was his relief. "You want to know what the first symptoms would be? I can tell you that," he said, and proceeded to do so, explaining that leprosy first manifested itself by an inability to feel heat or cold and then pain, usually in a hand or foot, followed by skin lesions, flat, pale ones called *maculas* in Latin or small, raised ones called *papulas*. Other possible symptoms were the sudden appearance of large bruises that looked white or livid, and swelling in the armpits or groin.

Baldwin said nothing, but the intent expression on his face told William that he was committing the symptoms to memory. To William, it almost seemed like a ghastly perversion of the lessons he'd taught during their years as tutor and pupil, and he could feel his control starting to slip. He fought to keep it from happening, for he owed Baldwin better than that. If the lad could show such courage even after being confronted with the unthinkable, he must, too. It was then, though, that Baldwin asked the question he'd been most dreading.

"Why?" Little more than a whisper. "Why me?"

William had been asked that before, of course, in the years since he'd become an archdeacon. A cry that must surely have echoed down through the centuries, every time a parent buried a child, a wife bled to death in the birthing chamber, a husband was struck down on the field of battle, a man or woman was faced with a wasting disease, an unbearable loss. He'd told them what he'd been taught, the words he'd offered to Maria when her daughter died, that it was not for mortal man to understand the ways of the Almighty. He'd quoted from Scriptures, "'Now we see through a glass, darkly; but then face to face,'" often having to explain the meaning to the illiterate, that whilst on earth, their knowledge was imperfect, upon that glorious day when they were admitted into the kingdom of God, all would become clear. He found now that he could not say that to Baldwin, and so he gave the boy an answer of wrenching honesty.

"I . . . I do not know, Baldwin."

Baldwin regarded him searchingly. "I know what men say of lepers. That they are morally unclean. That leprosy is the disease of the damned, punishment for their sins." His voice wavered, but then he broke William's heart by mustering up a small smile. "If it is indeed leprosy, I have not had a chance to commit any sins great enough to deserve this, William."

William shut his eyes tightly for a moment, waiting until he was sure he could keep his own voice steady. "It is true that some call leprosy the disease of sinners. But the Church also calls it the holy disease. The faith of lepers is tested as Job's faith was, and if they endure their suffering with grace, they will be rewarded with eternal life. One who endures purgatory on earth is ensured divine salvation, and it has been argued that leprosy is not a curse, rather a sign of God's favor. It is said that our Lord Christ often appeared as a leper to show his compassion for them."

Baldwin considered this for a time. "Could the Almighty not have found an easier way to bestow His favor?"

That was too much for William. Reaching out, he put his arm around Baldwin's shoulders. The boy stiffened for a heartbeat, and then relaxed against him. He could see the tear tracks on Baldwin's cheek now, and if the light had been better, he thought he might even see traces of those golden whiskers that Baldwin ostentatiously shaved off once a week. Fourteen was a challenging age for any youngster, poised between the borders of childhood and manhood. How could the Almighty expect Baldwin to bear the burdens both of kingship and leprosy?

He supposed Baldwin's disappearance would have become known by now; men would be out searching for him. But if Baldwin needed this time away from the world, by God, he'd have it. "You must remember, lad," William said huskily, "that all this talk of lepers is just that, talk. We do not know what the Almighty intends for you. Promise me you will keep that ever in mind."

"I will," Baldwin promised, with a flickering smile. When Asad lowered his head and nuzzled the boy's bright hair, Baldwin stroked his velvety muzzle, crooning softly to the stallion even as a tear trickled from the corner of his eye.

William's muscles were stiffening and he thought he could hear his bones creaking as he moved, yet he would stay there all night if that was what Baldwin wanted. He was not surprised that the boy was beginning to sound drowsy, for what he'd been through this day would have exhausted one of God's own angels. Baldwin's head was resting now in the crook of William's shoulder, and the boy was quiet for so long that William thought he'd dozed off. But then Baldwin said, "Has there ever been a leper king, William?"

"I do not know, lad. Probably not," William admitted, for if hope was to be Baldwin's shield, honesty would be his from now on.

"If I were to become a leper, that would be God's will?"

"Yes, that is so, Baldwin."

"As it was God's will that I became Jerusalem's king."

William had seen Baldwin approach problems in the classroom in just the same way, a step at a time until logic dictated the answer. If the Almighty did afflict him with leprosy, he'd have been given a divine mandate to rule despite the disease, for why else would God have allowed him to be crowned? Theology, faith, and common sense—an argument that would be difficult to refute if it did come to that. God had indeed made Baldwin a leper and then a king. Seeing that the boy's lashes were now shadowing his cheeks, William drew him closer. He was so grateful that Baldwin had not asked outright if he believed leprosy was already festering in his body. William had done his best to give Baldwin hope, but he had none himself. Gently, he brushed Baldwin's hair back from his forehead. *Ah, Baldwin, what a king you would have made.*

CHAPTER 7

June 1175
Jerusalem, Outremer

The High Court had convened in the solar of David's Tower. Chairs were positioned at the front of the chamber for Baldwin; Count Raymond; William, who was acting in the ailing patriarch's stead; and the king's mother. Some of the men showed surprise or indignation when Agnes took her seat, for most of them had been away with Raymond during the army's four months in the field. But William had warned Balian that Agnes had begun to attend the High Court sessions, which Baldwin had presided over in Raymond's absence. Balian waited to see if any of the lords would object to her presence, hoping Baudouin would not be one of them.

No one spoke up, though, and after William had given the invocation, Raymond rose from his seat. "I have good news to share. We have heard from the Holy Roman Emperor and he has suggested that the Lady Sybilla wed Guillaume d'Ameramici, the eldest son and heir of one of his most powerful vassals, the Marquis of Montferrat."

There were exclamations at that, more curious than either approving or hostile. The lords of the High Court were familiar with the genealogies and geography of France; many of them had family roots there and they were known as Franks in the rest of Christendom. The German empire was more alien territory and few knew much about Frederick's vassals. Some of them wanted to ask the most basic of questions, but hesitated lest they appear ill informed.

Baudouin had no such concerns, for his self-confidence was always flowing at high tide. Standing up, he said cheerfully, "Mayhap you ought to begin, my lord count, by telling us where Montferrat is."

That evoked some relieved laughter from the men and smiles from Raymond, William, and even Agnes. Balian noticed that Baldwin alone did not respond, shifting restlessly in his seat and stretching out his legs, crossed at the ankles. He wore knee-high leather boots, not shoes, for he'd been spending even more time lately on horseback, taking Asad out into the hills around Jerusalem. Balian had accompanied him on one of these rides and joked afterward to Baldwin that he must have been trying to outrun the Devil, for Asad's blazing speed soon left the young king's companions in the dust. Baldwin had merely shrugged. Balian had observed other changes in Baldwin in the past fortnight. Usually outgoing and quick to jest, he'd seemed withdrawn, even aloof at times. Balian kept his eye upon the boy now, wondering if his reticence was due to a dislike of the proposed match for Sybilla or just the moodiness of youth. For all that men tended to look back upon their early years through a golden glow of nostalgia, Balian remembered that the road to manhood could be a bumpy one.

Raymond explained that Montferrat was located in northern Italy and had been ruled by the current marquis's family for over two hundred years. "Guillaume will be an excellent husband for Lady Sybilla. Not only is he a first cousin to the Emperor Frederick, he is also a first cousin to the French king, Louis Capet. Few can boast better bloodlines than that."

That impressed them, for the kingdom would gain considerable prestige throughout Christendom by a marriage that linked their Royal House to the dynasties of Germany and France. The murmurs that reached Balian's ears were approving ones. But it was then that Walter de Brisebarre rose to his feet. Even before he began to speak, most in the audience were grimacing or rolling their eyes, for Walter was becoming an embarrassment. Raymond had refused to restore the fief of Beirut to him, just as Miles had done, and in recent months, he'd become even more embittered. Since some believed he was behind Miles's murder, he was no longer the sympathetic figure he'd once been. The general opinion was that he ought to count himself fortunate that he'd not been accused of Miles's killing and content himself with that.

Walter seemed to realize that the audience was not on his side, for he assumed a stubborn, almost defiant stance, arms folded across his chest, chin jutting out. "It is all well and good that this Italian lord has royal kinsmen. But is that truly our main concern? Can he govern? Can he lead men into battle?"

The solar was suddenly quiet, for Walter had come dangerously close to giving voice to what he'd belligerently called their "main concern," and the other men were not comfortable discussing that in Baldwin's presence. Raymond was frowning, as was William, and Agnes was glaring at Walter with such fury that few would have trusted her with a weapon at that moment. But it was Baldwin who was the first to react. His head came up sharply, blue eyes glittering.

"If you are asking whether Guillaume of Montferrat could rule if I were to become too ill to rule myself, yes, he could." He sounded much older than fourteen at that moment and Balian drew a sharp, dismayed breath, suddenly understanding. *God help him, he knows!*

While Walter was not the most perceptive of men, even he realized he'd misspoken, managing to offend the king, the regent, the king's mother, the chancellor, and half the barons on the High Court in one fell swoop. He subsided, slumping down in his seat to brood in silence.

Raymond did not often show his emotions, for the first lesson prisoners learn is self-control. He was clearly angry now, though, regarding Walter with a cold stare that did not bode well for the Brisebarre family fortunes under his regency. "As King Baldwin says, Guillaume of Montferrat is a worthy choice. At twenty-seven, he has already won a reputation for his valor on the battlefield. He is well educated and is said to be generous and openhanded, as great lords are expected to be. The emperor assures me he is proud but not arrogant, brave but not rash, quick-tempered but not one to hold grudges. And he and Lady Sybilla are not related within the forbidden degree, so there would be no need to seek a papal dispensation for their marriage."

Baudouin leaned over to whisper in Balian's ear that it was clever of Raymond to mention Guillaume's "openhandedness," for no one wanted a king who was miserly and loath to share his patronage with his lords. Balian merely nodded, not wanting to consider Guillaume as a future king, for that would not happen unless Baldwin was either dead or severely disabled.

Humphrey spoke next, expressing his approval of Guillaume of Montferrat as a husband for the king's sister, and in his own gruff way, he banished any lingering unease over Walter's blunder by saying forthrightly that of course they needed to choose a husband for Sybilla who was capable of ruling. She was the king's heir, and whilst theirs was a kingdom blessed by God, it was also one in which men did not live as long as the softer, more pampered males of other Christian realms. Had not King Baldwin's own father and uncle both died when still in their thirties?

"We do not often reach our biblical threescore years and ten here," Humphrey declared, "but so be it. I am grateful to live out my days, however many I have, in the land of the Lord Christ's birth." That went down well with them all, for they prided themselves upon being born in the Holy Land, a privilege granted to very few of their Christian brethren.

When both the Templar and Hospitaller grand masters also voiced their approval, it was obvious that Raymond's choice would prevail and it was soon agreed upon that Count Raymond would send envoys to Montferrat and offer Sybilla's hand in marriage to Guillaume. But those who hoped the session would conclude then were to be disappointed. Raymond announced he had another matter to bring before the High Court.

"I think we ought to extend the truce with Saladin," he said. "My spies tell me that he would be amenable to that and we could benefit from not having to worry for a while about Saracen attacks on our border strongholds or our supply caravans."

It was obvious to Balian that Raymond had already discussed this with William and Baldwin. William looked unhappy and so did his royal pupil, for he'd taught Baldwin that truces should be made only to promote Saracen disunity. He'd convinced Balian of that, too, and he was disappointed when William kept silent, even though he understood William's dilemma, torn between his beliefs and his benefactor. Balian did not have the stature himself to exert much influence upon the High Court and he hoped someone would speak out against Raymond's plan.

Only the grand master of the Templars did, and because the Templars invariably argued for war, his words did not have the impact they might otherwise have had. Balian was sorry that Denys de Grenier was not present. He'd surely have objected to a decision that could only enhance Saladin's power. Balian's hopes rose when Humphrey got to his feet but waned as soon as the constable began to speak, for he favored the truce. Glancing around the solar, Balian saw that many of the men viewed this truce as no different from others they'd made in the past with the Saracens. Leaning over, Balian asked his brother in a low voice, "You are not troubled by this?" When Baudouin shrugged, Balian reluctantly made ready to reveal his own misgivings.

Before he could rise to his feet, Baldwin spoke first. "Is there not a danger, my lord count, that Saladin will use this truce to strike at his Muslim enemies—the amirs of Aleppo and Mosul and the Assassins?"

Raymond looked surprised. "That is indeed a risk, my liege. But that is always true when truces are made. It is a sad truth that in time of peace, men continue to prepare for war."

"I understand that. Is this not different, though? We have never faced a foe as powerful as Saladin. If he gets full control of Aleppo, the rest of northern Syria will fall to him, and we'll find ourselves encircled on all sides but the sea. Once that happens, what will keep Saladin from seeking our destruction? The Saracens think this land is theirs no less strongly than we do."

That was an admirable summing up of William's teachings about the precarious balance of power that had existed in Outremer since the Christians had stunned the Saracens by taking Jerusalem in God's year 1099. William did not look proud, though; he was staring down at his clasped hands, color rising in his cheeks.

"Outremer will always be perched upon the cliff's edge, my lord king. Your kingdom is like an island in a vast Saracen sea, which is why it is so important that we get aid from the rest of Christendom. We are not numerous enough to hold off that swelling tide, need a constant flow of men who've taken the cross, men eager to fight for the Holy Land. And we need a powerful ruler to offer us his protection, one whom Saladin sees as a threat, which is why I have reached out to the Emperor Frederick."

"Saladin sees the Greek emperor Manuel as a threat," Baldwin parried, "and Constantinople is far closer to Outremer than Germany."

"That is so. But Frederick is more trustworthy than Manuel, my liege. Like us, he follows the true faith of the Latin Church in Rome. Moreover, he has often spoken of taking the cross and he cares about the fate of the Holy Land. In Constantinople, they deny the authority of the Pope and that Greek Orthodox religion of theirs is often hostile to the Church of Rome. Nor are their ways our ways. I do not believe the Greeks can be relied upon," Raymond concluded, and Balian saw that he'd carried the day, for most of the men did not trust the Greeks, either.

Baldwin did not continue to protest, for he'd done his best to articulate the argument that his father would have made and William should have made, and it had not been enough to sway the opinion of the High Court. William was looking more miserable by the moment, and Balian was not very happy, either, with the outcome. It was true that the Greeks and Franks were not natural allies. But Manuel was the first Greek emperor who appeared to be genuinely well-disposed toward their kingdom, and he was surely in a better position to come to their aid if the need arose. While Balian did not doubt the German emperor's goodwill, Frederick seemed to think that a man could never have enough enemies, and he was currently embroiled in a war with the armies of the Pope, the Italian city-states known as the Lombard League, and the Sicilian king. What if he lost? Who would protect Outremer then?

Baudouin and Balian were crossing the citadel bailey after the High Court session when they heard Raymond call out to them.

"Humphrey and I are going to head the delegation to discuss terms with Saladin. I thought you might want to join us, Baudouin."

Baudouin blinked. "Have you forgotten that I am a newlywed husband? Besides, I do not speak any Arabic. I cannot even curse in that infernal language!"

"That would not be necessary," Raymond assured him. "Both Humphrey and I speak it, and of course we'll have dragomen to interpret when need be."

Baudouin continued to shake his head. "I may have my faults," he said with a grin, "but I'm not daft enough to think Saladin would be better company than my Elizabeth."

Balian's eyes had brightened. "I speak a little Arabic," he said eagerly.

Baudouin stared at him in surprise. "You do? Since when?"

"For a while," Balian said evasively. He'd not told Baudouin of his lessons in Arabic, knowing how his brother would have teased him, unable to comprehend why he'd want to expend so much time and effort when dragomen were always available to communicate with the Saracens or the Franks' Arabic-speaking tenants. Baudouin's good-natured mockery was forgotten when Raymond agreed to include Balian in the delegation and he thanked the regent with such enthusiasm that Raymond bestowed one of his infrequent smiles upon him.

Raymond left them, then, having noticed that his wife was waving to him from the doorway of the great hall. As soon as he was out of hearing, Baudouin looked at Balian with puzzled amusement. "I know you do not approve of this truce, Little Brother. So why are you so keen to witness it? Will that not make you an accomplice of sorts?"

"I think it would be obvious. Who'd not want to meet Saladin face-to-face?"

"Me, for one," Baudouin retorted. "Whilst I might feel different if he was coming here to us, I am not about to spend days in the saddle for that privilege." When he headed toward the stables, Balian started to follow, but then he saw William emerging from David's Tower.

William looked so downcast that Balian did not have the heart to bring up the truce. The sound of laughter gave him another topic of conversation and he nodded his head in the direction of Raymond and Eschiva. "The count seems like a different man altogether when his wife is around. We should all be so lucky in marriage—a great heiress who is loving in the bargain."

"Raymond and Eschiva do appear to be well suited to each other," William agreed. "I am sure she is grateful that he is such a devoted stepfather to her sons, too." He was not interested in discussing the regent's marital good fortune, though, needing to unburden himself.

"I tried my best to convince Raymond that he ought not to make this truce with Saladin, but to no avail." William hesitated and then made a mumbled confession that testified to the strength of his friendship with Balian. "I should have spoken up again in public."

Balian was sorry that William was so ashamed of his silence in the High Court session, and sought to cheer him by saying, "Well, you've convinced Baldwin, for certes. And once he reaches his majority, he'll be much more likely to follow in your footsteps than in Raymond's."

William did not appear to take any comfort from that, though, and Balian said softly, "He knows, doesn't he?"

William did not reply, for that was Baldwin's secret to reveal or not. He suspected that the boy had done so with his mother and Count Raymond, but he'd not asked Baldwin, nor would he.

Balian realized that this was a question he should not have asked and he murmured an abashed "sorry" before saying, "Why is Raymond so set upon making this truce with Saladin?"

"Raymond was well treated during his long years as a prisoner of the Saracens. He learned Arabic and seems to have formed some friendships with his gaolers. I worry that his experiences in Aleppo may have made him more trusting than he ought to be. Judging from what he has said to me, I think he truly believes that a lasting peace with Saladin is possible."

"I assume you told him that Islamic law forbids Muslims from making peace with infidels, that they can only offer truces of ten years' duration or less."

William nodded morosely. "I did. He smiled and made a rare jest, saying he'd be willing to settle for ten-year truces that were continuously renewed. I fear he is too quick to dismiss both the Saracen belief in jihad and the Christian belief in holy war."

"I think many Poulains would be willing to make an accommodation with the Saracens if they believed it would be honored," Balian confided.

"The Poulains might, but not the men newly come to the Holy Land, afire with zeal to slaughter infidels. They are always horrified when they find we have adopted some of the Saracen ways, consult their doctors, and are more concerned with protecting our hard-won gains than with claiming new lands we'd not be able to hold for long. Can you imagine their outrage if they arrived to discover that we'd made a lasting peace with men they see as the Devil's spawn?"

"True enough," Balian conceded. "Many of them are already convinced that Poulains are questionable Christians, not worthy of being the defenders of the Holy City."

"And then there are the Saracens who are just as convinced that it is their sacred duty to drive us into the sea."

"Not all of their rulers have acted in accordance with jihad," Balian pointed out. "Like us, they have often done what was expedient or in their self-interest. Do you think Saladin has fully embraced jihad?"

"I would give a great deal if I knew the answer to that question, Balian, for it might well determine our kingdom's fate."

CHAPTER 8

Balian had looked forward to seeing Damascus, one of the world's oldest cities, according to William. He was sorry, therefore, to learn that they'd be meeting Saladin at his camp, set up at Marj al-Sufar, a large plain to the south of Damascus. He soon forgot his disappointment, though, for he was very curious about the enemies who were at once familiar and foreign, and he was sure this would be a memorable experience.

His first surprise was the sultan himself. Because Saladin loomed so large in their lives, Balian had envisioned the man as a physically imposing figure, one who was serious, single-minded, and intimidating. But the real Saladin was not at all like Balian's mental image of him. He was of average height and slender build, with dark coloring and a neatly trimmed beard. Nor was he aloof or reserved. He was quick to smile, approachable and affable, such a gracious host that it was almost possible to forget Saracen-Frank encounters were usually on the battlefield. Not all of Balian's expectations were wrong; he sensed a sharp intelligence at work behind those inscrutable black eyes, and he already knew Saladin could be ruthless if need be, having proved that in the past. He'd just not foreseen the sultan's charm.

Once the formal greetings were over, the ceremonial gift giving came next; Raymond presented Saladin with three very fine gyrfalcons and the sultan reciprocated with several valuable camels and a tent for the young king. If it was anything like Saladin's pavilion, Balian thought Baldwin would be delighted. Their kings had spacious, comfortable tents for campaigns, yet none were as impressive as this one; it easily accommodated well over a hundred men and even had an inner private compartment, where Balian assumed the truce negotiations would be held. But first they would break bread together, and Balian knew it would be an elaborate, lavish meal, for the Saracens took the obligations of hospitality very seriously.

Raymond had made sure that Balian was introduced to the sultan, a kindness Balian much appreciated. He did not expect to be seated with them at the diplomatic dinner, though, nor was he. Cushions were brought in and distributed, for the meal would be served on low tables or on the ground, a Saracen custom that many of the Poulains had quickly adopted themselves. Tablecloths were spread over the tent carpeting, and once Raymond and Humphrey had taken the seats of honor beside Saladin, they all washed their hands in basins of rose-scented water and settled cross-legged on their cushions. Balian had brought several of his knights along, and they looked surprised when he chose to sit next to one of Raymond's men rather than with them, for Gerard de Ridefort had not endeared himself to any of the Poulains on the journey to Marj al-Sufar.

While Balian did not know much about Gerard de Ridefort's background, he was sure the man must come from an influential family in his native Flanders, for he'd managed to attach himself to Raymond's household soon after his arrival in the Holy Land. On their way to meet Saladin, he'd also learned that the Flemish knight was hot-tempered and had the typical newcomer's suspicion of the native-born Christians. Knowing that this bias went hand in hand with a visceral hatred of all Muslims, Balian had been keeping an eye upon Gerard, not trusting him to stay on his best behavior once he found himself surrounded by Saracens.

Gerard was already showing signs of agitation and Balian knew from experience with other new arrivals to Outremer that their unease often expressed itself in anger. As soon as they sat down, Gerard began to complain about the lack of chairs or tables, asking scornfully if they were to eat on the ground like dogs. Even though he understood that the Flemish knight was distraught to be dining with men he'd sworn to kill, Balian still had to strive for patience.

"Once you become accustomed to it," he told Gerard, "you'll find it is a very comfortable way to eat. Many Poulains prefer it to the European way of dining."

"Why does that not surprise me?" Gerard muttered, sounding so sour that Balian suppressed a sigh, thinking it was going to be a long meal. Gerard next found fault with the liquid being poured by servants into their cups. Taking a grudging sip, he grimaced, and for a moment, Balian feared he was going to spit it out. "God's blood, what is this swill?"

After tasting his own drink, Balian forced a smile. "It is pomegranate juice, Sir Gerard, not hemlock. The Saracens do not serve wine, for their holy book says it is forbidden."

"'Holy book'? Most men would think it blasphemous to use words like that for vile infidel beliefs," Gerard snapped. Balian kept silent, hoping that would discourage him from continuing with his harangue. Gerard was quick to find another grievance, though, staring incredulously at the communal serving trays being placed on the tablecloth within reach of their plates. "Christ Jesus, you mean we are to eat out of the same dishes?"

Balian knew dishes were often shared at meals in the English and French kingdoms and he did not think it was any different in Flanders. What appalled Gerard, of course, was that some of the fingers being dipped into these dishes were Saracen fingers. Balian had hoped that he'd be able to ease the Fleming's discomfiture so he could relax and enjoy the meal. He realized now that he'd set an impossible task for himself, that the best he could do was to keep Gerard from making a scene that would offend their Saracen hosts and put all the Franks in a bad light.

"This is the first course, honey dates stuffed with almonds. I am sure you'll like them if you give them a try." Balian leaned over and put a date on the other man's plate. The knight let it lie there untouched. He was gazing at it as if it were offal, not a delicacy sure to please the most demanding palates, and Balian began to entertain a fantasy in which he held Gerard down and force-fed him every date in Outremer.

The main dishes were served next, brought out all at once instead of in separate courses, as was the custom of the Franks and their European brethren. Balian was pleased to see one of his favorites, *sikbāj*, a lamb dish marinated in vinegar, then cooked in olive oil with eggplant, onions, almonds, figs, and raisins. After helping himself, he offered to put some on Gerard's plate, only to get a curt refusal. More from stubbornness now than any hope of shaming the Fleming into remembering his manners, Balian continued to talk about the food, pointing out a dish called *zirbāj*, a sweet-and-sour fish dish fried in flour. All to no avail.

"You really need to try one of them," Balian persisted. "In this part of the world, it would be very rude to refuse to eat after being invited to dine. I think you'd like this dish. It is called *būrān*, made with eggplant fried in sesame oil, with yogurt, garlic, and chicken."

Gerard balked again. "Yogurt? What is that?" When Balian said it was curdled milk, Gerard muttered something in Flemish that did not need a translation, for the look of disgust on his face said it all. "How do you know so much about their food?" he demanded. "Do you have a Saracen cook?"

He'd meant it as sarcasm and was dumbfounded when Balian said that he did. That was not strictly true; the Ibelin cooks were Syrian Christians, but familiar with the Saracen style of cooking, which most Poulains preferred to the blander

Frankish cuisine. "You have an infidel cook?" Gerard was staring at Balian in genuine horror. "Christ Almighty, man, do you not fear being poisoned?"

"No, I do not. And lower your voice. Men are looking in your direction." Balian said that to embarrass Gerard into better behavior, but as he glanced around, he saw to his dismay that it was true. He'd not worried about any of the Saracens overhearing Gerard's rants, for very few of them understood French. Body language was universal, though, and Gerard's belligerence had attracted the attention of two of the nearest Saracens.

The younger one seemed faintly amused; his companion did not. Balian guessed the latter to be in his mid-thirties, wearing an elegant tunic called a *kazaghand* that was lined with mail and proclaimed his high rank. He was scowling, his dark eyes cutting from the Flemish knight's flushed face to his plate, empty except for that ignored lone date, and there was a fierce intensity in his unwavering gaze that put Balian in mind of a hawk first sighting prey.

"You think the Count of Tripoli will be pleased if you start a brawl in Saladin's tent?"

Balian's urgent undertone finally got through to Gerard, and he lapsed into a sullen silence after that, although he still refused to take a single mouthful of this alien, enemy fare. Balian devoted himself then to the pleasures of the meal, and the rest of it passed without incident. But each time he looked toward the Saracen hawk, the man was staring at Gerard.

After *qatāyif*, a sugared crepe baked with almonds, was served, basins of water and towels were provided again. As Saladin disappeared into the interior of his pavilion with Raymond and Humphrey, servants cleared away the remains of the meal. Gerard was already on his feet. "I need some air," he declared, and began to shove his way toward the tent entrance. To Balian's alarm, the hawk rose, too, and followed Gerard, shadowed by the younger Saracen.

Balian trampled some toes, but he got there in time, all three men converging at the tent entrance. "*Assalaamu 'alaykum*," he said, rather breathlessly. The hawk merely stared at him, although his companion responded politely to Balian's greeting with "And peace be upon you."

"My lord." Balian paused, hoping his elementary Arabic would be up to the task. "My friend is a newcomer to the East and has not yet become accustomed to the heat. He has been suffering from belly pains for days and so he was unable to eat any of this delicious meal."

Now that they were face-to-face, Balian thought the Saracen lord looked even

more like a hawk than he'd first thought. If he was placated by the apology, he gave
no sign of it; his mouth was set so tightly that it was impossible to imagine it ever
softening into a smile and his eyes caught the torchlight, a reddish flame reflected
in their dark depths. It was then that the other man leaned over and murmured
something in his ear, too softly for Balian to hear. The hawk was still for a moment
and then spat some Arabic at Balian, glaring at both men before he spun around
and stalked away.

Balian was indifferent to the insult, caring only that he'd not gone in search of
Gerard.

The other man had remained at Balian's side. "Did you follow what he said?"

Balian was by no means fluent in Arabic and he needed it to be spoken slowly
for full comprehension. He'd heard only one word clearly—*khanzeer*—and since
he knew the pig was considered an unclean animal to Muslims, that was enough.
"I think he called someone a swine," he said lightly. "Naturally I assume he was
not referring to me."

Although the Saracen's face was not easy to read, Balian thought he could
detect the inkling of a smile at that. He was curious about the other man, who'd
obviously been minding the hawk as he'd been minding Gerard de Ridefort. The
thought of the Fleming roaming the Saracen camp unsupervised was a disturbing
one and he beckoned to one of his knights, delegating that duty to him. "Come find
me if he seems likely to get himself killed. But if you think he'll only be beaten to
a bloody pulp, there's no need to hurry." The knight grinned and headed out as
Balian turned back to the Saracen.

"I am Balian, Lord of Ibelin. Thank you."

The other man did not pretend to misunderstand. "The sultan would not have
been pleased had his nephew started a brawl with one of the Franks," he said.
Balian was amused that his words almost exactly echoed his own warning to Gerard, but then he blinked in belated comprehension.

"The hawk is the sultan's nephew?"

"'Hawk'?" the man echoed, and this time the smile in his voice was unmistakable. "That suits him well. He is indeed the sultan's kinsman. You may have heard
of him—Taqī al-Dīn?"

Balian's eyes widened as he realized how close they'd come to disaster, for a
confrontation between two hotheads like Gerard de Ridefort and Taqī al-Dīn was
sure to have ended in bloodshed. Saladin's nephew had a reputation for being utterly fearless on the battlefield and just as aggressive off it, while his hatred of the
Franks was as well-known as his reputation for violence.

"Who has not heard of Taqī al-Dīn?" he said, for Arabic lent itself easily to such rhetorical flourishes. He casually looked around then, wanting to make sure that the sultan's fiery nephew had not slipped out in search of that dolt de Ridefort. He was relieved to see Taqī al-Dīn talking with two men who wore the yellow-gold colors of Saladin's elite bodyguard. But he was surprised, too, that so many of the Saracens were glancing in his direction.

"We seem to be attracting more than our share of attention," he said, not sure what to make of it.

"They are probably curious about you, for few of the Franks bother to learn Arabic."

"True enough," Balian conceded, although he was unable to keep from riposting, "yet even fewer of the Saracens bother to learn French."

He saw that he'd judged his man correctly by the gleam in those dark eyes. "That is also true. Do you know why?"

That was another challenge Balian could not resist. "I can hazard a guess. They do not think it is worth their while. They are sure the Franks are like unwanted houseguests, troublesome but temporary."

The Saracen grinned. "Come," he said. "Let's continue this conversation sitting down." Finding two vacant cushions, he signaled to a servant and they were provided at once with ornate cups that were cold to the touch. Even before he tasted it, Balian recognized the drink, for it was sprinkled with pine nuts, one of the ingredients of a *jallab*, which was made with date syrup, rosewater, and snow brought down from the mountains by carts covered in straw. Knowing he was showing off a bit, he said, "Ah, a *jallab*. Nothing better on a hot day like this."

The other man grinned again. "As troublesome houseguests go, at least you are very well-mannered."

Balian thought that applied to this Saracen Good Samaritan, too, for he was speaking slowly and distinctly so that his Arabic was easier to understand. He noticed that they were still drawing occasional glances, and then it all came together for him and he could only marvel that it had taken him so long. He was not the object of interest; it was his companion. It would take a brave man to risk antagonizing Taqī al-Dīn. It would also take a highborn one, for status mattered as much in the Saracen world as it did in his own. Deciding that the best way to satisfy his curiosity was by a direct frontal assault, he said candidly, "Not too many men would have challenged an acclaimed warrior like Taqī al-Dīn as you did, all the more so since he is the sultan's nephew. Is he likely to hold a grudge against you?"

He got a nonchalant shrug and then the answer he wanted, if not one he was expecting. "Not for long. He's my nephew, too."

Balian could hardly believe his good luck; how better to learn more about the enigmatic Salāh al-Dīn than from a close kinsman? "I am honored," he said, wishing he could remember some of the more flowery Arabic expressions used for such occasions. "And you are . . . ?"

"Al-Malik al-'Ādil Saif al-Dīn Abū Bakr Ahmad bin Ayyūb."

Balian sat up straight in astonishment, for the best-known of Saladin's siblings was al-'Ādil, the younger brother who'd so capably put down a rebellion against the sultan in Egypt that he'd been entrusted to govern there in Saladin's absence. He suspected that he was being gently mocked, for the Saracens knew the Franks were baffled by their naming practices, and most would have been lost as soon as al-'Ādil reeled off that string of names.

But William had studied Arabic nomenclature in order to write his Saracen history for King Amalric, and Balian blessed the archbishop now for having shared some of that knowledge with him. He knew that there were five elements in a Muslim name: the *ism* or given name; the *kunya* bestowed after the birth of a son; the *nasab*, which identified a man's father; the *laqab*, which was a title of honor; and the *nisba*, which he thought was similar to a surname. William had told him that Salāh al-Dīn was the sultan's *laqab*, meaning "righteousness of the faith," and his *ism* was Yūsuf, the biblical Joseph. While he'd forgotten a lot of William's lesson, he did remember that the *ism* was not used outside the family, so it would have been an insult had he called al-'Ādil by his *ism*, Ahmad. Knowing he was about to surprise the other man and relishing the opportunity, he smiled, saying blandly, "Please correct me if I am in error, but I believe I would address you by your *laqab*, Saif al-Dīn?"

Al-'Ādil cocked an eyebrow and when their eyes met, they both laughed, in that moment discovering that humor could briefly surmount the formidable barriers of religion and language and culture.

Now that they were no longer verbally jousting with each other, they found that conversation flowed easily. Al-'Ādil was willing to answer a few questions about his elder brother, and if his answers did not offer insight into the workings of the sultan's mind, Balian still found them interesting. The Franks used the terms "Saracens" and "Turks" to refer to all Muslims, but Saladin's family were Kurds, a tribe that was often viewed with suspicion by the caliphates of Egypt and Baghdad, and Balian thought that made his rapid rise all the more impressive. Saladin had been born in the Islamic calendar year 532 AH, and after al-'Ādil said he was thirty-seven years of age, Balian was able to figure out that would have been God's year 1138. Balian learned that the sultan did indeed excel at mall, that he liked poetry and hawking, that al-'Ādil was, at thirty, seven years his junior, and would soon be back in Egypt, so his meeting this July day with Balian was pure happenstance.

They found that they shared some common interests—a love of horses and hunting and music—and were soon getting along so well that al-'Ādil invited Balian to go hunting upon his next journey from Egypt, adding dryly, "Assuming that we're not back to killing one another by then." In times of peace, such hunts were not unusual occurrences, and Balian hoped it would come to pass, for he'd been fascinated once al-'Ādil revealed he hunted with trained cheetahs. He was telling the Saracen lord about Baldwin's cherished Arabian, Asad, when Saladin and his guests emerged from the inner tent.

All three men appeared to be pleased, so Balian concluded they'd come to mutually agreeable terms. While Raymond was his usual impassive self, Humphrey and Saladin were joking, so obviously comfortable together that Balian remembered something William once said—that Humphrey had met Saladin during one of Amalric's Egyptian campaigns, adding disapprovingly that they'd become quite friendly. At the time, Balian had been skeptical, given the power that both men wielded. As he watched them now, he decided they genuinely seemed to like each other. Was it friendship, though? Could the sultan of Egypt and the constable of the Kingdom of Jerusalem ever truly be friends? Casting a curious glance toward al-'Ādil, he wondered if friendship was possible between them, either. He wanted to believe it was so, yet he doubted it.

Denys de Grenier had joined his wife in Jerusalem for her son's Christmas court. They'd celebrated their reunion in bed, but afterward, Agnes could not sleep. As her husband snored peacefully beside her, she tossed and turned, listening to a cold rain beating down upon the flat roof of the palace before she finally pulled back the woven hangings enclosing the bed. Snatching up her mantle as a robe, she walked over to the window, where she watched drops of water streaking the cloudy pane. She'd heard that glass was a rare commodity in the rest of Christendom, that even the wealthy often had their windows blocked with oiled linen. She could not envision life in those distant lands, places that were only names to her, places where lepers were shunned and banished to lazar houses, cut off from contact with their family, friends, and neighbors.

Agnes left the window and began to pace. These dark thoughts assailed her only at night. During the daylight hours, she could keep them at bay. She was a fool to let them lay claim to her imagination like this, for they were mere shadows, lacking substance or reality. Her son did not have leprosy. She refused to believe that God would let that happen.

Seeking other concerns to occupy her restless brain, she concentrated upon Sybilla. The girl seemed happy enough with the proposed marriage. Especially after she'd been told Guillaume of Montferrat was said to be a handsome man. Agnes recognized that she was being cynical, but she did not have great confidence in her daughter's judgment. She'd been able to forge a bond with Baldwin as soon as Amalric died, although they could never make up for all that lost time together, and she fervently hoped that Amalric's stay in Purgatory would exceed a thousand years for keeping her from her son. Yet Sybilla continued to elude her. It was not uncommon to pass an entire day in the girl's company and come away feeling as if she'd spent those hours with a flighty stranger, one who flitted from one subject to another like a bee in search of nectar. Agnes reminded herself that the girl was young, just sixteen, that it was only natural for her to be a butterfly after being secluded for so long in the cocoon of the Bethany convent. But she knew she'd not been so naïve at Sybilla's age, already a widow, already learning that life was neither easy nor fair.

Her ladies were sleeping on pallets not far from the hearth; on the nights that Denys came to her bed to claim his marital rights, he left his squires back in his own bedchamber. Agnes considered awakening one of the women to play a game of chess or merels, anything to occupy the hours until sleep finally came.

Denys was still snoring. Passing strange that she'd found the greatest contentment in her fourth marriage. She could not recall much about her first husband, dead for more than twenty-five years. All her memories of Amalric were poisoned. Whilst she supposed they must have had some happy times, she could not remember any. Hugh, too, was fading away. She could only call to mind now his plaintive brown eyes, always wanting more than she could give.

Denys, bless him, asked nothing from her. He seemed to enjoy sharing her bed when they were together, yet she doubted that he missed her much when they were apart. He'd not complained that she spent so much time at Baldwin's court, as other husbands would have done. She occasionally wondered if he was as satisfied with their marriage as she was, more from curiosity than genuine caring. She saw their marriage as a bargain and felt that she'd held up her end. It was true she'd not given him a child. He'd known she was thirty-five at the time of their wedding and not as likely to conceive again as a younger woman would, so she felt she'd not cheated him. And he'd been nigh on forty then, with no bastards or by-blows of his own, so he could be as much to blame as she for the barrenness of their marriage; she'd never believed that it was always the woman's fault.

She'd talked to Sybilla about marriage, trying to make the girl see that the best ones were like hers and Denys's, a partnership in which both knew what was expected of them. She suspected, though, that Sybilla wanted the passion, the romance of those foolish minstrel songs. Well, she'd learn. Agnes doubted that passion survived most women's first experience of the birthing chamber.

Crossing to a table, she poured half a cup of wine, thinking that might help her to sleep. When the knock sounded suddenly, she was so startled that she almost spilled it, wine splashing onto her hand. Drawing the mantle tightly about her, she moved toward the door. "Who is it?"

The name given was familiar to her, one of Baldwin's servants, and she fumbled with the latch, so hastily that she caught her fingers as she slid back the bar. She never even felt that pinch of pain, in that moment aware only of the sudden pounding of her heart and the odd expression on the man's face—bewilderment mixed with fear.

Yves, Baldwin's squire, was awaiting Agnes in the young king's antechamber. He quickly cast his eyes down, blushing at the sight of her long blond hair, covered haphazardly by a hastily pinned veil, for a woman's hair was normally not seen in public, revealed only to her husband in the privacy of their bedchamber. "Forgive me for disturbing you, my lady," he mumbled. "I did not know what else to do."

"You summoned me, then? Not Baldwin?" He nodded, still keeping his eyes on his shoes, and she struggled with the urge to start shaking answers out of him. "Tell me what happened," she said as calmly as she could manage.

"The king did not want to go to the public baths because of the rain, so he decided to have a bath here. After the servants brought up buckets of hot water, I helped him undress and then went over to test the bathwater. Whilst it was very hot, my lady, I thought I could cool it by adding the water from the washing basin. When I turned around, the king was about to step into the tub. I cried out a warning and he jerked back in time. His toes were bright red, though, and there was more redness where the water had splashed onto his ankle. I hurried over to see

how bad the burns were, but he . . . he pushed me away. I said there was an ointment in one of the coffers. He did not seem to hear me. He just kept staring down
at that bathing tub . . . and then he told me to get out.

"I did as he bade, of course. The other servants went off to find places to sleep.
I did not feel right doing that, so I waited. For a long time, there was only silence,
and then I heard a crash. More noise followed and I tried to talk to him through
the door, asking if I could be of any help. I just heard a loud thud again, as if something had been thrown at the door. . . ."

Yves was a few years older than Baldwin, but he looked younger now, scared
and confused. "My lady . . . did I do something to make him angry with me? I did
not mean to. . . ."

"You did nothing wrong. Go off to bed now." Looking relieved, he fled, and
only then did Agnes approach the door. She felt no surprise to find it barred from
the inside. "Baldwin? It is your mother. Will you let me in?" There was only silence.
"There is no one else with me and I promise not to stay if you do not want me to.
Open the door . . . please."

What if he continued to refuse? He could not be left alone in there. But the door
could not be forced. She would not do that to him. "Baldwin, I beg you," she whispered, words that she'd never have thought to utter in this life. After another interminable silence, she heard the bolt slide back and the door slowly swung inward.

She'd never dreaded anything so much as she now dreaded crossing that
threshold. Closing the door behind her, she leaned against it, surveying the wreckage of Baldwin's bedchamber. The floor was strewn with shattered cups and flagons, a dented metal mirror, clothing, boots, a hairbrush, books, whatever he'd found
within reach. Almost at her feet lay a wooden bucket, staved in when it struck the
door. In the midst of all this destruction stood her son. The room was cold and at
some time during his rampage, he'd put his braies and shirt on again, but he was
still barefoot and she instinctively started to warn him about cutting his feet on
the broken glass, catching herself just in time.

She had no words, so she walked over and put her arms around him. She feared
that he'd pull away, but he simply stood there, limp and unresponsive in her embrace. He'd had a growth spurt in recent months, and when she remembered how
proud he'd been that he could now look down upon her, she felt such a stab of pain
that it took her breath away. "Come, my dearest," she said, and guided him toward
the bed, finding a path through the debris littering the carpet.

He sank down upon the edge of the bed and she sat beside him, clasping his
hand in hers as she waited until he could talk about what had happened.

"The water was hot enough to boil," he said at last. "But I did not feel the heat, would have been badly burned if not for Yves."

She stared down at his foot, wincing at the reddened skin. She wanted to ransack the chamber until she found the ointment Yves had mentioned and slather it upon his burned toes. She forced herself to sit still, although she could not keep her fingers from tightening around his. William had tried to tell her about the symptoms of leprosy. She'd refused to listen, as if hearing it would make it so. How she regretted that now! "You . . . you are thinking of your hand," she said, "how you lost feeling in it, and you fear this is the same. But you may just have been tired, Baldwin, or distracted, your thoughts elsewhere. This could be an accident, nothing more. . . ."

For the first time, he looked her directly in the face, and then he slowly shook his head.

"Let me prove it to you." Before he could react, she reached down, took his foot in her hands, and then dug her nails into his heel. "Did you feel that, Baldwin?" When he nodded, she could have wept, so great was the intensity of her relief.

"You see? There is no numbness. You felt the pain! It is not . . . not what you fear."

He was shaking his head again. "William told me that the first symptom is an inability to feel heat or cold," he said tonelessly. "Next I will be unable to feel pain, and then the foot will become so numb that I'll feel nothing at all. It is already starting. The burns hurt, but not as much as they ought. . . ."

Agnes wanted to put her hand over his mouth, anything to stop those awful words, so precise, so impersonal, as if he were speaking of someone else's pain. She'd even have welcomed another flare-up of wild rage, anything but this eerie detachment, this utter lack of hope.

"I am not willing to accept this! Nor should you, Baldwin. There are other doctors in the world, physicians more knowledgeable than that Syrian doctor of yours. We will find one, that I promise you, my dearest, someone who knows what is really wrong with you and how to treat it. We can go to Constantinople. The Greeks are skilled in medicine. . . ."

She got no further, for he was actually smiling, the saddest smile she'd ever seen. "I know what is wrong with me, Mother," he said softly. "I am a leper."

His words seemed to echo in the air between them. Agnes's throat closed, cutting off speech, as she was overcome by sorrow so overwhelming, so savage, that she truly thought she might die of it. Baldwin suddenly tensed and then recoiled, stumbling to his feet and backing away from the bed.

"You must not be here with me like this! Leprosy is contagious. Even the breath of a leper is said to be dangerous. Forgive me, I never thought—"

"Baldwin, no!" She rose so swiftly that she'd reached him before he could retreat, grasping him by the shoulders so tightly that her fingers would leave indentations in his skin. "I do not know if you have leprosy," she said in a choked voice. "But you will always be my son, always! And . . . and if it comes to pass that you are right, we will face this disease together and fight it together."

When she later looked back upon that moment, she would realize that her bravado and her faith had been equally false, that in the depths of her soul she'd always known this day was coming, that her beautiful, brave son was doomed. When had God ever shown pity on her and her own?

She saw now that Baldwin had desperately needed to hear what she'd just said—that he was not alone in this, that he was still worthy of being loved. He did not resist when she embraced him again, clinging to her as tightly as he'd done as a small boy, awakened from night terrors and in need of a mother's comforting arms. Neither spoke. Reaching up to stroke his cheek, she found that his skin felt hot against her fingers. And when she realized that it also felt wet, she could no longer hold back her own tears.

CHAPTER 9

January 1176
Jerusalem, Outremer

O h, poor Baldwin!" Sybilla's eyes filled with tears. She clapped her hand to her mouth and sank back in her chair as if overcome, a response that seemed deliberately dramatic to her mother's critical eye. But Sybilla's shock was very real. While she'd been aware that there was some mystery surrounding her brother's health, she'd never imagined he could be suffering from the ailment of those accursed by God.

"Are the doctors sure it is leprosy? There is no hope?"

"His chaplain says there is always hope." Agnes's mouth turned down, as if the very taste of the platitude was a bitter one. "His doctors do not agree."

Sybilla's thoughts were stampeding. Fumbling to catch one, she asked, "What happens now? What will he do after he abdicates? Will he join the leper knights?"

"He is not going to abdicate," Agnes snapped, and Sybilla flushed. She thought it was a perfectly reasonable question and she ought not to be faulted for asking it. It was true that she'd always been envious of her brother, for he'd been allowed to grow up at court whilst she'd been banished to that secluded, boring convent. She'd been a bit resentful, too, that he had a crown in the offing and the most she could hope for was an arranged marriage in which she had no say. Her jealousy had sharpened since their father's death, for her mother's partiality toward Baldwin was obvious to anyone with eyes to see. She felt a prick of guilt now as she realized why.

"He will continue to rule?" she asked dubiously, not seeing how that could be possible.

"Of course he will."

Sybilla glanced from her mother to her stepfather. She'd only gotten to know Denys since her return to court. She thought he was one of the ugliest men she'd ever seen and was baffled that her glamorous mother would have chosen him as a husband. But he'd always been kind to her and he was very clever, so she hoped he'd be more forthcoming.

"I do not understand. Leprosy is very contagious; everyone knows that. How could Baldwin keep . . . mingling with others? Surely the danger would be great that he'd infect—"

"Would you prefer to return to the nunnery, Sybilla, where you'd feel safer?"

Sybilla gasped. "That is not fair, Mother!"

Denys agreed with her and intervened before Agnes could lash out again at the girl. "It is true that people greatly fear leprosy, Sybilla. But it may not be as contagious as they think. Lepers are banished from society in Christian kingdoms like France and England, in part because it is a relatively new malady in those lands. It has been known for centuries, though, in Outremer, Syria, Egypt, and the cities of the Greek empire, so we've had more time to observe it. We've long had lazar houses set up for those stricken with leprosy, and we've seen that not all of the brave souls caring for them contract the illness themselves. You mentioned the knights of St. Lazarus. Did you know that not all of their order are lepers? Whilst their grand master must be one, they welcome others, too. Yes, some of those men become infected. There are also knights and serjeants who live with their leprous brethren for years and never do so. That would not be possible if leprosy were as contagious as so many think."

"I . . . I did not know that." Sybilla had an easy face to read, and Agnes was convinced she saw the moment when the girl began to consider how she'd be affected by this stunning revelation. "Does Guillaume know of Baldwin's leprosy?"

Agnes had an easy face to read, too, and Denys quickly stepped into the breach. "He was told there was a possibility that Baldwin might have a serious illness, no more than that." While there had been no mention of leprosy, the letter he and Raymond and William had draughted had made it clear, nonetheless, that Sybilla—and the man she married—stood next in line to the throne should the concerns over Baldwin's health prove justified. Denys did not doubt that Guillaume had understood that Sybilla's marriage portion might include a crown. But he was not about to say that in his wife's hearing, for her heart and head were still at war; he'd noticed that she had yet to speak the word "leprosy" and her son's name in the same sentence.

Sybilla wanted to believe he was right, that the healthy could not catch this dread disease by the mere touch of a leper's hand or by breathing in the same air. But what if he was wrong? She felt anger beginning to stir, for she ought to have been warned as soon as they'd begun to suspect it. Baldwin . . . a leper. The very thought was enough to make her shiver. She'd always heard leprosy was punishment for mortal sins, especially carnal ones. Yet what sins could her brother have committed? How could he deserve a leper's living death? Whilst she'd envied his crown, she'd never have wished this upon him. Surely God knew that. Did her mother, though?

"I am so sorry," she said softly. "What . . . what should I say to him?"

"Say nothing unless he does." Agnes leaned over and grasped her daughter's hand. "Say nothing to anyone else, either, Sybilla. We've told the members of the High Court and we will make it known throughout the kingdom in time—but not until Baldwin is ready."

Sybilla was relieved to be spared a talk with her brother, for she had no words for a calamity so great. As soon as Agnes's grip eased, she got hastily to her feet. "I shall pray for him," she promised solemnly. "I shall pray every night without fail."

Once the door had closed behind her daughter, Agnes got to her feet, too. "More fool I," she said acidly, "for thinking she might be of some comfort to Baldwin. We'll be lucky if she does not faint if his shadow even crosses her path."

Denys watched as she paced, her skirts whipping around her ankles. When she seemed to have burned off some of that angry energy, he said, "You cannot blame the lass for being frightened, Agnes. It is only to be expected. As little as we like it, we must face the fact that once Baldwin's leprosy becomes known, many will shrink from him, fearful of getting too close."

She whirled around to glare at him. "I never will!"

"I know you will not, my dear," he said, "but not all will have your courage."

No one had ever looked at her as he did now—with admiration. Suddenly so weary that she actually ached, she sat down beside him again on the settle. "I am afraid of leprosy, too, Denys. But when I am with Baldwin, I can think only of his pain and his fear."

"I know," he said again, reaching over to squeeze her hand in a rare gesture of affection. He considered himself a student of human nature and could usually predict how a man would react in any given situation. In truth, he'd not have thought Agnes capable of this sort of selfless love, and he suspected that she'd been surprised, too, by the fierce intensity of her maternal instincts. A pity she had none to spare for Sybilla, but then Baldwin's need was far greater.

"We have to talk about this, Agnes. It is true that Baldwin is likely to find more acceptance in Outremer than he would in other Christian lands. But the fear will always be there, too. Baldwin's squire Yves sought me out a fortnight ago. Baldwin is an honorable lad and he felt he had to tell Yves about his leprosy. Yves was stunned, then terrified. He was ashamed to face Baldwin and afraid to face you, so he came to me, pleading to be released from royal service."

Agnes was outraged. "Baldwin is well rid of that craven wretch! Let him go, then. We'll find Baldwin a squire who knows the meaning of loyalty, one who—" She cut herself off in midsentence as she finally comprehended what Denys was trying to tell her. "Dear God," she whispered. "No one will want to serve as his squire, will they? But he must have a squire, Denys. He cannot remove his boots with one hand and later, as his condition worsens . . ." That was a door she could not bear to open; she dared not look too far ahead. "What can we do?"

"I was at a loss, too," he confessed, "until William came up with an inspired idea."

"Did he, now?"

"Agnes, I know you detest him. That is an indulgence you can no longer afford, though. Baldwin is going to need all the friends and allies he can find."

She could not argue. "I know," she said grudgingly. "So, what is this 'inspired' idea?"

"The knights of St. Lazarus—"

"No! The last thing Baldwin needs now is to look daily upon a leper, to see what horrors await him! How could you even consider that, Denys?"

"As it happens, I agree with you—and so does William. He has in mind a member of the order who is not a leper but who is accustomed to living amongst them and does not fear leprosy as others do. He spoke with their grand master, who suggested a serjeant named Anselm. He's a Poulain, grew up in Beth Gibelin, and has been with the order for more than twenty years. William and I met with him and he said it would be a great honor to serve Baldwin."

While Agnes was resentful that William had set this in motion without consulting her first, she also felt a vast sense of relief. "Baldwin and I will have to approve him, of course." She fell silent then for a time. "Denys . . . must we tell Baldwin that Yves was too spineless to stay in his service? Could we not concoct a family emergency to explain his departure?"

"No," he said simply. "We cannot lie to Baldwin, Agnes, even if it is to spare him pain."

"I suppose you're right," she conceded. "I am sure he knows by now anyway, for I doubt that Yves is any better than Sybilla at hiding his fear." When Denys slid his arm around her waist, she leaned against him. "This might be for the best.

Having lived with lepers, Anselm must surely be knowledgeable about the disease. Mayhap Baldwin will be able to ask him questions that he'd not ask us or his doctors. And Anselm can reassure him that he may well remain healthy for years ere the leprosy gets worse. That may be a comfort of sorts to him. . . ."

Denys said nothing, unwilling to tell her that this comfort was likely a false one. When she'd confided in him after Amalric's deathbed revelation, his instinct had been the same as William's—to learn as much as possible about the disease that would kill his stepson. Although he did not speak Greek as the archbishop did, his Arabic was far better and he'd been able to consult Saracen treatises. They made grim reading, for the inevitable outcome was death. What he'd found most troubling was that some physicians believed leprosy was more virulent when it was contracted in childhood. If that was true, Baldwin would not have as much time as Agnes hoped. But after reading at length about the devastation that leprosy inflicted upon the human body, Denys knew that a shorter life span would be a mercy for the lad.

Salāh al-Dīn's enemies in Mosul and Aleppo continued to plot against him, and in April the sultan struck back. Taking advantage of his truce with the Kingdom of Jerusalem, he led an army across Outrejourdain and defeated the lord of Mosul in a battle at Tell al-Sultān. He then turned his attention to Aleppo, whose amir hastily sought an alliance with Bohemond, the Prince of Antioch. While Bohemond was quite willing to ally with Aleppo against Salāh al-Dīn, he set a high price for his support. Nūr al-Dīn had refused to ransom Agnes's brother, Joscelin, or Prince Bohemond's stepfather, Reynald de Chatillon. But Nūr al-Dīn was dead and at Bohemond's insistence, the amir of Aleppo agreed to free both men upon payment of large ransoms.

Once free, Reynald de Chatillon had hastened to Antioch and joined his stepson, Prince Bohemond. Joscelin de Courtenay chose to return to the kingdom ruled by his nephew, and plans were made to give him an elaborate welcome into Jerusalem. Agnes was unwilling to wait and on the day of his expected arrival, she and her husband and their household knights rode out to meet him on the watershed road a few miles from the Holy City.

Denys glanced curiously at his wife. The May sun was hot and the earth so parched that it was hard not to inhale the dust being kicked up by their horses' hooves.

She'd pulled her veil across her nose and mouth, but her skin was flushed with the heat and she was squinting against the sun's unrelenting glare. Catching sight of a small copse of tamarisk trees not far from the road, he suggested they halt for a time in the shade and she agreed so quickly that he wondered why she'd not chosen to await Joscelin with Baldwin in the comfort of the royal palace.

Denys helped her to dismount and she gratefully accepted his wineskin, taking a long swallow. Answering his unspoken question then, she said, after glancing around to be sure none of their men were within earshot, "I wanted to be the one to tell Joscelin about . . . about Baldwin."

He nodded approvingly, for Joscelin was bound to be stunned by the news. He'd not known Agnes's brother well at all, remembering him vaguely as a man who was brave on the battlefield, proud of his sister's prestigious marriage to the king's brother, and given to boasting when in his cups, but amiable, withal. "What is Joscelin like? Were the two of you close?"

"I suppose. . . ." After a moment or so, she said pensively, "He was just a year younger, yet I always felt protective of him, mayhap because he was so impulsive or because he was so often in our mother's bad graces. I can see now that she feared he'd turn out like our father, who was well meaning but weak. I do not believe Joscelin was weak, though, just carefree. . . ."

Denys did not think that was a trait likely to survive twelve years in a Saracen prison. Well, they'd soon see what changes time and captivity had wrought, for swirling dust clouds gave warning of approaching riders.

Agnes was shocked by her first sight of her brother, for this stranger did not match the Joscelin of memory. He was forty now and carried those years heavily. His prison pallor stood out sharply among the sunbrowned faces of his escort. His fair hair was cut unfashionably short and he still had the beard grown in captivity. He was much thinner than she remembered and looked as if it had been a long time since he'd gotten a good night's sleep, slouching in the saddle as if his bones were too weary to keep his spine upright. She could see none of the jubilation she'd expected, just the taut wariness of a man who'd long lived with daily danger. But when he saw her, he smiled, and for just a heartbeat, she caught a glimpse of the boy he'd once been.

Dismounting hastily, he tossed the reins to the closest rider and a moment later she was in his arms. "I never thought you'd be able to raise the ransom. I despaired when I was told they were demanding fifty thousand dinars for my freedom. But you did it, Sister, you did it!"

"Well, I had help from Baldwin," she said somewhat breathlessly, for he was crushing her ribs. "What Denys and I could not raise, we got from the royal treasury."

"Bless the lad for that!" Releasing Agnes, Joscelin embraced his brother-in-law next. "Bless you both."

"You might want to spare a blessing for the Count of Tripoli, too," Denys said, for he thought it would not be amiss to let Joscelin know he also owed a debt to Count Raymond. "As regent, his consent was necessary ere Baldwin could act."

"But not for long," Agnes said, with enough satisfaction to confirm Denys's suspicions that she did not share his favorable opinion of the count. "Baldwin reaches his majority next month," she said, for Joscelin's benefit, not sure if he remembered his nephew's age. He'd embraced her so exuberantly that his brimmed cap had been knocked askew, and she was saddened by the sight of his receding hairline. Had she not known better, she might have guessed him to be approaching his fifth decade. Informants had assured her that he'd not been treated as brutally as their father. It was painfully obvious to her, though, that his imprisonment had left some deep scars. And now she had to inflict yet another wound.

"Joscelin, there is no easy way to say this. There is something you must know. Baldwin is a son any mother would be proud of, courageous and clever and handsome. But he is very ill. He has . . ." Saying it aloud proved too much for her, and she looked imploringly toward Denys.

"The lad has leprosy, Joscelin," he said so quietly that it took a moment for his words to sink in.

When they did, Joscelin's jaw dropped. "Jesus wept!" Stepping back, he ran his hand through his hair, a gesture she'd often seen him make as a boy when under stress. She'd half expected him to protest, for he'd always been stubbornly optimistic, all of their family's life lessons to the contrary. She saw no disbelief in his eyes now, just horror, and she thought sadly that hope must have breathed its last sometime during those long years of confinement.

Joscelin was struggling to come to terms with what he'd just been told. "I'd heard rumors that the lad was ailing, but this . . . Holy Mother of God! Does the High Court know? And what of Sybilla? Will she be recognized as his heir?"

Agnes opened her mouth, but she said nothing, leaving it to Denys to reassure Joscelin that Sybilla was indeed Baldwin's heir. "Thank Christ for that," Joscelin muttered, and then, "Jesu, but I need a drink!" Before Denys could offer his own wineskin, the other man swung back toward his waiting escort, grabbed a proffered wineskin, and drank until he choked.

Agnes turned away, retreating back into the shade cast by the tamarisk trees.

Denys followed, saying softly, "You cannot blame him, Agnes. He does not know Baldwin, for the boy was just two when Amalric disavowed your marriage, barely three when Joscelin was captured. The lad is a stranger to him, so you cannot expect him to love Baldwin as you do . . . not yet. It is only natural that he'd want to know how your family will be affected by Baldwin's affliction."

She knew he was right, as usual, and resented him for it, for always being so dispassionate and logical. She did not want to be rational about Baldwin's tragedy, wanted to scream and swear and curse God. Joscelin was coming back and so she squared her shoulders, raised her chin, and reminded herself that at least she could trust Joscelin to be loyal. In a world in which loyalty was more often illusion than reality, that was not to be scorned.

The High Court was meeting in the great hall of the palace at Acre. Windows had been opened in hopes of enticing the breezes wafting in from the sea, for the summer had been a scorching one so far. Escorted by her brother, Agnes took one of the chairs that had been set aside as seats of honor. She thought Joscelin looked better after a month of freedom; he was clean-shaven again and had begun to put on weight. His nerves still seemed taut, however; he flinched at sudden noises and he'd confided that he could not sleep through the night. He had quickly embraced the role of uncle, winning Sybilla over with flattery and joking with Baldwin, although Agnes had noticed that he was careful to keep his distance. But so did all in the know; it was as if Baldwin was marooned upon a small island and only she and William were willing to reach across the void and make physical contact.

Baldwin was already seated, legs stretched out in front of him. He was wearing knee-high leather boots, indicating he'd either been riding before the High Court session or planned to do so afterward; she knew he spent almost all of his free time in the saddle, astride his beloved Arab. He looked so handsome and healthy that she found herself on the verge of tears. No one would ever guess that his body was being claimed by that insidious disease. At Easter, another symptom had surfaced—small skin lesions on his back called *maculas*—but the only obvious indication of impairment was the defiantly red linen sling cradling his right arm.

After the invocation, Baldwin rose to his feet. Once he was sure that all eyes were upon him, he looked toward Count Raymond. "Now that I am fifteen, the age of majority in our kingdom, the regency is at an end. I would like to thank my cousin, the Count of Tripoli, for his excellent service and loyalty." He and the count exchanged smiles that were perfectly polite but without warmth, before Baldwin turned back to their audience.

"There are some matters we must discuss. The seneschalship has been vacant since the death of Miles de Planchy. I want my uncle, Joscelin de Courtenay, to take that post."

That came as no surprise, and even those who disliked Agnes could not object, for Joscelin was his closest male kin. Baldwin was not sure how they'd respond to his next action, though.

"I want to make it clear that I hold Count Raymond in high esteem and I shall continue to value his advice as a member of the High Court. But I do not intend to ratify the treaty that he made with Saladin last summer. I do not believe it is in the best interests of our kingdom to assist the sultan in eliminating his rivals. Our truce allowed him to defeat the amir of Mosul and now our spies say he means to move again on Aleppo. We cannot permit him to gain control of that city, for if all of northern Syria falls to him, we will be encircled by our enemies. So I have spoken with Constable Humphrey, Count Raymond, and the grand masters of the Templars and Hospitallers about a summer campaign against Saladin."

Baldwin could not help looking then toward Raymond. The older man's face was without expression, but his hands were gripping the arms of his chair so tightly that his knuckles had whitened. Baldwin wished that there had been another way, one that would have spared Raymond's pride, for he did not doubt his cousin's sincerity. Raymond truly believed that they'd be better off by making peace with the Saracens. But Baldwin was just as sure there could not be a lasting peace with a man who believed in jihad.

While there were murmurings among the men, they seemed neither surprised nor dismayed. Truces came and went; war was a constant. Baldwin waited to give any of Raymond's loyalists a chance to object, and when none did, he said, "Next is the matter of my sister's marriage. Guillaume of Montferrat has written that he will be sailing with the Genoese fleet and he expects to arrive in Outremer in late September."

Again there were murmurings, and some frowns, most of them directed at Count Raymond. He'd convinced them that a marital alliance with the Holy Roman Emperor would benefit their kingdom, but in May Frederick Barbarossa had suffered a serious setback. When he'd confronted the Lombard League at Legnano, his army had been routed and he himself had been wounded. After such an overwhelming defeat, the imperial alliance lost much of its luster and, to many, it no longer seemed like such a good idea to marry Sybilla to one of Frederick's vassals.

Baldwin and Raymond were aware of this growing discontent, but they were not expecting outright opposition. Yet that was what they now faced, as several of the lords rose to argue that the plight troth should not be honored. Raymond scowled, starting to get to his feet. Before he could respond, Baldwin raised a hand for silence.

"I know that some of you now have misgivings about this marriage. That is understandable. But we cannot disavow the plight troth between Guillaume and Sybilla. Frederick would see that as a grievous insult and it is never wise to insult emperors. Even if he is less likely after Legnano to offer us military assistance, he remains a very powerful man. The French king would also be greatly affronted, for Guillaume is his kinsman, too."

Baldwin was pleased to see that they were listening intently, even the most vocal critics of the marital alliance. "I intend to reach out to the emperor of the Greeks in Constantinople, hoping to repair the damage done to our relations by the overtures made to Frederick. Yes, Manuel was wroth that we'd allied ourselves with a man he loathes. I still think he will be amenable to restoring diplomatic and military ties. It was not my doing, after all."

From the corner of his eye, he saw Raymond stiffen. It was the truth, though, so however bitter the brew, his cousin would have to swallow it. "There is another reason for honoring the plight troth. If we were to reject Guillaume, we'd have to start another search for a suitable husband for my sister, which would take time."

Baldwin paused, his gaze flicking toward his mother and William, for he was about to depart from the script, having told no one what he now meant to say. "And time," he said steadily, "is a luxury we cannot afford. You all know that when I was chosen as king two years ago, it was suspected that I might have leprosy."

There were stirrings in the audience and then, utter silence. "You have been told, too," Baldwin said, "that I developed other symptoms of this malady in December. So, there is no longer any doubt. I am a leper and it is only right that all in the kingdom are made aware of it."

His mouth had gone dry and he had to swallow before continuing. "I do not know why God has afflicted me with this dread disease. Nor do I know why He wants me to rule as a leper king. But He does and so I do not plan to abdicate. I will not endanger the kingdom, though. Upon that, you have my word. I will serve as long as I am physically able, and when I can no longer perform my duties as king, I will turn the government over to my sister and her husband."

It was very quiet once he was done speaking, and then someone started to applaud. It was soon taken up by the others. Baldwin was not the only one to see the irony in this standing ovation, but they did not know what else to do. Glancing toward his mother, then, he saw that she'd bowed her head, her face hidden. William was wiping away tears, and others were, too. Baldwin felt a flicker of pride that his own eyes were dry.

CHAPTER 10

August 1176
Bekaa Valley, Syria

A s Baldwin walked through their camp, he was followed by smiles. It meant so much to him that he'd won the approval of these seasoned soldiers and knights. He knew he'd done nothing heroic during their July incursion into the Damascus plain. It had been a successful raid, though; they'd advanced as far as the village of Dārayyā, just four miles from Damascus itself. There'd been little blood spilled, for the villagers and farmers had fled, taking what belongings and livestock they could, as word spread of Baldwin's army's approach. His men had torched the crops in the fields, returning to Sidon laden with plunder, and Baldwin supposed that was enough for them. Soldiers were always grateful for the opportunity to enrich themselves at the enemy's expense.

This second campaign was more ambitious. Upon learning that Saladin had departed for the north to assault Masyāf, the stronghold of the feared Assassins, the Franks took advantage of his absence to raid again into the sultan's lands. Baldwin led his men into the Bekaa Valley while Count Raymond attacked from the north. Their raiding parties spread devastation far and wide, although once again the villages had been abandoned by their inhabitants, who'd driven their cattle into the marshlands, then taken refuge in the hills. When the two armies joined forces, morale was high and the summer sky was stained with the smoke of burning fields and houses.

Baldwin continued to acknowledge the greetings and grins, thinking that if he'd had no chance for personal bravery, at least he'd not embarrassed himself on this, his first campaign. He'd yet to bloody his sword, though, and that troubled him. He knew this was how war was conducted by both sides. He'd been told that pitched battles in Christendom were rare, for few commanders wanted to risk all on one throw of the dice. Even in Outremer, where enmities were more intense because the Franks and Saracens were convinced they were fighting infidels, battles were not that common. Sieges and the lightning raids called *chevauchées* were the staples of warfare. But he could not imagine minstrels singing about stealing sheep or burning barns.

Baldwin would have liked to discuss his disappointment with someone more experienced than he in warfare, but who? He respected Count Raymond. He'd never warmed to the man, though, not finding him very approachable. While Humphrey de Toron was a fine soldier, one whom Baldwin admired greatly, his gruff nature did not inspire confidences. His uncle, Joscelin, was still a stranger. Baldwin had been willing to appoint him to high office and to give him a wealthy heiress, Agneta de Milly, but he did not feel comfortable confiding in Joscelin. His new squire, Anselm, had done his share of fighting before he'd joined the leper knights, yet their great disparity in rank kept Baldwin from choosing him as a confidant.

The day was waning and Baldwin had started back toward his tent when a familiar face caught his eye. He at once detoured in Balian d'Ibelin's direction.

Balian rose to his feet quickly, saying, "My liege," then sat back down on the ground after Baldwin joined him. By now Baldwin had gotten accustomed to the way others took such care to keep at a safe distance; what other choice did he have? It was isolating, though, as if he were alone on a desert oasis, able to watch as caravans passed by, unable to reach out to them. He was grateful, therefore, for the few who were able to hide their unease in his presence, and as Balian was one of them, that was another reason to seek out his company.

Baudouin had not accompanied the army, for his wife was about to give birth, and his hopes of a male heir had outweighed the opportunity for booty in the Bekaa Valley raid. Balian joked about his brother's absence now, revealing that Baudouin had promised to name a son after the sainted martyr Thomas of Canterbury. "From what I've heard of the slain archbishop, his besetting sin was pride, so mayhap the bribe will work and Baudouin will finally get a lad."

When Balian's squire approached with tin cups for his lord and his king, pouring from a large goatskin, he kept so far from Baldwin that he splashed half of the wine into the dirt. Balian frowned. Yet reprimanding Rolf for his blunder would discomfit Baldwin all the more.

Baldwin was learning to overlook such mishaps and ignored the fact that some of the spilled wine had splattered onto his boots. He was about to steer the conversation in the direction he wanted it to go when they were joined by Balian's friend, the Templar knight Jakelin de Mailly. Baldwin hesitated, then decided to include Jakelin in the conversation.

"I would ask you both a question about war. I understand that raids are done to deplete the enemy's resources, to weaken his resolve, to demonstrate to his people that he cannot protect them, and to reward the men who take part in these raids. But I found little satisfaction in harrying peasants and terrifying women and children. Am I foolish for feeling this way?"

Balian and Jakelin exchanged glances. Their first instinct was to respond with humor. The boy's question could not be shrugged off so easily, though. Such unsparing honesty deserved honesty in return.

Balian shook his head slowly. "Not foolish at all, my liege. We are taught that a knight's duty is to safeguard the weak and defenseless. That is the ideal, but the reality is that the weak and defenseless are always the first to die in war, whether we will it or not. Yet I doubt that many men, be they Franks or Saracens, take true pleasure in killing those who cannot fight back. And those who do are likely to pay for that pleasure in the hottest pits of Hell."

Baldwin was relieved that they did not seem to think he was being credulous or childish, that they'd taken his question seriously. "Does it get easier?"

"Yes," Jakelin admitted, "it does. Everything gets easier with practice, sire, even killing. We do what must be done, for God and for our kingdom. But it is on the battlefield that we prove our prowess, fighting men who also value honor and courage."

"Infidels, too?" Baldwin asked, and both men told him emphatically that this was so, that respect was given to those who'd earned it, even if they worshipped the wrong god. When Balian said that such respect was mutual, that all men of honor were willing to acknowledge bravery and valor, Baldwin found that comforting, for his belief in courage was stronger even than his faith. How else could he endure this most accursed of afflictions?

They could see that they'd told him what he needed to hear, and for the most part, it was true. War was more complicated than that, of course, as were the emotions it aroused. It was brutal and messy and exciting and awful. To men of their class, it was also a vocation, not a choice but something they'd been born to do.

Trying to lighten the mood, Balian said with a smile, "But even those who seek glory in battle can still be scared pissless if they have time to think about it beforehand. I've had moments when I felt as if my bowels had turned to water and I daresay our gallant Templar here has, too, whether he'll admit it or not."

Jakelin insisted that Templar knights never knew fear and feigned indignation when Balian hooted at that. While Baldwin smiled at their banter, his blue eyes were distant, gazing into an inner vista only he could see. "I do not think I'll be afraid," he said at last. Jakelin privately dismissed this as the natural bravado of youth. But Balian felt a sudden chill, realizing that he believed the lad. Why *would* Baldwin fear a quick death on the battlefield? Who would not prefer that to the long, agonizing death that a leper faced?

"My lord king!" One of Baldwin's household knights was hurrying toward them. "I was sent to find you by the constable. A scout has returned with news you must hear."

Baldwin got hastily to his feet, as did Balian and Jakelin. The latter knew his rank as a knight did not entitle him to a place in a council of war. He followed anyway, hoping that his appearance with the young king would gain him entry.

Humphrey de Toron was the actual commander of the expedition; Baldwin's authority was more titular than real. He had too much common sense, though, to feel slighted by that. Ducking into the constable's tent, he found Joscelin, Raymond, Denys, and the grand master of the Templars were already there. With Balian and Jakelin on his heels, he looked searchingly from face to face. "What has happened?"

"Tell him," Humphrey directed, and a man emerged from the shadows. He'd obviously done some hard riding, for his clothing and face were smeared with dust and sweat. Stepping forward, he knelt before Baldwin.

"Sire, Saladin's brother Tūrān-Shāh has left Damascus with an army and is heading toward the Bekaa Valley."

Baldwin looked from the weary scout to the others. "It is to be a battle, then," he said, so calmly that the men regarded him with approval and Balian silently vowed to stay close to his young king in the coming confrontation with the sultan's brother.

The sun was reaching its zenith. Soon the heat of the day would soak their gambesons with sweat and make them acutely aware of the weight of their hauberks. Baldwin had known he was not qualified yet to lead men, but he'd dreaded being left utterly out of the action, and so he'd been very pleased when Humphrey de Toron had given him command of the reserves. They'd taken up position on the wooded slope of the mountain called Jebel Liban by the Saracens, which offered a clear view of the valley below. To the north, Baldwin could see the peak of Mount Sannine and the rippling surface of the Litani River as it meandered toward the sea. He was blind to the beauty of the Bekaa Valley today, focused only upon the army lined up in battle formation, blocking the Damascus–Beirut road. They'd hastened south to intercept Tūrān-Shāh, arriving in time to catch the Saracens by surprise—or so they hoped.

There was a risk that Tūrān-Shāh had sent out scouts and was aware by now of the danger awaiting him. Good generals anticipated the actions of the enemy. Humphrey did not think Tūrān-Shāh was one of them. He was Saladin's elder brother, entrusted with authority because of blood, not ability, the constable said dismissively. Unlike the sultan and another brother, al-'Ādil, who was governing Egypt in his absence, Tūrān-Shāh was said to be impulsive, careless, and so jealous of his younger brothers that he was inclined to be reckless.

Their scout had reported that Tūrān-Shāh's *askar*, the soldiers sworn personally to him, had been augmented by local levies and men from the Damascus garrison. That meant the Franks would be outnumbered, which made the timing all the more crucial. Baldwin was anxiously aware that their knights would probably have just one chance to make a charge. The Saracens were more lightly armed and were very vulnerable to such an assault by mail-clad knights on destriers. But if they moved too early or too late, they gave the enemy time to break formation and scatter before the onslaught. It was very difficult to regain lost momentum and if they did not strike a lethal blow with that first charge, they'd be the ones in peril.

Baldwin's stallion snorted, as if sensing what was to come. "Asad will be very disappointed if he does not get to challenge other stallions," he said, glancing over his shoulder with a fleeting smile. "So will that evil-tempered beast of yours," he added, for Balian's destrier, Demon, was well named. "If we can only watch the battle, Balian, that will be poor repayment for your good deed. I know you joined the reserves because you believe I need looking after."

"Not so, my liege," Balian assured him mendaciously. "I know how important it is to hold men in reserve, for that can make the difference between victory and defeat. And when Count Raymond offered to augment the reserves with some of his own knights, I had to speak up. Otherwise you might have had to endure Gerard de Ridefort's blathering on and on. . . ."

As Balian had hoped, that earned him another smile from Baldwin, who found the Flemish knight irksome, too. But Baldwin had been right about his motivation. Balian was only eleven years older than the king, yet he felt as protective today as if he were sending his own son into his first battle. His eyes kept coming back to Baldwin's shield, with increasing unease. Their long, kite-shaped shields were almost as essential as their lances and swords, protecting a knight's vulnerable left side and able to be used as a weapon if need be.

Not for Baldwin, though, for he'd be wielding his sword in his left hand. He had tried putting the shield on his right side, even doubling the guige straps; it was just too heavy and cumbersome to manage with only one working arm. They'd finally resorted to a much smaller, round Saracen shield, but Balian feared it would offer little protection in close combat. Moreover, Baldwin could rely only upon his sword, for his handicap had proven too difficult when he'd attempted to master the lance. At fifteen, he was about the age of Balian's own squire, and squires were not expected to take part in battles. Yet Baldwin would if given half a chance. Balian never doubted that for even a moment.

His gaze resting now upon Baldwin's chestnut stallion, Balian tried to imagine going into battle without the use of reins. No matter how often he reminded himself that Baldwin was a superb rider, the boy had never faced a challenge like this. As well trained as Asad was, he was sure to be affected by the blood and noise and sheer chaos swirling around a battlefield. What if he took fright and bolted? Or shied away from the carnage, unseating his young rider?

Balian's morbid musings were interrupted by a sudden exclamation from Baldwin. "Look," he said, gesturing off to his left. "See the dust? They're coming."

What followed was an experience unlike any that either Balian or Baldwin had encountered before. Balian had participated in charges, but he'd never witnessed one as an observer, and Baldwin's combat lore was theoretical, not yet put to the test. They exchanged grins, delighted and relieved that Tūrān-Shāh was just as foolhardy as Humphrey had predicted. There was considerable confusion and alarm in the Saracen ranks when they saw the Franks waiting for them. Even then, there was still time to retreat. Pride prevailed over common sense and it soon became obvious that Tūrān-Shāh meant to give battle. The Saracens hastily attempted to get into battle formation, the air suddenly echoing with shouting and cursing and the throbbing drumbeat that was an integral part of Muslim warfare.

Humphrey and the Templar grand master gave them no time, striking hard and fast. As the men on the ridge watched, enthralled, their fellow knights smashed into the Saracen line, riding stirrup to stirrup, lances couched and their horses kicking up so much dust that they seemed to be trailing smoke. Balian felt a jolt of jubilation, sure that the day would be theirs.

Even though the Saracens were infidels, none of the Franks ever questioned their courage, and fierce fighting erupted in patches. Yet any army in disarray was at a mortal disadvantage, for once men realized that the battle was lost, the instinct for self-preservation took over. Soldiers were soon fleeing the field. A feigned retreat was a key strategy of Saracen fighting, and they'd often lured unwary pursuers into traps by such tactics. But not today. The Saracens had been scattered by the charge of the Franks and they lacked a commander strong enough to rally them. Now they sought only to save themselves.

Baldwin had been as fascinated as his men, for it was mesmerizing to see stories of combat suddenly brought to life before his eyes. But then he realized that some of the fugitives were seeking safety in the woods of Jebel Liban. "Cut them off!"

His men were eager to obey, welcoming this chance to enter the fray. Balian quickly spurred his destrier after Baldwin. He soon discovered that Asad was much faster than his own stallion and he was unable to keep pace. Nor could Baldwin's household knights, and they watched in horror as the boy rode straight toward a horse archer, his long plaits and his weapon proclaiming him to be a Turk. He reacted at once, grasping the sword that dangled from his right wrist and swinging it with lethal aim toward Baldwin's exposed right side. Asad swerved as gracefully as if he were a big cat, making a circle so tight that Baldwin was able to slash his sword down upon the other man's outstretched arm. He cried out, blood spurted, and his stallion reared. Unable to stay in the saddle, he hit the ground with such force that he lay stunned.

Baldwin had already turned Asad toward the closest foe, but by then Balian and the other knights had caught up with him. While more blood was spilled, many of the demoralized Saracens chose surrender over dying and the fighting soon ended. They would later learn that Tūrān-Shāh had been one of those able to escape, leaving behind a field strewn with his dead and wounded. This battle that the Saracens would call Ain al-Jarr was not a victory that would change the balance of power in Outremer. Yet for the Franks, it was a sweet win, and none of them cherished their triumph more than their king.

Baldwin turned in the saddle as Balian reined in beside him. Too breathless to speak, he simply raised his sword to show the blood smeared on its blade.

"You did well, my liege," Balian said, no less breathlessly, and Baldwin grinned.

By now he was surrounded by his knights and at first, he took great pleasure in their acclaim and exultant approval. Once his own excitement crested, though, their enthusiasm began to puzzle him. It was not as if he'd won the battle on his own, after all. Yes, the reserve under his command had contributed to the win and he'd taken his first prisoner, who was now sitting up groggily, raising his right hand in the Saracen gesture of surrender. But he saw his performance as more competent than heroic, and he felt a sudden unease, fearing that they were lauding him so effusively merely because he was the king and had not shown fear or fallen off his horse or committed any novice mistakes.

That concern tarnished some of the plaudits and as soon as he could, he signaled for Balian to follow him away from the others. Leaning over to stroke Asad's lathered neck, he said in a low voice, "Tell me the truth, Balian. Are they praising me so lavishly because they had such low expectations?"

Balian looked at the boy, not sure how to respond. He'd seen some daring exploits on the battlefield in the years since he was old enough to fight, as had the other knights. But he thought they'd never seen the sheer, raw courage that Baldwin had shown today, riding out to do battle with a crippled arm, lacking a lance or shield, whilst mounted on a stallion he could control only by the pressure of his knees.

Since he knew Baldwin would not thank him for stressing his handicap, he gave careful thought to his answer. "It is true they were not sure what to expect of you, my liege, not knowing you as well as I do. But this I can tell you for true: If courage were the coin of the realm, you'd be richer than Midas."

Baldwin had never gotten a compliment he valued more. He'd occasionally heard Jakelin call Balian a "silver-tongued devil" and he did that now himself, sparing them both any awkward sentimentality. But for the first time since he'd learned he was a leper, some of the anger he'd been secretly harboring against the Almighty eased, just a little. For if his leprosy was God's doing, so, too, was this victory.

When Salāh al-Dīn suddenly broke off his siege of the Assassin stronghold, Masyāf, many were surprised and puzzled, for the Assassins had twice attempted to murder the sultan. The second attempt just last May had come close to succeeding; he'd been slashed on the cheek and was saved from death only by the armor he'd worn under his tunic. He'd been so alarmed that he'd erected a stockade around his command tent and only those personally known to him were permitted access. All assumed he'd not rest until Masyāf was reduced to smoldering embers and rubble, and there was much speculation, therefore, about his reasons for ending the siege so abruptly. It was rumored that the Assassins had threatened the lives of his family; others concluded that his return to Damascus was motivated by the raid into the Bekaa Valley and the defeat of his careless brother at Ain al-Jarr. While only the sultan knew for sure, the young King of Jerusalem was happily certain that he'd be taken more seriously now by his Saracen foes.

CHAPTER 11

August 1176
Jerusalem, Outremer

A distant, muted cheer told those in the great hall of David's Tower that Reynald de Chatillon had entered the city. There were usually large turnouts for the return of liberated lords and knights. Most people had considerable sympathy for these men, even though a woman's homecoming would be far less joyful, for it was assumed that she'd been defiled, true or not. In the case of this particular freed prisoner, it was curiosity, too, that had lured the citizens of Jerusalem out into the hot August sun, for his notoriety had survived his fifteen years as a prisoner in the dungeons of Aleppo.

Balian had no memories of Reynald; he'd been only eleven when that controversial lord had been captured. "Are the stories told about him true?" he asked, hoping to engage his brother in conversation, for the usually gregarious Baudouin had been silent since their arrival at David's Tower. Not that Balian blamed him for his taciturnity; less than a fortnight ago, he'd suffered a great loss. Elizabeth had given him the son he'd long yearned for, but it had been a difficult birth and though the baby survived, she had not. While Baudouin had always been one for sharing his emotions with the world, his grieving had so far been very private, shutting out Balian and his seventeen-year-old daughter, Esquiva, who was now watching him with obvious anxiety.

Balian was fond of his niece and was pleased that she seemed to be content in her marriage to Amaury de Lusignan, despite the fifteen-year gap in their ages. It had been a good match for both sides, giving Amaury entrée into the Outremer nobility by a marital alliance with the powerful Lord of Ramlah, and securing for Esquiva a husband of good birth with a reputation for battlefield bravery. Esquiva had confided in Balian that she was with child, although she had not yet revealed this to her father, worrying that he'd fear for her so soon after Elizabeth's death in the birthing chamber.

"Papa, you knew Reynald de Chatillon ere his capture. Was he as wicked as men say?"

Baudouin had given no indication of hearing Balian's query, but he responded to the sound of his daughter's voice. "Wicked? I daresay there were many who thought so. The Patriarch of Antioch was one, for certes."

Amaury was showing signs of interest, too. "As I heard it, Reynald accompanied the French king Louis and his queen to Outremer, staying on after they returned to France. He then seduced and wed Princess Constance of Antioch, to the consternation of the citizens of that city and the emperor of the Greeks, who was always eager to meddle in the affairs of Antioch."

Baudouin seemed to be coming out of his dark reverie. "From what I heard of Constance, that lady was as strong-willed as any man, so I cannot see her taking Reynald into her bed unless she wanted him there. The marriage was not popular, though. Despite the claims of Reynald's legion of enemies, he is not lowborn, being the younger son of a French nobleman. Yet few thought him a suitable husband for the Princess of Antioch."

Esquiva was fascinated by the very thought of a woman daring to choose her own husband. "Did people try to end the marriage?"

"No, in part because Reynald and Constance were able to win over our king. Reynald even managed to placate the Greek emperor, who agreed to recognize the marriage if Reynald would rid him of an enemy, the lord of Armenian Cilicia. But when he did so, Manuel delayed in paying him the promised subsidy for his services." Baudouin smiled then, without much humor. "Did I mention that Reynald has the Devil's own temper? He did not take it well."

"Was that when he tortured the Patriarch of Antioch, Papa?"

"I am not surprised you know about that, Esquiva, for it created quite a scandal. Reynald was determined to avenge himself upon Emperor Manuel and saw a way to do so whilst turning a goodly profit, too. His plan was to raid the wealthy island of Cyprus, which was ruled by the Greeks. He needed money for this scheme and rashly sought it from Antioch's patriarch, who'd been one of the harshest critics of his marriage. The patriarch refused and was insulting in the bargain. He did not yet know the sort of man he was dealing with, you see."

Amaury was as mesmerized by this tale as his young wife. "Did he really torture the patriarch?"

"Reynald had him seized, dragged to the city's castle and up to the roof, where he was beaten and his wounds smeared with honey. It was a hot day and the old man was soon swarmed by hungry insects. He held out for a few hours before agreeing to give Reynald the funds he'd demanded. Reynald then sailed for Cyprus, where he and his men wreaked havoc, caring little that the Cypriots were Christians, too. According to all reports, they looted the island, raping and pillaging, not even sparing the nunneries or the nuns. Reynald returned to Antioch much the richer for his raid and heedless of the enemies he'd made or the bodies strewn in his wake."

Amaury was familiar with stories of lawless behavior by those in positions of authority, some of them involving his own turbulent family in France. But even he was impressed by the bravado and scope of Reynald de Chatillon's bold transgressions against both man and God. "He must have been pleasing to the eye if he won a princess for himself, and he surely did not lack for ballocks. He sounds rather dull witted, though, for any man with a grain of common sense would know the Greek emperor could never let such defiance go unpunished."

Baudouin was shaking his head. "You are wrong about that. Reynald has more than his share of flaws, but he is not stupid. It was arrogance that led him astray, that and the thrill of flouting those in power. I got the sense that he was too prideful to consider the consequences of his actions or even to conceive of defeat, sure that he could fight or talk his way out of any predicament. I imagine that cockiness did not long survive a Saracen dungeon, though."

That struck too close to home for Amaury; he'd spent time in a Saracen dungeon himself. He'd been fortunate enough to have been ransomed by King Amalric, but those were not memories he cared to dwell upon. His prison stint had been relatively brief; he could not begin to imagine how a man could endure fifteen years of captivity. Changing the subject slightly, he asked Baudouin how Reynald had managed to make peace with the Greek emperor.

"By a humiliating surrender. When Reynald heard of the approach of the Greek army, he hastened to Manuel's camp in the garb of a penitent, bareheaded and barefoot, and prostrated himself before the emperor. A stupid man would have chosen pride over survival."

"How was he captured by the Saracens?"

"Ah, that was simple greed mated to sheer recklessness. He'd staged a cattle raid into western Edessa, indifferent to the fact that he was stealing from fellow Christians. On his way back to Antioch, he was ambushed by the amir of Aleppo and taken there in chains. Nūr al-Dīn refused to ransom him, just as he had Joscelin, and both men would have rotted there till they breathed their last if Nūr al-Dīn had not died when he did."

Baudouin's gaze shifted toward the dais, lingering upon Joscelin de Courtenay. "Prison changes men," he said pensively. "Count Raymond emerged with knowledge of Arabic and the Saracen customs, believing that Muslims and Christians can live side by side in harmony. Joscelin was not treated as well as the count, and he came home with darker memories. Have you noticed that even his laughter is different now? It sounds hollow. He said Reynald's imprisonment was the worst of all, and I have no reason to doubt him."

He got no further, for all heads were turning toward the door to the great hall. Reynald was no longer Prince of Antioch, for Constance had died during his imprisonment. Yet he was not without royal connections even if he was now landless, for his stepson, Bohemond, ruled in Antioch and his stepdaughter, Mary, had wed the Greek emperor. The amir of Aleppo had demanded the staggering sum of one hundred twenty thousand gold dinars as his ransom, and few thought Reynald would ever be able to raise a sum so vast.

There were loud gasps as he entered the hall, so great was the surprise of the spectators, for in light of his age—over fifty by now—and his long, harsh captivity, they were expecting to see a man broken both in body and spirit. He had lost his prison pallor, having been freed during the spring, and while he was lean, he did not look in the least like a man so long locked away from the world. His dark hair was streaked with silver, yet it was still as thick as in his youth, and only a jagged scar above his left eye and shackle scars on his wrists testified to the years spent in that Aleppo dungeon. So often they'd seen freed prisoners appearing frail and unsteady on their feet, as if they'd aged decades in confinement. But Reynald de Chatillon's spine was straight, his shoulders squared, and as he surveyed the hall, his head was held high, his gaze raking the audience with an unspoken challenge, as if declaring to one and all that he was still a force to be reckoned with. He seemed remarkably fit, his step that of a much younger man, one who'd not lost his swagger. He halted until the hall had gone very quiet and then strode toward the dais to kneel before the king who'd been born in the same year of his capture.

Those watching felt free, then, to murmur among themselves, wondering how Reynald de Chatillon had endured such an ordeal without its ruining his health or dimming his wits. Baudouin thought that the secret of his survival must be his sheer obstinacy; he'd been too stubborn to die.

"No," Balian said at once, for there'd been a brief moment when he'd looked into those flint-grey eyes. "Hatred. Hatred was his shield and, then, his lifeline."

Baldwin was in good spirits, still reveling in the success of his strategic raids. They had driven Saladin to make a hasty truce with his foes in Aleppo and Mosul, thus avoiding Baldwin's greatest fear, that the kingdom could be surrounded by hostile Saracens.

Baldwin was also encouraged that he'd had no new symptoms of leprosy, not since the appearance of *maculas* upon his back and shoulders in the spring, and Anselm had shared reassuring stories of his leprous brethren who'd been able to serve for years after their ailment became known. Best of all, Guillaume of Montferrat had safely reached the Holy Land and was being escorted from Sidon by Baldwin's stepfather, Denys, having sent word ahead that they'd be arriving in Acre on this, the first Saturday in October.

The great hall of the palace was crowded with nobles and churchmen eager for their first glimpse of the man so likely to be their next king. There was an air of edgy expectation, for all knew how much depended upon Sybilla's husband-to-be, none more so than Baldwin. He liked what he'd heard of Guillaume, a man with all the prerequisites of leadership—high birth, battlefield experience, and a reputation for courage. He was said to be openhanded and outgoing, too; Baldwin thought he'd find it easier to win over the lords of Outremer, some of whom had been put off by Count Raymond's aloof demeanor.

It was in midafternoon that Baldwin had his first hint that there could be trouble ahead. Sybilla was the center of attention, which would normally have pleased her greatly. Today, though, she seemed preoccupied, short-tempered with her ladies and making little effort to engage others in conversation. Baldwin watched her with growing unease. Surely she was not going to balk at the eleventh hour? He admittedly did not know his sister all that well, privately considering her to be capricious and impulsive, without a true understanding of what would be required of her as queen. Had she decided that she did not want to wed Guillaume after all? The very thought caused Baldwin's pulse to speed up. He'd spoken the truth when he'd told his vassals he believed it was God's will that he rule their kingdom, despite being accursed as a leper. Yet he knew the day must come when his body would betray him, when he'd have no choice but to appoint a regent or to abdicate. In the past few months, he'd taken considerable comfort in knowing that there would be a competent man to rule in his stead once he could no longer do so.

He was not sure what to do, having always left Sybilla's whims and fancies to his mother. But Agnes had accompanied Denys to Sidon in order to give

Guillaume a royal welcome. And Baldwin had no desire to have a conversation with Sybilla that would be awkward at best. Yet if she were indeed having second thoughts about the marriage, he needed to know. Rising from the dais, he crossed the hall and said quietly, "Sister? We must talk."

Sybilla was so startled by his sudden appearance at her side that her hand jerked, spilling a few drops of wine. Thinking that she was drinking more wine than she ought, he suggested they go to the gardens and when he headed toward the stairwell, she followed slowly.

Neither spoke as they mounted the stairs to the roof. Much to his vexation, he had some difficulty in sliding back the bolt barring the door; as dexterous as he'd become in using his left hand, he was right-handed by nature and occasionally fumbled with ordinary tasks. At first, others would immediately offer their assistance, but they soon learned that Baldwin was fiercely independent. When he was finally able to open the door, he gave Sybilla credit for not rushing to help. As he glanced back at her, though, he noticed how much space separated them and realized she'd never have ventured close enough to risk physical contact. This was, he thought, the only time they'd been alone since she'd been told of his diagnosis.

The day was very warm, more like high summer than the beginning of autumn. The gardens were ablaze with crimson and purple flowers, the olive and palm trees swaying in the breeze wafting off the ocean. Baldwin liked to come up here by himself sometimes, gazing out at the waves rolling shoreward, just as they'd done since the dawn of time. Today, though, the gardens were not a refuge. Turning abruptly to face his sister, he said, "Are you loath to marry Guillaume, Sybilla?"

"No." She glanced at him quickly, and then away. "Why would you ask that?"

He was not sure he believed her denial. "Because your nerves are very much on the raw. Something is troubling you. If not the coming marriage, what, then?"

Color rose in her cheeks. She shrugged, saying nothing, but soon saw that he was not budging until she answered him. "If you must know," she said reluctantly, "I am nervous about meeting Guillaume."

Baldwin blinked in surprise, for that had never occurred to him. "Why?"

She shook her head impatiently. "How could I not be nervous? I am delivering my life and my destiny and the fate of our kingdom into the hands of a stranger. A wife surrenders so much in marriage, finds herself subject to her husband's will in all matters. What if Guillaume is one of those men who see women only as broodmares? Or what if I am not to his liking, if he is disappointed when he meets me?"

Baldwin could not imagine Guillaume being disappointed in Sybilla, not when she brought him a crown as her dowry. Knowing that was not what she'd want to hear, he paused to gather his thoughts. "Why would he not be pleased with you? You are very pretty, after all. Surely you know that?"

"So I have been told. But if Guillaume does not agree . . ."

Baldwin felt out of his depth, but he did his best to see this from her viewpoint. "Is it that you are uncomfortable with so public a first meeting?" He supposed he could see why that might make her anxious. Because he'd never lacked for self-confidence, he'd assumed that she was equally self-assured. Apparently not. "I have an idea," he said at last. "Stay here in the gardens. When Guillaume arrives, I will bring him up to you so you'll have some privacy."

Her eyes sparkled and at that moment, she looked very pretty, indeed. "Oh, yes, I'd like that!" Almost at once, though, her face clouded over. "People will gossip if we meet privately ere we are wed, Baldwin. It would not be seemly."

Baldwin doubted that she truly cared about strictly observing the proprieties; from what he'd heard of her girlhood in the convent, she'd shown a rebellious streak on more than one occasion. She must be even more nervous than she'd admitted. "That is easily solved. I will send one of your ladies up to the roof to wait with you."

Her smile was both radiant and relieved. "Thank you, Baldwin!" She reached out to him gratefully, her hand brushing his sleeve before she realized what she was doing and recoiled so violently that she stumbled, almost losing her balance.

For a long moment, neither of them spoke. Hot color flooded her face and when she willed herself to meet his gaze, he saw the shimmer of tears in the blue eyes so like his own. "I . . . I am sorry, Baldwin. . . ." Little more than a whisper. "It is just that . . . that I am so fearful of catching leprosy. . . ."

Baldwin felt no anger, just a weary sense of sadness and loss. "I know, Sister," he said softly. "I know."

Baldwin had spared no expense in giving his sister a splendid wedding. They had been wed in the courtyard of the Church of the Holy Sepulchre so that the throngs of spectators could witness the ceremony, then entered this most sacred of shrines for the marriage Mass. Afterward, there was feasting in the great hall of the palace, and now the trestle tables were being cleared away so the guests could dance.

Guillaume and Sybilla were the cynosure of all eyes, as bridal couples always were. They both seemed to be enjoying themselves, surrounded by the admiring and the curious and those eager to curry favor with a future king and queen. William thought they made a very attractive pair. Guillaume was as handsome as reported, tall and well built, with hair brighter than newly minted bezants and eyes as blue as the sapphire he'd given Sybilla for her bride's gift. Sybilla looked lovely in rose-colored silk embroidered with silver thread, and she blushed becomingly every time her new husband smiled at her. To judge by the expressions on so many faces, the Poulains were eager to believe that their kingdom's future was assured now that Guillaume had come to their rescue, for he looked and acted like a man born to wear a crown.

"Could it truly be as easy as this, William?"

He started, for he'd not heard Maria's quiet approach and her softly spoken words echoed his own thoughts with eerie precision; he, too, was wondering if Guillaume would be the savior of Outremer or a mirage, one of those false visions conjured up by the scorching desert sun.

"We can hope," he said, with a smile in which optimism warred with experience.

Maria looked fragile to him, the stark black of her mourning gown standing out against the vividly bright colors worn by the others in the hall. This was the first public appearance she'd made since getting word of her father's death in September at Myriokephalon in Anatolia, where the emperor of the Greeks had suffered a devastating defeat by the Sultan of Rum. While Manuel had survived the battle, Maria's father had not. Greek losses had been high; among the dead was Baldwin of Antioch, the son of Reynald de Chatillon and Princess Constance, dying in a heroic charge to break out of the trap sprung by the Seljuq Turks. William had no liking for Reynald, never having forgiven him for his torture of the Patriarch of Antioch or his ravaging of the island of Cyprus. He still felt a twinge of pity for the other man, deprived of the son who'd grown to manhood during his long years in that Aleppo dungeon. But his greatest sympathy was for Maria, having to grieve alone and far from her homeland.

"I wanted to thank you, William, for I am sure my invitation was your doing." Maria glanced across the hall toward the dais, where Agnes was glaring openly in her direction. She responded with a defiant smile.

"I did have a word with Baldwin," he admitted, "for I fear he is far too indulgent of that woman's whims and grudges. But it was not necessary; he'd already realized that it would not be wise to exclude Emperor Manuel's great-niece from a royal wedding, not at the very time he is seeking to restore his alliance with the Greeks."

As William followed the track of Maria's gaze, he suppressed a sigh, his eyes lingering upon the young king. "I do not imagine this was the easiest of days for the lad. Sybilla's wedding must surely have reminded him that he'll never be able to wed himself, never have sons of his own. He has handled it well, though, using his smile as his shield."

They did not need to worry about being overheard, for speaking in Greek thwarted even the most determined of eavesdroppers or spies, and so Maria felt free to say sadly, "We were never on good terms, Baldwin and I. I'll admit I even thought he was a brat."

"Ah, yes, the bat in your bedchamber," William said, thinking how far away that time seemed now, how innocent.

"That was only one of his practical jokes," Maria said, with a wry smile. "There was the time I found a frog in my bath, and I was always sure he was the one who'd put a very dead fish under my bed."

"He could be a handful for certes. I was surprised you never complained to Amalric about his pranks."

"Oh, I was tempted at times," she conceded. "I suppose I was too proud to ask for Amalric's help. But I think I knew even then that Baldwin was acting out of mischief, not true malice. I so wish that I'd made more of an effort with him. It is too late now, of course, for he'd assume that I was acting out of pity."

William nodded regretfully. "I think he fears pity most of all. But, Jesu, how lonely he must be. So few can seem comfortable in his presence. To give her credit where due, Agnes never shows the slightest qualm and Joscelin does try, even if he is not as bold as she is. Denys and Humphrey de Toron and the d'Ibelin brothers all manage to act as if leprosy is the furthest thing from their minds when they are with the lad, and to my surprise, Reynald de Chatillon does the same. I suppose a man who survived fifteen years in an earthly Hell does not find much to fear after that."

Turning his eyes away from the dais, he gave Maria a fond look. "You hide your unease well, too, and I bless you for that."

"I deserve no praise for that, William. It is easier for me than for many. In Constantinople, lepers were not shunned as they are in France and England, not forbidden to enter markets or churches. We were taught by the patriarchs that philanthropy is a great virtue and therefore lepers deserve our compassion and our care. I'll not deny that we fear leprosy, too, and it was to challenge this fear that leprosy is called the 'holy disease' in the empire. Our Church never preached that leprosy is a punishment for sinning."

Like most who followed the Latin Church, William had numerous misgivings about the branch of Christianity that looked to Constantinople rather than to Rome. He wholeheartedly embraced the concept of philanthropy, though, and now quoted approvingly from Scriptures. "'He hath dispersed, he hath given to the poor; his righteousness endureth for ever.'"

"But I will confess," Maria said after a long silence, "that when I brought Isabella forward to greet Baldwin, my heart was beating faster than a sunbird's wings. She'd practiced her curtsy until she could do it perfectly. Yet when she saw Baldwin, she forgot and would have run forward to embrace him had he not stopped her, hastily saying he had a cough he did not want her to catch. In those few moments, William, I felt sheer terror."

Remembering she had a cup of wine in her hand, she took a deep swallow. "She is old enough to understand that Baldwin and Sybilla are her brother and sister and she wonders why she sees them so rarely. I think it is lonely for her in Nablus. . . ."

William thought it was probably lonely for Maria, too; a life in exile was not what she'd envisioned for herself when she'd come from Constantinople as a bride of thirteen. He was about to speak when she suddenly smiled. Since she was gazing over his shoulder, he assumed the smile was not meant for him and turned to see Balian d'Ibelin coming toward them.

Balian kissed Maria's hand with such overdone gallantry that William suspected his friend had not stinted himself on the wine that had flowed so freely during the wedding festivities. Once greetings had been exchanged, Balian then expressed his sympathies for the death of her father, with such sincerity that Maria was touched; most of those at court had offered condolences that seemed perfunctory at best.

"There is one man I was looking forward to meeting at the wedding," she confided now to William and Balian. Since they'd switched from Greek to French, she had to choose her words with greater care. "Reynald de Chatillon has become something of a legend in Outremer, so I'd not think he was one to pass unnoticed, yet I've heard no mention of him all day."

"That is because he is not present." William smiled, for he knew his news was sure to startle. "Baldwin sent him to Constantinople after Martinmas to negotiate another alliance with Emperor Manuel."

Both Maria and Balian reacted with gratifying astonishment, for all knew of the bad blood between Reynald and the Greek emperor. Balian pointed out the obvious, that Reynald had never been lauded for his diplomatic skills, either, adding, with wine-flavored indiscretion, that wolves were rarely asked to watch over flocks of sheep.

William laughed. "That was my first thought, too. But once Baldwin explained his reasoning, I saw the sense in it. Reynald's stepdaughter is wed to Manuel, after all, and his son died trying to save the emperor at Myriokephalon. The son was said to stand high in Manuel's favor, so he is not likely to turn the lad's father away. And Reynald has become an almost mythical figure by now, with many thinking his suffering in Aleppo has absolved him of his past sins. Moreover, Reynald will be strongly motivated to succeed in this mission. He will want to prove to Baldwin that he can be trusted, that his talents are not limited only to the battlefield. Then there is that vast ransom to be paid. In the past, Manuel has shown himself to be quite generous in ransoming Christian lords, so it is very much in Reynald's interest to win Manuel's goodwill. For all of his fame, Reynald remains landless, after all."

"Ah, not so," Balian said, with a grin. "It is rare, indeed, when I am better informed than you, my lord archbishop. There is talk of a marriage between Reynald and Stephanie de Milly."

Maria and William were startled by Balian's news. With that marriage, Reynald de Chatillon would suddenly become one of the most powerful barons in Outremer, Lord of Outrejourdain, which included the impregnable strongholds of Kerak and Montreal. "How do you know this, Balian?" William asked, more sharply than he'd intended, for not only did he not like the prospect of seeing Reynald raised so high, he was irked that his sources had failed him like this.

Balian took no offense, playfully clinking his wine cup against William's and then Maria's. "Secrets seek me out," he joked. "It helps, too, that Stephanie and I are cousins."

William nodded, belatedly remembering that Stephanie's father and Balian's mother had been half brother and sister. He was not at all happy with Balian's news, for Stephanie had a temper of her own and nursed a deep resentment of Count Raymond, blaming him for the murder of her last husband, Miles de Planchy, merely because the count profited from it. He thought two stubborn, fiery souls like Reynald and Stephanie could feed off each other's anger, to the detriment of their kingdom's harmony.

They were interrupted, then, by the cries to clear the floor, for the musicians were in place and the dancing was about to begin. Balian would have liked to ask Maria to dance, but he realized a woman in mourning would certainly decline, so he suggested, instead, that he fetch her more wine. Since the floor was becoming crowded as people joined the circle for the dance, Maria chose to accompany Balian in search of a wine bearer. William was about to follow when he glanced toward the dais. Agnes and Joscelin had left to join the dancers and Baldwin sat alone, reduced to the status of spectator yet again. Since Maria seemed to be enjoying Balian's company, William felt free to leave her in his keeping and headed for the dais.

Baldwin welcomed him with a quick smile and a joke. "You are not going to dance?"

"That would be a sight to behold. It is bad enough that some of my clerical brethren disobey the Church's strictures against hunting or hawking without my scandalizing the patriarch by dancing." Taking a seat beside Baldwin, he said, "You gave Sybilla a perfect day, one she'll long remember."

"I hope so. She and Guillaume seem pleased with each other, too." When William agreed, Baldwin gave him a curious look. "So tell me . . . what do you think of him, William?"

William had indeed kept Guillaume under close scrutiny in the weeks since his arrival in Outremer. "Well, I have not detected any fatal character flaws," he said with an attempt at humor. "He gets angry too quickly but does not seem to bear grudges. He speaks his mind freely and, if his words hurt, that does not concern him overmuch. Men will always know where they stand with him, for good or ill. Most of the time, he is amiable and quick with a jest. He drinks to excess, although I have never seen him appear drunk or wine addled. Of his courage, there can be no doubt. I think he will treat Sybilla well, showing her the respect due her rank. I doubt, though, that he'll pamper or dote on her. As long as her expectations are reasonable, they ought to find contentment together."

Baldwin nodded. "A fair summing up of his character. However, you ever so tactfully avoided answering the crucial question—has he the makings of a king?"

"He'd not be as good a king as you, Baldwin. But, yes, I see no reason why he could not rule successfully. Whilst he'll need to win the other lords over, his affability and generosity will serve him well in that."

"Those are my feelings, too. It is a great relief, William, to know that when I can no longer govern, the kingdom will not be adrift, a ship without a rudder. Guillaume will have a steady hand on the helm."

They drank in silence, then, for this was a subject neither cared to dwell upon; its inevitability did not make it any more palatable. "I am glad the wedding festivities have gone so well," Baldwin said after a time. "Do you think Sybilla and Guillaume will mind if I do not stay till the evening's end?"

William felt a sudden quiver of alarm. "What is wrong, Baldwin? Are you ailing?" Even after Baldwin said no, William was not totally reassured and continued to study the boy intently until the answer came to him, so obvious that he wondered why he'd not seen it at once. Baldwin had spent the day watching his sister enjoy what would be forever denied him. Expecting him also to attend the ribald bedding-down revelries was too much.

Staring into his wine cup, William tried to marshal his thoughts. The Church taught that celibacy was an exalted state, holier than wedlock. But not all were convinced of that, especially fifteen-year-old boys. He remembered a theology lesson with Baldwin a few years ago. He'd related the story of St. Jerome, who'd reproached a grieving widow by saying that she should mourn the loss of her virginity more than the death of her husband. Baldwin had cocked a brow, saying dryly that she must have found that very comforting.

Since Baldwin had not mentioned the bedding-down revelries—he'd hardly complain about the burdens of chastity to an archbishop—William was tempted to divert the conversation into less turbulent waters. But there was an unspoken yearning in the boy's eyes that caught at his heart. "Baldwin . . . I never told you about a troubling discussion I once had with your lord father. He'd been laid low with a fever and was recovering when he asked me if, aside from the teachings of the Savior, there was incontrovertible proof of the Resurrection and the afterlife. I confess I was greatly agitated by this question, for it seemed to express dangerous doubts, and I assured him that the teaching of our Lord and Redeemer was all the evidence we needed."

Baldwin seemed very interested in this unexpected glimpse of his father's inner life. "What did he say to that, William?"

"He said that he himself believed, but he wanted to hear how I would convince one who did not accept the doctrine of Christ or believe in the Resurrection. This was what I told him. I asked if he believed God is just and he said he did. He agreed, too, when I asked if good should be repaid for good and evil for evil. I acknowledged, then, that in this life, that does not often happen. There are good people who suffer nothing but troubles and adversity in this world, whilst the evil flourish like the green bay tree. But since we know that God could not act unjustly, the scales must be balanced in the afterlife, with the good receiving their rewards and the wicked being punished as they deserve. I have no doubts whatsoever of that, Baldwin. In Heaven, the Lord God will embrace you and honor you for the grace and courage with which you've borne your affliction."

Baldwin's head was lowered; all William could see was a thatch of bright hair. "Was my father convinced?"

"He was, saying that I had wrested all doubts from his heart. If you have any such doubts . . ."

"I do not." Baldwin looked up at that, his expression not easy to read. Another silence fell and William hoped that his words had been of some solace to the lad. But then Baldwin said, "May I ask you a question about theology? Is it true that thinking about a sin is almost as bad as committing the sin?"

"Yes, that is so."

"Then if I gave thought to a very great sin, I would need to confess this to my chaplain and seek absolution?"

William was suddenly uneasy. "You have a good heart, Baldwin, so I doubt that your thoughts could put your salvation at risk," he said, trying to lighten the sudden dark tone of their conversation.

"No?" There was a challenging gleam in Baldwin's eyes. "What if I told you I'd thought about converting to the Muslim faith, that I found their view of Paradise more appealing than the Christian promise of Heaven?"

William was stunned. Could this accursed disease have affected the lad's brain? How else account for such madness? How was he to respond to this? "Saracens are damned, doomed for all eternity—" He stopped abruptly, the words dying in his throat, for he'd caught it, the slight curve at the corner of Baldwin's mouth, and he realized then that he'd been hoodwinked. He'd been offering reassurance that the loss of fleshly pleasures on earth would matter little when measured against the spiritual bliss of the afterlife, all without actually saying so. Not only had Baldwin understood the implied message, he'd seized this opportunity to bedevil his former tutor with some inspired mischief, using William's own teachings that Saracens believed they would enjoy carnal delights in Paradise.

William's relief was so great that he slumped back in his chair. "That was not amusing," he said, striving to sound both dignified and disapproving.

"Oh, but it was," Baldwin said, his grin breaking free. "If only you'd seen the look on your face, William!"

"Some matters are too serious to jest about, Baldwin, and the surety of your soul is one of them." But now that the shock had subsided, so had his distress, and he actually welcomed this sudden appearance of the Baldwin he'd once taught. A born tease, he'd loved to craft imaginative practical jokes, with Maria his favorite target, although William himself was not always spared. That carefree, playful youngster was only a distant memory, vanishing on the day that he'd learned he was a leper. To see him again, however briefly, was a gift from God.

"I am too old for such foolishness," he said, feigning indignation. Baldwin easily saw through his scolding and began to laugh, such a soaring, infectious sound that William could not help joining in. Their merriment attracted smiles from some of the dancers, pleased that their young king was enjoying his sister's wedding.

A sudden uproar on the dance floor signaled that the guests were eager to escort the bridal couple to their marriage bower. Like most churchmen, William did not approve of these raucous, bawdy revelries, but he was worldly enough to accept them as an inevitable part of every wedding. The dancing had stopped and the crowd was moving aside, revealing Guillaume and Sybilla; he was laughing and bantering with the other men while she assumed the modest demeanor expected of a virgin maiden, blushing even as she giggled when Guillaume leaned over to whisper something in her ear. They were approaching the dais and when William realized they were seeking him, he rose and went down the steps to meet them.

"My lord archbishop," Guillaume asked, "would you do us the honor of blessing our marriage bed?"

Flattered to be chosen when the hall was filled with other princes of the Church, William assured them that it would be his pleasure, pleasure that was enhanced by his glimpse of the sour expression on the face of Eraclius, the Archbishop of Caesarea, and the frowns with which both Agnes and Joscelin greeted this honor. As the other guests surged forward, William glanced over his shoulder toward the dais. But Baldwin had taken advantage of the commotion to make a discreet departure from the hall. The throne was empty.

CHAPTER 12

April 1177
Acre, Outremer

Isabella had rarely been so excited, for she'd been looking forward to her brother's Easter court for weeks. She had several new dresses made for the occasion and she'd been allowed to ride her own pony for the last part of their journey from Nablus. As they started toward the great hall, she took several skips to catch up with her mother, asking if the tall one would be there.

Maria seemed momentarily puzzled. "You mean . . . Lord Balian? Yes, I am sure he will, for no one will want to miss the king's Easter court."

Just as they reached the heavy oaken door, it swung back and Maria and Isabella found themselves face-to-face with Agnes de Courtenay. Isabella quickly moved closer to her mother, reaching for her hand. She knew hawks did not have blue eyes, but this woman's piercing stare always reminded her of a very hungry hawk. Since her mother was a queen, the other woman should have curtsied. Instead, she said in a voice that dripped scorn, "I would think you'd have too much pride to keep coming where you know you are not wanted."

Isabella knew that upset her mother, for although her face remained calm, her fingers tightened around Isabella's small ones. She smiled, though, saying, "Amalric often said that the happiest day of his life was the day he ended his marriage to you. It is easy to understand why."

The look on the older woman's face scared Isabella a little and she pressed closer to her mother's skirts. Agnes's lip curled and she brushed past them as if they were no longer there. Still holding her daughter's hand, Maria led Isabella into the hall.

Despite its being crowded, Maria saw at once that Baldwin was not present; the chairs on the dais were unoccupied. Nor did she see Sybilla and her new husband. Maria was disappointed that William was not here yet. Her entrance appeared to have gone unnoticed. She did not enjoy these visits to the royal court, where she was made to feel like an outsider—the Greek foreigner—even after nigh on a decade in Outremer. All knew Baldwin had no fondness for her and that she was bitterly resented by his mother, so few saw any advantage in cultivating her favor. She accepted these infrequent invitations nonetheless, for she was determined that Baldwin not forget he had another sister, one who deserved his protection and affection.

Across the hall, Raymond and his wife, Eschiva, glanced in her direction and, as their eyes met, acknowledged her with cool politeness; Raymond's antagonism toward the Greek emperor was a barrier neither he nor Maria had ever tried to breach. They were standing with a man unfamiliar to Maria, tall and imposing, well past his youth but still one to draw attention to himself. Stephanie de Milly was beside him, and when Maria noticed that her arm was linked in his, she realized this must be the notorious Reynald de Chatillon. She'd gotten a letter from her great-uncle, the emperor, telling her that he'd agreed to another alliance and would join in an invasion of Egypt that summer, so Reynald would soon be claiming his marital reward for his successful mission. Judging by the way Stephanie was looking at him, she would be a willing bride.

Maria had decided to withdraw, hoping their chambers would be ready, when the door slammed and a brisk wind blew into the hall, heading right toward her. Baudouin d'Ibelin's exuberant, tactless personality was utterly unlike her own nature. He was always friendly, though, and they shared a common loathing for his former sister-in-law, so she smiled as he kissed her hand with a flamboyant flourish and then made Isabella giggle by kissing her little hand, too.

Leading them toward the comparative privacy of a window seat, Baudouin signaled to a servant for wine and then grinned. "I was across the courtyard, close enough to see but not to overhear your exchange with Madame Hellcat. It looked to me as if you gave as good as you got. Tell me you drew some blood!"

That won him another smile. "I did," Maria admitted, "with a lie. I told her how happy Amalric was to be rid of her. He was as closemouthed as a clam about his feelings, though, and once her anger cools, she'll probably remember that."

"No, she will not," Baudouin said cheerfully. "Like as not, Amalric told her that himself more times than she wants to remember—"

He interrupted himself as a servant approached with the wine. He winked at Isabella after Maria refused to give her a cup, too, before saying more seriously, "Do not let your guard down with her, madame. Many women like to keep small dogs as pets and nuns are said to dote on cats. Agnes prefers scapegoats, especially Greek ones."

Maria wondered if it was as simple as that. Mayhap so, for Agnes had been hostile from the day of their first meeting. Not wanting to discuss Agnes in Isabella's hearing, she asked if Sybilla was here yet. Baudouin shook his head. "She's ever been one for making a dramatic entrance, so I expect they'll not arrive till the morrow." As if reading her mind, he added, "The Archbishop of Tyre is already here, though. Unfortunately, so is the Archbishop of Caesarea, Agnes's devoted lapdog."

Maria did not really know Archbishop Eraclius, but William disliked him and that was enough for her. She did not think it politic to be criticizing him so openly, however; Baudouin's booming voice could carry for miles. Changing the subject discreetly, she queried the whereabouts of the young king.

Baudouin's smile disappeared at the mention of Baldwin's name. "The lad took a bad tumble down the stairs this morning. Fortunately, he did not break any bones, just bruised his face and his pride. But the fear is that he is losing more and more feeling in his right foot and this is what caused his fall."

"He is under his doctor's care, then?"

Baudouin shook his head. "If his mother had her way, he'd have gone straightaway to bed whilst she summoned every physician in the kingdom. Yet the last thing he needed was time to dwell upon what happened and what lies ahead. Luckily, Balian was one of the witnesses to his mishap. Do not tell him I said this, but my little brother can be quick-witted. He ignored the fall and challenged Baldwin to a race. If looks could kill," he chortled, "Balian's blood would have been all over Agnes's hands. Baldwin jumped at the chance, of course. The only time the lad can outrun his troubles is when he is astride that Arab stallion of his."

Raised voices across the hall drew their attention, then. The conversation between Reynald de Chatillon and Count Raymond had become increasingly tense and now their smoldering antagonism burst into flames. Reynald had a voice almost as carrying as Baudouin's and all heard him clearly. "Christ, what a fool you are! You spent nine years as a prisoner of those accursed infidels and yet you learned nothing!"

Raymond's voice was lower-pitched, his reply reaching only those within immediate hearing distance. Yet the look upon his face made it abundantly clear that he returned Reynald's contempt in full measure.

Maria frowned, for an open rupture between these two powerful men was bound to have troubling consequences for the kingdom. She'd often seen Balian deftly defuse tensions with humor and she urged Baudouin to intercede, only to learn that he and his brother were not cut from the same bolt of cloth. "Intercede?

Why would I want to do that? This is the most entertaining thing that has happened at the Easter court so far!" He rose then, heading toward the combatants, and Maria hastily followed his example.

"You honestly believe Christians and Muslims can live side by side in harmony?" Reynald jeered. "Scriptures may claim that the day will come when the wolf will dwell with the lamb, but it will never happen in our lifetimes, my lord count!"

"Not if you have your way, my lord," Raymond said coldly. "Some men lust after blood the way other men lust after women and I think you are one of them."

Baudouin and Maria were not the only ones drawn by the commotion. Fire and ice, Maria thought uneasily, for there could be no common meeting ground between them. She felt some relief when she saw Joscelin de Courtenay striding toward the men. It lasted only until she saw Joscelin take up a position beside Reynald, glowering at Raymond. Archbishop Eraclius was also there by now and he, too, had moved to Reynald's side. Others were showing support for Raymond and as Maria watched in dismay, it seemed as if lines were being drawn in the sand, gauntlets flung down. When she saw Humphrey de Toron shoving his way through the crowd of spectators, she frowned again, for he might well have a vested interest in backing Reynald, who was soon to wed his widowed daughter-in-law.

She need not have worried, for Humphrey democratically directed his blistering glare at both men. "I suggest you take this show out into the street. Saladin's spies will have a better chance of witnessing it there."

Whether reacting to his own formidable presence or the message itself, neither Raymond nor Reynald challenged him. Maria was struck by the difference in the demeanors of their women. Eschiva seemed to be trying to soothe Raymond's anger, while Stephanie looked as if she were spurring Reynald on. Thinking that mayhap it was for the best that she and Isabella no longer lived at court, Maria's gaze happened to fall upon the youngster standing a few feet away. The other boys in the hall had reacted with excitement to the confrontation. But this boy was as tense as a drawn bowstring, watching Reynald so warily that Maria realized he must be Stephanie's son, Humphrey. She'd not seen him for several years and she reckoned he was about eleven now, still as handsome and shyly vulnerable as she remembered.

The expression on young Humphrey's face stayed with her and when she and Baudouin returned to the window seat, she heard herself wondering aloud what sort of stepfather Reynald would make. Baudouin glanced over at the boy and then shrugged. "I daresay Reynald will not be likely to coddle the lad. Humphrey needs to toughen up, though. He is heir to Outrejourdain, after all, not some timid clerk or scrivener."

Again they were interrupted by a sudden clamor, this time coming from outside. Baudouin got quickly to his feet, saying it sounded as if Baldwin and Balian were back. Taking Isabella's hand in hers, Maria accompanied him as he strode to the door. So did the other guests.

A nasty bruise was already darkening the skin along Baldwin's cheekbone. His face and clothes were splattered with mud, too, for they'd had an unusual April rainstorm the day before. But he was laughing as if he had not a care in the world.

"Not that I'd accuse you of cheating, my liege," Balian grumbled, "but it was hardly fair when you jumped that ditch."

Maria had never understood why men took such pleasure in this sort of barbed banter. It was obvious, though, that Baldwin was glorying in it, for he grinned and reminded Balian that he could have jumped the ditch, too.

"Tell that to Smoke," Balian said with a snort, patting his stallion's neck. "He'd not have attempted that jump unless a mare in heat was waiting on the other side, and even then, he'd have had to think it over."

Although Balian had appeared to give the spectators only a cursory glance, he'd homed in on Maria immediately, for he now doffed his cap in her direction. "What is that Greek legend, madame? The one about a winged horse? Mayhap that would be a better name than Asad."

"Pegasus." Taking her cue from Balian, Maria went on to mention another Greek folktale, this one about centaurs, mythical beasts who were said to be half man and half horse.

That clearly amused Baldwin, for he gave Maria an unusually friendly smile. His mother had materialized at his side, looking up intently at her offspring, her concern written plainly on her face for all to see. Agnes was wise enough to keep silent, though, contenting herself with a scowl of angry reproach, which she divided equally between Balian and Maria.

Maria was no longer holding Isabella's hand and the little girl suddenly darted forward to tug at Baldwin's boot. "Brother! Can you take me for a ride?"

Baldwin gazed down at the child, then slowly shook his head. Balian gave Isabella no time for disappointment, quickly offering her a ride on his palfrey, joking that Smoke was not as tired as Asad since he'd not run as fast. Baudouin lifted Isabella up into the saddle in front of Balian and, to her delight, he treated her to a slow, sedate canter around the courtyard.

Baldwin briefly met Maria's eyes and she inclined her head to express both her understanding of his refusal and her gratitude. She was surprised that he'd not yet dismounted, soon realizing why; he naturally preferred to dismount in the stables, where there would not be a crowd waiting to see if he stumbled or limped once he was on the ground.

"My lord king!" Baldwin's chaplain was hurrying across the courtyard, a sealed parchment held aloft. "This came from Ascalon whilst you were gone, a message from the Lady Sybilla."

Baldwin leaned down to take the parchment. "My sister is probably warning that they will not be at Acre for another day or two. I'd wager that she'd be late for her own wake."

Once Baldwin began to read the letter, his smile vanished. "My sister and her lord husband will be unable to attend our Easter court. He is ailing and does not feel up to such a long journey."

Those terse, carefully chosen words smothered all other conversation. Even after Baldwin told them that Sybilla did not think Guillaume's illness was cause for apprehension, those listening did not agree. As she glanced around, Maria saw that earlier animosities were forgotten for the moment, with all united by the same fear. As much as people worried about Baldwin's well-being, they were even more anxious about Guillaume's health, for Baldwin was their present and Guillaume their future.

Baldwin at once dispatched his personal physician, Abū Sulayman Dāwūd, to treat his brother-in-law. Joscelin accompanied him; while Agnes was torn, she decided to remain at Acre until she was able to evaluate her son's latest symptom. Within a fortnight, Joscelin was back, assuring the court that Guillaume would recover. The letter he brought from the doctor was not as optimistic, though, for he believed the illness was hectic fever, not an inevitable death sentence but still a very serious ailment. The Poulains offered fervent prayers on his behalf in the city's churches and almost convinced themselves that there was no need for alarm. Then another messenger arrived from Sybilla; her husband had taken a turn for the worse.

Rainfall was uncommon in May, so the sudden thunderstorm that rolled in from the sea took the travelers by surprise, and some saw it as a bad omen. Baldwin had insisted they depart Jaffa at dawn, for they had more than thirty miles to cover and he wanted to reach Ascalon by nightfall. It had been a dismal journey. Fear rode with them and spirits remained low even when the city walls came into view. They were wet and tired and their hopes hung as limply as the gold and silver banners of their kingdom, rain-sodden and slack in the humid ocean air.

Once they passed through the Jaffa Gate, they were struck by the eerie silence. Ascalon had over ten thousand inhabitants and its streets were usually crowded, loud and cheerfully chaotic. Now it seemed like a plague town, the marketplace all but empty, the cries of vendors silenced, and while a few of the passersby raised a dutiful cheer at the sight of their king, their faces were etched with worry.

When they crossed the drawbridge into the citadel's bailey, they saw Sybilla awaiting them on the steps of the great hall. Her eyes were red and swollen from too many tears and too little sleep. "Thank God you've come!"

Baldwin dismounted with deliberation, as if willing his body to do what his brain commanded, and William was not the only one to remember how easily he'd swung from the saddle just a few short months ago. Catching sight of his physician, Baldwin beckoned to him and they drew apart from the others, who were gathering around his sister. William had followed, for he knew they'd learn the truth of Guillaume's condition from his doctor, not his wife.

Baldwin wasted no time with formalities. "Are you sure it is hectic fever?"

The doctor nodded. "I have no doubts, sire. He has been exhibiting all of the classic symptoms of the disease—high fever, headache, chills, a rapid pulse, that telltale red rash on his chest and belly, and a constant thirst."

Baldwin swallowed with an effort. "Will . . . will he recover?'"

"I do not know, my liege. The third week usually is the most critical, for if the patient does not rally by then, his prognosis is not good. We are now into the fifth week and the count has shown no improvement. But he still lives, so we can hope . . . and we can pray."

Baldwin's reservoir of hope had long since gone dry. Yet he'd clung to the belief that God would not let Guillaume die, for that would be one burden too many to bear. He'd even made a lame joke about it, reminding William of that Saracen proverb about a camel's back being broken by one final straw. There was no humor in it now. "I want to see him," he said, with more determination than honesty.

Sybilla halted before the bedchamber door, saying nervously that some of Guillaume's days were better than others, so they were braced for what they would find—or so they thought.

The man in the bed was a stranger, gaunt and pallid, his eyes unfocused, his lips cracked and dry. They were horrified to see the toll that the disease had taken upon him, but what they found most disturbing was his lack of response as Sybilla said his name. He stared up at her dully, showing not even a glimmer of recognition. Lying on his back, he'd kicked off the covers. Before she tucked the sheet around him again, they could see that his abdomen was very swollen and his chest covered with blotchy red spots. When the doctor raised his head and tilted a cup to his mouth, he drank as if he could never get enough, then fell back against the pillows, mumbling words that made no sense to any of them. Approaching the bed, Baldwin leaned over, offering reassurances that he did not believe and Guillaume did not hear. He felt sick himself, as if he'd just taken a blow so powerful that it robbed him of breath and hope, of all but despair. *How could the Almighty let this happen?*

"He ought to sleep now," he told his sister, not knowing what else to say. She nodded, but then said she needed to speak with him in private. Baldwin, Joscelin, Agnes, William, and Archbishop Eraclius had followed Sybilla into her husband's bedchamber, Eraclius included at Agnes's insistence when she saw that William was coming. Now, as they exited into the stairwell, William hesitated, not sure if Sybilla's invitation was meant only for her family. But she gestured for him to follow. Eraclius would have followed, too, had Sybilla not stopped him, saying politely yet firmly that he must be weary after such a long journey and in need of rest.

William was not the only one who gave her a look of surprised respect at that; so did her mother and brother, all of them thinking the same thing—that Sybilla had found strength as Guillaume's strength ebbed away. Once they were seated in the solar, she remained standing. "He is not going to die," she said at last, sounding almost defiant.

William wondered if she truly believed that or if she was whistling past a graveyard; he did not know her well enough to judge. Agnes and Joscelin quickly made the appropriate responses, assuring her that Guillaume would recover, but they did not sound convincing. Baldwin roused himself to agree, although he never met his sister's eyes.

"There is something you all must know." For a young woman who'd always paid such heed to her appearance, Sybilla looked somewhat disheveled; her veil was askew and there were water stains on her bodice, even a smudge on her cheek. Vanity had obviously lost much of its importance during these past weeks as her husband fought for his life.

When she seemed to hesitate, Joscelin prodded gently. "What is it, sweetheart? You can tell us anything. Surely you know that?"

Her lips curved slightly in what was not quite a smile. "My news is good, Uncle. Guillaume and I were going to wait to share it, but you need to know now. I am with child. I missed my flux in mid-April and again this month. I consulted a midwife last week and she says the baby should be born in December—"

She got no further, for Joscelin let out a jubilant shout. Leaping to his feet, he embraced his niece so exuberantly that he actually lifted her off her feet. Agnes's response was just as elated. "I am so happy to hear this, Sybilla!" Taking her daughter into her arms, she kissed the girl on the forehead like a benediction. Baldwin was more restrained, staying in his seat as he said God had blessed her.

William alone was at a loss for words. He could only muster up a weak smile, too distressed to feign joy he did not feel. Sybilla's pregnancy was indeed a blessing— for the de Courtenays. Not for their kingdom, though. Did Baldwin understand that? While Joscelin and Agnes continued to express their happiness, William looked toward the young king. As their eyes met, he had his answer. Baldwin understood all too well.

Guillaume was dying; only a miracle could save him. Even if Sybilla gave birth to a healthy son, it would be many years before the lad would be old enough to rule in his own right. As soon as Guillaume drew his last breath, she would need a husband again. The search would begin for another Guillaume, but would such a man be willing to marry Sybilla now? If she had a son by Guillaume, he would take precedence over any son of theirs. How many highborn, ambitious men would find that acceptable? Where would they find a man whose Christian faith was stronger than his dreams of a dynasty?

May finally ended and June sidled in under cover of night. Baldwin's sixteenth birthday came and went all but unnoticed. Time seemed to have frozen for those trapped at Ascalon, watching helplessly as Guillaume edged closer and closer to death. By now, all knew the ending was as inevitable as it was disastrous for their kingdom, yet they had to join in Sybilla's pretense that there was still hope for her husband. Word soon spread that Sybilla was with child; William was sure it was Joscelin who'd spilled that secret. The de Courtenay allies welcomed the news gratefully, eager to see Sybilla rule once Baldwin could no longer do so. Others were not so pleased, seeing her pregnancy as William did, as another complication for a succession already in peril. As bad as things were, though, they were about to get much worse.

Agnes and William had noticed Baldwin's lack of appetite, for his health was an obsessive concern with them both. He'd shrugged off their questions and they reluctantly accepted his reassurances, knowing how deeply shaken he'd been by his brother-in-law's fatal illness. But then he began to cough. Within a few days, he was running a fever, experiencing chills and shortness of breath, in such discomfort that he had to take to his bed.

Their first fear was that he'd contracted Guillaume's hectic fever. Abū Sulaymān Dāwūd eased their minds, telling them he believed Baldwin's illness was one called peripneumonia by doctors and lung fever by laymen. Revealing yet another danger faced by lepers, he said that although he could not explain why, those stricken with leprosy seemed to become more susceptible to other ailments, too. While any disease seemed preferable to the one ravaging Guillaume's body, they soon realized that lung fever was just as capable of claiming Baldwin's life, for his condition quickly worsened. By then, Guillaume had lapsed into a coma, and once people learned that the young king was very ill, too, panic swept the city.

William and Agnes had been keeping vigil by Baldwin's bed, enemies temporarily forced into an alliance of expediency, their fear for him greater than their hostility toward each other. On this afternoon in mid-June, William was alone, for Guillaume had died during the night and Agnes was trying to comfort her grieving daughter. Rising, he leaned over the bed and put his hand on Baldwin's forehead. If they could not lower the lad's fever, he'd surely die. How could this be God's will? Guillaume and Baldwin, too?

William slumped back in his seat. When he glanced up again, he saw that Baldwin had awakened and was watching him. He hastened to fetch a cup of watered-down wine and slid his arm around Baldwin's shoulders, lifting him up so he could drink, and then settling the boy back against the pillows.

"I did not dream it. . . . Guillaume is dead?" Baldwin's voice was slurred, weakened by his continuing cough and the sharp pain that accompanied his breathing now. He'd been unable to eat, for that brought on bouts of vomiting, but at least he'd so far been able to keep liquids down. When William nodded, he closed his eyes, his hand moving in what William thought was an attempt to make the sign of the cross.

"Baldwin. . . . I must leave you for a time. Guillaume is to be buried in the Church of St. John in Jerusalem, and Sybilla has asked me to preside over the services for him." William found a thin smile. "She said Guillaume would want that, for he'd taken a liking to me. I will return straightaway after the funeral, that I promise."

Baldwin's lashes lifted and for a moment, his vulnerability showed so plainly that William's throat closed up. Then he lowered his gaze, saying softly, "My mother . . ."

"She is staying here with you, lad. Joscelin and Denys will escort Sybilla and Guillaume's body to Jerusalem." William reached out and covered one of Baldwin's hands with his own, thinking how few dared to touch the boy and grudgingly giving Agnes credit, both for her fierce maternal devotion to her son and for her courage.

Baldwin had fallen asleep again by the time Agnes returned. As William had done, she leaned over to put her hand on the boy's forehead, gauging his fever. "You can go," she said curtly, as if the archbishop were a servant to be dismissed at her whims. William was too weary to protest and did as she bade, leaving her alone with her son.

William had intended to go to his own chamber, but instead he found himself moving in the direction of the castle chapel. Approaching the altar, he sank to his knees, no easy feat for his stiffening muscles and aching bones.

It was hard, so hard, being torn between his love for the young king and his love for their homeland. For Baldwin, death would be a mercy, sparing him all the suffering and misery that lay ahead. But his death would be catastrophic for the Kingdom of Jerusalem. Even before he was buried with the honors he deserved, the struggle to choose his heir would already have begun—either his sister, Sybilla, or his cousin Raymond. It would seem to be an easy choice—an eighteen-year-old girl, widowed and pregnant, or a man well versed in the ways of war and statecraft. It was not, though. The de Courtenays would fight tooth and nail to gain the crown for Sybilla, and they would not lack for allies. Some would be opportunists like Archbishop Eraclius. Others would be men unwilling or unable to accept Raymond's belief in peaceful coexistence with the Saracens, men like Reynald de Chatillon. William feared that disaster would befall them all if Sybilla were chosen as queen. He also feared that if Raymond were chosen, a civil war was possible, even likely.

By now William's face was wet with tears. Lowering his head, he did what Baldwin would have expected of him. He prayed for the survival of their kingdom, for Baldwin's recovery.

CHAPTER 13

August 1177
Ascalon, Outremer

William sighed with relief as the walls of Ascalon came into view. He did not enjoy being on horseback for hours on end, and this was the fourth trip he'd made to Jerusalem since the young king had been stricken with lung fever. God had shown mercy to their kingdom and Baldwin was recovering from his illness, albeit very slowly. Since he was not physically strong enough yet to travel, William, as his chancellor, had been acting on his behalf in the Holy City.

He always became nervous as he passed through the barbican guarding the Jerusalem Gate, fearing that Baldwin's health might have regressed in his absence. But the townspeople were going about their affairs as usual, and the fear receded. At the castle, he waited to be assisted from the saddle, having no false pride about his riding abilities. He frowned, then, at the sight of the two men approaching. He was not pleased to see Reynald de Chatillon back at Ascalon again. Nor was he pleased that he seemed so friendly with Amaury de Lusignan, and he wondered if Baudouin d'Ibelin knew his son-in-law was on such amicable terms with Reynald.

Once they'd exchanged greetings, William smiled politely and offered Reynald his best wishes, for Baldwin had named him as regent during his illness. Reynald acknowledged his congratulations just as politely. But William caught the gleam of mockery in those unsettling grey eyes, for the new regent was well aware that he had no friend in the Archbishop of Tyre.

Baldwin was finding his long convalescence to be very frustrating. He'd grudgingly agreed to his doctor's insistence upon bed rest, but he was fully dressed and, in a small gesture of defiance, was even wearing riding boots. He was lounging on the bed as he dictated a letter to his scribe, whom he dismissed as soon as Anselm admitted William into the chamber.

"Anselm was about to go down to the kitchen to order my meal. Will you share it with me, William?" William said he would do so right gladly. Anselm's manners were not polished and he did not think to fetch the archbishop a cup of wine or to set a chair closer to the bed as most squires would have done. But William did not care that Anselm was lacking in some of the social graces; what mattered was that he seemed at ease in Baldwin's presence, apparently indifferent to the contagious disease that caused others so much fear.

After moving a chair beside the bed, William poured wine for them both while giving Baldwin what he hoped was an inconspicuous appraisal. The lad was pale, but that was actually good, for high color was a sign of the fever that had brought Baldwin so close to death. "I have letters for you," he said, gesturing toward his leather saddlebags, "and much to tell you. May I ask a question first?"

Baldwin looked wary and William understood why: questions about his health were not welcome. "You can ask me anything. I cannot promise to answer you, though, until I hear it."

"Fair enough. I have been wondering why you chose Reynald de Chatillon as regent and not Humphrey de Toron."

"Ah, I've been expecting that one." Baldwin took a sip of wine. "We all agree how important this attack on Saladin's power base in Egypt will be. You know that I have the greatest respect for Humphrey de Toron, both as a man and a battle commander. But I decided Reynald de Chatillon was a better choice to lead our upcoming campaign."

Baldwin looked away briefly then, and William ached on the boy's behalf, knowing how bitterly disappointed he was that he'd not be able to take part in that campaign. The Greek fleet was expected at Acre any day now, and he'd need weeks, possibly even months, to fully regain his strength. Baldwin would not want sympathy, so William offered none, saying instead, "I do not deny Reynald is utterly fearless on the battlefield. So is the constable, though. Do you think Humphrey is too old? I know he is nigh on sixty. . . ."

Baldwin shook his head. "Humphrey is a fine soldier and if age has slowed him down, he's hiding it well. But he has been very friendly with Saladin in the past, always willing to agree to truces, as the sultan well knows. Reynald, on the other hand, would barter his hopes of salvation for the chance to meet Saladin on the battlefield. So which man do you think is more likely to cause Saladin the greater concern? Who would make him lose the most sleep at night?"

William smiled at the boy, proud that Baldwin was showing such a talent for strategic thinking; clearly those childhood chess lessons had been worth the effort. While he was pleased that Baldwin had such practical reasons for his decision, it did have one drawback. "Your rationale for choosing Reynald over Humphrey would obviously apply to the Count of Tripoli, too," he conceded. "Even more so. But passing over Raymond in favor of Reynald carries a risk. Whilst Humphrey might not like it, he'd not take it as a personal insult. As Raymond is your cousin, he may well be offended at not being named regent again."

To his surprise, Baldwin merely shrugged. "I am sorry that you have never warmed to Raymond, lad, for he is a good soldier, a man of unquestioned integrity, one who would never put self-interest before the welfare of our kingdom, the way Reynald de Chatillon has done—"

He'd not meant to bring up Reynald's checkered past; the words seemed to flow into the conversation of their own accord. Realizing it was too late to backtrack, he was relieved that Baldwin did not appear angered by his criticism of Reynald, since it could be seen as doubting the young king's judgment. "I understand why you chose Reynald to lead the Egyptian campaign," he said quickly, "and I am not saying you are wrong. Who would not want Reynald fighting on our side? But I hope you will keep his lawless, rash history in mind, too. He may be a better battle commander than your cousin, yet he is neither as trustworthy nor as honorable."

"I agree with your opinion of Reynald's past, William. Whilst he called himself a prince, he was little better than a bandit back then, selfish and vengeful. Fifteen years in a Saracen dungeon changed him, though. He is a man motivated now by a burning hatred of the Saracens, a man who'd not prey on his Christian brethren as he once did." Baldwin paused before adding, "Or as my cousin Raymond did."

Seeing the shock on William's face, he held up his hand before the archbishop could object. "Do you know why Raymond has been so hostile to Emperor Manuel, so adamantly opposed to an alliance with the Greeks?"

"I assumed he did not believe such an alliance was in the best interests of our kingdom. Are you saying there is more to it?"

"Quite a bit more. I am not surprised you did not know, for it occurred whilst you were still pursuing your studies in Paris and Bologna. I only recently learned about it myself—that Raymond's sister was once plight trothed to the Greek emperor. Raymond was delighted, of course, with such an impressive marital alliance and he planned to send twelve galleys to escort her to Constantinople for the wedding. It never happened, for Manuel changed his mind at the eleventh hour and instead wed a princess of Antioch, Prince Bohemond's sister. Raymond was out-raged that his sister should be so shamed and she took it hard, dying not long af-terward."

"Who could blame Raymond for being angry?" William interjected. "It was a great affront, after all."

"I agree that his anger was justified. How he expressed it was not. He sent those twelve galleys to take vengeance upon the Greeks. They attacked Cyprus and the emperor's coastal towns, inflicting as much misery and destruction as Reynald did on his own Cypriot raid."

William did not want to believe Raymond was capable of Reynald's cruelty. "Are you sure of this, Baldwin? It sounds as if it came from one of Count Ray-mond's enemies."

"It did," Baldwin acknowledged, so blandly that William was suddenly sure that the lad had another surprise in store for him. "However, this is one enemy whom you are likely to find quite credible, William. It was my stepmother who told me about it."

Baldwin smiled, then, before explaining. "During my Easter court, my mother and uncle had gone out of their way to be rude to Maria, and I was not pleased, for if she complained of her ill treatment to Manuel, he'd not have been pleased, either. So I made a point of engaging her in conversation to show that she was welcome at my court. When Raymond's name came up, she enlightened me about the source of his animosity toward the Greeks. She was only a child at the time, but she said Manuel was enraged that the count should have dared to attack the em-pire. I saw no reason to doubt her word."

Neither did William. As much as he wanted to reject the story, if it came from Maria, it was true. But because he was grateful for all the count had done for his career, he reminded Baldwin that Raymond could not have been more than twenty-one at the time and the young were often prone to lapses in judgment. His heart was not in his defense, though, for he was disillusioned that the Count of Tripoli was not as high-minded as he'd once thought, that he was just as suscepti-ble as other men when the Devil whispered in his ear.

Servants arrived then with the meal. Because Baldwin's appetite was still lack-ing, the castle cooks had provided a variety of dishes to tempt him: an eel stew, a pottage of chicken and rice, roasted chickpeas, artichokes, and dates and oranges and quinces in syrup.

They chose to serve themselves so they'd not have to weigh their words. Once they were alone, Baldwin ladled some of the pottage onto his plate, regarding it without enthusiasm. He forced himself to swallow a spoonful, feeling William's anxious eyes upon him. "I am eating," he insisted. "Tell me how Sybilla is doing."

"About as well as can be expected. She has decided to remain in Jerusalem, saying it would be a good omen for the baby to be born in the Holy City."

Baldwin was not surprised. He said nothing and William continued, saying her nerves seemed ragged, but pregnant women were usually very emotional. "Moreover, it cannot be easy, carrying a child her husband will never get to see." Pausing to sample some of the stewed eels, he coaxed Baldwin into trying them, too, before resuming.

"Several members of the High Court approached Sybilla last week about the need to find her another husband." When Baldwin shook his head at that, William nodded in agreement. "I'd advised against it, yet they did not heed me. Sybilla not only balked, she reminded them sharply that our laws allow a widow a year of mourning. She said she is willing to marry again, but not until after her child is born."

"I can hardly blame her for that." Baldwin took a mouthful of the stewed eels to humor the archbishop. "I wonder who told her about her legal rights."

"Joscelin, most likely. He has been very protective of her." William tried to sound approving, though he was sure that Joscelin was as devoted to a future queen as he was to his niece.

Baldwin harbored the same cynical suspicions, but he supposed it was only natural that Joscelin would see Sybilla as a better investment. He still did not understand why the Almighty had let Guillaume die, a death as devastating to the kingdom as it was to his young wife. He'd made one attempt to discuss it with William, only to discover that even a prince of the Church could not explain the inexplicable.

They were finishing their meal when Agnes entered the chamber after a perfunctory knock. Although her gaze flicked to the uneaten food still on her son's plate, she refrained from commenting. William rose to give her a package of letters from Joscelin and Sybilla, and because she'd pointedly left the door open, he made ready to depart. Before he could, they heard footsteps in the stairwell and one of Baldwin's household knights appeared in the doorway, saying a message had just arrived for the king.

Breaking the parchment seal, Baldwin tilted the letter toward the light streaming through the closest window. He alarmed William and Agnes by drawing a sharp breath. But when he looked up, it was with a sun-drenched smile. "The Count of Flanders has arrived at Acre!"

As they exclaimed, he read the rest of the letter and then laughed, the first time they'd heard him laugh in weeks. "I'd about given up hope that he'd ever fulfill his vow. Yet he has even brought a small army with him." Glancing up at his mother and chancellor, he laughed again. "Mayhap our kingdom's luck has finally taken a turn for the better."

There was great excitement once word spread that Count Philip of Flanders was finally in Outremer. It had been more than two years since he'd taken the cross and many had begun to wonder if he meant to honor it. The news soon spilled over the castle walls into the streets of the city, and by the day's end the churches and taverns were filled with celebrants.

As the trestle tables set up for the evening meal in the great hall were taken down, William made himself comfortable on the dais. Snatches of conversation floated around him, almost all of them about the arrival of the Count of Flanders and what it would mean. William shared the general optimism, although he was not normally enthusiastic about crusaders, thinking they too often did more harm than good. They were filled with religious zeal but ignorant of the customs and history of the kingdom and too quick to pass judgment upon the Poulains for their willingness to make occasional alliances with the Saracens. They could not understand that the survival of the Holy Land depended upon such alliances, upon the ability of the Franks to pit one Muslim prince against another. And for more than seventy years, it had worked—until Saladin's rise to power.

William had never seen these foreign, highborn lords as the salvation of his homeland, for they had no intention of staying; they came to fulfill their pledges to God, to visit the sacred sites, to kill as many infidels as possible, and then to go back to their own homelands, sometimes with stolen holy relics. Outremer needed men like Guillaume of Montferrat, men who'd be willing to put down roots. This was why he was so hopeful about the Count of Flanders, for there was a chance that he'd agree to remain for a while, at least until a new husband could be found for Sybilla. His family's devotion to crusading could not be challenged; his father had made four pilgrimages and his mother had chosen not to return to Flanders after the last one, instead taking vows as a nun at the Bethany convent. Count Philip had also proved himself to be a very competent ruler, intelligent, ruthless, and bold. Of equal importance were his blood ties to the kingdom's royal family; Amalric and Philip's mother were the children of Fulk of Anjou, the Angevin count who'd become King of Jerusalem, so Baldwin and Philip were first cousins.

William was soon approached by the Bishop of Bethlehem. Neither Ascalon nor Jaffa had its own bishopric and both cities remained under the authority of Bethlehem, so Bishop Albert had been making frequent trips to Ascalon to visit their ailing king. They'd just begun to exchange pleasantries when they were interrupted by Abū Sulaymān Dāwūd and, even before he said a word, William was warned of trouble by the grim expression on the physician's face.

By the time they reached Baldwin's bedchamber, William shared the doctor's concern. As soon as they entered, they saw that the king's mother was also alarmed, so much so that she was even willing to accept the archbishop as an ally. "Tell him," she demanded. "Tell him how foolish it would be to attempt a return to Jerusalem on the morrow, how dangerous!"

Baldwin regarded the newcomers with resignation, saying reproachfully to the doctor, "I see you brought in reinforcements."

"You would not heed me or your lady mother, my liege, so I hoped you might listen to the archbishop."

Baldwin saw no point in continuing the argument with them and addressed himself to William. "I am not going to ride, will be using a horse litter, and I have promised that we will set a reasonable pace. No one runs races in a horse litter," he added, showing a flash of impatience.

"Even if you do not ride," Agnes interrupted, "a journey like that will be exhausting, one you are not ready to make!"

William was not sure his protest would help, for Baldwin seemed to have his mind made up, but he tried. "Your physician says that so much exertion could bring on a relapse of the lung fever. Why take such a risk? Summon the Count of Flanders to Ascalon."

"I need to get to Jerusalem as soon as possible, William, so I can call the High Court into session."

"Of course you'll want to discuss the Count of Flanders's arrival with them. But why the haste? The Egyptian invasion cannot begin until the Greek fleet arrives."

"I have more in mind than the Egyptian campaign. I need to meet with the High Court so we can discuss turning the government over to the Count of Flanders."

William blinked. "You mean . . . offer him the regency?"

"Yes, that is exactly what I mean."

"Baldwin, no!" Agnes was staring at her son in dismay. "These past two months have been hard, I know, but you must not do anything impulsive. Naming Reynald as regent is understandable, for you need a commander to lead troops into battle whilst you heal. Giving power like that to the Count of Flanders is a much greater risk. Who knows what he'd do with it? Do you truly want to entrust the hunt for Sybilla's next husband to a stranger?"

"Mother." Baldwin said no more than that, but there was something in his tone that stopped her words in midflow. "I am not offering the crown to Philip. I do think it is necessary to discuss a regency, though. My illness has shown me I may not have as much time as I hoped. And whilst we look for a suitable husband for Sybilla, how long might that take? At least another year, mayhap two. Think what could befall our kingdom if I die ere that happens."

"Baldwin, there is no reason why you cannot make a full recovery!"

"My doctor has told me that I am vulnerable to other ailments because of the leprosy. We cannot know what lies ahead for me. I do know that Outremer would be doomed if a civil war erupted between my sister and my cousin Raymond. I will not let that be my legacy. Philip's arrival seems like God's answer to our prayers."

Agnes was so worried that she appealed again to William for aid in changing Baldwin's mind. He could not do as she asked, though, for Baldwin's reasoning was as persuasive as it was unselfish. Time was not on their side.

Baldwin had never been so exhausted, but he was happier than he'd been in a long time, for as difficult as the trip to Jerusalem had been, it was all worth it. The members of the High Court had agreed that the Count of Flanders should be offered the regency and the command of the Egyptian campaign. If Reynald de Chatillon was angry at being replaced, he kept it to himself, saying that nothing mattered more than defeating Saladin. Philip had been welcomed enthusiastically by the citizens of the Holy City, who'd thronged the streets to cheer him and his men. The royal banquet given in his honor had been an unqualified success and now that it was over, Baldwin could at last yield to his urgent need for sleep.

After he let Anselm assist him in undressing, he climbed gratefully into bed. There he discovered that it was possible to be too excited to sleep, so he began to tell Anselm about the feast, knowing the squire would enjoy that. After he'd described the elaborate menu and the entertainment, Anselm asked him about the man whose future was soon to be inextricably entwined with that of their kingdom.

"I am told he is in his thirty-fifth year. Of all my male cousins, he most resembles me in coloring, although he is stockier than I am, and of course he has a golden beard, that being the fashion in his part of Christendom. French is his native tongue; I do not think he speaks Flemish at all even though half of his subjects do. He chooses his words with care and it is not easy to know what he is thinking. He is like my father in that," Baldwin added, and agreed when Anselm suggested wine might help him sleep.

"Do you want the draught mixed in it, my lord?"

"No, I should not need it tonight." Watching as Anselm bustled about the chamber, Baldwin found himself thinking how much his relationship with his squire had changed. At first, he'd been wary, unwilling to reveal too much to this stranger, and Anselm had been reticent, too, awed to be tending to the intimate needs of a king. Over time, though, Baldwin had slowly let down his guard, for he was desperately lonely, missing the friends he'd once had and never able to forget that he'd become an object of fear and revulsion to others.

With Anselm, it was different. He understood what lepers suffered, for he'd witnessed that suffering during his years with the knights of St. Lazarus. But he did not believe leprosy was as contagious as men thought, for otherwise why had he not gotten it, too? Once his initial shyness had ebbed away, he showed himself to be a talker, happy to ramble on for hours about past campaigns and skirmishes with Saracens before he'd joined the order. He'd even revealed why he'd joined it: because a cousin closer than a brother had been stricken with the disease. The cousin was dead. He'd offered no more information, though, and Baldwin had not pried.

As he became more comfortable with Anselm, Baldwin had slowly realized that the squire saw lepers in a way that others did not. William had often discussed the Church's teachings on that subject, insisting that lepers were blessed by God in that they'd be spared Purgatory, having already endured its punishments here on earth. Baldwin did not find much solace in that, and doubted if William did, either. But to Anselm, theology did not even enter into it. Lepers were accursed with a truly vile disease, yet the leper knights he'd known had faced it bravely and were therefore deserving of respect and admiration. To Baldwin, that was much-needed proof that there were men—however few—who could look past a leper's ravaged body and see into his unsullied soul.

He'd still been hesitant to trust Anselm with his own private anguish, for pride was his only defense. And then the terrible dreams had begun. Again and again, he'd be torn from sleep, drenched in sweat, his heart thudding like a Saracen war drum, his face streaked with the tears he would not shed during his waking hours. He'd even considered banishing Anselm from his bedchamber at night, shamed to be showing his fear so nakedly. The older man said nothing about these dreams. When they continued, though, he asked for leave to visit friends at the leper hospital run by the knights of St. Lazarus, and that night, he offered Baldwin a cup filled to the brim with a dark red wine that looked almost purple in the lamplight.

"Some of my brothers were prey to bad dreams, too. For those who wanted it, they could take wine mixed with these herbs to aid them in sleeping at night. It seemed to help." Baldwin had taken the cup, understanding in that moment that Anselm would never reveal one of his secrets, no matter what the temptation or the threats might be.

Anselm had poured a cup of watered-down wine after Baldwin had refused the sleeping draught and carried it over to the bed. "Do you think Count Philip will agree to act as regent, my lord? And if he stays, what of his men? Will they stay, too, after the Egyptian campaign?"

"I hope not," Baldwin confided. "They are horrified that I am both a king and a leper, which would be unheard of in Flanders. Philip is better mannered, but when he realized that he'd be expected to sit at the royal table during the feast, he looked truly greensick until he saw that I'd not be sharing any common dishes with the other guests."

Anselm snorted, muttering that foreigners were God's greatest fools, and Baldwin grinned, for he knew the squire was not saying that out of loyalty. Like many of the Poulains, he truly believed it.

"I think I can sleep now, Anselm, so you may make ready for bed, too."

Anselm sometimes startled Baldwin with unexpected insights. He was not well educated, yet he'd occasionally shown that he could read other men as easily as William could read Latin and Greek, and he did so now, saying suddenly, "It sounds as if you think the Flemish count should make a good regent. But you do not like him much, do you?"

Baldwin turned to stare at the squire. "Have you ever been accused of having second sight?" he asked, only half joking. "You are right. I do not find Philip very likable, and not just because he disapproves of a leper king. There is a coldness about him that puts me off. When I asked if he wanted to make a trip to the nunnery at Bethany so he could visit his mother's grave, it was obvious that had not even occurred to him."

After a moment to reflect, Baldwin smiled. "But what matters is that he is courageous and quick-witted and knows how to wield power. It is not necessary that I like him, too. Hellfire, Anselm, I do not like my cousins Bohemond and Raymond, either!"

CHAPTER 14

August 1177
Jerusalem, Outremer

The High Court session had not begun yet, but the palace great hall was already filling up. The Count of Flanders was to occupy a place of honor on the dais, and several of his highborn companions—the Flemish Advocate of Bethune, his two grown sons, and the English Earl of Essex—had taken the seats set aside for guests. As Balian moved toward the dais, he was not surprised to see Agnes in conversation with Archbishop Eraclius of Caesarea, for she often attended the High Court, much to the dismay of those lords who resented her involvement in matters of state. It was the first time he'd seen Sybilla in attendance, although he was not surprised by her presence, either; it was recognition of her importance to the kingdom now.

She was attracting a lot of attention; the favor of a future queen was an irresistible lure. Balian was sorry to see Baudouin among those gathered around her. He did not want his brother to be hurt and that was sure to happen, for Baudouin sought more than Sybilla's favor. He wanted to marry her and he'd convinced himself that such a marriage could happen, insisting to Balian that it made more sense to marry Sybilla to a Poulain when time was so urgent. A husband hunt abroad could take years, whereas he could wed her as soon as her baby was born. As Lord of Ramlah, he was one of the most important lords in the kingdom, a proven battle commander. Baldwin trusted him. And Sybilla liked him, so why would she not prefer to marry a man she knew rather than risk her future with a stranger?

Balian had stopped protesting once he saw it would accomplish nothing. There was just enough truth in Baudouin's contentions to give them a patina of plausibility. Baldwin did trust him and he had many friends on the High Court, men who'd be pleased to see Sybilla marry one of their own. As for Sybilla, she did seem to like him; she was laughing now at one of his jokes, gazing at him coquettishly through lowered lashes.

The problem was that Balian could have refuted each and every one of Baudouin's arguments without even pausing for breath. Baudouin had enemies as well as friends, above all his former sister by marriage. Agnes would never agree to wed her daughter to a man she despised. Nor would Baldwin reject the chance for a marital alliance with a highborn foreign lord, one that would benefit their kingdom diplomatically and militarily. And whilst Sybilla might be rash enough to marry for love—Balian did not have the greatest confidence in her judgment—he doubted that she harbored such feelings for his brother. She enjoyed flirting and might not have realized that she was giving him false hopes, but Balian thought it unlikely that she'd seriously considered Baudouin as her next husband. To make matters worse, as eager as Baudouin was to marry a queen, he liked the idea of bedding Sybilla, too, and that would make him all the more vulnerable when the inevitable disappointment occurred.

A sudden stir indicated that Baldwin had arrived and men hurried to take their seats. Balian was startled by the sight of the man accompanying the king and Count of Flanders, for Bohemond, Prince of Antioch, was not a member of the High Court and rarely paid visits to Jerusalem. Like his cousin, Count Raymond, he was in his mid-thirties, sharing the same dark coloring and lean build, their resemblance so pronounced that strangers sometimes guessed them to be brothers. But Raymond was known for his rectitude, deliberation, and self-control, whereas the stories Balian had heard of Bohemond indicated he had a very different temperament; he was said to be quick-tempered, impulsive, and too fond of the pleasures of the flesh.

Balian moved closer to get a better look at Bohemond. But he came to an abrupt halt as soon as he saw Baldwin. The king's cheeks had a feverish flush and he coughed several times as he made his way toward the dais. William followed him up the steps, for once again he was to act on behalf of the still ailing patriarch. As his gaze found Balian, it conveyed a troubling message. Baldwin had suffered the relapse that they'd feared; his lung fever was back.

Once all the lords were seated, William led the invocation and then turned the stage over to Baldwin. "Ere we discuss today's matters, I have good news to report." Baldwin's voice sounded hoarse, his throat raw from coughing. But he was determined to get through this, pausing to sip from the cup Anselm had placed on the arm of the throne. The water was icy, for his squire had filled it with the snow the Poulains used to cool their drinks. Baldwin was grateful for it now, feeling as if he were on fire. "I received word this morning that the Greek fleet has sailed into the harbor at Acre, seventy war galleys led by one of the emperor's own kinsmen."

There were pleased exclamations at that and Baldwin waited for them to sub-side before continuing. "It has been a sad summer for Outremer and we grieve still for my brother by marriage, may God assoil him. But your arrival, my lord count, has given us hope again. Because of my recent illness, I will not be able to lead our campaign into Egypt, so you could not have come at a more opportune time. After consulting with the High Court, it gives me great pleasure to offer you the regency. You will have control of the government, the treasury and revenues, and full juris-diction over all men until such time as my sister weds again."

Baldwin had delivered the offer with due solemnity, having practiced it before-hand, but now he flashed a smile that was indicative of the boy he still was, saying, "We all agreed that this would be in the best interests of our kingdom and you have no idea, Cousin, how rare such unanimity is in Outremer!"

Philip had clearly been expecting this. Returning Baldwin's smile, he said smoothly, "I am most gratified, my liege, that you think me worthy of such an honor. My family has always cared deeply about the safety of the Holy Land and the Royal House of Jerusalem. You and I are kinsmen and we all are worshippers of the cross. The infidels call us that in mockery, but I for one am proud to say it is so. Ours is the True Faith and it is surely God's will that Christians rule where the Lord Christ once walked."

Baldwin felt as if a great weight had just been lifted from his shoulders. Taking another swallow, he let the cold water trickle soothingly down his inflamed throat. But then the Count of Flanders said, "So I deeply regret that I cannot accept your offer of the regency."

Baldwin choked, his face reddening as he struggled to draw air into his lungs. The faces of the men in the audience reflected his own shock and dismay, and when he finally got his breath back, he eschewed tact or diplomacy and just blurted it out. "Why not?"

"I did not come here to acquire power of any kind, my lord king. My purpose in taking the cross was only to serve God. Moreover, I must be free to return to Flanders if necessary. Since I have no legitimate son to succeed me, I'd named my younger brother as my heir, but he died last year."

Baldwin was skeptical of the count's declaration that he sought only to do God's work, for such humility did not seem natural in a man so proud. But he did understand his cousin's concern for Flanders and, as disappointed as he was, he could not fault Philip for it. Summoning up a frayed smile, he said, "As much as I regret your refusal, Cousin, I realize that you have responsibilities to your Flemish subjects, too. We are grateful, though, that you will be able to lead our army to victory in Egypt."

"If you mean you are offering me the command of the Egyptian campaign, I fear that I must decline that, too. I have come to the Holy Land as a humble pilgrim, seeking God's grace, not temporal power."

There was a moment of deathly silence in the hall after that, broken only when Baldwin began to cough again.

Baldwin's fever burned higher and higher and within a day, he was confined to bed. Unable to continue negotiating with the Flemish count, he delegated William and his stepfather, Denys, to act on his behalf, for he feared that Philip might refuse to take part in the campaign, which would be disastrous. Not only did they need the men he'd brought with him, such a rift between the Poulains and a powerful western prince was sure to trouble the Greek envoys, who might begin to reconsider their involvement in the face of such dissension among the Franks.

Baldwin's doctor and Anselm had been bathing him all day in cool water in hopes of lowering his fever and by the time night fell, he was equally weary of their well-meaning, intrusive efforts and his mother's solicitous concern, wanting only to be left alone. But when he was told that William and Denys were asking to see him, he rallied and bade them enter.

Both men looked so grim that Baldwin closed his eyes for a moment, wondering what evil had befallen them now. "What . . . what is wrong?"

William was the first to speak. "Count Philip is not happy with your appointment of Reynald de Chatillon as regent again."

"What . . . he does not approve of Reynald?" While Baldwin could not deny that Reynald was a controversial figure, he thought it high-handed of Philip to meddle after turning down the post himself.

"Worse than that, I fear." Denys appeared as composed as always, hiding his distress at his stepson's haggard appearance. "The count does not think Reynald should act as your deputy during the campaign. He wants you to appoint a commander who would be willing to accept the blame if we fail and to receive the government of Egypt as his own should we succeed."

Baldwin stared at them. "That would make this commander the King of Egypt."

They nodded, pleased that he was so quick to comprehend what was behind Philip's demand. "We explained that we could not do that. Emperor Manuel expects to have suzerainty over any lands we conquer in Egypt and the lands themselves would become part of our kingdom." Denys paused, then said dryly, "That did not make Philip happy, either."

"How could—" Baldwin got no further, overcome by a fit of coughing so severe that it alarmed them all. When it finally ended, he sank back, exhausted. "So . . . Philip would not abandon Flanders to save the Holy Land, but he will abandon it right gladly for the chance to rule over the riches of Egypt."

They nodded again, neither one pointing out to Baldwin that he could not give in to anger; they knew by now that he understood the duties of kingship better than monarchs twice his age. He did not disappoint them. "Do what you can to placate him, give him no outright refusals. We need the bastard."

The fortnight that followed was one of the most wretched that William could remember. For days, Baldwin had hovered dangerously close to death, while they did all they could to get Philip to commit to the attack on Egypt. The air was so hot that the sky seemed blanched of color and even the birds were silent as William crossed the palace gardens in the direction of the king's quarters. The sunset was nigh and he hoped it would bring with it a cooling breeze. Baldwin's bedchamber must have felt like an oven all day. He was finally on the mend, although still not ready to deal with his cousin. William thought that was for the best; he'd have felt sympathy for an Egyptian asp if it slithered across the path of the Count of Flanders.

He was so caught up in his own grim musings that he did not at once hear his name called. Surprised to see Sybilla outside in such heat, he stopped to greet the king's sister. She was seated in the shade of a latticed arbor, being fanned by one of her attendants, but she did not look comfortable. Although he knew little about pregnant women, he thought it was only common sense that she'd feel more and more like a stranger in her own body as it swelled to accommodate the child growing in her womb.

Accepting her invitation to sit beside her in the arbor, he fumbled for a compliment since he assumed she expected one, finally saying that she looked very well. She dimpled at that. "If that is your idea of gallantry, my lord archbishop, it is for the best that you chose a career in the Church," she teased, amused when he actually blushed. She found it very entertaining that a man of such intelligence was so obviously ill at ease with women.

"I have been waiting for you," she confided, "for I knew you'd be coming to see

Baldwin after the High Court session." No longer playful, she turned to look directly into his eyes. "My uncle Joscelin told me that Count Philip meant to discuss my marriage. I want to know what happened." When he hesitated, she said firmly, "My lord archbishop, I have the right to know."

Yes, William decided, she did. He would normally have divulged nothing of their negotiations with Philip until he'd shared them with Baldwin. But word would soon be spreading as swiftly as any plague; the outrage of the High Court members would guarantee that. "As you will, my lady. Count Philip told us that he must be the one to select your next husband."

Her eyes narrowed. "Who does he want me to wed?"

William suspected the sweltering garden was about to get even hotter. "He was unwilling to tell us that. He demanded that we swear to accept his choice ere he revealed whom that would be, claiming it would be disparaging to such a highborn lord if we then rejected him."

Sybilla looked astonished and, then, enraged. "If he thinks I can be bought and sold like a mare at a horse fair, he will soon learn otherwise," she spat. "I would never agree to that!"

"Neither did the High Court. In fact, it got rather heated for a time. A number of the lords have lost all patience with the count and this was the proverbial final straw for many of them. Your stepfather and I were able to restore a semblance of order and even to soothe the count's pride, but it was no easy task."

He'd told Sybilla only part of the afternoon's high drama; Baldwin must hear it first. Rising, he excused himself. Before he could move away, she rose, too, reaching out and catching his sleeve. "I will never agree," she said again, and in that moment, her resemblance to her mother was startling.

Baldwin smiled at the sight of his chancellor, saying this was his best day in almost a week. His good spirits lasted as long as it took for William to tell him the Count of Flanders was insisting that he had the right to choose Sybilla's next husband. His fury was just as white-hot as his sister's had been, if under better control. "That is out of the question," he said flatly, spacing the words out like gravestones. "Even if I were deranged enough to agree to such an outrageous demand, the High Court would never give their consent."

"That is part of the problem. Philip does not understand that the High Court has the right to elect our kings and will fiercely defend that right. He sees them as lesser lords—they are Poulains, after all—who dare not defy him." That was such a gross misreading of political life in Outremer that William could only sigh. "There is more, Baldwin. He also wants to arrange a marriage for Isabella."

"She is five years old!"

"We reminded him of her age and that canon law prohibits the marriage of a child so young. He was not impressed by those arguments. He hears only what he wants to hear."

Baldwin shook his head slowly, as much in disbelief now as in anger. "To think I once saw this man as our savior." Settling back against the pillows, he said, "Tell me the rest."

William did. "We explained that Sybilla could not be required to wed until she'd observed a year of mourning. We told him that whilst we'd consider any man he put forward, we could not agree to the marriage without knowing his identity. Eventually, he realized that he had to make some concessions of his own and revealed that he wants Sybilla to wed Robert de Bethune and Isabella to wed the younger brother, William, both of whom are conveniently here, ready to race to the altar. Their father is one of Philip's greatest vassals, so the marriages would not be totally unsuitable. But he has so alienated the High Court that they'll never agree."

"Nor will I." Baldwin reached out to accept a cup of juice from Anselm. "So he came to the Holy Land just to do God's bidding, did he? I would never have guessed that the Almighty wants him to be King of Egypt and his handpicked puppets to rule in Outremer. How lucky we are," he added scathingly, "to have my cousin to interpret divine will for us."

A sudden knock sounded on the door and Anselm admitted Agnes and Denys to the chamber. "A pity my warning was not—" The touch of Denys's hand on her arm was enough and Agnes swallowed the rest of her words, realizing Baldwin did not need to hear her "I told you so" now that Count Philip had proven to be such a bitter disappointment. "Joscelin has gone to tell Sybilla," she said, approaching the bed to annoy her son by feeling his forehead for fever.

"I am getting better, Mother," he said crossly. "I wish you would stop watching over me as if you expected the Angel of Death to fly in the window at any moment." He at once felt a dart of remorse, seeing that he'd hurt her, and told Anselm to pour wine for his guests. "Fetch them seats, too, Anselm, for we have much to discuss."

Before the squire could comply, there was another knock on the door. When Baldwin nodded, Anselm ambled over to open it and, after a muffled exchange, stepped back to admit a young woman and a page of ten or so, clutching a large woven basket. The boy looked terrified but the girl seemed more curious and excited than fearful. Recognizing one of Sybilla's handmaidens, Baldwin sat up, carefully tucking the sheet around his chest. "Lady Gisele, is it not?"

"You remember me!" she exclaimed, favoring him with a surprised and very charming smile before making a graceful court curtsy that seemed incongruous in Baldwin's bedchamber. "The countess has a gift for you, my liege. Eudes, bring it to the king."

The boy gaped at her, as motionless as if he were rooted to the floor. It was painfully obvious to them all that he'd sooner leap into a river swarming with crocodiles before he'd approach the bed of the leper king. Anselm resolved the impasse by taking the basket and placing it within Baldwin's reach. The lid at once popped open, revealing a furry white head.

Agnes sighed in exasperation. What had possessed Sybilla? Guilt, probably, for not having come to see Baldwin. Dogs were troublesome creatures, dirty and noisy and into everything. Would the girl ever learn to think first? But then she saw the look on her son's face and her irritation melted away as if it had never been.

The puppy was looking around with great interest and then decided to climb onto Baldwin, nibbling his finger to see if it was edible, much to his amusement. "I had a dog once," he told Gisele, "a wolfhound almost as big as a mule. Bandit, I called him, for he was the best food thief in all of Jerusalem. He died when I was twelve and I vowed I'd never have another dog."

"Oh, but you must keep this one, my lord!" Gisele sounded truly distressed that he might refuse the puppy. "She is so sweet!"

"Very sweet," he agreed, but he was looking at her, not the dog. "What do you think I should name her, demoiselle?"

Flattered that he should want her opinion, she pretended to study the puppy. "Well, it would be good luck to give her an Egyptian name since our army will soon be marching along the Nile River. Babylon?" she suggested, for that was what the Franks often called the land of Egypt. Baldwin shook his head in mock horror, causing her to ask with a giggle, "Are there any famous Egyptian queens?"

"Cleopatra." Baldwin shot William a triumphant look, proud that he'd remembered those past history lessons so well. "That is a fine name for a dog, demoiselle, but alas, not for this one," he said, lifting the puppy up so she could see why.

She giggled again, and William felt such pain that he could almost believe he'd been stabbed. As he glanced around, he saw his own heartbreak etched on Agnes's face, too. It was simply too much, he thought, to be given this cruel glimpse of how life should have been for Baldwin, watching him react to a pretty girl the way any sixteen-year-old lad would.

He did not know if Baldwin suddenly realized that even this innocent flirtation was forbidden to him, or if he'd noticed that Gisele had ventured too close to the bed, for he was conscientious about keeping others at a safe distance. But Baldwin pulled back then, saying in a cool and very formal tone, "Thank my sister for the dog, Lady Gisele. Tell her I am pleased."

She seemed bewildered by the abrupt change in his demeanor. After a moment, she dropped another curtsy. "I will, my liege." When he did not reply, she turned toward the door, which Eudes opened with alacrity. She looked back once, but Baldwin did not meet her gaze.

After they had gone, the silence was so charged that William could barely breathe. Agnes had turned toward the window until she could regain her composure and Denys moved to her side. But Baldwin's face was so utterly inscrutable that William felt as if he were gazing upon the stone effigy that would one day adorn the boy's royal tomb.

It was Anselm who broke the spell. "So what will you name the little fellow, my lord? How about Saladin? The Saracens do not fancy dogs much, calling them unclean, so that would be a fine insult."

Baldwin looked up blankly, and then slowly came back from wherever he'd gone. "I do not want to think of the sultan every time I call him," he said, and while his voice was husky, it was also steady. "Mayhap Cairo."

They agreed that was the ideal name for the puppy. Almost as if understanding he was being talked about, Cairo began to bark, then scrambled onto Baldwin's shoulder to lick his face. And when his antics coaxed a smile from her son, Agnes silently blessed her impulsive, unpredictable daughter.

By the time Maria and her daughter reached Jerusalem, Isabella was tired and that made her cranky, so when she was told she must accompany her nurse, she insisted she wanted to see Baldwin first. As much as Maria loved her child, she believed in the need for discipline and she was not swayed by Isabella's pleading. Telling the steward that she must see the king straightaway, she was soon following a servant into the stairwell that led to the royal solar.

She'd hoped to find William with Baldwin, but her heart sank when she saw the others in the solar: Agnes and Joscelin de Courtenay, Reynald de Chatillon, and Archbishop Eraclius. As she came forward to greet her stepson, she could feel their eyes upon her, hostile, measuring, and predatory. Not for the first time, she wondered what would become of her and her daughter when Baldwin died and Sybilla and the de Courtenays ruled the kingdom.

Baldwin did not look well to her, pale and tired and gaunt; he'd lost an alarming amount of weight during his lengthy illness. She knew he was surprised by her appearance, for she did not attend the court unless invited to do so, but he greeted her with courtesy, and gestured for her to take a seat. "Did you bring Bella with you?"

She nodded, saying that Isabella was eager to see him. That seemed to please him. It did not please the others. Although nothing was said, their animosity blanketed the solar like woodsmoke. Ignoring them, Maria kept her eyes on Baldwin. "I am here," she said, "to talk to you about the Count of Flanders."

"I assume you wish to protest his marital plans for Bella. But he is no longer in the city, having decided to visit some of our holy sites, and I do not know when he will be back."

Despite his efforts to sound unperturbed, Baldwin was angry about the count's sudden departure while their plans for the Egyptian campaign remained unresolved; Maria caught echoes of that anger in his voice. And what she had to say would only add fuel to the fire. "He may well be planning to visit those sacred sites, but he came first to Nablus to see me."

Baldwin's court mask slipped, allowing her to see his surprise. Before he could respond, his mother and uncle spoke up.

"Why would he want to see you?" Joscelin asked in astonishment. Maria did not know if he meant to be offensive or was merely curious, but she took it as an insult. She was a daughter of the Greek Royal House, after all.

Agnes had been standing by Baldwin's chair, her eyes drilling holes into Maria's brain. "And you made him welcome?" she said in disbelief. "Surely you do not want your daughter married off to one of his vassals? God knows we have never agreed upon anything, but I would have thought we'd be united in this—wanting to see that man stoned in the marketplace."

"Half of Jerusalem would turn out for that," Reynald said laconically.

"Of course I do not approve of the count's outrageous marriage schemes," Maria said coolly, "and as Isabella's mother, I'd like nothing better than to pick up that first stone. But I could not turn the count away until I'd heard what he had to say. That is what queens do."

Baldwin's mouth twitched and Reynald looked faintly amused. But Agnes, Joscelin, and the archbishop were so obviously unamused that Maria felt a dart of satisfaction. Turning back to her stepson, she said, "For a man who claims that he came to the Holy Land only to honor God, Count Philip is spending an inordinate amount of his time on temporal matters. In addition to his plotting to marry your sisters to men of his choosing, he is here to fulfill a mission entrusted to him by the French king, Louis Capet. Louis wants to wed his youngest daughter to the Emperor Manuel's son and heir, and Count Philip asked for my help in bringing that about."

"And you agreed to help him?" Agnes's voice dripped scorn, and Maria decided the other woman probably was sincere in this if in nothing else—unable to understand how she would be willing to aid the man who'd have forced Isabella into a marriage at age five.

"Yes, I did," she said defiantly. "His mission to Constantinople has nothing to do with his selfish, lawless plans for my daughter. I considered whether my great-uncle would be interested in an alliance with the French king—and of course, he would be—so I advised the count how best to approach him with the proposal."

"I would not throw that man a rope if he were drowning," Agnes said proudly as Joscelin moved into Maria's line of vision.

"And you felt the need to make a trip to Jerusalem just to tell the king this? Are there no scribes left in Nablus, no messengers?"

"Uncle."

Baldwin said no more than that, but Joscelin subsided, and Maria was impressed by the quiet way her stepson asserted his authority. With the de Courtenays, it could be no easy task, she thought. "I have more to tell you, my lord king. During his visit, the count also spoke of the Egyptian campaign. He was surprisingly candid, mayhap because he saw me as an ally after I agreed to write to the emperor on his behalf. He said he had no intention of taking part in the attack upon Egypt because you refused to make it worth his while."

Even though Baldwin had already reached that conclusion, it was still infuriating to hear it confirmed in the count's own words. "Damn him," he said softly, "damn them all," and the others knew he meant the foreigners, the outsiders who were so sure they understood the Kingdom of Jerusalem better than the native-born Christians, so sure the Poulains were not worthy guardians of the Holy Land.

"I told him," Maria said, "that he'd be making a great mistake if he did not join the campaign. I warned him that if he remained in Jerusalem whilst you made war upon Saladin, his honor would suffer and the High Court would blame him if that war went badly. Although I doubt that he cares what the High Court thinks of him, he does not want to antagonize my great-uncle, who would blame him, too. He seemed taken aback by my speaking so bluntly, but he is an arrogant man, not a stupid one. He said he'd give it some thought, and the next day he told me that he would agree to join the campaign."

"Did he, indeed?" As Baldwin's eyes met Maria's, she experienced something she never had before, a moment in which she knew exactly what her stepson was thinking, and they exchanged a look of silent understanding.

Agnes saw it, too, and felt a quiver of fear. "Is that why you are here?" she snapped. "To claim credit for changing the count's mind?"

"No," Maria said, not taking her eyes from Baldwin. "I came to tell you that it does not matter what Count Philip says or promises. He cannot be trusted." She hesitated then, for she was about to venture into a quagmire of conflicting loyalties. Hers were dual. She was Greek to the marrow of her bones, would yearn for Constantinople until the end of her earthly days. But she would never go back, for she would never willingly leave her daughter and Outremer was Isabella's homeland, mayhap even her kingdom one day.

She knew that Baldwin was aware of the growing discontent of the Greek envoys. But he did not yet know how deeply suspicious they'd become; the Greeks had little confidence in Latin Christians in the best of times. She feared that if the Egyptian campaign was thwarted by Philip's intransigence, her great-uncle would not send his fleet to Outremer again.

She could not tell Baldwin what had been told to her in confidence by Manuel's envoys. She could warn him, though, that he faced opposition from within his own ranks. "You know, my liege, that the Count of Tripoli strongly disapproves of your alliance with the Greek empire. He mistrusts the Emperor Manuel and he'd not be disappointed if the Egyptian campaign were called off. Nor would your other cousin, the Prince of Antioch."

Baldwin was caught off-balance by that. They all were, even Reynald, who was Bohemond's stepfather. When Baldwin glanced in his direction, he shrugged. Agnes could endure no more and stepped in front of Maria. "What nonsense is this? Bohemond has no grievance against the Greek emperor. He wed a Greek princess last year, for God's sake!"

"Yes . . . my sister, Theodora." Maria had paid a visit to Antioch after the wedding, not having seen Theodora since her own marriage to Amalric a decade ago. She'd found a very unhappy young girl, homesick and miserable, who confided that Bohemond had not wanted to wed her, that Manuel had insisted upon it as part of his price for aiding the Franks. She'd not have expected him to be faithful, Theodora had sobbed, for he was a man, after all. But he was besotted with his longtime concubine, shamed her by flaunting the woman in public, and during one of their quarrels, he'd told her that their marriage would last only as long as Manuel lived.

Maria could not reveal any of this, though, could not betray her sister's marital misery. "I am not claiming that Bohemond shares Raymond's hostility toward the Greeks. But he has long viewed the Saracen castle at Hārim as a threat, for it is only twelve miles from Antioch, and he has been complaining that he'd rather besiege Hārim than sail for Egypt with the Greek fleet."

There, she thought; that ought to alert Baldwin to his cousin's unreliability whilst avoiding mention of his smoldering resentment of the marriage forced upon him by Manuel. Baldwin said nothing, but he looked so weary that Maria felt a twinge of regret for adding to the crushing burdens he was already laboring under. Yet he had to know. Rising, she said she ought to make sure that Isabella was settled in. Baldwin unexpectedly rose, too. "I'll walk with you," he said, "for I want to stop by the stables."

Reynald also got to his feet. As they all exited into the stairwell, Agnes heard her son tell Maria to bring Bella to his bedchamber that evening, saying he had a surprise for her. She knew what it was; he wanted to show his new puppy to his little sister, who would naturally be thrilled, bonding with him over that damned dog.

She managed to wait until the door closed, cutting off the rest of their conversation, before she exploded. "You see what she is doing, Joscelin? She is using that brat of hers to worm her way into Baldwin's good graces, and he has such a kind heart that it will work!"

Joscelin thought that his sister was rather irrational about Maria, for he did not see her as the threat that Agnes did. It would be different if she still lived at court, but she saw Baldwin only twice a year, at his Christmas and Easter celebrations. How much ground could she gain during such brief visits? "It is fortunate that she lives in Nablus," he said, hoping that Agnes would be satisfied with that.

Agnes knew him well enough to realize he was only humoring her, and she scowled, frustrated that he was blind to the danger that Maria Comnena posed. She was thankful that Archbishop Eraclius was more perceptive than her brother, as he proved now.

"I think we must be vigilant, madame," he said, nodding vigorously. "We dare not take that woman too lightly. She is Greek, after all, a race known to be as subtle as the serpent, and she is far too friendly with the Archbishop of Tyre, a man just as untrustworthy."

Joscelin had gone over to the table to refill his wine cup and quickly brought it up to conceal his grin. While many priests thought it was a minor sin to break their vows of chastity, openly taking hearth mates who were wives in all but name, the higher a man climbed on the Church ladder, the more cautious and circumspect he usually became. Even an archbishop's miter had not changed Eraclius's lustful habits, though; he was notorious for his indiscreet dalliances. Whereas Joscelin doubted that William of Tyre could be tempted even if a squirming, naked woman was thrust into his bed—the poor sod.

Agnes had begun to pace. Whilst it was true that she hated the Greek, she was also afraid of her. Maria had a powerful weapon—that child. Baldwin wanted the best for his sister and Maria was playing upon that, insinuating herself back into his life. If they could not find a suitable husband for Sybilla or—Jesu forfend—she did not give birth to a healthy son in December, her claim to the crown might well be challenged in a few years by Isabella, especially if Baldwin remained set upon this alliance with Constantinople. As Baldwin's health continued to fail, some might see the emperor's blood kin as a better choice than Sybilla, and Manuel had gold enough to buy half the members of the High Court. Even Isabella's youth might work to her advantage, for a long regency offered unlimited opportunities for unscrupulous, ambitious men to enrich themselves at the Crown's expense.

Her heart and pulse were racing. She could not fight for Baldwin whilst having to watch her back, too. Although she knew that was a battle she and her son were doomed to lose, she would never give up. Yet if leprosy could not be defeated, Maria Comnena could. She must find a way to banish the Greek bitch from court, to make Baldwin see her true colors. But how?

The city that the Franks called Cairo was not actually a city at all. Its proper name was al-Qāhira and it was a vast fortress, built two hundred years ago as a residence for the caliphs of the Fātimid dynasty, their wives, concubines, servants, slaves, court officials, and army brigades. Its Great East Palace was famed for its opulence, said to contain over four thousand chambers, although al-ʿĀdil wondered if anyone had ever actually counted them. After his brother had staged his bloodless coup against the caliph, they had discovered that the stories of its lavish accommodations were indeed true. The caliph's throne was of solid gold with silver steps, and the carved ceilings were inlaid with gold. There were marble pillars; pavements decorated with dazzling mosaics; curtains strewn with pearls; coffers overflowing with the finest brocades, silks, ivory, rubies, emeralds—riches beyond any man's wildest dreams. But none of it had the sultan kept for himself.

He had no craving for luxury, preferring to live as simply as a Sufi holy man, and he had laughed when it was suggested that he move into the caliph's Great East Palace. He'd chosen the more modest vizier's palace as his dwelling, turning the Great Palace over to his army commanders and giving the Lesser West Palace to his brother. The riches were distributed to his loyal followers, used for good deeds, and shared with his liege lord, for he'd not yet been ready to renounce his allegiance to Nūr al-Dīn. That inevitable confrontation had been avoided by the latter's death three years ago, and he then openly claimed what was already his, the sultanate of Egypt. It was a remarkable rise to power for a Kurd, for an outsider. But all that he'd accomplished was threatened now by the infidel invasion.

As he entered the gardens of Kafur, which adjoined the Lesser West Palace where he'd lived for the past six years, al-'Ādil paused to savor the tranquil scene that met his eyes, knowing how fleeting this moment of peace would be. The sun had begun its slow retreat from the waiting dark, trailing golden clouds in its wake and reflecting the blood-red sky in the canal and the distant waters of the Nile. He enjoyed living in the former pleasure-house of the caliphs, not sharing his brother's taste for austerity. Above all, he loved these gardens, shaded with tamarisk, willow, and sycamore trees, fragrant with flowers for much of the year, echoing with the cooing from the dovecotes and the songs of thrush, lark, and chaffinch. Would the day soon come when infidel boots sounded on its paved pathways?

The gardens covered a huge area, but he knew where to find Āliya, for she liked to watch the sunset from one of the marble pavilions near the canal. She was there, seated on a bench with her maid, Jumāna, while two of the household eunuchs hovered at a protective distance. She would never have ventured out in public unless she was modestly veiled, yet here in the privacy of their gardens, she had unfastened her veil to take advantage of the breeze wafting from the river, and al-'Ādil halted so he could watch her unobserved. Even though they'd been wed almost a year, she could still take his breath away. His pet name for her was "Ghazāla," for she had the grace of a young gazelle.

Āliya leaned over to whisper something to Jumāna and when both women laughed, al-'Ādil found himself smiling. He'd known from the first that Āliya was clever, for she'd taken pains to ingratiate herself with his first wife, Halīma, and she'd befriended his brother's favorite wife, Shamsa. But he'd not realized how clever she truly was until she freed Jumāna, the daughter of a household slave in Āliya's family household.

The girls had been raised together, and both intimacy and affection had developed between them, as often happened in such cases, for slaves were usually well treated in accordance with the teachings of the Qur'an.

But if Āliya was willing to share confidences, items of clothing, and perfume with Jumāna, she was not willing to share her new husband, and she'd soon noticed the way his eyes occasionally lingered upon Jumāna.

Al-'Ādil did find Jumāna desirable; he'd not deny that. He did not think he'd have acted upon that desire, though; at least he hoped not. But Āliya had made sure that he'd not give way to temptation. She did not let jealousy poison their marriage; nor did she blame Jumāna. She'd simply arranged for Jumāna's manumission, then innocently informed al-'Ādil of her good deed, for the freeing of slaves was always encouraged as an admirable act of piety. It also made it impossible for him to take Jumāna to his bed, for women taken as concubines could not be of free status; the Qur'an spoke clearly upon that, saying that a man could have sexual intercourse only with his wives or those possessed by his right hand—slaves. Al-'Ādil had been amused by her adroit handling of the matter, for he appreciated subtlety, knowing what a rare talent that was. Even as a youth, he'd seen that guile and indirection served as both a shield and a weapon, and he was pleased that Āliya understood this, too.

Āliya happened to glance in his direction then. Jumping to her feet, she glided toward him, her gold and silver ankle bracelets jingling with each step of her red leather slippers, turning her approach into a dance. "How glad I am to see you, my heart!" She did not embrace him, though, for in that, too, she was a proper wife, aware that open displays of affection belonged in the bedchamber.

Smiling down at her, he touched his fingers to her cheek in a light caress and acknowledged Jumāna with the formal courtesy he'd have bestowed upon a kinswoman, but not one of his own household. She made a respectful obeisance and withdrew a discreet distance so they might have privacy.

Tilting Āliya's chin up so he could look into her face, he said, "Are you well, Ghazāla? You had no morning queasiness again?" It was early in her pregnancy and he found that already he was worrying more than he had with any of Halīma's lying-ins.

"No . . . I ate so much that Jumāna said I must surely be carrying twins—two bowls of yogurt with cherries, dates, and almonds." The eyes he found so beautiful—as luminous as a fawn's, with lashes like silky fans—were searching his face intently, and he squeezed her hand reassuringly, then led her back to the pavilion.

He'd spent the day with his brother, who'd ridden in yesterday from his camp at Bilbais, where their army was waiting to repel the invasion by the Franks. Answering the unspoken question in those slanted dark eyes, he said that Yūsuf had heard nothing from his spies. "It is surprising that the Greek fleet has not sailed yet. The tension between the Poulains and that foreign count must be serious, indeed, to cause such a delay. But any day now . . ."

She cast down her lashes, but not in time; he saw her fear. All felt it, though. It was like waiting for a storm to break, wondering how severe it would be. "As soon as we get word that they have left Acre, I am sending you and Halīma and your households to Alexandria."

She gave a soft cry of protest, quickly stilled. "I would rather stay here with you," she said, "but I will do as you bid me—for the safety of our son." He saw one of her hands slide down to rest protectively on her abdomen, and he reached over to cover it with his own hand, for the gardens were cloaked in lavender twilight by now, creating the illusion that they were alone in their own world, one that held no dangers of death on the battlefield or in the birthing chamber. They sat that way in silence for a time, broken at last by Āliya. "Do you think Allah might see me as presumptuous for being so sure I will bear a son? I know it is not for us to say. It is just that I want so badly to give you a boy, Ahmad. . . ."

They'd been speaking in the Kurdish tongue that was native to them both, but he switched to Arabic then, saying, "*Insha'Allah*." For there was no greater truth; all was as Allah willed it.

"My lord!" The eunuchs had scrambled to their feet, hands dropping to their weapons, having heard what al-'Ādil had not, the thudding of footsteps on the pathway. Al-'Ādil was on his feet, too, as the man came into view, for he recognized a *khadim*, one who served the sultan.

Panting and red-faced, the man fell to his knees. "The sultan bade me summon you at once, my lord."

Given the size of al-Qāhira, al-'Ādil would normally have ridden, but it would take too long to saddle a mount, and so he chose, instead, to use the underground passage that connected the Great and Lesser Palaces. By the time he emerged into the east courtyard, he was out of breath, his heart hammering in rhythm to the urgency of his footsteps. He'd pressed a quick kiss into Āliya's palm, promising that he'd share with her afterward whatever he learned from his brother. They both knew the news would not be good. Obviously Yūsuf had gotten word that the invasion had finally begun.

Already filled with foreboding, al-'Ādil became downright alarmed when he was told that the sultan was in the stables. Did Yūsuf mean for them to leave for Bilbais this very night? If so, his spy must have brought dire news indeed.

Yet there was no air of exigency in the stables. Grooms were going about their chores as usual. Finding his brother in the stall with his new white stallion, al-'Ādil paused to draw air into his lungs and to study Yūsuf, who seemed as calm as the grooms. He was never one to panic in a crisis, but he definitely did not look like a man about to face an enemy army.

"Ah, there you are, Ahmad," he said, straightening up from an examination of his stallion's hoof and smiling over his shoulder. "Is he not splendid? Once he is trained for mall, your team will never be able to beat mine."

Entering the spacious stall, al-'Ādil gave the older man a probing look. "I was sure you were going to tell me that we'd soon be fending off the Franks on our own soil. But if you now have time for your new stallion, clearly that is not so."

They had no fear of being overheard by the grooms, for they were speaking in Kurdish. From habit, though, al-'Ādil lowered his voice. "I take it that the Greek fleet is still anchored at Acre."

"No, it has sailed . . . for home. The Greeks are on their way back to Constantinople, having grudgingly agreed to delay the invasion until next spring at the foreign count's insistence."

"Praise be to Allah! He has indeed blessed us, Yūsuf, by setting the Franks against one another. This will give us six more months to make ready." Al-'Ādil laughed, so great was his relief.

"No . . . there will be no invasion in the spring. My sources tell me the Greeks are so disgusted by the strife between the Franks and the foreign count that they are going to advise their emperor not to honor his commitment to the Frankish king, saying they are not to be trusted."

Al-'Ādil could scarcely believe their good fortune. "How thankful Āliya will be. She has been greatly troubled, as women are when breeding." This brief appearance of the husband yielded to the soldier again and he said with a grin, "Shall we send this foreign count some of our best camels in gratitude?"

"That is the least we owe him, Ahmad. Last week he and the Count of Tripoli rode north into Syria, where they mean to join forces with the Prince of Antioch to besiege Hārim."

Al-'Ādil was puzzled by his brother's complacent tone. Why was he so unconcerned about an attack upon their lands in Syria? "What are you not telling me, Yūsuf?"

"The Count of Tripoli has also summoned the levy from his wife's principality in Galilee, a hundred knights and two thousand men-at-arms. They were accompanied by the new grand master of the Hospitallers with all of his knights, and most of the Templars, may Allah curse them."

Upon first hearing, the assembly of such a large Frankish force did not bode well for northern Syria. But al-'Ādil at once grasped what his brother was really saying. "So the foreign count and his allies have stripped the kingdom of most of their men."

"The unbelievers are now protected by their ailing boy king, a handful of their nobles and their household knights, and less than a hundred of the accursed Templars."

"Allah be praised," al-'Ādil said again, astounded that the Franks could be so reckless. "So . . . now that we need not fear an invasion, we have thousands of soldiers camped on the infidels' southern border with nothing to do. That is never a good thing where soldiers are concerned, for they tend to get into trouble when they have too much free time on their hands."

"My thinking exactly, Ahmad," Salāh al-Dīn said, and when their eyes met, they shared a smile.

CHAPTER 15

October 1177
Jerusalem, Outremer

Sybilla had hoped that she might find a cooling breeze out on her balcony; the weather had remained unusually hot and humid for that time of year. She'd made herself as comfortable as any woman seven months pregnant could be, with pillows, a footstool, and cold drinks. Frowning down at her swollen ankles, she said irritably, "My legs look like tree trunks. I get these odd cravings for food I never liked, often in the middle of the night. My back throbs like an aching tooth. I cannot stray far from a chamber pot. My breasts are sore even to the touch. And I am as clumsy as a lame donkey. Yet someone dared to tell me yesterday that these are the happiest days of my life!"

"A man, perchance?" Agnes asked dryly. "Men and nuns tend to see pregnancy as a blessed time. But ask any woman who is familiar with the birthing chamber and if she's honest, she'll admit it was like doing nine months of penance for her sins. Every pregnant woman feels bloated and wretched and exhausted, whilst having to endure the foolish smiles of strangers and the stories that other women insist upon sharing about their own pregnancies. And most husbands are utterly useless, either underfoot all the time, wanting to know if she thinks she'll birth a son, or grumbling because she cannot whelp as easily as his best lymer bitch."

The words had no sooner left Agnes's mouth than she'd have called them back if she could. She was relieved to see that her daughter seemed to take those careless comments in stride, for there were days when her tears flowed like rain. Sybilla even managed a smile, albeit a sad one. "I am very glad that Guillaume lived long enough to know I was with child. He was so excited. . . ."

Agnes made amends by rising to fluff up her daughter's pillows. Sybilla squirmed in a vain attempt to find a more comfortable position, watching her mother all the while. One benefit of her pregnancy was that it had brought them closer; Agnes actually spoke to her woman-to-woman now, instead of scolding her as if she were still a wayward child. That awareness gave her the courage to seek answers to the mystery that was her parents' marriage. While she knew about the ill will that had existed between them, she had been too young to have her own memories of their years together. "Was my father pleased when you became pregnant?"

"Yes, he was . . ." Agnes paused to take a swallow of her drink, a sweet mix of orange and pomegranate juices, before adding, "in his own understated way."

Sybilla hesitated. "Mother . . . did you ever love him?"

"No."

Sybilla had not expected an answer so honest, so uncompromising. "Did you . . . love any of your husbands?"

Agnes was silent for so long that Sybilla wasn't sure she'd get any response at all. The older woman was not offended, however, merely considering the question. "No," she said pensively. "Oh, I may have thought I loved my first husband, for I was too young to know better. Yet within a year or two of his death, I could not remember what he looked like. As for Hugh, I was grateful to him for marrying me after Amalric cast me aside, for I do not know what would have happened to me had he not done so. But I did not love him. And I am very fond of Denys, although not in the way you mean."

Agnes paused again, wondering if she was misjudging her daughter. Yes, Sybilla had always seemed to be naïve and romantic, but in less than a year, she'd become a wife, a widow, and was soon to be a mother. Had she begun to mature? "And you? Did you love Guillaume?"

"Yes. . . ." There was something incomplete in that answer, though, and so Agnes waited, saying nothing. After a moment of silence, Sybilla continued. "Well, most of the time I did. Guillaume was very good company when he wanted to be. But he had a temper that the smallest spark could set off, especially when he'd been drinking. He was not very lovable in one of his rages. Fortunately, they never lasted long."

Seeing the expression on her mother's face, she said hastily, "Oh, he never struck me! He'd yell at me—at anyone within hearing range—but he did not raise his hand to me. I'd not have put up with that. After all, without me, he'd never be king."

Usually any mention of Baldwin's inevitable fate aroused angry despair in his mother, but now she nodded approvingly, pleased that Sybilla had the spirit to stand up for herself.

Sybilla finished her drink. "How is Baldwin's puppy?"

"He apparently thinks that if something fits in his mouth, God means for him to eat it. He is a wretched little pest most of the time. But he makes Baldwin laugh a dozen times a day and I thank you for that, dearest."

Sybilla went pink with pleasure, for compliments from her mother were as rare as summer rainstorms in the Levant. "How is Baldwin feeling?"

"He is regaining his strength, able now to take that Arab stallion of his out for rides. But he is worried sick about our kingdom's vulnerability, cursing his cousins and the Flemish count every time their names are even mentioned."

Sybilla knew, of course, that many of their men were away in northern Syria, besieging several Saracen castles. But she'd not realized it weighed so heavily on Baldwin's mind. "I can see why the border with Egypt is at greater risk. Yet surely the kingdom itself is not in peril?"

Agnes stared at her. Opening her mouth to remind Sybilla what had befallen Edessa, the county their family had once ruled, she stopped herself just in time. Sybilla did not need to hear again about the massacre of Edessa's Christians when it was taken by the Saracens. A woman soon to face the dangers of the birthing chamber had fears enough of her own.

Leaving her daughter to take an afternoon nap, Agnes returned to her own palace chambers, where she was surprised to find her brother waiting for her. She was even more surprised when Joscelin tersely dismissed her ladies. As soon as they were alone, he slid the bolt into place, locking the door. "I want to talk to you about Maria Comnena."

Irked that he'd taken it upon himself to give orders to her attendants, she shook her head. "Well, I do not," she said. "Now that she has finally gone back to Nablus, I need not speak of her or even think of her until she returns to ruin our Christmas court."

"She may have left the palace, but she did not go back to Nablus. She is still in the city. She has rented a town house in the Patriarch's Quarter, on St. Stephen Street."

Agnes had been about to pour them some wine. At that, she spun around to face Joscelin. "Jesus God! Are you sure?" When he nodded, she sat down suddenly upon the closest coffer. "Baldwin must have known. Why did he not tell me?"

Joscelin thought the answer to that was obvious; Baldwin wanted to avoid his mother's outrage. "I owe you an apology, Sister, for you were right about the Greek. She means to use her daughter as a weapon against us, as a means of winning

Baldwin's goodwill. She'll spend more and more time in the city, more and more time at the palace, reminding the High Court by Isabella's very presence that Sybilla is not Amalric's only daughter. What if—"

Joscelin cut himself off abruptly, for that was not a fear he could ever share with his sister. It was one that often tormented him, though, in the sleepless nights since Guillaume's death. *What if Sybilla dies in childbirth, she and the baby?* It was not that uncommon, after all. He had become very fond of his young niece, but her death would be much more than a personal grief. For their family, it would be catastrophic.

Agnes was already on her feet again, beginning to pace. "We need to turn Baldwin against her. She'll not find it as easy to entangle High Court members in her web if she has been sent away in disgrace. And if she is no longer welcome at court, then we'll see less of Isabella, too. Baldwin is always going to care about the girl because of their kinship, but if she remains at Nablus, he'll not be thinking of her that often, not with all he must deal with. . . ."

She could have been referring to the burdens of kingship. Joscelin knew what was really on her mind, for it was always on his, too—the inevitable decline of Baldwin's health as he fought a battle he could not hope to win. "I agree," he said. "We must outwit that scheming bitch ere it is too late. But how?"

Agnes came to a halt. "I do not know," she admitted. "But I will find a way. As God is my witness, I will."

It took her several days and the loss of some sleep, but Agnes did come up with a plan. When she revealed it to her brother, Joscelin responded with gratifying enthusiasm, laughing and giving her an affectionate hug. "That is brilliant, Agnes!"

"I think so, too," she said, eschewing modesty for candor. "The Greeks are Lucifer proud, so Maria is sure to take it as a mortal insult. And Baldwin will not forgive her for defying him. He is thin-skinned when it comes to his authority. . . ." Her smile disappeared then, for she well knew why Baldwin was so sensitive on that subject; he was acutely aware that his ill health made him more vulnerable to challenges than other kings.

Joscelin saw the shadow that crossed her face and acted quickly to banish it by embracing her again. "Let's drink to our success," he said, striding over to pour wine for them both. By the time he'd done so, though, some of his initial elation had begun to ebb away. "But will Baldwin agree to it? He knows how much you loathe the Greek, Agnes. Would he not be suspicious that you would come to him with a proposal involving Maria?"

"Of course he would. That is why the idea cannot come from either one of us. Fortunately, I have the perfect person in mind—Archbishop Eraclius. Baldwin truly likes the d'Ibelin brothers. So he is sure to be interested when Eraclius suggests that this would be an ideal way of rewarding their loyalty, and at no cost to the Crown. I'll tell Eraclius to mention the benefits to Isabella, too, for that will matter to Baldwin."

Joscelin nodded approvingly. "Very clever, Sister. And you are confident the archbishop will be willing to do this?"

"Very confident," she responded, with a cynical smile. "There is little that Eraclius would not do to earn our favor. And he can be quite persuasive, whilst being unburdened by any inconvenient scruples."

Convinced, Joscelin clinked his cup playfully against hers. "I suppose it is too much to hope that Maria might go back to Constantinople in high dudgeon?"

"Unfortunately, yes. So, I'll settle for making her unwelcome at court." Agnes smiled again at her brother. "The beauty of the plan, Joscelin, is that I will be avenging myself upon Baudouin d'Ibelin at the same time that we sink the Greek's hopes once and for all."

Joscelin raised his cup in a mock salute. "A pity that Balian has to go down with the ship, too. He's rather a decent sort."

Agnes shrugged, for while she bore the youngest d'Ibelin brother no grudge, in war, it was inevitable that the innocent would suffer along with the guilty.

The king's summons caused Baudouin and Balian some unease, for they feared Baldwin had gotten word of troop movements by the Saracens. But when they reached the royal palace, they found no sense of urgency or tension, reassuring them that Outremer was not in danger of invasion. As they crossed the courtyard, Baudouin came to a sudden halt. "There is Hugues of Galilee," he said in surprise. "I wonder why he is not off fighting in Syria with Count Raymond." He detoured, then, in the youth's direction, giving Balian no choice except to follow.

Baudouin was never one to deny his curiosity and once greetings were exchanged, he asked Hugues why he'd not joined his stepfather's campaign. Balian caught Hugues's look of discomfort and was quick to put the correct interpretation upon it. Because so many highborn women were made widows by war, it was not unusual for Poulain families to be headed by stepfathers. Often these relationships were rocky ones. Balian's own mother had remarried after his father's death and while he'd been too young to remember his stepfather, he knew his brothers had detested the man. Having seen young Humphrey de Toron with his new stepfather, he did not doubt that the boy was afraid of Reynald de Chatillon. But the four sons of Lady Eschiva were luckier than most, for they had forged a close bond with the Count of Tripoli after he'd married their mother. So, if Hugues was not in Syria with his stepfather, it must mean that he shared their concern for the kingdom's safety; he was the eldest of Eschiva's sons and the eventual heir to the principality of Galilee, after all. Yet if he confided his fears, it would seem as if he were being critical of Count Raymond, which the boy was clearly not willing to do.

Deftly seizing control of the conversation and thus sparing Hugues the need to answer, Balian explained that they had been summoned by the king. Hugues's expression lightened at that. "Then the king is no longer bedridden?" he exclaimed, alarming both the d'Ibelin brothers, for they'd not heard that Baldwin's lung fever had returned.

"Ah, no, it is not that," Hugues assured them. "He took another bad fall two days ago, even worse than the one back in April at his Easter court."

Hugues offered no details of the fall, nor did they ask for them. They understood at once what this latest fall meant: Baldwin was continuing to lose feeling in his right foot.

Baldwin shifted in his seat. The solar was shuttered, yet his eyes remained very sensitive to light and even the oil lamps seemed unnaturally bright. His head was pounding and, though he'd tried to hide it, he was still experiencing occasional bouts of dizziness. But he'd insisted upon being present at this meeting with the d'Ibelin brothers, for it was rare to have good news to impart and he needed to be able to do something that would bring joy to others. While his mother had finally stopped urging him to return to his bedchamber, she continued to watch him as if she were counting his every breath and he kept from lashing out at her with difficulty; both his temper and his nerves had been inflamed since his fall.

Archbishop Eraclius was keeping the conversation going, with some help from Joscelin. Baldwin had been surprised that he'd asked to be included. His mother was obviously here to stave off the Angel of Death. Baldwin hoped Joscelin was motivated merely by curiosity. Jesu forfend that both his mother and his uncle should start treating him as if he were a fledgling with a broken wing, too helpless to fend for himself.

When the d'Ibelins were announced, they came to an involuntary halt, their eyes drawn to the wide white bandage that covered the gash on Baldwin's forehead. Their responses were quite different, though. Balian chose diplomatically to ignore it; Baudouin gave a low whistle.

"I'd wager your head feels like a split melon, sire," he said sympathetically. "I still remember when my brother clouted me with a mallet. I not only saw stars, I saw the moon and sun, too, plus half a dozen comets."

"I did no such thing," Balian protested.

"Not you, lad . . . Hugh. You were still in your cradle then. I deserved it, though, for I'd been teasing Hugh all morning." Glancing back at Baldwin, Baudouin said, "You'll feel like a dog's dinner, sire, for a few more days, but you'll soon be on the mend. My mother used to insist that the male head is too hard to suffer lasting damage and I daresay she was right."

Baldwin found himself returning Baudouin's grin, preferring his brash joking to the smothering solicitude he was getting from everyone else. "Do sit," he said, and gestured for Anselm to pour drinks for them all. The squire served wine to the others, cold water to Baldwin, knowing that he continued to struggle with nausea. Baldwin gave him a grateful look, then nodded to the archbishop to begin; he wanted to keep his own talking to a minimum, for he feared that his speech was still slurred.

Archbishop Eraclius beamed at the d'Ibelins, looking so friendly that they were immediately on guard. "It is my honor to speak for the king in this matter. He wishes to discuss a marital alliance between the House of Ibelin and the Crown."

"Hallelujah!" Baudouin was on his feet, letting out a shout that reverberated like thunder, causing the others to laugh and Baldwin to recoil, for he was very sensitive to noise since his head injury.

Balian was astounded, for he'd been sure that Sybilla was beyond his brother's reach. As if reading his thoughts, Baudouin winked at him before saying, "I would be deeply honored, my liege, to wed your sister, and I will never give you cause to regret your trust in me."

There was a split second for Balian to realize something was amiss. Baldwin looked dismayed, but the de Courtenays were smiling, smiles he could only describe as smug. The archbishop leaned forward in his chair, saying earnestly, "Ah, my lord, I am indeed sorry if I gave you the wrong impression. The bride is not the king's sister. It is his stepmother, Queen Maria."

Baudouin dropped back into his chair, at a rare loss for words. Sybilla was the glittering prize he'd been pursuing even before her marriage to Guillaume of Montferrat. But he was far from a fool and despite his initial disappointment, he realized that marriage to Maria Comnena would transform their family fortunes, too, linking the d'Ibelins to the Royal Houses of Jerusalem and Constantinople. Looking over to get his brother's reaction, he was startled to see that Balian's face had drained of all color; even his lips were white.

Balian had never allowed himself to probe his feelings for Maria, for what would be the point? She treated him as a friend and he was realistic enough not to aspire to more than that. And now she was to be his brother's wife? He felt as if all the air had been driven from his lungs, a blow that had stolen both his breath and his power of speech. He knew he should offer Baudouin his congratulations, but he could not do it, not yet. He closed his eyes for a moment, willing the shock to subside, and when he opened them, he found they were all looking at him, Baudouin concerned, Baldwin frowning, and the others still smiling.

"You all right, lad?" Baudouin asked softly before returning his gaze to Baldwin and the archbishop. "Well, I cannot deny I had the Lady Sybilla in mind, but I've always had the greatest admiration for Queen Maria and so I—"

"My lord archbishop!" Baldwin's interruption was deliberate, an attempt to spare Baudouin further embarrassment. How could this have been bungled so badly?

Responding to the cold fury in Baldwin's voice, Archbishop Eraclius said quickly, with all the polished sincerity at his command, "My lord Baudouin, I must beg your forgiveness, for I seem unwittingly to have led you astray again. The marriage that the king has in mind is one between Queen Maria and your brother, Lord Balian."

Baldwin kept his eyes on Balian, not wanting to watch Baudouin's reaction, and some of his misgivings eased, for he'd never seen such a blaze of joy on anyone's face that he now saw on Balian's. Well, at least the archbishop had not been lying when he'd intimated that Balian was smitten with Maria. There was some consolation in that.

"Me?" Balian was too stunned for a moment to realize what a wound his brother had just suffered, and by the time he turned toward Baudouin, the older man had managed to pull himself together. Shooting Agnes a furious look—for he never doubted that she had set this up to shame him—Baudouin then rallied enough to muster up a weak smile.

"Good for you, lad." Adding, still with that sham smile, "So we'll be getting a queen in the family, after all, eh?"

Silently vowing to offer Baudouin the next great heiress who became available for marriage, Baldwin smiled at Balian. "You are agreeable to the match, then?"

Balian burst out laughing. "I think that is a safe assumption, sire." It was a strange sensation, like being drunk—not on wine, on happiness. He felt a stab of guilt that he could be so joyful whilst Baudouin was bleeding, yet he could not help himself. This is how an escaped falcon must feel when soaring toward the heavens, he thought, freed of all tethers, with nothing ahead but the beckoning horizon.

That poetic fancy gave way almost at once to a more skeptical voice, this one firmly rooted in reality. Whatever had possessed Maria to agree to a marriage like this? A marriage that would be considered disparaging, mayhap even shameful, back in Constantinople, for she was a daughter of the Greek Royal House and he was a minor baron at best. His fief of Ibelin encompassed less than a hundred miles, only a tenth the size of the lordship of Nablus.

"And Queen Maria . . . she is willing to wed me?" He found reassurance in the smiles of Baldwin and the archbishop, but the de Courtenays were watching him much too intently. Like cats at a mousehole, he thought, as a horrible suspicion began to form in the back of his brain. "She *has* agreed to this?" he said, so sharply that Baldwin and Baudouin blinked in surprise.

Baldwin merely nodded, for he was still trying to use his voice sparingly. When he glanced toward the archbishop for confirmation, though, he did not get it. "Actually, my liege, I've not yet spoken to the queen," Eraclius said calmly. "We were to meet earlier, but it was not convenient and so I suggested she come to the palace. In fact, she ought to be here at any moment, for Nones has just rung."

"You have not talked to her about the marriage?" Baldwin sounded so incredulous that Eraclius belatedly began to wonder if it had been wise to do the bidding of the de Courtenays.

"It was my understanding that the lady would be amenable to the match, sire," he assured Baldwin, whilst assuring himself that he'd not made a mistake. Even if the king were wroth with him afterward, he'd be able to convince the lad that his intentions had been good. The favor of Agnes and Joscelin de Courtenay was worth the risk, for how long could Baldwin rule? Either he'd become so disabled that he would be utterly dependent upon his mother and uncle, or he'd die, leaving Sybilla as his heir, who'd be even more reliant upon Agnes and Joscelin for advice. And with the backing of the de Courtenays, who knew how high he could rise? Mayhap even the patriarchy itself.

Baldwin did not appear convinced, though, and Eraclius was somewhat unsettled by the reaction of the d'Ibelins. They exchanged a meaningful look and then turned to stare at the archbishop and the de Courtenays, in a way he could only describe as threatening. They clearly were realizing what had really gone on here, and he did not doubt that he was witnessing a silent declaration of war. Eraclius did not lack for confidence, though, would never have gained an archbishopric if he shrank from conflict, and he continued to smile blandly at them, thinking that he had even more motivation now to make sure that the de Courtenays emerged triumphant from the coming power struggle.

As soon as she stepped across the threshold, Maria sensed danger. It was not just the unwelcome presence of the de Courtenays. There was palpable tension in the solar. Baldwin looked as if he ought to be in bed, almost as pale as the linen bandaging his head, the pupils of his eyes so dilated that most of the blue had disappeared. He was dealing not only with pain; the taut line of his mouth and the fist clenched on his thigh testified to a smoldering anger. Only the archbishop seemed to be his usual complacent self. His long, elegant fingers were adorned with splendid ruby and emerald rings and he was polishing them against his sleeve, putting her in mind of a peacock preening his gorgeous tail feathers, for Peacock was William's private name for him. She was expecting hostility from Agnes and Joscelin and they did not disappoint, regarding her coldly but with an odd intensity, too, almost anticipation.

It was her glance toward the d'Ibelin brothers, though, that caused her stomach muscles to tighten and her breath to quicken. Baudouin was a flaming torch, all but giving off sparks, not so surprising in light of his volatile temperament and his animosity toward the de Courtenays. But she'd never seen the equable, mellow Balian look as he did now. He was usually as adept as Baldwin at concealing his inner thoughts; today his defenses were down, his emotions overflowing like a river at flood tide. Whatever had happened to cause him such distress? She was not even sure if that was the right word to describe his agitation, for there was rage in his dark eyes, too, so much rage that she felt a flicker of fear. What had those accursed de Courtenays done now?

Approaching Baldwin, she said, "My liege," for she'd stopped calling him by his given name the day that he'd been crowned and he'd never invited her to shun formality, as he'd done with William. "The archbishop sent me word that you wanted to discuss something of importance with me."

"I do," Baldwin said slowly, enunciating his words with care, for he no longer trusted Eraclius to speak for him. "Please sit down, madame."

"Let me get you a seat, my lady." Balian had risen when Maria entered the solar, as had his brother. Picking up his own chair, he positioned it for her, and during the few moments that his back was to the others, he looked intently into Maria's face and silently mouthed the words, "I did not know, I swear."

Thoroughly alarmed by now, she settled herself in the chair, and gazed at Baldwin with what she hoped was a serene smile. "My lord king, how may I be of service?"

"It is my hope that you will give serious consideration to marrying again, madame." Seeing her eyes widen and then cut toward Baudouin, Baldwin said swiftly, wanting to forestall any further misunderstandings, "I believe that a marriage between you and Lord Balian d'Ibelin would be advantageous to you both, as well as to my sister Isabella. I am sure you'd agree that Lord Balian would be a caring stepfather to the little lass." Baldwin hesitated then, for he'd not prepared for this, assuming the archbishop had already secured her consent. Should he elaborate upon the political benefits of such a match? Yet surely Maria was capable of figuring that out for herself. He might not have liked his stepmother during her marriage to his father, but he'd never faulted her intelligence.

At mention of Balian's name, Maria's eyes had gone even wider. Her astonishment was so obvious to them all that no one spoke, scarcely breathing as they waited for her response. She took her time as she absorbed what she'd just been told, words she'd clearly never expected to hear. And then she smiled, first at Balian and then at Baldwin.

"Lord Balian is a man of honor, integrity, and courage, my liege. I have no doubts that he would be a kind husband and, as you said, a caring stepfather to my daughter. But marriage is a sacrament, one that ought not to be entered into lightly. I would ask, therefore, for time to think about this ere I give my answer."

That did not please either the de Courtenays or the archbishop. Before they could object, Balian said quickly, "Of course, my lady. That is a most reasonable request. Please take as long as you like." He was immediately backed up by Baudouin, both d'Ibelin brothers throwing down a gauntlet without a word being spoken, daring the others to protest.

"I think that is quite reasonable, too," Baldwin said, quelling any incipient rebellion by his mother or uncle.

Maria thanked him with another smile that gave away nothing of her thoughts, and allowed Balian and Baudouin to escort her from the solar. Baldwin rose, too, saying tersely that he was tired, a rare admission for him to make. When Agnes would have come with him, he stopped her with a level look, one that conveyed suspicion and frustration and a mute plea for privacy.

He glanced over his shoulder at the archbishop as he reached the door, the expression on his face promising a discussion in the near future that Eraclius would not enjoy, and then he disappeared into the stairwell, with Anselm trailing discreetly at his heels.

Agnes wanted to wait in the doorway, making sure he did not trip or have another dizzy spell. Knowing that would have angered him, she forced herself to trust Anselm's quick reflexes should Baldwin stumble again.

Joscelin moved past her to close the door. "Well, that did not go as planned," he said, giving Eraclius a look that made the archbishop begin to bridle.

"Surely you are not implying that is my fault? I did exactly as your sister asked."

Agnes was not satisfied with Eraclius's performance, either. She'd told him that she was looking forward to Baudouin's humiliation almost as much as to Maria's undoing. But she'd not expected him to be so heavy-handed. By deliberately dragging out the suspense to embarrass Baudouin, he'd aroused Baldwin's suspicions. She said nothing, though, for she did not want to alienate the archbishop; he was too useful an ally to lose. She was bitterly disappointed by Maria's surprising sangfroid, so sure had she been that the Greek would erupt like Sicily's famous mountain of fire. She still remained confident that Baldwin would be angered when Maria gave him a prideful refusal. Mayhap the archbishop's miscalculation might even work to their benefit. Baldwin had been truly indignant that Baudouin had endured such an affront to his dignity, and that could make him even more determined to see Maria and Balian wed, feeling he owed that to the d'Ibelins.

Her brother and Eraclius were continuing to squabble, and she intervened before it got out of hand. "Of course we hoped that the Greek would openly defy Baldwin. But she is never going to accept Balian and that is what matters." And when Joscelin asked nervously if there was any chance Maria might agree, she laughed. "Not a prayer in Hell, Brother. Not a prayer in Hell."

CHAPTER 16

October 1177
Jerusalem, Outremer

William kept the bulk of his library at the archbishopric palace in Tyre, and when his clerks could not find a Latin chronicle, he realized he'd forgotten to pack it. He'd intended to get some work done today on his history of the kingdom, but he needed to check a passage in Fulcher of Chartres's *A History of the Expedition to Jerusalem*. He looked now at the writing implements spread across his desk: a pumice stone for cleaning the parchment sheets, a knife to sharpen his quill, a boar's tooth for polishing the parchment to keep the ink from running, an inkhorn, a ruler to measure the margins. All he lacked was the missing book and motivation.

He was reaching for the quill when a servant entered with word that he had a royal visitor. Maria's unexpected arrival was a welcome distraction and he pushed his chair back, dismissing his clerk and requesting wine and wafers for three; he knew Maria would be accompanied by at least one of her ladies. For propriety's sake, they never met alone.

One glance at Maria's flushed face and he knew something was very wrong. Smiling at Dame Sophia, a matronly widow who spoke only Greek, he invited them to sit, but Maria shook her head. "I need to move, mayhap to throw things. What can you afford to lose, William?"

"Cushions are good for that purpose, unless you want to hear something shatter; in which case, I recommend holding off until the wine arrives." Retaking his seat, he said bluntly, "What have the de Courtenays done now?"

Maria startled him by spitting out a Greek curse, for she rarely swore. "I knew they would retaliate for my renting a house in the city, yet I never imagined they'd make such shameless use of the d'Ibelins to strike out at me. William, they convinced Baldwin that I ought to marry Balian!"

His eyebrows shot upward. "You mean Baudouin, do you not?"

She shook her head vigorously. "No, Baudouin's brother. Balian."

"Good God," he said softly. As Lord of Ramlah and Mirabel, Baudouin would have been the natural choice. Yet in Constantinople, even he was not likely to be considered a worthy husband for the emperor's kinswoman, once wed to a king. "This was a trap, then, with Balian as bait. And you say Baldwin was the one to propose this?"

"I spoke briefly with Balian and Baudouin once we left the solar and they told me that Agnes's lapdog had convinced Baldwin I would agree to the match."

William was relieved to hear that. He did not want to think Baldwin would have willingly been part of his mother's conspiracy, for conspiracy it clearly was. Easily identifying Agnes's "lapdog," he mentally marked up yet another grievance against Caesarea's ambitious archbishop. "That man is a disgrace to the Church. And Baldwin was their pawn. Damn them for that! He has enough woes without having to keep an eye peeled for his own family's double-dealing."

William was as alarmed as he was angry. *If Agnes and Joscelin would dare to do this now, whilst Baldwin is still capable and quick-witted, what will they dare once his health seriously begins to deteriorate?* A soft knock then announced the arrival of the food and wine and he waited until the servant withdrew before turning back to Maria.

"Let me guess what those fools had in mind. Once you were told of the proposed marriage to a man far below your own rank, you were supposed to react with outrage, defy Baldwin, and storm out. The de Courtenays do not know you at all, do they? What did you actually do?"

Maria smiled scornfully. "Agnes de Courtenay is more venomous than a desert scorpion, but she is not half as clever as she thinks she is. She assumed I would lash out in a fury because that is what she would have done in my place. Even if I were given to her sort of bad behavior, I would never have insulted Balian to his face like that. He and his brother were victims, too. So I smiled and politely requested time to consider the match, which Baldwin readily granted."

Maria chose her next words with care. "I do not know if Baldwin realizes yet that Eraclius is Agnes's accomplice in all of this. He might understandably be loath to acknowledge his mother's guilt." Seeing that William agreed with her, she said, "I think that he still wants the marriage to take place, for he saw it as a way of showing favor to the d'Ibelins."

"So what will you do?" William asked, confident that she'd already formed a plan to thwart the de Courtenays, for she'd been trained since childhood how to navigate the stormy waters of statecraft. Such a pity that Sybilla had not also learned the lessons of queenship.

Maria finally took a seat and, then, a sip of her wine. "I shall tell Baldwin that I cannot marry again without the consent of the emperor and I will promise to write to him straightaway. Alas, he will not agree to the match, forbidding me to wed Balian."

William nodded approvingly. "That is a diplomatic response and it has the advantage of being true. I do not imagine your great-uncle would be happy to hear you'd wed another Poulain, not unless he wore a crown."

Maria's smile this time was rueful, for she thought William had gone to the heart of the matter—that in Constantinople, the Franks were looked upon as barbarians and the Poulain nobility as parvenus, lords with questionable bloodlines and dubious backgrounds.

"I would welcome your help, William, in making my refusal acceptable to Baldwin, not as an act of defiance but one of obedience. And it is important to me that Balian understands this as well. I would not have him think he was rejected because I found him unworthy. He is a good man, deserves better than that."

"Yes, he does." William regarded her pensively. "I will do whatever I can to soften the sharp edges of your rejection. Would I be meddling if I offered an alternative course of action?"

"Please do. If you can see another way out of this snare, I would love to hear it."

"I would suggest that you accept, that you marry Balian."

Maria gasped. "You are serious?"

"I am quite serious. Whilst I realize this is not what you expected from me, I would ask you to hear me out." When she nodded slowly, he took a deep swallow of his wine and then another, for he was aware that he was in a position to change lives and even to alter history, a daunting responsibility.

"Maria, I have been worried about you and Isabella for some time now. The de Courtenays and their allies hate you and feel threatened by your daughter. You have been isolated, lacking allies of your own, and your vulnerability will increase as Baldwin's leprosy worsens."

He paused to gauge her reaction and saw that she'd been entertaining these same dark thoughts on nights when sleep proved elusive. "Once Baldwin . . . can no longer rule, you will be even more susceptible to Agnes's malice, for she does not care if the alliance with Constantinople flounders. I have no reason to think Sybilla bears you or Isabella any ill will. But she is eager to please her mother and uncle, so I fear she'd acquiesce if they tried to force you into another unsuitable marriage, this time to a man far less honorable than Balian. And if the Count of Flanders did not scruple to drag Isabella from the nursery to the altar, still less would the de Courtenays. I suspect their first priority would be to wed your child to a man of their choosing."

Maria said nothing, but she'd paled and he saw her hands tighten on the arms of her chair. "Sadly, you are still viewed as an outsider by some, Maria, as the foreign Greek queen. You need protectors, men willing to stand up for you. And if you marry into the d'Ibelin family, you'll have them. Not just Balian and Baudouin—the other members of the High Court, too, at least those who are friends to the d'Ibelins or who fear the de Courtenays. Many of them would see an attack upon the d'Ibelins as an attack upon them all."

He paused again to give her an opportunity to respond. When she stayed silent, he finished the last of his wine before continuing. "Agnes never even considered the consequences should you agree to wed Balian. Not only would you have a husband, then, to defend you, your marriage would transform Balian from a lesser lord to one of the most powerful men in the kingdom. As Lord of Nablus, he and his brother would suddenly wield enormous influence, both with the king and the High Court. I can assure you that was not a part of Agnes's calculations." He could not help smiling at the thought of the de Courtenays' reaction to such a dramatic alteration of the political landscape and he was gratified to see a faint smile cross Maria's lips, too.

"You are an eloquent advocate for Balian, William, and I cannot deny that what you say makes sense. But . . ."

When she hesitated, he nodded understandingly. "That would still not be enough to convince Emperor Manuel, would it? May I speak candidly? You must do what you think is best for you and your daughter, not what your kinsman thinks is best. I suppose he would insist that an emperor's protection is the strongest of all shields. It may not be true, though, when that shield is hundreds of miles away and the shield itself is held by a man long past his youth. He is nigh on sixty, no? What if he dies suddenly? What would that shield be worth then?"

Maria reached for her wine cup. "That is indeed plain speaking, William."

"I did warn you." Searching her face, he wished he could penetrate her own shield, divine her thoughts. "There are other considerations, too, Maria. Forgive me for asking so personal a question, but you are still a young woman. Have you not thought of marrying again? Of wanting more children, a brother or sister for Isabella?"

Her dark eyes were utterly unreadable. He chose to forge on, though. "You said yourself that Balian is a good man. I would say he is far better than most. There is no question that he would be devoted to Isabella, to any children you might have with him. But I also believe that such a marriage would bring you both happiness, more than most people can hope to find in this life. I know you think of him as a friend, so the door is already halfway open. He is also one of the few men in the kingdom who wants the woman as much as he wants the queen, and that is worth putting on the scales, too."

He caught a spark of emotion before she cast her eyes down, yet he was not sure how to interpret it. Surely she knew how easy it would be to claim Balian's heart? If even he, a man past his youth who honored his vow of celibacy, could see it, she must see it, too. Were women not supposed to have instincts about such matters?

Whatever was in her own heart, she was not going to share it. Realizing that, he felt some disappointment but was too wise to push. And so when she rose and thanked him rather formally for his advice, he responded in kind, rising to escort her and her maid as they turned toward the door. Returning to his desk, he settled back in his chair, ignoring the writing materials and stacked books, not stirring until one of his clerks entered.

"Your Grace, may I fetch anything for you? Are there any other books you need?"

"No, I am fine, Peter."

Peter was delighted by the archbishop's smile; they'd seen it rarely in recent weeks, banished by the Count of Flanders and then by the king's accident. "You seem in better spirits."

"Yes . . . I am." William regarded the young man fondly, for he tended to treat his clerks as surrogate sons. "You see, lad, I may have been able to do a good deed this afternoon for two people whose happiness matters to me. We can only wait and see."

As Balian could not afford to buy or rent a dwelling of his own in Jerusalem, he always stayed at Baudouin's town house whenever he visited the Holy City. Climbing the stairs to his brother's bedchamber, Baudouin halted, puzzled by the sound audible even through the closed door, a muffled thud coming at regular intervals. Giving a perfunctory knock, he pushed the door open just as an object flew past his head, struck the wall, and dropped to the floor at his feet. With admirable aplomb, he reached down, picked up the ball, and tossed it back to the man sprawled on the bed. He then took a conspicuous stance in the middle of the untidy chamber, looking around at the discarded clothing and dirty dishes with a pained expression. "A pig escaped from the market this morning and it occurred to me that he might have taken refuge up here with you, but I see not. Just out of idle curiosity, you do plan to let the servants in to clean in the next month or two?"

Since Baudouin's casual concept of housekeeping had driven both of his wives to despair, Balian ignored the jibe, throwing the ball this time at the door. Baudouin snatched the ball in midair and strode toward the bed to scowl down at his brother. "How much longer do you intend to drink and brood?" he demanded, nudging an empty wine flagon with his foot. "It has been two days, in case you've lost count."

Balian returned the scowl. "What would you have me do—challenge Eraclius or Joscelin to a duel?"

Baudouin had to smile at the image conjured up by his brother's sarcasm. "As entertaining as that would undoubtedly be, I have something more sensible in mind. I think it is time for you to go and have a talk with a young Greek widow of our acquaintance."

He was fortunate that he'd appropriated the ball, for Balian would have been tempted to aim it at his head. "I am sure she is looking forward eagerly to that discussion," he scoffed. "What could be more enjoyable for her than to have to tell me to my face just how unworthy a husband I'd be?"

"Aha! I knew it! That is what you fear—taking another blow to your wounded pride. I am beginning to think that priests are the lucky ones, at least those who actually honor their vows of chastity. For the rest of mankind, women can addle our wits with alarming ease."

Getting no response from Balian, he kicked aside another wine flagon and moved closer to the bed. "I came away from Wednesday's ambush with several interesting insights. Until then, I had not realized just how cool your Maria is under attack. And I say 'your Maria' because I know now how much you want her. No, do not bother insisting that you care only for her crown. Not being an utter fool, of course you'd want to marry a queen. But a man does not turn as white as a corpse candle, the way you did, unless he lusts after the woman, too."

Balian started to deny it, realized he couldn't, and kept silent, hoping that would discourage his brother from continuing the conversation. It didn't, of course. "If what you are dreading is being told you're too lowborn to marry, you ought to know her better than that. If she refuses you, she'll add so much sugar to it that you'll taste only the sweet, not the sour."

"If she refuses me? Surely you do not doubt that would be the outcome?"

"Probably so. But what if there is a chance, however slight, that you can convince her the marriage would be in her own interests as well as yours?"

Balian sat up, studying his brother intently. "Do you truly think there might be a chance of that, Baudouin?"

"To be honest, I do not know. I do know that you owe it to our family to make that effort. Our father made his fortune by pleasing a king enough to be given an heiress. That marriage carried him from obscurity to the nobility, allowing his sons to rise even higher. Think how high our sons might soar if you are able to marry a queen. The world is full of men who'd wed and bed a sow if she were a crowned sow. Few are ever as lucky as you, lad, for you could have it all—the woman you want, the lordship of Nablus, and an emperor for a kinsman. Not to forget that your stepdaughter might well be a queen herself one day. If that is not worth fighting for, what in Christ's name is?"

Satisfied that he'd gotten his message across to the younger man, he said, "Catch," and flipped the ball to Balian. Grinning, Baudouin sauntered toward the door, where he paused to share one final bit of brotherly wisdom. "God knows why, you've always had a way with women. Mayhap you can charm a queen, too, mayhap not. But if you do not at least try to win her, you'll take that regret to your grave." Pausing for maximum effect, he added, "And if you do not try, Little Brother, I'll never let you live it down."

He ducked as Balian sent the ball whizzing past his ear and then disappeared into the stairwell, echoes of his laughter lingering until Balian got up and closed the door.

By the time Balian had bathed, shaved, and changed into his best clothes, the sun had begun its slow retreat toward the western hills. It would have been quicker to walk, but he chose to make a more impressive appearance by riding Smoke and taking his squire, Rolf, along, too. As Maria's town house came into view, he reined in, ignoring Rolf's puzzled look. He could not remember the last time he'd been so nervous, for he'd discovered at an early age that girls liked him as much as he liked them. For a few moments, he gazed at the crowded street, thronged with pedestrians, priests, vendors, beggars, carts, and stray dogs. Finally he reminded himself he was not riding into battle and, mocking his own foolishness, he urged his stallion on.

He was admitted at once and escorted to the great hall while Rolf led their horses toward the stable, looking back wistfully over his shoulder. Balian was sure that all their household had some inkling by now of the week's amazing developments, for Baudouin could not keep a secret if his life depended upon it. And then he forgot about his curious squire, for Maria was coming toward him, smiling.

He refused to torment himself by reading any hidden meanings into her smile. Instead, he kissed her hand in his most courtly manner, saying, "My queen . . . I think we need to talk."

"Yes," she agreed, "I think we do, Lord Balian." As he followed her toward the door that led out into the inner courtyard, he caught no surreptitious glances being cast their way; apparently her household was better protected against gossip and rumors. Trailed by two of her ladies, they strolled toward the corner garden. It was much more modest than the palace gardens that had once been hers, but there was a small fountain, a few date palms, and a spreading tamarisk tree that offered shade. There was no need to seek shelter from the sun, though, for the day's heat was ebbing away, the light softening as it took on the golden haze of dusk.

Coming to a halt on the pebbled pathway, Balian paid no heed to their chaperones, knowing they spoke only Greek. Maria was tall for a woman, but he still towered over her, for he was above six feet in height. Gazing down into her upturned face, he wanted nothing so much as to kiss her. "I know I need not assure you that my brother and I were as surprised as you by the archbishop's ambush."

"I never doubted that for a moment."

"I want there to be honesty between us. So I will not deny that I very much want to marry you. We both know why I'd not have asked you had the de Courtenays not forced the issue." Smiles usually came easily to him, but not now; it felt fake, as if he were attempting to pay a debt in counterfeit coin. "On the ride here, I was rehearsing the arguments I might make on my behalf. Alas, it was much easier to think of the reasons why you would not want to marry me."

She seemed about to speak and he reached out, taking her hand. "Granted, there would be the pure pleasure of watching Agnes fall into the pit she'd dug for us. But I would not have you wed me merely to spite her, however tempting that might be for us both."

"I agree," she said, with the hint of a smile in her voice. "It is indeed tempting, yet not enough reason to wed." Turning then toward a marble bench, she led him to it, letting him keep her hand in his.

The delicate tamarisk blossoms swayed above their heads in a rustling pink cloud; it was like being enveloped in a feathery cocoon, one that swallowed up the sky and created the illusion of solitude, as if the world beyond its floral boundaries had ceased to exist. "This may sound like those honeyed words that men use to win a lady's favor, but never have I meant anything more. If the Almighty were to allow me to take any wife of my choosing, there is no woman in all of Christendom whom I would want more than you."

Maria was able to make a realistic assessment of her own attributes, considering herself to be pretty but not a great beauty as Agnes had been or Isabella gave promise of becoming. So it was a revelation to see that in Balian's eyes, she was very beautiful, indeed. "I should have spoken up ere this," she confided. "I had never been courted, though, and I could not resist experiencing it just once. The truth is that I'd already made up my mind. I am quite willing to marry you."

Although Balian was an optimist by instinct, he had not truly expected to hear those words. "If my brother were here, I know what he would do—tell me to rush you off to find a priest ere you could change your mind. And I may well regret this, but I have to ask. Why?"

Maria had always been one for advance planning, believing that gave her an advantage over those who raced ahead recklessly, heedless of what might await them. She was pleased to find that Balian shared that trait and thought his question was a quite sensible one under the circumstances.

"That is a story which begins with an emperor and ends with an archbishop—William, not that slimy hypocrite Eraclius. Your suspicions about my great-uncle are correct, Balian." This was the first time she'd used his given name, an act of undeniable intimacy, and she was surprised by the pleasure it gave her. "He would not approve our marriage; he'd not approve any marriage of mine that did not benefit his empire in some way. But William reminded me that Outremer is Isabella's homeland, and therefore it is now mine, too. He also argued persuasively that my position is a precarious one and marriage to you would offer me some protection against the malice of the de Courtenays. So I returned home to consider all that he'd said, and I made an unexpected discovery. The more I thought about marrying you, the more appealing the idea became."

She smiled then, almost shyly, and Balian could wait no longer. Putting his arms around her, he tilted her face up to his and kissed her. His mouth was warm, tasting of wine and the mint leaves he'd chewed to sweeten his breath, and she found she enjoyed it more than Amalric's kisses, which had always felt oddly impersonal, as if his were a need that any soft female body could satisfy.

When the kiss ended, Balian kept his arm around her shoulder, turning so he could caress her cheek with his free hand. "No one who dwells in the Holy Land can doubt the existence of miracles," he said with a smile so sunlit that it caught at her heart. "But I must confess that I never expected our Lord God to perform one for me." He began to laugh then. "My brother is going to be insufferable about this, for he was the one who prodded me into coming here today. I would have come eventually, just needed a bit more time to work up my courage. He will be convinced, though, that our marriage is all his doing!"

Maria laughed, too, blithely ignoring the dumbfounded faces of her ladies-in-waiting. It was a small shock to realize that Balian had just shared a confidence more personal and intimate than any she'd gotten from Amalric in nigh on seven years of marriage.

"For me," she said, "our history began on that day five years ago when I rushed into William's chamber and blurted out that Agnes de Courtenay was a bitch. I was mortified that a stranger had heard my intemperate words, especially a man kin to her by marriage. You gallantly came to my rescue and I soon learned to value your friendship greatly. Yet there is so much we do not know about each other. Your age, for one. Tell me some things about yourself that a wife ought to know."

"I turned twenty-seven on the ides of April," he said obligingly, letting his fingers linger on the curve of her throat. "My favorite color is emerald green. My favorite food is a Saracen dish, *sikbāj*. I've always had a special fondness for St. Philip the Apostle, mayhap because he was born in Galilee. I would barter the surety of my soul—almost—to own an Arabian stallion like Baldwin's Asad. And I very much want to kiss you again." Leaning over to nuzzle her cheek, he murmured, "Your turn now."

"I was twenty-three in June. My favorite color is a sapphire blue, which is also my favorite gem. I enjoy playing chess more than any other game. Isabella is so besotted with Baldwin's puppy that she coaxed me into getting one for her, so I hope you like dogs. And I want to kiss you again, too."

This time the kiss was different, not as tentative, and when it was over, they both felt as if a promise had been made, one to be fulfilled on their wedding night in the privacy of their bridal chamber. Maria was beginning to understand how different marriage to Balian would be. He proved that now by saying, "Will Isabella be happy about this? Mayhap it might help if she participates in the wedding?"

And it was only then that Maria could admit to herself how very lonely these past three years of widowhood and exile had been.

Baldwin's doctor would not let him take Asad out for runs yet, but he was hopeful it would be soon, for his symptoms were disappearing. He no longer suffered from nausea or dizziness or slurred speech and the headaches were greatly reduced.

"Good boy," he said as his stallion took the apple, his breath warm on Baldwin's palm. "Mayhap tomorrow."

His spirits were better this morning, for he'd had a productive meeting with the grand master of the Templars. Odo de St. Amand agreed that it would be wise to strengthen the garrison at Gaza Castle, their fortress close to the Egyptian border, and he would head out on the morrow with all of the Templars still in Outremer. Their spies had reported that Saladin had not dispersed his army even after learning there was no longer any danger of an invasion, and Baldwin often found it difficult to sleep at night, worrying what the sultan had in mind.

Asad enjoyed being groomed and whickered as Baldwin drew the curry comb along the Arabian's withers. Hearing footsteps approaching the stall, Baldwin said, "Did you get the hoof pick, Anselm?" The grooms usually made themselves scarce whenever he was in the stables, finding work as far away from him as they could, and rather than having to hunt them down when he needed something, it was easier to have Anselm accompany him on his visits to Asad.

When the squire did not answer, Baldwin glanced over his shoulder and straightened up in surprise, for his stepmother was standing a few feet away, flanked by the d'Ibelin brothers. She was resting her hand possessively on Balian's arm and all three of them were smiling.

Baldwin emerged from the stall, thinking that Balian looked like a man who was sure he was in the midst of a dream and was praying he'd not wake up. "I am going to make a wild guess that congratulations are in order," Baldwin said with a grin, and they laughed, for they were still in that blissful state when laughter came as easily as breathing.

Baldwin joined in their laughter, for this was a satisfying resolution on so many levels. Eraclius had insisted with great passion that he'd sought only to serve the Crown by rewarding the d'Ibelins for their loyalty, arguing that vassals were more devoted to a generous king than to a stingy one. While Baldwin still had doubts about the archbishop's good faith, he'd not pursued them. Nor had he let himself dwell upon his suspicions about his mother and uncle's part in it, for they seemed like paltry concerns when compared to the threat of a Saracen invasion or his newfound fear of falling. He could still appreciate the irony of such an ending, for someone's pigeons had surely come home to roost with a vengeance.

※

They found Agnes in the great hall, engaged in conversation with Stephanie de Milly. Reynald de Chatillon had just returned from a quick trip to his isolated fortress at Kerak, for he'd wanted to make sure it was prepared for a siege should Saladin raid into Outrejourdain. The fact that he'd brought his wife and stepson back with him showed the d'Ibelins that he, too, shared their unease about the sultan's intentions.

"Let me be the one." Baudouin's eyes were agleam with such anticipation that Balian and Maria could not deny him. They both were impressed by the grace he'd shown in accepting his younger brother's elevation at his expense, joking that he might yet snare a queen of his own since Sybilla was still free. Agnes and Stephanie had their backs to the door and had not yet noticed the new arrivals. That changed as soon as Baudouin strode across the hall, unsheathing a smile almost as lethal as his sword of Damascene steel. When Agnes whirled to stare at Balian and Maria, they waved cheerfully, savoring her look of horror as much as Baudouin did.

"I do believe," Balian said, "we've just received our first wedding gift, Maria."

Maria and Balian were wed in the splendor of the Holy Sepulchre, the marriage Mass performed by an archbishop and attended by a king, with a large, curious crowd gathered to watch as the bridal couple exchanged their vows at the church door. The celebration that followed the ceremony was much more private, for Maria had already had one formal, lavish wedding and Balian's chief concern had been to marry as soon as possible. Baldwin had excused himself after the service and a number of Balian's and Baudouin's friends were no longer in Jerusalem, off seeing to the safety of their own fiefs. So it was a rather small group that convened at Maria's town house to honor the newlyweds. Her cooks had not stinted on the food, though, offering numerous dishes cooked in the differing styles of the Franks, Saracens, and Greeks. The final course had included Lombardy custard, stuffed dates, plum and apricot fritters, and a special serving of marzipan for the youngest guest.

By then, Isabella could not do justice to it. She had been very proud to be part of the wedding, permitted to stand beside her mother as Maria plighted Balian her troth and he slipped the ring upon her third finger, declaring, "With this ring, I thee wed." She was almost as excited to attend her first feast. But her eyelids were at half-mast midway through the meal and she could no longer hide her yawns. When her mother suggested it was time for bed, she was too sleepy to object, and when her new stepfather lifted her up, she snuggled willingly into his arms, putting him in mind of a purring kitten. Heads turned their way as he and Maria rose from the table, for wedding guests were usually on the alert in case the bridal couple tried to slip away before the raucous bedding-down revelries. Their parental mission was so obvious that no one objected, although Baudouin reminded them that the dancing would begin once the tables were cleared away, so they ought not to tarry abovestairs.

As they left the hall, Isabella's new nurse caught up with them, for she'd been seated at one of the lower tables. Emma de Bāniās was an anomaly in Maria's household, for she spoke French, not Greek, and was a Poulain by birth, not one of the women who'd accompanied Maria from Constantinople. But Maria thought it was time for her daughter to have a French-speaking governess; while the child spoke both languages, French was her mother tongue.

As soon as Balian lay Isabella down upon her bed, Emma took over. Already half-asleep, Isabella did not even seem to notice as her shoes and stockings were removed. Maria reached over and gently squeezed a small bare foot, murmuring something in Greek as she kissed her daughter's cheek. Balian had asked William to teach him a few Greek phrases and was gratified to find that he understood "*matakia mou*" meant "my little eyes," which William said was a popular pet name for children in the empire.

As they stepped back from the bed, their eyes met and they experienced their first moment of wordless communication as a married couple, the same thought occurring to them at the same time. *Why go back to the hall?*

"You'd not mind missing the dancing and the minstrels?" Maria did not want to drag her new husband away from the festivities if he truly wanted to be there. But she had no desire to subject herself to the bedding-down revelries again, so she was pleased when he said he was sure they could entertain themselves without the help of harpists and jugglers. Leaving Isabella to Emma's care, they slipped out into the stairwell.

Their bridal bedchamber was ready for them, lit by white wax candles and fragrant with the last of the garden's autumn flowers. Wine was set out, even a plate of fruit, cheese, and comfits in case they hungered for food as well as each other. Balian crossed to the table and poured wine into a cup fashioned from Acre's famous red glass. Bringing it back to Maria, he said, "To our life together," and they took turns sipping the sweet, spiced wine.

While Balian bolted the door against any mischievous wedding guests, Maria removed her marriage belt of small coins and medallions; this was a Greek wedding tradition, and she'd been delighted when Balian had surprised her with one. She was accustomed to being dressed and undressed by her handmaidens, and she suddenly realized that she could not remove her bliaut without help. "This may seem like a strange question for a wife to ask her husband, but how are you at getting a woman out of her clothes?"

"One of my greatest talents," Balian assured her, which he proceeded to prove by turning her so he could unfasten her lacings with adroit fingers. Once she was free of the bliaut, he assisted her in taking off her gown, a green silk brocade with flowing violet sleeves; he'd been pleased that she'd remembered emerald was his favorite color. Clad only in her chemise, she sat down to loosen her hair. After her marriage to Amalric, she'd adopted the Poulain fashion, wearing her hair in two long braids, but for her wedding, she'd chosen to put her hair up, as a Greek bride would. Once the pins were out, Balian picked up her brush and began to pull it gently through her tousled, dark hair. "It is like polished ebony," he marveled, reveling in the silky feel and breathing in the faint scent of her perfume.

"You do not regret, then, that I do not have the flaxen hair and blue eyes so beloved by Frankish minstrels?" she teased, and when he responded by leaning down to kiss the nape of her neck, she sighed, thinking how different this night was from her wedding night with Amalric. "Balian . . . thank you for sparing me the bedding-down revelries. Enduring that once was more than enough."

"Ah . . . because you were so young," he said sympathetically, undoing the clasp of her elegant necklace, gold studded with garnets, sapphires, and pearls.

"It was not just my age. At home, we celebrated weddings, too, and the guests would escort the couple to their bridal chamber, but they did not come in. In Constantinople, male guests would never be permitted to enter a bride's bedchamber. The Greeks are not as strict as the Saracens in that way, but the women's quarters are barred to men unless they are family or eunuchs. Even at our wedding feasts, the men and women sit at separate tables."

"Truly? You did once tell me that highborn Greek women veiled themselves like the Saracens when they ventured out in public, but I did not realize they were so sequestered." He found himself feeling a rush of tenderness for that lonely little bride, naked in bed with a stranger, surrounded by raucous, bawdy drunks. "You must have thought that we really were the barbarians Greeks believe us to be."

She smiled at him over her shoulder. "I remember being greatly relieved when they finally left; I'd been half expecting one of them to snatch the sheets away. But worse was to come."

His hand tightened involuntarily upon her shoulder. "Amalric had his way with you? He ought not to have consummated the marriage that night, for you were only . . . thirteen? Bloody swine."

He sounded genuinely angry and Maria turned so she could see his face. "No, you are wronging him, Balian. He did not touch me that night, waited until I was fourteen."

Balian was relieved to hear that, even though he knew it was both foolish and futile to care about something that had occurred so long ago. "What, then? Surely you did not want him to . . . ?"

"No, I did not. But I expected him to, for a Greek husband would have claimed my maidenhead that night. I was afraid that I'd offended him in some way, or that he did not find me desirable. I was too proud to talk to my ladies about it, so I suffered in silence for months. By then, I'd become friends with William, yet I was surely not going to discuss that with him! I finally found out from Amalric himself that the Franks do not believe in bedding very young brides, and that did not happen until he'd decided I was old enough to be a wife. He was surprised by my ignorance, explaining that a girl of twelve or thirteen is more likely to die in child-bed and the baby, too, so it is just common sense to wait. In my case, he said, if he put me at risk by getting me with child too soon, he'd be putting his alliance with the emperor at risk, too."

"That sounds like Amalric—the soul of sentiment," Balian said dryly, shaking his head despite realizing how pointless it was to judge a dead man. "For certes, we will not allow Isabella or any of our other daughters to marry so young. I think they ought to wait until they reach . . . oh, at least thirty or so." And while he'd ended with a jest, he found no humor in his sudden awareness of a daughter's vulnerability.

Maria was touched that he sounded so protective of the young girl she'd once been. What mattered even more to her was that he already viewed Isabella as one of "our daughters." Rising, she looked up into his face, so intently that he felt as if she were seeing into his very soul. "I think," she said softly, "that William was right. We are going to have a good marriage."

She gave a surprised laugh then as he swept her up into his arms, almost as easily as he'd lifted Isabella, and carried her to the bed. She'd wondered if she might be nervous when this moment came, for she knew only what Amalric had taught her. She was reassured now when he showed himself willing to take his time, confirming her suspicions that her new husband had considerable experience in carnal matters. Removing her gold slippers and then her garters and stockings, he began an unhurried exploration of her body, his caresses so light that they made her yearn for more. Her chemise soon fluttered to the floor. By then she was sitting up, helping to rid him of his belt and tunic. When he pulled his shirt over his head, she startled them both by blurting out, "You are so beautiful, Balian!"

"I've been called many things in my life, Maria, but never that," he said, laughing.

"You are," she insisted, understanding for the first time how a man's body could stir a woman's desire. Amalric's heaviness had not been due to an unbridled appetite, for he'd been moderate both in drink and diet. But his excess weight had given him pendulous breasts that reached almost to his waist and she'd sometimes felt as if she were being smothered beneath a mountain of quivering flesh.

She felt some lingering loyalty to Amalric, having been both his wife and his queen, so she did not want to reveal this to Balian. She did want to caress and kiss his chest, to feel that firm, smooth skin against her breasts. Until now, she'd not had such an intimate view of the male body as it was meant to be, sinewy and lean, with the athletic grace that came from years of practice in the tiltyard, in battle, and on horseback. "Not beautiful, then," she conceded, knowing that was not a compliment men were likely to appreciate. "But if I'd seen you naked ere this, I'd have been the one to propose marriage to you."

He'd not been sure what to expect from her in bed, assuming there had been little passion in her marriage to Amalric and she might need time to overcome the inhibitions natural for a child bride who'd been an unloved wife. "Good God, woman," he said, only half in jest, "if you say things like that, all my good intentions will fly out the window and I'll not be able to pace myself."

In response, she reached out to stroke his chest, her fingers tracing the faint path of a scar that angled from his collarbone to his nipple. "Did you get this in battle?" she asked, frowning at the thought. It was one thing to know that all men were vulnerable in war, quite another to see the evidence with her own eyes.

Rising to his knees, he began quickly to undo the ties fastening his chausses to his braies. "I wish I could relate a story of my battlefield heroics that would have you dazzled by my daring exploits. The truth is that you're looking at a childhood injury. I've been blessed so far in battle, never suffering a serious wound, just the usual bruises and scratches and cuts."

She murmured something in Greek and, recognizing the word *Theos*, he assumed she was either thanking God for his past good fortune or asking Him to let it continue. This seemed an opportune moment to impress her with one of his Greek endearments, but she was helping him with the ties, and as her fingers brushed his thigh, he could wait no longer. Sliding his braies down over his hips so hastily that he heard the linen rip, he gathered her into his arms.

As familiar as he was with the physical ecstasy to be found in bedding a woman, he discovered that it was different—more intense and overwhelming—

when the woman was one who'd laid claim to his heart. He did his best to keep his urgency under control, but his body was no longer heeding his brain, and too soon he was crying out, spiraling into a swirling vortex of pure sensation, pleasure so acute it was almost akin to pain.

When he slowly returned to reality, his first coherent thought was concern for Maria. Although priests warned that females were more susceptible to lust than males, being sinful daughters of Eve, he'd learned that a woman's body was usually slower to catch fire, and he was not sure he'd given Maria enough time to reach her peak, not unless it had occurred during his own.

But when he raised himself on his elbow, he saw that she was smiling. "That was wonderful, Balian. Is it always like this?"

"If it is done right," he joked, glad that she'd found pleasure, too, in their first coupling. "I wanted it to last longer, but my cock had ideas of his own. Next time I'll try to rein him in a bit."

"If it gets better than this, I'll not want us ever to get out of bed." When he leaned over to kiss her, she nestled against him, pillowing her head on his chest. Amalric had never wanted to cuddle afterward, although in honesty, neither had she. It was different now. All in her life would be different with this man in it.

Balian threw the sheet aside, for they had no need of it, not yet. "Give me a chance to catch my breath and I'll show you that it gets better."

"Promise?" she murmured drowsily, turning her head to kiss the pulse beating in his throat. She knew she'd not experienced what he had, that moment when pleasure peaked and he'd spilled his seed into her womb. She also knew that women were capable of it, for many believed that a woman could not become pregnant unless she did. Her two pregnancies had disproved that myth, but she felt confident that this fulfillment would not keep eluding her, not with Balian sharing her bed.

"Promise," he said, smiling as he saw her lashes drift down to shadow her cheek, reminding him of Isabella at the wedding feast. "Sleep well, Marika."

She was surprised to find herself suddenly so sleepy. But at that, her eyes flew open. "That is a pet name for Maria. How did you know that?"

"I have my ways," he said, and she gave him another drowsy smile. She could not remember being as utterly relaxed as she was now, her bones so light that she felt as if she might float off the bed if she did not hold on to Balian. She could hear his heart beating against her ear and, lulled by its soothing rhythm, she soon slept.

He would eventually have to move, for he could not sleep on his back. But for now he was content to hold her in his arms, admiring the curve of her breast and hip, the softness of the thigh pressing against his. After a while, he laughed silently

at the sheer absurdity of it, that he should owe such happiness to Agnes de Courtenay of all people. When he finally turned onto his side, Maria rolled pliantly with
him, not awakening. He usually fell asleep soon after lying with a woman. But
tonight, sleep would not come. While his body was ready to let the day go, his
brain continued to race, his thoughts coming as fast and furious as a flock of birds
startled into flight. It took him a while before he realized why.

He had grown up in a land at war, had never known a peace that was not fleeting, as ephemeral as the morning mists, and he'd accepted that as the natural order of things. It was different now. From this night on, he was responsible for the
lives of the woman beside him and the little girl asleep in the chamber below.
Maria and Isabella and the children they would have, God willing, would all be
dependent upon him for their safety and their happiness. When he thought of his
new wife and daughter exposed to the dangers he'd always taken for granted, he
felt a hollow sensation in the pit of his stomach. To be a husband and father in
Outremer was to learn to live with fear.

CHAPTER 17

November 1177
Jerusalem, Outremer

Maria had been staring down at the parchment for some time. She'd decided to wait until after she was wed to break the news to the emperor, for then she'd not have to defy him should he forbid the marriage. But finding the right words was not easy. Her great-uncle would not be pleased; that she never doubted. When the Greek Royal House sent their daughters off to wed foreign princes, those daughters were expected to continue serving the empire. She could make a cogent argument that marriage to Balian would benefit her and Isabella; it was more of a challenge to convince Manuel that it would benefit him, too. By the time she finally completed the letter to her satisfaction, her fingers were cramping and she felt a headache coming on.

Laboring over her letter, she'd been vaguely aware of a murmured conversation at the far end of the solar, where her ladies were seated. She glanced up with a frown as their voices rose. Her women had been shocked by her marriage to a man of inferior rank, baffled that she would agree to such a mésalliance. They'd known better than to express their misgivings in her presence, of course, and Balian had shown her what a formidable weapon charm could be, for he'd soon won them over—with one notable exception. Eudoxia was indifferent to his smile, not impressed by his gallantry, and she was hard put even to be polite to him, so strong was her disapproval. Although Balian seemed untroubled by her coldness, Maria had taken Eudoxia aside and told her that her rudeness would not be tolerated. She'd expected Eudoxia to heed the warning, yet it was becoming obvious to her that the disgruntled widow was continuing to criticize Balian to the other women, no doubt angered that they had gone over to the enemy.

One more warning, Maria decided, only this time she would make the consequences clear to Eudoxia: unless she treated Balian with the respect he deserved, she'd be sent back to Constantinople in disgrace. Still scowling, Maria put the letter aside for her scribe to copy and then reached for another sheet of parchment. She had to write to her mother and brother, too, and she did not expect them to welcome her marriage, either.

For a moment, she found herself wondering how they'd react if she were to confide that she'd never been happier. She knew the answer, though; what mattered most to them was retaining Manuel's favor. She could not admit that her heart skipped a beat at the sound of Balian's voice or that she'd laughed more in her three weeks as his wife than she had in seven years as Amalric's queen. No, she must stress the political advantages of marriage into the powerful d'Ibelin family; that they could understand.

She'd just picked up the pen again when muffled noise echoed from the courtyard below. Rising, she moved to the window, wiping away the glass's condensation with her fist. "My lord husband has returned," she said, and her ladies started to rise, knowing she'd want to be alone with Balian. On several occasions, they'd scandalized her household by disappearing into their bedchamber during the daytime. The women were still gathering up their needlework when Maria heard the sound of boots on the stairs. She was surprised that Balian was back so soon, for he'd left only an hour ago to tell Baldwin that they would be riding to Nablus at week's end so she could formally introduce him to his new vassals. But his eagerness to see her was very flattering and she was already smiling by the time he burst through the solar doorway.

Her smile disappeared, then, for she was learning to read the subtle indicators of his moods. The tautness of his mouth, the set of his shoulders, his perfunctory acknowledgment of her women—all alerted her that something was wrong even before he said a word.

As soon as her ladies departed the solar, he strode to her side. "Maria . . ." He hesitated and she felt a sudden chill, for he always called her Marika in private. "I have bad news," he said, taking her hand in his.

"Has Baldwin's health taken a turn for the worse?"

He shook his head. "No . . . he got word this morning that Saladin has crossed the border with a large army."

Maria had known when she married Amalric that she'd be living in a land always at war. She'd not feared for the kingdom's survival while Amalric lived, but Baldwin's youth and leprosy had brought home to her just how vulnerable Outremer was. She'd never experienced the sort of fear that she did now, though, gazing up at her new husband and realizing that she could be widowed again ere the year was out. "Is it a raid or a full-scale invasion?" she asked, grateful that her voice sounded so natural, as if her heart had not begun to thud against her rib cage.

"Baldwin's scouts said it is too large a force for just a raiding party. Saladin clearly intends to take advantage of the absence of so many of our fighting men and inflict as much damage as he can."

Maria knew that Baldwin could call upon the services of less than seven hundred knights, and at least a hundred of those men were in northern Syria with Count Raymond and the Count of Flanders. So were all of the Hospitallers and most of the Templars. Doing some quick mental math, she came to a frightening conclusion—that even if every knight and serjeant still in Outremer responded to Baldwin's summons, he could not muster more than four thousand men. "How large is Saladin's army?" she asked, and this time her voice was not quite as steady.

Balian's hand tightened on hers. "We cannot say for sure," he hedged, but he'd promised there would be honesty between them and finally admitted that their scouts estimated the Saracen army at around fifteen thousand men.

Maria looked so horrified that he wished he'd lied. Knowing there were no words of comfort, none that she'd believe, he drew her into his arms and held her close as she struggled to maintain her composure. "What will Baldwin do?" she asked at last.

"He intends to gather as many men as he can and race for the coast. With luck, mayhap the Templars can hold Saladin at Gaza long enough for Baldwin to reach Ascalon, the next likely target." He had more bad news to share, delaying as long as he could before he told her that they would be facing Saladin without the most formidable battle commander in the kingdom, the constable, Humphrey de Toron. "He and his wife are both gravely ill, said to be near death."

Maria closed her eyes for a moment. She knew Baldwin would summon Count Raymond, the Hospitallers, and the Templars. She also knew they could never return in time. The defense of their kingdom rested upon the shoulders of a sixteen-year-old boy stricken with the worst of ailments and a handful of highborn lords. Balian was speaking again, saying that he wanted her and Isabella to remain in Jerusalem, and she quickly agreed, for at least she could spare him that worry; they'd be much safer in Jerusalem than in the unwalled town of Nablus.

"Promise me, Balian," she said, "promise me you'll take care of yourself." He nodded and she managed a wan smile, realizing how meaningless such a promise was under the circumstances. "Remember . . . I do not look good in mourning black."

"I'll bear that in mind," he said with a smile no more convincing than hers had been. And then, because there was no more to be said, he kissed her. Passion and despair and fear proved to be as combustible as Greek fire. They separated only long enough for him to bar the solar door and removed just enough clothing to feel flesh on flesh. The settle had none of the comforts of their marriage bed, but they could not wait. Their lovemaking was as intense as it was urgent, for they desperately needed this brief respite from reality, from what awaited them on the other side of the solar door.

The sky was the color of slate, but the day was dry; the winter rains had not yet begun. Balian and his men had set a demanding pace since sunrise, wanting to reach Ascalon by dark. His tension was growing with each passing mile. Would they be in time? It had taken him several days to ride to Nablus, summon the knights and serjeants who were now his vassals, and then head west to join the king. So much could have happened in those three days. Had Gaza fallen to the Saracens? What if Baldwin and his men had encountered Saladin's army on their way to Ascalon?

"We'll halt for a brief while," he called out, raising his hand. All around him, men were dismounting, taking out their waterskins. Balian handed Smoke's reins to his new squire, Piers, and looked around for Rolf. The youth had wisely stayed some distance from the others, as he was leading Demon, Balian's fiery black destrier, who was a formidable weapon in battle but a terror to deal with off the field, for he had never met another stallion he did not want to kill. Rolf looked relieved when Balian started in their direction; Demon was already baring his teeth at a nervous bay courser, who'd begun to shy away.

"No, you bloodthirsty brute," Balian admonished, taking the reins from Rolf, who marveled that Demon now seemed content to put aside his murderous plans until later.

"I do not know how you do it, my lord," Rolf confessed. "Just the sound of your voice can settle him down. Has anyone but you ever dared to ride him?"

"Actually, the king once did. My brother foolishly said in his hearing that I was the only one who could ride Demon. Baldwin was just thirteen, but none of us could talk him out of trying. They took off as if launched from a crossbow and by the time they came back, Baldwin was grinning from ear to ear and Demon was as well behaved as my palfrey, Smoke. Of course, that did not last long." Balian smiled, giving Demon a fond buffet when the stallion tried to mouth the sleeve of his hauberk.

It was a welcome memory of a more innocent time, but the pleasure Balian took in it soon soured, for he could not help comparing that carefree boy king with the Baldwin of today, a leper facing Armageddon. That was so troubling a thought that he at once tried to disavow it. To concede defeat already was the same as saying the Almighty had forsaken them in their time of greatest need.

As he glanced around, he saw that the other men were watching him, awaiting his will. He was not yet accustomed to his new status, and had to remind himself occasionally that he was more now than Baudouin d'Ibelin's younger brother. He was the Lord of Nablus, with eighty-five knights and three hundred serjeants under his command, plus his knights from Ibelin, soldiers urgently needed by their young king. Handing Demon's reins back to Rolf, he gave the order to mount up and ride on.

The sun was sinking into the sea by the time the outer walls of Ascalon came into view. Balian said a silent prayer of thanksgiving when he saw Baldwin's gold and silver banner streaming in the wind. They were not too late! As they approached the Jerusalem Gate's barbican, they were quickly given admittance. Balian knew Ascalon was the fourth-largest city in the kingdom, but as they made their way toward the castle, they were mobbed by so many people that he realized the town's population had swelled with refugees. Looking down at their frightened faces, he tried not to think about their fate should Outremer fall to Saladin.

Balian was glad to learn that his brother had ridden in that morning with his contingent of forty knights from Ramlah. He was about to go in search of Baudouin when he heard his name called. Turning, he smiled at the sight of the knight coming toward him; he'd not seen Jakelin for some weeks, not since he'd joined the Templar garrison at Gaza. "Are the Templars here with the king, then?"

"Not yet. Master Odo sent me to warn the king that Saladin has circled Gaza and is heading for Ascalon. So you're just in time to take part in our quest for glorious martyrdom."

Balian did not find that amusing; it held too much truth. "What lords are here?"

"Your brother. The king's stepfather, Lord Denys, and his uncle, Count Joscelin. Reynald de Chatillon. Hugues of Galilee and his brother Will. The lord of Caesarea, Guyon de Grenier, and his brother, Gautier. Amaury de Lusignan. Walter and Guidon de Brisebarre. The lords of Arsuf and Haifa and Montgisard. The viscount of Acre."

Balian grimaced. Not nearly enough. "I need to let the king know I am here."

Jakelin nodded and fell in step beside him as he entered the great hall. "I must return to Gaza on the morrow, but ere I leave, I want you to tell me how in God's name you managed to snare a queen."

Balian grinned. "I am still trying to figure that out myself."

"Balian!" Baudouin's voice rose above the noise in the hall like the bellow of a bull, and a moment later, Balian found himself enveloped in a brotherly bear hug. Snagging a cup from a passing servant, Baudouin thrust it into Balian's hand and, catching sight of Jakelin, claimed another cup for the Templar; he never bothered remembering when Jakelin could drink wine. "Over here," he directed, heading toward a window seat. "The king will be right glad to see you, lad. He needs every man he can get. Ere he left Jerusalem, he invoked the arrière-ban."

The arrière-ban required every able-bodied man in the kingdom to obey the king's summons. It was rarely used, reserved only for dire emergencies. Balian's weariness suddenly seemed to have increased a hundredfold. Sitting down in the window seat, he asked if there had been any word from Humphrey de Toron and felt no surprise when Baudouin shook his head.

"There is no hope in Hell that he could recover in time to join us. From what I hear, it will be a miracle if he even survives. Baldwin did what he must and named Reynald de Chatillon as commander of the army." Baudouin made a face. "I do not like the man much. But choosing him makes sense. Reynald fights like one possessed by a thousand devils and he knows killing the way a priest knows his psalter."

Dropping beside Balian in the window seat, Baudouin pointed across the hall. "That pompous ass Eraclius is taking his ease back in Jerusalem, of course. Fortunately the Bishop of Bethlehem has more steel in his spine than most of those pampered prelates. He chose to ride with Baldwin and has brought the Holy Cross with him."

Balian did not judge clerics as harshly as his brother. While there were bishops who'd won fame on the battlefield, most of them had not been trained in the ways of war. He would never have questioned William's courage, but he knew the archbishop would have been of no use in a fight. Gazing across the hall at Bishop Albert, he took some comfort from the knowledge that they would go into battle bearing the most sacred relic in Christendom.

Their first warning was the distant echo of Saracen war drums. Men in the great hall pushed away their plates and hastened to the battlements. They saw only billowing clouds of dust along the horizon, yet the air hummed with noise, with the very familiar sounds of an army on the move—a large army. They had already sought out priests to confess and be shriven. But if their souls were ready to face God, cleansed of their sins, their bodies were still tethered to the temporal world, to their earthly existence, and even the most battle-seasoned soldiers were not immune to a fear that was purely physical, the natural shrinking of bone and muscle and sinew from death-dealing blades and axes. By the time the order came to assemble, some of them had sampled the liquid courage to be found in taverns.

As long as they drank only enough to take the edge off their fear, their commanders did not begrudge them this combat aid. "Christ on the cross," Baudouin told his brother, "if ever there was a time to get stinking drunk for a battle, this is it. If I did not have to stay in the saddle, I'd have curled up to sleep in a wine keg last night."

Balian envied Baudouin his ability to joke at such a moment. He'd never been so nervous before a battle, but then he'd never had so much to lose. "Baudouin . . . can we win?"

"Of course we can, lad!" Baudouin followed up that reassurance, though, with a crooked smile. "But that is why I had to stop gambling. I was always so sure I could not possibly lose!"

❦

Baldwin had been living with fear since that day two years ago when he'd learned of the terrifying future he faced. But he'd never experienced fear like this, so sharp edged that he felt as if he were bleeding internally. So much was at stake—the lives of the men, women, and children who depended upon their king to keep them safe. If the reports about the size of Saladin's army were true, even the survival of the kingdom was in peril. What if he was not up to the challenge, if he failed them?

The townspeople turned out to watch as the men rode through the city streets toward the Jerusalem Gate. As Baldwin passed by him, an elderly man hobbled forward, leaning upon a crutch, and held up an object, crying, "For you, my lord king!" Reaching down, Baldwin attempted to grasp it without touching the outstretched fingers, but it dropped into the dirt, where it was trampled by the other horsemen. Glancing back, he could not repress a shiver, for it had been a small wooden cross. Was that an omen?

Outside the city walls, they formed the squadrons that would make up the vanguard and the rearguard. Baudouin expected that he and Balian and their knights would be in the vanguard, for he'd been fighting the Saracens for twenty years and Balian for ten, and he was not disappointed. They both were surprised, though, when Reynald showed unexpected sensitivity to the young king's pride by asking him to lead the rearguard, offsetting his inexperience with the presence of his stepfather and uncle. Reynald placed Hugues of Galilee and his younger brother in the rearguard, too, for they had even less combat exposure than Baldwin and most of the knights of their principality were fighting with Count Raymond in northern Syria. Once the battle formations were set, Reynald and Baldwin addressed the troops, keeping their speeches brief, for they both knew how challenging it would be to make desperation sound inspiring. Instead, they deferred to the Bishop of Bethlehem, who promised that salvation awaited all who died for the Lord Christ.

To the townspeople watching from the walls, they looked very impressive, God's army, in truth. The wintry sun gilded their armor, glinted off drawn swords and the jeweled reliquary that held the fragment of the True Cross, while their spirited destriers pawed the ground and snorted, their frosted breaths making it seem as if they were exhaling smoke. When they moved out, their banners catching the wind, the citizens of Ascalon cheered themselves hoarse and assured one another that victory was theirs, surely ordained by the Almighty. The men knew better, knew that nothing was ordained on the battlefield.

A scout had ridden in, reporting that the enemy was approaching, and they began a slow advance, keeping the city walls at their backs. The drums were getting louder. In Ascalon, the sounds of the sea were ever present and what they heard now was similar, a continuous, muted rumble like waves crashing upon the harbor rocks. Only this was a wave of men and horses, so many that the ground quivered as if a stampede were coming toward them.

Their soldiers had been engaging in the usual prebattle behavior—taunting the Saracen scouts, swapping rude jokes, camouflaging their unease with bravado. But they fell silent as the army of Saladin came into view—and kept on coming. Baldwin's breath caught in his throat. All around him, men were swearing, making the sign of the cross, gaping in disbelief as the Saracens continued to pour over the crest of a low hill and onto the plain.

Asad tossed his head and Baldwin instinctively tightened his hold on the reins with his left hand. Saladin's saffron banners unfurled against the sky, emblazoned with the eagle that was the symbol of his Ayyūbid dynasty. War drums kept up their throbbing cadence, augmented by the blare of trumpets, the clashing of cymbals, and the thumping of tambours, for a Saracen army used noise as a demoralizing weapon in and of itself. The deafening clamor grated on their nerves, but it

was the size of the enemy army that sent sweat trickling down their spines. They
thought they'd been braced for the worst, now discovered that was not so.

When his stepfather reined in beside him, Baldwin shifted in the saddle so he
could see the face half-shadowed by a wide nasal guard; as he expected, Denys
appeared outwardly calm. Swallowing with an effort, Baldwin managed to keep
his voice steady. "It seems to me," he said, "that our scouts erred. Surely there are
more than fifteen thousand men out there." He paused then, hoping that Denys
would tell him he was wrong, that his eyes were deceiving him.

But the older man nodded grimly. "I'd say we are outnumbered by at least five
to one," he said, and Baldwin slumped in the saddle, for that meant Saladin commanded more than twenty thousand men. And he had just four thousand at his
back, only five hundred seventy-five of them knights.

What followed felt like a childhood game of bluff to Baldwin. Both armies remained in place, watching each other. Saladin's men were drawn up in battle formation, but so far he seemed content to let the Franks make the first move. Now
that Baldwin knew they were so hopelessly outnumbered, he could not bring himself to give the command to advance, and apparently Reynald shared his misgivings, for he did not do so, either. There was minor skirmishing between the Saracen
scouts and Baldwin's turcopoles, mounted archers of mixed blood who were
viewed as apostates by the Muslims even though most of them were raised as
Christians. Foot soldiers surreptitiously took quick swallows from their wine
flasks and the arbalesters nervously fiddled with their weapons, making sure the
crossbows were cocked and loaded. Many of the knights were having trouble controlling their destriers, for the stallions were growing restless with the long delay
and keenly aware that some of the Saracens were riding mares. As the afternoon
dragged on, there were exchanges of taunts and insults, and a flurry of shower-
shooting by a few of the Saracen archers, but any injuries inflicted were minor. The
men were as edgy as their horses, not wanting to ride out to their deaths, yet finding it harder and harder to remain trapped in limbo like this. Both Denys and
Joscelin had quietly approached Baldwin, urging him to order a withdrawal into
the city. As daylight began to fade, Baldwin realized a decision must be made soon
and he called for a council.

They moved toward the rear, beyond the view of Saladin's scouts. Remaining
on their horses in case the Saracens suddenly launched an attack, they formed a

semicircle: Reynald; Baldwin; Denys and his cousin, the lord of Caesarea; Joscelin; and the d'Ibelin brothers.

Baldwin cleared his throat, wishing fervently that Humphrey de Toron was at his side, for his was the only advice the young king truly trusted. "I think we agree that we cannot engage them on the battlefield when we are so greatly outnumbered." He paused, relieved to see them all nodding, even Reynald. "We must decide now whether we set up camp here or go back into the city." He already knew which option seemed safer to him, but he respected the battle lore of these men and it seemed only right to let them have their say first.

Denys at once argued for withdrawing into Ascalon, pointing out how vulnerable they'd be to a surprise attack during the night. Joscelin was in full agreement. When it was their turn, Baudouin and Balian also declared themselves in favor of a withdrawal. All eyes then turned toward Reynald.

"We have no choice," he said tersely. "We'd be mad to force a battle with an army so much larger than ours. It would be only a little less rash to camp out here tonight like lambs to the slaughter. We can hold them off once we're behind Ascalon's walls, at least long enough for that Flemish whoreson and Saracen-loving count to get their arses and army back to Outremer."

Baldwin felt as if he'd passed some sort of test, his instincts validated by the unanimous agreement among his battle commanders. He'd heard horror stories of past sieges, ones in which the people starved, others that ended in fire and blood, for a city that did not surrender could expect no mercy when it finally fell. But a siege was surely the lesser of evils. "It is settled, then," he said. "Under cover of dark, we will withdraw into the city."

It was the spiritual duty of all Muslims to pray five times a day: in the predawn hours, at midday, in the afternoon, at dusk, and during the night. This could be problematic for Muslim soldiers, but their holy book permitted them to take their circumstances into account, stating, "When you travel through the earth, there is no blame on you if ye shorten your prayers for fear the unbelievers may attack you." Salāh al-Dīn rarely took advantage of this privilege. He'd had his tent set up behind the lines, where he'd performed the ritual ablution before the *salat al-maghrib*, the sunset prayer. When he finally emerged, twilight was falling and 'Īsā al-Hakkari was waiting for him.

"The Franks are sneaking back into Asqalan, my lord."

Salāh al-Dīn nodded. "I rather expected they would," he said, and 'Īsā grinned.

Although the sultan and the lawyer were separated by rank and age, they were bound by blood, for they were both Kurds. 'Īsā moved closer to the light cast by a nearby torch and studied the younger man's face intently, for all of the sultan's men were protective of him, knowing that he often pushed himself beyond his body's limits; he rarely got enough sleep and often had to be reminded to eat. He looked relaxed now, like a man at peace with himself, and 'Īsā felt a ripple of affection, so sure was he that Salāh al-Dīn would do what 'Īsā's former master, Nūr al-Dīn, could not—drive the infidels into the sea and reclaim the sacred city of al-Quds. Others were approaching; 'Īsā often thought that the sultan was a magnet for men, drawing them to him by the sheer force of his personality. But they hastily scattered as a rider on a magnificent roan Arabian burst through their ranks and reined in by the sultan's tent.

Taqī al-Dīn's teeth gleamed whitely in the flare of torchlight. "Uncle, have you heard? The cowards are fleeing back into Asqalan, not daring to fight us!"

"Not cowards," the sultan said mildly. "They just know how to count."

Taqī al-Dīn shrugged off the correction. "Whilst they cower behind their city walls, the road to al-Quds lies open to us. Allah has truly blessed us, Uncle, for the infidel kingdom is ours for the taking."

'Īsā did not fully trust Taqī al-Dīn. While he'd proved himself to be a fierce fighter, one without fear, 'Īsā thought he was too impulsive, too emotional, and too ambitious. But the sultan loved him, almost like a brother rather than a nephew, for they were close in age, and so 'Īsā kept his misgivings to himself. He watched intently now, worried that Salāh al-Dīn might embrace Taqī al-Dīn's reckless plan. With winter coming on, all-out war would not be a wise move. Nor had they planned on conquering the infidel kingdom, lacking the mangonels needed to lay siege to al-Quds. Much to 'Īsā's relief and Taqī al-Dīn's vexation, the sultan merely smiled, murmuring a noncommittal "We'll see."

CHAPTER 18

November 1177
Ascalon, Outremer

I mmediately upon their return to Ascalon, they began preparing for the
siege. The castle's larders were well stocked, but the townspeople had to be
fed, too, and how much food did they have stored away? Balian had heard
of sieges in France where the castle garrisons had expelled the civilians who'd
taken shelter with them once their provisions began to get low. He knew Baldwin would never give such an order, though he could easily see Reynald doing
so. At least the city had numerous wells. The sandstone double walls were in decent shape, too, buttressed by no less than fifty-three towers, which gave Balian
some hope.

When he reported to Baldwin after his inspection of the town walls, Balian
found the young king was too troubled to sleep. One by one, the other men excused themselves until only Denys and Balian and Anselm remained in the king's
bedchamber, watching as Baldwin paced back and forth, asking questions about
past sieges, asking if they thought Saladin would tunnel under the walls or try an
outright assault; if he'd brought mangonels from Egypt or would need to build
them; if he had enough supplies for a prolonged siege with so many men to feed.
They had no answers for him, but voicing his concerns seemed to calm his nerves
and so they smothered their yawns and let him talk.

It was very late before Balian retired to the bedchamber he was sharing with
his brother. When he opened his eyes again, light was seeping into the chamber
through the shutter slats and Piers was leaning over him, gently shaking his shoulder. "Wake up, my lord—please!"

Balian sat bolt upright in the bed. "Has the siege begun?"

The squire shook his head. "No, they are gone, my lord, they are all gone!"

Emerging onto the castle battlements, Balian saw that his brother, Baldwin, and Reynald de Chatillon were already there, staring down at the plain below. Instead of the sprawling siege camp they'd expected to see, there was only trampled grass and churned-up earth and emptiness. One of the largest armies to invade Outremer had vanished overnight.

Balian joined them at the embrasure. "They did not even leave scouts behind to keep watch over us?" he asked in astonishment.

Reynald spat out one of the Arabic oaths he'd learned during his long captivity in Aleppo. "Why should they? They think we pose no more threat than a convent of nuns!"

He sounded outraged, and Balian and Baudouin exchanged glances, grimly amused that Reynald was so offended by Saladin's cavalier dismissal of their small army.

Baldwin looked exhausted, but he was angry, too. "It is never wise to hold an enemy too cheaply," he said, and the d'Ibelin brothers realized that, like Reynald, he took the Saracens' scorn as a personal insult. "Is it a *razzia*, then?" he asked after a heavy silence.

Razzia was the Arabic word for the widespread raiding called a *chevauchée* by the Franks. The aim was to cause as much suffering as possible, laying waste the land of the enemy, burning his crops in the field, running off his livestock, plundering his towns and villages, and proving to his terrified subjects that they could not rely upon him for protection, a liege lord's first duty. Knowing how much pain a *razzia* would inflict upon his people, Baldwin was taken aback by Reynald's response.

"Let's hope so." Seeing Baldwin's surprise, Reynald said bluntly, "If it is not a *razzia*, then Saladin is marching on Jerusalem with twenty thousand men. Pick your poison, my liege."

Baldwin flinched, his gaze moving past Reynald toward the wide road that disappeared into the low hills to the east, the road that led to Jerusalem. "God would not let that happen," he said, but without much conviction. He'd once been sure the Almighty would never choose a leper to rule over the Holy Land.

The day dragged by. Quarrels broke out, for nerves were taut and tempers quick to kindle. Soldiers with nothing to do headed for the taverns, where townspeople were celebrating Ascalon's reprieve. Since most of the army had families scattered throughout the rest of Outremer, they took offense at the festive atmosphere. Some of these fights spilled into the streets and Reynald had to send serjeants out to restore order. Ascalon was not a city under siege, but they were still trapped, and without an enemy to unite them, the miserable men were turning on one another.

A noon dinner in the castle great hall went virtually untouched. Balian soon climbed up to the battlements again. The sun had burned away the last of the morning sea mist, so it felt more like September than late November. As a kestrel circled overhead, Balian tracked its flight until it went into a dive and disappeared from view. His spirits were plummeting like that hawk. He was turning away from the parapet when his eye was caught by a smudge along the horizon—smoke.

By the time Baudouin clambered up onto the battlements, the blue sky to the north of Ascalon was stained with billowing dark clouds. He looked so stricken that Balian hurried to his side. He started to assure Baudouin that it might not be Ramlah on fire, but the words wouldn't come. "You told them to flee if they saw the Saracens approaching," he finally said. "They'd have been on the road to Jaffa ere Saladin's men entered the town."

Baudouin said nothing. Over three thousand people lived in Ramlah and not all of them would have evacuated the town. Some would have been elderly or sick or just too stubborn to admit the danger until it was too late. They might have taken refuge in the castle, but it did not have enough men to fend off an assault for long. That was true for castles and towns all over Outremer, stripped of their garrisons by Baldwin's urgent summons. Baudouin slammed his fist against the stone merlon, skinning his knuckles and leaving a smear of blood. It didn't help. He began to curse then, long and loud; that didn't help, either.

Judging by the changing pattern of the smoke, there was more than one fire. Mirabel? Ibelin? Balian knew that only fourteen of Outremer's cities and towns had their own walls. The rest were like Ramlah and Nablus, protected by castles, often small ones. Balian thought of the villagers at Ibelin. Would they be able to reach the castle if a Saracen raiding party came swooping down upon them? Some of them were Muslims, but that might not save them, for men at war did not always take the time to identify the enemy. And what of Nablus? Would Saladin's army get that far inland? What would happen to the town and the ninety villages that depended upon him now for protection? He looked at the smoke spreading across the horizon, blotting out the sun, and he felt it was also blotting out all hope for his besieged homeland.

Men soon began to arrive at Ascalon, some bloodied, all deeply shaken, reporting encounters with Saracens as they made their way to the coast in response to the arrière-ban. They spoke of deaths and captures and narrow escapes, with those taken prisoner dragged along with the army, to be sold in the slave markets of Cairo. And they confirmed that the Shephelah plain was swarming with raiding parties, already laden with plunder and livestock.

Baldwin insisted upon hearing all of these stories for himself, even though each new account seemed to deplete more of his energy. By the evening meal, he looked absolutely greensick, not even making a pretense of eating. Few of the others did, either. They did drink, though, and that night Baudouin got very drunk. Nor was he the only one. Balian was greatly tempted, but he stayed sober to keep an eye on his brother and had another bad night, sleeping in snatches, jarred awake by nightmares he mercifully could not remember.

Dawn arrived with brutal inevitability and the castle was filled with men who looked like walking death, nursing bad hangovers. The only benefit from their drunken debauchery was that most of them felt too awful to squabble with one another. The great hall was unnaturally quiet as few were breaking their fast with bread, cheese, or thick slices of roasted lamb. Balian steered his groggy brother toward a table, but Baudouin veered away when the scent of meat roiled his stomach and instead collapsed on a bench near the open hearth.

When Balian thrust a cup into his hand, he drank in gulps. "If you had any mercy," he muttered, "you'd add hemlock to the beer to put me out of my misery."

"If I were going to poison anyone, it would be him." Balian looked across the hall, his gaze coming to rest on Joscelin de Courtenay.

Baudouin glanced up, then nodded approvingly. "Do not tempt me, Little Brother. I'd like nothing better than to rid the world of a de Courtenay ere I die."

Balian was no longer listening, his attention drawn to the table where Baldwin had been slouching, looking utterly desolate. He was on his feet now, though, rising so quickly that his chair teetered and crashed into the floor rushes. One of his household knights was at his side, gesturing toward another man standing nearby. Baldwin beckoned to him, then turned toward Reynald, seated at the same table. He rose swiftly, too, and as soon as the third man reached them, they headed toward the door.

Their path took them by Balian. Taking a few steps forward, he halted, watching as they strode past him. The man with them was a stranger. He was dressed like a Saracen, but many of the local Christians did so. Was he one of Baldwin's spies? A scout? Balian was sure only that the news he was bringing was not good.

They were not kept in suspense for long. Within the hour, Reynald returned to the hall. Stepping up onto the dais, he raised his voice in a demand for silence. The following lords were wanted by the king, he said tersely. As their names were called, men rose hastily to their feet. A few tried to question Reynald, but he ignored them. Spinning on his heel, he stalked toward the door, leaving the others to scramble to catch up with him. The d'Ibelin brothers followed at a more measured pace, Baudouin convinced that if he moved too fast, his head was likely to detach from his shoulders and Balian in no hurry to hear whatever Baldwin had to tell them.

Baldwin was slumped in a chair, his hand shielding his eyes. He got to his feet as they entered the solar, looking so distraught that they braced themselves for the worst. Wasting no time, he pointed to the stranger. "This is Bernard. I daresay most of you have heard of him."

Murmurs swept the solar, for Bernard was a legend in Outremer. That was not his real name, merely the one he used on his missions. He'd served Baldwin's father and now served the young king, beginning as a low-level spy and rising to command a ring that encompassed the entire kingdom. He was thought to be a Syrian Christian but could easily pass as a Muslim and often did. He was said to be fluent in Arabic, Kurdish, Syriac, French, and Greek, as well as several local dialects, and was utterly fearless, despite having a large Saracen bounty upon his head. At least that was what the Franks believed, trading improbable stories of his exploits in taverns and around campfires, no one really knowing the truth.

For such a celebrated figure, Bernard seemed quite ordinary. He was of medium height and slim build, a man to pass unnoticed on the street. Judging by his lithe body movements, Balian thought he was surprisingly young, in his late twenties or early thirties. But he could not be sure of that, for Bernard was wearing the Saracen turban called an *imamah muhannak*, which had a wide strip of dangling cloth its wearer could wrap around his mouth and nose in bad weather. Bernard was using it now to mask the lower half of his face; only his eyes were visible, so dark they were almost black, eyes that missed little and revealed even less.

"I have naught to tell you but bad news, my lords." He was so soft-spoken that they had to strain to catch his words. "Saladin has set his men loose to plunder and loot. Ramlah was burned. So were the closest towns and villages, Ibelin and Mirabel. When they attacked Lydda, the people fled to the fortified church, but the town itself was sacked. Any Franks unlucky enough to encounter them have been slain or taken as slaves if they are women or young and healthy. The countryside is shrouded in smoke, for they've been firing houses and barns and churches. The streets of Ramlah and Lydda are littered with the bodies of pigs and dogs, and they are stealing all the horses, cattle, and sheep they find. Never have I seen such destruction."

Bernard was not telling them anything they'd not already suspected. It was still devastating to have their worst fears confirmed. There were a few muted exclamations, some cursing, and someone in the back of the solar exclaimed, "How can people survive the winter if they've lost everything? They'll starve!"

"That is the least of our worries at the moment," Reynald said, so bitterly that the men fell silent again.

Bernard glanced over at Baldwin, who nodded for him to continue. "Saladin is in no hurry about it, but there seems little doubt of his intent. Whilst he may not have had it in mind when he left Egypt, once he discovered how weak we were, he realized what an opportunity he had. He is leading his army east—toward Jerusalem."

They stared at him, appalled. The loss of Jerusalem would mean the loss of their kingdom, too, the only world they'd ever known. And they would be blamed throughout Christendom for letting the Holy City fall to the infidels.

For some of them, the fear was more immediate. Balian felt as if his lungs were suddenly being squeezed in an icy grip and he had to struggle to breathe. Nor was he the only one with loved ones in danger; many men had left their families in Jerusalem, thinking they'd be safest there. Baldwin's mother and pregnant sister. Baudouin's two daughters, Esquiva and Etiennette, and his young son, Thomasin. Reynald's wife and stepson. William of Tyre. The elderly patriarch. Thirty thousand men, women, and children at the mercy of an infidel army.

Hugues of Galilee's first reaction was relief that his mother and younger brothers were at Tiberias, not Jerusalem. He at once felt guilty for that. Glancing toward Baldwin, he thought how dreadful it must be to preside over the death of their kingdom. He was seated closest to Baldwin's stepfather and he leaned over, asking Denys softly what Baldwin would do. Denys shook his head, for what could he do?

Seeing that Bernard had nothing more to say, Baldwin stepped forward, waiting until the solar quieted again. "I cannot and will not hide behind Ascalon's walls whilst my people are being killed and terrorized, their homes set ablaze," he said huskily. "Even if we cannot stop the Saracens from ravaging our lands, we have to try. You do see that?"

He was almost pleading, for he knew what he was asking of them. He did not blame them for being reluctant to ride out to certain death. But he'd shame them into it if need be, and raising his chin, he met their eyes unflinchingly. "I mean to depart Ascalon in search of Saladin. Who rides with me?"

"I will, my liege." The Bishop of Bethlehem got to his feet. Denys was the next to rise, followed by Baudouin and Balian. Joscelin looked so conflicted that Baldwin felt a spark of sympathy, knowing his uncle was haunted by those twelve years as a Saracen prisoner. But he still stood up. Amaury de Lusignan also rose, as did Denys's cousins. So did Hugues, torn between terror and pride. When his fifteen-year-old brother did, too, that brought more of the lords to their feet, for how could they let a youngster play a man's part whilst they stood aside?

Baldwin held his breath then, waiting. He felt deep gratitude when the bishop moved to stand beside him, saying firmly, "God will ride with us, my lord king."

Baldwin had hoped Bishop Albert's words would turn the tide. That was done, though, not by the prelate but by the man leaning against the wall, arms crossed over his chest, regarding the other lords with scornful eyes and a sardonic slash of a smile. "We are wasting time, my liege," Reynald said impatiently. "They'll come with us, for they have no choice. Any man who cowered behind Ascalon's walls whilst his ailing young king rode out to confront Saladin would never live down the disgrace." For a moment, his accusing stare targeted the Brisebarre brothers, both of whom flushed darkly and then slowly got to their feet.

Nor could any of the others hold out against Reynald's contemptuous challenge. Baldwin knew what had occurred here in the solar was a form of emotional extortion, but he was too desperate to care. "I will send word to the Templar grand master at Gaza," he said, "asking him to join us. Whilst I cannot order him, I am confident he will agree."

"The Templars can never resist a losing cause," Baudouin murmured in an aside to Balian, and those close enough to hear mustered up bleak smiles.

Reynald had overheard, too, and he laughed outright. "Dying as a martyr for Christ is not the worst way to go. But let's not measure ourselves for haloes just yet. The men who've been straggling into Ascalon have all told the same story—that Saladin's army has spread out over the Shephelah plain in search of plunder—and Bernard has confirmed those accounts. So, if we can find Saladin ere they rejoin him . . ."

Balian felt reluctant admiration, thinking that was adroitly done, offering a hint of hope without actually claiming they could win, which none of them would have believed. He looked over at his brother, then, wondering if the d'Ibelin family's spectacular rise would end on a November battlefield. Baudouin seemed to read his thoughts, for he punched Balian on the arm. "Do not look so woebegone, lad. Did you not hear Reynald? We'll likely be facing only twelve thousand Saracens now, so there is naught to fret about."

It was a game attempt at humor and Balian tried to match it. "I admit I was getting worried. Hoping for a miracle is not the best battle strategy I've ever heard. But you're right, Baudouin. Knowing we'll only be outnumbered three to one makes a world of difference."

Would Maria understand why he'd chosen to ride with Baldwin? After a moment to consider, Balian decided that she would, for honor and duty were concepts very familiar to his new wife. If only he'd insisted that she and Isabella seek shelter in Acre or Tyre! Their walls were in far better shape than Jerusalem's defenses. And if they'd taken refuge in a coastal city, they could have sailed for Constantinople if the kingdom fell to Saladin. He was trying to convince himself that even if they were captured by the Saracens, they'd be well treated, too valuable as hostages to be abused, when Denys's voice broke into his unhappy musings.

"We'd best shut down the taverns. Once they find out what awaits them on the morrow, every man in the army will want to get blind, raving drunk tonight."

"They'll not like that," Baudouin observed dryly. "So, if we close the taverns, we'd better leave the whorehouses open. Unless the men have something to do tonight, they might occupy themselves by plotting a mutiny."

That evoked some hollow laughter and a disapproving frown from the Bishop of Bethlehem, who said the men might better occupy themselves with prayer. Before the bishop could launch into a lecture about putting their souls at risk, Reynald raised his voice in a demand for quiet. "We are not waiting till the morrow. The less time that men have to dwell upon it, the easier it will be for them. We march as soon as the Templars arrive." Only then did he think to consult Baldwin. But the young king took no offense and quickly backed Reynald up, for slights to his royal dignity mattered little when they'd soon be fighting a battle they were sure to lose.

The stronghold at Gaza was only eight miles from Ascalon, so Baldwin was hoping for a quick response from the Templar grand master. He got one: Odo de St. Amand led his eighty knights into Ascalon in midmorning. Odo was notorious for his fiery temper and arrogance, traits that had not always served him well in the past, but they were ideally suited for a desperate last stand with their very survival at stake. Baldwin was heartened by the grand master's enthusiastic embrace of their plan. He was acutely aware that the lives of more than four thousand men were the stakes in the gamble he was about to take. Yet what choice did he have? It was better to die in the defense of their homeland than to watch helplessly as Outremer went up in flames.

They took the coastal road in hopes of avoiding Saladin's scouts and set such a punishing pace that they managed to cover twenty miles, reaching Ibelin well after dark. Even cloaked by night, the sight of the village tore at Balian's heart. He was thankful that the villagers had found shelter in the castle. But their houses and shops had been put to the torch, their livestock taken, and their future looked as bleak as the burned-out remains of their lives. William had once told Balian that three-quarters of the half-million inhabitants of Outremer were Muslims, the majority poor farmers and peasants who scrabbled out a hard living in a land inhospitable to men of any faith. Remembering that, Balian was reminded of an old folk saying, that when elephants fought, it was the ants who were trampled.

The next day was a Friday, the twenty-fifth of November, the feast day of St. Catherine of Alexandria, martyred for her faith at the age of eighteen, and many of the men were inspired to pray for her aid, believing they faced martyrdom, too. The sky had begun to cloud over and a chilly wind swept in from the sea. Smoke to the north and east spurred them on. Baudouin had asked for the command of the vanguard since they were advancing into his lands; that was a military tradition among the Franks, honoring the man whose lordship was under attack.

They were confident that they were close to the Saracen army by now. This was soon confirmed by one of their scouts, a Christian Syrian who nevertheless used the Arabic form of his name—Ya'qūb, not Jacob—for that was his mother tongue. At the sight of Reynald and Baldwin, he let out an excited shout. "I've found them, my lords! They are just a few miles away, southeast of Ramlah, near Montgisard!"

A break in the cloud cover had allowed Salāh al-Dīn to get a glimpse of the sun and he calculated it was nigh on two hours past noon. They'd been forced to halt when their baggage carts bogged down as they forded a stream, but there were still a few hours of daylight remaining and they ought to be able to reach Latrun by dark. He was sure that the Templar castle at Latrun would be abandoned, for their knights would be with their grand master at Gaza. He and his men would camp there for the night and in the morning, make their final push for al-Quds, which was just twenty miles to the east of Latrun.

When they'd crossed the border into the land of the Franks a week ago, he'd had nothing more ambitious in mind than a *razzia*, taking advantage of the absence of so many of the kingdom's defenders. But events had moved so quickly and their successes had been so easy that their *razzia* had become a triumphal procession. At first, he'd resisted his nephew's urging to target the city so holy to Christians and Muslims alike, for his army was not equipped for an extended siege, having left their heavy baggage in their border camp at al-'Arīsh. After the Franks had retreated into Asqalan, he'd been inclined to press north into Samaria, for Nablus and Nazareth were worth plundering and well-nigh defenseless. Taqī al-Dīn persisted, though, and eventually he prevailed, for the temptation was just too great to resist.

Unlike his nephew, the sultan did not expect them to be able to capture al-Quds. For a serious assault, he'd need siege engines and would have to recall the thousands of men he'd set free to pillage the countryside. Soldiers expected booty when they went to war, and this was a rare opportunity to reward them whilst greatly weakening the kingdom of the unbelievers. But by appearing suddenly before the walls of al-Quds, he would strike fear into Frankish hearts, showing them that not even their Holy City was safe, and making them more amenable to another truce when he was ready to move again against the amirs in Aleppo and Mosul.

"Will we reach al-Quds on the morrow?" When Salāh al-Dīn confirmed that to his young kinsman, Khālid responded with a jaunty smile, reminding the sultan how much he resembled his father. Khālid was Taqī al-Dīn's eldest son, nigh on twenty. Salāh al-Dīn's own sons were much younger, the oldest only seven, but Taqī al-Dīn's youth had been a wild one, resulting in fatherhood before he'd reached Khālid's age.

Ahead lay the hill called Montgisard by the Franks; it was crowned by a small, deserted castle, for its lord was with the leper king in Asqalan. They'd finally freed their baggage carts from the mud, but some of his men were still fording the stream, when the sultan heard shouting. Turning in the saddle, he saw one of Taqī al-Dīn's scouts racing toward them.

"The Franks! Their army is on the march along the coastal road!"

It was the panic in his voice as much as his message that spun heads in his direction. "Calm yourself!" the sultan said sharply. "Catch your breath, then tell me what you saw."

The scout was young, no older than Khālid, and very flustered, but he obediently tried to regain his poise. "Forgive me, my lord. The infidels have left Asqalan. I saw them with my own eyes, flying the banners of their king and the accursed Templars."

Salāh al-Dīn showed none of his inner agitation; he'd long ago mastered that aspect of leadership. But he was horrified by the scout's revelation, for his army was in disarray, with many of them off looting, others not even wearing their armor, and none mentally or emotionally ready for battle. He well knew that soldiers needed time to prepare themselves for combat; warfare went against the natural human instinct for self-preservation.

"Sound the trumpets to recall our raiding parties. Those of you who need to fetch your weapons and armor from the baggage train, do so at once." Glancing at the shocked men surrounding him, he sent several of them to find his nephew and his other battle commanders, then ordered others to post extra guards on their Frankish prisoners. His composure steadied them and they hastened to obey.

Khālid was shaken, but eager, too, for he was young enough to be excited at the prospect of proving himself in battle against the infidels. He'd learned enough of war, though, to recognize that they were caught at a disadvantage. "We still greatly outnumber them, do we not?" he asked, and felt some of his tension ease when his great-uncle assured him that even with so many off raiding, their army was much larger than the Franks'.

His father soon appeared and Khālid gave him a relieved smile. His feelings for his sire were complicated—respect and love and a desperate desire to please mingled with a little fear. But above all, he had utter confidence in his father's battlefield prowess and the last of his qualms faded away. They could not be defeated as long as Taqī al-Dīn was on the field.

Taqī al-Dīn, 'Īsā al-Hakkari, and Jawuli al-Asadi, who'd led the raid on Ramlah, were clustered around Salāh al-Dīn as they hastily drew up battle plans. It was agreed upon that they would anchor their line by the hill. But they ran out of time, then, for they heard the trumpets echoing on the wind, heralding the enemy's approach.

The small army of the Franks was already in battle formation, the squadrons led by their individual lords, with the overall command in Reynald's hands, the

Templars fighting under their own black-and-white banner, and the Bishop of Bethlehem riding with the men sworn to protect the True Cross and the cart that flew the standard of the Kingdom of Jerusalem—a gold crusader's cross on a field of silver, surrounded by four smaller Greek crosses. The foot soldiers and crossbowmen would usually march in front of the knights, trying to shield their horses from hit-and-run attacks by mounted Saracen archers. But today they marched in the rear, for all depended upon the element of surprise. Far behind came the squires of the knights and Templars, for they were not expected to take part in the battle.

They'd turned inland as soon as Ya'qūb located the sultan's army and were in better spirits thanks to Baudouin's exhortations. He'd been encouraged to learn that Saladin was near Montgisard, telling all within earshot that the area around the hill was crisscrossed with streams that fed into the Sorek and Ayalon Rivers, and even an ancient aqueduct. Reynald did not have Baudouin's familiarity with the region, but he saw at once that such a battlefield would not suit the usual tactics of the Saracens, who depended upon the speed and maneuverability of their horses to encircle and isolate their enemies. He quickly added his voice to d'Ibelin's, and midst the ashes of their extinguished hopes, a few embers began to glow.

It was then that Ya'qūb returned from a final reconnaissance, an arrow protruding from his boot. "They know we're coming! They were getting into battle formation, but then they started to shift positions. It looked like the left and right wings were switching places so they'd have the hill at their backs. There was a lot of confusion and I tried to get closer to see better—too close." He gestured toward the arrow with a grimace, saying it was only a flesh wound.

Despite his bitter disappointment that their attack would not be a total surprise, Baldwin still remembered to thank Ya'qūb. Reynald had already forgotten the scout, would not have noticed had he bled to death right before their eyes. "Christ Jesus!" he exclaimed, his face ablaze with sudden excitement. "Given half a chance, the Saracens will always retreat when we attack. Then they surge back ere we can get into formation for another charge."

Baldwin had no false pride; he truly wanted to learn from experienced warriors like Reynald. But this was so elementary that it was insulting. "I know that, my lord Reynald," he said coolly. "Even my sister knows that."

Reynald laughed, and to Baldwin's astonishment, he sounded genuinely amused. "You still do not see, do you? The scout said their left and right wings were changing places. If we can hit them whilst they are making this maneuver, they cannot retreat. We can cut through their ranks like a hot knife through butter!"

❈

The Saracens were still struggling to realign their left and right wings when the ground began to tremble, the air rang with hoarse shouts of "St. George!"—the war cry of the Franks—and an avalanche came thundering down upon them. Riding stirrup to stirrup, lances couched under their arms, the armored knights hit their enemies' line with such force that horses were knocked to their knees and men toppled from their saddles, their lighter armor unable to withstand the thrust of a lance traveling over thirty miles an hour. Confusion was always present on battle-fields, but now total chaos reigned.

For a few hectic moments, Balian truly thought they were going to prevail, for their cavalry charge had delivered a staggering blow, dozens of men dying before they could even unsheathe their swords. But their commanders managed to rally some of them and fierce fighting erupted. Balian loosened his hold on the reins, trusting in Demon's training and temperament. A Saracen soldier was looming on his left, and Balian smashed the man in the face with his shield. He'd fought in close quarters before, yet nothing like this, and he had a bad moment when Demon stumbled over a body. The stallion somehow kept his balance, even reaching out to rake his teeth across the rump of a wild-eyed chestnut, who screamed in rage and nearly threw his rider when he reared, hooves flailing the air. Balian's lance had shattered when he'd run it under the ribs of a *faris*, a Saracen knight. A nearby Templar's lance was still intact, though, and the Templar lunged forward, striking the chestnut stallion in the chest. Like most men of his rank, Balian loved horses and after every battle he lamented those slain or injured. For now, though, his only thought was to stay alive as long as possible. Raising his sword, he urged Demon toward the nearest foe.

Baldwin's life had just been saved by Asad; he'd nimbly swerved in time to keep the young king from being decapitated. Responding to the pressure of his rider's knees, Asad now veered to his right, allowing Baldwin to swing his sword at a man on a rawboned bay stallion. The Saracen managed to deflect the blow with his *duraqah*. Although Baldwin had the same round shield strapped to his right arm, his was a dead weight, like his arm. Sensing he was easy prey, the Saracen moved in for the kill. But Baldwin's household knights were staying as close to him as they could get, no less protective than Saladin's elite Mamluk bodyguard. One of them cut the Saracen down in a spray of blood that splattered Baldwin's leg and Asad's withers.

The momentum of the knights' charge had pushed the Saracen right wing into its center and the result was bedlam, with men being unhorsed by their own comrades when they careened into one another. Slashing his way into their midst, Reynald seemed indifferent to his own safety. He was known to some of the Saracens, having earned a grudging respect for his refusal to break during his long captivity, and he was a tempting target; slaying the man they called Prince Arnat would be a sure way to gain battle laurels. But Reynald forged ahead with reckless bravado, inspiring his knights to greater efforts as they struggled to reach his side. At one point, he was surrounded by three Mamluks, yet he was able to hold them off until several of the Templars came to his assistance. One of the Mamluks died; the other two let the tide of battle carry them away, for Templars were famed for their willingness to fight to the death rather than surrender.

The Saracen commanders had been able to send more of their men into the fray. One charge was led by Khālid, who did his father proud by killing the first knight who crossed swords with him. Some of his men were shouting "*Allahu akbar!*" but Khālid had no breath for that. Although he'd fought in a major battle once before, that was against fellow Muslims outside Aleppo. This was different, for this time they were facing the Franks, who'd dared to claim the holy city of al-Quds. A loss to the infidels would be unthinkable.

Time had no meaning on the battlefield. There was only the here and now, every man's world reduced to the most basic of needs—survival. Most of them were drenched in sweat, as if it were midsummer and not early winter. Balian's left leg was throbbing, for he'd taken a blow from a Saracen's mace. He was already exhausted. But instinct had taken over, drawing upon years of practice at the quintain and in the tiltyard. Training and luck would determine his fate, the fate of all who were fighting with such desperate courage as the afternoon light ebbed away.

Baldwin was taking as many chances as Reynald, for a death on the battlefield held no dread for him. Relying upon Asad's speed and agility to compensate for the lack of strength in his right arm, he'd so far gotten the better of his adversaries; he had no way of knowing if any of his blows had been lethal ones, but there was blood on his hauberk and sword, none of it his. He was not fighting without fear, though, for he was terrified that they'd fail and doom the kingdom.

Reynald was one of the few Franks who'd actually believed they could win. Their initial charge had been as devastating as he'd hoped, but the Saracens had fought back and the plain became a killing field, a seething mass of men and horses, hand-to-hand combat as savage as any of them had ever experienced. A Mamluk suddenly bore down upon him and Reynald spurred to meet this new foe, his mouth twisting in what was almost a smile, for the man's saffron tunic

identified him as a member of Saladin's *askar*, his personal bodyguard. Reynaud's
fatigue falling away as he realized he must be close to the sultan himself, he took
a hit on his shield that rocked him back against the cantle of his saddle. As the
Mamluk wheeled his mount to attack again, Reynald struck first, putting all
the force of his body behind the blow, and his sword severed the Saracen's arm at
the elbow. It was then that he sensed a change in the tempo of the battle. Slowly at
first and then more rapidly, the Saracens were giving ground.

"We have them!" he shouted. "For God and St. George!" Those close enough
to hear redoubled their efforts, energized with sudden hope. What had been a
trickle became a stream and then a flood tide as exhausted Saracens saw some
of their fellow soldiers abandoning the battle and joined them. Once the rout was
on, there was no stopping it, and Saladin's commanders sought in vain to hold
their men, eventually forced to flee themselves.

The battlefield was an appalling sight, soaked in blood and strewn with bodies,
with entrails, brains, bone, severed limbs, even heads. Everywhere Baldwin looked,
he saw the dead and wounded. Riderless horses milled about in panic. Other stallions were down, thrashing about in pain and fear. Now that the noises of combat
were stilled, the cries of the injured and dying filled the air, asking for help in
several languages. And for the first time, the survivors became aware of the smothering, stomach-churning stench of death.

Baldwin was too stunned yet to feel triumph, relief, elation, any emotion at all.
Others were not so numbed and they began to laugh, weep, and embrace one another, intoxicated by their reprieve, by the pure joy of deliverance. Reynald and
many of the knights had left the field in pursuit of the Saracens. Some of the men
had begun to heed the groans of the wounded, while plundering of the Saracen
dead had also begun.

Baldwin found himself surrounded by euphoric soldiers. He was searching for
familiar faces, feeling intense relief when he found them. His stepfather. His uncle.
The d'Ibelin brothers. Hugues of Galilee and his young brother, who'd fought in
his first battle before he needed to shave. There were missing faces, though, several
of his household knights. So many dead, so many crippled, so many widows and
orphans made this day. But God had rewarded their mad gamble. They'd saved the
kingdom.

He hastily dismounted when someone told him Asad was bleeding. Grateful
when Anselm stepped forward to offer his unobtrusive support, he saw that the
stallion had suffered a shallow cut along his flank, and he realized that there would
be time to celebrate their improbable victory, but not now.

So much to do. Wounded to care for, prisoners to chain up, horses to be put out of their misery or captured, bodies to be brought back to Ascalon, honorable funerals for their own, mass graves for their enemies, and messengers dispatched to Jerusalem and the other cities of the realm, spreading the word that Outremer was safe.

He was surprised and touched when his uncle rushed forward, enveloping him in an exuberant embrace, Joscelin's jubilation temporarily prevailing over his fear of leprosy. Baudouin and Balian had just ended a brotherly hug that would likely leave bruises. Wherever Baldwin looked, he saw nothing but smiles.

Baldwin began to delegate authority, asking Denys to organize relief for the wounded and the d'Ibelins to take charge of the prisoners. He felt a sudden jab of alarm, then, remembering that a Saracen army was most dangerous in retreat, often using it as a tactic to lure their enemies into an ambush. But when he voiced his concern, his stepfather reassured him. Reynald and the Templar grand master were in command of the pursuit, Denys said, and they would not let the hunt go on too long. Overhearing, Joscelin agreed, pointing out that Saladin's army was broken, his men concerned only with saving themselves. Baldwin at last let himself heed his battered body's message, that he was rapidly reaching the end of his endurance, and he did not object when Denys suggested he return to Ascalon with the wounded.

Some of the men encircling Baldwin began to step aside and he saw the Bishop of Bethlehem approaching. "The Almighty has indeed blessed us, my liege. It is only right that we give thanks for His goodness and mercy." Clad in a mail hauberk, a mace tucked into his belt, he looked very unlike a man of God at that moment. But he sounded like one and when he dropped to his knees, Baldwin followed his example, even knowing as he did that he'd likely need help getting to his feet again. The other men knelt, too, offering up their prayers for the miracle He had bestowed upon them on this St. Catherine's Day at Montgisard.

CHAPTER 19

November 1177
Al-Qāhira, Egypt

A l-ʿĀdil expected his brother to win a great victory over the Franks. At the least, their army would return with an abundance of riches. And Yūsuf could gain far more than the usual spoils of war. If the kingdom of the Franks was as poorly defended as their spies reported, he might even be able to threaten al-Quds. As time passed without word, though, al-ʿĀdil was growing impatient and even somewhat uneasy, for he'd fought in enough campaigns to understand how much could go wrong. What if their invasion was a success but Yūsuf died in battle?

When Āliya asked if he'd take her to the newly restored mosque of al-Amr, he welcomed the distraction. While many husbands preferred that their wives pray only in the privacy of their homes, he saw no harm in letting Āliya or Halīma visit a mosque. Women and men were segregated, after all, and the Prophet had said that a man was not to forbid his wife to go to the mosque if she asked for permission.

After the noonday *salat al-zuhr* prayers at the mosque, al-ʿĀdil agreed to take Āliya and Jumāna to see the progress being made at al-Gebel, where the sultan's new citadel would one day stand. Telling them that Yūsuf meant the citadel to be his residence once it was completed, al-ʿĀdil assured Āliya that they'd continue to reside at the West Palace, joking that the fortress would not be luxurious enough for her tastes. She laughed, knowing full well that he, too, liked living at the palace. She had enormous respect for his famous brother, and more than a little awe. But she was very glad that she was wed to Ahmad rather than Yūsuf.

Although no one would have known it to look at Āliya, for she was enveloped from head to toe in voluminous robes, she was now in her fifth month of pregnancy and tired easily. So, after a brief inspection of the citadel construction site, al-ʿĀdil escorted the women back to the West Palace. Dismissing his men, he helped Āliya out of her horse litter; Jumāna nimbly jumped out on her own. Turning his stallion over to a groom, he suggested to Āliya that they dine in the gardens, for Egyptian winters were the best time of the year, warm but without the sweltering heat of their summer sun. Jumāna volunteered to inform the cooks and al-ʿĀdil was about to lead his young wife toward a pavilion when he heard footsteps and a familiar voice called out, "My lord! A word with you, if you please!"

His brother's chancellor, ʿImād al-Dīn al-Isfahānī, was hurrying toward him. Āliya sighed softly, for the chancellor was not a favorite of hers. She acknowledged his intelligence and superior education, but she thought he was also very boastful, always with an eye out for the main chance. Al-ʿĀdil had initially been wary of ʿImād al-Dīn, too. He'd learned to appreciate the older man's sharp wits and pragmatism, however, for those were traits they shared.

ʿImād al-Dīn was carrying a wicker basket. Holding it out, he said, rather breathlessly, "A message has arrived from the sultan, my lord."

Al-ʿĀdil quickly raised the lid and lifted out a sleek carrier pigeon. Letters could be attached to a bird's leg, tail, foot, wing, sometimes even its neck. This message was fastened under a wing with thread. Gently stroking the pigeon, al-ʿĀdil cut the thread with the tip of his dagger, then handed the bird back to ʿImād al-Dīn. Carefully unrolling the small scrap, he scanned the few lines. "The sultan says he is safe and will soon be arriving with spoils. He instructs us to make his news public as swiftly as possible."

Āliya clapped her hands before taking a closer look at her husband's face. "Is that not good news?"

Al-ʿĀdil said nothing, leaving it to the chancellor to explain to Āliya the subtleties of official proclamations. "The sultan would not have assured us he is safe unless there had been a defeat."

Āliya gasped. "How . . . how could the sultan lose?"

"I do not know," al-ʿĀdil admitted, before adding grimly, "but I mean to find out."

Al-ʿĀdil chose to begin the search for his brother at their base camp at al-ʿArīsh, where the sultan had left the bulk of the army's baggage train. Here, an ancient city had once flourished by the sea, but it was long since abandoned, and the Saracen market town that had taken its place had not survived the arrival of the Franks. Al-ʿĀdil always found something vaguely melancholy about al-ʿArīsh, history's graveyard. He was shocked by what he encountered now—burned-out tents, overturned wagons, broken weapons, and some newly dug graves. His men were just as shocked, the same thought in all their minds: that the sultan's army must have been destroyed if the Franks had been able to assault his Egyptian base camp, too.

Shadows began to emerge from the ruins—wounded, gaunt, and ragged survivors of an army of thousands. They were pitifully grateful to see the sultan's brother, asking for food even before they asked for protection, for aid in returning to al-Qāhira. They all had horrific stories to tell and as he listened, al-ʿĀdil was stunned to realize the magnitude of the disaster that had overtaken Salāh al-Dīn.

The defeat on the battlefield at the hill called Montgisard was only the beginning of their suffering. Many had been slain or captured in the rout, when a soldier was at his most vulnerable, blundering into the nearby marshes. Those who'd escaped found that even the weather had become their enemy, for the winter rains had begun the next morning, icy torrents pouring from a sky that was dark even at midday. It soaked the men, turned the roads into quagmires, made it impossible to light fires even for those bold enough to risk discovery by the Franks. The infidels had been as unrelenting as the rains, they told al-ʿĀdil, the pursuit led by the accursed Templars and that son of a devil, Arnat. They'd had no food, their supply wagons seized by the Franks, and hunger and cold had driven many to surrender, preferring slavery to the perils they were facing. And those who'd forged on, expecting to find salvation at al-ʿArīsh, had instead found only desolation, for their camp had been plundered and burned.

When al-ʿĀdil cursed the infidels, they shook their heads, saying the camp had been raided by those treacherous dogs, the *Badaiyyin*. These nomads, also called *Aʾraab* by Saracens and Arabs or *Bedouin* by the Franks, were looked upon as an alien race by the sultan's followers even though they also believed that there was no God but Allah and Muḥammad was his messenger. Their name meant "desert dwellers," for they embraced the arid, barren wastelands that other men shunned, turning the sun-bleached sands of the Sinai into their private domain. They were fiercely loyal, but only to their own clans, and were notorious for siding with the victors, be they infidel Franks or their Muslim brethren. So, it did not surprise al-ʿĀdil that they'd have seized this tempting opportunity to loot his brother's lightly guarded camp. Yet if the *Badaiyyin* had taken advantage of Yūsuf's defeat, they had not caused it. What had?

The surviving soldiers had no answers for him, not at first, for they did not know why they had lost a battle to a greatly inferior force. Slowly, though, a pattern began to emerge, one that horrified al-ʿĀdil, for it indicated that his brother had been unforgivably careless.

Nor could these miserable, sickly, and starving men tell him anything useful about the sultan's whereabouts. They seemed sure that he'd survived the battle, although none of them reported seeing him on their flight from Montgisard. Al-'Ādil had a stroke of luck, then, for a wounded camp guard awoke from a feverish sleep and he revealed that as soon as the first fugitives from the battle arrived, the sultan's vizier, al-Qadī al-Fādil, had departed al-'Arīsh with a mounted force and supplies in search of Salāh al-Dīn. After he left, the *Badaiyyin* came, he whispered, and closed his eyes, too weak to speak again.

Just as the Franks relied upon Arabic-speaking Christian Syrians for scouts and spies, the Saracens made use of Muslim Syrians, men familiar with the roads, castles, and customs of their homeland. Leading his men north, al-'Ādil sent these local scouts ahead to search for the sultan. As they drew closer to the border with Outremer, they encountered the wretched winter weather that the soldiers had described so vividly—drenching rain, gusting winds, and cold that chilled them to the bone. Darkness came quickly at this time of year and al-'Ādil decided to set up camp for the night. Before he could give the command, a rider materialized out of the gathering dusk. He was plastered with mud and wet clear through to the skin, but his smile was triumphant. "I've found him, my lord! I've found the sultan!"

Al-'Ādil recognized some of his brother's *askar*, the elite soldiers sworn to lay down their own lives to keep the sultan safe, and he felt a swelling of gratitude for their loyalty. It was becoming very clear to him that Yūsuf could easily have ended up dead on the field or taken prisoner by the Franks. The small camp erupted into action at the approach of armed men, the Mamluks making ready to defend Salāh al-Dīn to the death if need be. When they realized the identities of the newcomers, they began to cheer. They soon parted to let a hooded figure pass through their ranks. For a moment, al-'Ādil thought it was Yūsuf, for he was of moderate stature, dwarfed by the towering Mamluks. But when he pulled his hood back, al-'Ādil saw it was al-Fādil, Yūsuf's vizier, who may well have been his savior, too. Had he not gone out in search of the sultan with food, tents, and soldiers, who was to say what might have befallen Yūsuf?

Swinging from the saddle, al-'Ādil drew the older man aside. "How is he?" he asked in a low voice. "Was he wounded?"

"His wounds are not of the body. . . ." When al-'Ādil asked if it was true that his brother had not ordered scouts to keep watch on the Franks at Ascalon, that he'd let his men loose to plunder the countryside, al-Fādil nodded reluctantly. "He'll want to tell you himself," he said, pointing toward one of the tents.

Al-'Ādil started to turn away, then stopped. "May Allah reward you with blessings. My brother may well owe you his life."

The vizier was not comfortable with such praise, so al-'Ādil was not surprised when he deflected it, saying it was fortunate that the sultan had ordered him to stay behind at al-'Arīsh, knowing he was a scholar, not a warrior.

The tent was small, meant for a soldier, not a sultan. It kept out the rain, but not the cold. A sole torch cast a feeble light, just enough to reveal the outline of a man seated in the shadows. He did not move as al-'Ādil ducked under the tent flap, so incurious he did not even turn his head.

"Yūsuf?" There was no response, not until al-'Ādil took a few steps forward and sat down beside him on the blanket.

Looking up then, he blinked in dulled surprise. "Is it truly you, Ahmad?"

When al-'Ādil reached out and touched his brother's hand, the skin felt like ice. Leaning over, he picked up another blanket and draped it around the other man's shoulders. Had al-Fādil not assured him otherwise, he'd have been sure Yūsuf was suffering from a serious wound, even a mortal one, for his face was grey, his cheeks sharply hollowed, his eyes dark pools of pain.

The silence between them was painful, too. There was so much al-'Ādil wanted to ask, so much he needed to understand. Why had they not kept the Franks at Ascalon under close watch? Why had his brother allowed discipline to flag so badly? Surely he knew that a soldier given license to loot had nothing on his mind then but the spoils he could claim for himself. Why had Yūsuf committed such massive mistakes and how many men had died because of them?

"My fault," the sultan said at last. "All my fault, Ahmad. Thousands dead or captured. Our army broken on the wheel of my arrogance. I brought us to ruin." He'd bowed his head and his words were so softly spoken that al-'Ādil barely caught them. "'He who has in his heart as much pride as a grain of mustard seed will not enter Paradise.'"

As boys, both brothers had learned to memorize the Qur'an, but in manhood, al-'Ādil did not have Yūsuf's extensive recall of their holy book. He did remember a hadīth dealing with forgiveness, though. "Allah's apostle said that whilst every son of Adam sins, the best of the sinners are those who repent."

Yūsuf's response would normally have been a teasing smile, feigning surprise that his younger brother could still call up any of those childhood lessons. Now he looked as if he'd never smile again. "'Īsā was taken prisoner."

"The Franks will ransom him, Yūsuf. You know that."

"We ought not to have tried to switch the left and right wings. There was no time. But 'Umar and the others urged it. . . ."

Al-'Ādil was not surprised that his nephew had gotten his way, for he knew Yūsuf usually heeded Taqī al-Dīn's battle advice. "Do you know if 'Umar escaped?"

"I think so. . . ." The sultan began to cough. When he finally got it under control, he said in a strangled voice, "His son Shāhanshāh was captured. Khālid—" He was interrupted by another fit of coughing, so severe that al-'Ādil winced to hear it.

"And Khālid? Was he taken prisoner, too, Yūsuf?"

The sultan was still struggling to get his breath back. Raising his head, he gave al-'Ādil an anguished look before dropping his gaze again. "No . . . he was slain during the battle."

Al-'Ādil froze. Tears stung his eyes and he closed them tightly as he sought to keep his grief at bay, not daring to give in to it, not yet. He did not know any in their family who did not love Khālid, who had inherited his father's high spirits but not his combustible temper. *To Allah we belong and to Him is our return.* Once he was sure his voice would not betray him, he asked if 'Umar knew of his son's death.

Salāh al-Dīn inclined his head. "He knows. Khālid's first charge into the midst of the Franks was successful. 'Umar bade him go again and it was then that he was killed."

After that, neither man spoke. Al-'Ādil had been aware for some time of a slow-burning anger, a fire half-smothered by his numbed sense of shock and disbelief. Yūsuf had been blessed with the power to inspire other men, a talent al-'Ādil knew he lacked. His brother was a visionary, albeit a pragmatic one, driven both by ambition and piety, a shrewd judge of character who excelled at statecraft and long-range planning. But al-'Ādil had long known that he was not a particularly skilled battle commander. He knew, too, that he'd never have made the mistakes that Yūsuf had made in the days leading up to Montgisard. Never underestimate the enemy. Yes, the Franks were infidels. They were also fierce fighters, with a history written in blood. Yet Yūsuf had greatly undervalued the young leper king and his knights. He'd forgotten that no one is more dangerous than a man with nothing left to lose.

He thought of Khālid, dead at nineteen, of the thousands of soldiers who'd died needlessly, of the great opportunity lost, of al-Quds, site of the al-Aqsa mosque and the Dome of the Rock. As he looked at Yūsuf, though, that clenched core of rage began to ease and then to ebb away. There was nothing he could say that Yūsuf had not already said to himself. He loved his brother and knew he could forgive him in time. Allah would forgive him, too. But could Yūsuf forgive himself?

"Yūsuf." Reaching out, he covered the sultan's hand with his own. "You could have died in that battle or on the flight back to Egypt. Many did, yet you did not. Allah spared your life for a reason. Now you must grieve for the dead, seek the forgiveness of Allah, learn from your mistakes, and remember that you and you alone can unite us to drive the infidels from our lands."

Salāh al-Dīn bowed his head again, his shoulders shaking. He no longer hid the tears trickling from the corners of his eyes. They sat together in silence for what could have been hours; al-'Ādil felt as if time no longer had any meaning. But when he heard his brother whisper, "'There is no strength nor power save in Allah,'" al-'Ādil permitted himself a brief smile.

As the walls of Jerusalem came into view, Baldwin sighed with relief. It had been a tiring journey from Ascalon even though they'd set a moderate pace to make it easier for the wounded. As much as he hated to admit it, Baldwin knew he was becoming more vulnerable to fatigue, his energy flagging after even moderate physical exertion. Yet another way that his body was sabotaging him. He would not let his demons spoil their homecoming, though, and he shoved them back into the far recesses of his brain. They'd break out after darkness fell and he was alone; they always did. *But not now, please, God, not now.*

"Look, my liege!" One of his knights was pointing to the large crowd that had gathered outside David's Gate. Baldwin had expected this, for whenever the True Cross had led men into battle, it was traditional for churchmen to escort it back into the city to its place of honor in the basilica of the Holy Sepulchre. But there were others besides clerics in this gathering, and although they were not yet within hearing range, it was obvious they were cheering loudly, waving banners and hats and scarves aloft in the chilly December sunlight. There were even a few trumpeters, blaring out the news of their arrival for the citizens waiting within the walls.

Baldwin smiled as he recognized faces in the crowd, yet he felt a prick of regret that even at such a time, his court was so divided. His mother; Joscelin's wife, Agneta; her cousin, Stephanie de Milly; and Archbishop Eraclius of Caesarea led the contingent on one side of the road, William and Maria and the anti-Courtenay faction on the other. Reining in his palfrey, Baldwin dismounted carefully, for the growing numbness in his foot was beginning to affect his balance. He was surprised to see Sybilla, seated on a stool, for she was less than a month from her due date. She smiled as their eyes met, gesturing toward the swollen belly hidden under her mantle as if to explain why she could not rise to greet him. He took a step forward and then his mother was there, holding on to him so tightly that he felt his ribs might crack; it was, he realized, one of the only times that he'd seen her weep from joy.

All around him, there was pandemonium as men flung themselves from their horses to embrace loved ones. Wherever he looked, he saw jubilant men and their blissful women and children. A few feet away, Balian was kissing his wife, and Baldwin smiled, thinking that he'd never expected to see Maria so indifferent to public decorum. Baudouin had found his daughters and Reynald was striding toward Stephanie, who ran into his arms; her son, Humphrey, hung back, though, regarding his stepfather with wary brown eyes. Joscelin had gotten a kiss from his wife and was now claiming a hug from his sister as Denys waited patiently until Agnes would find time for him. While his mother was occupied, Baldwin crossed the road toward the Archbishop of Tyre.

William was so proud that words failed him and with an utter disregard for protocol, he embraced Baldwin as if he were a son. When they finally stepped back to smile at each other, a man mobbed by children and his weeping wife pointed toward Baldwin, shouting out that he'd be on his way to the Cairo slave markets if not for the king. Baldwin acknowledged the praise with another smile, then explained to William that when the battle began, the hundreds of Franks taken prisoner during the *razzia* had seized their chance to overpower their guards.

William resisted the urge to give the young king another hug. "Jerusalem was terrified. When rumors spread that the Saracens were on the way, many people took refuge in the Tower of David, sure that the city would soon fall to Saladin. Panic was spreading like the plague. And then your messenger arrived with word of your victory. The citizens rushed out into the streets again, this time to give thanks in all the city churches. Many have begun to call it the Miracle at Montgisard."

Baldwin laughed. "That is as good a way as any to explain it, William. Some of the men claimed that they saw St. George fighting with us. I cannot say I saw him myself," he said wryly, "but then I was rather busy at the time."

"Your father would have been so very proud of you, lad," William said, and saw that he could not have said anything to give Baldwin greater pleasure.

"Well, he'd have been very happy with the spoils," Baldwin joked, for Amalric's avarice had been an open secret throughout the kingdom. "It was four days until all our soldiers returned to Ascalon, so heavily laden with plunder that they resembled a caravan. We gained tents, weapons, armor, clothing, drums, wagons of food. Thousands of horses and camels. And so many prisoners that I still do not know the total."

His smile vanished. "It was a great victory, William, but we paid a great price for it. Over eleven hundred dead—one of every four men lost his life on St. Catherine's Day. And seven hundred fifty wounded, so gravely that we put them in carts and brought them back with us."

William hated war for many reasons, despite recognizing it as a necessary evil. Above all, he hated the human cost, the lives sacrificed, the widows and orphans left to suffer. Their casualties were indeed horribly high, but it could have been worse, so much worse. He'd truly feared that the kingdom might be lost. "There is no better hospital in all of Outremer than the one run by the Hospitallers. The wounded will be well cared for there."

They were interrupted then by the Bishop of Bethlehem. "I understand the patriarch is awaiting us at the Holy Sepulchre," he said, once he and William had exchanged triumphal greetings. "Are you ready to enter the city, my liege?"

Baldwin nodded and when the bishop turned to stir the others into action, he looked again at William. "After we return the True Cross to its rightful place, William, I plan to accompany the wounded to the hospital of St. John. Will you come with me?"

"I would be honored, my lord king."

Anselm materialized out of nowhere to assist Baldwin back into the saddle. William had not come on horseback and he reluctantly accepted one at Baldwin's urging, eyeing the beast with faint suspicion, for the only horse he truly trusted was a dead one. It took a while to separate the men from their families, and as he glanced around, William saw that they'd be entering the city without either of the d'Ibelin brothers. Balian was still embracing his wife and had swung Isabella up into his arms, too. Baudouin had left his daughters and son and was gallantly devoting all his attention to Sybilla; she didn't seem to mind, although Agnes looked outraged. Once Reynald, Denys, and most of the other lords and knights were mounted, their soldiers surged forward, eager to reunite with their own families awaiting them in the city.

Jerusalem's main entrance was through David's Gate, and as the men rode across the dry moat and entered the barbican that opened onto David Street, it was like emerging from a tunnel into a sea of sound. People were packed into the open space where the grain market was held. They thronged both sides of the street, hung out of windows, and waved from the flat rooftops. Banners were draped from houses, fountains flowed with wine, shrieking children and barking dogs darted through the crowds, delighted to escape adult supervision. The noise level was painful, for every church bell was pealing wildly. But one sound rose above all the others, until it seemed as if the entire city was echoing with the name of their king.

Baldwin turned in the saddle, shooting a glance toward Reynald that was almost apologetic. "The cheers ought to be yours," he insisted, struggling to make himself heard over the continuing clamor. "You had the command."

Reynald shrugged. "You might as well get the credit, my lord king. Had we failed, you'd have taken all the blame."

"Yes, but then we'd have been dead." Baldwin grinned and gestured for Reynald to ride beside him.

William was puzzled that Reynald seemed willing to share the glory, for he'd not have thought the other man capable of compassion or magnanimity or even pity. But then he caught the look on Reynald's face as he glanced toward Baldwin and he understood. It was not empathy, the awareness that Baldwin needed this moment more than any of them. It was much simpler than that—respect for what men valued most highly in their world. William blinked rapidly, for his vision was beginning to blur. Courage—none could deny the lad that, especially Saladin. Not now, not after Montgisard.

Waves of cheering were breaking over them, a deafening roar unlike anything that William had ever heard before. He temporarily forgot his discomfort on horseback, forgot his fatigue, his fears for the future. For now, this was enough— watching as Baldwin was enveloped in cheers and euphoria, enveloped in the love and gratitude of his subjects, not caring that he was a leper, caring only that he'd saved their kingdom from the infidels.

Baldwin at once announced plans to build a Benedictine priory on the site of the battle, to be dedicated to St. Catherine of Alexandria.

Salāh al-Dīn reached al-Qāhira in mid-December and began the laborious process of rebuilding his shattered army and restoring their faith in his leadership.

CHAPTER 20

December 1177
Jerusalem, Outremer

Humphrey de Toron paused in the doorway of the great hall across from David's Tower. This was his first public appearance since he'd nearly died, stricken with the same ailment that had claimed his wife, and he looked like a man who still had a long convalescence ahead of him, pale, hollow-eyed, and gaunt. But his brusque, blunt-spoken demeanor had not been affected by his illness, and while he politely acknowledged the expressions of sympathy for the loss of his wife, he made it clear that he did not want to discuss either her death or his health. His prickly defensiveness eased only when Denys approached, for they were old friends. "I want you to tell me about the battle," he said with a smile, "and do not leave anything out. First, I must let the king know that I am here. Where is he?"

Denys caught the undertones of alarm, for they all were quick to read sinister significance into any of Baldwin's absences. "He is well, or as well as can be expected. He and Joscelin were called back to the palace. The Lady Sybilla's birth pangs began this morning."

"God keep her safe." Humphrey made the sign of the cross and dutifully echoed Denys's hopes that Sybilla would have a son. But he wondered if it truly mattered. Even if she was able to provide a male heir, he could not rule until he attained his legal majority. And although it grieved him greatly to admit it, Humphrey knew that Baldwin would be dead long before his sister's son reached his fifteenth birthday.

Baldwin and Joscelin soon returned with news that was warmly welcomed by the men and women gathered for the Christmas court: Sybilla had given birth to a son. But it was hours before they were allowed to see her and the baby. Following Agnes into the bedchamber, they found Sybilla sitting up in bed, cradling her infant in her arms. She looked surprisingly rested for a woman who'd so recently endured the travails of childbirth, and very pretty, her blond hair brushed to a golden luster, her smile triumphant. "Come and see my boy."

Joscelin hastened over to embrace her. Baldwin hung back, knowing how uneasy she must be to have him in close proximity to her vulnerable newborn and not blaming her at all. The infant was swaddled in a soft blanket and all Baldwin could see was a swatch of fair hair. Joscelin had earlier confided to Baldwin that all babies resembled prunes; his heiress wife, Agneta, had already given him a daughter. Yet he was insisting now that the prune was the very image of Guillaume, sure to be as handsome as his father.

"Uncle . . . I would like you to act as godfather to my son."

Joscelin declared that he would be honored and leaned over to kiss the new mother's cheek. She returned his smile, then gave Baldwin a sidelong glance that seemed abashed, even apologetic. When she started to speak, he quickly stopped her.

"I think Joscelin will be a fine godfather to the little lad." As the king and the baby's closest male relative, he should have been the natural choice to act as godfather, just as his own uncle had done for him. But he'd known Sybilla would never ask him; the godfather would have to hold the infant at the font during the baptismal ceremony.

Sybilla looked relieved that he understood. The baby began to cry suddenly and she gave a startled laugh. After trying unsuccessfully to soothe him, she handed him to the wet nurse, who carried him across the chamber and discreetly turned her back so he could suckle.

When Agnes suggested that Sybilla needed to rest, Joscelin and Baldwin hastily agreed, for neither one felt very comfortable in this ultimate female sanctum. Kissing his niece again, Joscelin bade her a good night, adding, "I assume you will name the babe after Guillaume?"

"No." Sybilla raised her head and for the first time met her brother's eyes. "I want to call him Baldwin."

Baldwin was touched by her gesture, although he wondered if their mother had suggested it, for Agnes was smiling approvingly. He decided then that he was being unfair to Sybilla; this might be her way of making amends for not naming him as the baby's godfather. He smiled and said the right things, said what was expected of him. But he could not suppress a prickle of foreboding, for Baldwin had not proved to be a lucky name for males in their family. His uncle had died at just thirty-three, and he knew that was an age he would never reach himself.

❧

Balian felt foolish, but he did not object when Maria insisted upon tying a blindfold over his eyes. He gladly indulged his wife's every whim these days, so attentive that his brother and male friends teased him mercilessly, reminding him that Maria was not the first woman ever to get with child. Baudouin and Jakelin were laughing at him now as he stumbled and he warned them not to let him walk into a wall. It was not even his birthday yet, he protested mildly. Maria merely laughed, confessing that she could not wait another day to give him his gift.

Maria led him through the doorway of the great hall, where he paused, feeling the sun on his face. Easter was less than a week away, but the weather remained chilly. Just then a small hand slipped into his and his stepdaughter announced that she would be his guide. Trying to slow his pace to match hers, he followed her across the courtyard. By now they'd attracted a crowd: their household servants and knights, Baudouin's men, and a few of the Templars who'd accompanied Jakelin to Nablus. They seemed expectant, too, and Balian tried to imagine what surprise could have them all so intrigued.

"Stop," Isabella said abruptly, and he made her giggle by saying, "Yes, my lady." When he asked if he could remove the blindfold, Maria told him to lower his head so she could unfasten it. He detected a whiff of sandalwood, her favorite perfume, and smiled at the touch of her fingers on his face, for they lingered in a brief caress, so discreetly that he alone noticed.

The sudden blaze of sunlight caused him to blink. He then caught his breath, for a groom was standing before him with one of the most splendid stallions he'd ever seen. A chestnut like Baldwin's Asad, this one had a distinctive flaxen mane and tail. He tossed his head, untroubled by the crowd of spectators, and regarded Balian calmly, displaying the equable temperament that made the Arabian so prized among horsemen in their world.

"How did you know, Marika?"

She laughed again. "I am not a soothsayer, Balian. That night in my garden, you confided that you'd barter your soul for an Arabian like Baldwin's, and I remembered." When she said that Baudouin had assisted her in finding the right stallion, he chimed in, declaring that he'd been happy to help as long as he did not have to pay for the horse himself.

"He cost your lady a bloody fortune, Little Brother, so for God's sake, do not let Demon kill him!"

Those familiar with Demon's diabolical temperament grinned. But Balian was no longer paying heed to their banter, intent upon letting the stallion become accustomed to his voice and scent and touch. After deciding he could safely mount, he spun around to give his wife an exuberant, grateful kiss, and then swung up into the saddle. Knowing he'd want to take his new horse out for a run straightaway, Baudouin and Jakelin had their own horses saddled and ready. They hastened to mount, assuring Maria that they'd keep him out of trouble.

The audience dispersed now that the drama was over, leaving Maria and Isabella to watch as the men rode through the palace gateway and out onto the dusty street that was Nablus's main thoroughfare. It had not been an easy pregnancy so far. Maria was suffering from the usual morning queasiness, swollen ankles, backaches, and fatigue. She'd begun to worry, too, that her womb had not yet quickened, for with her two earlier pregnancies, that had happened by now. But standing there in the April sun, she suddenly felt a familiar flutter. When it came again, she sighed with relief, marveling at the perfect timing. It was almost as if the baby wanted to take part in Balian's birthday celebration, too. That was a whimsical thought, not the sort of notion that would ever have occurred to her during her years as Amalric's wife. Marriage to Balian had unfettered her imagination, she decided, and pleased Isabella by laughing out loud.

Balian felt as if he were trapped in Purgatory, unable to do anything but endure. He'd been pacing back and forth for so long that he half expected to have worn a rut in the carpet. Work was out of the question, for he could think only of Maria, struggling to bring their child into the world. Several times he'd climbed the stairs to the birthing chamber. He was denied admittance, of course, but Dame Alicia, Maria's new French-speaking lady-in-waiting, would come out, assure him that all was going as it ought, and then disappear back inside. Once he heard Maria give a choked-off cry and the sound echoed in his ears for the next few hours. In desperation, he finally fled to the stables.

August was always the hottest month in Outremer and today the very air seemed to smolder, so intense was the heat. The sun was blinding, the sky bleached a bone white, and when he bit his lip, he tasted the salt of his own sweat. The birthing chamber must be like a furnace. It had been over fifteen hours since Maria's pains had begun, hours that seemed like years. He'd heard stories of women whose labor had lasted for days. "In sorrow shalt thou bring forth children." Never had that familiar scriptural verse sounded so ominous.

Knowing that Demon would sense his agitation and be infected by it, he chose to groom Smoke, his grey palfrey. By the time he was done, the horse's coat shone like silver, but there still had been no word from the birthing chamber. He moved on next to the stall of Khamsin, his cherished Arabian. His heart still leaped at the sight of the stallion, who looked like a living flame and could outrace the wind. With Demon, he always had to be on the alert; Khamsin greeted him as affectionately as a big dog, nuzzling him and then mouthing the scrip at his belt. Shaking several sugar lumps into the palm of his hand, he offered them to Khamsin, who was soon looking for more.

"That is enough for now, you greedy beast," he chided, reaching for a curry comb.

He whirled whenever he heard anyone entering the stables, for he'd made sure all knew where he was. Each time it was only a groom, though. But he did not detect the soft footsteps of the little girl and jumped at the sudden sound of Isabella's voice. "Why are you taking care of your horse yourself, Pateras?"

He had to smile, remembering how he and Maria had fretted about the proper way for his stepdaughter to address him. "Papa" was the name she had used for her father, and they did not think it appropriate that she call him that, too, even though she no longer remembered Amalric. While Balian had been fine with her making use of his given name, Maria had felt that was not respectful. Isabella had resolved the problem on her own, starting to call him *"Pateras,"* the Greek word for father.

I am grooming Khamsin to keep from going mad whilst I wait for word from the birthing chamber. As he could not very well admit that to Maria's daughter, he said instead, "Does Dame Emma know you are here, lass?"

"I hope not." Looking around, she overturned a bucket and perched on it. "We need to talk, Pateras," she said, sounding so serious that Balian could not help smiling again. "I know you cannot be with Mama, for men are not allowed in the birthing chamber. But why cannot I be there?"

"You are too young, kitten."

"I am six and a half! Why is that not old enough?"

"That is something you'll have to take up with your mother after she has the baby," he hedged. "It will not be much longer, Bella. Soon you'll have a little brother or sister."

"I already have a brother and sister," she pointed out, and he studied her more closely, wondering if jealousy was stirring. He was reassured when she continued. "I do not get to see Baldwin and Sybilla much. I will be able to see the new baby whenever I want?"

"Indeed you will," he assured her. "Your mother and I are relying upon you to help with the baby, to be a loving big sister." She seemed to like that, and he continued grooming Khamsin, keeping an eye on her, though, in case he'd misread her. After a few moments, she asked him again about the stallion's name, and he reminded her that *khamsin* was a hot, dry wind that swept up the coast from Egypt.

"I like *khamsin*," she said approvingly. "But I still wish you had let me name him."

He grinned at that, for she'd proven to be very creative about such matters. Probably because Baldwin had named his dog Cairo, she'd begun naming her pets after places, too. Her puppy was called Jordan, her tame lark was Bethany, and she'd decided upon Jericho for her new pony. "I dared not, Bella," he teased. "I feared you might name him Constantinople."

"I'd not have done that. It is too hard to say. Pateras . . . can I name the baby?"

"We've already chosen our names, kitten—John for a son, Helvis for a daughter."

She wrinkled her nose. "Helvis? I do not like that."

"It is not as pretty as your name," he conceded. "But they are family names. John is the name of your mother's father and Helvis is the name of my mother, may God assoil them both."

She considered that for a moment. "But your mama is with God now, so she would not know if you picked another name."

He laughed, telling her she'd have made a good lawyer. They were so caught up in their conversation that neither had heard Dame Emma's quiet approach. "I thought I'd find you here, Isabella," she said. She did not sound annoyed, though, and when she stepped into the circle of light cast by a hanging lantern, Balian saw her joyful smile.

Maria's women knew that Balian and Isabella would want to see her as soon as they learned she'd given birth, so before they dispatched Emma with the good news, they did what they could to make their lady and the bedchamber as presentable as possible, helping her to wash, brushing out her tangled hair, hiding the bloodied towels, and giving the afterbirth to the midwife to be buried later, lest it attract demons. The odor of blood still lingered, but they hoped Maria's husband and daughter would be too excited to notice, and that proved to be true.

"Mama!" Isabella catapulted into the chamber, with Balian and Emma right on her heels.

She almost flung herself onto the bed, Dame Alicia stopping her just in time.

"I am so happy it is over!" she blurted out, revealing how worried she'd been. "Where is my sister?"

Maria was exhausted; while the birth had gone as expected, it had dragged on for a night and half a day. She was still able to summon up a smile, first for Isabella and then for her husband, nodding toward the wet nurse, who stepped forward and handed the baby to Balian.

Holding his daughter for the first time, he felt so much tenderness that he found it difficult to speak. Isabella had no such problem. Rising on tiptoe to see, she exclaimed, "She has black hair like me! Oh . . . and blue eyes!" Emma explained that her eye color was likely to darken in time, but Isabella was not listening. "Can I hold her, too, Pateras? I promise I will not drop her."

None of the adults thought that was a good idea, and Emma interceded smoothly, suggesting that Isabella rock the baby in her cradle. Balian was surprised how reluctant he was to relinquish that small blanket-wrapped bundle. As soon as he placed Helvis in the cradle, he hastened back to the bed. Pulling a chair close, he took Maria's hand in his. "She is beautiful, just like her mother."

Maria studied his face, searching for clues to his real feelings. Looking across the chamber to make sure Isabella was not in hearing distance, she said softly, "You are not disappointed that it was a girl, not a boy?"

"Well, we'll just have to keep trying until we get it right," he joked, before realizing that she was serious. "No, I am not disappointed, Marika. I am thankful."

She so wanted to believe him, but her memories of her last birthing were too vivid for her to take him at his word. "This is my third daughter, Balian. What if I cannot give you a son?"

"That is in God's hands, my love." Reaching out, he ran his fingers along her cheek, troubled not by her fears but by her pallor, the dark shadows lurking under her swollen, bloodshot eyes, the small cut at the corner of her mouth where she'd bitten her lip to keep back her cries; he knew she was not a screamer. "Why are you so distraught about this? Have I not often told you that I cared only for your safety and that of the baby?"

"When Isabella was born, Amalric was gracious that I'd not given him a son. He seemed very taken with her, and assured me the next child would be a boy. But I birthed another girl and he could not hide his disappointment. He made it obvious that he thought I'd failed in my duty as his queen and wife, saying that he hoped I'd have better luck next time. Melisende was so tiny, so frail. . . ." Maria's eyes filled with tears. "Mayhap he saw what I could not, that she was not long for this world. . . ."

Balian had been surprised on his wedding night to discover he could be jealous of a dead man, resentful that Amalric had been so indifferent to the needs of his young bride. Now, though, he did not feel that flare of protective anger. "By the time Melisende was born, Amalric knew of Baldwin's symptoms. Even if he still denied the specter of leprosy, he had to be worried that Baldwin might never regain the use of his right arm. I think it was his fear for the future that caused him to blame you, Marika. That was easier than blaming God."

"That occurred to me later, after he was dead and we learned what Baldwin's doctors suspected. But even when a kingdom is not at stake, men want sons. I would not want you ever to feel cheated. . . ."

"Cheated? Marika, I thank God for each and every day that we have together, especially after Montgisard. When we parted, I truly thought I was riding out to die. I am so grateful that neither of us knew yet that you were with child. It would have been so much harder if I'd thought you'd have to face that ordeal on your own. To be given a reprieve from certain death and then to see my daughter born, to be able to hold her. . . . Well, that still seems downright miraculous to me, my love."

Maria expelled a breath, soft as a sigh, for she believed him. He saw Helvis as a blessing and even if Maria could never give him a son, he would not regret their marriage. "I think you are my miracle," she whispered, and he leaned over to kiss the corner of her mouth.

Glancing across the chamber, he saw that Isabella was still engrossed in rocking her baby sister. "She does not fancy the name Helvis very much. Mayhap we ought to call the little lass after the woman to whom we owe our happiness. Think how pleased Agnes de Courtenay would be to have a d'Ibelin as her namesake." As he hoped, that earned him a laugh from his wife. Soon after, she fell asleep, and he settled down to wait until she awoke, confident that her dreams would not be haunted by Amalric's dour, disappointed ghost.

The ship's master was not a happy man, for it was already October, late in the sailing season. Nor was he pleased to have so many clerics as passengers. He could not spit without hitting a bishop, he thought sourly, sure that they'd be demanding and judgmental, pampered princes of the Church who'd expect to be waited upon hand and foot and, likely as not, blame him and his crew for bad weather and the usual hardships of sea travel.

He did not know it, but he was not the only one who was loath to make this voyage. William of Tyre stood in the stern as the ship's anchors were raised. They had a long and arduous journey ahead of them, with Rome their final destination, summoned by Pope Alexander to attend the Third Lateran Council. It would not begin until March, but they had to leave now, for the winter months were too dangerous for ships to venture far from port.

Baldwin had accompanied them to Acre to see them off, along with many of the highborn lords of the realm, for he was moving his court north to Jacob's Ford during the construction of a castle at that site. William was vaguely uneasy about the plan to build a stronghold at Jacob's Ford, in part because it had originated with the Templar grand master, a man whose judgment William did not trust. It was true that Jacob's Ford had strategic significance, as it was the only crossing of the Jordan River for miles. But he feared that Saladin would do all he could to keep a fortress from being erected there, for it would be dangerously close to Damascus.

He was soon joined at the gunwale by Joscius, the young Bishop of Acre. Unlike William, Joscius was eagerly anticipating their visit to Rome, for it would be the first time that he'd traveled beyond Outremer's borders. He had also been entrusted with an urgent diplomatic mission upon the completion of the Lateran Council; he was then to continue to France, where he would seek to negotiate a marriage between the Lady Sybilla and the Duke of Burgundy.

William hoped that Joscius would succeed in that mission, for they desperately needed a king in waiting; Baldwin's health was deteriorating faster than they'd expected. In light of their unpleasant experience with the Count of Flanders and the deep divisions rending the kingdom, William was surprised that the High Court had been able to settle upon a candidate so easily.

It would have been difficult, of course, to raise serious objections to Hugh of Burgundy, for he seemed to be an ideal choice. He was thirty, experienced in warfare, having ruled Burgundy for the past ten years, and of noble birth, the nephew of the Queen of France. Baldwin had argued persuasively on his behalf, and Hugh appeared to be that rarity, a man acceptable both to the de Courtenays and to the rival faction led by the Count of Tripoli. Sybilla was agreeable to the match, too, an important consideration since she was no man's puppet. Only Baudouin d'Ibelin had protested, pointing out that Hugh of Burgundy already had a wife. But all knew that Baudouin had harbored hopes of wedding Sybilla himself and when assurances were offered that Hugh had put that wife aside and was thus free to wed again, it was quickly agreed upon that Sybilla and the crown would be offered to the Duke of Burgundy.

Joscius was thinking of that marital alliance, too. "If I may speak frankly, William, I've noticed that you do not seem to share my excitement about our journey. I would hope that you do not feel slighted that I was the one chosen to arrange the Lady Sybilla's marriage."

William blinked in surprise. "No, not at all. The king has entrusted me with a mission, too, after the Lateran Council ends. He wants me to travel home by way of Constantinople so that I may try to mend our alliance with the Greek empire. That was one of the many casualties of Count Philip's sojourn in the Holy Land, but we hope to convince the emperor that the failure of the Egyptian campaign was not our doing."

"I am pleased to hear you say that," Joscius confided, then glanced around to make sure no others were within earshot. "I get the sense that Archbishop Eraclius does feel slighted, for he has been treating me with conspicuous coolness ever since my mission was made known."

"Eraclius is a fool," William said bluntly. "If one of God's own angels appeared to assure us that the Holy Land's future was secure, Eraclius's nose would be out of joint unless he'd gotten a private visit from the angel beforehand."

Joscius laughed so loudly that heads turned in their direction, including the one belonging to the target of William's scathing assessment. Joscius smiled blandly in Eraclius's direction before turning back to William. "I take it then that your lack of enthusiasm for our trip is due to the company we'll be keeping for the next few months. I cannot say I am looking forward to having the peacock as our shipmate, either."

William was amused that others had taken up the disparaging name he'd given the prideful Archbishop of Caesarea. Joscius's conclusion, while logical, was not accurate, though. Eraclius's presence would be an annoyance, no more than that. What troubled William was far more painful and tragic.

Baldwin had come to the dock to see them off. He was astride a white palfrey, and William could not tear his gaze away from him. On horseback, Baldwin looked like any other youth of seventeen, handsome and healthy. His clothing hid the spreading lesions on his back and chest, and as long as he was mounted, none could tell that his balance problems were getting worse as he continued to lose feeling in his feet. At a distance, William could pretend that Baldwin was holding his own against the insidious disease that had already stolen away his youth. But William knew that was not so. The leprosy was advancing with alarming speed. For some lepers, it was a slow-burning fire that could smolder for years. With Baldwin, it would soon become a conflagration.

Baldwin gave a final farewell wave as their ship headed out toward the open sea. William continued to watch as Acre receded into the distance. Between the papal conclave, his embassy to Constantinople, and the inevitable delays involved in traveling such great distances, he would be gone from the kingdom for a long time, possibly as long as two years. What would he find when he returned?

CHAPTER 21

April 1179
Syrian Frontier

Although the Templars had christened their new stronghold Chastellet, most Franks called it the castle at Jacob's Ford, which had long been an important crossing of the Jordan River. Jakelin de Mailly preferred the Arabic name, Bait al-Ahzān, which translated as House of Sorrows, for there was something about the fortress that stirred in him an instinctive unease. The site seemed isolated, even desolate, to his eye. Many of the other Templars boasted that it would be invincible once construction was completed. Jakelin was not so sure, for he understood what a grave threat it posed to Saladin. Not only was this the only river crossing for miles, the stronghold would be just a day's march from Damascus.

He'd not been surprised when Balian confided that the Templar grand master had pressured Baldwin into agreeing to fortify Jacob's Ford, for he knew how forceful Odo de St. Amand could be; his men privately called him the Tempest. Saladin had soon revealed the depths of his own concern, offering one hundred thousand dinars if the Franks would abandon the new castle. Odo's response was a scornful refusal and the building continued. By April, one tower and the outer walls were completed and Baldwin formally turned it over to the Templars. Jakelin had spent several months at the site, helping to train the hundreds of horses that would be needed, for Chastellet would be garrisoned by eighty of his brother knights and nearly a thousand serjeants. Jakelin was glad that he was not one of them, for he had been attached for several years to their commandery at Acre, and he much preferred that lively coastal city to this bleak border citadel.

His return to Acre had to be delayed, though, once Chastellet's commander got word that Baldwin was planning a raid into the Huleh Valley to the north of their castle. Jakelin was entrusted with a message for the young king and was delighted when the commander gave him permission to join the royal raid before continuing to Acre.

He'd hoped that he would find Balian with the king, but upon their arrival at Baldwin's camp, he soon learned that this raiding party was composed of those men with northern lands: the young Hugues of Galilee, Joscelin de Courtenay, and a contingent sent by Denys de Grenier, although he himself was not participating. While Baldwin had the command, Jakelin was pleased that the man in actual charge was the constable, Humphrey de Toron. Jakelin doubted that any lord in Outremer was more respected than Humphrey; even the Saracens held him in high regard.

Humphrey smiled upon learning that Jakelin and his companions—six knights and a dozen serjeants—would be taking part in the raid. He explained that they'd learned the Saracens had driven their flocks and herds into the forest near Bāniās to forage. It was an irresistible opportunity to harass their enemies while gaining valuable spoils, and the mood in the camp was a cheerful one. The rules of the Temple forbade its members from owning any property, but the Templars welcomed the excitement that a raid offered. After making sure that his squires were taking proper care of his two destriers and his palfrey, Jakelin went in search of the king.

He found Baldwin in his tent, looking pale and drawn as Anselm changed the young king's blood-smeared bedding. Jakelin's initial alarm eased as he recalled what Balian had recently told him, that Baldwin had begun to suffer from severe nosebleeds. So he asked no awkward questions, instead greeting Baldwin as if he'd noticed nothing untoward. Baldwin gave him a grateful smile for that, interrupting when he started to introduce himself.

"Jakelin de Mailly, is it not? You're one of Lord Balian's friends."

"You have a good memory for faces, sire." Jakelin returned the smile, for it was always flattering to be remembered by the highborn, and handed over the letter.

Baldwin scanned it quickly, then looked up with another smile when Jakelin said that he and his brother knights would be accompanying them on their raid. "In that case, you'd best try to get a few hours' sleep. We plan to march tonight."

Jakelin did as he was bidden and returned to his tent, where he was soon napping, for he'd always had the enviable knack of summoning sleep like a well-trained dog. When his squire awakened him, darkness had infiltrated their camp and the sky above their heads was starlit, a pale waxing moon rising over the high plateau to the north. Had this been a battle march, one of his squires would be astride his second destrier, riding with the squires at the rear, ready to provide him with another mount should the first one be injured. But they did not think this would be necessary on a raid. One reason why they found the prospect of a raid so appealing was that the Templar rules for combat were both detailed and strict; obedience was a cornerstone of their order. Tonight they felt like boys escaping their tutors for a bit of fun.

Most of the men were mounted already. Jakelin noticed that they all glanced away when Baldwin approached his horse, trying to spare him embarrassment; his illness was progressing with such inexorable swiftness that he now needed help from Anselm to get into the saddle. Jakelin had long coveted highly prized stallions like Balian's Khamsin and Baldwin's Asad, and his eyes lingered admiringly on Asad's finely sculpted head and sleek red-gold coat. It took him a few moments to realize he was indeed looking at a chestnut Arabian, but not Asad.

"You are not riding Asad, sire?" he asked in surprise.

"This is Asad's younger half brother, Comet," Baldwin said, reaching out to soothe the horse, who sidestepped at Jakelin's approach. "He has blazing speed, may even be faster than Asad. But he is sometimes skittish, does not have Asad's calm temperament."

While Jakelin found it easy to praise Comet's striking appearance, he wondered why the king was not riding Asad. Baldwin seemed to hear the unspoken question, and after a long pause, he said, "Asad has foundered."

Jakelin was dismayed to hear that, for the ailment called "founder" or "fever of the foot" was a very serious one. Many horses never recovered. He expressed his heartfelt sympathy, all the while feeling a slow anger beginning to burn. Had Baldwin not lost enough? He knew Baldwin was still two months shy of his eighteenth birthday. But he found himself thinking that the king's youth was an illusion, for the blue eyes meeting his own seemed older than time.

Salāh al-Dīn's rise to power had been hindered by his Kurdish blood; to many, that marked him as an outsider and therefore suspect. His awareness of that had only strengthened his natural instincts, which were to trust his own. He relied upon family first and foremost, and he'd been fortunate, blessed with several kinsmen of uncommon ability. It was true his eldest brother, Tūrān-Shāh, had been a disappointment, so inept that he'd been banished to Egypt. But his younger brother, al-'Ādil, had shown flashes of brilliance, and his nephews, Taqī al-Dīn and Farrukh-Shāh, had proven themselves to be gifted battle commanders. It was Farrukh-Shāh who had accompanied his uncle when Salāh al-Dīn set up camp near Bāniās. Warned by one of his spies that the Franks were planning a raid, he dispatched Farrukh-Shāh to investigate, under orders to send word to him by pigeon if they encountered the raiding party and then to retreat.

With the tempestuous Taqī al-Dīn, Salāh al-Dīn could not be sure his orders would be obeyed. He had no such misgivings about Farrukh-Shāh, who was a cautious commander, much like the sultan himself. So it came as a shock when a pigeon came fluttering into camp with an alarming message: Farrukh-Shāh's advance guard been taken by surprise and defeated by the Franks. Farrukh-Shāh was going to their rescue and urgently requested his uncle's aid.

Farrukh-Shāh's men had not anticipated a night march by the Franks. When they materialized out of the dawn and swept down upon them in a thundering cavalry charge, the Saracen line broke and fled. Baldwin's knights eagerly took up the chase with jubilant shouts of "St. George!" Some stopped to plunder the dead, claim the wounded as prisoners, and turn the captured horses over to their squires. Most continued the pursuit, for their quarry was still in view.

The landscape was rugged, rocky, and strewn with boulders, its hills and canyons offering refuge for men lucky enough to reach them, and the Franks spurred their horses to overtake the fleeing Saracens before they could disappear into those crevices, caves, and ravines. Like the others, Jakelin was caught up in the excitement of the hunt. As they entered a deep, narrow gorge, though, he realized they'd advanced too far, their line dangerously strung out as the faster horses forged ahead. He urged his destrier after Baldwin, shouting to attract his attention, and saw that Humphrey de Toron was also calling out to the king, warning it was time to end the chase. Hearing them, Baldwin started to slow his stallion. It was then that the Saracens struck.

They were never to know if the men above them were fugitives from the battle who'd recognized the sudden vulnerability of their pursuers and rallied for a counterattack, or if Farrukh-Shāh had had the foresight to send archers to claim the high ground. They knew only that suddenly the air was humming with the unmistakable sound of arrows in flight, followed by screams as they found their targets. Saracen arrows rarely had the power to penetrate a knight's mail hauberk except at close range. So the Saracens aimed at their horses and within the span of seconds, all was chaos, the canyon echoing with the shouting of men and the shrill neighing of their terrified animals as arrows rained down upon them.

Baldwin had given the command to retreat, the trumpet's notes adding to the din as men struggled to control their panicked mounts. Triumphant cries of *"Al-lahu akbar!"* wafted from the heights above them, for the Saracen archers could see that Farrukh-Shāh was coming from the north with reinforcements. The Franks began a hasty, disorganized retreat, slowed by their efforts to save those who'd been unhorsed. The Saracen archers continued to shoot into the gorge, and when an arrow grazed the rump of Baldwin's stallion, Comet screamed, reared, and bolted. By now the knights were aware of Farrukh-Shāh's approach, for they saw dust being kicked up at the head of the canyon, and they milled about in confusion, unsure whether to follow the king or confront this new threat.

"Go after the king!" Humphrey shouted. "We'll hold them here!"

Since it was obvious that Baldwin's stallion was out of control, Jakelin had already taken off after him, followed by his fellow Templars. As Humphrey's knights hastened to his banner, most of the other men set out in pursuit of the king. Galloping after Baldwin, Jakelin soon despaired of overtaking him; his comments about Comet's blazing speed had been no idle boast. No matter how he urged his destrier on, Jakelin could not narrow the gap.

Comet had the bit between his teeth and Baldwin pulled on the reins to no avail, for he no longer had the strength in his left arm to bring the stallion to a halt. He'd almost been thrown when Comet bolted; only years of riding experience had enabled him to remain in the saddle, but he'd lost his sword. They were clear of the canyon now. Ahead of them, bodies of slain Saracens were sprawled in the dirt, the smell of blood adding to Comet's panic, as did the sight of several downed horses, thrashing about in pain. Baldwin had been taught that a runaway horse should be spurred on until exhaustion prevailed over fear. The stallion had veered from the road, though, onto ground so rough and uneven that Baldwin expected at any moment to hear the sound of a foreleg snapping like kindling. Unable to stop the Arabian's wild flight, Baldwin could only hold on and curse Comet, curse his own clumsiness in dropping his sword, curse their reckless pursuit of the Saracens, all the while knowing that what he really wanted to do was to curse God.

There was no surprise when Baldwin caught a glimpse of two Saracen archers angling to cut him off. There was no fear, either, even though he was utterly defenseless; in the bitterness of that moment, he didn't much care what befell him. They were closing fast and their approach spooked Comet again. He'd been shortening stride; now he summoned new reserves of energy, skimming over the treacherous terrain as if he'd suddenly sprouted wings. The Saracens were not about to give up the chase, though. Baldwin did not know if they'd recognized him or merely saw him as easy prey or if it was Comet they wanted. When he heard yelling, he glanced over his shoulder to see them wheeling about to confront charging Templar knights, who dispatched them both with the ferocity that made them so respected as fighters by friends and foes alike.

A steep hill was looming ahead and Comet, who was wheezing like a bellows by now, no longer had the strength or the heart for further mischief. Catching the change in his stride, Baldwin sought again to rein him in and this time managed to bring the stallion to a shuddering stop. Baldwin slumped back against the cantle, yearning to slide from the saddle but knowing his legs would not support him if he did. Then Jakelin de Mailly was there, mercifully asking no inane questions. Glancing from the lathered, heaving Comet, suddenly as docile as a carter's sumpter horse, to the king, his face deathly white with the sort of rage that scorched the soul, Jakelin instinctively knew there was nothing to be said. Unhooking the waterskin from his saddle, he watched as Baldwin drank in gulps, spilling as much as he swallowed.

Lowering the waterskin, Baldwin then said something that Jakelin never expected to hear from a king's lips. "I am sorry."

"For what, my liege?" Jakelin's puzzlement was not feigned, for he well knew that combat was never predictable, battles sometimes won or lost by luck alone.

"I put you all at risk, forcing you to break off the fight and ride to my rescue as if I were a green, witless stripling, all because I could not rein in my own horse."

Jakelin had no easy way with words, often finding himself tongue-tied at those moments when eloquence was most needed—like now. He wanted to say that he'd never seen anyone display the courage that Baldwin did, riding out to battle with a crippled arm on a stallion he could control only with his knees, rising each day to fight an enemy that gave no quarter, that never lost. He settled for pointing out truthfully that there was not a knight alive who'd not had a horse run away with him, whilst knowing that this would give Baldwin no comfort, Baldwin who'd learned to ride before he could walk, who'd always prided himself on his exceptional equestrian skills.

Simon de Garnier, the commander of Baldwin's household knights, had ridden up in time to hear their exchange, and quickly added his voice to Jakelin's, assuring the king that no harm had been done by Comet's bad behavior. "We were already retreating, sire. We just speeded it up trying to keep pace with that Arab of yours." He gave Baldwin a gap-toothed smile. "God's truth, I'd sooner try to run down one of those African cheetahs!"

Others were in view now, Joscelin giving a joyful cry at the sight of his nephew, alive and unharmed. Anxiety always made Joscelin garrulous and he could not stop talking, but Baldwin was not listening. "How many men did we lose?" he asked, bracing himself for the worst.

Not many, Joscelin assured him, while Simon de Garnier insisted that they'd lost more horses than men. Baldwin looked past them toward the Templar knights, for they were never ones for sugarcoating the truth. As their eyes met, Jakelin admitted that they would not know that until they got back to camp and the stragglers started coming in. Constable Humphrey and his knights had covered their retreat and were likely to have taken some casualties. Others were still roaming the countryside in search of plunder, unaware that another battle had been fought.

Baldwin flinched at this matter-of-fact reminder of how careless they'd been, overly confident, chasing after booty before victory was assured, and then rashly pursuing the Saracens despite knowing that a Muslim retreat was often a feint, bait for a trap. He said nothing, but they knew he was blaming himself and they sought to convince him that he was not at fault, Joscelin arguing that they could not have foreseen Farrukh-Shāh's arrival with more troops, Simon claiming that they'd been able to retreat ere they suffered many casualties, and Jakelin saying laconically that they'd all joined eagerly in the chase, even men as battle seasoned as Humphrey de Toron. Baldwin found truth in Jakelin's comments but no consolation, for he was the king and the ultimate responsibility had to be his.

Baldwin sent several men to ride to the top of a hill that offered a view of the surrounding area, and they soon returned with troubling news; billowing dust clouds to the north warned of an approaching army. The men exchanged grateful looks; had they not retreated when they did, they'd have found themselves fighting both Farrukh-Shāh and his uncle, the sultan. After dispatching scouts to keep the Saracens under surveillance in case they decided upon pursuit, Baldwin ordered some of his knights to escort the injured who could still ride back to their camp and to send wagons for their gravely wounded and their dead.

Joscelin was still shaken by Baldwin's near disaster and urged him to return to the camp, too. He backed off hastily, though, when Baldwin turned on him in a rare rage, for he usually kept his temper under a tight rein. Baldwin had dismounted by then, Anselm moving unobtrusively to his side should he need support, for his limp was more pronounced whenever he was fatigued. The sun was directly over their heads by now, and the heat was becoming uncomfortable for the armor-clad men. Thirsty and weary and soaked in sweat, they did their best to hide their unease, feeling very vulnerable with a large Saracen army so close at hand. Baldwin ignored the discomfort, keeping his eyes fastened upon the horizon. A sigh of relief swept through their ranks when they finally saw riders in the distance, their shields emblazoned with the arms of Humphrey de Toron.

They soon realized that something was amiss; the knights were holding their mounts to a slow canter, and as they drew nearer, those watching could see how many were injured. Baldwin's spirits rose as he spotted the constable. But then he was stumbling forward, his lameness forgotten, for the men riding beside Humphrey's destrier looked stricken. Humphrey was sagging in the saddle, holding tightly to the pommel as one of his knights led his stallion. His eyes were closed, his face livid, and the surcote covering his hauberk had a dark, spreading stain.

He raised his head once he realized they had come to a halt, his gaze focusing blearily upon Baldwin's anguished face. Making a great effort, he rasped, "Not as bad as it looks, lad . . ." But he was already swaying. As men ran to catch him, his eyes rolled back in his head and he toppled from the saddle into their outstretched arms, splattering his rescuers with his blood.

Humphrey was too weak to survive a journey to his stronghold at Toron; instead, he was taken in stages to the Templar castle at Jacob's Ford. Baldwin summoned his own physicians, and as word spread that the constable was dying, the lords of Outremer rushed to Jacob's Ford to say their farewells. Denys was the first to arrive. He was accompanied by his wife, for although she cared nothing about Humphrey de Toron, Agnes very much wanted to see her son. Roger de Moulins, the grand master of the Knights Hospitaller, was the next to arrive, followed by Balian d'Ibelin and his brother. Count Raymond had been holding his Easter court in Tripoli; upon learning of his friend's fatal wound, he took a galley south to Tyre and then hastened inland to Chastellet. But the one that Humphrey most wanted to see—his thirteen-year-old grandson and namesake—was far to the south, at his stepfather and mother's remote desert stronghold at Kerak, and it remained to be seen whether he could outrace Death.

Baldwin spent every waking hour at Humphrey's bedside, much to his mother's dismay. Despite her animosity toward the constable, she was not indifferent to his pain, telling Joscelin that she was not so heartless. But it was Baldwin's pain that she could not bear. She was convinced that her son was punishing himself by bearing witness to the dying man's suffering. She dared not say that to him, though. She could only watch and worry. As the days dragged by and Baldwin looked more and more like a lost soul, she began to pray for Humphrey's death.

Although she did not know it, those who loved Humphrey were also praying for an end to his earthly ordeal. He'd been shriven of his sins but there was little his doctors could do to ease his pain; only death could do that.

Upon his arrival at Chastellet, the Templar grand master demanded to be taken at once to the constable's bedchamber. Humphrey had fallen into a fitful doze and even Odo de St. Amand was not going to awaken a dying man, declaring he'd return later. No sooner had the door closed behind him than Humphrey's lashes flickered. "Is he gone?" he whispered. His mouth twitched in an attempt at a smile. "Damned if I'll waste my last hours listening to his blathering. . . ."

Baldwin moved his chair closer to the bed. "Is there anything I can do for you?"

That was a plea, not a question, and Humphrey rallied against the pain savaging his body, for there was one more service to be done for Baldwin. "Yes . . . stop blaming yourself, lad."

Baldwin looked away. "But it is my fault," he said at last. "You are dying because you were protecting me. . . ."

"Yes . . . and I thank God for it." Humphrey's voice was stronger now than it had been in days. "I am an old man, Baldwin, too old to fear dying. There can be no more honorable death than this . . . giving my life for my king. . . ."

"A crippled king, a weakling . . ." Baldwin had not meant to reveal his bitterness so nakedly, seeing it as self-pity. But Humphrey of all men deserved the truth. "I am not worthy of your sacrifice."

Humphrey did not reply at once, struggling to keep the pain at bay for a few moments longer. Then he reached across the bed and grasped Baldwin's hand in his. "Listen to me, lad. I have never respected any man as much as I respect you. You'd have been a great king if not for that accursed disease. . . ." His grip tightened. "I cannot even imagine how it is for you. There must be so many days when you yearn only for peace. . . ." His voice faltered, then steadied again. "But you must hang on a while longer, Baldwin, for we need you. You and you alone are holding the kingdom together. It is in danger of being torn asunder, with the de Courtenays and their supporters on one side of a crumbling wall and Count Raymond and his allies on the other. Only you can keep all that hatred and jealousy from breaking free and . . . and engulfing us all. . . ."

Baldwin entwined his fingers around the dying man's hand. When he could trust his voice again, he said softly, "I will do my best, I promise you. . . ."

Humphrey had expended the last of his energy and he could only nod. So much more he wanted to tell Baldwin. *Do not rely upon your mother, lad. Jesu, how that woman can hate. . . . Do not totally trust Raymond, either, for he has ambitions of his own. . . . So does Baudouin d'Ibelin. For all that I like the man, do not let him marry Sybilla. We need another foreign prince for her. . . . And watch out for Eraclius; he'd put a scorpion to shame. . . . Look after my grandson. He's a good boy, but too soft for this harsh, demanding land of ours. . . .* Closing his eyes, he felt tears trickling through his lashes. He hoped that Baldwin thought he was weeping for himself, for his grandson, and not for Outremer.

CHAPTER 22

June was the month when wheat and barley were harvested. When Baldwin learned that Saladin had sent raiding parties to ravage the lands around Sidon, he hastily summoned the lords of the kingdom to assemble at Tiberias. After Balian bade farewell to Maria, Isabella, and his young daughter, he and his knights headed north. The mood was somber, for although their aim was to catch the raiders, the men knew that a confrontation with the sultan was likely; their scouts had reported that Saladin was encamped with a large army not far from Bāniās.

It was sunset as they rode into the town of Tiberias; it had fewer than five thousand residents, but because so many of Jesus's miracles had been performed in and around the great lake known as the Sea of Galilee, it was a popular site for pilgrims, many of whom crowded the streets, casting curious glances at the knights as they passed. Ahead lay the citadel controlled by the Count of Tripoli since his marriage to the Lady Eschiva, Princess of Galilee. Most castles in Outremer were protected by deep, dry fosses; the one at Tiberias was sheltered on the east by the lake, and on the north, west, and south by a broad, water-filled moat. The drawbridge was already down and after identifying himself, Balian led his men into the outer bailey.

Dismounting from Smoke, he handed the reins to his squire Rolf; Khamsin was being led by his other squire. While destriers were normally ridden only into battle, an Arabian like Khamsin was as smooth gaited as any palfrey. But Balian preferred to save the stallion's energy for what lay ahead. Hearing his name shouted, he turned to see his brother coming toward him.

"I was afraid you were not going to get here in time, lad." Seeing Balian's puzzlement, Baudouin explained that they were marching on the morrow, and this baffled Balian all the more.

"Surely there are others still on the way? How could Reynald de Chatillon have gotten to Tiberias ere I did? Kerak is much farther to the south than Nablus."

"By the time Reynald gets here, we'll be long gone—which he'll not take well. Even Baldwin's stepfather is going to be left out of the action, for Denys has not yet arrived, either."

That made no sense to Balian. "Why would Baldwin insist upon departing ere all the lords answer his summons?" The answer came to him then. Not Baldwin. The grand master of the Templars. "This is Odo de St. Amand's doing."

Baudouin confirmed his suspicions with a sigh. "That one would not be willing to wait for his own execution. But I think there is more to this than his natural impatience. Because he gets to command his Templars as if they were serfs, he assumes that all men should be so quick to heed his orders. And we both know that Reynald listens to no voice except his own."

"And Baldwin agreed to this?"

"Well, the Count of Tripoli supported Odo's argument, claiming that the longer we delay, the more of our harvests will be lost to Saladin's raiders." Baudouin liked the count well enough. That did not keep him, though, from pointing out that Raymond would not want to share a command with Reynald de Chatillon any more than Odo de St. Amand would.

Balian frowned, for it was becoming harder and harder to convince himself that these petty rivalries posed no threat to the stability of their kingdom. He still did not understand why Baldwin had consented to this. While Baldwin had always been respectful of the greater battle lore of the older men, he'd never been shy to voice his own opinions. "Why did Baldwin agree?" he asked again.

"Damned if I know, Balian. The lad has not been himself, not since Humphrey's death. I think he still blames himself for that."

Balian nodded. It was, he thought, as if Baldwin's confidence in his own judgment had ebbed away with Humphrey's lifeblood. The Templar grand master was not easy to rein in; he'd even dared to defy Baldwin's autocratic father. But Baldwin was the king, not a Templar knight sworn to obey Odo. Baldwin needed to learn to trust his own instincts again. The trouble was that Balian had no idea how to make that happen. *If only William were not still in Rome!*

As they entered the great hall, Balian headed toward the dais where Baldwin was seated with Joscelin, the Templar grand master, Count Raymond, and Eschiva's son Hugues. Balian wondered if it was too late to argue against the decision to depart on the morrow, his gaze locking upon the big-boned man in the white mantle. Odo de St. Amand was gesturing emphatically, dominating the conversation as if he were the one holding court.

Baldwin seemed somehow diminished next to the imperious, overbearing

Templar. Balian thought Baldwin looked very tired, dark shadows hovering under his eyes like bruises, his useless right arm cradled in a black sling instead of the defiant, dramatic red one he'd worn in the past. He'd celebrated his eighteenth birthday earlier in the week and Balian doubted that it had been a happy one. The young king smiled, though, at the sight of Balian, and he returned the smile as he strode forward, wishing that Humphrey were not such a faithful ghost.

The Franks knew that Saladin would have scouts watching the low road that led to the head of the Huleh River basin, so they chose instead to swing west through the mountains. On June 9, they reached the hill overlooking the plain known as Marj Ayyun and camped for the night. As the darkness faded and the sky began to take on the glowing hues of a summer sunrise, a spectacular panorama unfolded below them. In the distance, they could see the snow-crowned peak of Mount Hermon, to their left the blue sheen of the Mediterranean Sea. The Litani River flowed down the center of the valley before making a sharp turn to the west. Perched on a cliff high above the river, Beaufort Castle looked impregnable. To the south, they could see the smoke of the sultan's campfires, and to the west, more smoke, which set them to cursing, for they knew it marked the path of the Saracen raiders.

They reined in on the crest of the hill as they gazed down upon the plain. As Balian moved closer to the king, Baldwin's eyes lingered upon Khamsin with a naked hunger. Asad was still recovering from founder and he'd been forced to admit Comet could not be trusted in battle. As much as he yearned to prove that he could handle the high-strung stallion, he could not put the lives of his men at risk again. He was astride a dark grey destrier called Charcoal, well trained and sturdy but lacking the speed and intelligence of his Arabians, and he could not help wondering if he'd ever ride one of those splendid stallions again. Balian was joking about Demon, his infamously bad-tempered destrier, saying he'd put the horse at stud if he were not afraid his foals would have cloven hooves, when Odo de St. Amand called out to the king.

"The whoresons have no idea that we're here. So, what are we waiting for?"

Their descent of the slope was so rapid that the infantrymen soon fell behind. The knights had to wait for them to catch up, and while they were waiting, they sent out scouts in search of Saracen raiding parties. The scouts soon returned with good news: raiders heavily laden with booty, stolen livestock, and their own baggage were in the process of fording the Litani River, unaware of the presence of the Franks.

The Saracens had no warning; some had already crossed to the east bank, while others were still in midriver. The sudden appearance of their enemy threw them into utter confusion, which then turned into panic and they were quickly vanquished by a knightly charge. Well before noon, the Franks could claim an easy victory.

The sultan had decided to move his army north to the Bekaa Valley. He'd dispatched men under the command of his nephew Farrukh-Shāh for one final raid around Sidon, and was returning to camp when one of his archers came galloping up on a lathered horse. Salāh al-Dīn listened in disbelief as the man called out that he'd run into several frightened herdsmen who claimed an infidel army had just defeated a Saracen force by the Litani River.

"That is not possible." His scouts would have warned him had the Franks been on the march. Yet when the herdsmen were brought before him and swore in the name of the Prophet that they spoke the truth, he had to believe them. His scouts had been watching the road to the east, not the western mountain passes, while the Metullah Hills lay between his camp and the plain of Marj Ayyun. Just as their night march had caught Farrukh-Shāh by surprise back in April, the Franks had slipped through his net again. He was furious with himself for this lapse but wasted no time on self-recriminations, grateful that he'd been given this warning.

Balian was not happy with the way their campaign was being waged. It had been foolhardy not to wait for Reynald de Chatillon and Denys de Grenier. Their foot soldiers had been exhausted trying to keep pace with the riders. And now they'd split their force in two, the knights off in pursuit of the fugitives from the battle while the infantrymen busied themselves plundering the captured baggage wagons and searching the bodies of the dead. Balian had been given command of the rearguard and by the time he'd made sure their prisoners were securely bound and their wounded tended to, the rest of the riders were long gone.

"My lord?" Sir Fulcher de Hebron, the captain of his knights, reined in beside Khamsin. "What now?"

"We catch up with the king." Balian spared a glance over his shoulder as his men rode out. He'd ordered the infantrymen to post guards on higher ground so they'd not be taken unaware by another raiding party, but he did not have much confidence in their vigilance. Welcoming this chance to rest after that mad scramble down the mountain and delighted by the richness of their spoils, they were relaxing on the riverbank, squabbling good-naturedly about their shares of the plunder, pleased to take their ease until the knights returned. Balian uttered a few choice Arabic curses—somehow they sounded more impressive in that language—and rode on.

Farrukh-Shāh was horrified to learn that one of his raiding parties had been attacked and defeated by the Franks. As he listened to a survivor of that battle, he realized that he and his men were trapped on the wrong side of the Litani River. They had to ford the river to reach the sultan's camp, yet how could they do that with an enemy army awaiting them on the opposite bank? He hastily sent scouts out to locate the Franks. When a scout reported that some of the Franks were camped by the river downstream, he led his men upstream to find a safe crossing.

Balian found the king and the knights at a small spring, watering their horses. His relief waned, though, as he drew closer, for Baldwin was accompanied only by his own household knights, those led by his uncle, and the men charged with guarding the most sacred of the kingdom's relics, the Holy Cross. *Where in bloody Hell have the rest of them gone?* Balian managed to phrase that question more tactfully, but Baldwin flushed as he said that the Templar grand master and Count Raymond had continued their pursuit of the fleeing Saracens.

Baldwin's presence here showed that he did not think it wise to advance so close to Saladin's camp. But Balian knew why he'd not forbidden it. Odo de St. Amand would not have heeded such an order and Raymond was not likely to obey a command from the king, either, for he was a ruler in his own right, seeing Tripoli as an ally of the kingdom, not a vassal state. Exchanging curt nods with Joscelin, Balian guided Khamsin closer to Baldwin's grey.

"This is not going well, is it?" Baldwin said in a low voice. "They all seem to think we've won this great victory and there is nothing more to fear." His blue eyes met Balian's dark ones, reflecting the same memory: an April day that began with a victory and ended with Humphrey de Toron mortally wounded by a Saracen spear.

Joscelin did not like his nephew turning to one of the d'Ibelins for advice and forced his stallion between their horses. "The king and I were discussing whether we should return to the infantry or follow the Templars and the other knights."

Neither choice was a good one and they knew it. Baldwin reluctantly concluded that they ought to try to catch up with Odo and Count Raymond. Balian concurred, no less reluctantly, for what was not debatable was the danger in having their army divided like this. Signaling to his men to fall in behind him, Balian could not help muttering "The damn fools" under his breath.

Joscelin was close enough to hear. "One of those 'damned fools' is your brother." Balian had already realized that; if Baudouin was not with the king, he must be riding with the Templars and Count Raymond. He said nothing, refusing to let Joscelin know his gibe had hit home, and they moved out, the silver and gold banner of Outremer unfurling in the summer breeze.

They'd covered only a few miles when two knights came into view, spurring their mounts mercilessly. They shouted at the sight of Baldwin's banner but did not slacken their pace. "Go back!" one yelled. "Saladin's army!" Pointing south toward the Metullah Hills as if words alone were not enough to convey the danger. By now Baldwin and his men could see that one of the knights was bleeding from a shoulder wound. They would have galloped right past if Baldwin and Balian had not urged their stallions out to bar the road.

"Tell us what happened! Where are the Templars? Count Raymond?"

"Cut to pieces," the bleeding knight gasped. "We ran right into them, had no warning. No time to form battle lines ere they were upon us. . . ."

The second knight continued on, calling over his shoulder that he could not afford a ransom and did not want to end up in the Cairo slave markets. The injured man paused long enough to plead with Baldwin, "Save yourselves whilst you still can. It is too late for the others. . . ." And with that, he, too, was gone.

By now they could see dust rising to the south, kicked up by hundreds of horses. Baldwin's expression was anguished, yet he did not hesitate, for he was responsible for the lives of these men. He gave the command to retreat and they wheeled their horses, galloping after the two fleeing knights.

Balian was no less anguished, but like Baldwin, he could not give in to his emotions. No matter what had befallen his brother and Jakelin, he had ninety-five knights under his command. This was not terrain that was kind to horses, with rock-strewn ridges, hollows, and defiles, the earth cracked and dry after years of drought. But if they could reach the more level ground in the Marj Ayyun plain, they ought to be able to find safety at Beaufort Castle. They were greatly relieved, therefore, when they saw the distant shimmer of the Litani River.

It was then that the attack came. Suddenly they found themselves under assault by Saracen archers, and as horses swerved in fear and men raised their shields to deflect the hail of arrows, Farrukh-Shāh and his men swept down from the hills to take the offensive.

"To me! To me!" Balian shouted to his knights, for their only chance was to fight as a unit; one-on-one, they'd be surrounded and slain. There was little room to maneuver, and their Saracen foes had the advantage in such close-quarter fighting, for their horses were much nimbler and more agile than the heavier Frankish destriers. Balian's knights were able to rally to him, and when they launched an attack, the Saracens gave way. Unable to withstand a charge, they sheered off, hoping to surge back before the knights could regroup. Their retreat gave Balian a chance to survey the battlefield. Joscelin's men had taken the brunt of the assault. But Baldwin's banner still flew, for his knights would fight to the death to protect him.

"To the king!" As his men joined Baldwin's knights, Balian thought they would be able to fight their way free. It was then that the army of Salāh al-Dīn arrived on the scene.

Balian had learned that battles had tides, ebbing and flowing. Now they found themselves engulfed in a wave too powerful to resist. Faced with a choice of dying, surrendering, or fleeing, the Franks chose flight and scattered.

Balian sought in vain for a glimpse of Baldwin amid the seething mass of men and horses that the battlefield had become. Turning, he confronted a Kurd wielding a sword with a wickedly curved blade. Khamsin swerved and the sword found only air. Balian slammed another attacker with his shield, then narrowly avoided a Saracen knight on a screaming black stallion. For a moment, he wished he was astride Demon, who turned into a killing machine in combat. Then Khamsin spun away from a Mamluk clad in the sultan's saffron and Balian decided that speed mattered more now than ferocity. With half a dozen Saracens in pursuit, he sent Khamsin flying up the slope of a barren hillock. But not even Khamsin could outrun an arrow and one struck Balian in the leg just as he reached the summit of the hill, slicing through the mail greaves to lodge in his calf. He felt the impact of the blow but there was no pain, not yet. Giving Khamsin his head, Balian rode for his life.

The Saracens did not abandon the chase, for they had the advantage in numbers and need not fear an ambush by the men they were hunting. Many of the fleeing Franks were overtaken and slain, or made prisoner if they looked as if they'd be worth ransoming. Others were luckier and outraced their pursuers. Some splashed across the river and headed for Sidon and Tyre. But most of them sought closer refuge in the stone stronghold more than nine hundred feet above the west bank of the Litani—Beaufort Castle.

Balian caught up with some of his knights once they reached the Marj Ayyun plain. They gratefully banded together and urged their spent stallions on, for there were five more miles to Beaufort Castle. As their horses scrambled up the narrow path leading to the citadel's southern gatehouse, they paused occasionally to gaze at the plain and hills far below them. Each one of them still clung to the forlorn hope that they would see Baldwin's banner streaming aloft as he and his knights galloped toward the fortress. All they saw were Saracen riders swarming over the countryside like bees from an overturned hive, searching for Frankish fugitives. None dared to speak it aloud, yet the same thought was in every man's mind: *Where is the king?*

Baldwin hit the ground with such force that he lay stunned for a time. As his wits cleared, he opened his eyes. All around him was a scene of desolation: the bodies of men and horses, the moans of the wounded, blood seeping into the arid earth and splattering the crumpled banner of the kingdom. Beside him, Charcoal lay still, a Saracen spear protruding from his chest. It came as a shock to Baldwin to realize that he was alone on a field with the dead and dying.

His sword lay a few feet away and he reached for it before struggling to his feet, swaying like a sapling in a high wind. He dared not stay here. His men—those who'd not been slain or captured—would soon be searching for him. The Saracens would come first, though, to recover their wounded and their dead and to strip the bodies of the Franks. Several loose horses remained on the battlefield and Baldwin eyed them yearningly. Yet he made no attempt to catch one, for he knew he could not get into the saddle on his own. They were in a ravine and boulders higher up on the slopes might offer hiding places. Could he get there ere the Saracens returned?

Squaring his aching shoulders, he began to limp across the field, detouring around bodies and averting his gaze from the blind stares of the slain. He faltered when he recognized one of his own knights, his face swarming with flies, his intestines spilling out in a puddle of clotted dark blood. It was then that he heard a horse snort, heard the thud of hooves on the hard, sunbaked soil. Dropping to the ground, Baldwin lay still, scarcely breathing.

It was a lone rider. The man was out of Baldwin's line of vision and he could not risk shifting his position. Time seemed to have stopped and then he heard a cry of despair—in French. Sitting up, he saw the rider had dismounted to recover their trampled banner and was holding it to his chest as if it were a precious relic. With an effort, Baldwin managed to regain his feet just as the soldier turned in his direction. Recognition was instantaneous and mutual.

"Anselm!" Baldwin stumbled toward him as his squire flung himself forward. Then they were embracing, holding each other like drowning men trying to stay afloat.

"I've been searching for so long. . . ." Anselm's weathered face was smeared with dirt and tear tracks. "I feared you were dead, sire!"

"You are lucky that you are not," Baldwin said with a shaky smile, realizing what a great risk Anselm had taken, venturing alone into the midst of the victorious Saracen army. Looking abashed by the praise, the older man whistled to his mount. He was saying that his horse could carry them both when the wind brought to them the sound of voices.

With seconds to spare, they flattened themselves on the ground as riders came into view. Pressing his cheek against the dirt, Baldwin listened as his enemies joked and laughed; though he spoke no Arabic, the language of victory needed no translation. Through his lashes, he saw one of them discover his banner, flaunting it with a triumphant cry. Anselm's courser was quickly claimed, as were the other loose horses. He knew they'd soon dismount, eager to rob the bodies of the slain knights. They would recognize him, of course, his youth and paralyzed arm offering irrefutable testimony to his identity. He did not doubt that he'd be treated with respect; they'd know the worth of their royal hostage. But would they see Anselm's life as valuable, too?

Beside him, Anselm had inhaled dust and was trying not to sneeze as they waited to be discovered. It did not happen. Instead, another Saracen rider galloped into view, one of Saladin's Mamluks. After he shouted, the other men turned their horses and followed him. A command from the sultan? Had they flushed more fugitives from the battle? Baldwin and Anselm knew only that they'd gotten a brief reprieve and they'd not be likely to get another one.

As soon as the Saracen soldiers were out of sight, they got to their feet. Anselm agreed with Baldwin that their best chance was to climb the rocky incline rising to the west. But they soon realized that Baldwin was not going to be able to scramble up that steep slope.

"Lean on me, sire," Anselm insisted, and Baldwin had no choice but to abandon pride and accept the older man's support. They continued to struggle, though, for Anselm was only of average height and well past the prime of youth. Both were soon winded, having to pause often to catch their breath, all the while listening for the return of the Saracens. Several times they slid on the loose gravel and almost fell. After the last stumble, they were suddenly peppered with more gravel, this time coming from above them. Squinting into the sun, they saw the figure of a man at the top of the ridge.

"Wait there," he called, and started down. He was young and agile and made his descent look easy. After reaching them, he actually started to kneel before Baldwin stopped him. His sunburned, freckled face looked vaguely familiar and when he identified himself as Sir Thomas de Caymont, Baldwin recognized him as one of his uncle's household knights. He did not appear to be injured and seemed embarrassed by that, for his account of being thrown when his horse shattered a foreleg sounded almost apologetic.

"I found a cave up there," he said, gesturing toward the hilltop, "and meant to hide till the Saracens were no longer hunting for us. We must hurry, though, for I saw more dust clouds off to the south. If you'll permit me, sire . . . ?" Reaching out, he grasped Baldwin's left arm and gestured for Anselm to take up position on Baldwin's other side.

They made more progress with Thomas to help, but as they climbed higher, the going became more treacherous. By now, Baldwin was so exhausted that he dangled limply between them, his feet dragging on the ground. Thomas soon stopped. "This is not going to work." His forehead furrowed as he considered their options. Dropping to his knees, he asked Baldwin to put his arm around his neck, reaching down to clamp Baldwin's legs around his waist. He staggered as he sought to regain his feet, then slowly straightened up with a triumphant grin. With Baldwin clinging to his back and Anselm following closely in case Thomas stumbled, they made their way up the slope, one cautious step at a time.

Thomas did not stop once they finally reached the top, lurching forward until they were sheltered by the boulders. After bending down so Baldwin could dismount, he flopped on the ground with another grin. "You're heavier than you look, my liege," he panted.

Baldwin could only look at him in wonderment. Torn between mortification at his own helplessness and deep gratitude, he hesitated. But he had to ask, "Were you not afraid?"

Thomas did not pretend to misunderstand. "I'd be lying if I said no, sire. I told myself that leprosy cannot be so easy to catch, else Anselm there would have been stricken long ago. Still . . ." He shrugged, a wordless admission that fear was not rooted in logic or even common sense. "But how could I not have come to your aid? You are my king."

Baldwin found the semblance of a smile for the young knight and then turned his head away so they'd not see the tears glimmering behind his lashes.

The Saracens were soon back for their dead, leaving the stripped enemy corpses at the mercy of the vultures. They were still searching for fugitives, but the sharp incline of the ridge discouraged the few who glanced speculatively in its direction, and eventually they departed. Emerging from the damp, musty cave, Baldwin and his two companions watched as the sun sank below the horizon and the night stole in, mercifully cloaking the battlefield below. With darkness, the temperature dropped sharply, and they returned to the dubious shelter of the cave, huddling together to pass what promised to be a very long night. They had no food, only two half-filled waterskins, which Thomas and Anselm tried to give to Baldwin and which he firmly refused, insisting that they share equally. First Thomas and then Anselm fell asleep. Baldwin stayed awake, alone with his regrets.

At first light, Thomas volunteered to go in search of help and bounded down the slope with the resiliency of the young and healthy. Within the hour, he was back, astride a borrowed bay gelding, accompanied by a dozen armed knights. Sir Simon de Garnier was in the lead. Unable to wait as Baldwin and Anselm began their slow descent, he clambered up to meet them. He was grinning from ear to ear, and Baldwin realized that they'd given him up for dead.

From Simon, Baldwin learned that his uncle and Balian d'Ibelin had been able to reach Beaufort Castle with most of their knights, and men were continuing to show up. It seemed almost miraculous that the Holy Cross had not fallen into infidel hands. But when Baldwin asked him about the missing lords and Templars, Simon could only shake his head.

The light was fading by the time Balian and his men slowly rode up the winding path that led to Beaufort Castle's gatehouse, exhausted and numbed by the events of the past two days. They'd found a few men still living amid the dead, found a few more in hiding. But they were overwhelmed by their losses and haunted by the fate of their missing.

Dismounting in the bailey, they assisted the wounded from their saddles and turned their horses over to their squires. As Balian limped into the hall, he came to a halt and then smiled for the first time since they'd looked down from the heights upon the peaceful meadows of Marj Ayyun. Baldwin refused to let him kneel and insisted that he take a seat on the dais. Ignoring Joscelin's baleful glare, he sank down into a chair next to the king, but neither one spoke, for there were no words to describe the catastrophe that had befallen them and their kingdom.

Soon after dark, they were surprised by the arrival of Baldwin's stepfather. Beaufort was his and the castellan had immediately dispatched a messenger to Sidon. Denys had already learned of the defeat, though. Leading an armed force to join Baldwin at Marj Ayyun, having received word that they'd not waited at Tiberias, he'd encountered men fleeing the battle, and their stories were so harrowing that he'd turned around and returned to Sidon, assuming there was nothing more to be done. Now that he realized he might have saved some of the fugitives from capture had he only continued on, he was deeply shaken.

Baldwin refused his apologies. "I doubt that you could have changed the outcome, Denys," he said in the flat, toneless voice of one still in shock. "It was already too late."

Sleep proved elusive for many at Beaufort Castle that night. Balian finally gave up and rose to dress hours before dawn would disperse the darkness. He was trying to take hope from his failure to find either his brother's body or Jakelin's, trying to convince himself that they could still be out there, awaiting their chance to make their way to safety. Yet he knew the likelihood was that they were dead or captured. Ransom was usually possible for a man taken prisoner by the Saracens. But not always. And how likely was Saladin to ransom a Templar?

In this way, Balian tormented himself in the solitude, silence, and darkness that proved to be fertile soil for despairing and desperate thoughts. He was preparing to go out with another search party when a rider arrived with a message from the Count of Tripoli. Raymond had managed to escape the battle and, with a few companions, had been able to reach safety in Tyre. But his messenger had no word of the fate of those still missing, for the battle had quickly turned into a rout. Balian rode out again to look for his brother and his friend.

It was another futile quest, made dangerous by several near encounters with Saracens out hunting, too, for Franks. His knights were so obviously drained and his leg was aching so badly that he ended the search before darkness had fallen. It was only upon his return to the castle that he finally learned what had happened to his brother.

Another survivor of the battle had been found, Baldwin told him, so somberly that he knew the news would be not be good. The wounded man was a Templar, struck down and left for dead by the Saracens. But he'd not died and now he gave Balian an eyewitness account of the end of the battle—when those still alive realized they must either yield or fight to the death. Nigh on three hundred knights and lords had been taken prisoner by the infidels, he whispered, amongst them the Templar grand master, Lord Baudouin of Ramlah, and the Count of Tripoli's stepson Hugues of Galilee.

CHAPTER 23

July 1179
Tell al-Qādī, Syria

The day was hot, the air so still that the red and gold d'Ibelin banner and the white flag of truce drooped like willow leaves. Balian could see the tension on his men's faces as they came in sight of the sultan's camp. He'd taken only a few of his knights, those whom he could trust to remain calm no matter the provocation. Beside him, his dragoman, Yūnus, shifted awkwardly in his saddle, then offered Balian a strained smile. "With your permission, my lord, I wish to be called by the French version of my name whilst we meet with the sultan."

"Of course—Jonah." Balian understood the older man's unease. As Arabic was their native tongue, Syrian Christians often took the Arabic form of their given names. But Muslims viewed apostasy as a sin deserving of death and Yūnus did not want any of the Saracens to doubt that he was Christian by birth, not by converting.

They'd been spotted. Riders were coming out to challenge them. "I am Balian d'Ibelin, Lord of Nablus, under a safe-conduct to meet with the sultan," Balian said slowly and carefully. As usual, the riders were startled by Balian's ability to speak Arabic, which worked in his favor.

The man in command gave an order too fast for Balian to catch, and the Franks found themselves surrounded. Their arrival created a stir in the camp. As they waited with their guards, Balian glanced around curiously. Men were repairing weapons and armor, bantering with one another, seeking shade from the summer sun. Aside from the absence of wine or games of chance, which were forbidden by the Qur'an, Balian could have been looking at a Frankish army camp. Soldiers were the same the world over.

A man was approaching, escorted by several of the sentries, but he was clearly not a soldier. He was no longer young—Balian guessed him to be in his fifth decade—and garbed in civilian clothing: a finely woven cotton tunic and matching turban, leather sandals rather than riding boots, and no sword at his hip. Introducing himself as 'Imād al-Dīn al-Isfahānī, the sultan's chancellor, he said, "The sultan will see you."

They were attracting a lot of attention, and some jeers were flung their way. Balian's Arabic was good enough by now for him to understand the taunting. They were called dogs and demons of the cross but the slur that struck him as ironic was *kafir*, for it meant "infidel," the same insult that the Christians hurled at their Muslim foes.

Balian had to surrender his sword once they reached the sultan's tent, for Salāh al-Dīn had begun taking precautions for his safety after the second attempt on his life by the Assassins. The knights were disarmed, too, but 'Imād al-Dīn said only Balian and his dragoman could enter the tent's inner section. Giving his men a silent warning to be on their best behavior, Balian took the saker and falconer's glove from one of them, then moved to meet his brother's gaoler.

Salāh al-Dīn was seated cross-legged on a large cushion. Balian remembered how surprised he'd been to find that the sultan was of modest stature and amiable demeanor, for he'd envisioned their greatest enemy as a colossus among men, fierce and prideful. He'd soon realized, though, that the sultan's power was not in his sword. It was the spirit that burned within him, the depth and breadth of his ambitions, his utter certainty that he was Allah's instrument, fated to destroy the Christian kingdom of Jerusalem.

Bowing, Balian offered the traditional Arabic greeting, "Peace be upon you." As much as he wanted to get right to the purpose of his visit, he knew there were proprieties to be satisfied first; hospitality was taken seriously by the Saracens. Stepping forward, Balian offered his gift, saying it would please him if the sultan would accept this token of his respect.

The token ruffled her feathers, her talons digging into the leather of his glove. Although she was hooded, all her senses were alert and she turned her head toward the sound of Balian's voice. Sakers were prized by the Saracens, who loved hawking as much as the Franks did, and this bird was a rarity, whiter than the snow still capping Mount Hermon.

The sultan thanked him for such a splendid *hurr*, using the Arabic word for a female saker, and then paused. "How much of our tongue do you speak?"

"I do speak some Arabic. But I thought it best to have my dragoman accompany me so that there can be no misunderstandings between us, my lord."

The sultan gestured to a large cushion. "Sit," he said, "and we shall talk."

❧

Salāh al-Dīn had not accorded Balian the honor of a private audience, but he was attended only by 'Imād al-Dīn and two other men, both of whom bore such a marked resemblance to him that Balian was not surprised when they were introduced as his nephew Farrukh-Shāh and his first cousin, Nāsir al-Dīn. The saker had been turned over to the sultan's falconer and Balian had been provided with more cushions for his injured leg after Salāh al-Dīn noticed his discomfort.

It was only after the amenities had been observed that the sultan took another sip of his juice and began their negotiation. "You are here on behalf of your brother, of course."

Balian swallowed the last of his own drink and set it on the ground. "I am, my lord."

"We have met before, have we not? I believe you accompanied Humphrey de Toron and the Count of Tripoli when they sought a truce with me."

Balian was impressed with the sultan's memory. While he'd had an extended conversation with Salāh al-Dīn's brother al-'Ādil, he'd only exchanged greetings with the sultan. "Can you tell me if my brother is well?"

"His pride was badly bruised," the sultan said, with a slight smile, "but he was not otherwise injured."

Balian made no attempt to disguise his relief. "It is my hope," he said, "that you are willing to ransom him."

"I am willing to consider it. You are not the first one to make such a request. The Count of Tripoli and his wife are very eager to gain her son's freedom. We have been discussing a ransom of fifty-five thousand dinars."

That was a steep price, but one Raymond and Eschiva could afford. It was also one Baudouin might be able to afford, and some of Balian's tension began to ease. It was then that the sultan said, "The ransom for the Lord of Ramlah would be much higher, of course, since he will become a king if he weds the leper king's sister."

Balian stiffened, and signaled to Yūnus to translate for him. "Tell the sultan that he is mistaken. My brother has no hopes of kingship. The Lady Sybilla is betrothed to a French lord, the Duke of Burgundy."

As the dragoman spoke, the sultan and the other men began to look amused. "There is no betrothal, not yet. And until the lady is actually wed to another man, your brother's 'hopes of kingship' remain alive and well."

Balian barely listened to Yūnus's whispered words, for he'd understood the sultan's reply, understood, too, the underlying message—that the Saracens were very well informed about Baldwin's court and the rivalries that were dividing it. "I do not deny that my brother has long wanted to wed the Lady Sybilla. It is not going to happen, though. If our king thought Baudouin would make a suitable husband for his sister, he'd have said so after she was widowed."

The sultan shrugged. "Even if he does not become your king, the Lord of Ramlah is a man of considerable importance in your kingdom, courageous on the battlefield and outspoken in the council chamber." Nāsir al-Dīn leaned over to speak, too swiftly for Balian to follow. Salāh al-Dīn listened before turning back to Balian. "My cousin thinks it might be best if we do not release him, pointing out that he is sure to give us more trouble once he is free. There is some truth in that. I am still willing to ransom him, though, provided that we can agree upon the terms. We will discuss this matter with him and inform you when a decision has been made."

That was the common practice when a prisoner was highborn; he would usually be released to arrange for the ransom's payment, so it was necessary that he agree to the amount demanded. Balian's emotions were as conflicted at that moment as their court's loyalties, deeply thankful that the sultan was willing to accept a ransom while chilled by the fear that it might be so exorbitant that they'd never be able to raise it.

"Thank you, my lord. Would it be possible for me to see him?" He felt no real surprise when the sultan refused, explaining that all of the prisoners had been taken to Damascus. "My brother's freedom is my main concern, but not my only one. Seven of my knights were captured by you, my lord." Nodding toward Farrukh-Shāh. "I wish to ransom them, too."

The sultan's nephew looked to be in his thirties. He was a younger brother of Taqī al-Dīn, but did not have the latter's reputation for ferocity or hatred of the Franks. He proved that now by saying, "Your knights fought bravely, my lord, and brave men deserve to be ransomed. You may gain their freedom if you are able to pay a thousand dinars for each one."

Ransoms were such an established custom in the Levant that the amounts had become set over the years. For an infantryman or civilian, the price was thirty-three dinars, for a knight a thousand dinars, and for a lord or prince, whatever the market might bear. Balian quickly agreed to the sum and when asked for the names, Yūnus produced a parchment scroll. Farrukh-Shāh smiled when he saw that the script was in Arabic and handed it to 'Imād al-Dīn.

Seeing that the sultan was about to end the audience, Balian said swiftly, "My lord sultan, there is one more matter to discuss. I also wish to ransom a man named Jakelin de Mailly."

"Another one of your knights?"

"No, my lord. He is one of the Knights Templar."

Until now, his reception had been courteous, even cordial. The atmosphere changed, though, with the admission of Jakelin's identity. The sultan's eyes narrowed, his mouth tightening. "The Templars are the enemies of Allah, the scourge of my people. Why would I want to set one of them free to spill more Muslim blood?"

Balian leaned forward, the ache in his leg forgotten. "Say this to the sultan," he told his dragoman. "Ask him if he admires courage."

Salāh al-Dīn blinked. "Of course I do."

"I am sure the sultan knows that the order of the Templars does not ransom their brethren if they are taken prisoner. Ask him to consider what courage it takes for a man to ride into battle knowing that if he is captured, he will have no hope of regaining his freedom. Knowing he will be doomed to pass the rest of his earthly days as a slave or in a dungeon so dark it is impossible to distinguish night from day."

That was clearly not the argument the sultan had been expecting. His face was difficult for Balian to read. The other men were more transparent: Nāsir al-Dīn was frowning, while Farrukh-Shāh's mouth softened in what may have been a smile. Balian kept his gaze upon Salāh al-Dīn, scarcely daring to breathe as Jakelin's fate hung in the balance.

"I've heard it said that you Franks are lawyers at heart," the sultan said after an eternity. "I think you would have made a good one, Lord Balian. I daresay I will regret it, but you may ransom your Templar friend for the sum of five thousand dinars."

As they followed 'Imād al-Dīn from the tent, Balian nearly collided with a man striding toward it. Stepping back, they regarded each other in mutual astonishment. "I thought you were in Egypt, my lord!" Balian exclaimed. Did al-'Ādil's presence here mean that the sultan planned another offensive against the Franks?

Al-'Ādil shook his head, thinking that his brother had been no less taken aback by his unexpected arrival four sunsets ago. But when he'd gotten the request for fifteen hundred fresh troops, he'd yielded to the temptation to bring them himself, for he had family matters to discuss with Yūsuf. Realizing that Balian d'Ibelin must be here in hopes of ransoming his brother, he told 'Imād al-Dīn that he would escort the Franks to their horses.

Balian fell into step beside al-'Ādil, who gave him a sidelong smile. "Lord of Nablus. You have come up in the world since we last met."

Balian took no offense, for it was true. "God has been good to me."

Al-'Ādil nodded approvingly, for the Qur'an said that whatever of blessings and good things a man had, it was from Allah. Not all men were wise enough to understand that. "And what of my brother the sultan? Has he been good to you, too?"

"He has." As they walked, Balian related what had occurred in the sultan's tent. Al-'Ādil had expected that Balian's brother and his knights would be ransomed. Between the expense of keeping a large army in the field and the damage that the drought had done to their economy, Yūsuf greatly needed the money. But he came to an abrupt halt when Balian said that the sultan would also ransom his Templar friend.

"You are not joking?" He looked at Balian in amused amazement. "You must have made a very good impression upon my brother if he agreed to free a Templar!"

Balian was still not sure how he'd managed it. "If you knew Jakelin de Mailly, my lord, you'd agree with me that he is a brave and honorable man." Al-'Ādil looked so skeptical that Balian had to laugh. He stopped, though, when he realized that he'd not asked the sultan about the fate of the grand master of the Templars. As far as he was concerned, Odo de St. Amand deserved to rot in a Damascus dungeon. Whilst it was true that Count Raymond and even Baudouin deserved some of the blame for the disaster at Marj Ayyun, the lion's share belonged to Odo. But when it was learned that he'd seen the sultan, men would want to know what was said about the Templar grand master.

"I forgot to ask the sultan about the grand master of the Templars," he confessed; only later would he wonder at the ease he felt with the sultan's brother, as if they had a long history instead of a few hours together nigh on four years ago. "Try not to laugh at me if I ask you whether your brother would consider ransoming him."

Al-'Ādil grinned. "Actually," he said, "the sultan offered to free the grand master in exchange for one of his amirs, captured at the battle you Franks call Montgisard."

Balian was astonished. "But he loathes the Templars. Does he not fear releasing a man he calls the scourge of Muslims?"

Al-'Ādil's grin widened. "Just between us, I think he sees the grand master as our secret weapon."

Balian could not help grinning, too, thinking that Saladin might well be right; Odo had never been one to learn from past mistakes.

Al-'Ādil was finding this conversation very enjoyable. "Alas, the prisoner swap will not take place. Odo de St. Amand refused to agree, saying he would never pay ransom to infidels and no 'pagan prince' was the equal of the grand master of the Templars."

"Jesu!" Balian had to admit, however grudgingly, that Odo de St. Amand was that rarity, a man who practiced what he preached. He still could not muster up sympathy for the Templar; his recklessness had caused the death and capture of hundreds of men, men the kingdom could not afford to lose.

By now they'd reached their horses. Al-'Ādil stood, watching, as Balian and his knights mounted. "Do you want me to send some of my men with you until you reach the lands of the Franks?"

Balian thanked him, saying that was not necessary. For a moment, their eyes held. "I do not suppose that we will ever get to take that hunting trip together," al-'Ādil said at last.

"No," Balian agreed, "I do not suppose we will."

Maria had not argued when Balian told her he must try to ransom his brother; loyalty and duty were the underpinnings of her moral code. But when she threw herself into his arms as soon as he'd swung from the saddle, Balian realized how fearful she must have been for his safety, as she was not given to public displays of affection. He had no such inhibitions himself and kissed her, so long and so passionately that his knights began to cheer.

Maria was flushed when he finally let her go and swept Isabella up into his arms. He turned next to Helvis. Just learning to walk, she wobbled unsteadily toward him, her wet nurse hovering to catch her if she fell. He knelt so he could embrace her and when he lifted her onto his shoulders, she giggled and held on to his hair. Maria watched, smiling. Balian could still breathe in the scent of her perfume, could still feel the softness of her curves as she'd clung to him, and he wanted nothing so much as to take her into the palace and straight up to their chamber. When they lay together in bed, their bodies entwined, he could forget for a time their kingdom's peril, the court feuds, Baldwin's failing health, Saladin's commitment to jihad.

He could not do that, of course, for his daughters were clamoring for his attention, his knights were bombarding him with questions about Saladin, and they had company. Amand, the Viscount of Nablus, and his wife were family, for he was wed to Baudouin's youngest daughter, Etiennette, and Ralph, the Bishop of

Sebaste, was a friend and neighbor. But the other guests were strangers: the abbot of the Greek Orthodox monastery of St. Elias, a baron from Armenian Cilicia and his entourage. Wellborn pilgrims and those traveling on Church business relied upon the hospitality of castles and monasteries rather than the inns that catered to all classes. Heaving a martyr's sigh, Balian headed off to their chamber to make himself presentable for their guests.

After bathing, shaving, and changing into clean clothes, Balian hastened down to the hall to play the role of gracious host. He was the center of attention and over their meal, he related his experiences at the sultan's camp. His knights were elated that their captive comrades would be freed and gave Balian grateful looks, for not all liege lords were so conscientious about the men who'd sworn fealty to them. There was rejoicing, especially by Etiennette, that Baudouin would be ransomed, and they all marveled that Balian had been able to rescue Jakelin, too. None of them were interested enough to ask about Odo de St. Amand's fate.

The conversation then turned to Maria's news—that a contingent of highborn French lords had landed at Acre. They included the French king's brother, the Count of Champagne, and the bishop-elect of Beauvais. Almost as an afterthought, she remembered to mention the arrival of Amaury de Lusignan's younger brother . . . Guy, she believed his name was.

Balian was very pleased when Maria assured him that these lords had brought many knights with them, for their kingdom's chronic manpower shortage had become critical after the debacle at Marj Ayyun. She'd saved the best news for last—that Bishop Joscius's marital mission had been successful. The Duke of Burgundy was willing to marry the Lady Sybilla and would sail for Outremer after he'd arranged to turn his duchy over to his fifteen-year-old son.

"God be praised," Balian said softly. Hugh of Burgundy was said to be a fine soldier, a man accustomed to command, whilst Baldwin was a candle fast burning down to its wick, kingship becoming a cruel burden for him. Once Hugh married Sybilla, Baldwin would be able to abdicate, to live out his remaining days away from the curious eyes, the constant scrutiny, the pity.

After the meal was done, Maria briefly excused herself to put her daughters to bed. Balian usually joined in this bedtime ritual, but tonight he manfully stepped into the breach to entertain their guests until his wife returned. When she did, Maria paused in the doorway, watching as he did his best to bridge the language gap; not all of the Armenian pilgrims spoke French and the abbot's Greek accent was so thick that he was not easy to understand. Maria smiled, deciding Balian had earned a reprieve. So, instead of retaking her seat on the dais, she gave Balian a concerned look, one filled with wifely solicitude. "My lord husband . . . is your wound bothering you again?"

Balian almost denied it from force of habit, for he was as reluctant as most men to admit to any infirmities. Catching himself in the nick of time, he confessed that his leg had indeed begun to ache. The ploy worked: Amand, Etiennette, and Bishop Ralph soon departed and the other guests were escorted by servants up to the chambers set aside for them. Balian's energy had been flagging as the evening wore on, for he'd been in the saddle since dawn. His fatigue was forgotten, though, when Maria caught his eye and winked.

As soon as they'd reached their bedchamber, Balian set about untying the lacings of Maria's gown as he backed her toward the bed. She cooperated at first, but once he'd stripped her down to her chemise, she caught his hand in hers. "Wait, my heart. We must talk first."

The only conversation he had in mind at that moment was carnal. "Talk fast, then," he urged, pressing his lips to the hollow of her throat. Choosing actions over words, she placed his hand over her abdomen, pleased when he was quick to comprehend. "You are with child again?"

"I am," she said, tilting her face up for his kiss. It was a gentle one, as she'd known it would be. When he'd learned she was pregnant with Helvis, he'd been the same way at first, acting as if she were suddenly as fragile as newly blown glass. She'd been able to reassure him with gentle humor, pointing out that Scriptures called wives the weaker vessels, not the breakable ones, and by showing him that pregnancy and passion were perfectly compatible. She reminded him of that now by returning his kiss with such ardor that he drew her even closer, murmuring something about "cloven tongues of fire" and carried her the few steps to their bed.

Afterward, they talked and she revealed that she'd missed two of her fluxes, the first whilst he was on the way to Marj Ayyun and the second that past week, after he'd departed for Saladin's camp. "I did not say anything after the first, for I wanted to be sure. But I've missed two in a row only when I was carrying Isabella and Melisende, and then Helvis."

"We have truly been blessed, Marika." She knew he was happy that she was with child again, but she caught the undertones of unease in his voice. Understanding that he feared for her safety, she confided that she'd already begun praying to the patron saint for women in childbirth, and that seemed to reassure him somewhat. She did not tell him that she was praying to a Greek Orthodox saint, not a Latin Catholic one. Amalric had insisted that she convert to Catholicism, saying she would seem less alien and foreign to his subjects if they worshipped in the same way. Once she was widowed, she could have gone back to the faith of her childhood. She'd decided, though, that this would be confusing to Isabella, who must be raised in the Latin Church as she might be queen one day.

Maria knew she could have confessed this to Balian, who was as unlike Amalric as chalk and cheese. But every marriage had a secret or two and this was hers. It was too hot to cuddle so she settled for placing his hand again on her belly and was soon asleep.

Balian was not as lucky. As tired as his body was, his brain was racing like Baldwin's runaway stallion. He very much wanted more children. He could not deny, though, that for women, the birthing chamber could be as dangerous as the battlefield was for men. And underlying the natural anxiety of a man for his wife, a greater fear loomed. If Maria gave him a son, what sort of future would he have? Their world seemed more dangerous now than it had when Helvis was born nigh on a year ago. What if their kingdom did not survive? What sort of legacy would they be leaving their children?

Maria awoke a few hours later and was concerned to find he was still awake. "Are you fretting about your brother's ransom?" Propping herself up on her elbow, she was able to study his face, for they'd forgotten to quench the oil lamps in their haste to reach the bed. "You fear that Saladin will ask for a ransom so great that Baudouin and you cannot raise it? Should that happen, I will ask the emperor for help in paying it."

"You would do that, Marika? Would the emperor agree, though?"

"He has helped to ransom other Christian lords held captive by the Saracens. He sees it as a religious duty to aid the afflicted . . . and of course such public displays of magnanimity and piety greatly enhance his prestige." Maria's smile was both affectionate and worldly-wise, for she was fond of her great-uncle but under no illusions about him. "Moreover, our marriage has linked you to the Greek Royal House and this is your brother. Manuel could well see this as a matter of family pride, especially if it were presented to him in that way."

Balian kissed her, laughed, and kissed her again. Maria was delighted that her offer had eased his anxiety about Baudouin's ransom and it had. But he'd also remembered that if the worst did happen, if he died defending Outremer and the kingdom fell to Saladin, Maria and their children would be far more fortunate than most Poulains. They could always find safety in Constantinople.

CHAPTER 24

August 1179
Jerusalem, Outremer

Agnes had realized that Balian and Maria would join the court in Jerusalem to meet the newly arrived French lords. But she'd not expected them to bring Isabella and she glowered as she watched them maneuver their way through the crowded hall toward the dais. "Damn that Greek witch," she hissed. "She never misses a chance to flaunt that brat of hers in front of Baldwin, to remind him and all the other Poulains that they share the same blood."

Sybilla had a throbbing headache, for she'd slept little the night before, worried by her son's coughing. His doctor had insisted it was a mild case of the croup, no cause for anxiety, but the little boy was miserable. She was in no mood today to listen to one of her mother's familiar rants about Maria Comnena. "Well, they *do* share the same blood, Mother. Nor do I see anything sinister in Isabella's occasional visits to the court. She is just a child, after all."

"That 'child' could claim a crown one day—your crown!"

Sybilla usually took the path of least resistance, not finding it easy to stand up to her formidable mother. Today, though, an imp seemed to have taken possession of her tongue. "All in Outremer know that I am Baldwin's heir, and then my son. Isabella is a distant third, and she will be pushed even farther from the throne by the children I will have with Hugh of Burgundy."

Agnes's frustration and fear and the bitter grudge she bore God for Baldwin's suffering had honed her temper to a razor-sharp edge. She glared at her daughter, wondering how she could have given birth to such a foolish, frivolous creature. "How can you be so naïve? The crown is elective in Outremer, or have you forgotten that?"

"No, of course I have not. But the High Court's confirmation is only a formality—"

For a moment, Agnes was speechless, not hearing the rest of Sybilla's words, hearing only Amalric's voice as he told her that their marriage was over, that the High Court would not proclaim him king unless he put her aside. She'd lost everything that day—her crown, her children, her faith in the future. "What a fool you are, Sybilla!" she snapped, loudly enough to turn heads in their direction. "God help you, for you will not help yourself or your son . . . not until it is too late, until our enemies have staged their coup and placed that *child* on your throne!"

Sybilla's cheeks burned with mortification and she glanced around hastily to see if any were within earshot of Agnes's diatribe. How dare her mother treat her like this, as if she were still a child. She was a grown woman of twenty, a widow, a mother, and in time a queen. But her indignation was no match for her mother's scorched-earth furies, so once again she backed off, saying nothing, hating herself for being so weak willed, so easily intimidated.

Agnes yearned to grab the girl by the shoulders and shake some sense into her. Why could she not see how precarious her position was? Why could she not understand that nothing in this world came to the meek or the timid? Agnes slowly shook her head and then turned away, intent upon reaching Baldwin's side before Balian and Maria did.

Sybilla felt as if every eye in the hall was upon her. Crossing to a window seat, she stood with her back to her audience, pretending to gaze out the window as she waited for her breathing to steady and her angry color to fade. Her emotions were in a hopeless muddle. As much as she resented her mother's lectures and rebukes, she desperately wanted her approval. Even with a child of her own, there were times when she felt unbearably lonely. In truth, she'd been lonely for most of her life. Somehow, she must make sure that her son never felt so alone.

"My lady . . ." She'd been so caught up in her own unhappiness that she'd not heard the approaching footsteps. Whirling around, she found herself face-to-face with a stranger. Holding out a wine cup, he offered it to her with a tentative smile. "If I am not intruding . . . ?"

Her first impulse was to rebuff him as she'd not dared to rebuff her mother. But as she subjected him to a haughty scrutiny, she realized that he seemed vaguely familiar. He was also quite handsome. His hair was a bright shade of chestnut and cut shorter than was the fashion in Outremer. The neatly trimmed beard offered further proof that he was not a Poulain, for in the kingdom, men of rank were clean-shaven. There was something appealing about that smile, too. She was accustomed to seeing her desirability reflected in male eyes. This man was also according her the respect due a queen and that sort of deference was rare. Accepting the wine cup, she sat down, then gave him permission to sit beside her. "Do I know you, sir?"

"I would not expect you to remember me, my lady. I was but one of many who paid our respects to you and to King Baldwin upon our arrival in the Holy City. You do know my brother, though—Lord Amaury de Lusignan."

"Of course," she said, prodding her recalcitrant memory to produce his name. Giles? Gilbert? When it came to her, she smiled graciously and added, "Sir Guy," as if she'd known it all along, for her mother was always nagging her about the importance of remembering names. "It is not often a knight acts as my cupbearer. What made you think I was in need of wine?"

"It gave me this chance to speak with you, did it not?" That charming smile appeared again, but then he said, in all seriousness, "The truth, my lady, is that I could not help noticing your distress after your conversation with your mother."

"You were eavesdropping upon us?" As she started to rise, he quickly shook his head.

"I heard nothing, I swear it. You caught my attention only because I'd had so many arguments of my own with my father, may God assoil him."

Sybilla sat down again, suddenly curious. "You and your father were often at odds?"

"As far back as I can remember," he admitted, startling her by his candor. "I was a younger son and nothing I did seemed to please him. He was constantly berating me for not being more like my older brothers. I well knew they were not paragons of knightly virtue; they were just more skilled at hiding their escapades from him. Yet I could hardly defend myself by pointing out their sins, could I?" With a rueful smile and a shrug.

Sybilla was surprised by the sympathy she felt for that little boy who could do nothing right. That he would confide something so personal was unusual in and of itself, for she was accustomed to men who were as taciturn as the holy hermits on Mount Carmel when it came to discussing their emotions. For certes, Guillaume would never have revealed any childhood memory that cast him in less than a heroic role. Unknowingly, Guy de Lusignan had shone a light upon her darkest secret—her jealousy of her brother. She was ashamed of it and would never have revealed it to another living soul, not even her confessor. How could she begrudge Baldwin their mother's unconditional and exclusive love? He was dying of leprosy, and what fate could be worse than that? She would have to be a monster to envy him that maternal devotion. And yet there were times when she did.

"Did you and your father make your peace, Sir Guy?"

"Alas, we did not. He took the cross and died in a Saracen dungeon ten years ago, whilst my brothers and I were back home in Poitou."

"I am so sorry!" And this was more than a polite expression of regret. She truly meant it. He seemed to sense that, for he smiled again, saying that sympathy from a beautiful woman would heal any wound. Flirtation was Sybilla's favorite game. Pleased that she was on familiar ground again, she smiled, too.

Isabella had been practicing her curtsy all week, for she wanted to get it right. When she straightened up, she saw that Baldwin was smiling and that gave her the courage she needed. Instead of returning to her parents, she hastened up the dais steps.

"My mama and Pateras . . . they told me," she said solemnly. "I am so sorry." Baldwin started to speak, then stopped, for what was there to say? "I did not understand," Isabella continued, "for people say lepers are being punished for their sins. But my mama said that was not so. She said leprosy is proof of God's love, for lepers will not have to go to Purgatory and can go straight to Heaven. I was glad of that, only . . ." She paused, biting her lip before blurting out, "Only I wish God had loved you less, Brother."

Baldwin regarded her in silence for a moment and then he began to laugh. "So do I, Bella, so do I."

It had been so long since Agnes had heard Baldwin laugh like that. But she was alarmed, too, at this unexpected moment of camaraderie. At times, she found herself wondering how her family could have offended God so grievously; how else explain their litany of sorrows? Her son was dying slowly and painfully, and they had enemies, so many enemies. And of them all, she feared a seven-year-old girl the most, for she offered an alternative to those who hated the de Courtenays, those who did not want Sybilla as queen.

Isabella curtsied again when she saw a lord was waiting to speak with Baldwin and rejoined her parents. She sensed their pride and felt a warm glow. Some of it faded as she looked around, for the woman with the hungry hawk eyes was staring at her. By now she knew this was Baldwin's mother, but she did not know what she'd done to earn such disapproval. She moved closer to Maria, then remembered that she'd not told Baldwin about her new mount, a white mule. Thinking he might like to pick the name for her, she started back toward the dais. But Agnes barred her way, saying curtly that she must not take up any more of the king's time, that there were others waiting to speak to him.

Before Isabella could say anything, her mother was there, smiling down at her as she suggested to Isabella that her stepfather escort her over to greet her sister,

Sybilla. Isabella brightened at that, turning to slip her hand into Balian's large one. As he led her away, though, she heard her mother say to Baldwin's mother, "Stay away from my daughter!" Her eyes widened, for she'd never heard Mama sound like that.

Agnes had never heard Maria sound like that, either, and she was momentarily taken aback. After giving the younger woman a look of utter disdain, she turned her back and joined Baldwin on the dais. But she had to watch helplessly, then, as her daughter chatted amiably with Balian and the Greek's brat. In the brief time since they'd parted, Sybilla had managed to find another male admirer; she collected them the way a miser hoarded gold bezants.

These flirtations did not disturb Agnes unduly, for she refused to believe Sybilla would be reckless enough to take a lover, and she had to admit that her daughter was adept at offering encouragement without actually committing herself. She'd even snared Baudouin d'Ibelin, may he rot forever in that Damascus dungeon. Agnes had been furious at first that Sybilla should be so friendly with d'Ibelin, but once she assured herself that the girl's emotions were not engaged, she came to enjoy watching as Baudouin made a fool of himself over her daughter. She did not doubt that he lusted after the crown as much as he lusted after Sybilla. Fortunately, both would be out of his reach once the Duke of Burgundy arrived to marry Sybilla. She knew that for Baldwin, the wedding day could not come soon enough.

After they'd been introduced to the French lords, Maria excused herself to take Isabella back to their town house, and Balian and Denys withdrew to the palace gardens. The sun was at its hottest and the olive trees provided only a modicum of shade, but they were willing to endure the heat in the interest of privacy. When Balian asked about the most conspicuous absentee at the court festivities, the older man shook his head, assuring him that Count Raymond was in Jerusalem. "Yesterday he got into a nasty public quarrel with Reynald de Chatillon over who was to blame for Marj Ayyun. Fortunately, Raymond's wife is coolheaded, so Eschiva managed to draw him away ere he and Reynald went for each other's throats."

"For once, I agree with Reynald," Balian admitted. "That battle was a debacle from start to finish. You say the Lady Eschiva interceded. Not Baldwin?"

"He was not in the hall at the time. Nor was he there when another squabble erupted after Raymond had stalked out. Reynald was still fuming and he loudly proclaimed to all within hearing that the count would be no match for a bawdy house filled with whores, much less the Saracen army. Reynald's wife and his knights thought that was hilarious. Gerard de Ridefort did not and objected on Raymond's behalf. With two such hotheads, it is a wonder it did not lead to bloodshed. But the Bishop of Bethlehem and I were able to intervene ere it came to that."

"Why would Gerard de Ridefort meddle like that? I know Raymond showed him favor upon his arrival in Outremer, yet de Ridefort has never struck me as a man who holds gratitude to be a virtue."

"Ah, but Gerard looks upon Raymond as his patron now. He has been boasting all week that the count has promised him the next eligible heiress in Tripoli or Galilee."

That was the customary means of rewarding a man for loyalty or good service; the d'Ibelin family's own rise began with the marriage of Balian's father to the heiress Helvis of Ramlah. Balian understood that daughters of privilege were raised to accept their fate as marital pawns. But he knew Gerard de Ridefort well enough to pity any wife of his. "Why was Baldwin not in the hall? He's not ailing again?"

"No . . . he's just not been sleeping well of late." Even though he knew Balian was very sympathetic to the young king, Denys did not feel comfortable discussing his stepson's health with others. Instead, he asked if Balian had heard anything from his brother or Saladin.

Balian shook his head. "But I did get an unexpected request from Baudouin's daughter about his son. Since the lad's mother is dead, Esquiva took him in after Baudouin was captured. Now she has asked if Maria and I can care for Thomasin until Baudouin is freed. Of course, we agreed. I was puzzled, though, and she reluctantly admitted that this was her husband's doing."

As their eyes met, Balian saw that Denys understood the significance of Esquiva's plea. For some time, it had been rumored that Amaury de Lusignan was becoming quite friendly with Reynald de Chatillon and Joscelin de Courtenay. If he no longer wanted Thomasin in his household, that was his dramatic declaration of a shift in loyalties, letting it be known that he was throwing his lot in with the court faction. Balian felt sorry for his niece, caught between her husband and her father, and he knew Baudouin would be furious when he found out. From what he'd seen of Amaury de Lusignan, the other man was a pragmatist through and through. So for him to switch sides like this, he must have concluded that the de Courtenays would win the power struggle likely to erupt after Baldwin's death.

On the following day, Baldwin held a feast in honor of his French guests. Christians from other countries were always surprised by the very comfortable lives led by the Poulains. Many embraced it enthusiastically, while others regarded these luxuries with suspicion. They looked askance at the exotic fruits, the savory dishes enhanced by Arabic spices, the carpeted floors. The silks, brocades, and fine cottons, worn only by the highborn throughout the rest of Christendom, were in Outremer worn even by lesser lords and their ladies. And the elaborate bathhouses were unlike any they'd encountered back in France or England, with sweating chambers, heated water, and servants or slaves on hand to provide scented soap or shaves. To some of these crusaders, there was a decadence about it all and they were quick to conclude that the Poulains were not worthy to live in the land of the Lord Christ's birth.

Since the kingdom was dependent upon these foreign realms for money and men, it mattered that westerners returned to their own homelands with positive stories about their time in the Levant, especially when they were kin to kings. Baldwin was pleased, therefore, that the dinner—and the visit itself—seemed to be going well.

After the meal, they were entertained by minstrels as the trestle tables were cleared away for dancing. Balian was about to lead Maria out to join the circle when he happened to notice two men unobtrusively making their way toward the dais. One was a palace official. The second man was clad in Muslim garb, the folds of his kaffiyeh headdress deliberately draped to cover the lower half of his face, but it was his graceful gait that drew and held Balian's eye. He seemed to glide across the floor of the hall, almost as if he'd leave no footprints, and a memory stirred, followed by unease. If this was indeed Baldwin's legendary spymaster, Bernard, it was not likely that the news he was bringing was good.

Balian was no longer in the mood for dancing. He and Maria were soon joined by Denys, who thought he'd recognized Bernard, too, and they watched in tense silence as Baldwin hastened from the hall with the mysterious stranger at his side. When Baldwin returned, he limped up onto the dais and signaled for the music to stop.

"I have just gotten troubling news from a very trustworthy source. Saladin is planning to attack the Templar castle at Jacob's Ford. He has gathered a large army and he has sworn that he will raze it to the ground. I plan to muster as many men as I can and come to the aid of the Templars. We will gather at Count Raymond's castle at Tiberias, and from there we will march to Jacob's Ford." Baldwin raised a hand then, silencing the murmurs sweeping the hall as he looked for the French king's kindred. "My lords, will you ride with us?"

Guy de Lusignan was the first to respond, giving a loud and emphatic "Yes," although, as a younger son lacking lands either in Poitou or Outremer, he had only a few knights under his command. But the other French lords all joined in, too, pledging their men and their honor to defeat this infidel foe, and Baldwin permitted himself a small sigh of relief; after Marj Ayyun, they needed every able-bodied man they could get.

Maria said nothing, although she could not keep from tightening her hand on Balian's arm. This would be his third battle in less than five months. By chance, her gaze came to rest on Agnes de Courtenay. Agnes had never learned to hide her emotions, and her fear and despair were there for all to see as she looked at her son. Maria's hatred of the other woman was like a river flowing toward the sea, too deep and too swift to permit even a ripple of pity to break the surface. She did feel an odd, impersonal sense of kinship, though—with Agnes, with the other wives and mothers and daughters, with all the women down through the ages who'd been left behind as their husbands, sons, and fathers rode off to war.

The Franks had derived no benefit from Bernard's advance warning, for they'd encountered unexpected delays in mustering their army, and by the time they reached Count Raymond's stronghold at Tiberias, Saladin was already at Jacob's Ford. Fortunately, the beleaguered stronghold was well prepared for an extended siege; it had provisions enough to last a year or more and such a vast cistern that they'd not run out of water. So the Franks had no fear that it could not hold out until their arrival. Their greatest worry at the moment was a logistical one; they'd forgotten the True Cross and now had to decide how long they could wait for it to arrive from Jerusalem.

There was no consensus among the men gathered in the castle solar on this last Thursday in August. Joscelin and the French noblemen were adamant that they did not want to go into battle without the True Cross. Raymond, although not overly pious himself, was also willing to wait, for he thought its presence would encourage their men. Baldwin and Reynald were in favor of marching on the morrow, whether the cross had arrived or not. Denys and Balian eventually sided with

Baldwin; while they did not doubt the power of holy relics, they did doubt that its presence alone could determine victory or defeat. It was finally agreed that they would continue to wait, but only for one more day.

They were in accord on the next issue, though—that the failure to bring the cross was due to the death that past spring of the constable Humphrey de Toron. After agreeing that the post must be filled upon their return to Jerusalem, they relaxed with the snow-cooled wine sent up by the Lady Eschiva. Baldwin was not looking well: his color was off, his eyes were bloodshot, his voice hoarse. He still made an effort to keep the conversation going, asking Balian and Raymond if there had been any word about the ransoms of Baudouin and the count's stepson.

Balian became the focus of all eyes when he revealed that he'd gotten a letter from his brother. "He says the ransom demand is so outrageous that he told Saladin he might as well ask for the sun, moon, and stars. He would not even tell me the sum, saying the bargaining had just begun."

Raymond took center stage next, telling them of the efforts he and Eschiva were making to raise Hugues's ransom. Balian rose to refill his wine cup, then wandered to the window to gaze out at the Sea of Galilee, now an inky blue as the last of the day waned. Joining him, Denys helped himself to wine, too, before saying quietly, "How is Baudouin holding up?"

"You know my brother. He'd make light of it if he woke up in Hell, joking that at least he'd save money on firewood. He said little about how he is being treated, only that it could be worse, that he could be cellmates with Odo de St. Amand."

They shared a smile that held more sadness than humor. The view from the window was so tranquil that it was almost possible to forget two armies were camped under this star-spangled twilight sky, soon to meet in a battle that would leave grieving widows and orphans no matter who won. Balian found it hard to turn away, wanting a few moments more of that deceptive peace. But as he glanced from the lake to the shadow-cloaked hills, he drew a quick breath.

"Look at the sky, Denys. Do you see that glow to the north?"

Denys did. "Holy Mother of God," he whispered as their eyes met in appalled understanding.

Baldwin had struggled to climb the stairs to the castle battlements and he was panting by the time he reached the embrasure. All around him, stunned men were looking toward the north, unable to believe what their own eyes were telling them. Clouds of billowing smoke were rising to blot out the stars and the sky was turning an eerie shade of orange along the horizon, as if dawn were coming hours before its time. Some of the watchers cursed, others wept. But all knew they were witnessing the death throes of the Templar castle at Jacob's Ford.

Salāh al-Dīn's first attempt to undermine the castle walls failed and he sent his sappers back to enlarge the tunnel, then to set fire to the struts holding it up. When part of the wall collapsed, the garrison built fires to block the breach, but the wind blew the flames back at them. The fighting that followed seemed like a foretaste of Hell. Salāh al-Dīn himself would later describe the doomed castle as "a ship in a flood of fire." The Templar commander threw himself into one of those fiery pits rather than be taken alive, and of the fifteen hundred men of the garrison, only seven hundred survived to be made prisoners. Salāh al-Dīn freed one hundred Muslim prisoners who'd been forced to do hard labor and had the Frankish crossbowmen and those he considered to be apostates executed at once. Most of the captives were slain on the way to Damascus by some of the sultan's unruly volunteer troops; those still alive were then sold as slaves. The castle itself was utterly destroyed, as the sultan had sworn to do, leaving nothing but rocks and rubble and charred wood.

On October 9 of that year, Odo de St. Amand died in a Damascus dungeon. Salāh al-Dīn exchanged his body for the release of one of his amirs. As the Templar grand master had been widely blamed by the Franks for their catastrophic defeat at Marj Ayyun, few mourned him.

CHAPTER 25

March 1180
City of Tripoli

On this sunlit Monday in early March, the Countess of Tripoli had ordered the cooks to roast a goose for dinner; in just two days, they would have to adhere to a meatless Lenten menu and she wanted her family to indulge themselves while they still could. Eschiva also hoped that a bountiful meal might tempt her eldest son's indifferent appetite. She'd expected Hugues to return home in high spirits, savoring his freedom. Instead, he'd been surprisingly subdued, saying little about his time in Saracen captivity, shrugging off her solicitude and his brothers' curious questions. She was puzzled enough to seek out her husband in the palace solar, asking him to dismiss his scribe so they might talk in private, always challenging in a household of hundreds.

Not all men would have been pleased by the interruption, but Raymond had always taken her concerns seriously and he listened attentively as she confided her worries about Hugues's uncharacteristic reticence. When she was done, he moved from his chair to the settle and drew her down beside him. "It is only to be expected, Eschiva, that Hugues was affected by his captivity. Ere that happened, he'd felt invincible. The young always do, sure that evil might befall others, never them. Now he feels vulnerable and it is unsettling to him. Just give him time."

Eschiva was grateful for his insight; even as the mother of four rambunctious boys, she'd never truly understood the workings of the male brain. "You assured me that he'd not be hurt by his captors. But he seems so withdrawn now, so unlike his old self . . ." She hesitated before confessing, "I started to wonder if you were wrong, if he *had* been maltreated. . . ."

"I doubt it, my dear. He would have been worth too much to risk harming him. Highborn prisoners are ill-treated only if they prove troublesome or if they balk at the ransom demanded. Hugues was one of the luckier ones, for Saladin knew we'd not haggle over the price set for his freedom."

Eschiva smiled when he slid his arm around her shoulders; even after more than five years of marriage, she did not take their marital harmony for granted. Studying Raymond's profile, she could not help thinking of his own years as a prisoner. He'd once said that he'd learned patience in confinement. He'd learned Arabic, too, and had emerged from captivity with a firm belief that peace was possible between the Franks and the Saracens. She was leaning over to kiss him on the cheek when a knock sounded at the door and Raymond's steward entered, saying that the Prince of Antioch had just ridden in.

Raymond and Eschiva exchanged surprised looks. Bohemond and Raymond were first cousins and quite friendly; Raymond was even the godfather of Bohemond's eldest son. Yet they were so different in temperament that they did not socialize frequently. Raymond rose, intending to go down to the hall to welcome Bohemond. But his cousin had not waited, following the steward into the solar.

After an exchange of greetings, Raymond ordered wine and wafers and invited the other man to be seated, sure that he was not just paying a friendly visit. Bohemond confirmed his suspicions by remaining on his feet and smiling dismissively at Eschiva, explaining that he needed to speak with her husband in private.

Eschiva would not normally have taken offense. But it vexed her to be banished from her solar like an errant child by Bohemond of all men. He treated his own wife so shabbily that he'd caused a minor scandal, for Theodora was highborn, great-niece to the Greek emperor and sister to Maria Comnena. Having been coerced into the marriage by the emperor, Bohemond was taking out his resentment upon Theodora, deliberately shaming her by flaunting his concubine in public as if she were his consort. Despite her annoyance, Eschiva did not want to make a scene, and she would have risen had Raymond not put his hand on her arm.

"My wife and I have no secrets, Cousin," he said calmly, and although she did not show it, Eschiva greatly relished the bemused look on Bohemond's face.

"As you wish," he said with an unconvincing smile. Claiming a seat close to the settle, he leaned forward. "I have troubling news, Raymond. As you know, I have sources at the Greek court. As you also know, Manuel has been cultivating ties with the French now that his son is to wed the French king's daughter. He has gotten word of serious unrest in that country after their king was stricken with apoplexy last autumn."

Raymond had already heard that the French king was seriously incapacitated, paralyzed and barely able to speak. Before he could respond, Bohemond launched into a patronizing lecture on French politics, presumably for Eschiva's benefit. It was their custom for a king's heir to be crowned in his lifetime, he explained, and they went ahead with the coronation of Louis's fourteen-year-old son, Philippe. But the lad had soon fallen under the malign influence of the Count of Flanders, who'd contrived to wed Philippe to his ten-year-old niece. This outraged Philippe's mother and her brothers and France hovered on the verge of a civil war.

When Bohemond at last paused for breath, Raymond was able to get a word in, saying that they knew of the troubles besetting the French court. Bohemond shook his head slowly and dramatically. "No, Cousin, I fear you do not know the worst of it. The Duke of Burgundy has decided that he cannot turn his duchy over to his son as he'd planned, concluding that it is too dangerous to entrust governing to an untried youth whilst France remains in such turmoil. He will not be coming to Outremer to wed Sybilla."

Raymond and Eschiva stared at him. "How have we offended the Almighty that He should punish us like this?" Raymond's query was not a rhetorical one; he was genuinely stunned by this turn of events. Eschiva was no less horrified. Not willing to abandon all hope, she asked if the duke might still come if peace was made between Philippe and his family.

Bohemond shook his head again. "From what I was told, I think not. This sudden strife has made the duke rethink his plans, for he does not want to put his son's heritage at risk—" He stopped abruptly, for a servant had entered with wine and wafers. Ignoring the food, Bohemond drained his wine cup in several deep swallows. "So the husband hunt begins again, and how long will it take this time? It has been nigh on three years since Sybilla was widowed. Can we endure another three years with a cripple's hand on the ship's helm?"

Raymond frowned. "You sound as if you are blaming Baldwin for his declining health."

"No, I am just stating the obvious. Our young cousin is far sicker now than he was at the time of Guillaume's death. Dare we squander another two or three years trying to find a suitable husband for Sybilla? Who is to say that Baldwin will even be alive by then? If you think that France is in turmoil, imagine what will befall the Kingdom of Jerusalem should Baldwin die with only a convent-bred girl and a child as his heirs. We well know who'd be pulling Sybilla's strings. And what of Saladin? You think he would not seize his chance to set the kingdom aflame and march on the Holy City?"

Bohemond rose abruptly to his feet. "We cannot stand idly by whilst Armageddon looms, Cousin. Sybilla must be wed to a man who is a battle-seasoned commander and it must be done as soon as possible."

"You mean a Poulain? That makes sense. But Baldwin is bound and determined to forge a marital alliance with a western lord, one with ties to the kings of France or England."

"And what is more important, Baldwin's wishes or the survival of his kingdom? It is well and good to seek a highborn husband for Sybilla. But that is a luxury we can no longer afford. It must be one of us, for time is as much our enemy now as Baldwin's leprosy."

"I agree with you, Bohemond, about the need for urgency. But whom do you have in mind? There are few candidates who'd be acceptable to Baldwin and the High Court. Whilst my wife's son is of noble birth, Hugues is just eighteen and lacks the battlefield experience we so desperately need. So does the late constable's grandson, Humphrey de Toron, and he is even younger than Hugues. Even if Humphrey were suitable, I'd never agree to have Reynald de Chatillon's stepson become a king in waiting. That man is a lunatic."

By now, Raymond was on his feet, striding back and forth. "There is only one man who meets your criteria—Baudouin d'Ibelin. Men would right willingly follow him into battle and he is known to us all, not a stranger who is ignorant of our ways. But the de Courtenays would never accept him as Sybilla's husband. Nor would Baldwin. If he wanted Baudouin to wed his sister, he would have arranged the marriage after Sybilla ended her year of mourning. He prefers a prince and an alliance in the west."

"That is why Baldwin and the de Courtenays cannot be allowed to choose Sybilla's next husband. We must make the choice for them."

"When you say 'we,' do you mean the High Court? Or you and I?"

"I think the High Court will be willing to accept d'Ibelin as their next king."

It did not escape either Raymond or Eschiva that Bohemond had not really answered the question. After a heavy silence, Raymond said warily, "And how do we convince Baldwin to accept the marriage? What exactly do you have in mind, Cousin? Forcing him to abdicate?"

"I do not believe it will come to that. Once Sybilla has a husband capable of governing and defending the realm, it is likely that Baldwin will want to give up his kingship. It has brought him little joy and much sorrow. I think he would welcome the chance to put that burden aside and live out his remaining days in peace and privacy. But we can be sure that the de Courtenays and their allies will balk, so I think it wise that we both bring enough men we can trust with us when we go to Jerusalem to meet with Baldwin."

Enough men we can trust. In other words, an army. Raymond gained some time to think while pouring more wine. "And what of Baudouin d'Ibelin? I think we can safely say that he'd be more than willing to marry Sybilla. But what if he remains Saladin's prisoner?"

Bohemond's smile was complacent, almost smug. "Ah, you have not heard, then? Baudouin and Saladin have come to terms. Once he provides hostages, Baudouin will be set free to raise his ransom."

After another fraught silence, Raymond said that he must think upon all that Bohemond had related, and the other man seemed content to accept that, for he went willingly when the steward was summoned to find lodgings within the palace for him and his knights. He departed with the cheerful observation that no one would think it unusual if they arrived in Jerusalem as Easter drew nigh. What could be more natural than wanting to worship at the Church of the Holy Sepulchre during this most sacred of seasons for Christians?

Once they were alone in the solar, neither Raymond nor Eschiva spoke, for what was there to say? Bohemond was right. Now that the Duke of Burgundy was not going to be the kingdom's savior, what else could they do?

Balian was awaiting word from Saladin, at which time he would journey to Damascus and escort his brother home. He did not expect that to happen for another fortnight, though, and so he was very surprised when Baudouin arrived in Nablus at dusk on Palm Sunday. For a time, all was joyful chaos. After the brothers embraced, Baudouin kissed Maria and Isabella next, with an exaggerated gallantry that made them both laugh. Scooping up his young son then, he explained that once his hostages had reached Damascus, there was no reason to delay his release. And since his captive knights were being freed with him, he had no need of an escort.

His arrival had interrupted their supper and the meal was going cold by the time they trooped into the great hall. Baudouin seemed in high spirits, bantering with Balian, bragging that he'd learned some choice Arabic curses, delighting Isabella and Thomasin with a comic tale of a chameleon he'd befriended during his confinement. Even they did not believe him when he claimed he'd taught the lizard more tricks than Isabella's dog, but they shrieked with laughter when he confided that he'd named the chameleon Balian.

Had a stranger witnessed the boisterous scene, he might have concluded that the man at the center of attention must have been an honored guest of the sultan, not a prisoner. Balian knew better. He noticed that although Baudouin was talking nonstop, he was saying very little, and there was a brittle edge to his laughter. So

Balian asked no questions, listened and smiled and kept the wine flowing. Once the meal was finally over, he brought his brother up to date on happenings in the kingdom during his absence. Highborn French lords had come and gone, he related, and Bishop Joscius and Archbishop Eraclius had returned from their sojourn in the west. Archbishop William was still in Constantinople, negotiating with the emperor on Baldwin's behalf. The French king had suffered a seizure and was not likely to recover, resulting in unrest throughout his realm, but they still expected the Duke of Burgundy to sail for Outremer sometime that spring. Baudouin grimaced at that, making a dubious jest about the duke's ship going down in a squall. He was among friends here, though, who were willing to overlook his reluctance to see Sybilla wed to another man.

Balian had been judicious in what he'd chosen to share, feeling that Baudouin need not be confronted with bad news immediately upon his return. So he did not tell his brother that the odious Gerard de Ridefort had managed to gain the post of marshal, proving Fortune could favor the unworthy as well as the deserving, or that Baldwin's health continued to deteriorate.

After Isabella and Thomasin had been ushered off to bed and pallets were being set up in the aisles of the great hall for Baudouin's knights, Balian rose, saying he had a surprise for his brother. Baudouin had retained a childlike love of surprises and the fact that he did not bombard Balian with guesses offered further proof that his jovial mood was camouflage. But once he'd been led abovestairs to a small room below Balian and Maria's bedchamber, there was genuine joy in his exclamation as he saw the cradle.

"Good for you, Little Brother!" Slapping Balian on the back, he almost awakened the baby with his elated shout when Balian revealed that Maria had given him a son, named John after her father.

The wet nurse had discreetly disappeared, giving them a rare moment of privacy. For a time, the two men stood by the cradle, gazing at the sleeping infant, swaddled in linen and cocooned in innocence, mercifully unaware that he'd been born in a land under siege, at a time when the future of their kingdom had rarely seemed so precarious. Baudouin leaned over to stroke the baby's wispy dark hair before crossing the chamber to the window seat. "I am glad for you, lad," he said, suddenly sounding very tired. "Thank God you listened to me when I told you to go and claim your queen. You should make heeding me a habit from now on."

Balian joined him in the window seat, his eyes intently searching his brother's face, for he thought he'd glimpsed a gap when Baudouin had smiled. "You lost a tooth?"

Baudouin studied him in silence for a moment. "I did not 'lose' it," he said grimly. "It was taken from me, as was this one." Pulling his lip back to reveal a second empty space where a tooth had once been. "I balked at the ransom Saladin demanded, knowing it would have been my ruination and mayhap yours, too."

Balian was not surprised that Baudouin had been so loath to pay the ransom, for he'd been staggered by the size of it—two hundred thousand dinars and the release of a thousand Muslim prisoners, including 'Īsā al-Hakkari, who'd been captured at Montgisard. Balian had not expected the sultan to resort to torture, though, and some of his rising anger was directed at himself for being so trusting. "What happened?" he asked, even though he did not really want to know.

"Saladin was angry when I continued to refuse his extortion. He finally lost patience and told his amir *jandar*—the officer responsible for carrying out such orders—to convince me that it was in my best interests to pay the ransom. That accursed swine decided to see what I valued more, my money or my teeth." Baudouin slumped back against the wall. "I did my best," he said softly, sounding almost apologetic, "but after they pulled the second tooth, I gave in. I do not think I'd ever experienced pain like that, not even when I was hit by a crossbow and they had to cut the bolt out. . . ."

Balian had too vivid an imagination for his own good and he felt as if his brother's pain had become his own. Reaching over, he grasped the other man's arm, hoping the gesture would convey what he could not put into words. He knew Baudouin would be embarrassed if he tried to express what he was feeling at that moment.

"I am sorry, lad," Baudouin said after a long silence. "Even if I sell every acre I own, every horse and sheep and camel on my demesnes, I cannot raise a sum so vast. It is likely to impoverish us both and it still will not be enough. And it is not just our family that will suffer. What of the liegemen who pledged their freedom for me? Hostages are treated better than prisoners of war, yet if I cannot pay . . ."

"There is another way, Baudouin. Maria thinks that her great-uncle can be persuaded to pay the greater part of your ransom." Balian had entertained a few misgivings about Maria's offer, for Baudouin's pride could assert itself at the most inopportune moments. He saw now that he need not have worried; Baudouin looked like a drowning man who'd just been thrown a rope.

"God bless her!" Leaping to his feet, Baudouin pulled Balian up, too, and into an exuberant embrace. The hug was punctuated by a wail. Torn from sleep, John was making his unhappiness known—to all within hearing range. Both Balian and Baudouin were at a loss, for although they had six children between them, neither man had much experience in soothing screaming babies. When rocking the cradle did not placate John, Balian picked him up; that did not work, either. But the baby's shrieking had been heard by Dame Rohese, his wet nurse. Balian gratefully surrendered John to her as she hastened into the chamber.

Eventually, calm returned to the nursery. Announcing that he must find Maria and declare himself her paladin forever and aye, Baudouin headed toward the door. His spirits had soared now that he knew he was not facing penury and he began to laugh. "I am feeling like one of Dame Fortune's favorites of a sudden. Mayhap she will even see to it that the Duke of Burgundy has a change of heart and leaves Sybilla at the altar, a jilted bride in need of a groom."

Anselm had rarely felt so helpless. He'd come to love the young king, awed by his rare courage and unflagging sense of duty, and he ached to see Baldwin so heartsick. There was nothing he could do, though. He could not even express his sympathy, for that would not be seemly. Watching as Baldwin limped around the bedchamber, picking up and discarding items at random, he knew that Baldwin was delaying going to bed, dreading the nightmares that had returned with a vengeance. They'd come back after Humphrey de Toron's death, but they'd never been as bad as this, turning Holy Week into a sleepless ordeal from dusk to dawn, for Baldwin began to fear them as soon as daylight began to wane.

Anselm had been with the king two days ago when the letter from the Archbishop of Tyre had arrived. He remembered how pleased Baldwin had been when he saw William's familiar wax seal and, then, the moment when Baldwin learned that the Duke of Burgundy would not be marrying Sybilla, for he'd gone bone white, gasping, "Jesu, no!" There had been so much anguish in that cry that the mere memory was enough to bring tears to Anselm's eyes. More than anyone else, he understood how much Baldwin had been relying upon the duke's arrival. He'd joked once or twice that it would be like getting a reprieve on the steps of the gallows, humor so dark that Anselm had surreptitiously made the sign of the cross. And now the noose was back around Baldwin's neck, so tight he could scarcely breathe.

Anselm tensed when Baldwin stumbled, his shambling leper's gait so unsteady that he was always in danger of falling. This time he kept his balance and hobbled toward the closest chair. "My fever has come back," he said, and Anselm hurried to add an herbal potion to Baldwin's night wine. He'd suspected that Baldwin was ailing again, for his appetite was off and he was coughing more than usual. Anselm knew that most people shared the usual misconceptions about leprosy—that it was highly contagious, that it was either punishment for carnal sins or God's blessing in disguise, that it was always fatal. His years with the leper knights had taught Anselm that it was no more infectious than other maladies and it was not lethal. Lepers died from the ailments that followed in leprosy's wake—pleurisy, consumption, the bloody flux, lung and hectic and quartan fever, the red plague. People of all ages and classes were stricken by these contagions, but it seemed to Anselm that they preyed upon lepers more than the healthy. He'd once asked Baldwin's doctor why this was so, getting no satisfactory response, and he'd eventually concluded that mayhap it was God's mercy, ending a leper's suffering so he could be rewarded in Paradise.

"What are you thinking, Anselm? You've the oddest look on your face."

Anselm was startled to see Baldwin regarding him with a quizzical smile. "Nothing of importance, sire," he said hastily, holding out the cup of medicated wine. Baldwin made a face, but he dutifully took a few swallows. Their fingers brushed as he handed the cup back, and Anselm was pleased that Baldwin did not recoil as he'd once done. Whenever he watched the king struggle to avoid putting others at risk, Anselm always felt a dart of sadness, thinking his young lord must be starved for the touch of a hand on his, for the daily human contacts that others took for granted.

It was Anselm's awareness of that need which changed his opinion of the king's mother. He'd heard nothing but evil of her prior to entering Baldwin's service, and he'd soon decided that she'd earned her notoriety; she was sharp-tongued, suspicious, and arrogant . . . save with her son. With him, she seemed to have infinite patience, boundless reservoirs of maternal love. A Templar had once told Anselm that soldiers often cried out for their mothers as they lay dying. He'd been skeptical, for his own mother had chased after him and his brothers with a broom and doled out praise with a miser's stinginess. After viewing Baldwin and his mother together, he was no longer so dubious.

When the door opened suddenly and he saw the king's mother standing there, Anselm drew a sharp breath, for it was almost as if he'd conjured her up from his own thoughts. She was no figment of his imagination, though. Brushing past Anselm as if he were invisible, she hastened across the chamber toward her son. "Thank God you are still awake, Baldwin!"

"What is wrong, Mother?" Baldwin added "Uncle?" for Joscelin had entered the chamber after Agnes. While he did not like them bursting in like this, he did not object, for they both were visibly shaken.

"We must talk with you in private, Baldwin." Glancing over her shoulder, Agnes said curtly, "You are dismissed, Anselm."

"No, he is not."

Agnes had learned not to argue with Baldwin whenever she heard that steeliness in his voice. Instead, she swung around on Anselm, who was so startled that he took a backward step. "Swear on the surety of your soul," she hissed, "that you will never repeat to a living soul what you hear tonight."

"I . . . I do, madame," he stammered, torn between wanting to be of help to Baldwin and wanting to be out of range of those icy blue eyes.

Baldwin sat upright, squaring his shoulders as he braced for yet more calamitous news. The commotion had awakened his dog, who'd been napping under his bed. Scrambling out, Cairo began to bark loudly until Baldwin silenced him. His mother was usually annoyed by the dog's barking; that she did not even look his way now was not a good sign. "Pour wine for us, Anselm," he said, sensing they were going to need it. "What has happened?"

"Do you know a man named Sir Gervase Vernier?" When Baldwin shook his head, Agnes seemed to straighten her own shoulders, lifting her chin. "He is one of the Count of Tripoli's household knights and stands high in Raymond's favor. He is also my spy and has been for years."

Agnes could not keep defiant color from staining her cheeks, for she knew Baldwin did not approve of her personal spy network. But he did not comment upon that now, instead saying tersely, "Go on."

"Raymond and the Prince of Antioch are on their way to Jerusalem. Gervase avoided accompanying them by feigning illness. As soon as they were gone, he saddled his best mount and took another route. A lone rider can always outrace an army and he reached Jerusalem tonight, coming straight to me. After this, he cannot return to Raymond's service, but that is how urgent his message was."

"An army? Or an escort? Which is it, Mother?"

"An army, Baldwin."

Baldwin was silent for a moment. There was no real surprise, for he'd never fully trusted either of his cousins. "What does Gervase say they intend to do once they reach Jerusalem?"

"He told me that they mean to compel Sybilla to marry a man of their choosing now that the Duke of Burgundy has repudiated their betrothal. I am sure you can guess whom they have in mind—Baudouin d'Ibelin, God rot him!"

"And what do they have in mind for me?"

"Gervase says they expect you will abdicate, allowing Baudouin and Sybilla to be crowned in your stead."

Baldwin's composure was beginning to unsettle Joscelin. He did not really understand his nephew, which made it difficult to predict how Baldwin would react in a crisis. And what could be a greater crisis for their family than this? His eyes searched Baldwin's face intently, but he could not penetrate that inscrutable court mask and his unease grew. What if Baldwin saw this as a chance to escape the yoke of kingship? If he did, could he be blamed for it? Yes, by God, for if Sybilla wed Baudouin d'Ibelin, they would lose all that they'd gained during Baldwin's kingship. Determined that he would not go down without a fight, Joscelin moved as close as he dared get to his nephew and said almost accusingly, "Baldwin, they mean to stage a coup! Are you going to let them force you from the throne?"

Baldwin realized in that moment that he did not always like his uncle very much. He did trust him, though, and he supposed that mattered more. "No, Uncle," he said coolly, "I am not. I do not know why God wants me to rule as the leper king and I will not pretend it has been easy. But it is not for mortal men to challenge the Almighty's will. I mean to do as God bids me and I do not believe He wants me to surrender my crown to men without honor or loyalty."

Anselm broke into a wide grin, resisting the urge to cheer. Instead, he hurriedly passed wine cups around, pleased when Baldwin told him to pour one for himself. Agnes waved her cup away, keeping her gaze locked upon her son. "I have never been so proud of you," she said, her eyes catching the candlelight so that they seemed to glow like sapphires. Baldwin rarely initiated physical contact with her, for he could never shake a sense of guilt, fearing he was exposing her to his accursed malady. Now, though, he reached for her hand and held it tightly, wanting her to know that without her unconditional love and support, he'd have been lost and alone in the darkness of his earthly purgatory.

"We must summon the High Court on the morrow . . ." His words trailed off, though, as he faced a frightening truth. How many of those lords could be trusted? How many were allied with his cousins against him?

CHAPTER 26

April 1180
Jerusalem, Outremer

They gathered in the palace solar the next morning, disheartened that there were so few of them. Baldwin had sent word to Reynald de Chatillon and, at his mother's urging, to Eraclius, the Archbishop of Caesarea. Sybilla was present, of course. Denys's inclusion had been a contentious one, for Joscelin was opposed to his presence, arguing that he was too friendly with the d'Ibelins and Count Raymond to be trusted. But Agnes insisted that Denys would never betray Baldwin, and Baldwin agreed with her. The invitation to Roger de Moulins, the grand master of the Hospitallers, had been controversial, too, for Eraclius and Reynald de Chatillon both disliked him. Since Baldwin felt Roger was an honorable man, he prevailed.

The council had begun with Sir Gervase Vernier, summoned to tell them all what he'd already shared with Agnes. He did not look like a man who thrived on attention, lacking the swagger or bravado that would have made him memorable, but they realized that his unobtrusive manner was the hallmark of the successful spy. He repeated his story concisely and convincingly, and then withdrew, for his part was over.

Joscelin and Eraclius at once began an animated discussion of the High Court members, arguing about which lords could be trusted. Baldwin soon called a halt, realizing they were wasting time. He had not slept and it showed on his face. His voice was steady, though, and while his dispassionate demeanor continued to vex Joscelin, the others were reassured by his self-control. Kings were expected to remain calm even as others panicked.

"At first I thought to summon the High Court." Baldwin felt a tickling in his throat and swallowed with an effort, hoping he'd be able to ward off a coughing fit. "I no longer think that would be wise. My uncle is convinced that many of its members are already allied with Bohemond and Raymond. But what I fear is that if my cousins are given the chance to address the court, they could make a credible case for themselves. Few know yet of the Duke of Burgundy's betrayal. That dramatic revelation alone could sway men in their favor. None will be willing to wait another two years to select a new husband for my sister."

His honesty was met with silence, for as much as they wanted to refute his bleak conclusion, they could not. Reynald was the only one present who seemed at ease. "I think it is time to discuss the number of men we can muster and how quickly they can get to Jerusalem."

The grand master of the Hospitallers looked appalled. So did Denys. The others seemed willing to entertain the idea, and Baldwin moved swiftly to quash it. "You are talking about a civil war, Reynald. There has to be another way than that."

"I am waiting with bated breath to hear what it is," Reynald drawled. "We are lying to ourselves if we think blood need not be spilled. They mean to seize power, to force you from the throne, my lord king, and to replace you with a man of their choosing, a man who will owe his crown to them. If that is not reason enough to go to war, what in Christ's name is?"

The Hospitaller grand master stood. "My knights and I will have no part in this." Before the others could react, Roger de Moulins bowed to Baldwin, turned, and strode toward the door.

Reynald was unimpressed by his dramatic departure. "One gone. Who will be next to abandon the sinking ship? My money is on you, my lord," he said, aiming a sardonic smile in Denys's direction.

Denys was known for his equanimity, but now anger crossed his face, a lightning flash that briefly illuminated his interior landscape. Before he could retaliate, Sybilla rose to her feet, drawing all eyes. "There is a better way," she said. "Their plot depends upon my marriage to Baudouin, does it not? Well, then, why cannot I simply refuse to wed him?" Glancing around, she was both puzzled and disappointed by their lack of response. "They cannot drag me to the altar, after all," she insisted. "Surely my refusal would put an end to their treachery."

Baldwin saw that it would be left to him to reply, and he sighed softly, not wanting to bruise her pride. "In theory, you are quite right, Sister. But I think you do not realize how much pressure would be brought to bear upon you. Not just from my cousins—from the High Court, from the patriarch, many of his bishops, even people in the streets, all of them desperate to see you wed now that you're no longer betrothed to the Duke of Burgundy. It would be argued that you must make this marriage if the kingdom is to survive, that if you balked, you'd be inviting Saladin to launch jihad. They'd give you no rest and eventually, you'd have to yield."

"No . . . no, I would not." But her denial did not sound convincing even to Sybilla herself, and she hesitated, then returned to her seat.

Another silence fell. But Eraclius had been awaiting just such a moment. "I believe I have a solution to this dilemma," he said, and all heads swiveled in his direction. "Their plot depends upon Lady Sybilla's marriage to d'Ibelin. The Lady Agnes's spy said nothing about them claiming the throne for themselves. They are trying to give their coup a semblance of legitimacy, for they prefer to cast themselves as kingmakers, not rebels or traitors. So, to thwart them, we need only find another husband for the Lady Sybilla, taking her off the marriage market, so to speak," he concluded with a satisfied smile. Yet like Sybilla, he did not get the response he'd been anticipating from his audience.

Agnes was shaking her head impatiently, as if she'd expected better from him. Denys seemed grimly amused. Joscelin heaved a theatrical sigh. Reynald's smile looked suspiciously like a smirk to Eraclius; they might be political allies, but there was no love lost between them. Sybilla was frowning thoughtfully and Baldwin just looked bone weary.

Unable to summon the energy to soothe the archbishop's vanity, Baldwin said what the others were thinking. "That idea has already occurred to me, my lord archbishop, to all of us. It is a solution both simple and elegant—find my sister a husband and the problems go away, slinking back to Tripoli and Antioch with their tails between their legs. There is just one drawback: Where do we find this new husband for Sybilla?"

"I will not make a disparaging marriage," Sybilla said abruptly. "I will not wed a man who is not wellborn—not even to save the kingdom!"

"I agree, Sister." Baldwin tried to give her a reassuring smile. "Sybilla has the right to make that demand. So we would need a man of the nobility, one with battlefield experience. He could not be related to her within the forbidden degrees, for there would be no time to seek a papal dispensation. And he must be here in Jerusalem, ready to marry her ere my cousins arrive in the city. So you tell me, my lord archbishop. Where do we find such a man?"

Eraclius scowled. "Surely we could find someone suitable, mayhap amongst the men who accompanied those French lords who arrived whilst I was in Rome."

"Now, why did we not think of that? What of the Count of Grandpré? Or the Viscount of Provins?" Reynald sounded as if he were enjoying himself. "Ah, but they both left with the Count of Champagne." He reeled off the names of a few more French lords, pretending to remember then that they, too, had departed the kingdom. "No, wait . . . you are right, my lord archbishop. There is *one* man who meets all of the king's qualifications—Baudouin d'Ibelin."

Eraclius rose to his feet, glowering at Reynald, and Baldwin sought to keep the council from disintegrating into chaos by saying, "Enough! Our enemies are not in this chamber. They are out on the watershed road, leading an army toward Jerusalem." Unfortunately, the authority in his rebuke was weakened when he was then seized by a prolonged coughing fit, so severe that Agnes hastily poured him a cup of wine and the others shifted in their seats. It was never comfortable to bear witness to the king's losing battle with his mortal malady.

Alarmed by his stepson's labored breathing, Denys stepped into the breach. "Whilst we could have done without Lord Reynald's sarcasm, he is right about the scarcity of worthy bridegrooms. I can think of only two possible candidates, excluding Baudouin d'Ibelin, of course." The irony, he thought, was that Baudouin would actually have been the best choice, but he knew better than to make that argument. He did not see how Baudouin could have been a part of the conspiracy. There simply was not enough time, for conspiracies were not committed to parchment and then sent to Damascus for Saladin to read first. It did not matter, though, not now.

Rising, Denys moved to stand beside Baldwin's chair. "The late constable's grandson, Humphrey de Toron, is of good birth. He is also fourteen and has never even seen a battle. You are his stepfather, Lord Reynald, but I think you will agree that he is not yet capable of leading our army against Saladin."

"Fourteen or forty, it makes no difference. Men would not follow that milksop out of a burning building." Reynald's brutal honesty aroused a prick or two of pity for his stepson and it occurred to Sybilla that a callow fledgling like Humphrey would be as malleable as wax, easily molded into a husband so bedazzled that he'd be eager to do her bidding. But she agreed with Baldwin and the others that she must marry a man grown, a man who knew how to wield a sword, both on the battlefield and in the bedchamber. An idea had been taking shape as she'd listened to them argue, and she let it solidify as they moved on to discuss and eliminate Hugues of Galilee. He was Raymond's stepson and that alone disqualified him.

"It is actually quite simple, my liege. If you want to keep your crown, you have to fight for it. If you are not willing to do that, you need to start practicing your abdication speech."

"It is *not* that simple, Reynald," Baldwin snapped. "The Lord God wants me to fight the Saracens, not my own people." But his anger was diluted by despair, for he saw no way out of this trap. It was then that his sister rose again, this time addressing herself to him alone.

"Baldwin . . . there is one possible candidate. He is not a Poulain. But he is of good birth, has experience in combat, and he is here in the city." They were all staring at her now, and she paused, then threw the dice. "Amaury de Lusignan's younger brother . . . Guy."

Baldwin felt the faintest spark of hope beginning to stir, a lone ember almost smothered by ashes. "Amaury is a seasoned battle commander," he said slowly. "And Sybilla is right; the de Lusignans are an important family in Poitou, vassals of the English king. But Amaury is wed to Baudouin d'Ibelin's daughter."

Sybilla almost reminded him that they were considering Guy, not Amaury. She caught herself in time; better not to seem too eager. She could have kissed Joscelin when he assured Baldwin earnestly that Amaury was no longer in the d'Ibelin camp, that he was utterly trustworthy, a man of prowess, which was one of the highest compliments that could be bestowed upon a knight, encompassing courage and fighting ability and leadership skills. Sybilla allowed herself the smallest of smiles as she saw what was occurring. Whilst Guy was not really known to them, Amaury was—a proven soldier, a man capable of inspiring confidence in others, a man capable of ruling Outremer had he only been free to wed Sybilla. But if they could not have the older brother, why not the younger one? Why should they not be arrows from the same quiver?

Baldwin tried to dampen his rising excitement, for this was too important a decision to be made impulsively. "What do you all think of Guy de Lusignan?"

"Well, he is here and he has a pulse," Reynald said dryly. "I suppose we could do worse."

"If a man afoot is offered a horse, he'd be a fool to bicker over its color," Eraclius said sententiously. Joscelin's friendship with Amaury had colored his assessment of the younger de Lusignan, and he did not hesitate, declaring himself in favor of the marriage. Denys had more reservations, but that was because Guy de Lusignan was a stranger to him and, given the exigency of their circumstances, that did not seem reason enough to argue against the man.

Having gotten a tepid approval from Denys, Baldwin turned toward Agnes. "What of you, Mother? Would you be comfortable with it if Sybilla were to wed Guy de Lusignan?"

Agnes glanced over at her daughter and then shrugged. "What else can we do? If the choice is between a civil war and Guy de Lusignan . . ."

Sybilla was bewildered by her mother's reaction, for she'd expected Agnes to have strong views about the selection of a son-in-law. Yet she'd sounded almost . . . indifferent. Sybilla looked from Agnes to Baldwin, and then she understood. What mattered the most to her mother was not her marriage. It was safeguarding Baldwin's kingship. As always, his needs came first.

Joscelin volunteered to fetch the de Lusignan brothers and departed with such eagerness that his enthusiasm proved contagious. There was a palpable easing of tension in the solar, and Sybilla realized that would work to Guy de Lusignan's advantage. The others wanted to find him acceptable and that made it more likely that they would do so. She was touched when Baldwin asked her if she had any misgivings about the marriage; he was the only one who'd given her feelings any thought. She was glad that she could reassure him of her willingness to wed Guy. She would do what she must for the kingdom, she said, striving to sound dutiful and brave.

When Joscelin returned with the de Lusignans, it was obvious that he'd briefed them on Baldwin's plight. Amaury looked as they would expect a man to look after being informed that his brother was to wed a queen, like one scarcely able to believe their family's good fortune. Guy seemed dazed. Striding toward Baldwin, Amaury bowed deeply and then offered an eloquent avowal of loyalty and gratitude.

Guy started to follow him, but swerved at the sight of Sybilla. Reaching her side, he dropped to one knee and kissed her hand, his eyes blazing with such joy that she felt as if he'd set her body afire with that one glance. Only then did he rise and turn back to the king. Amaury was frowning at this breach of etiquette, obviously irked that Guy had not first expressed his thanks to the man who was making this miracle possible. It occurred to Sybilla that Guy had never been able to escape from his brother's shadow. Not until now, she vowed, giddy with the triumphant euphoria surging through her veins, the intoxicating sweetness of knowing she had taken her fate into her own hands, no longer a pawn in this game of kings.

Sybilla would remember little of what followed. Guy said all the right things, making a favorable impression upon an audience already predisposed to approve him. Baldwin had then given his consent, but only after making it clear to Guy that power still rested in his hands and Sybilla's son by Guillaume of Montferrat would stand closer to the throne than any sons he and Sybilla might have, conditions that Guy accepted without hesitation. It seemed to Sybilla that time had speeded up, for before she knew it, they were discussing her wedding, wanting it to take place that very day. That in itself was extraordinary, as marriages were not performed during

Holy Week. This obstacle was brushed aside by Eraclius, who offered to officiate himself.

Agnes bestirred herself at that, seeing that her daughter seemed unable to take charge of her impending wedding. "We must find you a gown fit for a bride. I suppose it would not be seemly to wear the gown from your wedding to Guillaume. No matter, we will do right by you." For the first time, she considered the marriage not as Baldwin's salvation but as a life-changing event for her daughter. "You do not mind forgoing the usual wedding revelries?"

Sybilla let her mother steer her toward the door, where she glanced over her shoulder, her eyes meeting Guy's. He smiled, and for a moment, it seemed as if they were the only two people in the solar, in the kingdom, mayhap even the world. "No, Mother, I do not mind," she said, and for once she did not even notice that she'd earned her mother's unqualified approval.

Raymond and Bohemond rode through Jerusalem's St. Stephen's Gate before dusk on Good Friday. Bohemond had wanted to reveal their intentions before the High Court, but Raymond did not think it would be fair to ambush Baldwin like that. He deserved to be told first, he'd argued. Moreover, that would give the lad time to accept the inevitable. Bohemond grudgingly agreed and they headed for the palace.

There, they were told that the king had already retired for the night and could not see them. They'd not heard that Baldwin was ailing again, but their cousin's illness would work to their advantage, proving the precarious state of his health. All seemed to be going their way when they learned that there would be a High Court session on the morrow. That fit perfectly into their plans, and this delay would give them time to let Baudouin d'Ibelin know that his future was about to include a queen and a crown. In good spirits, they returned to Raymond's town house to prepare for the coming confrontation with Baldwin and the de Courtenays.

Balian and Maria and Baudouin had traveled together from Nablus for the Easter court, separating to their respective town houses upon their arrival in the city. Although Balian was rather surprised that a High Court session had been called for Holy Saturday, he did not expect it to last long and promised Maria that he'd soon be back. He'd tried to coax her into accompanying him, reminding her how much her presence would vex Agnes, but she preferred to visit the public baths with her ladies, assuring him there would be other opportunities to irritate Agnes.

The High Court was meeting in the upper chamber of the citadel keep, and it was already crowded when Balian entered. While Baldwin had not yet arrived, Count Raymond was present and—to the surprise of many—so was Prince Bohemond of Antioch. So was the aged patriarch, who looked as if he were living on borrowed time. Baudouin was the center of attention, for most of the men had not heard that he'd regained his freedom and they were giving him a noisy welcome. But as soon as he spotted Balian, Baudouin disengaged himself and propelled his brother toward the stairwell that led up to the battlements, saying they must talk.

The sun was so bright that it seemed to be bathing the Holy City in waves of white-gold light. But Baudouin gave Balian no chance to admire the dazzling view. "Few know what I am about to tell you. I am not even sure if Baldwin knows yet. If he does, that is why he has summoned the High Court on such short notice. I met last night with Prince Bohemond and Raymond and they told me the Duke of Burgundy will not be coming to Outremer to marry Sybilla."

"God help us. . . ." Balian felt as if he'd taken a physical blow. "Are they sure of that? Why did he change his mind?"

"That is not important. What does matter is that Bohemond and Raymond believe no more time can be wasted chasing after a foreign prince. They intend to tell Baldwin that Sybilla must wed one of us, a Poulain lord—me!" Baudouin burst out laughing then. "You look as if you've been poleaxed, lad. Are you not happy for me?"

"Of course I am! Nothing would give me greater joy than to see you wed to Sybilla. But will Baldwin agree to the marriage?"

"Raymond and Bohemond are confident that he will see this is for the good of the kingdom. Once Sybilla and I are wed, the lad can finally find some peace, mayhap retreat to a monastery."

"Is that what they think he should do?" The pieces were beginning to fall into place and Balian did not like the pattern they were forming. "Do they mean to force him to abdicate?"

"No! I would never have agreed to that. I owe Baldwin. He was willing to free 'Isā al-Hakkari and a goodly number of Muslim prisoners for me. He has done his best to rule, has more courage than any man I know. But his body has become his enemy, Balian. Soon he'll not be able to ride or even to walk—and we know what that accursed disease does to its victims, the disfiguring ulcers and misshapen limbs. . . ." Baudouin gave an involuntary shudder. "You think Baldwin wants us all to watch as that happens to him?"

They'd deliberately propped the door open and the noise now coming from the stairwell alerted them to Baldwin's arrival. Baudouin hastened down the stairs with Balian following, hoping that all would go as his brother expected, for Baldwin's sake as well as for Baudouin's.

Baldwin was seated in a cushioned high-backed chair, his cane within reach. Baudouin had not seen the king in nigh on ten months and so the changes in Baldwin's appearance were more noticeable to him than to men who'd observed them over a period of time. As always, the sight of such old eyes in a young face jarred, and he felt a sharp jab of pity when he saw that Baldwin had tried to comb his hair to cover welts and lesions on his neck and forehead. He wanted to make sure Baldwin understood how grateful he was for assisting with his ransom, but Baldwin interrupted him, saying the court session was about to start.

Chairs were positioned by the window for Agnes and Sybilla. There was a third guest, a stranger to Baudouin. He nudged Balian and his brother whispered that this was Guy de Lusignan, Amaury's brother, shrugging when Baudouin asked why he'd been included since he held no lands in Outremer. Baudouin was furious with his son-in-law, for Balian had warned him of Amaury's shift into the de Courtenay camp, and as he watched Amaury's brother being treated as an honored guest by Sybilla and Agnes, Baudouin decided he did not much like this de Lusignan, either—another crusader from the West whose woeful ignorance of Outremer would be matched only by his disdain for the men who actually called it home.

Archbishop Eraclius offered the benediction. As soon as he had retaken his seat, Raymond rose, saying he and the Prince of Antioch had an urgent matter to bring before the court.

"You will have to wait, Cousin, for I need to address the court first," Baldwin said, and Raymond had no choice but to sit down again. Baldwin seemed in no hurry, though, his eyes sweeping the chamber, lingering for a moment upon the faces of his cousins. Only when puzzled murmurs began to rustle through the audience did he raise his hand for silence.

"Several days ago I received a letter from the Archbishop of Tyre in Constantinople. He'd heard very disturbing news from the Emperor Manuel regarding the ongoing unrest in France. The Duke of Burgundy fears that it might lead to civil war and so he has decided to repudiate his betrothal with my sister. He will not be sailing for Outremer as promised."

Knowing how the men would react to that, Baldwin allowed them time to express their shock and outrage and dismay before continuing. "It is well-known that I hoped to make a marital alliance for my sister with a highborn lord from the West, the vassal of a powerful king. But we no longer have the time to negotiate such a marriage. Every lord in Outremer knows that my health is failing. So I am sure you all will agree that nothing matters more than marrying my sister to a man able to defend our kingdom, to govern when I am no longer able to do so."

Baldwin paused again, shifting his gaze back to his cousins. Bohemond had a smile playing about his mouth, but Raymond's brows had drawn together, as if wondering if all was going too well; Baldwin knew he thought Fortune was a fickle bitch, always on the lookout for new conquests. *Well, for once you are right, Cousin. She has moved on.*

Baldwin glanced then toward his sister and her new husband. They were practically glowing, he thought, and he felt a sorrowful stirring of envy for all that he'd never get to experience when a man took a woman into his bed. Turning back to the audience, he said, "We still face a formidable enemy in Saladin and the years ahead will not be easy. But we need no longer fear that upon my death, my sister must rule on her own. She will have a husband by her side to share her burdens and to do what she cannot—lead our army to war. Two days ago she was wed in the palace chapel to Sir Guy de Lusignan, brother to Lord Amaury de Lusignan, a vassal of the English king, and now the new Count of Jaffa."

He'd expected chaos to erupt. Instead, his revelation was met with a stunned silence. All eyes turned toward the newlyweds, who smiled and reached over to clasp hands. For what seemed like forever to those in the chamber, no one moved and nothing was said. Archbishop Eraclius finally broke the spell by saying impatiently, "What . . . are none of you going to offer your congratulations to the happy couple?"

The High Court members shifted uncomfortably, waiting for one of the highborn lords to take the lead. But the Prince of Antioch and the Count of Tripoli seemed frozen in their seats. The Lord of Ramlah appeared even less capable of speech and while his brother, the Lord of Nablus, did not look as shocked, he did look unutterably sad. When the silence dragged on, the Bishop of Bethlehem rose reluctantly to his feet. "Of course we wish them well," he said firmly. "We were just taken by surprise. I am sure that God will look with favor upon their marriage."

Gilbert de Flory, the Viscount of Acre, was the next to rise. "As the bishop says, we were not expecting such momentous news—first that the Duke of Burgundy had reneged upon his promise and then that the king's sister was hastily wed to a man few of us know, and during Holy Week when marriages are not performed. We simply need time to comprehend it all."

Men began to nod, relieved that someone had dared to point out how unorthodox this sounded. Joscelin glared at Gilbert for implying there was something furtive and therefore suspect about the wedding. Before he could lash out at the viscount, Baldwin said, with a razor-sharp smile that few had seen before, "Under the circumstances, we had little choice. The sooner my sister could be wed, the better for the kingdom. Would you not agree, my lord cousins?"

Neither Bohemond nor Raymond replied, and their continuing silence only added to the growing unease. Few of the men understood what had happened, but they sensed that there were undercurrents in this chamber deep enough to drown in. It was Denys who eased some of the tension by crossing the chamber to offer his congratulations to Sybilla and Guy. Others followed then, wanting to learn more about this stranger who'd wedded and bedded the king's sister and become a king in the making, all in the span of days.

Baldwin reached for his cane and lurched to his feet. He did not bother to call the session to order, for he'd accomplished what needed to be done. Halting in front of his cousins, he said, startling them by how much he suddenly sounded like his father, "I assume you both will be attending the Easter vigil tonight at the Church of the Holy Sepulchre. You are welcome to do so. I would suggest, though, that you make ready to return to Antioch and Tripoli on Monday. You brought so many men with you that there is simply no room to lodge them in the city."

By now a large crowd had gathered around Sybilla and Guy. As the shock receded, most were avidly curious to learn more about Guy, for he'd not attracted much attention since his arrival in Outremer as a landless young knight. Not long after Baldwin departed, his royal cousins did, too, ignoring all the questions flung their way by men hoping they could shed some light on this astonishing turn of events.

Watching them go, Balian felt anger catching fire, scorching the boundaries of his self-control. He could understand why they'd felt the need to meddle in the matter of Sybilla's marriage, for the stakes could not be higher. But they'd made a fatal mistake. They'd only thought of Baldwin as a leper. He was a king, too, and kings did not surrender power willingly. Whilst Baldwin had often said that he would abdicate when he could no longer rule, it would be on his terms, not terms forced upon him.

Balian's anger, though, was not for their miscalculation. It was for involving his brother in their scheme. They'd infected Baudouin with the insidious disease of hope, making him believe that he could have it all—the woman, the queen, the kingdom. And when Baldwin struck back at his cousins, the blood spilled was Baudouin's.

After a time, Baudouin rose and left the chamber, not even glancing at Sybilla and Guy, surrounded by well-wishers. Balian caught up with him as they emerged into the tower bailey, and they headed for the stables to retrieve their horses. It was only then that Baudouin broke his silence. Standing beside his stallion, he said in a low voice, "Who is this Guy de Lusignan?"

Balian did not make the obvious response—younger brother of Amaury—for he knew what Baudouin was really asking. *What sort of king will this man make?* And no one knew the answer to that, he thought, not Baldwin, not Sybilla, mayhap not even Guy himself.

CHAPTER 27

After seven months at the Greek emperor's court in Constantinople, William, the Archbishop of Tyre, was coming home. He was honored by Manuel with an escort of four imperial galleys and, accompanied by several Greek envoys, he landed at the port of St. Simeon in the principality of Antioch on the twelfth day of May. Their ships then rowed up the Orontes River to the city of Antioch, where he was welcomed by Bohemond and his Greek wife, Theodora.

Antioch had an impressive citadel, Antakya Kalesi, but Bohemond preferred the greater luxury of the palace, a splendid residence with gardens, pools, balconies, and dazzling columns of red and white marble. After their long sea journey, William was not loath to spend some days as Bohemond's guest. He soon confided to Bohemond and Theodora the reason for his visit. The emperor was very ill and did not expect to recover, he reported with regret, for he had a genuine respect for Manuel, who'd ruled in Constantinople for almost four decades.

Knowing that his earthly days were dwindling, Manuel was determined to assure the succession of his eleven-year-old son, and he wanted Prince Bohemond to recognize the boy's right to the imperial throne. William had not been impressed with the lad during his stay in Constantinople, for he'd shown none of Baldwin's precocity and maturity. But if he was given good counsel, William hoped that he'd learn how to rule by the time he reached manhood—and that he'd share his father's goodwill toward the Kingdom of Jerusalem.

Bohemond assured William that he would offer his support to the emperor's young son. Pleased and a bit surprised that Bohemond was being so cooperative, William gladly retired to his guest chamber to rest after a very tiring trip.

After the evening meal, Bohemond suggested to William that they take a stroll in the gardens. Realizing that the prince was seeking a private conversation, William was both curious and uneasy, for Bohemond's earlier responses to his queries about Baldwin's health had seemed evasive. As they followed a paved path into the gardens, the sun was setting in a blaze of fiery color. William was too nervous to enjoy the scenic splendor, though, fearing that Bohemond was going to tell him Baldwin was grievously ill again.

The prince paused by a marble fountain and they sat on a nearby bench. Bohemond finally broke the taut silence by asking if William knew what had happened in Outremer at Easter. When William shook his head, the younger man seemed to sigh.

"As I feared. You'd left Constantinople by the time the news would have reached the Greek court. I regret that I must be the one to tell you—"

"Baldwin . . . he is not dying!"

"Calm yourself, my lord archbishop. He is not on his deathbed. But his accursed malady may have begun to affect his wits. I do not know how else to explain what he did at Easter. Without even consulting the High Court, he suddenly married his sister to a French newcomer to Outremer, a man little known to the rest of us—Amaury de Lusignan's younger brother, Guy."

William sucked in his breath, for the de Lusignans *were* known to him. "How . . . how could this happen?"

Bohemond shook his head sadly. "The young king is listening to the wrong people these days and they have poisoned his mind against my cousin, the Count of Tripoli. From what we later learned, they convinced Baldwin that an Easter visit by Raymond and me was cover for a coup attempt, that we intended to depose him and marry Lady Sybilla to a man of our choosing. You know Raymond to be a man of honor. Can you believe that of him?"

"No, I cannot! These 'wrong people' you accuse—the king's mother and uncle? The Archbishop of Caesarea?"

"Who else? As the king's health has deteriorated, their baneful influence has expanded. Baldwin heeds no one else these days. Raymond and I were indeed concerned about arranging a new marriage for Sybilla. We'd learned by then that the Duke of Burgundy had reneged on his promise to wed her. We intended to discuss the matter with Baldwin and the High Court, hoping to persuade them that Baudouin d'Ibelin ought to be chosen. What could be more reasonable than that? But we never got the chance, were met with the news of this sudden, secret marriage—performed during Holy Week! Just as troubling was Baldwin's hostility. He clearly does not trust us any longer, even though the same blood flows in our veins."

William was horrified both by the choice of a de Lusignan as their next king and by this dangerous breach between Baldwin and two of the most powerful lords in the Levant, his own kindred. "God help us all if Agnes and Joscelin de Courtney and Eraclius are the ones with their hands on the royal reins," he said bitterly. He refused to believe that he could not get through to Baldwin. But there was no undoing what had been done. For better or worse, after Baldwin's death their kingdom would be given over to a man unworthy to rule.

After leaving Antioch, William intended to sail down the coast to Tyre and then to escort the Greek envoys inland to Jerusalem to meet Baldwin. These plans were abruptly changed as they approached Beirut and saw the royal banner flying above the castle, for that meant the king was in residence. William hastily told the ship's master that they would go ashore in Beirut.

Beirut Castle was not one of the most comfortable of the royal residences and William was surprised by Baldwin's presence there, for he had rarely visited Beirut in the past. This mystery was solved when the castellan explained to William that the king had gotten reports of Saracen ships set to attack Beirut and hastened to the city's defense. But once the Saracen ship masters learned that the sultan had just concluded a truce with the kingdom, they'd sailed away.

When he was told that the king had not yet emerged from his private quarters, William found that somewhat alarming, for it was almost noon. Putting his concerns aside, he saw to it that his Greek guests were properly accommodated. He'd just sent his clerks off to his own chamber when he heard a voice call out, "My lord archbishop!"

Anselm was hurrying toward him, his face aglow; he was very grateful to the prelate who'd arranged for him to serve the young king and changed his life so dramatically. "How pleased the king will be when he learns you are here, my lord! He was just saying the other night that he hoped you'd soon be returning from Constantinople."

William grasped the other man's elbow and steered him toward the closest door. "Let's find a place where we can speak in private." That was no easy quest in a crowded castle and they eventually had to slip into the chapel, where William immediately asked if Baldwin was ailing. "No, my lord. He remains abed this morn because he had a bad night." Anselm grinned unexpectedly. "He drank enough wine to fill the moat and he's paying the price for it today."

William's initial relief ebbed away, for this had long been a secret fear of his. He'd known too many men who'd turned to wine or ale when their lives did not go the way they wanted, and who would have a better reason for blotting out reality than a youth facing the cruelest of all fates? Baldwin had always drunk sparingly in his presence. He'd not seen the young king in almost two years, though, and he well knew the inroads Baldwin's leprosy could have made in that time.

"Does . . . does he make a habit of this?"

Anselm blinked in surprise. "Not at all. This was the first time I've ever seen him drunk." A puzzled look crossed his face. "I think something happened when he went into town yesterday. He was whiter than chalk when he returned to the castle and retreated to his bedchamber. I gave him time to himself, but when I came back to assist him at bedtime, he told me to fetch wine. He was not used to drinking so much and he soon became dog sick, the poor lad."

"And you have no idea what caused this?"

"No, my lord. He was not in the mood for talking. . . ." Anselm lowered his voice. "I've seen my share of drunkards and usually you just watch over them to make sure they do not harm themselves or others and put them to bed after they pass out. But my young lord got so sick that I feared he'd puke his guts out and then he just lay there like a log, ignoring me, even ignoring his pup and he thinks the world of that dog. I did not know what to do. . . ."

Anselm hesitated, for he knew the archbishop would not like what he was about to say. "By God's grace, the king's mother had accompanied us to Beirut—"

"There is nothing about that woman which can be associated with God's grace," William snapped, for his emotions were still roiling from Bohemond's shocking revelation.

Anselm shuffled his feet, looking uncomfortable. "She was asleep when I sought her out, but she'd instructed her servants that I was never to be turned away, no matter the hour. Once I'd led her to the king's bedchamber, she told me to sleep in the antechamber. I could hear them talking for a long time. . . ." Gnawing his lower lip, he said softly, "When she finally left, the king seemed more peaceful, my lord, I swear he did. And he soon fell asleep."

William was not impressed with this testimonial to Agnes's maternal skills. What did it matter if she loved her son when her advice was so dangerous? There was nothing more to be said and they returned to the great hall, where Anselm hurried off to inform Baldwin of the archbishop's arrival and William engaged in polite conversation with the castellan, disappointed to learn that neither d'Ibelin brother nor Denys de Grenier had accompanied the king. Nor was he cheered to be told that Joscelin de Courtenay was also in Beirut. He had no time to ponder this, for Anselm was soon back. The king wanted to see him straightaway.

William had occasionally heard someone say his heart had been in his throat, but he'd never experienced that himself until he stood before Baldwin's bedchamber door, dreading to see the damage that leprosy had done in the twenty months since their last meeting. He was deeply grateful to God to find that Baldwin was not yet showing any of the worst manifestations of his disease. He did look somehow different, although it took a moment for William to realize why—he'd lost most of his eyebrows and his eyelashes had thinned dramatically, making his eyes look oddly exposed and vulnerable. His voice was hoarser, too, than William remembered. He stumbled a bit as he came forward, revealing how unsteady his gait had become, and then they were embracing, clinging together like fellow shipwreck survivors or a father and son reunited against all the odds.

"How gladdened I am to see you, William!" The smile at least was the same, brighter than the noonday sun. William expressed his joy, too, and followed Baldwin to a window seat. "I heard from the emperor. He said you'd convinced him to renew the treaty with Jerusalem. Well done, my lord archbishop, well done! I knew I was right to entrust this mission to you."

William could feel a flush of pleasure warming his cheeks, for Baldwin's praise was worth more to him than all the gold in Montpelier. Not wanting to poison this moment with talk of the de Lusignans and Baldwin's duplicitous kindred, he asked instead about the truce. He'd been troubled to learn of it from the castellan, for this was the first time in their kingdom's history that the Franks and the Saracens had come to the bargaining table as equals; whenever peace had been made in the past, the Saracens had paid a price for it. But Baldwin explained they'd had no choice, for they were still recovering from their disastrous defeat last summer at Marj Ayyun. That battle had cost William dearly, too; his brother, Ralph, had been among the slain. In the months since learning of Ralph's death, he'd often cursed the Templar grand master in language ill befitting a prince of the Church and he felt an unchristian satisfaction now when Baldwin told him that Odo de St. Amand had subsequently died in a Damascus dungeon. Forgiving his enemies was the only one of the Lord Christ's teachings that William continued to struggle with.

Remembering his duties as host, then, Baldwin asked William if he wanted food sent up from the kitchens. "You must be hungry since you missed dinner. Nothing for me, though, Anselm." Baldwin's smile was sheepish. "I drank more than was good for me last night."

William insisted he was not hungry, either, knowing the mere sight of food could unsettle a queasy stomach. At that moment, a servant knocked on the door, holding a hemp sack, saying it was for the king. Baldwin took the sack and opened it. He pulled out several swaths of cloth and held them up, appearing puzzled. It took them both a moment to realize they were looking at the Saracen headdress known as a kaffiyeh and the turban called an *imamah muhannak*. When they did, William caught a strange expression on Baldwin's face, as if he did not know whether he wanted to laugh or to cry.

Choosing the first option, Baldwin gave a chuckle, studied William for a moment, and then dispatched Anselm to walk Cairo. Once they were alone, he said, "My mother sent these. I know you and she have never gotten along, William, but I also know you are a fair man and you cannot deny that she has been my mainstay more times than I care to count. Last night for certes."

"What happened last night, Baldwin?"

"Last night was one of the worst I've endured since learning I was a leper. But it began in the afternoon, when we were riding past the souk," Baldwin said in a low voice, using the Arabic word for market. "It was then that I saw him . . . a beggar, being berated and cursed by several shopkeepers. When I sent one of my knights to stop them from throwing stones at him, they insisted they were just trying to get him to leave, that he was scaring their customers away. He was wrapped in a long cloak despite the heat, its hood hiding his face, and I had not realized he was a leper. I told the knight to give him a few coins to leave the souk, not knowing what else to do. He did not reach out for the coins, though. I did not understand . . . not until I saw his hands. They were so crippled that they looked like claws, the fingers deformed and curving inward toward his palms."

Baldwin turned sideways in the seat so that William saw only his profile. "Yet the worst was still to come, when his hood fell back and I saw his face. . . ." He managed to keep his voice level, but he could not suppress a convulsive shudder. "It was covered in crusted nodules, William, his cheeks, his forehead, his chin, like . . . like huge warts. He was clearly blind in one eye, for it looked as if it were filled with blood and the . . . color was all clouded over."

"Ah, lad . . ." William's voice choked up. To his surprise, Baldwin found that the other man's obvious anguish was somehow bracing, helping him to cling to his own self-control. In an odd role reversal, he reached over and laid a comforting hand on William's arm.

"You need not say anything, William. But I knew I was looking at myself a few years from now, mayhap sooner, and I . . . I felt as if I were drowning in despair." Baldwin forced a wan smile at that, saying, "I hope that does not sound too over-wrought." Standing abruptly, he said, "I think I might need some wine after all." Limping to the table, he poured with a hand not as steady as his voice. "I am ashamed to admit that I did not think of that poor wretch till later, after we'd re-turned to the castle. I sent out several of my knights then, with orders to convey him to a lazar house. They said they could not find him. . . ."

Baldwin took a sip of the wine and made a face, setting it down on the table. "It tastes like goat piss. Will I ever like wine again, William?" With another of those small smiles that unraveled the archbishop's composure. "Not that I need any, for I probably have more wine than blood in my veins today. What I did was foolish and you need not worry that I'll do it again. But . . . but it was not even the thought of looking like that poor, accursed soul that I found so unbearable. It was that I am the king, unable to hide myself away from other eyes. Yet how could I go out in public once I am that deformed? How could my subjects look upon me and not be sickened, as I was sickened when I looked upon that leper in the souk?"

It all came together for William then. "The kaffiyeh," he said, holding up one of the headdresses.

Baldwin nodded. "I confided that fear to my mother after Anselm brought her to my chamber. She usually tries to assure me that I will not suffer the deformities and horrors that other lepers do, as if I am somehow immune to the worst of that accursed affliction. Last night she did not do this. She said if it came to that, I could wear a kaffiyeh the way my spymaster Bernard does. This may sound crazed, Wil-liam, but that actually gave me some comfort. At least I need not fear frightening small children."

William found Baldwin's game attempts at humor even more excruciating than tears would have been. All he could think to do was to promise Baldwin that he'd find that crippled beggar and see that he was taken to a leper hospital, where at least he'd not go hungry.

Baldwin had never used his illness as an excuse to shirk his royal duties. Nor did he let a hangover keep him from welcoming the Greek envoys, having supper with them that evening, and doing his best to play the role of host. He'd given the archbishop the place of honor on his right, but his mother was seated to his left and kept intruding into the conversation with the envoys, much to William's barely suppressed fury. This wicked woman had lied to her son and cruelly maligned the Count of Tripoli so she could marry her daughter to a de Courtenay puppet, a man not fit to rule, and now she dared to play the role of queen? He did not know what angered him more: that she cared so little for the future of their kingdom or that she was so shamelessly willing to use Baldwin's illness to her own advantage.

None of the Greek envoys spoke French and they'd brought along a translator, but Baldwin preferred to rely upon William and he spent much of the meal facilitating the exchange of pleasantries between the king, his mother, and their Greek guests. Joscelin, seated farther along the dais, occasionally joined in, too. William was hard put to hide his dismay when he learned that Baldwin would be sending Joscelin to Constantinople to finalize the new treaty.

His worst moments came when one of the Greeks asked about the king's marital plans for his sister now that she'd not be marrying that French duke. Baldwin hesitated and then asked William to tell them that the Lady Sybilla had been wed to another French lord, Guy de Lusignan, in April. The Greeks looked pleased, for now that they were allies again, their emperor would want to see the succession settled in the Frankish kingdom, and they politely proposed a toast to the newlyweds. William raised his cup as the others did, but he could not drink to a marriage that he believed was a calamity for his homeland. When he set the cup down, untasted, he saw that Baldwin and his mother were both watching him, Baldwin's expression inscrutable and Agnes's face bright with triumph.

After the meal was over, Baldwin excused himself, asking his mother to entertain their guests. William soon offered his own excuses and withdrew to his chamber. He'd not yet made ready for bed when he received an unexpected message: the king wished to see him.

Their meeting got off to an awkward start, for William was loath to discuss Sybilla's marriage. Baldwin was not looking forward to that discussion, either, sorry he would have to shatter William's illusions about the Count of Tripoli, so at first they made meaningless small talk about the evening and their Greek guests. Listening to their desultory conversation, Anselm concluded that the young king wanted privacy and concocted an errand to run.

His departure spurred Baldwin into action. "I regret that you had to learn of Sybilla's marriage the way you did, William. It must have been a shock to you."

William's shoulders twitched in a noncommittal shrug. "I'd already heard about it."

"I know you are not pleased with it." Baldwin smiled slightly. "Your face has always given you away. I understand your disappointment, for I'd hoped, too, that we could make a marital alliance with one of the great houses. But once I tell you how it came to be, I am sure you'll approve."

It may have been his fatigue. Or his fear for the future. Or the memory of Agnes de Courtenay's smug smile. But William found he could not do this. With so much at stake, he owed Baldwin the truth, unpalatable as it might be. "Accept it, I must. But I will never approve of it, for Guy de Lusignan is undeserving of the great honor you have conferred upon him. He is not worthy to be king."

Baldwin's eyes widened. "That is a harsh judgment upon a man you've never even met."

"It is true that I've yet to meet him. I know about him, though, far more than you do, I fear." Now that he'd crossed the Rubicon, William had no choice but to forge ahead. If Baldwin could not undo what had been done, at least he could be forewarned. "Do you remember one of the English lords who accompanied the Count of Flanders to Outremer—William de Mandeville, the Earl of Essex?"

Another man might have seen William's question as a non sequitur, an odd digression. Baldwin merely nodded. "I do. Go on."

"I was taken aback by the deliberate rudeness that the earl showed to Amaury de Lusignan and finally confronted him about it. De Mandeville was quite willing to tell me why he held the de Lusignans in such contempt. It is no secret that they have always been troublesome vassals, too ambitious and unscrupulous to be trusted. King Henry kept a close eye on them, reining them in when need be. But that all changed with the attack upon his queen."

"What? Are you serious?"

William nodded grimly. "The English king had seized Lusignan Castle as punishment for yet another rebellion. Queen Eleanor was riding from Poitiers to Lusignan, under the protection of the Earl of Salisbury, when they were ambushed by the de Lusignans. I suppose they thought they could hold her hostage until the castle was returned to them. She was able to escape, though, thanks to the heroics of her men. Amongst the dead was Salisbury, slain by a lance in the back ere he could put on his hauberk."

"Good God Almighty! Was this Amaury's doing?"

"No, the raid was led by his elder brother, Joffrey, and his younger brother. The man who is now wed to your sister—Guy de Lusignan."

Baldwin was quiet for some moments. "When did this happen?"

"Twelve years ago, in April of God's year 1168."

"I will not deny that I find this very troubling, William. But Guy must have been quite young at the time, not more than eighteen or so. Not that his age excuses him . . . yet the greater blame must rest with his brother."

William shrugged again, letting the gesture speak for itself. Baldwin pushed his chair back, then remembered his cane was out of reach. "I see now why you are so distressed by this marriage. In truth, we knew we'd be taking a gamble with Guy. I had no choice, though. Had Sybilla not married Guy, she'd have been forced to wed Baudouin d'Ibelin and I would have been deposed. I will not pretend to understand why the Almighty would have a leper king rule over the Holy Land, but I am king by His will and I must believe that He has reasons for all that He does. Surely you see that, William?"

"Of course I do. None of this is your fault, Baldwin. You were misled by those who knew better, who took shameless advantage of your strong sense of duty, your faith in—"

"No! That is not how it happened. My cousins were plotting my overthrow, meaning to rule through Sybilla and d'Ibelin. Had we not been warned in time—"

"And how were you warned? How was this *plot* exposed?"

"My mother had a spy in Count Raymond's household and he alerted us that Raymond and Bohemond were marching on Jerusalem with a large army. He told us . . ." Baldwin stopped speaking then, for the expression on William's face was both sorrowful and skeptical.

"They were lying to you, lad. It was a cleverly laid trap, one that allowed the Archbishop of Caesarea and the de Courtenays to wed Sybilla to a man of their choosing whilst making sure that you'd never trust the Count of Tripoli again, that you'd heed no voices but theirs. But it may not be too late, Baldwin. Can you not annul Sybilla's marriage to de Lusignan? Find a more worthy husband for her? Must we let that woman and Eraclius win?"

Baldwin lurched to his feet, blue eyes blazing. "'That woman' is my mother! You dare to accuse me of being their pawn? You are the one who sounds like a puppet, your strings being pulled by the Count of Tripoli!"

"Baldwin, that is not so! I am seeking only to help—"

"And I am sure Count Raymond is grateful for it. No—do not speak. You've said enough, my lord archbishop. More than enough."

William's every instinct was to argue until Baldwin understood the great mistake he'd made and the even greater mistake he was making now. His words died in his throat as he realized he was not looking at the youth he'd tutored and mentored and loved like a son. He was looking at an angry king.

On July 6, William returned to his archepiscopal city of Tyre. What followed was the most wretched summer of his life. After he'd reluctantly withdrawn from Baldwin's bedchamber, he'd consoled himself with the belief that he could explain once Baldwin calmed down, that he could find a way to make the young king see that he'd spoken the truth. But he soon discovered that Baldwin's anger had congealed into ice. He was given no opportunity to raise the subject of Sybilla's marriage. Even though there were times when Baldwin was close enough to touch, the distance between them grew with each passing day. And once Agnes and Joscelin realized that he was no longer in Baldwin's favor, they rejoiced openly, missing few opportunities for baiting him. When Baldwin left Beirut with the Greek envoys, William did not accompany them. Instead, he went home to Tyre, where he tried to lose himself in Church matters, tried to pretend that his heart was not broken.

William was grateful that his days were so busy, for constant activity kept him from dwelling upon his estrangement from Baldwin. Sooner or later, though, he would have to return to court, for he was still the chancellor . . . unless the de Courtenays convinced Baldwin he should be removed from that post. He trusted Baldwin's sense of fair play, but he dared not underestimate the malice of his enemies—a prince of the Church who brazenly embraced sins of the flesh and a woman detestable to God.

And so his summer days dragged by. But in August, everything changed, for he had an unexpected visit from Balian d'Ibelin. He'd accompanied Baudouin to Acre, he explained, where his brother took ship for Constantinople, armed with a letter from Maria, urging her great-uncle to pay the vast ransom owed to Saladin. William was grateful beyond words that the younger d'Ibelin had been willing to continue on to Tyre, no easy journey in the heat of high summer. He desperately needed what Balian could provide—friendship and answers.

They had much catching up to do and at first confined themselves to personal news. Balian offered his condolences for the death of William's brother at Marj Ayyun and William expressed his delight upon hearing that Maria had given birth to a son. Balian then thanked the archbishop for writing to Maria about the Greek emperor's grave illness, leaving unspoken the concern in both men's minds—that Manuel's death could make Maria and Isabella more vulnerable to the machinations of the de Courtenays.

"Maria and I also want to thank you, William, for your diplomatic success in Constantinople. It matters greatly to her that there is peace between her land of birth and the land that became hers by marriage. Baldwin must be very proud of you."

William paused in the act of reaching for a wine cup. "Did . . . did he say that?"

Balian thought that an odd question. "Maria and I have not been at court since Easter, so, no, I did not hear him say it. Surely he told you of his pleasure when you met him at Beirut?"

"Yes, he did. But I am not sure if he still feels that way, for we had a serious quarrel whilst we were in Beirut and I have not heard from him since that quarrel." Balian was too discreet to probe as Baudouin would have done. William did not doubt, though, that he had a sympathetic ear and so, haltingly at first, he began to relate what had happened on that terrible night in Baldwin's bedchamber. He felt a great sense of relief when he was done, for there was solace in sharing his pain. That lasted only until he looked up and saw Balian's face.

"Ah, William . . . Baldwin was speaking the truth. Prince Bohemond and Count Raymond did indeed lead an army to Jerusalem with the intent of marrying Sybilla to Baudouin and then crowning them after Baldwin abdicated."

William reeled back in his seat. "That cannot be! Raymond would never do that! Why would you believe the de Courtenay lies, Balian? I do not understand."

"I can only tell you what I was told, William, by one who was there when Agnes's spy related what he'd learned of their plans. He believed the spy's story and I believed him when he came to us afterward, for he is a man I call my friend. So do you—Denys de Grenier."

William was stunned. "I do not think Denys would lie," he conceded. "But he could still be wrong, Balian. Bohemond told me that he and Raymond did intend to discuss the matter of Sybilla's marriage with Baldwin and the High Court. He never denied that. He did deny very forcefully that either he or Raymond had even considered forcing Baldwin to abdicate."

"Then why did they come to Jerusalem with an army, William?" Balian paused, saw that William had no answer to that. "I cannot tell you for a certainty that they meant to depose Baldwin after marrying Sybilla to Baudouin. But Baldwin believes it and that is not an unreasonable belief under the circumstances. Denys did insist that this was not a conspiracy by the de Courtenays. He swore that Agnes's fear was very real, that she was more concerned about protecting Baldwin's kingship than about choosing a husband for Sybilla. In fact, it was Sybilla who first mentioned Guy's name."

William leaned forward, burying his face in his hands. "What have I done? Baldwin tried to tell me, but I would not listen. I was so sure that Raymond was being maligned, that this was a de Courtenay plot. . . ."

"Well, we rarely go wrong believing the worst of the de Courtenays," Balian said dryly. "Unfortunately, Baldwin now harbors suspicions of Baudouin and those suspicions may have spilled over onto Maria and me, too. We tried to talk to him after Denys told us why Baldwin had wed his sister to Guy de Lusignan. He heard us out as we swore we'd had no part in any plot against him. It was impossible to say whether he believed us or not and he was rather cool to us during the remainder of the Easter court."

William raised despairing eyes to Balian's. "Do you think Baldwin will forgive me?"

"Of course he will. He loves you, William. But he also loves his mother."

"I know," William admitted, "I know. . . ." He slumped in his seat, excoriating himself for blundering so badly in Beirut. After a time, he said wearily, "Even if this marriage was not the result of de Courtenay conniving, we are still stuck with a highly questionable king-in-waiting. You've met him, Balian. What is your opinion of the man?"

"In truth, I do not know him well enough to have formed an opinion yet. What you told me about the ambush of the English queen does not inspire much confidence. But as you said Baldwin pointed out, he was young then. We can only hope that he has matured in the intervening years."

"What of the other Poulains? What do they think of him?"

"I doubt that many were overjoyed by the selection of another foreigner. Whilst he is wellborn, he does not have the royal connections that the Duke of Burgundy has, and there is some resentment that Baldwin did not consult with the High Court beforehand. I suspect that they'd have welcomed a marriage between Sybilla and Baudouin with greater enthusiasm. But I think most men are willing to give Guy the benefit of the doubt, at least for now."

Balian smiled, then, without any humor whatsoever. "Not my brother, though. No matter what Guy de Lusignan says or does, he will never win Baudouin over."

CHAPTER 28

September 1180
Jerusalem, Outremer

Asad had begun to nuzzle his master's tunic and Baldwin pushed him away with a laugh. "Sorry, boy, nothing for you to eat." Taking the comb from Anselm, he began to untangle the stallion's mane and Asad reluctantly abandoned his search for treats.

Anselm watched for a while, thinking that the only time the young king seemed at peace was when he was in the stables. What would the lad do when he could no longer ride at all? "Do you think Asad can ever be ridden again, my lord?"

"Not likely. But he is no longer in pain." For a moment, Baldwin had a vision of the stallion racing the wind. Though the memory hurt, he still found a smile for Anselm. "He will not miss his old life, for he has his own harim now and several of his mares are in foal." Asad nudged him again and this time he won; Baldwin sent Anselm off to the kitchens to get sugar.

A stable cat sauntered over. This one seemed to have formed a bond with Asad, for Baldwin often found her sleeping in the stallion's stall. She stretched and then leaped onto the top of the stall door. When Asad snorted, Baldwin leaned for a moment against the Arabian's withers, inhaling the familiar, comforting smells of the stable. "Was I right, boy?" he murmured. "Are the mares enough for you now?" *Yet how could a crippled hawk not yearn for the skies?*

His balance had become so unsteady that he could no longer groom Asad properly. He still enjoyed brushing the stallion and thought the Arabian enjoyed the contact, too. He'd forgotten to ask Anselm for a soft cloth to clean Asad's eyes and nostrils. Seeing some piled on a nearby bench, he opened the stall door; this annoyed the cat, who jumped off with a hiss. He'd only taken a few steps before he stumbled and, unable to catch himself, he went down hard.

For some moments, he lay still, the breath knocked out of him. When he touched his forehead, his fingers came away bloodied and he realized he'd cut himself on the edge of a bucket. Rolling over, he managed to sit up. In the past few years, he'd taken falls beyond counting. It was only recently, though, that he'd found he needed help in getting to his feet. Wiping the blood from his eyes, he saw two grooms standing not far away, staring at him. When neither one moved, he felt a sudden rage, sparing neither himself nor these frightened grooms nor the God who'd brought him to this. He wanted to lash out, to punish them for their fear and for witnessing his humiliation, sprawled in the dirt like a turtle turned on its back. But he held on to the shreds of his self-control. Ordering them to fetch Anselm, he slumped down again and listened to their fleeing footsteps.

His head was still bleeding and his cheek was throbbing. It was the injury to his pride that he found hardest to bear, though. He was God's anointed, a crowned king who'd bloodied his sword at fifteen and then won a miraculous victory at Montgisard. Yet now he was lying here as helpless as a mewling babe. How could he accept this? How could any man? Why would the Almighty demand so much of him?

"My lord!" Baldwin had been so caught up in his own misery that he'd not heard these new footsteps. He tried to sit up again and then arms were encircling him, struggling to help him rise. It was not easy, for his rescuer was slightly built and was panting by the time Baldwin was able to lurch to his feet. "Over here," he gasped. "Lean on me, sire."

It was a young voice and vaguely familiar. Baldwin did as bidden, let himself be steered toward the bench. He sank down upon it gratefully, for his legs felt like jelly. Only then was he able to identify his Good Samaritan—the late constable's grandson, Humphrey de Toron. As always, he was struck by the boy's uncommon beauty and by his vulnerability, both of which made him seem younger than his fourteen years. His wide-set dark eyes, fringed by improbably long lashes, were regarding Baldwin anxiously. "I'll be right back," he said, and quickly returned with a water bucket.

Picking up one of the cloths, Humphrey dipped it in the water, then averted his gaze as Baldwin scrubbed the blood and dirt from his face, sensing that the king's greatest need was for privacy. Reaching for another cloth, he offered it shyly. "You are still bleeding, my lord. . . ."

Baldwin applied pressure to the cut as Humphrey hurried over to retrieve his cane, then paused before the overturned bucket. "This is what must have caused your fall, sire! The grooms ought to be reprimanded for carelessly leaving it out like this."

"I did not trip over it, Humphrey," Baldwin said wearily. "I fall easily, for I can no longer feel the soles of my feet when they touch the ground. That is why lepers so often stagger around like drunkards." He was not sure why he felt the need to explain this to the boy, nor why he then confided that he could not brace himself when he went down because of his dead arm. He did not reveal, though, that he was losing strength in his left arm, too, for that was a secret he'd shared with no one, not even his doctors.

Humphrey looked stricken and Baldwin realized that the youngster had not fully understood just how difficult daily life was for a leper, even one with servants on hand. Humphrey surprised him then with honesty of his own. "Where do you find the courage, my liege?"

Baldwin shrugged off the compliment, for he did not think courage was all that commendable if there was no other choice. "I could well ask the same of you, for few men would have dared to come to my assistance as you did. That took considerable courage."

Humphrey's expression was so dubious that Baldwin wondered if he feared he was being mocked. The boy's response was almost inaudible. "I'd not say that in front of my mother and stepfather, sire, for they'd likely laugh themselves sick."

Baldwin remembered Reynald de Chatillon's contemptuous quip. "Men would not follow that milksop out of a burning building." He shifted on the bench, not trusting his legs. "I could tell you the opinions of others do not matter, Humphrey. We both know that is not true, though. Unless a man is a hermit or a saint, they matter. But this is a bedrock truth—that it is your own opinion of yourself that matters the most. And after today, you need not doubt your courage. You proved it by rushing to my aid, by being willing to lay hands upon a leper."

Humphrey's sudden smile was sunlit. It was also brief. "But I *was* afraid," he confessed. "I just did not give in to it. . . ."

"Courage is not a lack of fear, lad. It is overcoming fear." It seemed odd to call Humphrey "lad," for there were only five years between them. Yet Baldwin felt a lifetime older than this unhappy youth and the pain from an old wound began to stir. Never had Humphrey needed his grandfather more than now, trembling on the cusp of manhood. The wound inflicted by the constable's death was still unhealed, both for his only male heir and for the king he'd died trying to protect.

"My lord! Are you hurt?" Coming to a halt, Anselm gave a gusty sigh at the sight of his king seated on the bench. "I ought to take a strap to those lackwits for scaring me pissless!" Hastening forward, he subjected Baldwin to a critical scrutiny. "What happened, my lord?"

"I took a fall, Anselm. Fortunately for me, Humphrey was here to help." And when Baldwin glanced over at the boy, he saw that those casual words of praise meant more to Humphrey than a hoard of golden bezants.

After changing his clothes, Baldwin sat at his desk. He did more and more of his work in the privacy of his bedchamber now, away from prying eyes. He began with the packet of letters brought that noon by an imperial messenger from Constantinople. He tensed as he broke Joscelin's seal, fearing that he'd be told the emperor was dead, for their alliance might well die with him. Scanning the letter, he was so relieved that he shared the good news with Anselm.

"My uncle says that they are making progress in the negotiations." Joscelin would never give William credit for laying the groundwork so well, but Baldwin's innate sense of fairness compelled him to admit that Joscelin's task had been made much easier by the archbishop's skilled diplomacy during his long stay in Constantinople. Setting Joscelin's letter aside, he was surprised to find one from Baudouin d'Ibelin, reporting joyfully that the emperor had agreed to pay his ransom and thanking Baldwin again for all he'd done to secure Baudouin's release.

When he shared this news with Anselm, the squire did not comment. Baldwin knew why—Anselm was not sure how the king felt about Baudouin d'Ibelin now. Baldwin was not sure himself. He did not see how Baudouin could have been an active participant in the coup, for he'd not regained his freedom until Holy Week. Both d'Ibelin brothers had sworn to him that Baudouin would never have agreed to usurp his throne, and Baldwin wanted to believe them. Yet a nagging doubt remained, for he knew how easy it was for men to convince themselves that what they wanted was also for the greater good. If the plot had succeeded and Baudouin had wed Sybilla, would he truly have objected when Bohemond and Raymond then insisted that the next step must be the king's abdication?

Picking up another letter, he told Anselm that it was from his sister and the squire stopped playing with Cairo to ask if she and Lord Guy were staying in Ascalon much longer; they had retreated there after Easter and there was growing impatience about their absence from Jerusalem. Men were eager to learn more about their future king.

"Yes, they are still in Ascalon," Baldwin confirmed. "She promises, though, that they will be here for my Christmas court." Like his subjects, Baldwin found it frustrating that Guy remained such a stranger. Yet he could not blame his sister for wanting time alone with her new husband. He knew that most men were withholding their judgment until they got to know Guy better. He was, too, especially after hearing William's troubling account of the de Lusignan attack upon the English queen. But Sybilla had already reached her own verdict, for never had she sounded so happy. They could only hope that her assessment of Guy de Lusignan was right.

He had just opened a letter from Joscius, the Bishop of Acre, when Cairo barked sharply.

Anselm hurried over to open the door, listened briefly, and then glanced toward Baldwin. "My lord, the Archbishop of Tyre has arrived at the palace and is requesting an audience." He took care to keep his voice neutral, for he did not know if this was welcome news or not.

Baldwin hesitated before replying. He'd been hurt by his estrangement from William; as far back as he could remember, the older man had been his rock and his anchor. He wanted to mend their rift. But he was in no mood to resume their quarrel about the Easter conspiracy, not after the morning he'd just had. Yet how could he refuse to see William? "Tell the seneschal to escort the archbishop to my bedchamber."

As soon as William entered the chamber, Anselm found an excuse to depart, escaping after he'd poured wine for them. There was an awkward formality about the first moments, as William waited respectfully for permission to sit. But protocol was forgotten as soon as he saw the young king's face. In a day or so, Baldwin would have several spectacular bruises as a result of his fall. The skin along his cheekbone was only reddened now, yet that was enough for William's sharp eye. He opened his mouth to express his concern, catching himself just in time. Tearing his gaze away from that proof of yet another mishap, he cast court decorum to the winds and said simply, "I have come to ask your forgiveness."

Baldwin reined in his initial pleasure; wariness had become second nature to him by now. "Forgiveness for quarreling with me? Or for not believing me?"

"Both." William leaned forward in his chair, clasping his hands so tightly that Baldwin could see his knuckles whitening. "Bohemond swore to me that he and Raymond had never plotted against you and he was very convincing. That was no excuse, though. I ought never to have doubted you."

Baldwin agreed wholeheartedly with that; he'd been shaken by William's apparent willingness to give Raymond the benefit of every doubt. "How did you learn the truth?"

"From Balian d'Ibelin. He assured me that what happened at Easter was no de Courtenay plot, that it originated in Antioch and Tripoli."

Baldwin had not fully realized how heavy a burden their estrangement had been, not until he suddenly found it easier to breathe. "I am glad that you know what really happened."

"And you forgive me?"

"Of course I do."

"Then we can put this behind us?" William's relief was overwhelming when Baldwin assured him it was already forgotten. But he sensed it would leave a scar. And as their eyes met, he saw that Baldwin feared that, too.

After a long illness, Emeric, the elderly Patriarch of Jerusalem, died on October 6 and all eyes turned toward the canons of the Church of the Holy Sepulchre, for they had the responsibility to select a new patriarch. There were two obvious candidates—William, the Archbishop of Tyre, and Eraclius, the Archbishop of Caesarea. Others were allowed to address the canons on behalf of the candidates and Agnes de Courtenay made a passionate speech in which she urged them to choose Eraclius. William also asked to speak, and riveted the canons in their seats as he argued against the election of Eraclius, pointing out that the archbishop's immoral life was an open secret, citing his notorious liaison with Pasque de Rivieri, the wife of a Nablus mercer.

Although William was not a particularly eloquent speaker, no match for Eraclius in that regard, few doubted that he was speaking from the heart. But no one expected what he did next. Instead of advocating his own election, he pleaded with them not to choose a prelate from Outremer. The kingdom would be better served, he insisted, by the selection of a wise man of God from elsewhere in Christendom.

The canons were impressed by his willingness to sacrifice his own ambitions to keep the patriarchy from going to Eraclius. But they were not convinced by his plea that they look beyond the sea for their next patriarch; most of them preferred to elect a man already known to them. Yet when they gathered in the chapter house to vote, they discovered to their dismay that they were split into equal factions between the two archbishops, and none could come up with a compromise candidate.

Denys was not looking forward to the unpleasant task he'd taken upon himself, but William was an old friend and he thought he should be the one to deliver the bad news. He was quickly ushered into the solar of the archbishop's town house, where he was warmly welcomed. "How is the king?" William asked as soon as greetings had been exchanged. "Is he still ailing?"

Baldwin had been running a fever all week, troubled with a sore throat and cough, but Denys was able to assure William that so far the illness showed no signs of flaring into a more serious ailment. "He ought to have heeded his doctor's advice that he stay in bed for a few days. You know how stubborn the lad is, though."

William's smile was sad. "I've never known another soul with a will as strong as Baldwin's." He waited until a servant had served them wine before resuming the conversation. "Is it true that the canons are stalemated over the choice for patriarch?"

Denys was not surprised that William had heard the news already. "The canons were unable to choose between you and Eraclius. When they could not break the deadlock, they came to Baldwin with both names and implored him to make the choice." The sudden hope on William's face was hurtful to see and he said hastily, "Alas, Agnes was present and she asked Baldwin to let her choose, reminding him that this had been done in another election for patriarch, when the king allowed his mother, Queen Melisende, and her sisters to make the choice."

"And . . . and Baldwin agreed?" William sank back in his chair as if all the energy had suddenly been drained from his body, leaving only an empty husk. When Denys nodded somberly, he closed his eyes for a moment, struggling to maintain his composure. His disappointment was like a finely honed blade, too sharp to handle. But his fury was even greater, for what could be more outrageous than that accursed woman's willingness to take such selfish advantage of her son's sickness? He could not let his anger loose, though, had to remember that Agnes was Denys's wife. When he finally felt that he could trust his voice, he said, "Again and again I've counseled Baldwin that he must accept God's will, no matter how difficult that is. It seems that the time has come for me to drink my own poison, Denys."

Upon his return to the palace, Denys learned that Agnes had wasted no time. After announcing that she would follow the example of Queen Melisende and consult with other ladies of high birth, she held a hasty meeting with Stephanie de Milly and Joscelin's wife, Agneta, selecting Archbishop Eraclius as the next patriarch of the kingdom. Denys was a student of history, so he knew that many considered that earlier election to be irregular because of the queen's participation. He was sure that Baldwin knew it, too, and decided that, if only from morbid curiosity, he had to know why the king had agreed to Agnes's proposal.

Despite the lateness of the hour, Denys made his way to Baldwin's private chambers, knowing that his stepson often found sleep to be an elusive quarry. His gamble paid off and he was admitted at once. Baldwin was lying on his bed, fully dressed except for his shoes. He seemed grateful for the company and when Denys refused the offer of refreshments, he asked Anselm to take Cairo for a walk, for this would not be a discussion for other ears.

Denys did not temporize. Pulling a chair up to the bed, he said simply, "Why?"

Baldwin regarded the older man in silence for a time, his expression pensive and not easy to read. "Ere I answer that, tell me your opinion of the two men."

"Well . . . they are both qualified to serve as patriarch. They are well educated and whilst Eraclius is not a Poulain like William, he has been here long enough to learn our ways and to understand the dangers we face from Saladin. William is a good man, a far better man than Eraclius, but the latter is the better politician. Is that what tipped the scales in Eraclius's favor?"

"My mother hates William. And he detests her and Joscelin. The animosity between them does not matter whilst I live, but what would happen if William were the patriarch when I die and the crown passes to Sybilla? William cannot dissemble to save his soul. Whether he willed it or not, he would become a rallying point for all who mistrust the de Courtenays, who are loath to accept a foreigner as king. The court would be split asunder, far worse than it is now, for I can keep peace between the two factions. Sybilla could not. If we have any hope of keeping Saladin at bay, we must be united, Denys. Dissension would doom us."

Denys was impressed by the unsentimental and unsparing clarity of Baldwin's thinking. Nor could he argue with Baldwin's reasoning. Amalric would have been proud of the lad, for he had learned well the harsh lessons of kingship. But he knew Baldwin found it far harder than Amalric to heed his head and not his heart, for he loved William.

He yearned for the right words, for some comfort to offer. "I saw William a few hours ago and I'll not deny that he was distraught. Yet you made it easier for him, Baldwin, by letting Agnes choose the patriarch. By being able to blame her and not you, he need not fear that the friendship between you has waned, and I think that is as important to him as the patriarchy itself."

"Yes," Baldwin said softly, "that was my hope."

CHAPTER 29

Reynald and Stephanie had wholeheartedly embraced Agnes's proposal. It had never occurred to her that they would not, for she was offering them a rare opportunity—if she could make it happen. Stephanie was still flying high, showering Agnes with lavish, grateful praise. But Reynald had a soldier's mind and he was already assessing their enemy's strengths and weaknesses. "I can see one flaw in this plan," he said. "What happens if Maria appeals to the Greek emperor for aid? Baldwin values that alliance. Would he risk alienating Manuel?"

"We need not worry about interference from the Greeks. The news has not gotten out yet, but two days ago Baldwin received word from Constantinople. The emperor died on September twenty-fourth."

Reynald smiled, then, giving Agnes the approval he reserved for a skilled military strategist, while his wife laughed and clapped her hands. "What perfect timing!"

Agnes liked Stephanie. She did not see Reynald's wife as a deep thinker, though, and was not surprised that the other woman did not immediately recognize there was nothing accidental about the timing of her scheme. "We've known since the spring that Manuel's illness was mortal. I admit patience has never come easily to me, but this was worth waiting for. The new emperor is Manuel's eleven-year-old son, Alexios, and we can be sure the boy will have far more to worry about than a complaint from a kinswoman he has never even met."

"I assume Mary will be acting as regent?" Reynald had a connection of his own to the imperial court, for Alexios's mother, Mary, was his stepdaughter, one of the children of Constance of Antioch's first marriage. He wondered now if Mary would be up to a challenge of this magnitude. She was a virtual stranger to him; she'd been just thirteen when she'd been sent off to wed Manuel, the same year that he'd been cast into that accursed Aleppo dungeon. Whilst they'd reunited briefly during his diplomatic mission four years ago, all he could say for certes was that she was beautiful and unpopular with her Greek subjects, who scorned her as a foreign barbarian. No, he would not wager money on her chances of steering through the stormy waters ahead. Glancing over at Agnes, he asked if she wanted him to approach the king.

Agnes quickly shook her head. "No, it is better that I be the one to talk to Baldwin. I have the best chance of gaining his consent."

Baldwin and Anselm were playing merels. At the sight of Agnes, her son smiled. "Do you have time for a game of chess, Mother?" He'd taught the basics to Anselm, but his squire's grasp of the game remained too rudimentary to offer much of a challenge.

"Of course." Agnes smiled back, glad to see him in good spirits. "We need to talk first, though." She moved to the window until they finished their game, gazing out at the darkening sky. Anselm won and whooped in glee as he aligned all three of his pieces in a row. Initially, she'd disapproved of the deepening intimacy between them, but no longer. She'd finally recognized that Anselm was utterly devoted to her son and this mattered more than his low birth.

Anselm always found excuses to exit the chamber when she visited and he volunteered now to take Cairo for his evening walk. Once he was gone, Agnes sat on the settle and waited until Baldwin joined her, averting her gaze from his uneven gait. His pallor troubled her, but at least he was no longer running a fever and she took what comfort she could from that. They chatted idly for a while, agreeing that it was past time for Sybilla and Guy to return to Jerusalem and discussing how Manuel's death would affect Joscelin's stay in Constantinople, for they thought it likely that he'd have to renegotiate the treaty with the new government.

Baldwin was already on the alert, for it rarely boded well when his mother announced, "We need to talk." Positioning a cushion behind his back, he braced himself both physically and mentally for whatever was to come. "What do you need to discuss?"

"Isabella. I think it is time to consider a marriage for her."

Baldwin managed to suppress a sigh. "You do remember that Bella is just eight?"

"Of course. I am talking of a plight troth now, marriage once she is older."

"Now, why do I think this is not going to please Maria?" He smiled but she caught the sarcastic undertone and realized she must be utterly honest with him about this marriage. Lying to Baldwin rarely worked.

"I do not deny that Maria's distress will not displease me. I loathe that woman, Baldwin. Yet I swear upon the surety of my soul that our feuding is not the motivation for this plight troth. There is far more at stake than my mistrust of the Greek." Moving closer, she rested her hand on his arm. "You know that I've always seen Isabella as a danger. But I thought that she posed a threat to Sybilla, not to you. That changed with the exposure of the Easter plot by your treacherous cousins. Whilst they failed with Sybilla, that was only because we were warned in time. Why would they not try again with Isabella?"

He did not argue, proving to her that he harbored some of the same anxieties. "What I most fear, Baldwin, is that Bohemond and Raymond might try to wed Isabella to Raymond's stepson Hugues. If they were willing to dethrone an anointed king, why would they have any scruples about her age?"

"That had occurred to me, too," he confided. "I reassured myself that we need not worry about that just yet, given her youth. That may have been foolish, as you point out. I suppose I did not want to think that Maria and Balian might plot against me."

Agnes's relief was so intense that she actually felt light-headed; for once, he was truly listening to her. "What mother would not want her daughter to be queen? Even if we could be sure Maria would never conspire with your cousins, what if they simply abducted the girl? Think how many heiresses have been forced into marriage against their will. It is just too great a risk, Baldwin. Fortunately, there is a way out of this snare, one that secures your kingship and protects Sybilla's position as your heir. It will even protect Isabella."

Baldwin did not exactly roll his eyes at that last comment, but he came close. "And of course, your concern for Bella's welfare is paramount. So . . . tell me, Mother. Whom do you have in mind for her bridegroom?"

"Humphrey de Toron. He is of high birth," she said quickly, "the grandson of a man you and the other Poulains revered. Only Maria and those overweening Greeks would see it as a disparaging union. Our people would be delighted to see Isabella wed to one of our own."

She paused to see if he'd object, was encouraged when he did not. "Moreover, he'd make a good husband for Isabella. He is quite handsome and from all I've heard, he is a kindhearted lad, one who'd treat Isabella very well."

The corner of Baldwin's mouth quirked at that. "Such a 'kindhearted lad' might well make an excellent husband. But few would see that kind heart as a kingly attribute."

"No, they would not," she agreed, so readily that he blinked in surprise. "A marriage to Humphrey would discourage malcontents from rallying around Isabella as a rival to you or Sybilla. He lacks the steel in his spine that a king needs to achieve the mastery of other men. This is why he is such a perfect choice for Isabella. With this marriage, we'd keep her from being used as a pawn against you or Sybilla at the same time that we'd be assuring Isabella's future happiness. I will not pretend that matters to me. I know it matters to you, though. Marrying her to Humphrey will give her a loving, handsome husband whilst sparing our kingdom the risk of a civil war."

"When you put it like that, Mother, who could possibly object? Well, Maria for one, Balian for another."

She never liked it when he used that very dry tone, for it evoked sardonic echoes of Amalric. It hurt to know that her son did not fully trust her. "What can I say, Baldwin? I admitted to you that I will take pleasure in outwitting Maria and sabotaging her ambitions. But what truly matters is that we safeguard your kingship and your sister's right of inheritance. Surely you know by now that there is nothing I would not do for your sake?"

His mouth softened. "Yes, I do know that, Mother."

"There is another reason why I thought this marriage might be agreeable to you, quite apart from its political advantages." She saw his eyebrow arch in a familiar mannerism; only now the eyebrows, like his lashes, had been claimed by the evil that was ravaging his body and she suddenly found herself on the brink of tears. "I remember," she murmured, "what you told me about your deathbed vigil with the constable. You promised him that you'd look out for Humphrey, that you'd do your best for the lad. Do you not think he'd have been pleased to have his grandson marry into the royal family?"

Baldwin did not reply at once, gazing down so she could no longer see his face. "Yes," he said after a long silence. "I think it would have pleased him very much."

Maria and Balian welcomed Baldwin's summons. Yet they were wary, too, for they knew their relationship with the king had been damaged by Baudouin's unwitting involvement in the Easter plot. Now that they were a family of five, travel was more complicated and it took them a while to settle their children after their arrival at their Jerusalem town house. They sent word to the palace that they'd be there in the morning and then decided to pay a visit to William, for he could bring them up to date on happenings in the city and at the court.

Maria nodded gravely as William offered his condolences. Her great-uncle's death was not a deep personal loss, for she'd not seen Manuel since she was thirteen. But it was a political loss for certes. Stripped of the emperor's protection, she felt suddenly vulnerable, and was very grateful to William for having urged her to marry Balian. Not only had that marriage brought her more happiness than she'd ever expected to find in this life, it provided a shield against the de Courtenays' malice.

They had heard, of course, of the recent death of the ailing patriarch, and were dismayed when word reached Nablus that Eraclius had been chosen over William. They did not know more than that, though, and listened indignantly as William told them how Agnes de Courtenay had taken advantage of Baldwin's failing health to gain the patriarchate for her ally.

"That detestable woman has no conscience," William said with a bitterness that they felt was justifiable under the circumstances. "In her own warped way, I do think she loves Baldwin. But she will never put the needs of Outremer before her own selfish ambitions. She is bound and determined to do all she can to make sure the crown passes to Sybilla, and Baldwin seems to pay her more and more heed. Now she is urging him to appoint Amaury de Lusignan as constable."

Balian knew that would infuriate his brother, for Baudouin viewed Amaury's move into the de Courtenay camp as a betrayal. But none could deny that Amaury was well qualified for the post, and it had been vacant far too long, since Humphrey de Toron's tragic death last year. "Well, Amaury is a good commander," Balian pointed out in an attempt to reconcile William to the inevitable. "Whatever their other failings, the de Lusignans seem to make fine soldiers."

William was not impressed. "We can only pray that will prove true for Guy, too."

Baldwin had suffered another serious nosebleed that morning, for his nasal passages were being eroded by his disease. He knew that eventually the cartilage would collapse, yet he dared not let himself think too far ahead; lepers had to learn to take one day at a time if they hoped to save their sanity. Although he was still exhausted when Maria and Balian arrived, he did his best to hide his fatigue and greeted them warmly. He was well aware that they would not welcome his plans for Bella. Whilst he had not been able to banish all his doubts about Baudouin, he had no misgivings about Balian's loyalties and he did not want them to think the proposed plight troth was punitive in any way. If only he could make them see that this was for the good of the kingdom. They could never survive a civil war, not with Saladin awaiting his chance to strike. There were so many nights when he lay awake, fearing what could happen after he died. He was sure that Balian and Maria understood the dangers that Outremer faced. But they were likely to react as parents and how could he blame them?

Once they were seated and courtesies exchanged, Baldwin expressed his sympathies for the emperor's death and they spent some time discussing the ramifications of Manuel's demise. Chaos in the Greek empire would inevitably affect life in Outremer, adding one more worry to the many that weighed him down. One of those worries perched on his shoulder now, reminding him that he could delay this unpleasant task no longer.

"There is no way to ease into this," he said, "for I realize that what I am about to say is bound to come as a shock to you both. That attempted coup at Easter has forced me to think about what lies ahead for us. My cousins in Antioch and Tripoli came dangerously close to succeeding and I do not think they've given up. Now that they can no longer use Sybilla as their pawn, I fear that they may try to use Bella. If they managed to wed her to Raymond's stepson, we could find ourselves facing a civil war. I cannot let—"

"But I would never agree to that marriage!" It was the first time Baldwin had seen Maria's poise crack like that, and he wondered if she realized what was coming. Remembering her manners then, she apologized for interrupting him, then continued quickly before he could respond. "My liege, I can see why you'd feel some unease after what they tried to do with Sybilla. I can put your mind at rest, though. Neither my husband nor I would ever permit Isabella to become entangled in one of their webs."

"I do not doubt your good faith, madame. But sometimes choice does not enter into it. If she were somehow to fall into their hands—by treachery or by force—there would be little you or Lord Balian could do about it. I cannot allow our kingdom to be destroyed by internal conflict. Nor would I ever want to see Bella put at risk. To safeguard her future, to keep her from becoming a pawn, I mean to remove her as a chess piece, to take her off the board."

Maria and Balian exchanged alarmed glances. The convent was not always a refuge; sometimes it offered a cloistered confinement for young women who'd made powerful enemies. Neither of them could envision Baldwin forcing his little sister to take holy vows. But marriage was not an option, either, because of her youth. "I do not understand," Balian said, choosing his words with care. "If you want us to take greater measures to see to Isabella's safety, to make sure she cannot be abducted, we would naturally be quite willing to do so . . ." His sentence did not so much end as trail off, for he sensed that Baldwin had something else in mind.

"I fear that would not be enough. We were able to thwart my cousins' coup only because we wed Sybilla to Guy. If Bella were no longer free to wed—"

This time the protest came in unison, Maria and Balian both exclaiming, "No!" in virtually the same breath. "My daughter is only eight, far too young for marriage!" Balian at once followed Maria's cry from the heart with the reminder that the canonical age for consent was twelve, and Baldwin found himself thinking that they functioned well as a team.

"I know that," he said gently. "I am speaking of a plight troth now, marriage later."

Maria had to draw upon the teachings of a lifetime to maintain her composure. "And who is the man willing to plight his troth to a child?"

"Not a man, a lad of fourteen. Humphrey de Toron."

Maria got to her feet so abruptly that her chair rocked. "I do not want my daughter marrying into that family!"

Baldwin frowned. Assuming she thought a Poulain was not worthy of Bella, he was about to retort that she'd willingly wed Balian, who was a Poulain and not of royal blood. But Maria's objections lay far closer to home. "Humphrey's mother is Agnes de Courtenay's puppet and your mother has always detested Isabella!" Head high, she stared challengingly at Baldwin, as if daring him to deny it and he felt a reluctant twinge of admiration. It was hard to fault a woman for wanting to protect her child.

"I know," he said, with disarming candor. "My mother has always felt irrationally threatened by Bella. But her misguided animosity is not relevant, for I am not doing this to please her. You may not believe me, Maria, when I say that I would never have chosen a husband for Bella who would make her unhappy. It is true, though. I care for my sister and not just because the same blood flows in our veins. She is a sweet, clever child who deserves the best that our world can offer. I believe this marriage will be good for Bella and Humphrey and good for our kingdom. I hope that once you've had time to think upon it, you will see that."

"I do believe you care for Isabella." Maria crossed the few steps separating them and then took Baldwin aback by kneeling before him. "Baldwin, I implore you. Do not do this. Isabella is too young. Look into your heart and then tell me that you truly want to end Isabella's childhood and yoke her to a boy not old enough or strong enough to protect her."

As he listened to her plea, his court mask crumbled. "Of course I do not want to do this," he said softly, sounding so soul weary that she could only listen mutely, mesmerized into silence. "Any of it. I do not want to suspect men I have always thought to be my friends. I do not want to fight battles I cannot hope to win. I do not want the world to watch as my body rots and my own people shrink from me in horror. I do not want to be a crippled king, forced to cling to power when I yearn only for peace. But God gave me no choice, Maria. He placed upon my shoulders the blessed burden of Christ's kingdom. Nothing matters more than the survival of Outremer. I vowed to safeguard it from the day I was anointed with the sacred chrism until the day I draw my last mortal breath."

Baldwin paused then, for this was the only consolation he could offer Maria—utter honesty and the gift of his private pain. When he spoke again, it was in the quiet, controlled tones of the king. "I truly believe that this plight troth will help to keep our kingdom at peace. So there is nothing more to be said."

Balian dismounted in the courtyard, then stepped forward to assist Maria from her mare. As she straightened up, she heard an eager cry of "Mama!" and turned as her daughter came flying from the hall. "I learned how to spin the top! I saw Pateras's squires playing and they said it was not a game for girls but I asked them to teach me." Isabella grinned. "And I beat them at it!"

Maria opened her mouth, but as she looked at her daughter—cheeks flushed, dark eyes sparkling with excitement, a smudge of dirt across her nose—the words caught in her throat. Unable even to fake a smile, she merely nodded and hastened toward the hall. Balian quickly followed, pausing long enough to tell the bewildered Isabella that her mama had a headache and she could show them how to spin the top after dinner.

By the time he reached the hall, Maria had already disappeared. He headed toward the stairwell that led up to their bedchamber, taking the stairs two at a time. Maria was standing in the middle of the room, as if she'd forgotten why she'd rushed abovestairs. As they'd ridden home, she'd not spoken a word, but her rigid

posture, her ashen complexion, and her blank stare had communicated more elo-
quently than any words could have done. She did not respond when he said her
name now; he was not even sure if she'd heard him.

She turned only when he reached out and touched her arm. "We cannot allow
this to happen," she said, sounding like a stranger. He did not know what to say,
for he knew full well that there was no way they could stop it, and the dulled, flattened tone of her voice told him she knew it, too. All he could think to do was to
embrace her, hoping she could find some comfort in sharing their pain.

That was a mistake. She pulled away from him so vehemently that she stumbled. "So you have nothing to say? You are just going to accept it? Would you be so
accepting if it were Helvis?"

He was so shocked that he needed a moment to respond. When he did, it was
with a flare of rare anger. "Isabella is as much my daughter as Helvis and just as
greatly loved. Do you truly doubt that, Maria?"

Sudden color flamed in her pallid cheeks, making her look feverish. She closed
her eyes for a moment, then shook her head. When she swayed, he caught her just
in time and she crumpled against his chest, sobbing so convulsively that her entire
body was trembling. He was more disturbed by her collapse than he'd been by the
unfairness of her accusation, for in the three years of their marriage, not once had
he seen her lose control. Never had he felt so helpless. He could only hold her as
she wept, gently stroking her hair, murmuring despairing endearments, and silently cursing himself for failing her, for failing Isabella.

Isabella was wearing a special gown; it was her favorite color at the moment—
lilac—and was made of silk, the first time she'd been allowed to wear such a luxurious fabric. Normally, she'd have been delighted by this new acquisition; today it
seemed unimportant. She and her nurse, Emma, were sitting in a window seat of
the palace great hall, trying to ignore all the curious eyes upon them. Abovestairs,
her parents and Humphrey de Toron's parents and her brother were going over the
final details of her marriage contract. She was not sure what that involved, knowing only that she'd soon be summoned to plight her troth with a stranger.

She supposed that Humphrey was not truly a stranger since she'd met him
before. But she did not know him. Her mama and Pateras had been trying to pretend that this plight troth was a good thing, that they wanted it for her. She knew
they were lying. On the day they'd returned from the palace, she'd been shaken by
the odd way her mother had acted and she'd followed them, slipping into the

stairwell and trying to listen outside their door. Whilst she was unable to hear what was being said, she could hear their raised voices and she'd never heard them yelling at each other before. What happened next was even more alarming—the sound of her mother's sobs. She could not remember ever hearing Mama cry and now she was weeping as if her heart would break.

Afraid she'd be discovered, Isabella had then crept downstairs. Later they tried to act as if nothing had happened, but she knew something was wrong and it scared her. When they finally told her about this plight troth, she understood why her mother had been crying. Mama and Pateras did not want her to marry Humphrey de Toron. She did not want that, either. She decided she'd talk to Baldwin, tell him that. She'd had no chance to do that, though, for he got sick again. When he felt better, he'd summoned them all to the palace for the plight troth, and now she could only wait with Emma to be recalled to the solar.

She was finding it hard to sit still. Emma understood why she kept squirming and patted her hand, saying it would not be much longer. That did not comfort Isabella, for she did not want to go back up to the solar. She began to chew on her thumbnail even though she'd promised Mama that she'd stop doing that; Mama said it was a bad habit. And then she sat up straight, hiding her bitten nails within the folds of her skirt, for *he* was coming toward them.

Humphrey greeted them both very courteously, even kissing Emma's hand. Isabella thought he might kiss hers, too, so she kept it out of sight. He asked Emma if he could sit with them, but when he noticed how Isabella was fidgeting, he suggested instead that they walk in the gardens whilst they awaited the king's summons. Emma hesitated. Isabella did not, for she did not like the way everyone in the hall was staring at her. Jumping to her feet, she said, "Let's go."

It was a warm autumn day, too warm for cloaks or mantles. Isabella's spirits lifted a little as soon as they escaped the hall. They began to walk along one of the garden pathways, Emma on Isabella's left, Humphrey on her right. Isabella came to an abrupt halt, though, when she saw *that woman* coming toward them. It was the first time that Baldwin's mother had ever smiled at her. Isabella did not find it reassuring and she became even more nervous when she saw that Agnes was stopping. She smiled at Humphrey, too, as if she were truly happy to see him, and offered her congratulations on their plight troth, confusing Isabella, who did not understand why that should matter to Agnes. But Agnes was beaming at them both, saying that they would have such beautiful children together. Humphrey thanked her politely and to Isabella's relief, she then continued on toward the hall.

They resumed walking. Isabella was surprised when Humphrey said, "You do not like Agnes de Courtenay much, do you?"

"I do not like her at all," she said emphatically, and saw him smile.

"I do not like her, either," he confided.

She eyed him curiously. "Do you like my brother Baldwin?"

"Very much," he said, so warmly that she found herself smiling, too. "There is no man in all of Outremer more courageous than King Baldwin." He asked Emma then if he could show them the fish ponds, and she agreed. They walked in silence for a few moments, Isabella glancing at Humphrey from time to time. Catching her at it, he said, with another quick smile, "We do not know each other yet, but I am sure we will find that we have many things in common."

"What things?"

"Well, we both lost our fathers when we were very young. Both of our mothers married again, so we have stepfathers. I've actually had two. Reynald is my mother's third husband."

Isabella was not too interested in his family. "What else do we both like?"

"I love horses and dogs and I've heard that you do, too." She brightened at that, for she enjoyed talking about her pets, and he soon learned that she had a dog called Jordan, a pony named Jericho, and a white mule named Cyprus, and she'd had a lark named Bethany, but it died. Humphrey in turn told her about his greyhound, Robyn, and his palfrey, Smoke, smiling again when she interrupted to say that her stepfather had a palfrey named Smoke, too.

By now they'd reached the fish ponds and Humphrey explained that they were usually stocked with Saint Peter's fish, which were found in the Sea of Galilee, but fish stews often held bream, too, even pike, though they would eat the smaller fish if put in the same pond. "Fish are no different from men," he said, puzzling Isabella, for fish and men seemed utterly unlike to her.

Seeing that Isabella seemed comfortable with Humphrey, Emma had lagged behind. When Humphrey noticed that, he gave her a grateful look, for he had something to say that was meant only for Isabella's ears. "We are alike in another way, Isabella. We are both pawns."

"What is a pawn?"

Picking up a small pebble, he tossed it into the pond. "Do you know how to play chess?" When she shook her head, he promised to teach her. "In a chess game, the pieces are named after the king, queen, bishop, knight, and rook. Pawns are the weakest, least important pieces and are the ones most often sacrificed."

She still did not understand, but nodded when he asked if she did. "We may be pawns, Isabella, yet that does not mean we cannot be friends and allies. I hope that we can."

Isabella thought that over before nodding again. "I would like that."

Just then, they heard running footsteps and a moment later, a man came panting into view. Neither Humphrey nor Isabella had seen him before, yet he'd obviously been searching for them, for he gave a sigh of relief when he spotted them by the fish pond. "The king sent me to find you, my lord Humphrey. You and the Lady Isabella are wanted in the palace solar."

Emma paused at the door, leaving Humphrey and Isabella to enter on their own. Humphrey's mother immediately began to scold him for disappearing, saying sharply that they'd been looking everywhere for them. He flushed and mumbled that he'd been showing Isabella the fish ponds, looking so uncomfortable that Isabella found herself feeling sorry for him. Her parents offered no reprimands, but she found no reassurance in their frozen smiles and anguished eyes. Isabella felt an icy knot forming in her stomach. It had gone away during their walk in the gardens; now it was back. Baldwin looked to her as if he had a stomachache, too, and she thought that the only ones who seemed glad to be here were Humphrey's parents.

Her mother hugged her tightly, explaining that she and Humphrey must clasp hands and repeat the words, "I plight thee my troth." Isabella said she understood, although in truth she did not understand any of this. If this plight troth was making them all so unhappy, why was it being done? But she did not balk, for she sensed that would do no good.

Humphrey took her hand in his and, turning to face her, said slowly and clearly, "I, Humphrey, do plight thee, Isabella, my troth." His back was to the others now and as Isabella dutifully echoed the vow, he winked suddenly and squeezed her hand, reminding her that she was not utterly alone, that they were in this together as friends and allies. Isabella was surprised to find that she could take some comfort from that secret message.

CHAPTER 30

When he received the king's summons, Reynald de Chatillon knew it was because of the turmoil in Antioch. No longer fearing the wrath of the Greek emperor, Prince Bohemond had repudiated his wife, Theodora, and married his longtime concubine, to the dismay of the Church and his vassals. Since he was Bohemond's former stepfather, Reynald expected Baldwin to ask him to intervene, for political unrest in Antioch would inevitably affect the other two Christian realms, Outremer and Tripoli. Upon his arrival at the palace, Reynald ran into Eraclius, for the new patriarch had also been summoned, yet more proof of the depths of Baldwin's concern.

They were escorted up to the king's bedchamber, which usually meant that Baldwin was ailing again. As they expected, he was lying on the bed, although fully dressed. What did startle them was that the chamber was deep in shadows. The windows were still shuttered and only a few candles and a sputtering oil lamp provided illumination. Eraclius and Reynald exchanged a puzzled look, then came forward to greet the king and Agnes, for no one else was present.

They could not make out Baldwin's face, for his bed was situated in the darkest corner of the room. But his voice sounded as it always did, level and dispassionate. "There have been new developments in Antioch. When Bohemond refused to put his concubine aside and take Theodora back, their patriarch excommunicated him."

Eraclius nodded approvingly, not seeing what else the patriarch could have done in the face of Bohemond's defiance of the Church. Reynald was surprised that the patriarch had already gone to one of the Church's most lethal weapons; they were usually the last resort. Thinking that was a sign of weakness, he said skeptically, "And did this bring Bohemond to heel?"

"It only spurred him to greater outrages," Baldwin said grimly. "He retaliated by seizing Church property and carrying off holy relics. Their patriarch responded by laying all Antioch under an interdict." Baldwin shook his head sadly, for the denial of all sacraments except baptism was sure to cause great suffering to the people of Antioch. "The patriarch then retreated to his castle at Cursat, only to have Bohemond lay siege to it."

"Bleeding Christ!" During his fifteen years in an Aleppo dungeon, Reynald had learned who the true enemy was, and he'd vowed to devote the rest of his life to fighting the Saracens if only God would set him free. Before Aleppo, he'd been indifferent to oaths; this one he would never betray. He was furious that Christians would be squabbling amongst themselves like this whilst Saladin continued to consolidate his power. "The damned fools! We have to put a stop to this madness ere it is too late."

"I agree." Baldwin glanced from Reynald to Eraclius. "My lord patriarch, I want you to lead a delegation to Antioch and try to make peace between Bohemond and the Church." His gaze flicked back to Reynald. "I would like you to be part of the delegation, too, my lord, since you were once wed to Bohemond's mother."

Reynald knew how little that would mean to Bohemond, and was sure that Baldwin knew, too. But desperate men grasped at hope the way drowning men gasped for air. "I will do whatever I can."

Eraclius rose to his feet. "There is much to be done. I will take the Bishop of Bethlehem with me." He paused to consider. "The Archbishop-elect of Caesarea, too."

The men were well-respected churchmen, but there was one obvious omission. When he realized that Eraclius did not intend to include the man most qualified for such a diplomatic mission, Baldwin opened his mouth to object, catching himself just in time. He must let Eraclius handle the task as he saw fit, even if that meant unfairly excluding William.

Eraclius's eyes came to rest upon the king's mother, who until now had taken no part in the discussion. He knew neither she nor Baldwin would like what he was about to say, but so be it. Whilst he was grateful to Agnes for her help in securing the patriarchate, he did not feel he was beholden to the de Courtenays, and it might be best to show her that early on.

He bade them farewell, saying he would notify Baldwin when he was ready to depart. Then, he paused. "There is one thing you should know, my lord king. I intend to stop in Tripoli and ask Count Raymond to accompany us to Antioch."

Baldwin's bed was shrouded in shadows. His voice revealed what his face did not, though. "I do not think that is a good idea, my lord."

"Indeed it is not!" Agnes shot Eraclius a look that could have kindled a fire in the hearth. "That man is not to be trusted!"

"I did not say I trusted him, madame," Eraclius said with patronizing patience before turning his attention to the king. "Sire, I understand your misgivings. But the count and Bohemond are more than cousins and friends. They were conspirators in that Easter plot against you. Who would Bohemond be more likely to heed than Raymond?"

Agnes was not convinced. She realized, though, that this was not an argument she could win and she reminded herself that what mattered now was restoring order to Antioch.

Eraclius and Reynald soon departed; Agnes remained behind. She wanted a private conversation with her son, for they'd only had a few moments to talk before the others arrived. She had accompanied her husband back to Sidon after the Christmas festivities and so had not seen Baldwin for nigh on a month. When they were apart for any period of time, she dreaded what she would find upon her return. He was usually evasive about new symptoms and, because of the darkness in the chamber, she'd not even been able to judge for herself how he looked.

"Have you eaten yet, Baldwin?" In the past, when she hovered too much for his liking, he would playfully cluck to remind her that she was acting like a mother hen. Now she got only a noncommittal sound that could have been a yes, a no, or merely the clearing of his throat. But she was determined not to be put off; she knew that some days were harder than others for him, and she feared that today was one of them. Why else would he shut out the sun like this?

"Where is Anselm?" she asked, wanting to send him down to the kitchens for some of Baldwin's favorite foods. When Baldwin said he was walking Cairo, she frowned, thinking this was typical of Anselm, underfoot when he was not wanted, disappearing when he was needed. Well, at least she could do something about this depressing darkness. Striding over to the closest window, she slid back the bar latching the shutters.

"No!" There was such panic in Baldwin's cry that she froze. He'd flung up his arm to shield himself from the surge of sunlight, shouting at her to close the shutters. She complied with difficulty, for her hands had begun to shake. Once darkness had been restored to the chamber, she hastened toward him, but he turned away when she leaned over the bed.

"Baldwin . . . what is wrong? For the love of God, tell me!"

She feared he was not going to answer her. Then he shifted his position, rolling over to face her. "I cannot abide the light."

They were so close now that she could finally see his face; it was deathly white and one of his eyes was obviously inflamed. "Please," she whispered. "Tell me what has happened."

Using his left arm to brace himself, Baldwin sat up. "It began two days ago. I'd been having some discomfort in my right eye and my vision occasionally blurred, but it never lasted long. Then I woke up on Wednesday and when Anselm opened the shutters, I felt as if a dagger had been driven into my eye. It is tolerable as long as I am not exposed to strong light. . . ."

"What did Abū Sulayman Dāwūd say?"

"He confessed that he'd long feared this day might come, though he'd said nothing to me. Whilst lepers often suffer from eye ailments, it does not happen to them all, and he hoped that I'd be spared this. Sometimes a leper loses the ability to blink and the eyes dry up. Sometimes the colored part of the eye—called the iris—becomes infected, as with me, and causes great pain in sunlight. He says there is a Saracen ointment that will ease the pain and he is getting it for me. But he warned that . . . that eventually both eyes will be infected and I will go blind."

Baldwin had spoken without emotion, his voice toneless, his words without inflection, just as on that night when he'd been burned by hot bathwater and realized he did have leprosy. But as he raised his head, she could not keep from crying out, for his eyes betrayed him, revealing the depths of his despair and his terror. She sobbed and then she was clinging to him as if they were both drowning, holding him tightly as he wept against her shoulder.

Baldwin had been determined to celebrate his Easter court in spite of his deteriorating health. With the exception of the Count of Tripoli, who was not welcome in Outremer, and Joscelin and Baudouin, who were still in Constantinople, all of the kingdom's lords and their ladies were in attendance. None commented upon their king's lack of eyebrows or the eye patch he wore during the daylight hours or his shambling gait, at least not in public. And Baldwin soon received positive proof that his vassals remained loyal to him. In Holy Week, word reached Outremer of Pope Alexander's encyclical to his bishops throughout Christendom, in which he'd called for a new crusade. But what reverberated throughout the court and kingdom and generated much anger were the Pope's comments about Baldwin:

> *The king is not such a man as can rule that land, since he, that is to say*
> *Baldwin who holds the government of the realm, is so severely afflicted*

by the just judgment of God, as we believe you are aware, that he is
scarcely able to bear the continual torments of his body.

Upon reading that, Baldwin felt as if he'd been punched in the stomach without warning. Since he'd been stricken with the scourge of leprosy as a child, he'd
never believed that the Almighty was punishing him for past sins. Yet now the
Pope himself was proclaiming that his suffering was the "just judgment of God."
Baldwin forced himself to go about his usual duties, and soon saw that his subjects
were united in their outrage, utterly rejecting the Pope's harsh verdict. Even their
prelates and churchmen and priests shared the universal condemnation, and when
he was cheered as he rode through the city streets, Baldwin was deeply thankful
that his people understood even if the Pope did not.

Sybilla and Guy did not arrive until Easter eve, and while some faulted them
for missing the solemn ceremony of Tenebrae, the Maundy Thursday almsgiving,
and creeping to the cross on Good Friday, most were happy to see them, late or not.

It was Baldwin's hope that with this visit, he could at last take Guy's measure.
Why was Guy so hard to read? The outer packaging was reassuring, for he was
handsome and well-mannered and had so far shown few of the flaws so common
to sons of Adam. But what of the man's heart and mind? Baldwin supposed they
must wait until Guy's mettle was tested in the council chamber and on the battlefield, trying to ignore the seditious inner voice whispering that by then, it would
be too late, that it was already too late for second thoughts or belated qualms.

Baldwin smiled at the sight of his sister, for Sybilla radiated a bridal glow even
after a year of marriage. She'd brought her son, Baldwin's namesake; he was in his
fourth year and bore a distinct resemblance to his late father. Baldwin refused to
let himself dwell upon what might have been had Guillaume not succumbed to
hectic fever and welcomed them with as much energy as he could muster up. Sybilla returned his greetings warmly, although she took care to make sure young
Baldwin did not get too close to his royal uncle. Baldwin did not fault her for that
and they were all relieved when the little boy's nurse ushered him from the
chamber.

Agnes and Denys had trailed in after Sybilla and Guy. Anselm could offer them
nothing to eat or drink as Holy Saturday was a strict fast day, so they plunged at
once into animated conversation. After Sybilla and Guy had related a lighthearted
account of their journey from Ascalon, finishing each other's sentences in the habit

of the long married or the still infatuated, Baldwin told them of the news from Antioch.

"Patriarch Eraclius and the delegation had some success. Eraclius convinced their patriarch to lift the interdict and Reynald talked Bohemond into returning the Church property he'd confiscated." Baldwin paused, yet fairness compelled him to add reluctantly that Count Raymond had been of considerable help in gaining Bohemond's cooperation.

Baldwin then revealed that a stalemate existed over Bohemond's marriage. "He still refuses to repudiate his concubine and take Theodora back. Until he does, the patriarch will not absolve him from the excommunication edict. Bohemond apparently finds that acceptable, although few of us could imagine sacrificing salvation for the sake of a woman."

"It would depend upon the woman," Guy quipped and Sybilla gave a low, throaty laugh. Agnes, Denys, and Baldwin did not share her amusement; while a happy marriage might be the ideal, people preferred not to have one flaunted in their faces by the fortunate husband and wife.

"I wish I also had good news to share from Constantinople," Baldwin resumed. "But their boy emperor is running into trouble even faster than we'd all feared. Last month a plot was discovered against his government, led by his own half sister. The *protosebastos* and the emperor's mother, Mary, ordered the arrest of the plotters. The lad's sister and her husband then sought sanctuary in Sancta Sophia Cathedral."

Sybilla and Guy declared their sympathy for the young emperor, but Baldwin was worried that they did not fully grasp the ramifications of this tumult in the Greek empire. The Emperor Manuel had cast a protective shadow over Outremer. Now that there was no longer hope for military aid or money from Constantinople, Baldwin was acutely aware of his kingdom's vulnerability and he wished he could be sure that his sister and brother-in-law also understood that. He'd already discussed this with them during his Christmas court, though, and he did not want to appear as if he was lecturing them.

It was then that his mother spoke up. "Did you hear what the Pope did, Sybilla?" Agnes was still seething; the mere mention of Alexander's name could send her into a wild rage. Needing to share her indignation with her daughter, she quickly told Sybilla and Guy about the Pope's cruel attack upon her son.

Sybilla was shocked and then, furious. "How dare he say that? Baldwin was ten years old when he was infected with leprosy. What mortal sins could a ten-year-old commit?"

Baldwin wished his mother had not brought up the Pope's condemnation. He wanted only to forget those hateful words, even though he knew they were engraved upon his heart. But he was touched by his sister's robust defense. How lucky he was that his family and friends and most of his subjects had never seen his disease as God's punishment.

Sybilla and Agnes were taking turns denouncing the Pope for his lack of mercy and common sense. When she realized that her husband had so far remained quiet, Sybilla sought to bring him into the conversation. He was part of their family now, and she wanted her mother and brother and stepfather to value his opinions as much as she did. "Did you ever expect to hear such mean-spirited foolishness coming from a Pope's mouth, darling?"

Guy hesitated, then agreed that the Pope had indeed misspoken. But for the span of seconds, his guard had been down and Baldwin thought he saw something troubling in the other man's eyes. Did Guy agree with the Pope? Did he also see leprosy as a "just judgment" from God? Striving to be fair, Baldwin told himself that Guy could hardly be blamed if so, for that view was commonly held in other Christian lands and Guy had grown up in France. Baldwin found it so upsetting, though, that he chose to believe he was wrong, that he'd been led astray by his own feverish imagination. Guy was his brother by marriage now, the man who would rule with Sybilla after his death, and surely he deserved the benefit of the doubt.

Balian had paid a courtesy call upon the commander of the Templar commandery at Acre and was pleased to encounter Jakelin afterward. Jakelin was leaving to deliver a message to the city's viscount and Balian offered to accompany him, as this would give them a chance to catch up; Templars led such structured lives that they had little free time for themselves.

When Jakelin wanted to know what had brought him to Acre, Balian explained that he was there to await Baudouin's arrival from Constantinople and would be in the city for about a fortnight. "My brother wrote that he expected to reach Acre in mid-August. I brought his little lad with me, for he's missed his father sorely; Baudouin has been gone for nigh on a year."

Balian smiled, then. "Thomasin is a handful. I hope that my Johnny will not have such a talent for mischief when he reaches Thomasin's age. I left my squires to watch over him today until I get back, much to their horror. How is it that women make caring for children seem so easy?"

Jakelin still found it hard to envision Balian as the father of three. "Your lady did not accompany you?" he asked in surprise, for he knew Balian and Maria were rarely apart.

"Alas, no." Balian eased his palfrey as a beggar appeared beside him, fumbling in his scrip to toss the man a coin. "Maria is with child again and did not feel up to making such a long journey, especially in the heat of summer." He was no longer smiling. "In truth, Jake, it has not been an easy pregnancy so far. Her morning sickness has been much more severe than when she was carrying Helvis and Johnny."

Jakelin knew little of pregnancies, but he caught the echoes of anxiety in Balian's voice and offered the only comfort he could, a promise to pray for Maria's health and a safe birthing when her time came. They were on Cypress Street by now, skirting the Venetian Quarter. They were about to turn onto the street that led north toward their destination, the city citadel, when they heard a sudden, shrill cry. Glancing in the direction of the sound, they saw a woman waving wildly to attract their attention.

As they reined in their mounts, she picked up her skirts and ran out into the street to intercept them. "Lord Balian, oh, thank God! I could scarcely believe my good fortune when I saw you ride by!" She was past her youth and her gown was of good-quality cotton, but her profession was obvious, for no respectable woman would show so much décolletage or use so much rouge and powder. She looked vaguely familiar to them both. Balian had a sharper memory than Jakelin and he was the first to remember; this was the bawd who'd run one of Acre's better bordels during the early years of their friendship, long before Jakelin had taken holy vows as a Templar and he had wed a queen. After a moment, he even remembered her name: Clarice.

"Please help me, my lords! He has been swilling wine for two days and he's so drunk there is no reasoning with him! He has destroyed all the furniture in his chamber and when another customer complained about the noise, he threw the man down the stairs. None of my girls are willing to go back in there, but he'll soon want one again and what can I tell him?"

Balian and Jakelin exchanged bemused looks. "I am sorry, Clarice," Balian said politely, for he'd never thought that courtesy was only for those of high birth. His brothers and friends had occasionally teased him about his misguided chivalry, but it had made him very popular during his youthful forays into bawdy houses. "I do not see how we can help. You need to ask the authorities to deal with this disruptive drunkard. Brother Jakelin and I are on our way to see the viscount. If you like, we can ask him to send a few of his men to restore the peace."

"I dare not do that, my lord. He is not just another customer but a man of great importance." Glancing around uneasily, she edged closer to Balian's palfrey before revealing the identity of the "disruptive drunkard," the marshal of the kingdom, Gerard de Ridefort.

Balian bit down on his lip to stifle a laugh and Jakelin suddenly had to cough. Clarice waited tensely as they sought to camouflage their mirth. "You can see why I cannot have him arrested. He'd never forgive me for shaming him like that and I cannot afford to have him as my enemy. But if we cannot get rid of him, he's bound to start more fights with my other customers or hurt one of my girls. Please, Lord Balian. Who else can I turn to?"

She clasped her hands, gazing up imploringly into Balian's face, her mouth trembling, her eyes moist. Balian was not naïve; he well knew that softhearted bawds were as rare as dragon's teeth. But he'd never learned how to resist a woman's tears. Heaving a sigh, he swung reluctantly from the saddle. "Come on, Jake, let's get this over with."

"Have you lost your wits?" Jakelin was staring at him, incredulous. "I am a Templar, Balian, cannot go into a bawdy house!"

"Even on a mission of mercy?"

"That does not matter. If I were to be seen entering a bordel, I could be expelled from the order. At the least, I could lose my habit and have to do a year of harsh penance. I cannot take a risk like that, Balian."

Balian sighed again. "No, I do not suppose you can," he agreed, handing his reins to Jakelin, and signaling for Clarice to lead the way. He just hoped that Baudouin would not find out about this, for his brother would never let him live it down.

The common room was crowded with Clarice's whores and their customers, intent upon the drama at hand. Balian did not recognize any of the women, but he'd not been here for years and there was surely a high turnover in their precarious profession. "I assume you have a hireling to help you handle the drunks," he said and Clarice gestured toward two men, one heavyset, the other tall and skinny, neither showing any enthusiasm for facing down a powerful lord. When Balian beckoned, they approached slowly, going no farther than the stairwell. Clarice had told him which chamber was Gerard's and Balian shoved the door open, then waited. Nothing happened and he stepped inside. The stench hit him at once: the musky scent of sex mixed with vomit, sweat, urine, and wine. The light was poor, for the window was shuttered, and the August heat was stifling. The bed was rumpled, the sheet stained and ripped. Near the door, a chamber pot had been overturned, broken furniture lay scattered in the sodden floor rushes, and empty flagons were everywhere. Gerard had been holed up in this sty for two days?

Moving farther into the room, Balian called out Gerard's name, then whirled as he thought he caught movement in the shadows. A figure was slumped against the far wall, legs spread out, head lolling back, mouth agape. For a moment, Balian feared the man was dead, but then he heard the wheezing. Not dead, dead-drunk. "Why me, Lord?" he asked aloud. Getting no answer from the Almighty, he braced himself for the unpleasant task at hand.

Gerard did not stir even when Balian leaned over and shook his shoulder. Striding to the door, he shouted for Clarice's hirelings. Once they saw that Gerard was unconscious, they responded to Balian's orders with alacrity, eager to get the marshal out of their bordel before he woke up. One man went to fetch Gerard's horse from the stable while the other one helped Balian drag Gerard to his feet. He mumbled a few times, but he did not seem fully aware of his surroundings or the men holding him upright. He was a dead weight, and both Balian and the hireling were swearing and sweating by the time they maneuvered him down those narrow stairs.

Once they reached the common room, Balian shoved Gerard onto the closest bench, grabbing him in time to keep him from toppling to the floor. Balian accepted a cup of wine from Clarice as they waited for her man to bring Gerard's horse around to the street, and decided he'd stop at the public baths, wanting to wash away the stink as soon as possible.

"I've never seen a man drink so much. It was like he was a bottomless pit." The speaker was so scantily clad that Balian lost control of his eyes for a moment. She grinned and he could not help grinning back. She was young, with a tumble of ash-blond hair, a sharp intelligence gleaming in the depths of greenish-blue eyes, and an ugly bruise angling across one cheekbone. When Balian asked if Gerard had done that, she gave a nonchalant nod.

"My face got in the way of his fist. He'd never done that on past visits. But he'd never gotten so besotted before." She regarded Gerard impersonally, with neither hostility nor sympathy, showing more interest as her eyes appraised Balian. "You want to go abovestairs for a quick one? Clarice said there's no charge."

"I think I'd best get Gerard out of here ere he comes to and starts another brawl."

She shrugged and her gaze shifted back to Gerard, who'd begun to snore. "When he sobers up, tell him he is still welcome here." She caught Balian's expression and shrugged again. "I've been with worse. He pays for what he gets without trying to want more for free like some do. But he was already in his cups when he showed up, raving and ranting like a madman about being betrayed, cheated of a rich heiress by some count."

Balian studied her with sudden interest, for her words had triggered a memory of old gossip about Gerard. What was it? Ah, yes, that Count Raymond had promised to give Gerard the next available heiress in his domains. "This count . . . was it the Count of Tripoli?"

"Yes, that's the one! It was quite a tale. As best I could make out, a lord died and Gerard expected to marry his daughter. But a Pisan merchant wanted her, too, and he offered the count the girl's weight in gold. So the count gave the girl to him instead of Gerard." She laughed at the sheer absurdity of a world in which such things could happen. "I can see why the count would snatch at that offer. Yet it may be a bad bargain, for he's earned himself an enemy he'll not want. That one," she said, pointing to Gerard, "will nurse a grudge to the grave and beyond."

Balian agreed with her, but that was Count Raymond's concern. Clarice was signaling to let him know Gerard's horse was outside. On impulse, he reached for the girl's hand and kissed it in his best courtly manner. She looked startled and a little pleased, giving him a come-hither look that was almost sincere, waving as he and the hireling hauled Gerard toward the door.

Jakelin was still waiting, not happily, grumbling impatiently as Balian and Clarice's men tried in vain to rouse Gerard so he could mount his horse. "How do you always manage to drag me into craziness like this, Balian? Just throw him over the saddle and let one of the men ride behind him so he does not fall off."

Jakelin's suggestion actually worked and Gerard was soon draped over his horse like a large sack of flour with one of the men perched on the palfrey's haunches, no longer an unwilling accomplice after Balian tossed him a few coins. Then Jakelin asked an awkward question. "Now what? What do we do with him?"

That gave Balian pause. After a moment to reflect, he flashed a wicked smile. "Amaury de Lusignan has a town house in Acre. Since Gerard has just joined the de Courtenays' feud against the Count of Tripoli, we'll let Amaury deal with his new ally."

Baudouin returned from Constantinople with a promise from the new government to honor Manuel's agreement to pay his ransom. He also brought gossip that was undeniably entertaining but troubling to those hoping for stability and peace in the Greek empire. Manuel's will had compelled his widow to take holy vows in order to retain custody of their son, and Mary had soon shown herself to be a very unwilling nun. The new *protosebastos* was Maria's uncle. He was also arrogant, avaricious, and excelled at making enemies, who then became Mary's enemies, too, for it was widely believed that they were lovers. Baudouin's assessment of the Greek empire was both pithy and alarming. It was, he said, "a sinking ship." Joscelin reached Outremer not long afterward, and he was equally pessimistic, warning Baldwin that their kingdom could expect no help from the Greeks in their struggle against Saladin.

It had been a brutal summer for the Egyptians, one of searing heat and continuing drought. The coming of winter at least offered a respite from the soaring temperatures, if not from the drought, and made it easier for people to observe the holy fast during the month of Ramadān, when all devout Muslims must refrain from food and drink from sunrise to sunset. Fasting was one of the Five Pillars of Islam and a cause of concern to al-ʿĀdil, for his young wife Āliya was in the fourth month of a pregnancy that had been difficult so far.

Returning to his residence in the Lesser Palace at al-Qāhira, he found her resting in her bedchamber, attended by Jumāna and Jawhara, a new slave skilled in midwifery and childbirth. Āliya's face lit up at the sight of her husband and she would have risen to greet him had he not objected. Even her heart-stopping beauty could not hide the signs of stress; she was very pale, her eyes deeply shadowed and narrowed, as they did whenever she was stricken with a headache. Having two wives and several concubines, al-ʿĀdil had considerable experience with pregnancy. A woman with child usually had a round, full face, but Āliya's was drawn, almost gaunt. Leaning over the bed, he took her hand, yet refrained from kissing her, for that was forbidden during the hours of fasting. Despite the warmth of the room, her skin was cold to the touch and he felt a throb of relief that he'd realized her danger in time.

"I spent the morning consulting with imams, Āliya, and they all agree that a pregnant woman need not fast during Ramadān if that fast could harm her or her child." When she started to protest, he gently put his finger to her lips. "I also spoke to several doctors, and they, too, agreed that it can be dangerous for a woman with child to go from dawn till dusk without even a sip of water. They told me that the symptoms of severe thirst include headaches, cramps, fatigue, and dizziness, all of which you've suffered since you began the fast."

Āliya could deny none of it, nor that her body desperately craved fluids. But fasting was a sacred obligation for all Muslims. "Other women have been able to do it, Ahmad." Although she got along well with his first wife, she occasionally felt a rivalry pang, and she could not help adding, "Halīma has fasted during Ramadān whilst she was with child."

"And you may be able to do so, too, but not this time, Ghazāla." As he hoped, his use of that pet name made her smile. Thinking it was lucky that she'd given birth to their daughter a fortnight before Ramadān began and that the timing of their son's birth had also spared her a Ramadān fast, he told Jawhara to have the cooks prepare a meal for Āliya and to fetch dates and pomegranate juice at once. Then, he tried to ease Āliya's qualms by reminding her that those unable to fast during Ramadān could make it up later and, although she need not pay the *fidyah*, he would right gladly do so, feeding the hungry for each missed fast day.

Her conscience assuaged, Āliya lay back against the pillows, and when Jawhara returned with the dates and drink, she gratefully gulped the juice, even nibbled at a few dates to please Ahmad, although food had become the enemy in this pregnancy. He soon had her laughing, relating the latest rumors he'd heard in the souk, and teasing that people were saying women were giving birth to twins in unusually high numbers this year.

After drinking another glass of juice, Āliya confided that she was feeling better. "Will you be seeing Yūsuf this afternoon? When do you think he'll be hearing that Aleppo is ours?"

Aleppo was on al-'Ādil's mind, too. The news had caught them by surprise. When Nūr al-Dīn had died, leaving his eleven-year-old son, al-Sālih, as his heir, Yūsuf had seized his chance and was soon the sultan of Egypt. Whilst al-Sālih was too young to offer a serious challenge, he remained a threat, a rallying point for Yūsuf's enemies. But al-Sālih had suddenly been taken ill two months ago and died eighteen days later. On his deathbed, he'd bequeathed Aleppo to his cousin, 'Izz al-Dīn, amir of Mosul. Yūsuf had acted swiftly, ordering Taqī al-Dīn and Farrukh-Shāh to keep 'Izz al-Dīn from reaching Aleppo. He had set up relays of carrier pigeons to get word as soon as possible and then the most difficult part began—the waiting.

"We ought to be hearing soon," al-'Ādil assured Āliya, smiling, for once they controlled Aleppo, the Franks would be surrounded, and after Yūsuf defeated the last of his Muslim enemies, he could turn his attention to fulfilling his promise of jihad against the Franks. Al-'Ādil did not share his brother's zeal for jihad; he was a pragmatist at heart and thought it was easier to coexist with the infidels than to try to destroy them. But he understood that Yūsuf's frequent use of jihad as justification for attacking fellow Muslims had run up a debt, one that would eventually become due. Already there were those who questioned why he'd continued to make truces with the Franks, others who called his sincerity into question because of those truces.

Al-'Ādil began to discuss the coming nuptials in the spring, at which time four of his daughters would be wed to four of Yūsuf's sons, demonstrating to all that the bond between brothers went beyond blood. This public proof of Yūsuf's trust would discourage the overly ambitious from seeking to undermine his position as the sultan's governor in Egypt, and he'd been honored when his brother had suggested it. Āliya was just as pleased, for their daughter was to be one of the brides. Given the extreme youth of the children, the marriages would not affect their lives for years to come. But these unions were a powerful pledge of unity, a means of protecting the future of their dynasty, one founded by Kurdish outsiders who'd once been scorned by the caliphs of Egypt and Baghdad.

He saw that Āliya was tiring and he had risen to go when a eunuch came in search of him, saying he had been urgently summoned by the sultan. Al-'Ādil and Āliya shared a smile, the same thought in both their minds: At last! This would be a historic day, one that would long be remembered—the seventh day of the ninth month of Ramadān in the year 577. He paused to mentally calculate the Christian calendar, for this would be a significant day for their kingdom, too. The fourteenth day of their month of January in the year 1182. The date that marked the beginning of the end for the Franks now that Aleppo had fallen to Yūsuf.

The sultan was not alone, attended by 'Imād al-Dīn, his chancellor; al-Fādil, his vizier; and 'Īsā al-Hakkari, who'd only recently regained his freedom after his capture at Montgisard. Al-'Ādil's excitement faded, for he was sensitive to his surroundings and there was no joy in this room. His brother was standing by a window, his back to the door. He turned only after al-'Ādil said his name, and the younger man drew a sharp breath. "Yūsuf, what is wrong?"

"Seventeen days ago, 'Izz al-Dīn rode into the city of Aleppo, where he was acclaimed as its lord and given control of the citadel and the treasury."

Al-'Ādil gasped. How could that have happened? Taqī al-Dīn was not always reliable, too headstrong and hot-tempered. But Farrukh-Shāh was as dependable as the tides and the moon. How could they both have failed to keep 'Izz al-Dīn from claiming Aleppo?

He saw the pain in his brother's face and realized he must be suffering from one of his periodic attacks of colic. So he put his questions to the others and they were the ones to tell him. Farrukh-Shāh had been unable to provide Taqī al-Dīn with the expected reinforcements, for he'd had to race south into Outrejourdain to deal with the Frankish lord they called Prince Arnat, Reynald de Chatillon. And without his brother's aid, Taqī al-Dīn did not have enough men to intercept 'Izz al-Dīn.

Al-'Ādil glanced from one grim face to another, then back toward his brother. As great a disappointment as this was, it was a setback, not a defeat. "Although this is regrettable," he said slowly, "'Izz al-Dīn can still be dealt with. Unless . . . is there more to this than you've told me?"

His brother moved away from the window and he saw that he'd misread the older man's expression. It was not pain. It was rage, a rage he'd never seen Yūsuf display before. "Farrukh-Shāh made the right decision," he said, and al-'Ādil blinked in surprise that he'd not called their nephew by his family name, Da'ud. This was the sultan he was facing, not the affectionate brother or indulgent uncle.

"Arnat dared to do what we once thought unthinkable. He led a raid across the Sinai and into the Hijāz, the very heart of Islam. He advanced as far as Tabuk and was on the road to Medina and Mecca when he learned that Farrukh-Shāh had invaded Outrejourdain and was burning and pillaging around al-Karak to draw him back to defend his own lands. Allah be praised, it did."

Al-'Ādil was stunned. Their spies had warned them months ago that Arnat was planning to break the truce, but they'd never imagined he had an undertaking so audacious, so outrageous in mind. If he'd not been forced to return to protect al-Karak, could he have reached Medina, where the Prophet was buried? Or Mecca, the holiest of cities, birthplace of the Prophet, site of the most sacred of mosques, al-Masjid al-Haram, and the Kaa'ba, the House of Allah? The loss of Aleppo, great as it was, paled into insignificance when compared to sacrilege like this.

"What will you do now, Yūsuf?"

The sultan was silent for a time, almost as if he were listening to a voice only he could hear. "This man Arnat is the most dangerous of all the infidel Franks and he will answer for his infamy. This I swear by the greatness of Allah, that the day will come when I slay him with my own hand."

CHAPTER 31

February 1182
Nablus, Outremer

H umphrey de Toron's nervousness increased as they approached Nablus. He'd done all he could to avoid inconveniencing Isabella's parents; he'd waited until after her actual birthday so he'd not intrude upon their family celebration and he planned to lodge his men in a local inn rather than expecting Balian and Maria to provide shelter for them. Yet he knew that his visit would not be welcomed. They would be civil; Balian might even be amiable. But the marriage was as distasteful to them today as it had been fifteen months ago. He could only hope that Bella did not share their reluctance. At least they would not attempt to poison her mind against him, as his own mother would have done in similar circumstances.

He glanced over at his squire, who was carrying Bella's birthday gifts. Not all squires were young or apprentice knights; Ivo was a dour man of middle age, chosen for Humphrey on his fifteenth birthday. He was sure that Ivo acted as his mother's informant; he doubted that his stepfather would have bothered to spy on him. He hoped Bella would be pleased with her presents, pleased with him. He very much wanted this marriage to take place, for it would be a great honor to be King Baldwin's brother by marriage. He knew, too, that his parents would blame him if the plight troth was broken. He'd also become very fond of his young betrothed. Bella was a sweet little lass and he wanted her to be willing to wed him when that day eventually arrived. It would be wretched to have a wife loath to share his life and his bed.

After sending his men to the inn, he continued on to the palace, accompanied only by Ivo. Balian was awaiting him on the steps of the great hall. After dismounting, Humphrey launched into a hasty explanation of his visit, gesturing toward the wicker birdcage and the chess set wrapped in a linen cloth. "Bella told me that she'd once had a tame lark, so I thought she might like another one. And I promised that I would teach her to play chess. . . ."

As always, the boy's unease evoked a flicker of sympathy. But Balian wanted to respect Bella's future husband, not pity him. "I am sure Bella will be delighted with the gifts." Taking Humphrey into the great hall, he dispatched a servant to fetch Isabella. Humphrey had also brought a gift for his hostess, several jars of Maria's favorite wine, and Balian offered thanks on her behalf before explaining, "My wife will not be able to bid you welcome, Humphrey. Her birth pangs began during the night and she is sequestered with the midwife and her ladies."

Humphrey stared at him in dismay. While he'd known that Maria was pregnant, he'd not realized that she was so close to the birthing. "I am so . . . so sorry," he stammered. "I will not stay, of course, for you've no need of guests at such a time. I will leave the gifts and—"

"Actually, lad, your arrival is a blessing of sorts. At ten, Bella is old enough to understand the dangers of the birthing chamber. I'd be grateful if you can distract her, keep her from dwelling upon her fears for her mother."

Humphrey nodded solemnly. "Of course I will." He hesitated then. "Lord Balian . . . may I have a few moments in private with you first? There are some things you need to know."

It had been Balian's experience that no good ever followed a sentence that contained the words "things you need to know." But he also knew that such revelations were almost impossible to avoid and so he led Humphrey toward the stairs.

Humphrey waited until they were alone in the solar. "You know, of course, about the raid that my stepfather made into the Hijāz. At that time, he also captured a rich Saracen caravan on its way from Egypt to Damascus and Saladin has demanded its return, reminding King Baldwin that their truce is still in effect. When the king ordered Reynald to release those taken prisoner and to make restitution for the goods seized, Reynald balked. King Baldwin is understandably furious at his defiance, but Reynald . . . he does not care."

Humphrey's distress was obvious in his reluctance to meet Balian's gaze. What was equally obvious was the reason for his anxiety. The boy feared that Baldwin might be angry enough to punish Reynald by repudiating the plight troth.

Balian frowned. If Reynald could get away with defying a royal command, other lords would be tempted to do the same if their own interests were threatened. He was not surprised by Reynald's boldness, merely surprised that it had not occurred sooner. How long could a dying king command obedience from his vassals?

"Baldwin will neither forget nor forgive. But Reynald's disgrace will not affect you, Humphrey, for the plight troth was not meant to please Reynald and your mother. The king sees it as a way to honor the memory of a man he greatly respected."

"My grandfather?" When Balian nodded, Humphrey drew his first easy breath since his stepfather had dared to flout the royal will. "So I need not fear that the king will blame me for Reynald's betrayal?"

"I am sure you do not," Balian assured him, for Baldwin knew full well that the lad was utterly under Reynald's thumb even though he was now of legal age.

"Thank God," Humphrey said, so softly that Balian could not tell if the words were meant for him. But then the youngster raised his head, meeting Balian's eyes for the first time. "There is more, my lord. My inheritance concerns you and Queen Maria since it will one day affect Bella, too. You have the right to know that the king has commanded me to exchange my hereditary lands of Toron and Chastelneuf for a money fief of seven thousand Saracen bezants."

Balian's eyes narrowed as he considered Baldwin's action. It would not be detrimental to Isabella's future, for the money fief was a generous one, and Humphrey would still inherit the lordship of Outrejourdain from his mother, one of the largest fiefs in Outremer. But why would Baldwin do this? "Did Baldwin explain to you why this must be done, Humphrey?"

The boy nodded. "He said the kingdom's northern borders could be better defended if Toron and Chastelneuf joined Beirut as Crown lands."

Balian supposed there was some truth in that. But as he called up a mental map of the castles, it occurred to him that Beirut, Toron, and Chastelneuf formed a barrier between Tripoli and Tiberias. Jesus wept! Could Baldwin's action be aimed not at Saladin but at Count Raymond? He knew Baldwin no longer trusted the count. Could his distrust go as deep as that?

No woman ever faced the birthing chamber without some fear. During her past lying-ins, though, Maria had been blessed to have a midwife in whom she had complete faith. When she was pregnant with Isabella, she'd asked Amalric to find a midwife whose native tongue was Greek. Dame Agathe had safely delivered Isabella and then the doomed Melisende, helping to ease Maria's grief after the baby's death. So, after she married Balian, Maria had arranged for Agathe to come from Jerusalem for her lying-ins with Helvis and John, and she'd wanted Agathe to attend her again when this baby was due. But the older woman had been stricken with a recurring ague fever, leaving her unable to travel, and forcing Maria to engage a stranger.

Dame Odile was a well-spoken, handsome woman who was said to be the most popular midwife in Nablus. She was pleasant, reassuring, and seemed very knowledgeable. It was just that they had no history, and Maria had not yet learned to trust her. Nor was Maria pleased by the presence of Mary de Brisebarre, sister to the notorious Brisebarre brothers, Walter and Guidon. Mary meant well, making a special trip to Nablus so she could attend Maria during her lying-in; she was a talker, though, and her nonstop chatter soon wore on Maria's nerves. But she was family now, Baudouin's new wife and therefore Maria's new sister-in-law.

Fortunately, Maria was attended, too, by Balian's niece, Etiennette; by Dame Alicia, her French-speaking lady; and by Isabella's governess, Dame Emma. Realizing that Lady Mary was more of a hindrance than a help, they took turns distracting her while Odile monitored the dilation of Maria's womb and assured her that it would not be much longer, even predicting she would be delivered of a son. So far, all had gone as expected. The pangs had progressed as they ought while Maria paced, sipped wine mixed with feverfew, and prayed silently to Greek Orthodox saints said to protect women in childbirth.

Maria was relieved when her waters broke, for that usually meant the birth was drawing nigh. Her women stripped her of her wet chemise, replacing it with a dry one, and placed a blanket around her shoulders when she sat back on the birthing stool, for she'd begun to feel cold. Odile knelt and raised Maria's skirt. "The mouth of your womb will soon be fully opened, madame." She sounded so pleased that Maria knew she was already anticipating the benefits she'd gain once word spread that she had a queen's favor.

Odile had anointed her hands in thyme oil and her touch was gentle; Maria still found it intrusive. Bracing herself for those probing fingers, she closed her eyes. But then she heard the midwife's gasp. "What? Is something wrong?"

Odille's face had gone the color of newly skimmed milk. She tried to offer a reassuring smile, but it turned into a grimace that sent a chill up Maria's spine. "The baby has shifted position in your womb."

Now it was Maria who gasped, for every woman knew babies must be delivered headfirst, that when one was malpositioned, the birthing could result in the death of both mother and child. "What . . . what happens now?"

Odile's initial shock had eased and this time her smile was more convincing. "I must nudge the little one back into the proper position," she said, making it sound like a foregone conclusion, and Maria grasped gratefully at her certainty.

Ignoring the frightened looks on the faces of the other women, she told Odile to do what she must. The pain was greater than she'd expected, different from birth pangs, and she had to bite her lip to keep from crying out. Odile made two attempts to shift the baby, both attempts failing. She finally sat back on her heels when blood began to trickle down Maria's thighs. "It is no use. He will not budge."

Maria found it hard to swallow. "Can the baby still be delivered?"

Odile summoned up another smile. "Of course, my lady! I've usually been able to turn them in the womb, but I've also delivered babies that came rump first, even feet first."

"And the mothers, the babies? Did they all live?"

Odile's smile held firm. "They did." But as their eyes met, Maria knew that she lied.

Balian hated the tradition banning men from the birthing chamber, for he found it impossible to wait patiently for word, not when his wife's and child's lives were at risk. So, as a compromise, Emma or Alicia would periodically seek him out to assure him that nothing was amiss. But it had been a while since he'd gotten one of these reassuring updates, and when he could endure it no longer, he left the hall and swiftly mounted the stairs to Maria's chamber. An apology for the intrusion was already forming on his lips as the door opened a crack. When it opened wider and the midwife slid out to join him in the stairwell, his heart skipped a beat. Why had she not sent Emma out? Why would she leave Maria unless something was wrong?

"I was about to call for you, my lord. Your lady's baby has turned in the womb and I could not get it back into the natural position." Not sure how much he understood of the birthing process, Odile hesitated before confessing, "It is very dangerous to deliver a baby like this. Often the baby dies and the mother can die, too. I need you to go into the town for another midwife, my lord. Maud is the only one I know who has had much luck in delivering malpositioned babies. But . . . but she might not come if I ask, for she resents me for my success. Her practice has fallen off since I moved to Nablus and she thinks I've spread falsehoods about her, which is not true—"

"Enough! Just tell me where I can find her."

"She has a house by the new hospital of the Hospitallers, across from the souk." Odile wanted to warn him that Maud could be difficult. He gave her no chance, though. Leaning against the wall, she listened to the thud of his boots on the stairs. He had to bring the old woman back with him; he had to convince her! Having to ask her rival for help was so very hard. But if the baby or—God forbid—the queen could not be saved, at least she'd not have to bear all the blame; it would be Maud's fault, too.

When Odile reluctantly admitted she'd sent for a second midwife, Maria's initial reaction was a jolt of fear, for that sounded as if Odile was giving up. But she soon realized that if this were true, she wanted another midwife. Although Odile did her best to sound optimistic, insisting that the baby would be born safely, Maria no longer believed her.

Maria had no idea how much time had elapsed. During her other birthings, she'd yearned to be told her womb was fully dilated. Now she feared hearing that; as long as the baby remained in her womb, it was safe. The contractions were stronger, but they were different from her past labors. She'd never experienced such severe back pain, nor such waves of nausea. Odile urged her to drink powdered mint mixed with wine to settle her stomach; Maria could not keep it down. Etiennette hurried over so she could wash her mouth out with water and then gently wiped the perspiration from her face. Maria leaned back against Alicia, trying to get a few moments' rest between contractions. The sudden thump upon the door startled them all. Mary gave a stifled scream, Etiennette spilled some of the water, and Maria jerked upright on the birthing stool just as another contraction struck. By then, Odile was already at the door, flinging it open.

At the sight of Balian standing there alone, she clasped a hand to her mouth. "She would not come?"

"She is here. One of my men is helping her mount the stairs." When he brushed past her, she made a half-hearted protest at his intrusion into this female sanctum, but that was for form's sake; all she cared about was that he'd fetched Maud.

Balian never even heard her objection. In two strides, he'd crossed the chamber to Maria's side. "I have brought the midwife, Marika." He spoke swiftly, for he had not much time to persuade her before Maud entered the chamber. Maria was a daughter of the Greek Royal House and Maud did not look like a woman fit to serve a queen, a blunt-speaking, rough-hewn peasant with no education, no longer young. "She does not make a good first impression, my love. But I spoke with her at length and she convinced me that she knows the art of midwifery as few others do. I believe she can save you and our baby and I beg you to let her try."

Maria needed no urging. Having lost faith in Odile, she saw Maud as her only chance of survival. "Yes," she whispered before another contraction took away her power of speech. She felt her husband's lips on her forehead, and then he was forgotten as she was engulfed by the pain again. When she opened her eyes, he was gone and a stranger was hobbling across the chamber toward her.

Maria's first thought was that Balian had been right to alert her, for she'd rarely seen a woman so unprepossessing. Squat and stoop-shouldered, she leaned heavily on a cane, and the wisps of hair escaping her veil were well salted with grey. The paternoster looped at her belt proclaimed her to be a Christian, but the darkness of her skin proclaimed some Saracen blood. Her clothes were threadbare and faded, her shoes caked with mud, and the contrast to the elegant Odile could not have been more dramatic.

Ignoring Odile's stilted attempt at welcome, Maud slowly sank to her knees before the woman on the birthing stool. "I am not as crippled as I look, lady. My knees are bad, but my hands have been spared the joint evil," she said, holding them out for Maria's inspection. Her French was underlaid with an odd sibilant hiss, for like most of the poor, age had claimed many of her teeth. "Did your husband tell you about me?" When Maria shook her head, she shot Odile a sardonic glance. "That one neither, I'd wager. My mother was a midwife, too, and I learned at her knee as she'd learned from her mother. I've been delivering babies for nigh on forty years and what I do not know is not worth knowing."

Odile looked indignant and Mary and Etiennette were regarding Maud as if she were an apparition. But calm and confidence were what Maria desperately needed now, even coming from such an unlikely source. If this woman could offer hope, she would willingly overlook her rough edges and her low birth. Her mixed blood might even be a boon. Saracen medicine was more advanced than the medicine of the Franks; Maria had lived in Outremer long enough to have no doubts about that. It made sense, then, that Muslim midwives might know secrets their Frankish sisters did not. "Was your mother a Saracen?"

Maud hesitated before admitting with a hint of defiance, "She was, lady."

"Good. . . ." That shocked the other women, but Maria cared nothing for their disapproval. "Have you delivered many babies like mine? Did they live?"

Maud did not reply at once, her small, dark eyes intently searching the younger woman's face; it was, Maria thought, as if she were trying to see into her very soul. "I need the truth," she said tautly, and Maud nodded slowly.

"Aye, I can see that. Not all of them lived, lady. A babe lying crosswise in the womb cannot be delivered alive." Maria knew—all women knew—that if it came to a choice, midwives always chose the mother over the child. She was glad, though, that Maud left that unsaid, for she could not bear to think of it, not now.

Maud had reached into a sack, pulling out a glass vial. "But babies need not come headfirst, not if the midwife knows what she is about. This is a mixture of linseed oil and fenugreek. It will make it easier for me to reach into your womb and see what's what." Pouring the oil into her palms, she then raised Maria's chemise and began to probe. Almost at once, she expelled an audible breath and then she grinned. "Bless him, your little one wants to come butt first and with the legs up around the ears. I've never lost a baby willing to come out like that, nary a one!"

Maria found herself blinking back tears, for that old woman's toothless smile was surely one of the most beautiful sights of her life. Maud was rummaging in her sack again, this time pulling out something small and metallic. "I always have my mothers hold on to this whilst the babe comes," she said, pressing the object into Maria's hand. Before she could examine it, she was hit with another contraction. While she writhed on the stool, Maud began to snap out instructions, telling the other women to add wood to the hearth and to move that brazier of coals closer, saying the chamber had to be warm for the baby. They bridled a bit at taking orders from Maud, but obeyed. Once she'd gotten her breath back, Maria examined the talisman. It was a pendant, made of lead, showing the figure of a woman; she held a book in one hand, a cross in the other, and was standing on a dragon.

"St. Margaret of Antioch," she said softly. The patron saint of women in childbirth, at least in the Latin Church. Bringing the pendant to her lips, she kissed it reverently, and when the next pang began, she did as Maud bade and held on to it tightly.

Maud had not lied to Maria; over the years, she had delivered babies that were malpositioned in the womb and the position of Maria's baby was indeed the safest of these births. She well knew, though, that much could go wrong even when the baby presented headfirst. Maria had given birth to other children and Maud took comfort in that. Nor did Maria seem likely to panic and that, too, was reassuring. Still, it was daunting that this woman had been Queen of Jerusalem. Maud had never attended a mother of such high rank and she had a natural suspicion of those in power. But it was too late to worry about the consequences if this ended badly and she set about delivering Maria's baby.

The first danger was the risk that the navel cord could wrap itself around the child's neck or be squeezed between the baby's body and the mother's womb, so she was very relieved when another inspection eased that fear. Since Maria's womb was still not fully dilated, she insisted that the queen not bear down yet, much to the latter's dismay. Maria acquiesced after Maud explained that the mouth must be at its widest in order to deliver her baby's head. Maud then had Emma soak a towel in hot water and place it against Maria's lower back, which eased the intensity of her pain. Mary agreed to keep the hearth fire going and Maud took a certain grim amusement in seeing a highborn lady performing a task usually done by servants, by those like herself. "Soon now, lady, soon," she said soothingly and hoped she was right, for prolonged labor could sap a woman's strength at the time when she'd need it the most.

Once Maria could bear down, it was not long before the infant's bottom became visible. The baby's legs slid out with only a little guidance from Maud's nimble fingers. The other women cried out joyfully as the little body emerged, thinking the worst was over. Only Maud knew this was actually the most dangerous moment, for if the queen could not deliver the baby's head quickly, the child would die. Maud's mother had admitted she was not sure why this happened, saying some midwives thought the baby started to breathe as soon as its skin and cord touched the air. That presented no problems if the baby came out headfirst, but in a birth like Maria's, the child would suffocate if delivery was delayed too long. Maud did not speculate about the reason for such deaths, caring only that they not occur on her watch, to one of her mothers.

"Bear down again, lady," she urged. "You're almost done." She wanted to cheer when she saw the nape of the baby's neck, and then Maria gave one final push, groaned, and her daughter entered the world, sliding into Maud's outstretched hands. Carefully laying that slippery little body upon her mother's belly, she announced it was a girl, hoping that Maria would not be too disappointed. To judge by her smile, she was not, and Maud smiled, too, then let Emma and Alicia help her to her feet. Steered toward a chair, she sank gratefully onto its cushion, willing to let Odile take over now, to clean the baby, cut and tie the cord, then deliver and dispose of the afterbirth. Her knees were throbbing and she felt so stiff that she wondered if she'd ever be able to straighten up. She was getting too old for this. But as she watched the queen cuddle her daughter, she thought that if this were indeed her last delivery, it was a most memorable one.

Maria awoke with reluctance, for never had she felt such exhaustion; it took an effort even to lift her lashes. But she remembered, then, what had happened and the need to see her baby vanquished her fatigue. As soon as she stirred, she was the center of attention, and once she'd been propped up in bed, the wet nurse placed her daughter in her arms. She was a beautiful baby, almost as perfect as Isabella had been, showing no signs of her perilous entry into the world. Maria brushed her lips against the infant's silky cap of dark hair, delighted that her little legs were no longer oddly upraised. Maud had assured her they would soon lower of their own accord and by then, she accepted whatever the old woman said as gospel. It was still a relief to see her baby's legs now safely tucked into their cocoon-like swaddling.

Balian soon appeared, looking more rested. Kissing her and then their daughter, he pulled a chair over to the bed, and for a time they were content to remain silent, savoring this precious moment of family harmony. When Maria realized she was hungry, her admission unleashed a torrent of activity and she was given a cup of pomegranate juice to sip as they waited for food to be sent up from the kitchen. The baby still slept peacefully and Maria and Balian exchanged smiles. After he leaned over to kiss her again, she observed that he needed a shave and he acknowledged that with another smile, rubbing his chin ruefully.

"Last night you said you no longer wanted to name her after your mother. Are you still sure of that, Marika?"

She nodded. "I want to name her Margaret."

"Ah, after the saint? Mayhap we ought to name her Maud," he joked half seriously, and Maria laughed, for a memory had suddenly surfaced—her husband jubilantly seizing the astonished midwife and giving her a grateful hug after his first glimpse of his new daughter.

Another memory came to the fore. "Balian . . . you said Humphrey de Toron is here?"

"He arrived yesterday with gifts for Bella's birthday." Seeing her brows draw together, he reached over to give her hand a reassuring squeeze. "I was glad to have him here, for he was a great help in keeping Bella occupied. She seems to like him very much, Marika." He was not surprised when her expression remained skeptical, for he knew how strongly she opposed this marriage. He understood her reluctance to see Bella sent off to a household headed by two people so hostile to her; he shared it. But he was enough of a realist to hope that she'd come to accept what could not be changed. "He is a good lad, Marika, kindhearted and eager to make Bella happy. She could do far worse. You know that is so, my love."

Maria was silent for a moment. "Yes," she said at last, "I do. But tell me this, Balian. Do you think he will ever be strong enough to protect her?"

He would not lie to her, not even to offer comfort. "No," he admitted. "No, I do not."

CHAPTER 32

March 1182
Jerusalem, Outremer

Balian and Maria were not planning to attend Baldwin's Easter court. Because Margaret was too young to travel, Maria did not want to leave her, and Balian did not want to leave his wife, who was still recovering from her childbirth ordeal. The choice was taken away from him, however, by the arrival of a terse message from William, urging him to hasten to Jerusalem.

The roads were muddy from the winter rains at this time of year and travelers usually took two days to cover a distance that could be ridden in a day during the summer. But Balian was racing both the sun and his apprehensions, and as sunset turned the sky into a celestial cauldron of fiery color, the walls of the Holy City slowly came into view against the horizon.

Knowing that Balian had been in the saddle all day, William wanted to send to the kitchen for a meal, but Balian refused, suspecting that what he was about to hear would chase away his appetite. Baudouin and Denys arrived soon afterward, and to Balian's surprise, they were accompanied by Hugues of Galilee. Although he would one day inherit his mother's rich principality, Hugues had not yet taken an active role in the political life of the kingdom, content to defer to his stepfather. His presence here tonight indicated that might be about to change.

Once greetings had been exchanged and William ordered wine for the newcomers, it was Denys who took command of the conversation. "We summoned you because the kingdom is in crisis, Balian," he said bluntly. "Baldwin has made a grave error and it is up to the High Court to make him understand that he has blundered. You know that he remains very suspicious of Count Raymond and I cannot blame him for it."

Balian saw Hugues sit upright as if he meant to protest. Denys noticed that abortive movement, too. "Mayhap you should be the one to tell him, Hugues."

Hugues hesitated and then turned so he was facing Balian. "It has been two years since my stepfather has set foot in the kingdom. He knew the king bore him a bitter grudge and he thought it best that they had time apart. But he could not stay away from Galilee any longer and he and my mother intended to celebrate Easter at Tiberias. We'd only gotten as far as Jubyal when we were intercepted by the king's men, ordering Raymond not to enter Outremer."

"Christ Jesus," Balian said softly; this was worse than he'd feared. "What did he do?"

"He was loath to spill blood, so he went no farther. I hurried to Jerusalem and sought to convince the king that Raymond had no evil intent, that he'd meant only to deal with matters in Galilee and posed no threat. Baldwin did not believe me."

Balian understood now why Denys was here, throwing in his lot with the barons even if that put his relationship with Baldwin at risk. With so much at stake, he'd been forced to choose sides. "What does Baldwin mean to do? He cannot keep Raymond out of Galilee forever."

"He can if he charges Raymond with treason," Denys said somberly. "We think he intends to do that and then turn Galilee over to Hugues."

"My stepfather is an honorable man." Hugues sounded defensive, as if expecting them to argue with him. "Yes, he plotted against the king, but he truly believed it was for the best. He was thinking only of the good of the kingdom. He does not deserve this."

"What do the other members of the High Court say? Who supports Baldwin in this?"

"Who do you think, Little Brother?" Baudouin gave a harsh, humorless laugh. "Joscelin and Agnes have been pouring poison into Baldwin's ear for nigh on two years now, seeking to convince him that Raymond is not to be trusted, that this time he wants the crown for himself. Guy and Sybilla have also been urging Baldwin on. So have Agnes's lapdog Eraclius and that arrogant whoreson de Chatillon and of course Gerard de Ridefort, who swears Raymond is the Antichrist since he reneged on his promise of that heiress. The rest of the lords are horrified, including the grand masters of the Templars and the Hospitallers."

"Reynald de Chatillon is here? He is no longer defying the king?"

"Oh, he still balks at compensating Saladin for that captured caravan. But he'd not miss a chance to stab Raymond in the back and Baldwin accepted his support, for he knows he'll need all the allies he can get."

Balian found himself wishing that Maria could have accompanied him, for he trusted her judgment. "What happens now?"

"Two days hence, the king is meeting with the High Court," William said, sounding as unhappy as he looked, "and we must try to convince him that he is in the wrong."

Balian did not ask the obvious question, for he already knew the answer. If they failed, their kingdom could be facing a civil war.

Baldwin was already in the upper chamber of David's Tower when his lords began to arrive, for he did not want an audience as he staggered toward his chair; walking was becoming more and more of a challenge even with a cane. Agnes and Sybilla had both been given seats on the dais even though they could not participate in the debate. Sybilla was so radiant that she was attracting admiring glances from many of the men. Baldwin was one of the few who knew the reason for her radiance; she was in the early stages of pregnancy.

Baldwin's vision was slowly failing him, yet he still had enough sight in one eye to study the men as they took their seats. And he realized that of all the people in this chamber, only his mother and his chancellor, William, truly understood why he clung so tenaciously to his kingship—because he knew he alone could unify their divided kingdom and because he needed to believe that there was a reason for his suffering.

The High Court session was going to be an unpleasant experience. William and Denys had pleaded with him to let the Count of Tripoli enter the kingdom, warning that they'd have to speak out against him if he did not. But he was convinced that Raymond was untrustworthy, that if the count must choose between integrity and ambition, he would always choose self-interest.

He soon saw that his sense of foreboding had been justified. One by one, his lords rose to argue that he'd wronged the Count of Tripoli and his banishment must be lifted. They insisted there was no proof that Count Raymond was plotting against the Crown, and when Reynald and Joscelin angrily reminded them of the count's failed Easter coup, some of them even seemed skeptical of that, saying he'd never been charged with any crime. It was obvious to Baldwin that many of the men were concerned with their own lands, fearing that if even the king's cousin could be deprived of his wife's principality, they were also vulnerable. But others were sincere in their concern for the peace of the kingdom and that was obvious to Baldwin, too.

He was particularly impressed by Balian d'Ibelin's speech, for Balian did not try to defend Raymond's honor as some of the lords did. He spoke instead of how strife amongst the Franks would embolden Saladin, asking how they could hope to fend off a Saracen jihad if they were fighting amongst themselves. That was an argument Baldwin could not easily refute.

What finally compelled Baldwin to concede defeat was the realization that almost all of the men in the chamber were adamantly opposed to his action, siding with Raymond against the Crown. The High Court would never agree to charge the count with treason or to exile him from the kingdom. Yielding would lacerate Baldwin's pride. Nor had any of them been able to overcome his deep misgivings about his cousin's loyalties. But he knew he had no choice.

The relief was palpable when he told them that. William offered to act as peacemaker between the king and his cousin and Baldwin agreed, wanting only to end this wretched business as soon as possible. He was thankful when the men did not linger once the session had ended, shepherded from the chamber by his stepfather and chancellor, who were perceptive enough to understand that privacy was the only balm they could offer for the wound they'd inflicted.

Once he was alone with his family, Baldwin allowed himself to slump back in his seat. He could sense his mother's eyes upon him, but when he raised his head, he saw no reproach in her gaze, only concern for his dwindling strength. Joscelin did not look happy, yet he knew enough to hold his tongue. Guy did not show the same restraint.

"How could you give in to them like that? Surely they did not convince you that Raymond can be trusted?"

Baldwin discovered that the last of his patience had ebbed away during the ordeal he'd just endured. "No," he said, with unwonted sharpness, "of course I do not trust Raymond!"

Guy seemed honestly baffled. "Why did you yield, then? Why let your enemies win?"

"Because I had no choice, Guy."

"But you are the king!" Guy strode forward, stopping in front of him. "You weakened the Crown's authority by surrendering to them. You damaged your kingship. Do you not see that? The English king would never have allowed his vassals to challenge him like this!"

"Nor would I if I were King of England!" Baldwin snapped. "But in Jerusalem, the king's power is not absolute. He must share that power with the High Court." He was suddenly very angry. "You are not a newcomer to Outremer, have dwelled amongst us long enough to have learned our customs and our laws. One day my sister will be queen and you will rule with her. God help us all if you remain as ignorant then as you are now!"

Guy flushed deeply, and for a moment, he seemed about to lash out at Baldwin. Before he could do so, Sybilla jumped to her feet. Baldwin thought she meant to intercede, to ease the tension. But when she moved to stand beside Guy, linking her arm in his, Baldwin realized that she was declaring her loyalties were with her husband, not her brother. The one who did intervene was Joscelin, saying hastily, "Our nerves are all fraying after that court session. I am sure Guy did not mean to insult you, Nephew. He knows how much he owes you, after all."

That heavy-handed reminder served its purpose, prodding Guy into a terse apology. He and Sybilla soon found an excuse to depart, followed by Joscelin. Alone with his mother and Anselm, Baldwin no longer had to dissemble, for with them, he dared show his body's weakness. "I must rest ere I can manage the stairs," he confessed, and Anselm hurried over to the sideboard to pour him a cup of watered-down wine.

Agnes wanted to help, too, and when she noticed a cushion in the window seat, she snatched it up and placed it behind Baldwin's back. "It is fortunate for Guy that he is so pleasing to the eye, for he has sawdust where his brains ought to be." She regretted the words as soon as they'd left her mouth, for she knew Baldwin needed to believe Guy de Lusignan would be a capable king. They all needed to believe that. "I will speak to Sybilla," she said quickly. "She must see to it that Guy reads the legal codes and learns the customs of the realm."

Baldwin had begun to find it difficult to grasp objects and feared that his fingers would eventually curve inward toward his palm, like the maimed hands of that leper he'd seen in the souk at Beirut. At least he could still touch his mother's hand and he did so now, wanting her to know how much her support meant to him. He fervently hoped that no choice need ever be made, yet if it did, his uncle would stand with Sybilla, not with him. By coming to Guy's defense, Joscelin had made that painfully clear. But by criticizing Guy so harshly, Agnes had shown that her loyalties lay with her dying son, not the daughter who was their family's future.

William had arranged for the meeting between Baldwin and Raymond to be private, not wanting witnesses if it became as acrimonious as he feared it might. He'd also been very honest with Raymond, making sure he understood the depths of Baldwin's hostility. But as they were ushered into the palace solar, he realized that he'd forgotten to warn Raymond of the ravages wrought by leprosy in the two years since Raymond had last seen the king. Too late now. He could only pray that Raymond did not inadvertently reveal either pity or revulsion. As they entered the chamber, he heard the count's sharp intake of breath as he saw Baldwin's eye patch, his cane, the lack of eyebrows and lashes, the nose flattened by the collapse of his nasal cavity, the raw lesions upon his forehead. By the time they reached Baldwin, though, Raymond's face was impassive again and, as William blessed his self-control, he knelt before his sovereign, showing only the respect due the king.

Baldwin gestured for him to rise and then to be seated, and William was relieved that he did not intend to use his rank as a weapon. Neither did he pretend that this meeting was a social one. "You know you are here not by my doing. I was compelled to defer to the High Court. But since we have been yoked to the same plow, we must find a way to move forward together. Have you any suggestions as to how we can manage that?"

Raymond was not thrown off-balance by Baldwin's candor, responding with candor of his own. "There was nothing sinister in my wish to return to Tiberias, my liege. There were matters in Galilee needing my attention. I know you were told I am aiming to claim your throne, but that is not so. I am innocent, and will swear that upon the True Cross if it will ease your mind."

Baldwin's lips twitched in a cold smile. "And are you also willing to swear upon the True Cross that you did not mean to usurp my throne two years ago?"

"No," Raymond said calmly, "for we both know I was guilty then. Bohemond and I did intend to wed your sister to Baudouin d'Ibelin, whether you wished it or not. And I did hope that you would be willing to abdicate in their favor after their marriage, although I did not want to force your abdication. You have been a good king, Cousin. If not for the leprosy, you might even have been a great one. But you *are* a leper and there can be only one ending to your story. When the Duke of Burgundy balked at marrying Sybilla, we concluded that we dared not wait a year or two to find another husband for her. That is what spurred us to take the action we did."

Baldwin studied Raymond in a silence that seemed interminable to William. "And now?"

"I was not seeking the throne for myself, neither then nor now. You have nothing to fear from me, for Sybilla is no longer free to wed. Would Guy de Lusignan have been my choice? No, for I know little about the man, whereas Baudouin d'Ibelin is one of us and a proven battle commander. But there is no undoing the marriage, so we can only hope you chose well."

William thought Raymond had made as good a case as possible for himself under the circumstances. When Baldwin did not challenge him further, William decided that he thought so, too. He doubted that Baldwin would ever truly trust Raymond again, for he knew that his young king was not one for forgetting or forgiving a wrong done him. He would be fair, though, in his dealings with Raymond, and to William, that was enough. Whether it would be enough for Raymond, only time would tell.

It was going to be an exceedingly hot summer; the days were already stifling, and it was only May. The bedchamber's windows were open, but although the sun had set an hour ago, the heat still lingered. Neither Balian nor Maria noticed, for they were generating heat of their own. His barber had been ill for the past week and Maria had begun to complain about his stubble; despite growing up in a culture in which beards were a symbol of masculinity, she'd discovered that she enjoyed making love to a man who was clean-shaven. Balian had laughed at her when she'd suggested that she shave him and she'd taken that as a challenge. One thing led to another, until he found himself stretched out on their settle, his head in her lap and a razor at his throat.

"I must have been mad to agree to this. I very much doubt your lessons at the Greek court involved learning how to shave a man."

"I will try to keep the bleeding to a minimum," she assured him. When she finally did nick his chin, drawing blood, he did not object, for she apologized with a kiss. He returned it with enthusiasm, but she insisted upon finishing the shave. By now they were both enjoying this game of delayed gratification, anticipating its culmination in the bed conveniently close at hand. They never reached it, though, for just as their caresses were becoming more intimate, there was a sudden knock at the door.

"Can we pretend we're not here?" Balian whispered, but Maria was already sitting up, adjusting the bodice of her gown, and he got reluctantly to his feet. After a brief exchange with someone on the other side of the door, he turned back to Maria. "William has just ridden in!"

Maria was equally surprised, for the archbishop always sent word ahead of a planned visit. With a wistful glance back at their bed, she repinned her veil, replaced one of her earrings, and followed Balian down the stairs to welcome their guest.

As soon as they saw William's face, Maria and Balian braced themselves for trouble. He was traveling with an unusually large entourage, too; leaving their unexpected guests to their steward's care, they led William up to the solar. He sank down upon the settle with a sigh that revealed both his weariness and his reluctance to unburden himself.

"I am on my way to Jerusalem to see the king; I have news he must hear straightaway. But it is news that you must know, too, and I did not want you to hear it from someone else."

Maria's heart began to beat faster, for he was gazing sadly at her, not at her husband. "What has happened, William?"

"There is no easy way to tell you, Maria. Last month, there was a coup in Constantinople and much bloodshed. Manuel's cousin Andronicus Comnenus has seized power and the boy emperor and his mother are his prisoners. Your uncle, the *protosebastos*, was also captured, then blinded and maimed. There was no resistance, the citizens welcoming Andronicus, the commanders of the royal troops and the fleet all going over to him. For now, Andronicus is claiming he acted only to protect the young emperor and is showing him respect, at least in public, although Mary is being maltreated and few expect her to survive for long. Manuel's daughter and her husband are already dead, believed to have been poisoned at Andronicus's orders."

Maria was suddenly finding it hard to breathe. "What of my mother and my brother? Do they still live?"

"Yes, I was assured of that," he said quickly, even though he knew how little that assurance meant, and Maria did, too.

Maria got unsteadily to her feet, moving toward the window. Looking blindly out at the encroaching darkness, she struggled to recall a lifetime's lessons in self-control. After a few moments, she sensed that Balian was standing behind her. He said nothing, but by his very presence, he reminded her that she was not facing this alone, and she found that more comforting than any words he might have offered.

"My country is doomed," she whispered, and when Balian put his arm around her shoulders, he felt her trembling. He feared that she was right. Andronicus Comnenus was notorious throughout the Levant, a charming and ruthless scoundrel. He'd caused a great scandal in Outremer by eloping with the young Queen of Jerusalem, the late King Baldwin's widow, fleeing with her to the Saracen court. He'd eventually managed to be restored to Manuel's favor, for he'd always been able to talk himself out of trouble. It was only a matter of time before he murdered the twelve-year-old emperor and claimed the crown for himself. From what Balian had heard of the boy, he was spoiled and lazy, more interested in games and chariot races than in lessons of statecraft. He still felt pity for the lad and for his mother, Mary, despised by the Greeks as a "Latin," their disparaging term for those who followed the Church of Rome. But he felt sorriest of all for the little French princess who was to have been Empress of the Greeks, for she was close in age to his step-daughter, Isabella. What would become of her now?

Some of Maria's shock was ebbing and she frowned as she recalled the archbishop's words. "You said there was no resistance to Andronicus, William, that he was welcomed by the people and the army. Yet you also spoke of 'bloodshed.' What did you mean by that?"

This was the moment William had been most dreading. "As soon as Andronicus seized power, the city went quite mad. Mobs rampaged through the streets, killing any Latins they could find. They burned the Latin quarter to the ground and murdered thousands, most of them Italians. Women, children, the aged, the ailing—none were spared. They invaded the Hospital of St. John run by the Hospitallers, killing all who were too sick to flee. Monks and priests fared the worst, for they were tortured ere they were slain. They even dared to murder a cardinal of Rome, a papal legate unfortunate enough to be in Constantinople at the time."

Balian and Maria were staring at him in horror and William found he could not continue. The stories he'd heard from the Latin survivors of the massacre would haunt his sleep for years to come. The Latin cemetery dug up, the bodies thrown into the Bosporus. The mothers pleading in vain that their children be spared. The people burned alive, thrust back into their flaming houses. He did not want Maria to have images like that branded into her brain.

Her skin was ashen, her lips rimmed in white. For one so proudly Greek, hearing of the atrocities committed by those of her blood must rock her world to its very foundations. He had more to share, though, proof that the Greeks had no monopoly when it came to cruelty.

"I've heard the death toll is in the thousands," he said bleakly. "But not all the Latins were slain. Some of them were warned by Greek friends and were able to flee to the ships in the harbor, where the Italian merchants had forty-four galleys. Instead of rejoicing in their reprieve, they chose to take vengeance—not upon the killers in Constantinople but upon the innocent Greeks living along the Hellespont. They raided towns and villages and monasteries, killing and looting. Not all of the Latin survivors joined in this orgy of revenge and they sailed for the Holy

Land. That is how I learned of this, when their ships reached Tyre. I am escorting them to the king so Baldwin may hear their stories for himself."

Maria leaned back against her husband, grateful for the strength in the arms encircling her waist. She could not imagine being able to endure this without him. "I must tell Isabella," she said, and shivered at the prospect. How could she make Isabella understand? Would she be ashamed of her Greek blood now? Thank God their other children were too young to be told!

"Do not worry about that now, Marika. We will tell her together on the morrow."

"Yes, that would be best. . . ." She found it hard to focus her thoughts; there was an eerie sense of unreality about this night, almost as if she were listening to a fable from a foreign land, one that could not possibly be true. "I want to go to the chapel," she said at last, for that was all she could think to do; mayhap prayer could staunch her bleeding.

One glance was enough to tell Balian she needed this time alone with God. Kissing her forehead, he slumped down in a nearby chair as the door closed quietly behind her. "When word of this spreads, there will be great anger against the Greeks, William. Do you think there might be outbreaks of violence, attacks on the Orthodox monasteries in Outremer?"

"No. Baldwin will take measures to keep the king's peace. But it is good that Maria is now the wife of a Poulain lord, no longer the alien queen, the outsider. We know how quickly Agnes would have taken advantage of her sudden vulnerability."

Balian nodded in weary agreement. "I've never admitted this to Maria, not wanting her to know my fears for our future. But I've taken comfort from her ties to the Greek royal family. I've told myself that if I were to die fighting the Saracens and our kingdom fell to Saladin, Maria could take our children and seek safety in Constantinople."

William feared for their future, too. He loved Outremer, as the cradle of Christianity and as his homeland. But as he looked at Balian, he found himself thinking that a man's need to protect his family was one of mankind's most powerful, primal urges, and he was sorry he could offer Balian no solace. Whatever happened in Outremer, Maria dared not go home again.

The Poulains had little time to consider the ramifications of the Greek coup. On May 11, Salāh al-Dīn again entrusted the government to al-ʿĀdil and led a large army out of Egypt, ready to resume warfare against the Franks.

Baldwin hastily assembled his army at Kerak in Outrejourdain, hoping to prevent the sultan from advancing any farther into their kingdom. But their plan to confront Salāh al-Dīn at Kerak failed when he outflanked them, heading into the eastern hills. By June 22, he'd reached Damascus. He soon was on the march again, and by July 11, the Saracen army was encamped on the east bank of the Jordan River, threatening Tiberias. Although Raymond was very ill at the time, stricken with a tertian fever, he was able to send for help and Baldwin led a relief force north.

On July 15, the royal army had taken up position on the plain near the Hospitaller castle of Forbelet. There they discovered that they were greatly outnumbered by the sultan's forces. The heat was even more of a danger than the Saracens; in William of Tyre's history of their kingdom, *A History of Deeds Done Beyond the Sea*, the archbishop reported that "fully as many in both armies perished from sunstroke as by the sword." Baldwin could no longer lead his army on horseback, but he insisted upon being present upon the battlefield and his men were inspired by his courage. It was a battle the Franks should have lost, for they faced a much larger army. They managed to break free after fierce fighting, and were able to withdraw to the castle at Forbelet.

The battle was inconclusive, but the Franks considered it a victory against overwhelming odds. The Archbishop of Tyre would proclaim proudly in his history of the kingdom: "We proved superior to our foes. Baudouin of Ramlah and Balian, his brother, showed magnificent prowess that day and fought with vigor and courage." Many of Baldwin's subjects saw the battle at Forbelet as proof that he still enjoyed God's favor, for it was fought upon the eighth anniversary of his coronation.

Salāh al-Dīn was not discouraged by his failure to destroy the Frankish army at Forbelet, and in August he launched a two-pronged attack upon the kingdom. He ordered al-'Ādil to lead a raid into the southern regions around Ascalon and Gaza and to send the Egyptian fleet of forty ships to assault Beirut. He then led a land assault upon that city.

Baldwin realized he could not defend both areas under attack. Since the loss of Beirut would be the greater blow, he hastened to Tyre, where he managed to gather a fleet of thirty-six ships, most owned by the Pisans who'd fled the slaughter in Constantinople. Dispatching this fleet to Beirut, he sent word to the beleaguered city that he was leading an army to lift the siege.

At Beirut, the citizens had put up such a spirited resistance that the Saracen army had been repulsed. Salāh al-Dīn had no siege machines with him, and when his men captured Baldwin's courier and learned that the Franks were coming to the aid of Beirut, he ended the siege after only three days. Realizing that once again he'd underestimated the young leper king, he decided to postpone the day of reckoning with the Franks while he dealt with his Muslim enemies in Aleppo and Mosul. In September, he led his army into northern Syria.

The Franks attempted to force Salāh al-Dīn to abandon his siege of Mosul with military action in Outremer. In December, Baldwin and Raymond led raids into the lands around Damascus, burning the harvest. But Salāh al-Dīn considered the capture of Mosul to be of greater importance than any damage they'd inflicted and remained in Syria. Not even the grief of losing his nephew Farrukh-Shāh to a sudden illness interrupted his campaign. Baldwin reluctantly disbanded his army and accepted William's invitation to celebrate Christmas at Tyre.

Sybilla could have traveled to Tyre, for her pregnancy was over. More than two months ago, she'd delivered a healthy daughter, and if Guy were disappointed that she'd not given birth to a son, none knew it; he bragged to anyone who'd listen that his little lass would be a beauty like her mother and Sybilla loved him all the more for that. She and Guy chose to remain at Ascalon and, since many saw it as their first Christmas court, it was well attended by lords and their ladies, eager to win the favor of the couple who would one day rule over them.

Balian and Maria decided to spend Christmas at Tyre, an easy choice in light of their friendship with William and their respect for Baldwin. So did Baudouin and his wife, for he'd sooner have passed the holiday in Hell than with Guy de Lusignan. Upon their arrival at Tyre, Balian took particular note of those present, evidence of the deep divisions rending the court. He found it significant that Agnes and Denys were at Tyre, as was the new Lord of Caesarea, Denys's cousin, Gautier de Grenier, who'd inherited the family fief upon the recent death of his brother, Guyon. But Joscelin was at Ascalon with Sybilla and Guy. Patriarch Eraclius, an astute politician, came to Tyre first to show respect for the current king, then hastened down to Ascalon, where he could insinuate himself into the good graces of the king-to-be. Count Raymond and Eschiva had gone to Antioch to offer solace to his cousin, for Bohemond had received tragic news about his sister Mary; she'd been strangled in her cell, Andronicus forcing her young son to sign his own mother's death warrant. The grand masters of the Hospitallers and Templars were at Tyre, as were many of the prelates and clerics. Reynald de Chatillon, always one to blaze his own trail, was welcoming Christmas at Kerak. His stepson, Humphrey, was at Tyre, though, escaping from Reynald's shadow to show his loyalty to Baldwin; Balian suspected that his wish to see Isabella was a factor, too, in his presence at Tyre.

Baldwin had already retired for the evening. He'd limited his attendance at the Christmas festivities, and Balian realized that he might not hold any more Christmas or Easter courts, restricting his public appearances to those that he could not avoid. But the revelries continued without him, Balian thought sadly, gazing around the hall at the great lords and ladies celebrating the birth of the Christ Child.

Isabella had been allowed to stay up past her normal bedtime, having reminded her parents that she was almost eleven, surely old enough for the Christmas festivities. Balian had kept a paternal eye upon her until he saw that Humphrey was no less protective of her. They were laughing now and, as he watched, he could not suppress a sigh, for he genuinely liked Humphrey. But he agreed with Maria; in a world so dangerous, a girl of royal birth needed a man strong enough to defend her, to keep others from exploiting her for their own benefit.

He finally spotted Maria across the hall, engaged in conversation with Joscius, the Bishop of Acre, and one of the Pisan merchants who'd managed to escape the massacre of his countrymen in Constantinople. They looked so serious that he was sure they were discussing the Empress Mary's gruesome fate. Her murder and the plight of the little French princess had intensified Maria's concern for her eldest daughter, making her even more reluctant to see Isabella wed to Humphrey de Toron.

Balian had begun to weave his way in his wife's direction when he was intercepted by William. The archbishop had been in high spirits all week, delighted to have this chance to play host to the king, to show his enemies that his friendship with Baldwin remained intact. "I think I could use some air," he said. "Come along with me."

Balian knew that meant he had something to share that he did not want overheard. It was a mild evening and neither man bothered to retrieve his mantle. Stepping out into the moonlit courtyard, they strolled toward a marble bench. William was the first to break the silence. "Did Humphrey de Toron say anything to you or Maria about Reynald's absence?"

"No . . . why?"

"He confided to Baldwin that he thinks Reynald is up to no good again, that he has some sort of scheme in mind, for he has been very secretive of late, spending most of his time at his castle at Montreal and refusing to let Humphrey accompany him. Baldwin is understandably concerned after Reynald's raid last year into the Hijāz and his seizure of that Saracen caravan."

"It would probably be wise to keep an eye on Reynald," Balian agreed. "His reckless nature is one of the reasons Maria and I do not want to see Isabella married into that family."

"I wanted to talk to you about that, too, Balian. As you requested, I discussed the plight troth with Baldwin. I went over all of your misgivings and Baldwin politely heard me out. But he said he has no intention of changing his mind, that he is still set upon the marriage."

Balian had not really expected a more favorable response; it still stung, though. He said nothing and William resumed, trying to make him see Baldwin's point of view. "Whilst he did not say this in so many words, Balian, I am convinced he believes he will not live much longer. He fears what will happen to the kingdom after he dies, and he fears, too, for Isabella—that unscrupulous men could use her as a pawn in a struggle over the crown. He truly believes that nothing would be more disastrous for Outremer than a civil war, so he wants to see Isabella safely wed ere he dies, both for her own sake and for the sake of the country. You and Maria can discuss this again with him, but I very much doubt that anything will change."

Balian rose and began to pace. He'd not tell Maria till the morrow, he decided, for she would take it hard, still having some hope that Baldwin might reconsider. At least he could give her one more peaceful night. William attempted to assuage his disappointment by reminding him that Humphrey was a good lad, decent and honorable and God-fearing, but he soon saw that his consolation was falling flat. When he rose, too, they started back toward the great hall.

They'd almost reached the door when William stopped suddenly. "I almost forgot! Earlier tonight, I was speaking with the Templar grand master. A man of refined tastes and subtleties, a great improvement over that lout Odo de St. Amand," he said, making Balian smile when he felt obligated to add "May God assoil him" even though he thought Odo would be trapped in Purgatory for centuries to come. "But he told me the most astonishing story, Balian. Do you remember when Gerard de Ridefort was stricken with a high fever this summer?"

Balian nodded; he'd been glad of the other man's illness, for it had kept him from joining the army during their July campaign or taking part in the battle of Forbelet. "I was sorry he recovered, if you want the brutal truth, William. Why?"

"It seems de Ridefort was greatly shaken by that near-mortal illness. When he regained his health, he decided that the Almighty must have spared him for a reason, wanting him to mend his ways, to repent his past sins, and lead a more godly life."

"How long do you think that will last?" Balian asked skeptically. "Assuming he has not already shattered that resolution a hundredfold in a certain Acre bawdy house."

"He seems to be sincere, at least for now. The grand master said he has taken holy vows as a Templar."

Balian stared at him. "God in Heaven," he said at last, and then, "Poor Jakelin!"

CHAPTER 33

Baldwin had hoarded his dwindling energy in order to attend a general assembly that February and then to preside over a High Court session at Acre in mid-March. But his devotion to duty had forced him to spend the following fortnight in bed. Although he was up and dressed on this mild April morning, Anselm had to coax him to the table where fruit and bread were waiting. He'd stopped eating in public after losing most of his sight and even with Anselm, he remained self-conscious, so the squire usually made himself scarce after the food had been served. Yet today he hovered by the table, for he had a surprise for the king.

"I've smeared honey on the bread, sire. It is on the left side of your plate, the dates and figs and almonds to your right. I have already poured a cup of grape juice for you."

The corner of Baldwin's mouth turned down. He hated to have Anselm hold a cup to his lips so he could drink, but his hand was no longer able to grasp it securely. Anselm did not raise the cup, though, instead placing something long and thin between his fingers. "What is this?"

"A hollow reed, my lord. If we put it in the cup, you can suck up the juice through it whilst leaving the cup on the table. I know that sounds odd, but it really does work."

Baldwin was skeptical. But when he tried it, he smiled. "I'll be damned if you're not right, Anselm! Wherever did you learn of this trick?"

"I remembered a story I heard when I was still with the leper knights. One of the men claimed he'd had to hide from Saracens in a patch of river reeds, cutting a reed and breathing through it whilst he sank below the water so he'd not be seen. I'd not want to rely on one for air, but a reed can be used for drinking. If you like it, we could ask a silversmith to make one so you can keep using it."

Anselm was obviously trying to sound matter-of-fact, even nonchalant, but Baldwin could sense his excitement. He was, of necessity, learning to read voices as he'd once read faces. "Thank you. I truly do not know what I'd do without you, Anselm."

Anselm flushed with embarrassment and pride. "It was nothing," he muttered, "just a notion of mine." A knock suddenly sounded and he hurried toward the door, smiling over his shoulder as he saw Baldwin lower his head to use the reed. When he turned back toward his young lord, though, his smile had vanished. "It is *him*, sire . . . your spy."

Baldwin fumbled for a napkin to wipe his mouth, suddenly cold despite the spring sun pouring in through the unshuttered windows. Saladin had remained in northern Syria throughout the winter. Having failed to capture Mosul, he was now targeting Aleppo again and Baldwin lived with daily fear that this time he would succeed. But among his master spy's many talents was an apparent ability to read minds, or so it often seemed to Baldwin. As soon as Bernard saw his king's face, he said quickly, "I have no word of Aleppo, my lord."

"Thank God." Baldwin told Anselm to serve Bernard, too. The spy tucked into the meal with enough enthusiasm to reassure Baldwin that for once he was not bringing news to steal sleep and destroy appetites. "What have you come to tell me, Bernard? Can I hear it sober?"

He was only half joking, but Bernard chuckled. "In truth, my lord, I have a most remarkable tale to share with you. I discovered what Reynald de Chatillon was plotting and I must confess it was not something I'd ever have guessed. Say what you will of the man, he does not lack for either ballocks or imagination. Whilst his grand scheme failed, we may be sure it sent waves of fear and horror sweeping through all the lands where men worship Allah."

"Knowing Reynald as I do, I doubt that anything he'd do would truly surprise me."

Bernard soon proved him wrong and Baldwin listened in amazement as his spy related what Reynald de Chatillon had done that past December. He'd had five galleys built at his castle at Montreal and then disassembled, packed upon camels, and transported through the Sinai Desert to the Gulf of Aqaba. He'd led an attack upon the Saracen garrison at Eliat while the galleys were put together again. Two of them remained to blockade the garrison and the other three galleys sailed out into the Red Sea. There they wreaked havoc on Muslim shipping. Sixteen merchant vessels were seized and plundered and a pilgrim ship was captured. They'd ventured as far as the port of Rābigh, where some of the men went ashore. They were within a day's journey of Islam's holy city of Medina when they were finally caught.

"How did Reynald escape?"

"He did not join in the Red Sea expedition, returning to Kerak after leading the raid on Eliat. He was luckier than he deserves, for if he'd been captured, there would have been no ransom demand, only death. My sources tell me that the Saracens are utterly outraged, viewing his raid as sacrilege. They are convinced that his men were heading for Medina where they meant to steal the body of the Prophet, Mohammed."

"Would Reynald be that crazed?" Baldwin thought about it and concluded he would. "For sheer bravado, it is hard to match this Red Sea raid, but aside from adding fuel to the jihad fire, what did it accomplish, Bernard? Even if Reynald had captured the fortress at Eliat, the Franks could not have held it for long; we've not enough men to expand our influence into the Sinai. And the raid would have been profitable only if they'd gotten back to the kingdom with their booty and prisoners, which they did not."

"Well, they might have, sire, if not for the quick action of Saladin's brother. Reynald probably expected the Saracens to be slow in responding with Saladin still away in Syria. But as soon as al-'Ādil got word of the attack on Eliat, he borrowed a page from Reynald's own book, ordering galleys from Alexandria to be carried overland to the Red Sea. He put these ships under the command of the former admiral of the Egyptian fleet. They soon captured the Franks' galleys and then tracked the men down as they fled inland. There was fierce fighting and many died, with one hundred seventy Franks surrendering to save their lives. Saladin refused to honor that promise and ordered them all put to death. Whilst al-'Ādil was troubled by this, Saladin overruled him."

"God pity them," Baldwin said, wondering if Reynald would care that he'd sent hundreds of men to their deaths. "You constantly surprise me, Bernard, by how easily you uncover the secrets of other men. This time you've truly outdone yourself. How did you learn all this?"

Bernard's smile held a touch of pardonable pride. "Al-'Ādil wrote to Saladin in early March, telling him of the raid and the capture of Reynald's men. I managed to get my hands on a copy of that letter. As for the quarrel between the brothers over the fate of the Franks who'd surrendered, that came from one of my Syrian spies."

Baldwin was impressed; he'd not realized that Bernard had sources so highly placed in the Saracen camp. "Whatever I pay you, it is not enough," he said and

Bernard laughed, for a king's praise was valued almost as much as his coins. Once he departed, Baldwin lapsed into a brooding silence, paying no heed when Anselm urged him to finish his breakfast. "I can no longer lead our army into battle," he said at last. "We desperately need a man who can, a man like the late Humphrey de Toron, may God assoil him, one with both courage and common sense. Reynald de Chatillon is utterly without fear and in a fight to the death, I'd want him at my side. But his Red Sea raid proves why I could never entrust him with our kingdom."

Anselm agreed, for the fastest stallion was of no use unless he could be broken to the saddle. Looking at his doomed young king, he yearned to offer comfort, even if it was a lie. "At least you were able to find a husband for your sister, my lord. If you sickened of a sudden, you could take to your bed knowing he can act in your stead."

Baldwin found little reassurance in that thought, for even after three years of marriage to Sybilla, Guy remained an enigma to him. Baldwin did not doubt his bravery on the battlefield; the de Lusignans did not breed cowards. But a king needed more than courage and Guy's judgment was still untested. He did not let himself express such doubts, not even with Anselm, and so he merely nodded, silently sending another prayer winging its way to God's ear, that the Almighty keep his beleaguered kingdom safe from infidels, overly ambitious lords, and fools.

In May, Salāh al-Dīn finally lay siege to Aleppo. Its citizens put up a fierce resistance but were betrayed by their own amir, who secretly came to terms with the sultan and agreed to surrender the city. On June 11, the Franks' greatest fear came to pass and Aleppo fell to Salāh al-Dīn. Baldwin hastily ordered their army to muster at Saforie, and they prepared to defend their kingdom.

Soon after arriving at Saforie, Baldwin had been stricken with a fever. Since he'd begun going blind, his mother had rarely left his side and she insisted that he withdraw to Nazareth until he recovered. He reluctantly agreed, only because it was just six miles from the army camp at Saforie, enabling him to stay in close touch with his scouts and battle commanders. Virtually every lord in the kingdom had answered his summons, as had Count Raymond of Tripoli. By now they'd heard that Saladin had left Aleppo, heading for Damascus. War was looming.

On August 17, the barons were suddenly summoned to Nazareth. Balian and

Baudouin wondered if Baldwin's spies had discovered where Saladin meant to strike first; many of the men were convinced he would besiege Beirut again, while others were sure that he intended to attack the strongholds of Toron and Chastel-neuf. The uncertainty was abrading men's nerves and the d'Ibelin brothers hoped that Baldwin would be able to end the suspense. They also wanted to know whom he would name to command the army.

The Archbishop of Nazareth had invited Baldwin to stay in his palace, even giving up his own bedchamber for the ailing king's comfort. Balian and Baudouin expected to be ushered toward the archbishop's great hall and they were alarmed when they were led, instead, into his private quarters. They'd not been surprised to be told that Baldwin's illness had taken a turn for the worse; by now his lords were accustomed to his ongoing battles with one malady after another. But knowing how proud he was, they realized that he'd never have held a council in his bedchamber unless he was too weak to leave his bed.

Their first glimpse of Baldwin confirmed all of their fears. He was so deeply flushed that he seemed sunburned, his eyes glazed with fever and sunken back in his head. The windows had been opened to combat the stifling August heat, but Baldwin's bed was piled high with blankets and as they approached it, they could see that he was shivering. He looked far younger than his twenty-two years and so vulnerable that Balian was not surprised to see Agnes, Joscelin, Denys, and William surrounding the bed, sentinels vainly seeking to ward off Death.

The Archbishop of Nazareth and the patriarch, Eraclius, were also present, and Balian recognized several of Baldwin's doctors and his confessor. He was startled to see Guy de Lusignan, too, for he'd not heard that Baldwin had summoned Guy from Saforie ahead of the others. As men continued to file into the chamber, Guy signaled to catch the eye of his brother, Amaury, with a grin so jubilant that Balian stiffened. Beside him, he heard Baudouin mutter, "Sweet, suffering Christ," and he knew his brother shared his sudden suspicion.

Although Archbishop Lethard's bedchamber was a large one, it was still a tight fit for all the lords jockeying for position. Rank prevailed and space was cleared by the bed for Count Raymond, Reynald de Chatillon, the d'Ibelins, and the grand masters of the Templars and Hospitallers. There was some grumbling when Amaury de Lusignan forced his way to the front, but men grudgingly let him by, sensing that Guy's star was finally on the ascendancy.

When Baldwin began to speak, the men had to crowd in even closer to hear, for his voice was slurred and too faint to carry far. "Once I was sure that . . . that I was a leper, I promised that I would rule only as long as my health permitted. . . . That day has come, for I am too ill to lead our army into battle against Saladin. . . . After much thought, I have decided to name my sister's husband, the Count of Jaffa, as regent of the realm. . . ."

Baldwin had to pause often for breath. "I will retain the kingship, the city of Jerusalem, and an annual income of ten thousand gold bezants. . . . All else will be given over to Count Guy. He will rule the kingdom with the advice and consent of the High Court and he will command the army. . . ."

He paused again, this time as he struggled to suppress a coughing spasm so severe, he sounded as if he were strangling. Those watching could only wait helplessly until it passed. The chamber was strangely silent, aside from Baldwin's ragged breathing and the occasional shuffling of feet. All had known since they'd learned of Guy's marriage to Sybilla that this day was coming, yet it somehow caught most by surprise. Some still saw Guy as an alien interloper and remained resentful that he'd swooped in to claim such a prize for himself. Even those most enthusiastic about Guy's appointment as regent were motivated more by self-interest than by confidence in his abilities. Others were not yet convinced that he would be equal to the challenges of kingship at a time when the very survival of Outremer was at stake.

"I want my vassals to swear fealty to the Count of Jaffa." Baldwin could not see the joy that lit Guy's face. The other men did and many of them did not like it. Baldwin had halted to catch his breath. What he said now wiped Guy's smile away. "But first I would have Count Guy swear an oath of his own. . . . I want him to avow that whilst I still live, he will not aspire to the crown or alienate from the royal treasury any of the cities or castles still in my possession."

It was obvious to them all that Guy had not expected such a stipulation and that he resented the implication—that Baldwin did not fully trust him. He frowned and glanced toward his brother, who nodded almost imperceptibly. Their eyes held for a moment and then Guy nodded, too, saying that of course he was willing to take such an oath if the king requested it. But when William at once stepped forward, holding out a jeweled reliquary, the look Guy gave the archbishop was not a friendly one. He solemnly swore upon those holy relics, though, that he would not attempt to usurp the king's crown. His smile reappeared, then, as one by one, the lords of the realm came forward to swear fealty to him as regent and to acknowledge that the command of the army and the government and the future of their kingdom were in his hands.

Once they'd exited Baldwin's bedchamber, the men broke into small groups to discuss this dramatic development, some clustering around Guy, others gathering to hear Baudouin and Raymond openly express their doubts about Baldwin's decision. Balian preferred to confide his misgivings in privacy and he and William slipped away in search of it. They eventually found the solitude they sought in the cathedral cloisters and sat down on a bench in one of the carrels.

"I assume you argued against this, William."

The archbishop sighed. "I tried. Baldwin pointed out that he had no real choice, for the crown will pass to Sybilla and Guy when he dies."

"Were you responsible for that *sine qua non* oath Baldwin demanded of Guy?"

William was amused by Balian's unexpected use of that Latin legal phrase. "No, that was Baldwin's idea. But he decided to demand it of Guy after I told him of the rumors I'd heard, that Guy has been seeking out lords of the realm and promising to make it worth their while if they'd support his claim to the crown." Anticipating Balian's next question, he shrugged. "Were those rumors true? I cannot say for a certainty. Guy would hardly have approached me or you or Baudouin or Raymond, after all. All I could tell Baldwin was that such rumors had been circulating for a while. Since he felt the need for such an oath, Baldwin obviously gave some credence to them."

Balian did, too. Unlike his brother, he could not fault Guy for wanting to be king. But he found it troubling that even after three years, so many remained dubious. Why had Guy not been able to win over the other lords? Jealousy alone could not account for it.

It was then that he heard his name being called. Anselm was striding up the cloister walkway, waving to attract his attention. "I've been searching everywhere for you, Lord Balian! The king wants to see you straightaway."

Agnes glowered at Balian as he entered the bedchamber, as if he had barged in, uninvited. "Do not overstay your welcome," she snapped. "The king is very tired."

Balian merely looked at her. It was Baldwin who responded, saying, "I am going blind, not deaf, Mother. Now, if you'll pardon us, I need to speak privately with Lord Balian. . . ." There was such obvious affection in the rebuke that Agnes did not object. Leaning over the bed, she kissed her son on the forehead, then gave Balian one more admonitory glare before reluctantly departing the chamber.

Balian thought Baldwin looked even worse than he had during the council. "Sire, I can come back after you've rested. Surely whatever you want to tell me can wait for a while."

"No, it cannot. . . ." Baldwin tried to sit up, sank back against the pillows. "Balian, Bella and Humphrey . . . they must wed, as soon as possible. . . ."

"Sire, no! Bella is too young!"

"She . . . is in her twelfth year. . . ."

"But she'll not be twelve for nigh on six months, and twelve is the canonical age for marriage. Sire, you know that. This makes no sense."

"Balian, I am dying. . . ." Little more than a whisper, but the words echoed in Balian's ears like thunder. Why had he needed to be told?

"My liege, surely your doctors can . . ." *Can do what? Prolong his suffering?*

"The doctors do not even know what is causing my fever. . . . They urged me to make my peace with God." When Anselm put a cup to his lips, Baldwin managed a swallow or two. "For Bella's sake and for the sake of the kingdom, she must be wed ere I die. . . . I'd not have her become a pawn, used as a weapon against Sybilla. . . . She deserves better and . . . and if we war amongst ourselves, we are well and truly doomed. . . ."

"Sire, I promise you that we'll see her wed to Humphrey. I give you my sworn word. But let the marriage wait until she is older, at least fourteen. Eleven is too young!"

Baldwin no longer had breath for persuasion, even for speech. Nor did he see any point in it. He understood why Balian and Maria would resist, did not blame them. But as long as Bella was free to take a husband who might become king, she'd be too much of a temptation for many men. For better or worse, the crown must go to Sybilla and Guy. It was the last thing he could do for Outremer—avoid a disputed succession. "There is no other way," he said hoarsely. "They must be wed. . . ."

Balian opened his mouth to protest further, then saw the futility in it. How could he badger a dying man? He could not even argue that this was too high a price for Bella to pay, not when Baldwin had sacrificed his health, his youth, and now his life to defend the kingdom that was their homeland and the beating heart of Christendom.

Salāh al-Dīn left Damascus on September 17 and struck the first blow of his campaign against the Franks on September 29, attacking Bethsan. The garrison of the castle and the townspeople had gotten advance warning of his approach and fled to safety at Tiberias, leaving the town to be plundered by the Saracens. The next day a contingent of soldiers coming from Kerak under Humphrey de Toron's command was ambushed by some of the sultan's Mamluks and over a hundred of Humphrey's men were taken prisoner. On that same day, Guy de Lusignan led their army out of Saforie toward a looming confrontation with the sultan's forces.

CHAPTER 34

September 1183
Nazareth Hills, Outremer

The constable of the realm, Amaury de Lusignan, was leading their vanguard through the hills surrounding Nazareth. So far they had not come under attack, but he knew that would not last, for he'd lived in the Holy Land for more than a decade, time enough to have mastered the strategies of war as practiced by the Franks and Saracens. While he'd often bloodied his sword in France, he'd had to learn about the forced marches, for they were unique to Outremer. Nor had he encountered fighters like the Saracens before. They swooped in like hawks and then flew away to safety, harassing and infuriating the Franks with their hit-and-run tactics. He thought it was fortunate that they were so vulnerable to the Franks' greatest weapon—a coordinated charge by well-armored knights and their heavier, fiery-tempered destriers.

Yet the charge had to be perfectly timed, not unleashed until the commander felt it would do the most damage. It was a constant challenge to exert that sort of control over prideful knights, men whose natural instincts were to strike back when attacked. Amaury had seen even highly disciplined Templars and Hospitallers break ranks when they could endure no more, and he was determined that none of the men in his squadron would shame themselves like that. Because he'd proven himself at Montgisard, at Marj Ayyun, at Forbelet, and in *chevauchées* beyond counting, men knew he'd not been chosen as constable just because he was Guy's brother. He'd earned their respect where it counted, on the battlefield.

But he often found himself wondering if they would accord Guy that same respect. Guy had never fought in a pitched battle or commanded an army; until now, his greatest accomplishments had taken place in Sybilla's bed. Amaury thought it only natural that the Poulains would harbor doubts about Guy. He shared them, for he knew something about his younger brother that few did—how easily he was influenced by the opinions of others.

They'd been on the march for about two hours when the attacks began. Mounted archers appeared on both sides of the road and the infantrymen protecting the knights' horses reeled back under a withering barrage of arrows. Men began to die. Amaury shouted for his men to keep moving, to hold the line. Some of the Saracens were heading for the vanguard's rear, hoping to encircle them. As long as his men did not break formation, though, they would win this skirmish.

Those infernal Saracen war drums were throbbing, making a hellish racket, and the air was vibrating with shouts and curses and insults. Up ahead he saw that the road was curving and it occurred to him that this would be a very nasty place for an ambush. But he was proud of his men for showing such discipline . . . until they did not.

It happened without warning. Several knights could take no more and suddenly spurred their stallions against their tormentors, shouting the battle cry of St. George. Amaury yelled a warning; it was already too late. Others joined in the charge, a few infantrymen almost getting trampled when the knights shot past them. Within moments, all was chaos. "To me! To me!" Amaury shouted till his throat was raw. But he saw with horror that they were being separated from one another and would soon be overwhelmed by sheer numbers.

It was then that he heard it—the clarion call of trumpets, sounding like Heaven's own harps—and he turned in the saddle in time to see the knights thundering toward them. It was as perfect a charge as he'd ever seen, the Franks riding stirrup to stirrup, lances couched, catching the enemy by surprise. Horses reared, going back on their haunches, and then the Saracens who were not down on the field were in flight, veering off in all directions to thwart pursuit.

Amaury soon corralled his scattered squadron. There were bodies on the ground, most of them wounded, a few riderless horses milling about in confusion. Yet the losses they'd suffered could have been far worse. Sheathing his sword, Amaury rode over to thank his rescuers.

But at the sight of that familiar red cross on their shields, he swore under his breath, for he most definitely did not want to be indebted to his estranged father-in-law; Baudouin would enjoy lording that over him until Judgment Day. The d'Ibelin brothers moved their stallions forward to meet him; recognizing Balian's infamous Demon, Amaury reined in at a discreet distance.

"I am fortunate that you happened to be in the neighborhood," he said, with a tight smile.

Baudouin regarded him coolly. "Count yourself lucky that I thought my daughter is too young to be a widow."

Balian was friendlier. "A scout reported that the vanguard was under attack and we did not want you to have all the fun."

"Well, I am glad that you were so eager to join in the revelries."

Baudouin shrugged. "Your bones would be bleaching by the side of the road by the time your brother decided who should come to your aid."

Amaury frowned at this insult to Guy, but Balian also caught the curve of his mouth, as if he'd suppressed an involuntary smile. He found that quite interesting; so Amaury had some misgivings about Guy's leadership, too. He watched as Amaury turned away, giving orders to deal with the wounded and the dead. His men obeyed him with alacrity, which was also interesting. Glancing over at Baudouin, he said, "I think Sybilla married the wrong de Lusignan."

Baudouin was staring after Amaury. "You mean Amaury would have made a better king than Guy? God save us, your new squire, Ernoul, would make a better king than Guy!"

Balian had often heard Baudouin aim scathing comments at Guy's handsome head. He'd never heard him sound quite so bitter, though, and he did not like it. Baldwin's doctors were no longer sure that his fever would prove fatal; he had actually improved enough to make a slow journey back to Jerusalem by horse litter for further treatment. But all knew this reprieve would be fleeting. Baldwin was dying and when he did, the crown would pass to Sybilla and Guy. Baudouin must find a way to accept that, for what other choice did he have?

Salāh al-Dīn withdrew his army downstream. The Franks then set up their own camp at Ain Jālūt. They had the largest force ever mustered in Outremer, thirteen hundred cavalry and over fifteen thousand foot soldiers, and the Saracens numbered even more. These two great armies were now separated by only a mile, as the men waited to see what their leaders would do.

Jakelin de Mailly found that a large crowd had already gathered outside Guy's command tent, hoping to overhear some of the heated discussion going on inside. Several of Jakelin's fellow Templars were standing by the tent and he started toward them before recognizing Gerard de Ridefort. They'd not noticed his approach yet, so he was able to veer away in time and took up an inconspicuous stance amid the German crusaders; their liege lord, the Duke of Louvain, was taking part in Guy's war council. The others within the tent were the lords of

Outremer, the cleric in charge of the True Cross, the Count of Tripoli, and the grand masters of the Templars and Hospitallers. Only Prince Bohemond of Antioch was absent.

The men were a diverse group: knights and their squires, foot soldiers—all the Poulains who'd responded to Baldwin's summons. There were a number of pilgrims, too, who'd been about to depart the Holy Land, and when they heard of the Saracen invasion, they'd immediately hastened to join the army at Saforie. So had many of the Venetian, Pisan, and Genoese sailors on the ships waiting to take the pilgrims back to their homelands. Jakelin admired their courage and piety, for the safe sailing season was ending and they'd be stranded in Outremer until the following spring. He just wished they'd come better prepared for a campaign; they had weapons, but few had thought to bring food with them and there were already serious shortages reported throughout the camp.

Within the tent, voices were rising again. Reynald de Chatillon's was easily identified, so Jakelin assumed the second one belonged to the Count of Tripoli; Balian had told him that the two men had been at each other's throats since their arrival. He knew what was causing such dissension; by now, all in the camp did. The council was split in twain, torn between those who wanted to take the war to Saladin and those who wanted to adopt the traditional military tactics of Frankish armies: avoiding a pitched battle whilst shadowing the Saracen force, thus keeping the invaders from laying siege to any of their towns or castles.

To no one's surprise, the man arguing so fiercely for battle was Reynald de Chatillon, supported by Joscelin de Courtenay; Amaury de Lusignan; the grand master of the Templars, Arnaud de Torroja; and the crusading noblemen. The men who favored a more conservative, cautious approach included almost all of the Poulain lords and the grand master of the Hospitallers, Roger de Moulins. Both sides were deeply entrenched and their angry debates had been going on since their arrival at Ain Jālūt four days ago. Meanwhile, their supplies dwindled and the patience of the army eroded by the hour, for the majority of the men sided with Reynald. They wanted to fight.

When the council finally broke up, Jakelin waited until Balian emerged and then fell in step beside him. "Nothing has changed, I take it? By now we know what most of the council members think, Balian. But what of Guy? What does he think?"

"God alone knows, for I do not. He began well, Jake, by giving us all a chance to speak. It soon became obvious that the council was stalemated and it was for him to make the decision: war or wait. Since we have remained in camp, you might think he has sided with Raymond and the Poulain lords. But I honestly do not know what his true thoughts are. It is almost as if he is so fearful of making the wrong decision that he can make no decision at all."

"Well, if he heeds Count Raymond and you, he's made the wrong decision for certes," Jakelin said with a grin, for he, too, wanted to fight.

"Do you truly think there is a right decision, Jake?"

Jakelin halted in surprise. "You do not?"

"I have been doing my best to convince Guy that we should not take the field against Saladin, that it would be foolhardy to risk the destruction of our army against a larger force, for a defeat would mean the death of our kingdom, too. But I could argue just as persuasively that we ought to do battle with Saladin, for we're not likely to ever muster so many men as we have now and this chance might not come again."

"Jesu, Balian, what are you saying? That it does not matter what we do, that we are doomed whether we choose to fight or not?"

"I do not believe we are doomed!" Balian snapped, sounding as angry as Jakelin had ever heard him. "The Almighty will not forsake us in our time of need. But prayers alone will not be enough. We need to stop fighting one another and unite against Saladin."

"You would not happen to know how we can manage that miracle?"

Jakelin's wry tone took the edge off Balian's anger. "I'm working on it," he said, and they exchanged rueful smiles. They continued on in silence. Jakelin knew Balian was heartsick about Isabella's wedding and wished he had comfort to offer. But he could think only to ask how Maria was bearing up.

Balian was silent for a time; he found it painful to talk about the looming marriage that would bind Isabella to a family he and Maria loathed. "About as well as you'd expect," he said at last. "Once Maria realized that she could not change Baldwin's mind, she swallowed her pride and wrote to Humphrey's mother, asking Stephanie if Bella could continue to live at Nablus for a few more years after the wedding. It was a very reasonable request since Bella is only eleven. But Stephanie knows nothing of a mother's love and she insisted that Bella's proper place must be with her husband at Kerak."

Jakelin started to say how sorry he was, then realized how hollow those words would sound. "This is probably not the best time to give you more bad news, Balian. But you'll hear about it soon enough. My order needs a new seneschal and I fear our grand master will choose Gerard de Ridefort."

Balian stared at him. "You are not joking? Has your grand master lost his wits?"

Jakelin could only shrug. "Gerard is very good at currying favor with powerful people. Remember how he weaseled his way into Count Raymond's household? Then he got the de Courtenays to vouch for him as the kingdom's marshal. So it should be no surprise that since joining our order, he has done all he could to make life easier for the grand master, always eager to volunteer and offering support and praise for Master Arnaud in our chapter meetings." After making a face, Jakelin added glumly, "And here's a thought to keep us all awake at night. If Gerard does become our seneschal, we'd best pray for the health and safety of our grand master. If he dies suddenly, his seneschal will be likely to succeed him."

Balian found that prospect so appalling that words failed him and he could only shake his head in disbelief. Before he could question Jakelin further, they heard shouting and turned to see one of their best turcopole scouts galloping into the encampment. After recognizing Balian, he reined his stallion to a sudden stop. "My lord, where can I find the Count of Jaffa?"

"In his tent. What has happened, Ilyas?"

"Saladin has dispatched raiding parties to ravage and plunder the countryside. They have already burned the village at Jenin and taken Forbelet and they are now heading toward Mount Tabor to attack the monasteries there."

The October sky was aglow with the vibrant colors of an Outremer sunset and Balian paused for a moment to watch the dying of the day. Then he braced himself for an encounter he did not expect to enjoy and, approaching one of Guy's household knights, announced that he needed to speak with the Count of Jaffa.

Guy's tent was both spacious and luxurious, even having an inner partition like the tent of Saladin that Balian had seen years ago. He thought Guy would have done better to choose more modest accommodations for his first command; he knew many had been put off by Guy's obvious glee in his rise to the regency. After a delay that he suspected was deliberate, he was finally ushered into the tent's inner section, where he found himself met with hostility.

He was not surprised by Joscelin de Courtenay's blatant animosity, but he had not expected Guy to be so openly antagonistic, for they'd never quarreled. Apparently just being Baudouin's brother was damning in Guy's eyes. Only from Amaury did he get a polite greeting.

Guy gestured impatiently when Amaury offered wine, cutting off his brother rudely in midsentence. "What do you want, d'Ibelin?"

Balian allowed himself to raise an eyebrow at the truculent tone, no more than that. "I want to talk to you, my lord count, about this campaign and what I think we should do."

"I know what you've advised, that we not do battle. What more is there for you to say?"

"That I have changed my mind." That got their attention. Amaury looked interested, Joscelin skeptical, and Guy oddly angry. "I did indeed urge caution, for reasons we've already discussed in council. We must always weigh the risks ere we commit our men to battle, especially when the enemy is so eager for that battle. I've found," Balian said, with a faintly ironic smile, "that it is rarely a good idea to do what the Saracens want us to do."

"So why are you now arguing the opposite? What new game is this?"

Balian was at a loss to explain Guy's attitude, but he was determined to have his say. "I have changed my mind because circumstances have changed. In the past two days, the Saracens have wreaked havoc upon the kingdom. They have destroyed Jenin and Forbelet and plundered the Greek monastery of St. Elias, and now we hear that they are threatening Nazareth."

For the first time, Balian acknowledged Joscelin's presence. "You were at Ascalon when King Baldwin decided not to engage Saladin's army. You agreed, as we all did, that it was the right decision by the young king, for we were hopelessly outnumbered. But when Saladin turned his raiding parties loose upon the countryside, the king changed his mind. He told us that he could not watch and do nothing whilst his people were slaughtered, their houses burned, and their livestock stolen. That, too, was the right decision, resulting in our great victory at Montgisard. But even if we'd lost that battle, it still would have been the right decision."

Guy raised his hand, as if he'd heard enough. "You need to consult with your fellow conspirators, d'Ibelin. They continue to insist that we must refuse to do battle with Saladin."

"'Fellow conspirators,'" Balian echoed. "What are you talking about?"

Guy and Joscelin exchanged knowing glances, and then Guy deliberately turned away, moving to the table and picking up a pair of dice. "Jos? Amaury? Who's for a game of hazard?"

Balian was too astonished for anger. After a moment, he turned and walked out. Exiting the tent, he headed back toward the area where the men of Nablus were camped. He soon heard hurried footsteps behind him and swung around to confront his pursuer.

It was Amaury de Lusignan. "I will likely regret this," he said, "but we ought to talk."

"About what? Whether your brother has gone stark, raving mad?"

"He should have heard you out, not dismissed you as if you were a servant. But he'd just learned he's been betrayed and men tend to lash out at any and all targets when that happens."

"What betrayal? And what did he mean when he called me a conspirator?"

"This morning, Guy summoned Count Raymond and your brother. He wanted to know if they were still unwilling to do battle with Saladin. Unlike you, they have not changed their minds. But later Joscelin came to us with rumors his spies had picked up in camp. Trusting soul that he is, he spies on others besides the Saracens."

"What are these rumors he claims to have heard?"

"That some of the Poulain lords have ulterior motives. They do not want us to win a great victory over Saladin, for the glory would go to Guy as commander of the army, and then they'd have no hopes of getting the regency away from him or keeping him from becoming king."

"Jesus, Mary, and Joseph," Balian said wearily. "And Guy believed that?"

"Is it really so far-fetched, Balian?"

"Yes!"

"I wish I could say that, too. But I wanted you to understand why Guy's nerves were so taut and why he acted like such a horse's arse with you." Amaury started to turn away, then stopped. "I argued for a battle because I believe we have a chance to rout Saladin's army the way we did at Montgisard. And, yes, I was also aware how much Guy needs this win, how much he needs his first command to be a success." He did not wait for Balian to respond and walked back toward his brother's tent.

Balian watched him go. *How could Guy believe such arrant nonsense? How could any man of honor be willing to let our kingdom suffer just to deny Guy the victory? Surely Count Raymond could never countenance that? Or Baudouin?*

Salāh al-Dīn's attempts to lure the Franks into battle came to naught, and after an eight-day standoff between the two armies at Ain Jālūt, he stopped trying. On October 13, he broke camp and headed toward Damascus. The Franks were still fearful that he might launch another attack and so they marched back to Saforie to keep watch. But they soon received an urgent message from the king, summoning his lords to Jerusalem.

CHAPTER 35

November 1183
Jerusalem, Outremer

Balian had disregarded the king's summons, for if war was no longer looming, he was determined to put his wife and daughter's needs first, and
he returned to Nablus so he could escort Maria and Isabella to Kerak for
the wedding. Having to leave them there was as difficult as anything he'd ever
done, but Baldwin was awaiting him in Jerusalem. Promising Maria that he would
come back to take her home after the wedding, he and his men settled into their
saddles for another long journey, all those endless miles stretching between Kerak
and the Holy City.

Upon his arrival in Jerusalem, Balian and his knights stopped at one of the
public bathhouses to wash away the grit of the road and then continued on to his
town house, where he changed his clothes before setting off for the palace. Baldwin
might well be angry with him for missing a High Court session, so he went first to
the Archbishop of Tyre's town house to learn the lay of the land; William would
know what sort of reception he'd get if anyone would.

"No, you've not missed the High Court session," William assured him. "Baldwin
has scheduled one for week's end, so you're just in time. He has been conducting a
very thorough investigation, interrogating Guy and all of the lords who were with
the army at Saforie and Ain Jālūt, trying to piece together what happened. Like me,
Baldwin does not understand how we could have assembled the largest army in
the history of the kingdom and yet failed to strike a single blow at the enemy. Nor
do the people understand. Guy has been booed whenever he rides through the city
streets," he said with a touch of malicious satisfaction.

So public opinion has turned against Guy, judging his first campaign to be a failure, just as Amaury feared. Balian agreed with that conclusion, but not for the reasons that men were debating in taverns and on street corners. He was too weary to argue with William, though, nor did he see any point to it, for William was no soldier. Gratefully accepting a cup of wine, he sank back against the settle cushions, feeling as if every bone in his body was aching. "Should I expect a cold reception from Baldwin?" he asked, thinking it was no small feat to be able to have offended both the current king and the future king at the same time.

"No, not at all. Baldwin told me that he'd expected you to accompany Maria and Isabella to Kerak. He also said he was eager to hear what you had to say about the campaign. Why look so surprised? Baldwin has always respected your opinions, Balian."

Balian took a swallow of his wine. "It sounds as if Guy has few friends left at court."

"You do not know the half of it, lad. I'd often wondered if the man had any talents aside from seducing Sybilla. Well, it turns out he has a gift for making enemies. I am sure you will agree that his position is a precarious one, as even he ought to realize. Whose favor should matter the most to him? Whom should he be most concerned about pleasing?"

Balian assumed that was a rhetorical question, yet William seemed to be waiting for an answer, so he provided one. "First and foremost, he needs to keep Sybilla happy since his claim to the crown depends upon hers. And to have Baldwin on his side, of course. After that, mayhap the patriarch, Eraclius, and then as many members of the High Court as he can win over."

William nodded. "That is just common sense, no?"

Balian regarded the other man curiously. "What has Guy done, William?"

"When Baldwin conferred the regency upon Guy, he kept for himself Jerusalem and an annual revenue. His doctors told him that it would be better for his health if he resided in a coastal city, so he requested that Guy exchange Tyre for Jerusalem. Guy refused to do it."

Balian was truly shocked; stupidity always astounded him. "I assume Guy felt Tyre was more profitable than Jerusalem because of its trade," he said after taking a moment to reflect. "But I cannot think of a more blatant example of a man cutting off his nose to spite his face." Swallowing the last of his wine, he stretched his cramped muscles, saying that he'd best be on his way. "You said there is a High Court session scheduled?"

William nodded. "Not just the members of the High Court. The grand masters of the Templars and Hospitallers will be there, too, even Prince Bohemond; he arrived from Antioch a few days ago. Only Reynald de Chatillon will be absent. I assume you saw him at Kerak?"

"I did." Balian's mouth tightened. "In truth, I was surprised to find him there. I am sure he cares only that Humphrey and Bella are legally wed, so I did not expect him to give a fig for the wedding festivities themselves." He stopped then, for the archbishop's face was as transparent as spring water. "William?"

"I would have said something, but I was sure you knew, that Reynald would have told you. He is there because a spy warned Baldwin that Saladin is considering an attack on Kerak."

Balian was already on his feet. "That cankered, treacherous whoreson! He said nary a word about a planned attack on the castle. He knew that if I learned Saladin was leading an army to Kerak, I'd never have left Maria and Bella there, would have taken them to Jerusalem with me, the wedding be damned!"

"We do not know for sure that Saladin is planning an attack," William said, as reassuringly as he could. "Baldwin's spy could be wrong. Even if he is not, you need not fear for Maria and Isabella. Reynald may be the Devil's own, but he is a superb soldier. And Kerak is the most formidable citadel in all of Outremer. It could never fall to the Saracens."

Balian had retrieved his mantle and was on his way to the door. "Men said that, too, about the castle at Jacob's Ford."

"Come in, Balian, and sit beside me at the table. Anselm will get you some wine."

Balian was surprised that Baldwin's voice sounded so strong, not at all like a man who'd been on his deathbed just three months ago. It was significant, too, that they were meeting in the palace solar and not Baldwin's bedchamber, more proof that his doctors had vanquished his mystery fever.

Balian sat as bidden, but almost at once, he rose again, too edgy to sit still. "I need to know what your spy told you about the Saracens' planned attack on Kerak. How reliable is your man? Do you expect Saladin to lay siege to the castle?"

"Whilst I cannot tell you for a certainty that it will happen, it makes sense, given how much Saladin hates Reynald. Moreover, the wedding itself would be a tempting target, offering up some very highborn hostages, including my sister. That is why I sent so many knights with Reynald as soon as we got my spy's report—to make sure Kerak would be well defended. Since it would take a messenger so long to ride from Kerak, I gave Reynald two of my own pigeons to take with him. So far they have not come back to Jerusalem."

That eased Balian's mind a bit. While the Franks had never relied upon the use of messenger pigeons to the extent that the Saracens did, some of the Poulains had become convinced of their value, including the Hospitallers and Templars. "I still wish to return to Kerak, sire, as soon as possible after the High Court's session."

"Of course. I have also sent out scouts, under orders to return to Jerusalem at once if they discover the Saracen army is on the move toward Kerak. If that happens, I will personally lead a relief force to raise the siege. On that, you have my word. Now . . . do sit down again."

"How did you know I was not sitting down?"

"There is nothing wrong with my hearing," Baldwin said with a slight smile. "I heard your chair scrape the floor as you pushed it back and then your pacing whilst you listened to me. I fully understand why your nerves are on edge, but I need to hear your view of what happened at Ain Jālūt. Guy is claiming that he is being unfairly criticized for making a decision—not to fight—that was urged on him by most of the Poulain lords."

Balian conceded there was some truth in that. "I was one of those who counseled Guy to avoid a battle." When Baldwin asked why, he took his time in framing his answer, for it was obvious that a military decision had taken on political ramifications, too. "Historically, we have always been cautious about battles with the Saracens and I explained to Guy that Saladin could afford to lose an army, but we could not, that a loss on the field would mean the loss of the kingdom, too. Also, Saladin was trying very hard to bait us into a battle. Lastly, we were outnumbered and some of his men could have attacked us from the rear if we'd engaged his army."

Anselm had placed a cup at Balian's elbow and he paused to drink. "I changed my mind, though, when Saladin sent out raiding parties, for our people have the right to expect us to protect them." Baldwin nodded and Balian knew they were both thinking of Montgisard.

"So, you are saying Guy's initial decision not to do battle with the Saracens could be justified on military grounds, but once circumstances changed, he failed to take that into account."

"Exactly so, my liege. A failure of judgment can be forgiven unless it is utterly reckless and that was not the case at Ain Jālūt. His other mistakes and blunders cannot be as easily dismissed. Guy sent out an urgent summons to Acre and Tyre for aid, and the pilgrims about to sail responded heroically, as did the crewmen of their ships. Yet Guy made no provisions to feed all these extra mouths. In fact, he neglected to make sure we had enough supplies for the thousands of our foot soldiers. The Templars and Hospitallers and most of the Poulain lords had seen to it that their own men were provided for. But Guy had arranged to take only enough food for three days and men were soon going hungry. It was a failure of leadership and not the only one."

Baldwin's face was expressionless. "What others?"

"He did not take any measures to protect our holy sites even though they would be natural targets for the Saracens. As a result, the Greek monastery of St. Elias was plundered, all of its sacred relics stolen, and the abbey on Mount Tabor was almost overrun, saved only by its walls and the stout defense put up by the monks and villagers. When our food began to run out, Guy asked local villages and towns to provide supplies, but he failed to send out men to protect their wagons and some of them were captured by the Saracens. Even after word reached us of the suffering being inflicted by Saladin's raiding parties, he did nothing."

Balian paused again. "I told Guy what you'd said after learning that Saladin's men were ravaging the countryside, killing and looting—that you could not remain behind the walls of Ascalon whilst your people suffered. But he was not willing to listen to me at that point, convinced that I was his enemy and seeking to lead him astray. His greatest failing, though, was his inability to inspire respect or loyalty or to gain mastery over the other men. When it became obvious that the council was so divided, he should have taken control and made the decision himself."

"He claims the Poulain lords like Raymond and your brother thwarted him from doing that. He accuses them of wanting him to fail and insists he could not give battle to the Saracens because he feared they would not fight for him."

"He never told the council that he wanted to fight. Would some have balked? Mayhap they would. The Count of Tripoli is fiercely independent, as we know. And the Hospitallers and Templars rarely miss an opportunity to remind us that they are accountable only to the Holy Father in Rome. These are men to be persuaded, not commanded. If Guy does not understand that after four years in Outremer, it does not bode well for his regency, much less his kingship."

Balian wished he found it easier to read Baldwin's face. He'd always been able to shield his thoughts and he was even more inscrutable now that he'd gone almost blind. "To be fair to him, sire, Guy is in a difficult position. Likely any man would find it a challenge to overcome the jealousies and suspicions that most Poulains harbor against outsiders. But Guy is floundering as if he has been thrown into water over his head and he does not know how to swim."

"I appreciate your honesty, Balian," Baldwin said, no more than that. Balian was sure, though, that Baldwin was not happy with Guy's first command and that he was understandably furious with his brother-in-law for rejecting his request to exchange Jerusalem for Tyre. He supposed the king could reprimand Guy for his blunders. That would help only if Guy was able and willing to learn from his mistakes. Yet what else could Baldwin do?

As the lords filed into the upper chamber of David's Tower, they saw that Baldwin was already present, seated on the dais with his mother on one side and William on the other. Guy, Sybilla, and Joscelin were nearby, all three of them looking so distraught that some of the men hoped this meant Guy was expecting a humiliating public rebuke.

Once they were seated, the patriarch offered a prayer and then all eyes turned to Baldwin. "Ere we begin the session," he said, "I have bad news to share. Late last night a messenger arrived from Reynald de Chatillon. Kerak is under siege by Saladin."

Balian was on his feet before the words were out of Baldwin's mouth. "When did the siege begin?"

"A fortnight ago." Baldwin anticipated Balian's next question. "They set my pigeons loose ere the start of the siege. Both were shot down by Saracen bowmen, and the first man that Reynald entrusted with an appeal for help was captured and killed. The second messenger managed to get through their lines and outraced his pursuers, for which he will be well rewarded."

"Sire, when did this man escape the castle?"

Baldwin turned toward the sound of Balian's voice. "Nigh on a week ago," he said, and in the silence that followed, Balian was the object of many sympathetic glances, for they all knew how much could happen at a siege in the course of a week.

"We will ride to the relief of Kerak as soon as possible," Baldwin continued. "But there is a matter of grave importance to discuss first. My doctors had expected the worst when I was stricken with a high fever this summer. As you can see, I made a full recovery. Therefore, I am no longer in need of a regent and I am removing the Count of Jaffa from that position."

Like waves racing shoreward, amazed murmurs swept through the chamber. Those who'd hitched their hopes to Guy's chariot looked dismayed. But most of the men appeared relieved or downright joyful. Baldwin waited for the furor to subside before resuming.

"So, I will be the one leading our army to Kerak. I will, of course, expect all of you to take part in that rescue mission."

Joscelin had been conferring with Guy and Sybilla while their audience reacted to this unexpected news. He kept shaking his head, but Guy apparently could keep silent no longer and strode toward the dais. "I am going to speak bluntly," he said, adding "my liege" almost as an insulting afterthought. "I think you are making a great mistake. We all know it is merely a matter of time until you fall gravely ill again, unable to fulfill the duties of kingship. Even though you are now fever free, you can no longer lead troops into battle and will need a horse litter. You still have need of a regent. As my wife and I are your heirs, I am the only logical choice."

There was a moment of shocked silence, for none had expected Guy to throw the gauntlet down like that. Then the lords began to talk among themselves, their voices rising until Baldwin called for quiet.

"My lord Count of Jaffa." He'd invested those five words with such contempt that Guy flushed and Sybilla glared daggers at her brother. The Poulain lords leaned forward intently, sensing something momentous was occurring.

"It does not surprise me that you seem to have forgotten it is the High Court who selects the king, for you have remained ignorant of the history of Outremer. I had not intended to raise your fitness to rule during this session, for we have more important matters to discuss—our plans to raise the siege at Kerak. But if you would have me say it now, so be it. You have not shown yourself capable of commanding our army or governing our kingdom and I have come to realize that turning the realm over to you would be the greatest gift Saladin could ever get."

With that the audience erupted, exclamations of amazement, anger, and joy reverberating across the chamber, some of the men jumping to their feet, others embracing one another triumphantly, a few benches toppled over in the confusion. Balian felt a stab of regret that Baldwin could no longer see the faces of his vassals, for many of them were regarding their king with the same fierce pride they'd bestowed upon him after their victory at Montgisard. As he glanced around, Balian knew he was not the only one thinking that Baldwin, blind, crippled, and doomed, still had more steel in his spine than Guy de Lusignan.

Guy looked as stunned as his supporters and Sybilla seemed on the verge of tears. Recovering quickly, she came forward to stand beside her husband, linking her arm in his as she stared defiantly at her brother. Guy acknowledged her support by squeezing her hand, but then his rage broke free. "I know what this is about. This is a petty attempt at retaliation, punishing me for my refusal to yield Tyre!"

Baldwin's own anger seemed encased in ice. "I am thinking of the welfare of our kingdom. But I would not expect you to understand that."

By now, Amaury de Lusignan had shoved his way to Guy's side, obviously seeking to keep his brother from making a bad situation even worse. So were Joscelin and the patriarch, but Guy paid none of them any heed. Instead, he spun around and stormed from the chamber, with Sybilla right on his heels. Amaury followed hastily. Joscelin hesitated, then he, too, hurried after them. The rest of the men retook their seats, marveling at what they'd just witnessed.

When relative calm had been restored, Roger de Moulins, the grand master of the Hospitallers, rose to speak. "I can find no fault, my liege, with your judgment upon the Count of Jaffa. But does this mean you intend to disinherit your sister the Lady Sybilla? If you are now giving consideration to the rights of your other sister, the Lady Isabella, we cannot do so as long as she remains in danger of becoming a hostage of the Saracens."

Baldwin had realized that someone was likely to raise the issue of the succession, and he could only hope that they'd be satisfied with an ambiguous response. The truth was that he had determined to remedy the mistake he'd made in wedding Sybilla to Guy by having the marriage annulled. He was not yet ready to reveal that, though, so he said only that there would be time enough to discuss the claims of his sisters after they'd raised the siege at Kerak.

At first, it seemed as if they'd accept that. But then his cousin rose to speak and Baldwin sensed that Bohemond was about to dip his oar into troubled waters. "You have proven this day, my lord king, why you are held in such high regard by your subjects despite the accursed disease ravaging your body. You have done us all a great service in removing Guy de Lusignan from the regency and the succession. Yet as much as it pains me to say it, your need for a regent cannot be dismissed as easily as de Lusignan's pretensions. So, I would suggest that we appoint the Count of Tripoli to hold that post, a man of honor and courage who has royal blood running through his veins, a man who has already proven himself to be very capable of command."

Baudouin jumped to his feet before Bohemond was done speaking, for like Bohemond, he'd seen what an opportunity they had with Raymond's most vocal enemies—Reynald de Chatillon, Joscelin, and both de Lusignans—not present for deliberations. "I am sure I speak for many on the High Court when I say we could have no finer regent than the Count of Tripoli."

Hugues of Galilee was the next to speak, offering a heartfelt testimonial on

Raymond's behalf. The count's adherents had seized the momentum and Baldwin was not sure he'd be able to deflect it. He feared that if the proposal to make Raymond the regent carried the day, his allies would then try to get him named as the heir apparent. He was given a brief reprieve when Balian objected to a discussion of the regency at this time, reminding them how they'd argued for days about the succession after Amalric died, a luxury they could not afford as long as Kerak was in peril. It was then that Agnes leaned over to whisper urgently in her son's ear. He listened in surprise, and then laughed softly before calling out for quiet again.

"It was not my wish that we discuss the succession during this session. In that, I am in full agreement with the Lord of Nablus. The safety of those trapped at Kerak must come first. But my lady mother has made an intriguing suggestion, one that deserves to be heard."

When she saw that Baldwin was according her the honor of making her own argument, Agnes rose and turned to look out proudly upon an audience of skeptics. "I understand why so many of you are uneasy about leaving the succession unresolved. You fear that if the king were to be stricken again with another fever, Guy de Lusignan would attempt to lay claim to the regency, even to the crown itself. That fear is not unfounded. I would strongly advise the High Court, therefore, that we recognize the right of the king's nephew to succeed him."

This was as great a surprise as the brutally decisive action Baldwin had taken against Guy and it generated a lively, loud discussion, with everyone wanting to have his say. It soon became apparent that this was a brilliant counterstroke, a compromise that satisfied those who'd not wanted to disinherit Sybilla, those who preferred virtually anyone over Guy, and even those who harbored hopes that Raymond might rule after Baldwin's death, for there would be time to advance his claim once the kingdom was faced with a child king. Only those who still supported Guy were disgruntled and they'd always been in the minority. With surprising unanimity, a decision was made to crown Baldwin's five-year-old nephew and namesake as soon as possible.

On Sunday, the twentieth of November in the tenth regnal year of the king, Sybilla and Guillaume of Montferrat's small son was crowned as the fifth King Baldwin in the Church of the Holy Sepulchre. The citizens of Jerusalem turned out to watch the procession to the church, but the crowd was subdued, their cheering muted. While many were overjoyed that Guy had been barred from the succession, they found it difficult to celebrate the prospect of a long minority. Even those who were illiterate and unfamiliar with Scriptures had still heard that ominous biblical prophecy: "Woe unto thee, O land, when thy king is a child."

Night had fallen when Balian and Baudouin mounted the stairs to the roof of David's Tower. As they watched, the huge bonfire was lit, the first in a series of warning beacons, a fiery promise to the besieged of Kerak that relief would soon be on the way. Baudouin moved closer to the crackling warmth, for a winter chill had set in, then tried again to console his brother. "You need not worry, lad. Reynald would never let himself fall into Saladin's hands. He'll hold that castle until Judgment Day." Balian did not answer and they stood together in silence as the white-gold flames soared up into the black, cloud-smothered sky.

CHAPTER 36

November 1183
Kerak Castle, Outrejourdain

On the morning of her wedding, Isabella awoke to the sound of screaming. Sitting up, she rubbed the sleep from her eyes, not sure if she'd been
dreaming. Her mother was up and dressed already; so were Alicia and
Emma. Isabella was very grateful that Emma had been willing to accompany her
to Kerak. At least she'd not feel utterly alone after her mother departed. She knew
Humphrey, of course, and liked him very much, but she was not sure she could
confide in him the way she could talk with Emma. Her mother saw she was awake
and was turning toward the bed when the shouting began again.

"Mama, what is wrong?" After a brief hesitation, her mother told her that Saladin's army had arrived. That was not a total surprise, for they'd known for days
that Saladin was encamped at al-Rabba, just six miles from the castle. Isabella had
not expected that the siege would start today of all days, though.

Maria sat beside her on the bed and did her best to sound reassuring, reminding Isabella that Kerak was one of the most formidable strongholds in the entire
kingdom, on a high ridge bordered on three sides by steep slopes that led down to
the ravines known as wadis. It could easily hold out until Baldwin arrived with
their army.

"Why are people screaming, then, Mama?"

"Reynald has chosen to defend the entire ridge, so he is refusing to let the
townspeople bring their goods and livestock into the castle, insisting that they
remain in their homes."

Despite the neutrality of the words, Isabella sensed that her mother did not
approve of Reynald's decision. From all the noise, it was obvious that the townspeople were unhappy with it, too, and she felt pity for them, denied the safety of
Kerak's stone walls. But then she saw her wedding clothes laid out on a nearby

coffer and her own reality blotted out all else. Her life was about to change dramatically, even though neither she nor her parents wanted that to happen.

The inner bailey of the castle was so crowded that one of the knights had to clear a path for the women, which he did none too gently, for he was dealing with the lowborn peasants who'd fled from the countryside with their meager belongings. Their goats and sheep had been lowered on ropes into the deep, dry moat that separated the town from the citadel, and their mournful bleating had become so familiar that Isabella no longer noticed it. The refugees looked miserable even though they'd been allowed into the stronghold, fearing that they'd return to their villages to find them burned to the ground.

Other knights came to escort them toward the keep at the south end of the bailey. The great hall occupied the entire first story and was already decorated for the wedding feast, with carpets spread upon the floor and white linen cloths covering the trestle tables; many Poulains had adopted the local practice of eating at low tables while seated on cushions, but Reynald scorned any custom associated with the Saracens.

As soon as they entered the hall, Archbishop Guerricus of Petra came forward to greet them, as did Isabella's aunt by marriage. Mary d'Ibelin had insisted upon accompanying them to Kerak, feeling it was her duty to offer her sister-in-law moral support at such a difficult time. Her good intentions notwithstanding, her presence was no comfort to Maria or Isabella, for neither one liked her all that much.

Isabella politely submitted to Mary's kiss on her cheek. Archbishop Guerricus was assuring her mother that they were in no danger, making the siege sound like a minor inconvenience. Smiling at Isabella, he said that they'd had to change their plans and she and Lord Humphrey were now to be wed in the castle chapel instead of in the cathedral church in town. When he admitted that he was not sure all the wedding guests could fit into the chapel, Isabella thought there were not that many guests. She did not say that aloud, for she knew Humphrey's mother was angry that so many of their expected guests had sent their regrets.

All of the kingdom's highborn lords except Reynald and Humphrey were in Jerusalem attending Baldwin's great council, and most of their wives had chosen not to come without their husbands, not after rumors spread of a Saracen assault upon Kerak. Joscelin's wife, Agneta, was naturally present, as Stephanie's cousin. A modest, unassuming woman quite unlike the flamboyant Stephanie,

Agneta did not look happy to be there. She'd been friendly to Isabella, who found herself wishing now that Agneta and not Stephanie was to be her mother by marriage.

The others on hand were Reynald and Stephanie's vassals and their wives. There were numerous knights, some from Reynald's household, others ordered by Baldwin to accompany him when they'd first heard the rumors of a Saracen attack. Then there was the garrison, castle servants, the wretched refugees from nearby villages, and the entertainers. They'd begun arriving weeks ago—musicians and jugglers and minstrels, even a man with trained dogs; Isabella was looking forward to seeing them perform. But they were in low spirits, fearing both for their lives and the loss of all the money they'd expected to make; weddings of the highborn were usually very profitable.

Humphrey soon appeared and headed in their direction. He amused Isabella by gallantly kissing her hand and was very respectful to Maria, as always, but she still showed no signs of thawing and accorded him no more than cool courtesy. He took solace, though, in the warmth of Isabella's smile. She thought he looked quite handsome in a red and gold tunic and opened her mantle to show him her wedding gown, a brocaded silk the color of ripe plums, and her slippers of green felt, pleased when he praised them extravagantly.

When Humphrey said that Reynald was up on the battlements, Isabella wished she could also do that, for she wanted to see what was happening. She'd never been in a castle with so few windows. Those in her bedchamber were very small and faced the inner bailey, while the only other sources of light were the arrow slits in the outer wall, and the great hall lacked the customary window alcoves; the keep was constructed for war, not comfort.

Isabella had been too young to remember life in her father's Jerusalem palace. She'd been told it was much more elegant than their palace at Nablus. But she'd learned to love their Nablus home. Built around a garden courtyard that was the heart of the household, the house was spacious and sunlit, so different from the bleak frontier fortress at Kerak. And as she stood there in the great hall, just hours away from becoming Humphrey's wife, she knew she did not want to spend the rest of her days in this secluded stronghold, perched high on a mountain within sight of the barren Salt Sea.

Wedding vows were normally exchanged before the bridal couple entered the church so there would be as many witnesses as possible. But Stephanie herded them all into the chapel, for it had begun to rain, unusual in November at Kerak, and Isabella hoped that was not a bad omen.

Isabella would remember only fragments of the ceremony or the nuptial Mass that followed. Her most vivid memory was of kneeling with Humphrey before the altar, dutifully pledging her troth after he did, then holding out her hand to him. When he slid the ring onto her third finger, he said, "With this ring, I thee wed," and Isabella became his wife.

Reynald had missed the ceremony. He put in an appearance at the wedding feast in the great hall, although he was obviously distracted, his thoughts on the Saracen army that had now taken up position around the castle to the south and north; the east and west slopes were so steep that an approach was impossible. Isabella and Humphrey had the seats of honor on the dais, with Stephanie sitting next to her son and Reynald next to the bride.

Reynald made no effort to engage Isabella in conversation, but she was fine with that. Knowing that Humphrey feared him and her mother and Balian distrusted him, she felt very uncomfortable in his presence. She wished her mother had not been seated so far down the table; she was a queen, after all. Stephanie had spared no expense and the menu was a lavish one. The guests were served a soup of almond milk and onions, quail stuffed with herbs and grapes, rice, lentils, roasted wild boar, a cream custard, carobs, and fruit-filled wafers. Isabella was accustomed to Syrian and Greek cuisine, and she thought many of the dishes were rather bland; Humphrey had confided that Reynald would rather starve than eat any food with Saracen seasoning.

Kegs of wine had been brought in from vineyards around Bethlehem and barley beer brewed by alewives in the town. Fruit juices were also provided; Humphrey made sure that Isabella's cup was kept filled with almond milk. He drank very little himself. Male guests were expected to drink themselves into oblivion at wedding revelries, but wine was not flowing as freely as was usual. Isabella guessed many of the men were wisely pacing themselves under the circumstances. She found it passing strange to be celebrating whilst an infidel army surrounded the castle and she thought that surely others must feel that way, too.

Reynald had disappeared in midmeal, rising quickly when one of his knights entered the hall and signaled to him. Stephanie was obviously annoyed that he'd left without saying anything to her, as she was not one for concealing her emotions.

A handsome woman with red hair and green eyes, she bore no resemblance to her son; Isabella assumed Humphrey took after his late father, who'd died when he was seven. Humphrey did not talk much about him, or about his mother, either. He had told Isabella a lot about his grandfather, the constable, though. It had been four years since he'd died defending Baldwin in that Saracen ambush, but it seemed clear to her that Humphrey still missed him very much.

The dishes in the last course had been served and the musicians were performing when there was a sudden loud crash and the building seemed to shake. People jumped to their feet with a hastiness that revealed the state of their nerves. Sir Yvein, one of Reynald's knights, soon entered and strode toward the dais. "You need not worry, my lords and ladies. The Saracens set up two mangonels on the south side of the castle and they are testing them, trying to find the right range." He grinned then, saying that they were wasting their time. "Only one stone cleared the wall and struck the keep. All the others splashed down into the berquilla."

"What is a berquilla?" Isabella asked Humphrey, who explained that was the name for the outside cistern, which functioned as a moat in wartime and a water source in peacetime. He started to elaborate on that answer, to tell her that the castle's greatest vulnerability was at the southern end of the ridge and the cistern had been dug there to keep attackers from tunneling under the walls. But his mother was calling for silence.

Stephanie had gone over to the sideboard and selected a covered silver dish, which she then handed to a servant. "I am sending this out to Saladin," she announced. "I'd not want anyone to go hungry on the day of my son's wedding."

The guests at once began to cheer and clap. Isabella noticed that even her mother smiled. The only one who did not seem impressed by Stephanie's bravura gesture was the servant who would have to venture from the town out to the Saracen camp under a flag of truce.

The tables were quickly cleared away and Isabella participated in her first dance; Emma and Maria had taught her the steps and she was soon enjoying herself. Whenever she caught her mother's eye, Maria smiled, but it was the saddest smile Isabella had ever seen.

It was not long before the servant returned. The dancing stopped, all eyes upon him as he approached the dais and bowed before Stephanie. "I did as you bade, my lady, delivered the dish and your message to the sultan. He thanked you and then he asked in which tower the bridal couple are being lodged. When I told him, he said that he would refrain from aiming his siege engines at that tower."

A silence fell and as Isabella looked around at the guests, she saw that she was not the only one thinking that Saladin had gotten the better of her mother-in-law in that exchange.

It was then that an inebriated male guest asked loudly if it was time to escort the bride and groom to their marriage bed. Isabella blushed, but her mother was already saying, in a clear, carrying voice that was colder than ice, "There will be no bedding-down revelries."

Some of the guests looked disappointed. Archbishop Guerricus quickly agreed with Maria, reminding them that such raucous revelries would be most unseemly since the bride was just eleven. And with that, Isabella's wedding festivities came to an abrupt end.

Isabella and Humphrey knelt in his bedchamber as Nicolas, the chaplain, blessed their marriage bed. He and Humphrey were then ushered out by the women. In the usual wedding, many of the women guests would have been involved in making the bride ready for her groom; on Isabella's wedding night, she was attended only by her mother, Emma, and Mary. It did not take long. As she sat on a stool, her mother brushed her long black hair and Emma turned back the covers. Since people normally slept naked, Isabella was surprised when Maria stopped her as she started to remove her chemise.

Isabella was already giving promise of the beauty she would one day become. Her flux had not begun, though, and her body was still slim and childish, not yet showing any womanly curves. But Balian had told Maria that lads of seventeen were in a constant state of arousal, so she worried that the sight of Isabella's bare skin might tempt Humphrey into forgetting his good intentions.

At a soft knock on the door, Mary crossed the chamber to admit Humphrey. Maria leaned over the bed and hugged Isabella tightly, whispering, "*O Theos na sas kratisei asfali,*" for there was nothing more she could do for her daughter except entreat God to keep her safe. When Isabella murmured, "*Kalinikta, Mitera,*" Maria's throat tightened. It was not just that she'd said "Good night" in Greek, but that for the first time she'd said "Mother," not "Mama."

Humphrey was standing by the bed, politely waiting for them to leave. Taking his sleeve, Maria drew him aside, pitching her voice for him alone. "Remember what you promised my husband and me—that you will not consummate the marriage until Isabella is old enough."

Humphrey was insulted that she'd felt the need to remind him of that promise.

Why would she not believe that he'd never hurt Bella? "I gave you and Lord Balian my word, madame," he said, with a flash of rare resentment, and Maria had to be content with that.

As soon as the women departed, Humphrey closed the door and slid the bolt into place. It occurred to Isabella for the first time that he had the right to do that, to shut out the rest of the world, for she belonged to him now, and she felt a prickle of unease.

"I have your bridal gift, Bella," he said, and was surprised by her look of dismay.

"I have nothing for you, Humphrey! I am sorry, I did not know. . . ."

"That is not customary," he assured her. "The bride's gift to her husband is herself."

Opening a coffer by the bed, he pulled out a cushioned wicker basket. "For your dog . . . Jordan, right? I know you've missed him, but once the wedding and siege are over, he need not stay in the kennels and he can sleep with you in your bedchamber."

Isabella gave him a radiant smile, pleased with the gift and delighted by his revelation. "Thank you! I will have my own bedchamber, then?" When he confirmed that she and Emma would have a private chamber until she was old enough to share his bed, she lay back against the pillows, feeling some of her tension ebbing away.

Moving to the brazier, Humphrey checked to make sure the coals were still smoldering, for November nights could be quite chilly at such an altitude. He crossed next to the table, where he extinguished the candles, all but one in case either of them had to use the chamber pot before morning. Returning to the bed, he undressed quickly, tossing his wedding finery onto a chair. Isabella watched through her lashes, saw him start to pull his braies down his hips, stop, glance in her direction, and keep them on. Realizing that he'd done that for her sake, she smiled again. Her new husband had a kind heart and, as young as she was, she still understood the value of that. Getting into bed, he leaned over and kissed her on the forehead, as her mother and Pateras so often did. She suddenly felt very tired and soon afterward, he saw that she was sleeping. He watched her for a time and eventually fell asleep with a smile on his face.

Their first night of marriage was surprisingly peaceful, given the circumstances, but Isabella and Humphrey's awakening the next morning was not. They were jolted back to reality by screaming, shouting, cursing, the sounds of running feet on the tower roof, and the crashing of mangonel stones against the south wall. Humphrey dived from the bed, opened a coffer, and snatched up the first clothing at hand. "I must see what is happening," he explained as he headed for the door. "I'll send Emma in to help you dress, Bella." And then he was gone.

Isabella slid out of bed, padded barefoot across the chamber to peer out of an arrow slit. All she could see was part of the eastern castle wall and the man-made sheer slope that lay below it; it was called a glacis, for the rock had been smoothed to a glass-like surface, making it impossible for invaders to scale. It was Emma who brought the bad news, telling her that the Saracens were attacking the town. Unlike Nablus, Kerak had walls, but they were neither as high nor as thick as the castle walls and Isabella hated to think what could befall the townspeople who'd pleaded in vain to enter the stronghold.

Isabella and Emma stood, frozen, in the tower doorway, never having seen a scene so chaotic. People were panicking. The noise level was so high that it hurt their ears. The sounds of the mangonels' stones striking the walls almost drowned out the cries of the frightened animals—the stabled horses and the castle livestock in the lower bailey and the villagers' sheep and goats huddled in the moat. Some of the refugee children were wailing loudly; others crouched down in the dirt, made mute by their fear, while their mothers sobbed and their fathers prayed. Wounded men were being helped across the inner bailey. Others ran along the battlements, clutching crossbows and bolts. It was like watching a torrent of humanity and neither Isabella nor Emma dared to venture out into that swelling tide.

They were rescued by the chaplain. Father Nicolas dragooned two of the stable grooms into helping and the three of them formed a battering ram, Isabella and Emma sheltering behind them as they shoved and pushed their way toward the keep. There Isabella was reunited with her mother and Mary. Stephanie was not one to be daunted by war and her nervous servants were soon scurrying back and forth between the great hall and the kitchen, bearing bread and fruit and slices of pork so the wedding guests could break their fast. Isabella joined Stephanie, Maria, Mary, Agneta, and the archbishop at a table on the dais, but no one had much appetite.

When Humphrey entered the hall, Isabella looked so happy to see him that he flushed. Would she smile like that if she'd heard what Reynald had said? After he'd asked how he could help, his stepfather had snarled, "Stay with the women where you will not be in the way," loud enough for others to hear; he'd seen the grins and smirks on the faces of nearby soldiers. He'd rather have been tortured than repeat those demeaning, scornful words to Isabella or her mother, so he feigned a smile, telling them that Reynald had instructed him to take care of his bride.

The hours dragged by. Reynald and his knights and men-at-arms repulsed the first two assaults fairly easily, but the Saracens kept coming, and they held the advantage in numbers. Humphrey escorted Isabella and Emma back to his bedchamber while Maria assisted Agneta and Stephanie in making ready for the likely flood of wounded. Despite Isabella's pleading, Humphrey refused to take her up onto the roof, saying it would be too dangerous. She'd begun to sulk, in part because she truly could not see anything from the arrow slits and in part to test their boundaries. He seemed so distressed by her disappointment that she began to feel guilty, and she found herself assuring him that she was not really that distraught. It was then that the shouting changed; suddenly they heard nothing but screaming.

Rushing to the window, Humphrey called to a soldier in the bailey below. Sprinting toward the steps leading up to the ramparts, he yelled over his shoulder that the Saracens had broken through and were in the town. Humphrey, Isabella, and Emma stared at one another in horror, and then he rushed for the door, saying that he had to help and ordering her to stay in the bedchamber, where she'd be safe. He did not take the time to put on his armor, needing his squires' help for that, just grabbing his sword and scabbard as he disappeared into the stairwell.

As soon as he was gone, Isabella started for the stairs, too. But she went up, not down, and emerged onto the roof of their tower, with Emma protesting a few steps behind. Earlier, she'd seen men up there. They were gone now, joining the desperate fight to save the town. To Isabella's frustration, her viewpoint was still limited. While she could see the town, the gate was not visible, blocked by the northeast tower above it. She could see the bridge over the moat, though, and it was packed with people, shoving and pushing and screaming as they tried to escape into the castle. "God help them, Emma!" she cried, for it was obvious that not all of them were going to make it.

Men on the battlements were trying to shoot crossbows and throw down stones, but they risked hitting the terrified noncombatants or some of their own soldiers, for there was fierce fighting in the streets. Isabella thought she caught a glimpse of Reynald, his sword bloodied up to the hilt. She did not see Humphrey and she began to pray silently, asking God to spare him.

Emma had been urging her to go back to the bedchamber. She paid no attention, mesmerized by what she was watching. Bodies were sprawled in open doorways and dead dogs seemed to be everywhere, struck down while defending their owners' homes. A few fires had broken out and smoke was coming from the cathedral. Their knights and soldiers had begun to retreat, trying to make an orderly withdrawal toward the castle, and it was only then that she realized the town was lost.

"Isabella!" She whirled at the sound of her mother's voice, for she'd not heard Maria's entrance onto the roof. "Foolish girl, do you not know how perilous this is?" Grabbing her arm, Maria pulled her toward the shelter of a merlon. Isabella did not protest, for she could still see the battle through the embrasure. Isabella had begun to tremble and Maria jerked off her own mantle and draped it over her shoulders. She'd seen dead bodies before, but nothing like this, and she gasped as a Saracen soldier was pushed into the moat and fell screaming to his death.

Those crowding the bridge were soldiers now, no longer civilians, and Maria told her the townspeople had reached the safety of the castle. Not all of them, though. The bodies in the streets and female screams offered grim testimony that some had been too slow, too unlucky. What Isabella did not understand—but Maria did—was that the fate of Kerak hung in the balance. Saracens were racing onto the bridge, too, intent upon forcing their way into the castle with the fleeing soldiers. If they succeeded, the stronghold would fall to Saladin, for its defenders would be greatly outnumbered.

Turning away, Isabella hid her face in her mother's shoulder, unable to watch anymore. The Saracens surging onto the bridge had suddenly halted and were being jostled and bumped by those following them. Maria was the first to realize what was happening. "Some of our knights must be making a stand on the bridge," she told Isabella, feeling deep gratitude toward the brave men willing to sacrifice their own lives to save the castle.

Now that the Saracens were massed on the bridge, the men up on the battlements were shooting crossbow bolts down into their midst, and several fire arrows hurtled through the air to thud into the railing. One of Reynald's knights came into view, advancing onto the bridge with a torch. When he flung it like a lance, it struck a Saracen soldier, who recoiled and then began to slap frantically at his clothing as it caught fire. The knight had been handed another torch and when he threw this one onto the bridge timbers, it started to smolder. With great courage, the knight held his ground long enough to throw another torch and then hastily retreated when he heard a warning shout from the castle battlements.

As soon as he reached safety, a pot came sailing over the wall. It shattered on impact, spilling liquid onto the bridge, the smoking torches, even splashing some of the enemy. And then with a blinding flash, the bridge burst into flames. The

Saracens were already in flight, but one of the oil-splattered men was not fast enough and became a human torch. By now burning wood was falling into the moat, where it showered some of the bleating goats and sheep. As the women watched in shocked silence, the bridge was fully engulfed in flames, stopping the Saracens from entering the castle, yet also cutting off its inhabitants from the rest of the world.

CHAPTER 37

November 1183
Kerak Castle, Outrejourdain

I sabella was alarmed to see blood on Humphrey's tunic and was very relieved when he assured her that it was not his, that he'd helped several injured townsmen and soldiers into the castle. It puzzled her that neither Humphrey's mother nor his stepfather offered any praise for what he'd done; she thought saving lives was just as admirable as taking them. But the hero of the hour was Sir Yvein, the knight who'd almost single-handedly held the bridge until it could be destroyed. The meal in the great hall that evening was celebratory in tone because of Yvein's courage and he was the subject of so many congratulatory wine toasts that by the time he'd reeled off to bed, he'd needed help in finding it.

The triumphal mood in the great hall did not extend to other areas of the citadel. It had already been crowded; now, with the influx of the townspeople, there was no space to accommodate them all. The peasants found themselves treated with even more disdain, uprooted to make room for these new arrivals. They were no longer allowed to sleep in the vaulted halls of the stables and storerooms, evicted so the more affluent apothecaries and chandlers and farriers could settle their families there, and told brusquely to find places to sleep along the walls of the inner bailey.

The townspeople were just as wretched as the villagers. At first, they'd been thankful that their lives had been spared. But some became bitter as they realized they'd lost all of their possessions; their homes would be stripped bare by the Saracen soldiers, their larders emptied, and the houses themselves might well go up in flames before the siege ended. Others were grieving for lost loved ones, for the friends and neighbors who'd not been able to reach the safety of the castle. As they talked among themselves, most agreed that Lord Reynald should not have tried to hold the ridge, the castle, and the town, too. They'd been undone by his arrogance. If he'd permitted them to shelter within the citadel from the first, at least they could have taken their movable goods with them, and no lives would have been lost—unless Kerak fell to Saladin. That was a prospect so frightening that none of them were willing to dwell upon it, for they knew what their fate would be then: slavery or death.

Isabella had heard some of the knights expressing the same anger with Reynald's strategy, although no one dared to say it within Reynald's hearing. He remained very much in command, stalking the ramparts like the lions in the bestiaries that Maria had read to Isabella when she was younger. When he was not directing their defense or rebuking the garrison for not showing more zeal, he was up on the walls, shouting challenges and obscene taunts in Arabic. Isabella marveled at his bravado, for if the castle was captured, he could count his life in the span of breaths. All knew that Saladin had sworn a holy oath to behead him personally because of that raid into the Red Sea.

There were many wounded, both soldiers and townsmen, and Stephanie set up an infirmary in one of the vaulted halls above the stables. The town doctor was among the wounded, so she pressed the women into service, for every lady of a manor or castle needed to have some knowledge of the medical arts and herbal lore. Kerak had been targeted so often by the Saracens that Stephanie had become quite skilled in treating war wounds. Isabella was proud when her mother agreed to tend the injured. She offered to help, too, but Stephanie brushed the offer aside, saying she was too young.

When Stephanie was not supervising the infirmary, she was conferring with the kitchen cooks, checking the storerooms to monitor the supplies, setting up schedules for meals; it was a logistical challenge just to see that so many mouths were fed. Isabella did not like her new mother-in-law at all, finding her to be almost as intimidating as Reynald, but she had to admire her for her energy, confidence, and capacity for command.

The first two days after the town fell were not that bad. The primary problem was the overcrowding, for with so many people underfoot, most of them unable to fight, just crossing the bailey was onerous. But on the third day, the Saracens set up more siege engines—six mangonels within the town and two to the south. They soon turned life into a nightmare for those trapped in the castle.

The air became thick with the dust and debris that swirled into the sky whenever a mangonel hit its target and the constant thudding against the stone walls soon stretched nerves to the breaking point. There was no respite after dark, either, for the sultan kept them operating in shifts day and night. And once they'd calibrated the range of their siege engines, some of the heavy rocks began to crash into the inner and lower baileys, adding a new terror for the besieged. People huddled as close to the walls as they could get, afraid to venture out into the open, for that rain of rocks occasionally proved lethal. They could not even prevent the slaughter of the animals in the moats, had to watch helplessly as daring young Saracens slid down into the deep ditch on ropes and butchered the sheep and goats, sending the meat up to feed their troops.

The stench of blood and death overhung the citadel like a smothering miasma. The horses were terrified, and even the most docile of animals began kicking against their stalls. The destriers became even harder to handle now that they were deprived of their daily exercise; Reynald's favorite war horse, a bay stallion with as evil a reputation as Balian's Demon, trampled a careless groom. Isabella smuggled her small dog from the kennels up to their bedchamber and tried not to think of the stories she'd heard of past sieges, when food ran out and the desperate besieged were reduced to eating the castle's dogs and cats and finally, even the horses.

On the seventh day of the siege, Reynald attempted to set up a mangonel of their own on the roof of the northeast tower, over the gate. But the Saracens targeted it immediately, aiming all six of their mangonels at the tower roof, and they reduced the mangonel to kindling.

Isabella was finding it hard to sleep at night. Even with pillows pulled over her head, she could not block out the rumbling of the mangonels, thunderstorms that never slackened or moved on. She'd placed her dog's basket nearby and once Humphrey fell asleep, she invited Jordan to jump onto the bed, cuddling with him for comfort. And she kept reminding herself that help was on the way. They'd caught sight of a beacon on a distant hill, which meant that a bonfire had been lit in Jerusalem, sending a fiery message across the miles that relief was coming.

But would they arrive in time? Was Baldwin strong enough to lead a rescue mission? And even if their army was able to break the siege and drive off the Saracens, she found little solace in thoughts of what would happen next. Once the infidels retreated, she would be reunited with her brother and her stepfather. Then Baldwin would return to Jerusalem and Pateras and her mother would go home to Nablus, leaving her behind in this desolate desert citadel with Humphrey's sharp-tongued mother and swaggering stepfather.

On the morning of November 22, the groggy castle inhabitants awoke to excited shouts from the battlements; keen-eyed soldiers had spotted the dust clouds rising above the horizon. A large army was approaching. There was great rejoicing—until the riders were close enough for them to see the banners taking the wind. This was no rescue force from Jerusalem. It was another Saracen army arriving from Egypt, led by the sultan's brother al-'Ādil.

It was not until the arrival of Saladin's brother with the Egyptian reinforcements that Maria seriously began to fear that Kerak would fall to the Saracens. She was not afraid for her daughter's life or for her own. They'd be such valuable hostages that their good treatment would be guaranteed. She knew, too, that Saladin had a reputation for being chivalrous with women. But much more was at stake than mere survival. The lives of her household knights. The hundreds of noncombatants who'd be doomed to the slave markets of Cairo or Damascus. The price of the ransoms demanded, for they could be high enough to bankrupt a family's fortunes. And for women, the loss of their honor.

A woman held captive by the Saracens emerged tainted in the eyes of many, for people assumed she had been violated during her captivity. A husband often put such a wife aside, even if she swore she'd not been raped. The perception almost always proved stronger than the reality. Even a queen had been repudiated, the wife of Jerusalem's second king. So, for women, ransom did not end their troubles; often it was just the beginning. A wife cast aside for her "failure to preserve the sanctity of the marriage bed" had little choice except to withdraw to a nunnery. Balian had told Maria that Muslims and Jews were more realistic. They recognized that a woman prisoner could not prevent being raped, and so she was not judged as wanton, not harshly blamed in the way that Christian women were. Yet even in their societies, it was believed that death was preferable to dishonor for a female captive, so it was still not easy for a Muslim or a Jewish woman to return to her former life.

Maria did not fear that she would ever face such a fate. A queen was not cast aside, not if she was an heiress, too. In her case, ending her marriage would also have ended the d'Ibelin claim to her Nablus fief. But she was confident that Balian would not have repudiated her even if she had been violated, even if Nablus were not balanced in the scales. She did not doubt that he loved her. Moreover, he was the fairest man she'd ever known, and unlike so many of his male brethren, he saw the injustice in blaming a woman for being raped. They'd occasionally discussed the plight of female captives and he'd always expressed sympathy for such women.

Maria's fears were for her daughter. As certain as she was that Saladin would never permit Isabella to be carnally abused, she knew that was almost irrelevant.

Balian seemed convinced that Humphrey had a good heart, but who could say what a seventeen-year-old boy might do in such circumstances? Most likely it would be Stephanie who'd make that decision, for Reynald would never survive Kerak's fall. And whilst Isabella would be freed to return home if she was rejected by her young husband or her mother-in-law, that would be a short-term blessing, for her captivity and repudiation could damage her chances of making another marriage. Her beautiful, clever, loving daughter might find her only future lay within the cloister.

Maria consoled herself with the meager comfort that Isabella did not realize her danger. The other woman at Kerak did, though. She saw the fear on their faces. The women of lesser rank were even more vulnerable, their futures more uncertain. At least highborn women could expect ransom. Would the wife of a knight be so lucky? Only Stephanie seemed impervious to the threat, for she was such a great heiress that, besmirched honor or no, there'd be no shortage of men eager to wed the woman who was the Lady of Outrejourdain.

Al-'Ādil had received an enthusiastic welcome in the Saracen camp, for he'd also escorted a caravan of Egyptian merchants with goods they were eager to sell and the soldiers eager to buy. The soldiers were even happier with the arrival of fresh troops. Not only would their numbers speed up the capture of the castle, they'd then take over for the veterans, who'd be able to go home to their families. Resuming the siege with renewed energy, they kept the siege engines going without pause, denying the besieged any rest. But unless their mangonels could shatter the south walls, they could not launch an assault, so they began the laborious task of trying to fill in the moat. Since it was almost one hundred feet deep, they joked about how many years it would take, with men pledging the services of their sons after they'd died of old age.

Twilights were sudden in the Levant and once the sun disappeared below the western horizon, night staked its claim. By the time al-'Ādil and his brother had completed the sunset prayer of *salat al-maghrib*, the sky was as black as polished ebony or Āliya's raven hair, lit by as many stars as there were soldiers with sins to repent.

When the sultan stopped to chat with several of his Mamluks, al-'Ādil paused to admire the formidable silhouette of al-Karak, holding the darkness at bay with flaming torches along the battlements. It posed such a danger to the caravans traveling between Egypt and Damascus that many Muslims wanted to see it razed to the ground, reduced to sheer rubble, preferably with the infidel Arnat's body buried under the stones. Al-ʿĀdil thought that would be a great waste of a strategic site and intended to ask his brother for the castle when it was taken.

If it was taken, he amended, for he knew al-Karak would be no plum ripe for the picking. He supposed it could be starved into submission—eventually. But the Franks would not give them that much time. Their young leper king had never failed to respond to one of their invasions. He'd come to al-Karak's defense even if he had to drag himself from his deathbed.

Upon their return to Salāh al-Dīn's tent, they were joined by his vizier, al-Fādil, and al-ʿĀdil's chancellor, al-Sanīʿa b. al-Nahhāl. Seated on cushions, they sipped fruit sorbets while al-ʿĀdil studied his brother. He'd seemed distracted all day and it was time to find out why. "You still mean to give me control of Aleppo?" Assured that Aleppo was still his, he said, "What is preying on your mind, then, Yūsuf?"

"It involves ʿUmar. I've written to tell him that you will be governing in Aleppo, and he is not pleased."

Al-ʿĀdil was not surprised. He'd known for a long time that their nephew had a soul shriveled by envy, never pleased to see the fortunes of other men rise. But Taqī al-Dīn's discontent could not be dismissed out of hand; he was too good a soldier for that. Moreover, Yūsuf loved him. "How much trouble does he plan to cause?"

"He is complaining about the loss of Sinjār, and when I told him I was giving you control of Manbij, too, he objected strenuously, for he'd long held the *iqta* for that fortress and town."

Al-ʿĀdil was willing to concede that his thin-skinned nephew had a legitimate grievance about Manbij. "So, he wants to be compensated for his losses."

Salāh al-Dīn sighed, for there were times when it seemed as if the entire world was seeking money from him, with their blood kin at the head of the line. All but Ahmad, who'd loaned him one hundred fifty thousand dinars for his campaigns. "I've been giving it a great deal of thought. Now that you will no longer be governing for me in Egypt, I will need someone competent and trustworthy to replace you. I am thinking of sending ʿUmar."

Al-ʿĀdil considered that in a pensive silence. ʿUmar was competent. Trustworthy? More or less, he supposed. And he was the sultan's nephew, no small matter when blood counted for so much. Glancing toward the vizier, he saw a faint smile on al-Fādil's face. Al-ʿĀdil trusted his judgment and if he thought it was a good idea to send ʿUmar to Egypt, it probably was.

His brother had put aside his sorbet. "My old friend will accompany ʿUmar to Egypt," he said, with a fond glance at al-Fādil, "at least until he feels comfortable in his new role."

"An excellent idea," al-ʿĀdil agreed, reassured to see that Yūsuf's affection for Taqī al-Dīn had not blinded him to the need to keep their nephew under scrutiny. "You said that ʿUmar would be joining us at the siege. Does he know yet that you'll be naming him as my replacement in Egypt?"

"No, I thought we could tell him together," the sultan said blandly, and al-ʿĀdil grinned, thinking that he was a better battle commander than his brother and a better administrator, but Yūsuf was a more skilled politician.

He excused himself soon afterward so his brother could get some sleep. As they headed toward his own tent, his chancellor cleared his throat several times, a sure sign that something was on his mind, and he gave the younger man an encouraging glance. "I am listening."

"My lord, will you retain my services once we are settled in Aleppo?"

"Of course. Why would I not? You've been with me for years."

Al-Sanīʿa was surprised that he needed to remind his lord of his controversial background. He'd been born and raised in the Christian faith, but he'd converted to Islam after falling in love with a Muslim girl, so there were always people who looked at him askance, doubting his faith. Neither the Muslims nor the Christians ever put much store in conversions. "Some of those in Aleppo might be suspicious of me," he explained, "once they learn of my history."

"You have my trust," al-ʿĀdil said, "and that is all that matters. In fact, I want you to take charge of my chancellery in Aleppo."

"Thank you, my lord! I am greatly honored and will justify your faith in me. There is one more thing. . . . Several of my clerks are Christians. Have I your permission to continue employing them?"

"If the sultan can consult a Jewish doctor, I see no reason why we cannot hire Christians now and then, provided they are the most qualified." Al-ʿĀdil's step slowed and he turned to stare at the fortress of the Franks, shrouded in darkness but not silent, for their mangonels continued to slam rocks down upon it. His chancellor's mention of Christians brought a particular one of them to mind, the amiable Lord of Nablus, whose wife and stepdaughter were trapped within al-Karak. He stood there for a time, puzzling al-Sanīʿa, who did not know he was imagining his fear if Āliya or Halīma or his children were caught in a siege led by that devil, Arnat.

The weather turned very cold on the morning that marked the first day of December to the Franks and the thirteenth day of Sha'ban to the Saracens. A knife-sharp wind was coming from the mountains of Moab and the sky was blotched with leaden rain clouds. Salāh al-Dīn had been awakened at dawn by one of his scouts, bearing information that was unwelcome but not unexpected. Dressing hastily, he summoned his brother and vizier, and they spent some time discussing how they should respond. Then, Salāh al-Dīn sent for his nephew, for he would have to break the news to Taqī al-Dīn before sharing it with his army.

Once they were seated on cushions, an oil lamp's flickering flame losing its battle against the encroaching gloom of a coming storm, the sultan wasted no time. "I have bad news. One of my scouts has reported that the army of the Franks is coming to the defense of al-Karak and they have already reached the town they call Hebron."

Taqī al-Dīn glanced around the tent and did not like what he saw. "What of it? We are supposed to fear their leper king? A man so crippled that he cannot even ride a horse, must be carted around like a sack of flour."

"His knights can ride," al-'Ādil said, keeping his tone mild.

Taqī al-Dīn scowled, but before he could reply, the sultan leaned forward, his hands resting on his knees, his body language conveying composure. "I have decided that there will be no battle. We will withdraw ere the Franks arrive."

As he expected, his nephew erupted in outrage. "I thought you wanted to fight the Franks! How are you to drive them into the sea if you are unwilling to face them on the field?"

"It will happen in Allah's time and by Allah's will," the older man said calmly. "I think it makes sense to postpone the day of reckoning. Our men are tired, eager to go home. Discipline is always a problem with our soldiers, as you well know. And the holy fast of Ramadān is approaching. We can afford to wait."

Taqī al-Dīn could not recall ever being so angry. He glared at his uncle, thinking that he was becoming an old man, with no more ballocks than the eunuchs that guarded their harims. But he managed to swallow those words. He could probably have gained Yūsuf's forgiveness for speaking his mind; he'd always been able to do so. Ahmad was less forgiving and he had Yūsuf's ear. So did al-Fādil and he was slowly shaking his head in an unmistakable warning.

"I do not agree," he said at last, knowing he sounded sullen, not really caring. "But it is your decision, Uncle, not mine."

It was not a graceful concession, but Salāh al-Dīn was sure of his own authority and did not need subservience from others to prove it. "My brother and I will depart in a few days' time for Damascus. I want you to ride for Egypt, where you will rule in my stead."

Taqī al-Dīn inclined his head, still angry, but somewhat mollified by the reminder of the power that awaited him in Egypt. He could not resist one last parting shot, though, warning his uncle that he was losing a chance to make the infidel Arnat pay for his sins against Muslims, one that might not come again.

"You need not fear, Nephew. That is a debt that will be paid." Although the sultan did not raise his voice, Taqī al-Dīn was suddenly glad that he'd kept his temper under control.

Once they turned east toward Kerak, the army of the Franks took up battle formation, compelling Baldwin's litter to withdraw to the rear. He was one of the last, therefore, to hear the report from their scouts. Alerted by the sudden shouting, he leaned out at the approach of the Count of Tripoli and several other lords. Reining in beside the litter, Count Raymond slid from the saddle with one of his fleeting smiles. "Good news, sire. Our scouts say that the Saracens are gone. Clearly, they heard of our approach, for they have retreated. The siege is over."

The abandoned Saracen camp had a forlorn appearance. They'd taken everything of value, possessions and plunder, but there was always stuff left behind when an army moved out. Campfires had been extinguished with sand. Latrine ditches scarred the rocky ground and litter was being blown about, collecting wherever tattered tents still stood, judged too weathered to be packed up.

The men slowed their mounts as they approached the town walls and most of them grew quiet, for they were looking upon a scene of tragedy and abject misery. The town of Kerak was no more, its bones picked clean. The cathedral church rose up from the ruins like a shattered tombstone, its roof fallen in, a few charred pillars still standing in the nave. Doors of houses were kicked in, shops ransacked, discarded trash everywhere. Wine kegs had been dragged from taverns and axed open, so much wine spilled into the ground that the odor still lingered. No dogs had survived, but a few hungry cats had emerged from their hiding places, only to fade away again as the men entered the town. They rode slowly through the streets toward the moat, warned by the stench of what they would find: the bodies of men and carcasses of animals thrown down into the ditch to rot.

But across the moat were the living and they were joyfully embracing their deliverance and eager to embrace their rescuers, too. Men were hanging over the citadel's walls, cheering and gesturing. The gate soon opened, the Lord of Kerak striding out to welcome them. Reynald looked tired, otherwise none the worse after a month-long siege, and he had a cocky grin on his face, as if he were the one responsible for driving the Saracens away.

Riding to the edge of the moat, Balian swung from the saddle, laughing from sheer relief when he recognized Maria among the women now emerging from the castle to greet them. Isabella was already there, waving wildly to attract his attention. He was looking appraisingly at that deep moat when he heard his brother's voice behind him. "Do not even think of doing it."

"What?"

"You know what, Balian—lowering yourself down by rope and then trying to climb up the other side. You'll just break your damn fool neck."

Balian could not argue with that, but he still said, "You could help me, Baudouin. After all, you've a wife over there, too."

"True enough," Baudouin said, then grinned. "But I'm not that desperate to be reunited with her." Giving a sudden shout, he caught the attention of the jubilant knights congregating across the moat. "So, we cannot get into the castle until you lazy drones build another bridge?"

That sparked laughter, for the garrison found humor in everything at that moment; a reprieve from death could be as intoxicating as the strongest wine. "Go back to the berquilla!" one man yelled, gesturing toward the southern end of the castle. "Swim across it and we'll lower a ladder from the wall for you. Or you can try to make your way around the cistern—as long as you're not as clumsy as you look."

Baudouin cheerfully told him to do something anatomically impossible, setting off another wave of raucous laughter. The rest of the rescue force were studying the sheer angle of the slope and the dizzying drop down into the wadi below, while wondering how badly they wanted to enter the castle.

When they'd reached the Salt Sea, Baldwin had been compelled to turn the command of the army over to the Count of Tripoli. He was still given such a warm welcome when the people spotted his horse litter that he found himself fighting tears. It meant more than he could ever say that his subjects understood how much he'd sacrificed for them, understood that he'd clung to royal power only to keep them and the kingdom safe.

Despite being hailed as their savior, Baldwin did not linger at Kerak, remaining only long enough to give his men and horses a much-needed rest. He preferred to spend Christmas in Jerusalem, where he'd have greater comfort and greater privacy.

His lords were eager to return to their own homes, too, after four months in the field. Balian and Maria intended to accompany the king back to Jerusalem, then to continue on to Nablus and hold their own Christmas there. They knew the days were gone when Baldwin would be presiding over a Christmas or Easter court. In the past year, he'd appeared in public only when his royal duties demanded it and he'd begun to wear the Saracen headdress, the kaffiyeh, which enabled him to shield his face from curious or pitying eyes.

On an overcast morning in mid-December, the army left the ravaged town, where the devastated residents were trying to pick up the broken pieces of their lives as best they could, and descended into the wadi that bordered the castle on its eastern side. Isabella and Humphrey hastened across the bailey toward the keep, racing each other up the stairs to the roof so they could watch until the riders were out of sight. Isabella had told Balian and her mother that she'd be there and so they kept turning in their saddles to wave until Kerak had receded into the distance and Maria could no longer hold back her tears.

Guy de Lusignan was not among those heading for Jerusalem. He'd seethed during their march to Kerak, complaining angrily to his brother that the other lords were shunning him as if he were the accursed leper, not Baldwin. He did have one ally left, and Patriarch Eraclius privately warned him that he believed Baldwin had it in mind to annul his sister's marriage, thus neatly solving the problem posed by the brother-in-law he'd judged and found wanting.

Guy was stunned by this warning. Privately, he'd always dismissed Baldwin as a helpless cripple. He'd never imagined that the leper king would prove to be such a lethal enemy. He was appalled to think that Baldwin could take away all that mattered to him—his marriage to a woman he loved and the kingdom that belonged by rights to them both. So, as soon as he could, Guy had gathered his household knights and rode swiftly to his stronghold at Ascalon, quickly putting it on a war footing. He then sent an urgent message to Sybilla, telling her to leave Jerusalem at once and join him at Ascalon, which she was willing to do, even though it meant she had to leave her young son behind.

CHAPTER 38

January 1184
Ascalon, Outremer

The wind was coming now from the west, carrying the scent of the sea and alerting them that they were not far from Ascalon. When Baldwin's horse litter came to a halt, his lords and knights reined in their mounts, too, and began to murmur among themselves, for they were not sure what to expect upon their arrival. Guy had repeatedly defied the king, refusing every summons to Jerusalem by claiming he was ill. But they still found it difficult to believe that they were actually facing a rebellion. Could Guy truly be that crazed?

At Anselm's signal, a squire brought a horse up from the rear. Baldwin struggled from the litter, but despite Anselm's help, he could not mount. Most of the knights averted their eyes, for even the least sensitive among them could find no humor in their king's humiliation. To men he'd fought with, he'd never be a laughingstock.

"Let me give you a hand, sire." Dismounting swiftly, Balian came forward to balance Baldwin while Anselm guided his boot into the stirrup. Taking advantage of his height, Balian then boosted Baldwin up into the saddle, all the while trying not to remember that the young king had once ridden like those mythical Greek centaurs in Maria's bedtime tales to their children.

Reclaiming his reins from Baudouin, Balian swung back up into Smoke's saddle. As their eyes met, he saw that his brother also understood the significance of Baldwin's action. Unlike most of his men, he *did* expect Guy to defy him and he was determined to have that confrontation as a king, not an invalid.

They halted again once the walls of Ascalon came into view. They would normally have entered via the Jerusalem Gate, but its complex defenses would be too challenging for Baldwin to navigate on his own. They chose, instead, the Jaffa Gate. Baldwin could still distinguish some light and shadow in his left eye and he'd joked to Anselm that it would be hard to miss a walled city. But now that he was astride a horse he'd never ridden and acutely aware of his body's weakness, his fear of making a fool of himself was as strong as any fear he'd felt on the battlefield. Some of his anxiety eased when he realized that he was not alone: Denys was riding on one side, Anselm on the other, ready in case his horse balked or, Jesu forfend, bolted. So far, the gates stayed shut and although he could not see them, he was sure that men would be lining the battlements, staring down at him.

When they reached the square tower protecting the Jaffa Gate, Denys adroitly maneuvered his horse so that Baldwin's mount shifted sideways. When he felt his leg brush a hard surface, Baldwin leaned from the saddle and slammed his left hand against the wooden door. "Guy de Lusignan! As your king and liege lord, I demand that you give me entry!"

He could hear voices now from the men up on the walls, echoes of alarm and excitement running through their ranks. He waited and then struck the gate again, repeating his formal demand for entry. He did this three times, following the protocol for dealing with a rebellious vassal. There was no response from within; the gates of the city remained closed to him.

From Ascalon, Baldwin rode to Jaffa, the other city under Guy's command. At Jaffa, his reception was quite different; the citizens and castle garrison came out to welcome him into the city. He quickly appointed a new governor for the citadel, thus depriving Guy of one-half of his fief. When he resumed his journey, he continued up the coast to Acre, where he'd summoned a general assembly. They'd been planning to discuss sending another delegation to the West with a plea for help. But his lords knew that he also meant to strip Guy of all his holdings in the Holy Land, to turn this would-be king into an outlaw or an exile.

The general assembly was held in the great hall of the palace at Acre. With the exception of Guy, all of the lords of the kingdom were in attendance, even Count Raymond and Amaury de Lusignan. When challenged by Baudouin and others, Amaury calmly retorted that unless the king relieved him of his duties, he meant to continue serving as Baldwin's constable. While that did not satisfy his critics, it did silence them. After the invocations were completed, the patriarch and the grand masters of the Templars and Hospitallers rose and approached the dais.

Eraclius declared that they had a matter to discuss, so urgent it must take precedence over other business. The patriarch was known to be an eloquent speaker and he launched into a well-rehearsed presentation, saying they all agreed that the king had good reason to be wroth with his disobedient vassal, the Count of Jaffa. But they'd come to entreat the king to forgive Count Guy, insisting he must pardon the count for the good of the realm.

Baldwin heard them out in a stony silence that should have warned them. Apparently, it did not, though, for all three of them seemed genuinely surprised when he said, turning words into weapons, that he had no intention of pardoning the Count of Jaffa, not even if the Archangel Gabriel himself were to plead on the count's behalf. They did not argue with him, realizing it would be in vain. Instead they shocked the audience by turning and stalking out.

Their angry departure threw the assembly into chaos. Since the planned delegation to the West was to be led by the patriarch and the grand masters, there could be no decisions made in their absence. Once calm had been restored, Baldwin called for silence. "We must postpone discussion of the delegation until another time. We can discuss, though, the rebellion by the Count of Jaffa and the consequences of his rebellion."

"What do we need to discuss?" Baudouin rose to his feet. "De Lusignan has forfeited his rights to the lordships of Jaffa and Ascalon by his defiance of our king."

It had been a long time since Baudouin had found such favor with Baldwin. "The Lord of Ramlah has gone to the heart of the matter. Guy de Lusignan has proven himself unworthy to be a king, a regent, or a lord of this realm. I would strip him of his title and his fiefs and ask that the general assembly support me in this in accordance with the assize governing liege homage."

Like the High Court sessions, general assemblies required patience, for each man was determined to have his say. At first, Baldwin was gratified by what he heard, for Guy found none to defend him; even his brother held his peace, a silent observer as Guy was judged and found guilty. But gradually it became apparent that few of the lords were echoing Baudouin's demand that Guy be dispossessed. They were willing to condemn Guy in the strongest language possible, yet stopped short of taking the next step—to pass the judgment that Baldwin wanted.

It was Denys who finally spoke for them, taking on that burden as the king's stepfather. "We are in agreement, my liege, that Guy de Lusignan deserves to lose the lands and honors he gained through marriage to your sister. But we are caught between a wall and a very sharp sword, for de Lusignan will not willingly relinquish Ascalon. We shall have to go to war to rid ourselves of him, and that we dare not do. If we fight amongst ourselves, we are giving Saladin the keys to the kingdom and I think you know that as well as any man here."

"I cannot pardon a vassal who has defied me as de Lusignan has done. No king could."

"I know," Denys said sadly, "I know. . . ."

Baldwin slumped back in his seat. He could not even muster up anger, for whilst he was right, so were they. He dared not let Guy get away with his defiance, not if he hoped to hold on to any shreds of royal power. But neither could they risk a civil war.

Baudouin was one of the few willing to take that risk, so convinced was he that Guy de Lusignan's very presence was poisoning his homeland. The danger was too great that Guy and Sybilla would seize power when Baldwin died, he argued with impassioned candor. Eventually even he subsided, realizing that Saladin cast too great a shadow for most of the men.

It was then that Balian came up with a way to end the impasse. "Sire, if I may speak? We are in agreement that we cannot uproot Guy from Ascalon by force. But neither can he be allowed to escape the consequences of his lawless behavior. May I suggest that we wait, bide our time? Guy will not dare to venture from the safety of Ascalon's walls, fearing he'd be seized and dragged to Jerusalem for judgment. For now, he is a defanged snake. Let him cower in his lair whilst we deal with the greater danger, the threat Saladin poses to the kingdom."

At first it seemed too simple a solution. Once they considered it, they realized its brilliance lay in that simplicity, offering them a path out of the wilderness. None were happy with it, Baldwin least of all, but this was the best they could do for now and they knew it.

"I do not understand, Humphrey." Isabella fought back a wave of panic, for she'd not been prepared for this. "Why can we not spend Easter with my family?"

Humphrey no longer met her eyes. "Easter is one of the most sacred days on the Church calendar and my mother and Reynald want us to observe it together."

That made no sense to Isabella. She could have been invisible for all the notice Stephanie and Reynald took of her, and the only time they paid any attention to Humphrey was when he'd somehow incurred their displeasure. "You know how disappointed I was when I was not allowed to visit my family last month on my twelfth birthday. I did not make a fuss, though, did I? But I can wait no longer, Humphrey. I've not seen them since November and it is now near the end of March! You must talk to them again, make them understand that."

Humphrey did not know what to say. Emma did, though. Stepping forward, she regarded him with ill-concealed contempt. "My lord, is it not time you finally tell her the truth?"

Isabella swung around to stare at her. "Humphrey would not lie to me, Emma. Would you, Humphrey . . . ?" He looked so stricken that she faltered. "Humphrey?"

"Forgive me, Bella. I was just trying to spare you hurt. . . . I did not know how to tell you that my mother and Reynald have forbidden you to visit your mother and Balian."

"But . . . but why?"

"They say that . . . that your mother is an evil influence upon you."

With that, Isabella's shock gave way to anger. How dare these hateful people malign her mother like that? She started toward the door, stopping when Humphrey did not move. "Are you not coming with me? We must talk to your parents, make them understand."

Humphrey well knew how futile that would be. But he also knew that he could not let her venture alone into the lion's den.

Stephanie sat on a coffer while her maid brushed out her hair; it reached to her hips and attracted an admiring glance from Reynald as he entered their bedchamber. "Leave it loose," he said, and she gave him a knowing smile, for that meant he wanted to swive her that night.

"A courier has arrived from Antioch," he said. "The news about Constantinople is bad."

"It could hardly get worse," Stephanie pointed out, for the Greek empire had begun to resemble a doomed ship, water pouring in from a hole in its hull while its rigging burst into flames. The news had reached Outremer in December that Andronicus had done what all had feared he'd do. He'd ordered that the boy emperor be strangled and his body thrown into the Bosporus. He'd then wed the boy's twelve-year-old widow, surely the most ill-fated of any French princess.

"Bohemond thinks it will indeed get worse. He says Andronicus will prove more bloody-handed and depraved than any of the Roman emperors, including Nero and Caligula."

Stephanie had no idea who Nero and Caligula were and suspected that Reynald did not know, either. "Does Bohemond think Andronicus might be overthrown?" she asked. Before Reynald could respond, a knock sounded at the door, and they both were surprised when her maid ushered their daughter-in-law into the chamber, trailed by Humphrey.

Isabella was never sure how to address her in-laws. Even though she was of higher rank as a king's daughter and a potential queen, they seemed to want her to show deference and so she did, sensing it was better to humor them. She dropped a perfunctory curtsy now, trying to act as if there were nothing unusual about her presence in their bedchamber.

"I apologize for the intrusion, my lord, my lady. But Humphrey has told me that you do not want me to go to Nablus to see my family and surely he must have misunderstood. . . ." Isabella's heart was racing and she paused for several deep breaths, not wanting them to see her unease. "I have not seen them in nigh on four months and I miss them very much."

Stephanie and Reynald were staring at her in astonishment, which quickly turned into annoyance. "You will adjust, Isabella," Stephanie said briskly, "for this is the way of our world. I am not saying that you can never see your parents. But you cannot go running off to Nablus whenever the whim takes you. A wife's place is with her husband, as Humphrey ought to have explained to you."

"But I miss them very much, madame! Not just my mother and stepfather. I miss my brother, Johnny, and my sisters Helvis and Margaret. They miss me, too, and they are too young to understand why I have not come to see them—" Isabella stopped then, for Stephanie was glaring at her the way she usually glared at Humphrey.

"Will there be anything else, Isabella? If not, we bid you good night."

Stephanie's tone was so icy that Isabella shivered. "But I do not understand," she said so plaintively that Humphrey winced. His mother was not moved, however.

"It is not necessary that you understand," she snapped, "merely that you do as you are told."

Isabella hid her hands in the folds of her skirts so Stephanie would not see that they were trembling. "I have a right to know why you are forbidding me to see my family."

Reynald had been faintly amused by the girl's obstinacy, for he knew his wife was accustomed to unquestioning obedience from Humphrey. But this had gone on long enough and he said brusquely, "You want an answer, girl? We think your mother would not be a good influence upon you. There you have it. Now, off to bed with you."

Isabella was still afraid, but she was furious now as well. This man had defied her brother, defied his king. He was no better than a brigand. How dare he insult her mother? "I love my mother very much," she said, and Stephanie lost all patience.

"I am not surprised that Maria has raised a spoiled brat, but you will mind your manners here or suffer the consequences!"

No one had ever spoken to Isabella like that and she took an involuntary backward step. One glance toward Humphrey told her that she could expect no aid from that quarter. Forcing herself to meet her mother-in-law's angry eyes, she said as steadily as she could, "My mother is a queen. She taught me the lessons of queenship, too, for I might well be a queen myself one day. She told me that queens must have long memories."

There was a moment of utter silence. Stephanie took a quick step forward and Isabella flinched. But then Reynald burst out laughing. "By God, you've got spirit, girl," he said with a grin. "Seems like there are some ballocks in your marriage, after all." With a scornful glance toward Humphrey, who flushed darkly, staring down at the floor.

Although Stephanie frowned, Reynald's was the hand on the helm of their marital ship, and she held her tongue. He crossed the chamber, halting in front of Isabella. He towered over her, for he was almost as tall as Balian, but he was smiling. "You've given us much to mull over, lass."

Isabella knew he was lying; they were not going to reconsider. She also knew there was nothing she could do about it, not yet. She murmured a thank-you that meant as little as his own words, curtsied, and let Humphrey lead her from the chamber.

Neither spoke as he escorted her across the bailey toward her bedchamber in the southeast tower. Just as they reached the door, he put his hand on her arm, for he knew Emma would be waiting within. "I am sorry," he said softly, "so very sorry. . . ."

Isabella felt very sorry, too, in that moment, sorry for his misery and his shame and his inability to give her what she most needed—strength. She'd become quite fond of him in these past few months, but she felt a new emotion stirring now, almost maternal, an instinct to protect him as he could not protect her. "I do not blame you, Humphrey," she assured him. "None of this is your fault." She found a smile for him, then slipped inside, where she could share her heartache with Emma, where she could weep for her family and the end of her childhood.

There could be no estrangement between the Crown, the patriarch, or the Templars and Hospitallers, and since all involved knew that, a peace was soon patched up between Baldwin and Eraclius and the two grand masters. In June, a delegation

sailed for the West, led by Eraclius, the Hospitaller Roger de Moulins, and the
Templar Arnaud de Torroja, their mission to appeal for military and financial aid
from the Pope and the kings of England and France. They were instructed to offer
the keys to Jerusalem, the Holy Sepulchre, and the Tower of David to any king
willing to return with them and undertake the defense of the Holy Land. Eraclius
snubbed William, the senior churchman in his absence, by naming the Bishop of
Lydda as his vicar until his return. For Jakelin de Mailly and his Templar brethren,
the departure of their grand master had more immediate consequences. The command of their order now rested in the hands of their seneschal, Gerard de Ridefort.

It had been a hot July. Isabella had opened her window after the sun had flamed
out, but her bedchamber was sweltering. She'd talked Emma into playing chess.
Under Humphrey's patient tutelage, she'd soon mastered the basics and hoped that
practice would hone her skills; she was nursing a fantasy in which she challenged
Reynald de Chatillon to a game and soundly defeated him. She was frowning at
the chessboard when a knock sounded at the door.

When Emma started to rise, Isabella stopped her, for she had noticed that her
dog was sniffing at the door, tail wagging wildly. "Come in, Humphrey!"

Entering the chamber, Humphrey paused to play with Jordan, who was jumping around like a furry whirling dervish. As much as he loved dogs, he knew he
was using Jordan to delay the inevitable, and he straightened up reluctantly. Isabella was smiling at him, genuinely glad that he was here. She was so trusting that
it well-nigh broke his heart. He'd wanted nothing but her happiness, yet he'd
brought only misery into her life. If depriving her of her family was not bad
enough, he'd put her safety at risk, too, for as long as she lived at Kerak, she'd be
in danger. Saladin hated Reynald as much as he did, and Kerak would be a target
until the Saracens finally succeeded in capturing it.

"Bella, we may face some difficult days ahead. One of Reynald's scouts rode in
a while ago with bad news. Saladin is on his way to Kerak with a large army."

Even in the wavering light cast by the oil lamp, he could see that she'd lost
color; her eyes were so wide and dark that he could think only of a fawn, trapped
and helpless as Death moved in. Crossing swiftly to the table, he took her hand in
his and swore that she need not fear. Kerak was well prepared for a siege, and this
time Reynald would not be so reckless, would not try to hold the town, too. They'd
have their mangonels set up before Saladin arrived. And as soon as Baldwin

learned that the castle was under siege again, he'd come to their rescue just as he'd done last November.

For once, Humphrey and Emma were on the same side and she hastened to echo his comforting words. Isabella thought that between them, they made a siege sound like a way to liven up the summer, a petty annoyance at worst. She did not know how much truth there was in their assurances. But in this game of grown-ups, she was learning how to play her part, so she smiled and nodded and pretended to believe there was no reason to be afraid.

CHAPTER 39

August 1184
Al-Jawwār, Syria

A l-Sanī'a b. al-Nahhāl's clerk, Ibrāhīm, heard the insult quite clearly and knew it was meant for him; *kafir* was Arabic for unbeliever and he was the only Christian in al-'Ādil's camp. He supposed it could be meant for al-Sanī'a, too, since many Muslims regarded his conversion to Islam with a jaundiced eye. But al-Sanī'a paid no heed, continuing on toward their lord's tent. Ibrāhīm wished he could be as nonchalant, for his post was a well-paying one and he did not want to lose it.

Ibrāhīm was wrong in thinking that al-Sanī'a had not heard the slur. He'd also taken notice of his new clerk's unease and as they approached al-'Ādil's tent, he said, "I am sure you've heard the proverb, Ibrāhīm: 'Let the dogs bark; the caravan continues on.' You need not fret over behind-your-back grumbling. As long as I stand high in my lord's favor, nothing else matters."

Ibrāhīm hoped he was right. "May I ask you something, lord? Why were so many scouts sent out to watch the roads? Does our lord fear an attack by the Franks?"

"The Franks are too busy gathering an army to relieve the siege at al-Karak to send out raiding parties. No, my lord's concern is closer to home. He wants his family with him in Aleppo, yet it was too dangerous for them to take the caravan road to Damascus because of that devil, Arnat. But he saw a chance to bring them safely from Egypt whilst Arnat was defending al-Karak. When the sultan ordered Taqī al-Dīn to join him at the siege, he agreed to bring al-'Ādil's household with him. The sultan is sending them on to our camp as soon as they get to al-Karak and our scouts are out watching for them."

Ibrāhīm uttered a heartfelt, "God willing, they have a safe journey."

Al-Sanī'a smiled. He did not doubt that the God of the Muslims and the God of the Christians was one and the same. He knew better than to share that conviction with any others, and he contented himself by echoing Ibrāhīm's "God willing" with a devout "*Insha'Allah.*"

Al-ʿĀdil strode forward as the caravan came into view. By now he could see the domed, curtained litters of his wives and concubines; their handmaidens rode behind them on gold-plated saddles, well veiled against intrusive eyes and surrounded by soldiers, for women always rode in the middle of a caravan for safety's sake. His children were too young to ride horses or camels, and they were already tumbling out of their litters. Not waiting for help and unfazed by their falls as they jumped to the ground, they scrambled up and ran toward al-ʿĀdil.

"Papa!" His eldest, seven-year-old Muḥammad, outran his younger brothers, Mūsā and ʿĪsā, and was the first to be caught up in his father's embrace. They clustered around him, such handsome, healthy little boys that he felt a rush of gratitude; how greatly Allah had blessed him.

His women were still waiting in their litters, wanting him to be the one to help them onto the ground, and he entrusted his sons to al-Sanīʿa's watchful eye, for they could get into mischief in a heartbeat. His chancellor adroitly held their attention now by promising to show them a rare white camel they'd gotten from the *Badaiyyin*.

Al-ʿĀdil's wives greeted him with proper decorum, but they both communicated with their eyes how much he'd been missed. One of his little daughters toddled toward him, holding out her arms, and he lifted her up, feeling a pang of regret that his children had grown so much in the nine months he'd been away.

ʿĪsā had escaped al-Sanīʿa's eagle eye and darted to al-ʿĀdil's side. Handing his daughter to Halīma, he reached down to ruffle ʿĪsā's cap of dark hair, and then he turned, for his soldiers had begun to laugh, pointing and joking, elbowing one another to get closer. Al-ʿĀdil could not see the object of their interest and he glanced, puzzled, toward his wives for enlightenment.

"I imagine it is Zirafah attracting so much attention," Āliya said and stifled a laugh at the startled look on her husband's face.

"You brought Zirafah with you?" Al-ʿĀdil shook his head, astonished that Taqī al-Dīn had agreed to let them take his children's tame giraffe on that long journey from Egypt.

"We could not leave her, Papa!" ʿĪsā was only four, but he already had a mind of his own. He'd been smitten with Zirafah from his first look at her spindly legs and long, sweeping eyelashes, and al-ʿĀdil could well imagine how he'd pleaded and cried to make sure Zirafah accompanied them to their new home in Aleppo. ʿĪsā caught his hand and he let the little boy pull him toward the circle of soldiers surrounding the young giraffe. She was a remarkably placid creature, ignoring the crowd of men in favor of the acacia leaves her handler was feeding her.

"My lord?" Āliya had followed and stood beside al-ʿĀdil, watching as their son insisted that he be the one to feed his giraffe. Switching to Kurdish for privacy, Āliya asked softly, "You are not vexed with us for bringing the beast, Ahmad?"

"No, I am not vexed," he assured her, "though ʿUmar will likely never let me live this down. I could not have resisted the boys' pleading, either." He had another reason for not objecting to the giraffe's presence, but it was not one he could share with Āliya. As he watched his men jesting and gawking at Zirafah, he was glad that they were enjoying this moment of levity, for he knew that some of them would die at al-Karak.

Salāh al-Dīn warmly welcomed his brother and then escorted him into the town to show him the progress they'd so far made. Al-ʿĀdil was impressed, for the sultan's nine mangonels were operating day and night, inflicting considerable damage upon al-Karak's walls and northern towers. He ventured close enough to the fosse to peer down into its depths and gave an appreciative whistle, for their men had filled in much more than he'd expected. "It will not be long until we can make a frontal attack, Yūsuf."

"Especially now that you've brought more siege engines with you," his brother agreed. "Once we set them up, the Franks will not dare to show themselves on the battlements and we can target their remaining mangonels. We've already destroyed the ones on their roofs, as you can see," he said, pointing toward the castle's damaged north tower.

The sultan's chancellor, ʿImād al-Dīn, had joined them and at that, he gave a triumphant laugh. "The infidel Arnat's day of judgment is finally upon him!"

Al-ʿĀdil was not yet ready to claim victory, for he never underestimated their enemy. "Where is the army of the Franks?" he asked, and his brother shrugged.

"So far our scouts have no word of their whereabouts." While ʿImād al-Dīn continued to lavish praise upon the sultan for this great triumph, the brothers paid him no heed, for they knew the leper king would come to al-Karak's rescue. The only question was whether the castle would fall before he got there.

In early September, Salāh al-Dīn finally heard from his scouts. The army of the Franks was on the move, but instead of riding along the west bank of the Salt Sea as they had done the year before, they'd crossed the Jordan and were marching south through territory held by the Saracens, endangering Salāh al-Dīn's lines of communication with Damascus. The sultan then raised the siege and headed north to confront the enemy. When they reached the ruins of the ancient city of Hisbān, they halted to wait for the Franks, blocking the road to al-Karak.

The Franks soon arrived and camped at Ain Awāleh, just six miles from Hisbān. They'd chosen the site well, for the rough terrain offered protection against attack. Salāh al-Dīn waited, hoping to lure them out to do battle, but they remained where they were, and after a few days of frustration, he ordered his army to withdraw.

Taqī al-Dīn was almost sputtering, so great was his outrage. The other men in Salāh al-Dīn's command tent—al-'Ādil, 'Īsā al-Hakkari, al-Fādil, and 'Imād al-Dīn al-Isfahānī—were glaring at him. The sultan himself remained composed, showing no emotion as his nephew ranted.

"We've let ourselves be outwitted by an accursed leper, an infidel! He waited until you summoned Ahmad with your reserves so he need not fear being attacked from the rear, and then he got you to abandon the siege merely by getting between our army and Damascus. We ought to have stayed at al-Karak and continued the siege. We could have forced the Franks into combat with us there. Instead, we did what he wanted, let him win without a blow being struck!"

'Īsā and 'Imād al-Dīn did not think Taqī al-Dīn was entirely wrong, but they offered no support, for he'd angered them by speaking so disrespectfully to the sultan. Al-'Ādil thought his brother's decision to retreat was proof that he'd seen his attack on al-Karak as a *razzia*, a raid rather than the start of jihad against the Franks, and since he was not in favor of all-out war, he was not about to challenge Yūsuf on this. He did think their hotheaded nephew needed to be put in his place, and he waited now to see how Yūsuf would do it.

"Are you done, 'Umar?" The sultan's voice was clipped and cool, underlaid with authority rather than anger. "It is true that the Franks have broken the siege at al-Karak without shedding a drop of blood. I always understood, though, that time was not on our side at al-Karak and we had to take the castle ere the Frankish army arrived. I hoped to force a battle at Ain Awāleh, but they were too wary to take the bait."

Taqī al-Dīn looked even more outraged, if that were possible. Before he could speak, his uncle raised his hand for silence. "We have lost a chance to fight them. I admit that. But all is not lost. With their army on the march to al-Karak, that leaves much of their kingdom undefended, including the rich lands of Samaria and Galilee."

The army of the Franks camped outside the town of Kerak while they waited for the bridge to be rebuilt. Once that was finally done, Baldwin moved into the castle. Joscelin and Denys did, too; so did Balian, since staying in the citadel would give him more time with Isabella. But Count Raymond and Baudouin declined the hospitality of a man they despised and remained in the camp. Baudouin did agree to shelter some of their horses in the vaulted stone stables against the north wall, and it was there that Balian found him.

"What is wrong with Merlin?" he asked, for Baudouin was examining the stallion's hoof.

"A stone bruise; it does not look too bad, though." Baudouin beckoned to his hovering squire, telling him to fetch a bucket of warm water from the castle kitchen so they could soak Merlin's foot. "I do not know about you, Little Brother, but I think these annual rescue trips to Kerak are getting tiresome. Are we supposed to pull Reynald's bleeding chestnuts from Saladin's fire every damned year?"

"I hope not. I am sure Baldwin feels the same, but he needs Reynald to guard our southern borders."

Baudouin acknowledged that with a shrug. Merlin had begun to whicker, and Baudouin moved to the stallion's head. "By now you've had some time with Bella. How is she faring. . . . truly?"

"She insists she is well, but she'd not tell me even if she was utterly wretched, not wanting us to share her misery."

"You're sure the little lass is only twelve? She sounds more mature than the pair of us and you're thirty-four and I'm nigh on forty-five."

Balian smiled bleakly. "I think she's probably taking it better than Maria, who is as bitter as she is heartbroken."

"If Amaury de Lusignan had ever tried to forbid me to see my daughter, I'd have showed up at his gate and dared him to deny me entry."

"Esquiva is a woman grown, Baudouin. Bella is a 'little lass,' as you said. We discussed doing that, but we were afraid they would make it worse for Bella after we'd gone."

"You're right," Baudouin conceded. "But what is wrong with that de Toron cub? Why does Humphrey not speak up for Bella? Is he mute as well as spineless?"

"I tried to instill some spirit in the lad," Balian admitted, "to no avail. He's as skittish as a dog that's been kicked so often he expects nothing else."

"You're too softhearted, Balian. De Toron is . . . what? Eighteen? That's old enough to have grown a pair." Baudouin gave Merlin a final pat before moving from the stall. "We both know who is truly to blame. Stephanie has never needed an excuse to be nasty. But this is the hell bitch's doing. Agnes loathes Maria fully as much as I detest that swine de Lusignan."

Balian was in full agreement with his brother. "Ever since Stephanie's cousin married Joscelin de Courtenay, Stephanie has been doing all she could to ingratiate herself with Agnes and Joscelin. And after being rewarded with a royal marriage for her son, she'd likely walk barefoot on burning sand if she thought it would please Agnes."

"I assume you've had it out with Reynald and Stephanie by now?"

"For all the good it did. I do not think Reynald truly cares whether Bella sees Maria or not; he is just humoring Stephanie because she asked it of him. And Stephanie is hoping to curry favor with Agnes. She even dared to warn Bella not to say a word to me or Baldwin!"

"She does not know Bella very well, does she? So how did Baldwin react?"

"Just as you'd expect. Baldwin has never had patience with pettiness, now less than ever. He heard me out, then summoned Stephanie and Reynald into his bedchamber and snarled, 'For Christ's sake, let Bella see her family!' Stephanie was foolish enough to try to argue with him, which did not go well for her. At least Reynald knew enough to keep his mouth shut."

Baudouin laughed. "I wish I'd been there to watch that with you. Do you think his tongue-lashing will help?"

Balian did not reply at once. "It might, but for how long?"

Baudouin merely nodded, for what was there to say? Balian was really asking how long Baldwin would live. If the Almighty were merciful to Baldwin at last, that would not be long. But Baldwin was the glue holding the kingdom together. "We can only hope," Baudouin said grimly, "that Baldwin outlives that treacherous weasel de Lusignan."

"My lord, wake up!"

Opening his eyes, Balian blinked up at his squire. "Ernoul, what in hellfire . . . ?"

"The king has summoned you, my lord. You must go to him straightaway."

By the time he'd dressed, Balian was fully awake. Why would Baldwin want to see him in the middle of the night? He got no answers from Anselm, who escorted him silently up the stairs to the bedchamber set aside for the king's use. Within, oil lamps were still burning. Baldwin was sitting in a high-backed chair; he'd obviously never been to bed. "Is he here?" he asked as soon as the door opened, then beckoned Balian to come forward and take a seat.

"Balian, I am sorry to have you awakened like this, but it could not wait. An urgent message has arrived from the Archbishop of Nazareth." Baldwin paused, hating what he had to do. "We thought Saladin was returning to Damascus. We were wrong. Archbishop Lethard says that he has dispatched raiding parties who are ravaging Samaria, burning and pillaging."

Balian stared at him. "Christ Jesus . . ." His mouth had gone so dry that he could not force the words out, but Baldwin did not need to hear them.

"Yes," he said, "the archbishop says Nablus was one of the towns attacked and overrun."

The week that followed was the longest of Balian's life. Baldwin had promised that the army would follow as soon as possible, but between Balian and Baudouin's men and the knights provided by Baldwin, they had a large enough force should they encounter Saracen raiding parties. They did not know what they would find and that was the fear that drove them on, hour after relentless hour from dawn till dark. The d'Ibelin brothers rode side by side, but without speaking, neither man sharing his fears. At night, they slept poorly, tormented by dreams in which Balian's wife and children and Baudouin's daughter Etiennette and her young son were trapped in flaming buildings, crushed under mangonel bombardments, or dragged off into captivity by jubilant Saracen soldiers.

It was all too easy to follow the trail of a marauding army. Villages were deserted, the inhabitants dead, hiding in the hills, or enslaved. Crops had been torched or stolen. No livestock grazed in the fields, just the carcasses of slain pigs and hogs.

Worst of all was the eerie silence. No dogs barked; they had either fled or been killed. Even the birds were quiet, though they did see vultures soaring above their heads, looking to feast upon the carrion that soldiers invariably left in their wake.

Most of Balian's men also had families in Nablus, and some still clung to hope that the archbishop had been wrong, that their town had been spared. That hope lasted until they approached the orchards and olive groves that surrounded Nablus, saw trees stripped of fruit, others charred and blackened. This was nothing new to the men riding with Balian, for their *chevauchées* and the Saracen *razzias* were similar both in their aims and tactics, meant to inflict as much suffering as possible upon their enemies. But when it was their own homes that had been plundered and torched, their own kinfolk victimized, war took on a terrible immediacy. With a growing sense of dread, they braced themselves for their first view of Nablus.

"Christ on the cross!" The words were ripped from Baudouin's throat by the sight that met their eyes: what looked to be the skeletal remains of Nablus. The fires had burned out by now, although the acrid smell of smoke still lingered and each gust of wind sent cinders and ashes swirling into the air. The new Hospitaller hospital had been partially burned, as was the Church of the Passion and Resurrection. Shop doors had been kicked in, the houses still standing were as bare as plucked chickens, shattered wine kegs littered the streets, stove in by axes, and, just as at Kerak, evidence of people's overturned lives was everywhere.

When he saw the ruins of the palace that had been his family's home, Balian bit his lip until it bled. While it had not been burned, it had been thoroughly ransacked, looted of all valuables, leaving only memories. He reined in Khamsin, staring down at a child's toy, a small wooden cart. Had that been Johnny's?

The citadel was situated west of the city, a relatively simple structure consisting of a tower keep and a walled-in bailey. It was the town's only refuge; had it survived? Balian urged Khamsin along a haunted street, peopled only by ghosts. And then he saw the grey stone walls rising up in the distance. The castle still stood! Baudouin had caught up with him by now and together they galloped toward it.

As they approached, the gate swung open and a man emerged onto the road. They were close enough for recognition; it was Amand, the viscount of Nablus, Baudouin's son-in-law. Sprinting toward them, he shouted, "They are alive and well!"

By the time they reached him, the viscount was red-faced and out of breath.

"Your lady saved the town! She was uneasy after you left, worried that the garrison at Damascus might take advantage of the absence of our men to stage raids as they've done in the past. She asked me to post guards in the hills to keep watch. Whilst I saw no need for that myself, thank God I heeded her! We thought danger would come from the north, not the south, but our sentries spotted Saladin's army ere they reached Nablus. Some towns were taken by surprise. We were not."

"How many of the townspeople were able to take shelter in the castle?"

"Almost all of them. Queen Maria dispatched men throughout the town, warning them that the Saracens were on the way and telling them to get to the castle straightaway. There are always a few fools who will balk, not wanting to leave their houses, but we insisted—"

"What happened? Did they attack the castle?"

"That they did. They made several attempts, but we were able to fend them off. They had no siege engines, and once they saw we were going to fight to the end, they contented themselves with plundering the town. I am sorry; they stripped the palace bare. . . ."

Balian was no longer listening, gazing over the viscount's shoulder at the castle. Amand jumped aside as Balian sent Khamsin racing for the woman coming through the gate. Flinging himself from the saddle, he gathered her into his arms and for a time, neither spoke; they just held each other. After a while, Maria said, somewhat breathlessly, "My heart, if you squeeze me any harder, you may break a rib."

He reluctantly eased their embrace. "If you or our children had come to any harm, Marika, I was going back to Kerak and send Reynald de Chatillon to Hell everlasting."

She gave a shaken laugh. "That sounds more like your brother than you."

"Johnny and the girls? How bad was it for them?"

"Thankfully they are too young to fully understand what we were facing. In truth, I think they were more excited by the novelty of it all than fearful. Of course, they have not seen the palace ruins yet, or all the damage done to the town. We feared some of the Saracens might be watching, so we thought it safer to stay in the castle until you arrived. As I knew you would," she said, with such utter confidence that he kissed her again. When they came up for air, Baudouin was standing beside them, his arm draped around his younger daughter's shoulders.

"Amand said the other towns were not as lucky as Nablus. Zar'īn and 'Ain Jālūt were burned well-nigh to the ground. They took Jenin, too. At Sebaste, Bishop Ralph got them to spare the town by releasing eighty Saracen prisoners, and then—"

"Papa." Etiennette squeezed Baudouin's arm. "I do not think they hear you."

He took a closer look at his brother and sister-in-law, saw the way they were gazing into each other's eyes, and grinned. "I think you're right, lass."

Balian arrived in Acre on a rainy afternoon in late November. He and his men stopped first at a public bathhouse to soak away what felt like pounds of mud, and then rode on to Baudouin's town house. Balian was accompanied by an English knight named William Marshal and soon afterward, they were being admitted to the quarters in the palace that were always set aside for the Archbishop of Tyre on his visits to Acre. William was very pleased to see Balian and insisted that they join him for the evening meal. After they settled down in the solar with wine, a servant showed the Englishman the way to the privy chamber and Balian took advantage of his brief absence to share his background with William.

"Will arrived in the Holy Land this summer. We met after he joined the Kerak relief force. He is making a pilgrimage on behalf of his late lord, the English king's eldest son, the one they called the young king. He'd taken the cross on a whim, never followed through on it, and when he realized he was dying, he entreated Will to go in his stead."

"Such loyalty is commendable," William said approvingly. "If only it were as contagious as the plague, for it is in short supply in Outremer these days."

"Will would very much like to pay his respects to the king and I told him that if any man can arrange that, it will be you."

"Ah, Balian . . . I am sorry. Baldwin is ill again and I doubt that he is up to seeing strangers. He had very troubling news last week about that treacherous spawn of Satan, de Lusignan. Have you heard what Guy did?"

When Balian shook his head, William set his wine cup down with a thud. "That man is no better than a bandit. He ventured out from Ascalon and launched a raid upon a Bedouin camp near Dārūm. They are under the protection of the Crown and thought themselves safe, so they were caught off guard. Guy and his men stole all of their camels and horses, burned their tents, and carried off some of their women and children as slaves."

Balian was listening incredulously, for the Bedouins were invaluable allies, often assisting the Franks against the Saracens even though they, too, followed the faith of Islam. "How could Guy be so stupid? We cannot afford to turn the Bedouins into enemies!"

Neither man had heard Will Marshal's quiet reentry into the solar and they jumped at the sound of his voice. "This is what the de Lusignans have always done in Poitou. They claim to be lords, but more often than not, they act like brigands, as lawless as they are greedy."

"I have no doubt of that," William said grimly. "But in Outremer, the stakes are much higher. De Lusignan's shameful raid can undermine the Crown and keep other Muslims from making alliances with us. Our king was outraged by Guy's attack on the Bedouins. It was a foul, cowardly act and it will not be easy to mend the damage done."

Balian leaned forward, gesturing toward the Englishman. "I think the king will want to talk with Will, for he knows firsthand what the de Lusignans are capable of doing. Remember what you told me about the de Lusignans attacking the English queen and almost taking her captive? Well, Will was one of her men on that ill-fated day. They were led by his uncle, the Earl of Salisbury, and he and Will and a few others held the de Lusignans off until the queen could escape. Will was wounded and taken prisoner and—"

"And they murdered my uncle, the earl." The Englishman's voice was without emotion, a judge delivering a verdict. "Guy and his brother Joffrey later claimed they'd not meant to harm him, that it had been an accident. They lied. A man is not stabbed in the back by accident."

William studied the other man and then smiled at Balian. "You are right. The king *will* want to talk with him."

They continued their conversation over supper. Will Marshal insisted that Guy de Lusignan was totally unfit to rule and must never be allowed to claim the throne. With Balian and William, he was preaching to the converted and they listened intently to his stories of de Lusignan family misdeeds in Poitou. There were enough to take them through the meal. It was then that William shared more unwelcome news. When he'd asked after Maria, Balian explained that she'd not accompanied him because she was with child. The archbishop expressed his delight upon hearing that, but then he told Balian that he'd heard Sybilla was pregnant again, too.

"I will be very sorry if that turns out to be true, William." Seeing that Will Marshal seemed puzzled, Balian elaborated upon his answer. "If Sybilla would agree to leave Guy, I am sure the king could find a compliant bishop to declare her marriage invalid. But we need Sybilla's cooperation for that to happen and so far, she has clung to Guy like a barnacle to a ship's hull. If she is pregnant again, that will be one more reason for her to balk at leaving him."

"She does not need a reason, Balian," William said bitterly. "Sybilla is utterly besotted with the man, as she's proven again and again. God may in time forgive her, but I never shall. She has put loyalty to her husband before loyalty to our kingdom."

Agnes had been having a very bad week. She was extremely worried about Baldwin's declining health. He insisted he was just tired, but his doctors were quite concerned by the discovery of foam in his urine, for that often signified a kidney ailment. She'd also just passed a stressful night with her grandson, summoned by the little boy's nurses when he'd awakened shrieking in pain. His doctor had diagnosed an earache, mixing up an herbal concoction that eventually worked. Before it did, the child had wept until his pillow was sodden with his tears, crying for his mother. Agnes had comforted him as best she could, not knowing what to tell him.

He was a quiet, self-contained child most of the time and it was not easy to know what he was thinking. But in a crisis—when he was ill or could not sleep or had been grieving over the loss of his pet dog—he invariably called out for Sybilla, for the mother who'd abandoned him. He was not yet seven and Agnes could not bring herself to tell him the truth—that Sybilla had chosen Guy over her own flesh and blood.

Once young Baldwin had finally fallen asleep, Agnes had managed to get a few hours' sleep herself. She'd been plagued with a throbbing headache since midmorning and felt more and more fatigued as the afternoon dragged on; she'd even endured a sudden and embarrassing attack of hiccups. This was, she now thought, the perfect ending to such a dismal day—trapped in a corner of the palace courtyard by Balian d'Ibelin, having to listen as he blamed her for his family's woes.

When he finally paused for breath, she said sharply, "Balian, if you have any complaints about the way Isabella is being treated, take it up with Stephanie and Reynald, not with me!"

"Your fine hand is all over this, Agnes. Despite being commanded by the king, they are still refusing to allow Bella to come to Nablus, not even for Christmas. Maria has not seen her daughter in over a year."

"And I should care about Maria's misery because . . . ?"

"Because this is your fault. Stephanie is your pawn, either following your orders or doing what she thinks will please you. However much you dislike Maria, you ought to be the last woman on earth who'd want to see a mother separated from her child. Do you truly need reminding how Amalric cut you out of Baldwin and Sybilla's lives?"

"I did not tell Stephanie to do this," Agnes insisted. Raising her hand to her aching temples, she tried to massage away the pain. "I do not blame Stephanie, though. She says Maria and you have raised a brat and she is just trying to teach the girl some manners."

When Agnes tried to maneuver around him, he held his ground. "I know Baldwin is ill again and I do not want to burden him with this. But I will if you do not call off your dogs."

"Do not dare to bother Baldwin with this nonsense!" But she saw that he was not bluffing, that he would do exactly as he threatened. "Whilst I cannot promise that they will heed me," she said at last, "I will talk to them about letting the girl visit her mother. In return, you must promise not to drag Baldwin into this. He . . . he is fighting off another infection."

Much to her dismay, her voice cracked. She had trouble swallowing and no longer met his gaze, not willing to show any weakness, not to the man who was Maria Comnena's husband and Baudouin d'Ibelin's brother. He'd always been too perceptive, though, and seemed to sense her vulnerability. How else explain what he said then, quietly and without anger. "Let's do what is right for our children, Agnes."

She acquiesced by her silence, moved around him, took several steps, and stopped. She could not explain the impulse that overtook her, could only yield to it. "You have always been loyal to Baldwin," she heard herself say, the words slightly slurred, as if she were listening to someone else's voice, "and I thank you for that." She walked away then, and did not look back.

Baldwin was too tired to continue, telling his scribe that they'd resume in the morning. He heard rustling as the man gathered up his ink, pen, and other supplies, then made a discreet departure. He'd been dictating letters to the Pope, the Holy Roman Emperor, and the kings of England and France, once again pleading for aid. The last he'd heard, their delegation had safely reached Sicily and were going to meet with the Holy Father. He did not have much hope that they'd succeed, any more than he expected his own pleas to touch the hearts of his fellow Christian kings. It was impossible to be both an optimist and a leper. He could not admit it, not even to his confessor, but he felt Outremer had been abandoned by the rest of Christendom. Far worse, there were times when he felt they'd been abandoned by God, too. How else explain the kings they'd been cursed with, a leper, an often sickly child, and a selfish lordling whose greatest military triumph had been an attack upon a camp of unsuspecting Bedouins and their families?

Almost as if sensing how dark his thoughts had become, Cairo padded across the chamber and nudged Baldwin's hand with a cold nose. He'd noticed years ago that the dog never touched his right hand, the one without feeling; it was always the left, crippled but still capable of sensations. *How did Cairo know?*

"Cairo has had his nightly walk, sire. Are you ready for bed yet?" Like Cairo, Anselm had learned to read his lord's moods. "Shall I prepare a potion to ease your sleep?"

"Yes, I fear I have need of that tonight," Baldwin admitted, then raised his head, hearing a knock on the door. It was very late for visitors, but it was never too late to receive bad news, a lesson he'd learned early on in his kingship. He leaned back in his chair, listening to the murmur of voices, then the sound of Cairo's thumping tail, which meant this was no stranger.

"My lord king . . ." Anselm's voice sounded oddly muffled. "It is the Lord of Sidon."

Baldwin's tension eased, for his stepfather knew he kept late hours and occasionally stopped by to visit after others were long abed. "Come in, Denys. Shall I have Anselm fetch wine?"

"No, I . . . no." Denys's voice sounded as scratchy as Anselm's. "I do not know how to tell you this, Baldwin. Your mother . . . she is dead."

Baldwin heard the words, but it took a moment for them to sink in, for him to understand. "How?" he whispered. "How?"

"She'd not been feeling well for a day or two, complaining of tiredness, a bad headache. After supper, she had a dizzy spell and I convinced her to go to bed early. We were in our bedchamber when . . . when she suddenly cried out and collapsed. We summoned the palace doctor straightaway and . . . and our chaplain. There was no time to send for you; it was over so fast. Ere the doctor even got there, she'd lost consciousness. She breathed her last an hour ago . . ."

Denys's eyes were stinging and swallowing was suddenly painful. He let his words trail off into oblivion and waited for Baldwin to speak. There was only silence.

❊

William followed Anselm up the stairs to Baldwin's bedchamber. When they reached the door, he asked, low voiced, if Baldwin had been able to sleep at all; he felt no surprise when the other man shook his head. He was dreading what lay ahead, his emotions in turmoil ever since Denys's dawn visit. He did not mourn Agnes; how could he? But he could not bear to think of Baldwin in such pain. After a long moment, he signaled for Anselm to open the door.

The chamber was still dark, for no lamps had been lit and the shutters remained closed. Reminding himself that Baldwin had no need for light, William waited by the door until he heard Baldwin tell him to enter. He was seated on the settle, Cairo lying at his feet, his face in shadow. William sat beside him, reaching out to take Baldwin's maimed hand in his. Desperate to offer solace of some sort, he said, "Denys assured me that she'd been given the Sacrament of the Faithful by her chaplain."

From what Denys had said, he doubted if she'd been able to coherently confess and repent her sins. But he knew that few priests would quibble about formalities at such a time; Christians on their deathbeds were usually given the benefit of every doubt. As much as he'd hated Agnes, he'd not have denied her salvation. He was not even sure he still hated her, for she'd chosen Baldwin over Sybilla, chosen her dying son over her family's fortunes. He'd seen her as selfish and vindictive and grasping, yet she'd put Baldwin's needs first and for that alone, she deserved to be spared damnation.

"I am sorry, lad," he said, tightening his grip on Baldwin's deformed fingers, "so very sorry. . . ."

Baldwin did not reply and William forced himself to be still, to wait until the younger man was ready to speak. He was close enough to hear the hitch in Baldwin's breathing. "Did you know Queen Melisende, William?" Baldwin asked softly. "I never knew her myself, for she died the year I was born. My father told me that she suffered an apoplectic seizure, and when she awoke, she could neither walk nor talk. He said she lingered for months in a half-dead state, tended only by her sisters, who allowed no one else to see her like that."

Another silence enveloped them, as suffocating and dense as winter fog. "I am glad my mother was spared that, William. . . ." Baldwin's voice was husky, and though he could not see them, William knew tears had begun to spill from those blind blue eyes. "It is just that . . . that I never thought she'd be the one to die first. I even took a bittersweet comfort in it, thinking at least I'd not have to mourn for my dead. . . ."

CHAPTER 40

Nothing in Outremer was as William Marshal had expected. He'd assumed that he'd be fighting the infidels, but he'd yet to engage the enemy despite taking part in two campaigns: lifting the siege of Kerak and then riding to the rescue of Nablus. He'd imagined there was a constant state of war between the Franks and Saracens; that was not so. Even while Saladin was assaulting Kerak, trading caravans continued their journeys to Acre, Tyre, and Damascus. And now the newly appointed regent, the Count of Tripoli, had just made a four-year truce with the sultan, which meant that Will might well return home without ever bloodying his sword.

Nor were the Poulains as he'd expected. In England and France, they were spoken of disparagingly, mocked as men seduced by the sinful luxuries of the Levant, soft and even effeminate with their love of baths and fine silks and Saracen cuisine, their shameful trust in Muslim medicine. Will soon discovered that he liked the Poulains. There was nothing soft about men like the d'Ibelin brothers, no matter how often they frequented the public bathhouses. And if Saracen doctors were more knowledgeable than Christian physicians, why not consult them?

Will's views on leprosy had changed, too. He'd known, of course, that their king was a leper, which was madness since one could contract the disease merely by breathing the same air as a leper. Yet if that were true, how had Baldwin ruled for nigh on eleven years without infecting anyone, not even his devoted squire? How could healthy men serve with the leper knights and never catch that accursed ailment? He was told that leprosy was an old and familiar foe in the Levant, not a new and terrifying menace as it was in other parts of Christendom, and he soon concluded that the Franks, Saracens, and Greeks were right and his countrymen wrong—that leprosy was not so contagious that those stricken must be shunned without mercy. And if leprosy was punishment for earthly sins, why had Baldwin contracted it as a child?

He'd admittedly been nervous when the Archbishop of Tyre had arranged his initial audience with Baldwin. That unease soon passed, replaced by admiration. They'd established a connection from that first meeting, but the rapport that developed between them went beyond their shared loathing for Guy de Lusignan. Will was honored to be accorded these occasional private visits, for Baldwin rarely ventured out in public anymore.

When he was ushered into Baldwin's bedchamber, he was not surprised that it was so poorly lit. Baldwin did not want others to look upon the ravages of his disease, nor did he want to wear a kaffiyeh in the privacy of his chambers. Even though he knew Baldwin would not know if he stared, Will avoided doing so, feeling that would be a betrayal. Once greetings had been exchanged, Will let his curiosity guide their conversation and asked if it was true that the little king's grandfather had arrived in the kingdom. "People are all talking of it, but I thought sea travel was not done during the winter months."

Baldwin confirmed that the Marquis of Montferrat had indeed reached Outremer. "Ordinarily, men prefer to wait until the safer sailings in the spring, yet we do get messages or visitors if the need is urgent enough. In the marquis's case, I doubt he fears much, be it storms or Saracens. He is approaching his biblical threescore years and ten, has come to devote his final years to the service of God and his grandson, and may God bless him for that."

Will knew that Baldwin feared Guy de Lusignan would attempt to weasel his way back into power once he was dead and a child ruled, a fear Will shared, knowing the de Lusignans as he did. Remembering now that the delegation headed by the patriarch and the grand masters had stopped in Italy to see the Pope, he asked if the marquis had brought any letters from them.

"No letters, just news and none of it good. They met the Pope at Verona and whilst he gave them a warm welcome, he offered no tangible help for the Holy Land. The marquis said the delegation then headed north, to France and England. But they suffered a grievous loss at Verona, the death of the grand master of the Templars, Arnaud de Torroja. He was an experienced diplomat and his skills would have been very useful in their dealings with the English and French kings. His loss will be sorely felt here, too, Will. The Templars will have to elect a new grand master and I've been told that Gerard de Ridefort might well win that election."

Will had met Balian d'Ibelin's friend, Jakelin de Mailly, who'd become the order's marshal in the past year, and through Jakelin, he'd become acquainted with a number of other Templars, spending enough time with them to develop a deep respect for these soldiers of God. He said that now, adding, "I've liked all of the Templars I've met so far."

"Then you must not have met Gerard de Ridefort yet," Baldwin said very dryly.

"I take it you do not think highly of the man, sire?"

"He is arrogant and obstinate, with a diabolic gift for detecting another man's weakness and using it against him. Above all, he is not one to be trusted with the sort of power that their grand master wields. But if I tried to interfere in their election, all of the Templars would react with outrage, even those utterly opposed to de Ridefort, for they are fiercely independent."

Seeing that Baldwin was troubled by the likelihood of de Ridefort's becoming grand master, Will fumbled for another topic of conversation. "I confess I was surprised to hear that the Count of Tripoli had made a truce with Saladin." He'd been surprised, too, when Baldwin had named Count Raymond as regent, but he would not presume to question the king about his decision. He thought Balian d'Ibelin's explanation was likely the correct one—that Baldwin had no other choice under the circumstances. Guy de Lusignan had proven unworthy and Reynald de Chatillon had proven too reckless.

"Saladin wants this truce so he can move against the last Muslim ruler holding out against him, the amir of Mosul. And, yes, it can be said that we are making it easier for him to conquer Mosul. But we desperately need this truce, too, Will. We cannot fight off the Saracens whilst dealing with the accession of a child king."

Will was taken aback by how calmly Baldwin spoke of his own death. Did he truly believe it was so close? It was true that the loss of his mother had inflicted a wound that still bled. But rumor often had him at Death's door and he'd always rallied.

"Will, I asked you here tonight because I have some questions for you. Your loyalty to the man they called the young king is commendable. You served him well in life, and in death, too, by making this pilgrimage for him. Because you were one of his inner circle for so many years, you also got to know his father and his younger brothers. Since our kingdom's future might depend upon what they decide, I want you to tell me about them."

Will did know these men well enough to answer Baldwin's questions. But he feared his would be answers the king would not want to hear. "What do you want to know, my liege?"

"We need not fear Saladin if my cousin Henry would accept the crown. Be honest, Will. Think you that he might take the cross and accompany Eraclius back to Outremer?"

"No, sire. He is too busy fighting his own sons and keeping a wary eye on the French king."

"What of those sons? He still has three. Surely he could spare one of them for us?"

Baldwin's face was in shadow, but Will could hear the hope in his voice, and he did not know what to say. The youngest, John, would gladly come if he thought there was a crown in the offing; he was just eighteen, though, a battle virgin, and Henry would never let him go. The middle son, Geoffrey, had no more interest than Henry in crusading. The eldest son, Richard, was a superb soldier and he cared greatly about the fate of Jerusalem. But he was at war with his father and feared that Henry might disinherit him while he was in the Holy Land.

He'd waited too long to answer. "You do not think any of them will come, either," Baldwin said softly, "do you?"

"Richard will come once he is king. I know the man, sire, and can promise you that."

Baldwin knew what Will did not—how quickly time was running out. Others might see glowing embers capable of being coaxed back into flames again; he saw only a cold hearth, nothing but ashes and cinders.

There was so much sorrow in his silence that Will cursed himself for not lying. "Why do you think aid from the West is so crucial, my liege? You've thwarted that swine de Lusignan, and have gotten your lords to swear allegiance to your nephew. Surely your people will rally around young Baldwin once he becomes the king. Unless . . ." He paused, struck by an ugly thought. "Do you not trust the Count of Tripoli to be loyal to the little lad, sire?"

Baldwin surprised him by saying that he did trust Raymond not to usurp the throne from his nephew. "He thinks of himself as a man of honor and there'd be no honor in betraying a child, a child he'd sworn to protect. But if the lad dies ere he reaches his legal majority, I think Raymond would be sorely tempted to make his own bid for the crown. He'd have a strong blood claim, so why not? I daresay he is sure that he'd rule better than either Sybilla or Bella."

"Most of us would rather see a man on the throne than a woman, sire. Is it that you do not think Count Raymond would make a good king?"

"In truth, I do not know what sort of king he'd make. It would not be easy to rule a land as divided as ours is. But I'd rather see Raymond crowned than Sybilla, for she will never agree to part from Guy. And if Guy ever becomes king, I fear Outremer would not survive for long."

Will could not argue with that chilling judgment, for he agreed with it. He could see that Baldwin was tiring, so he made his excuses and departed soon thereafter. Jerusalem was rife with gossip about the king's latest illness. The most alarming rumor was that Baldwin's kidneys were failing. While only doctors knew how these organs functioned, Jerusalemites still understood that, if this were true, it boded ill for their king and for them. Will had yet to meet anyone who was not praying fervently for Baldwin to fend off Death again. He shared their fears and when he spotted a church, he stopped. Not even caring if it was Latin, Greek Orthodox, or Armenian, he slipped inside and lit a candle for the stricken King of Jerusalem.

It was the first week in April but a fire burned in the hearth. There was even a brazier heaped with coals, for Baldwin had begun to suffer from chills. He was propped up on pillows, the bedcovers concealing his nudity from visitors, for he no longer had the strength to dress. He smiled when the archbishop was announced, but William was dismayed by how much ground the king was losing from day to day. His skin had taken on a greyish cast, and although he'd lost a great deal of weight in recent weeks, his face was puffy and swollen around his eyes, which William now knew was a common symptom of kidney ailments.

"You . . . are . . . just in time, William, for the . . . others will . . . soon be here."

William's smile did not waver, for he'd learned by now to disguise his distress at the erratic pattern of Baldwin's speech; constantly short of breath, he often had to pause between words as he struggled to draw more air into his lungs. They were not alone. In addition to the ever-present Anselm, Denys and Joscelin were there. Joscelin looked so wretched that William felt a surprise stirring of pity. As much as he disliked Baldwin's uncle, he could not deny Joscelin's misery; he'd yet to recover from his sister's sudden death and seemed overwhelmed by the realization that Baldwin, too, might soon be dead. After greeting the men, William approached the bed. "Are you sure you feel up to this, lad?"

Baldwin was learning to expend his energy—and his breath—cautiously, so he merely nodded. Feeling a small warm body pressed against his hip, he clumsily stroked the dog's head and Cairo's tail thumped a loving rhythm against the blankets. He must have dozed off then, for when he awoke, he heard other voices.

William was leaning over the bed, saying that the most important members of the High Court had arrived and were awaiting the king's will.

Baldwin waited until he heard them approach the bed. "My lords . . . my doctors tell me . . . I am dying. I summoned you to . . . do homage again to my nephew . . . and to choose a regent to rule . . . on his behalf . . . until he reaches legal age. . . ."

He heard only silence. Surely this was not a surprise to them? When they finally began to speak, they sounded shaken, uncertain. Several were talking at once, making it difficult for him to identify the speakers, and he realized he'd gone as far as he could; it was up to them now. "I would choose the Count . . . of Tripoli as regent, but the . . . choice must be yours. Discuss it and tell me . . . your decision." He sank back then, exhausted even by this brief exchange.

There was another murmur of voices, then a closing door, and he slid gratefully into oblivion, painfree and peaceful.

When he awoke again, he sensed he was not alone. "Anselm?"

"Here, my lord. Have you need of a chamber pot?" He shook his head, for his urination flow had decreased drastically in the past week, and drank from the cup Anselm provided, wondering if a man had ever been knighted for providing his king with a river reed.

"My lord, the archbishop and Lord Denys are here to tell you about the High Court session. Do you want to talk with them now or later?"

"Now. . . ." Baldwin heard footsteps and then a familiar hand had closed around his own.

"It is William, lad. The session went very well. They discussed the various candidates for regent and were all but unanimous in choosing Count Raymond as regent for the little king."

The corner of Baldwin's mouth curved, hinting at a smile. "William . . . surely it is a mortal sin to lie . . . to a dying man."

He heard the older man's ragged intake of breath. When William finally spoke, his voice was unsteady. "I ought to have known better. . . ." His words trailed off in an unspoken apology and Baldwin tried to squeeze his hand to show he understood.

Denys cleared his throat. "William was right. They did choose Raymond. But you were right, too, Baldwin, for there was nothing peaceful or even civil about it. Whilst most of the members of the High Court voted for Raymond, he was fiercely opposed by a very vocal minority, led by Joscelin, Reynald de Chatillon, and the new grand master of the Templars."

"Why . . . ?"

Denys understood what Baldwin wanted to ask. "Why was de Ridefort there? He talked his way in, insisting that he had a right to be present, for his Templars had a stake in the outcome. Since he was not a member of the High Court, he ought not to have participated in the discussion; of course, he did. Not even a gag could shut that man up. And Reynald and Joscelin were glad to have an ally. They launched one verbal assault after another upon Raymond, each one more vitriolic than the last, accusing him of wanting the crown for himself and even of being hand in glove with Saladin. He angrily denied all of their accusations, but they were unrelenting and he finally declared that he'd accept only the regency, not the personal guardianship of the young king, too. He said that he would not give his enemies the opportunity to blame him if the little lad were to die ere he reached fifteen."

Denys and William exchanged glances. They did not know if Baldwin had been told just how often his young namesake and nephew was ill. The lad might well outgrow these childhood ailments, and most thought it was likely that he would. But none of them ever forgot that the mortality rate for children in the Levant was alarmingly high.

Baldwin did not know how to interpret their sudden silence. "What happened then? I would hope they selected Joscelin to act as the boy's guardian, for he'd be the natural choice. He and his wife have been caring for the lad since my mother's death."

They were able to reassure him, saying all had agreed Joscelin ought to have the boy in his care. Raymond had then wanted to be compensated for the expenses he'd incur as regent and it was decided to give him the royal fief of Beirut. There was some turmoil when it was proposed that all of the royal castles in the realm be placed in the keeping of the Templars and Hospitallers. Raymond took that as a grave insult, but it passed when even some of his supporters saw it as a harmless concession, albeit one that called his honor into question. The session ended after authorizing a formal crown-wearing ceremony for the little king, to be followed with another oath-taking by the lords of the kingdom, pledging their fealty and loyalty to the lad.

Baldwin thought that between them, surely Raymond and Joscelin could protect his nephew's rights. "And Guy?" He sighed with relief when they reassured him there was no support for Guy de Lusignan amongst the members of the High Court and no one had proposed that he be named as regent or guardian for young Baldwin despite being the boy's stepfather.

"Thank God for that much. . . ." Baldwin could feel another wave of fatigue sweeping in, too powerful to resist, reminding him of the riptides that could carry unwary swimmers out to sea. But something was not quite right, something they ought to have mentioned. . . . His brain was as exhausted as his body and it took a few moments to realize what had been omitted. "What happens if . . . Baldwin dies ere he reaches fifteen? What provisions . . . were made for . . . that?"

Another silence followed, telling him that they'd hoped he'd not ask that question. He waited and Denys eventually said in a very neutral tone of voice that if such a tragedy occurred, they agreed that the regent would be the one with the best claim, which most took to mean Raymond. This regent would rule until there was a decision about the succession from a special royal commission consisting of His Holiness the Pope, the Holy Roman Emperor Frederick, the English King Henry, and the French King Philippe. They would determine amongst themselves whose claim to the crown was stronger—Sybilla's or Isabella's.

God have mercy. Baldwin wondered who'd proposed this lunatic, unworkable plan, clearly drawn up out of desperation by men unable to agree on the most logical heir, Raymond.

All they could do was pray that young Baldwin reached his majority and proved himself to be a worthy king. If not, they could only hope that Humphrey de Toron would finally show some backbone, show that he had the constable's blood flowing in his veins.

Baldwin noted with drowsy surprise that he could consider their kingdom's future with something almost like detachment, as if his head and not his heart were engaged. Was that because he could do nothing to change what would happen? That he'd done all he could and Outremer was now in God's keeping? Or just that he was so very tired?

"Thank you for telling me. . . ."

They held their breaths, for they'd been sure he'd be angry and upset by even the possibility that Sybilla—and therefore Guy—might have an opportunity to claim the crown. They were taken aback when he said nothing more. Moving closer to the bed, they saw that his eyes had closed and they realized he'd fallen asleep again. It was only then that they could admit to themselves there would not be another miraculous recovery. Baldwin was truly dying.

CHAPTER 41

April 1185
Jerusalem, Outremer

The fifth King of Jerusalem to be named Baldwin had his crown-wearing ceremony in the Holy Sepulchre. The crown was so large that it had to be padded to fit and was so heavy that he'd soon developed a pounding headache. The churchyard was crowded and he hesitated at the sight of this sea of strangers, blinking like a baby owl as he emerged from the dimly lit church into the bright April sunlight. He was a handsome child, with the fair coloring of his parents, but of slight build, looking even younger than his age to the spectators, especially the women.

It had been planned for him to walk from the Holy Sepulchre to the Temple of Solomon so he could be seen by the citizens of the city. But because of his small size, there was some concern that he'd not be visible to the crowds thronging the streets, so it was decided that he'd be carried to the temple. Balian was chosen for that honor, both because he was the tallest of the lords and because he was Isabella's stepfather.

Baldwin had not balked when he was told of this change in plans, yet it was obvious to Balian that the boy did not want to be carried as if he were a toddler. He knew his son, Johnny, would have hated that and he was two years younger than Baldwin. Kneeling so their eyes were on the same level, he suggested that Baldwin ride on his shoulders so he could better see his subjects. Baldwin considered this and then nodded. But when he realized that he would tower over all of them, he grinned, the first time Balian had seen him react like a typical seven-year-old.

People had been gathering since midmorning along the planned route: the two major thoroughfares of the city, the Street of the Patriarch and the Street of the Holy Sepulchre. They soon saw in the distance the round silhouette of one of Jerusalem's most distinctive buildings, on a site sacred to three religions, Islam,

Christianity, and Judaism. Known to Muslims as the Dome of the Rock, where Muḥammad was said to have ascended to Heaven, its fate had hung in the balance when Jerusalem fell to the men of the first crusade. Its leaders had decided not to destroy it and converted it into a church, the Templum Domini, the Lord's Temple. The nearby al-Aqsa mosque was renamed the Temple of Solomon and turned over to the new order pledged to protect pilgrims in the Holy Land; they would take their name from it—the Knights Templar. It was here that young Baldwin's coming kingship would be celebrated with a great feast.

Although the procession had attracted large crowds, their enthusiasm was muted. While some waved and clapped, others watched in somber silence. Cheers seemed perfunctory and Balian was glad that Baldwin was too young to notice, too young to understand why so few rejoiced, too young to realize what a burden had been placed upon his frail shoulders.

Balian sealed the letter with wax, then handed it to the messenger. By now the man knew the routine, for his lord and Queen Maria had been exchanging letters almost daily since he'd been summoned to King Baldwin's deathbed.

No sooner had he left than Baudouin arrived. "What are we having for dinner?"

"I thought I was to join you today," Balian reminded him, and his brother shrugged.

"You have a better cook than mine." Baudouin fished some dice from his scrip. "Let's play hazard. Without something to occupy your brain, you'll do nothing but brood about Maria."

"Of course I worry about her, Baudouin. She is just a month away from giving birth!"

"You'll be back with her by then. Surely God will finally show Baldwin some mercy and not let him linger much longer."

Balian started to confide how much he feared for Maria each time she entered the birthing chamber, catching himself in time. Baudouin was the last man who'd need to be reminded of the dangers of childbirth. As their eyes met, he saw that his brother was thinking, too, of Elizabeth, the wife who'd died to bring his son, Thomasin, into the world.

With an effort, Baudouin banished Elizabeth's ghost. "I see an empty table," he said and started across the hall toward it. "What shall we wager to make it interesting? How about putting up Khamsin as the stakes? I'll offer that new palfrey of mine."

"You have a droll sense of humor, Brother. Khamsin? When pigs fly."

Baudouin grinned. "It never hurts to try. I've been thinking that one of us ought to look after Anselm. Should we ask him to join your household or mine?"

"As usual, I am two jumps ahead of you," Balian joked. "I've already spoken with Anselm. He said Baldwin has provided very generously for him and he plans to rent a small house in the city for himself and Baldwin's dog, then offer to help at the leper knights' hospital."

"I'm gladdened to hear that. We ought to have known that Baldwin would assure Anselm's future. He's always been openhanded, a fine quality in a king. Did you hear that he has given a royal fief to the little king's grandfather?" But Balian was no longer listening, watching the cleric cross the hall toward them.

"My lords." He bowed respectfully "The archbishop has sent this message for you."

Balian broke the letter's seal. When he looked up, his face showed no surprise, only sadness. "William says we must come at once."

William looked so devastated that Balian fumbled for words of comfort and asked if Baldwin had been shriven yet, hoping it might give the archbishop some consolation to remember that Baldwin was assured entry into Paradise.

William nodded, making a game attempt to smile. "I heard his confession myself. He . . . he said he was sorry that his sins were so boring."

There were others in the chamber—Denys and Joscelin and several doctors. But they saw only the man in the bed. Balian wanted to tell Baldwin that he'd never met anyone who'd shown such courage. His throat had closed up, though. Baudouin had no such trouble. "It is Baudouin of Ramlah, sire. Balian is with me, too. I promise you this—that we will never let that treacherous turd de Lusignan even get within sight of your throne."

That was not the usual deathbed promise or prayer. But they were sure they saw Baldwin smile.

Baldwin felt as if he were underwater, swimming up toward the light. He was surprised how bright it seemed near the surface and he wondered if he'd already died. So he whispered William's name, sure that the archbishop would be with him until his heart stopped beating. If William did not answer, he must be dead. As simple as that.

"I am right here, lad."

Baldwin felt a twinge of disappointment. He was ready for it to end. "Who . . . else?"

"When you fell asleep, I told Denys and Joscelin to get something to eat. They will be back soon. Your chaplain is here and your doctors." William hesitated, then said that people were weeping in the streets. Baldwin did not reply. He seemed to be drifting, an odd sensation that put him in mind again of water. Once, as a boy, he'd accompanied his father to Kerak and slipped away to splash in the Salt Sea. He'd cut his foot on the rocky bottom, but it had been fun to float in the warm water, even if William had scolded him for that bit of folly afterward.

"Anselm . . ." Knowing what he wanted, the squire bent and lifted Cairo onto the bed.

William leaned over and kissed the younger man's forehead. For a moment, time seemed to fragment and he was back in that stable stall on a June evening nigh on ten years ago, holding Baldwin as the boy wept. The memory was so vivid that it was as if he were reliving it, inhaling the scent of horses and straw, feeling Baldwin's head against his shoulder, hearing the uneven rhythm of his breathing after he finally fell asleep, and then echoes of his own whisper, "Ah, Baldwin, what a king you would have made. . . ." He could think of no better epitaph for Baldwin than that.

Baldwin died on April 15 in the eleventh year of his reign as King of Jerusalem. He was buried beside his father in the Church of the Holy Sepulchre. He was not yet twenty-four.

Balian awoke to the chiming of the city's churches, reminding him that it was Easter morn. Ernoul had already laid out his clothes. As Balian pulled his shirt over his head, he heard the youth ask when they'd be returning to Nablus. "There is a High Court session on Tuesday that I must attend. Then we'll go home."

Balian had crossed to a washing basin and was splashing water onto his face when his other squire, Brian, burst into the chamber. "My lord," he panted, "a messenger from Nablus!"

The man's clothes and face were streaked with dirt, evidence of hard riding. "Your lady . . . she wants you home, lord, for her birth pangs have begun!"

Khamsin seemed to sense his master's urgency, for he summoned up so much speed that Balian's men had trouble keeping up with him. The messenger had told him that Maria had gone into labor at sunset, but more than that, he did not know, only that the baby was not due until sometime in May. And this was April 21.

Dusk was falling by the time they saw the orchards and olive groves that surrounded Nablus. In the months since the Saracen attack, the resilient townspeople had made impressive progress in rebuilding their homes, shops, and lives. Normally that was a source of pride to Balian, for he and Maria had done all they could to aid in the town's recovery. Now he saw none of it, the buildings passing in a blur as he urged Khamsin through the city streets toward the palace. The gates were opening by the time he reached them. His stallion came to a halt in the middle of the courtyard and he slid to the ground as his niece hurried toward him.

"You need not fear, Uncle!" Etiennette's smile was like a sunrise. "She gave birth this morning to a son, small but healthy."

Maria was propped up by pillows, looking pale and tired. Sitting on the bed, Balian took her in his arms, not yet having the words to express his relief.

Maria felt the prickle of his stubble against her cheek, showing her he'd not taken time that morning to shave. She reached up to brush his windblown hair back from his forehead, aware that not all husbands would have responded with such urgency to her plea. "Your son is going to be a handful, my love. Not only did he insist upon arriving nigh on a month early, he peed on Etiennette and Maud swore it would have been easier to swaddle an eel."

Fear had ridden pillion behind Balian all the way to Nablus, had still trailed after him as he'd taken the stairs two at a time to Maria's bedchamber. But Maria's teasing tone stopped it in its tracks and it had made an ignominious retreat by the time a wet nurse entered the chamber, giving Balian his first glimpse of his new son. He did not stir even as he was settled into his father's arms; by now, Balian was an old hand at cradling newborns.

"Is Maud still here?" he asked, thinking that if Scriptures said a virtuous woman was more precious than rubies, so, too, was Maria's elderly Saracen midwife. He well knew that not all premature births had happy endings.

"I made her go home, for she was even more exhausted than I was." The skin under Maria's eyes looked bruised, but the smile she gave Balian held so much love that it took his breath. "Do you still want to name our lad after Philip the Apostle? Whilst I know he is one of your favorite saints, would you rather we name our son in Baldwin's honor?"

Balian gazed down at their sleeping son, already at home in this brave new world beyond his mother's womb. "No, Marika," he said sadly, "Baldwin is not a lucky name."

Eraclius and the grand master of the Hospitallers landed at Acre in mid-July. Joscelin had taken the boy king to Acre after Baldwin's funeral, hoping the sea air might prove healthful for the delicate child, so he was the first lord to welcome the patriarch and the first to tell him what had occurred in the kingdom during the two years that their delegation had been in the West.

Much of what Joscelin related was not only unknown to Eraclius, it was shocking. He'd already heard of Guy de Lusignan's abrupt fall from grace and he was not surprised to learn of Baldwin's death. The election of the Count of Tripoli as regent was unexpected and alarming, but he was thankful Joscelin had retained custody of the little king.

What stunned him was the disclosure of Agnes de Courtenay's sudden death that past November. She'd been forty-nine and while many saw that as elderly, Eraclius was five years her senior, so he thought that was much too young to die. Nor was he pleased by the rest of Joscelin's family news. Guy and Sybilla rarely ventured from Ascalon and public opinion remained hostile to him. Sybilla showed no signs of discontent with the marriage that had cost her so much—her son and most likely a queenship. She'd given birth to a second daughter that spring, Joscelin reported, and Eraclius wondered why the Royal House of Jerusalem sired so few sons; how different their history might have been if only Baldwin had brothers instead of sisters.

Momentarily distracted by these musings, he focused again on Joscelin. The other man was telling him that Guy and Sybilla were very bitter, convinced the crown ought to have passed to her, not to her son. Eraclius was relieved that Joscelin was still on good terms with his niece and her husband. He prided himself on his pragmatism and that required looking to the future, making contingency plans in case the boy king did not grow to manhood. He'd heard of the marriage of Baldwin's sister Isabella to the de Toron stripling during his sojourn in the West and had concluded that he'd rather have Sybilla than Isabella on the throne.

Neither Guy nor Humphrey were likely to inspire soldiers to fight for them, but at least Guy's courage was not in question. Moreover, if Isabella became queen, she could no longer be kept away from the baneful influence of the Greek and the d'Ibelins. She'd have the backing of the Poulains, too, whereas Guy and Sybilla would be desperately in need of allies. They'd naturally turn to him for counsel and support, grateful to have the patriarch on their side. There would be a price for such support, of course, and he and his Church would be the beneficiaries of that royal largesse.

God willing, it would not come to that. Far better to have the opportunity to instruct and guide little Baldwin, to mold him into a king who would be devoted to the Church—and to the man who headed it. It was fortunate that the young were usually as malleable as clay. A stray phrase from Scriptures popped into his head then, something about a fly in the ointment. Their fly was named Raymond de St. Gilles and they must never forget how dangerous he was. If the boy king died, Raymond would strike like a horned viper.

The patriarch paused to imagine a kingdom ruled by the Count of Tripoli, finding that a deeply troubling vision. Thankfully, Raymond did not lack for enemies. Joscelin de Courtenay would be adamantly opposed to him. So would Reynald de Chatillon. And the new grand master of the Templars. Eraclius had mixed feelings about Gerard de Ridefort. He was unpredictable, as reckless as Reynald, and so consumed with hatred for the Count of Tripoli that Eraclius sometimes wondered if that grudge of his had driven him half mad. It was natural to want to avenge himself upon the man who'd wronged him. But he suspected that de Ridefort would willingly see the world go up in flames as long as Raymond was amongst those charred to ashes and blackened bones. He would be useful, though, even if he did require careful handling.

"There is more to tell you." Joscelin leaned forward eagerly. "Whilst there was no way to keep Raymond from claiming the regency, he did lose one of his most steadfast allies. The Archbishop of Tyre resigned the chancellorship not long after Baldwin's death."

Eraclius rarely shared his emotions with the world; why give ammunition to rivals? But he was so startled by this that he could not hide his astonishment. "Why?"

Joscelin shrugged, for he had no interest in why William had relinquished the post; it was enough that he had. "I do not know," he admitted. "He has seemed downcast for months, even ere Baldwin's death. I suppose he is grieving for Baldwin. Or he could be ill. I heard that he has stopped writing that history of his, too."

He dismissed the Archbishop of Tyre's soul struggles with a wave of his hand. "What matters is that we now have a chancellor who is not in Raymond's thrall, one who would right gladly support Guy de Lusignan and Sybilla should it ever come to that. The new chancellor is Peter, the former archdeacon of Lydda."

Eraclius smiled, for Peter of Lydda was indeed no friend to the Count of Tripoli. But why had Raymond agreed to Peter's appointment? "Did Raymond not oppose this?"

"Well, actually, he was quite reasonable about it," Joscelin conceded. "I'd suggested Peter, expecting resistance, but Raymond said he'd defer to my judgment in this matter. I suppose he is trying to get his regency off to a good start even if that means cooperating with a de Courtenay."

"Or else he is trying to win you over to his side," Eraclius said thoughtfully. "From what you've told me, his powers as regent are not unlimited, so he'll need allies." Something else was nudging his memory, something Joscelin had said earlier. He'd not followed up on it, disconcerted by the news of Agnes's death, but after a moment, he remembered. "You said you thought it would be more beneficial for the little king to live along the coast. Is there a reason for you to be concerned about his health, Joscelin?"

Joscelin hesitated. "He is a good lad, tries to do what is expected of him. I've become very fond of him, and my wife . . . she thinks the world of the boy. But he is not robust, is often ailing. Sybilla used to claim that if there was any contagion within a hundred miles of Ascalon, he'd be the one to catch it."

"Is that so unusual?" Eraclius knew nothing of childhood ailments and preferred to keep it that way.

"Mayhap not. But in the past year or so, he's started to suffer from lung infections that cause prolonged coughing and sometimes shortness of breath. Agneta and I grew concerned enough to consult that Syrian doctor of Baldwin's, Abū Sulayman Dāwūd, swearing him to secrecy, of course. He examined the lad and diagnosed a malady called asthma."

Eraclius had never heard of it. "Is it serious?"

"It can be. But he said it can be managed with diet and by inhaling certain herbs and getting enough rest. According to him, Saladin's eldest son has this malady and the sultan's doctors have had success in treating him."

Joscelin sounded hopeful that Baldwin's asthma could be managed, too. Eraclius was less sanguine for he'd long ago learned that it was usually better to prepare for the worst. "I think," he said, "that it would be wise if you accepted Raymond's overtures of friendship. Do it gradually so you'll not arouse his suspicions. Support him in council meetings, do not join de Chatillon and de Ridefort in their feud against him. Make him believe that the two of you can work together for the good of the little king and the realm. Can you do that, Joscelin?"

Joscelin did not reply at once and Eraclius thought that was an encouraging sign, showing he was giving serious consideration to this proposed plan of action. "I think so. My sister could not have done it. God love her, Agnes's every emotion was always emblazoned across her face for all the world to see. But I had years in which to learn how to keep my thoughts hidden, lessons that I dared not fail."

Eraclius was pleasantly surprised that Joscelin was proving to be such a valuable ally. He was puzzled, though, by his last cryptic comment. It was only later that he understood, remembering that Joscelin had been held prisoner by the Saracens for twelve years.

It was a week before Michaelmas when Balian and Maria received an urgent message from Denys: William was very ill and they needed to get to Tyre as soon as possible. They'd last seen William in July and had agreed that he seemed very disheartened. But they'd not thought he was ailing, so they did not know what to expect when they reached Tyre.

Upon their arrival, they realized how serious this illness must be, for Joscius, the Bishop of Acre, was there and so was Count Raymond. If the regent had been summoned, William must be dying. This distressing conclusion was confirmed even before they spoke to Denys, for how else explain the abject, obvious misery of the archbishop's clerks and servants, or the solemn crowds gathering outside the archbishopric palace? .

Denys knew this was no time for false optimism and as soon as they followed him into the archbishop's solar, he told them that William's doctors held out little hope for his recovery. They were both shaken, for William had been an important part of their lives since Maria was thirteen and Balian only a few years older. Denys answered their shocked questions as candidly as he could, no easy task since he considered William a dear friend, too. "The doctors say it is a liver ailment, likely a cancer. His liver is swollen and his skin has taken on a yellowish tinge."

Maria sat down suddenly in the closest seat and Balian put a supportive hand on her shoulder. "Why did he not tell us he was so ill?"

"I do not think he realized it. At first the symptoms were easily dismissed: loss of weight, feeling very fatigued. We know he is still mourning Baldwin, so I think he assumed his tiredness and waning appetite were only to be expected as he grieved. But even if he'd alerted his doctors earlier in the summer, it would not have changed the outcome. Cancers are very difficult to treat."

Denys let his words fade away, thinking of an old superstition that deaths often happened in threes. First Agnes and then Baldwin and now William. Rallying then, he said, "He will be so glad that you arrived in time. He wanted very much to be able to bid you farewell."

William had been sleeping and awoke with reluctance, for his dreams were far more pleasant now than his reality, carrying him back into his past where he was united with his parents, both long dead, and his brother, Ralph, slain at the battle of Marj Ayyun. Baldwin often frequented these dreams, too, the son of his soul, miraculously restored to health and happiness. Ever since William had taken holy vows, he'd struggled, like most men and women, to embrace the Lord's will rather than his own. But now that he knew it was God's will that his earthly time would soon be over, it was surprisingly easy to accept.

He saw that his friends were still at his bedside: Balian and Maria, Denys, Joscius, and Raymond. He'd been blessed in his friendships, for certes. He was sorry they were grieving for him, wished he could assure them he did not mind dying now. It might even be an act of mercy by the Almighty, sparing him from having to bear witness to the coming apocalypse that he so feared. He could not tell his friends that, of course. Especially not Balian and Maria, for they had young children and that gave them a vested interest in Outremer's survival. He must say or do nothing that might take away their hope or their faith in their family's future.

He must have fallen asleep again, for when he opened his eyes, he could tell that night had fallen. Balian and Maria were still keeping sentinel by his bed, Denys dozing in one of the window seats. He hoped Raymond had gone; he was too busy to spend days with a friend who was taking too long to die. At least he was the regent now. If any man could save their kingdom, surely it was Raymond? But he was a swimmer surrounded by sharks.

William still remembered his first sight of sharks on his initial trip to the West, all the more terrifying because only their fins were visible, leaving him to imagine the sleek deadly bodies hidden by the waves. They'd appeared as if by magic when a sailor fell overboard, attracted by his panicked splashing. He'd been saved from them, though, scrambling up the rope ladder thrown down by other sailors.

Raymond might escape his sharks, too. He might be able to thwart Reynald de Chatillon and de Courtenay, mayhap even outwit the spider who spun his webs from the patriarch's palace. But what of Saladin?

"William . . . you're awake. Can we get you some wine? Are you hungry?"

He shook his head, managing to find a reassuring smile for them. How wonderful that their marriage had brought them such blessings. He'd gladly take credit for the part he'd played in it. "Balian . . . I've told my clerks to make copies of my history of the kingdom. I want you and Maria to have one. You, too, Denys."

They thanked him so sincerely that he felt sure they were not humoring him, that they understood the significance of his work. *A History of Deeds Done Beyond the Sea* would be his legacy. No matter what happened to Outremer, he'd told its story. Its kings and queens and its valiant, stubborn people would be remembered. A private smile touched his lips at that, for he might even be remembered, too.

William died on Michaelmas, September 29, at age fifty-five, and was buried in Tyre's great cathedral. He died before word reached Outremer of the bloody end to Andronicus's usurpation in Constantinople, for that had occurred earlier in the month. Andronicus had decided to execute a distant cousin, Isaac Angelus. Isaac, an unassuming man who'd seemed an unlikely candidate to spearhead a rebellion, found the courage of desperation, resisting arrest and fleeing to sanctuary at Sancta Sophia Cathedral, where he called upon the people to overthrow the tyrant. His cry became the spark to ignite a bonfire and the citizens of Constantinople rose up against the man they'd grown to hate and fear. Andronicus tried to flee with his little French empress and his favorite concubine, but they were soon captured. While the women were not harmed, Andronicus was mutilated and tortured before being turned over to the people who'd suffered under his erratic cruelties for the past three years. They put him to a prolonged and public agonizing death. Isaac, the man who'd almost inadvertently brought about his downfall, was then proclaimed the next emperor of the Greek empire.

The death of Baldwin and the accession of a child were welcome developments to the Saracens. But in December, Salāh al-Dīn fell ill with a quartan fever, what later ages would call malaria. His illness dragged on for months and on several occasions, he was feared to be dying. The empire he'd created suddenly seemed in peril, as many of his amirs and allies began to consider what they would do if he were no longer in power. Al-ʿĀdil hastened from Aleppo with Syrian physicians and Salāh al-Dīn slowly began to convalesce. He did not fully recover until early March 1186, when he came to terms with ʿIzz al-Dīn, the amir of Mosul, who swore allegiance to the sultan. Salāh al-Dīn was now free to fulfill his promise to launch jihad against the kingdom of the Franks.

CHAPTER 42

August 1186
Acre, Outremer

Joscelin's wife had dropped to her knees by the bed and her sobs were convulsing her entire body. None of the men seemed to know what to do. The doctors were already edging toward the door, as if wanting to flee the scene of their failure. The Bishop of Acre tried to offer some words of comfort; Joscelin doubted that Agneta even heard him. Raymond was obviously at a loss. Joscelin felt that way, too, even though this was his own wife. They were all mourning Baldwin's death, both for his tragically brief life and for the terrifying void that suddenly loomed ahead of them. But Agneta's visceral grief cut to the bone, too painful to witness. When he could endure it no longer, Joscelin tried to assist her to her feet. She resisted, though, and he was grateful when Raymond's wife took charge.

"Let her be," she told Joscelin. "I'll stay with her whilst she grieves for the little lad."

Joscelin willingly surrendered the responsibility to Eschiva. For a moment, he hovered beside Agneta, his eyes filling with tears as he gazed down at the small body in the bed. Baldwin had not even reached his ninth birthday. Moreover, his death could be catastrophic for the kingdom. Remembering that time was of the essence, Joscelin glanced over at Raymond and then toward the door. Raymond understood and followed him from the bedchamber.

After they'd settled themselves in the palace solar, they waited until a servant withdrew after bringing them wine. Joscelin noticed that the count's eyes were red rimmed, proof that he, too, grieved for the little king. Taking a deep gulp of wine, he thought that Raymond's regency had gone far more smoothly than he'd expected. Following the patriarch's instructions, he'd done his best to get along with the count and Raymond had showed himself willing to compromise. That past December, he'd even agreed to return the fief of Jaffa to Guy and Sybilla, an act that outraged some of his own supporters. Joscelin had actually begun to think that he and Raymond could work in tandem to protect the kingdom until Baldwin reached manhood. But then the boy's asthma attacks grew worse and during this last one, his heart apparently stopped.

Raymond was the first to break the fraught silence. "I could not tell you how many men I've seen die over the years. But none of those deaths were as bad as this one."

Joscelin was in full agreement. He feared that he'd be haunted for the rest of his life by the look of panic in the boy's eyes as he struggled to get air into his lungs. "At least he is no longer suffering. Yet I cannot help wondering why God took Baldwin and not Saladin's son. Where is the fairness in that?" When Raymond said that he'd heard al-Afdal's asthma was milder and more easily treated, that seemed unfair to Joscelin, too. But he was prodded into action by this reminder of how knowledgeable the Count of Tripoli was about their Saracen foes, knowledge that his enemies found quite suspicious.

"It seems callous to talk about the succession when the little lad is just hours dead. But we dare not wait, not when the very future of the kingdom is at stake."

"The succession is settled," Raymond said coolly. "We all swore on the True Cross that if the boy king died prematurely, a regent would rule whilst a royal commission decided who had the stronger claim, Sybilla or Isabella."

"And when we swore, we all silently prayed that it would never come to pass, for even then we knew how difficult it would be to enforce. Just notifying the Pope, the kings of England and France, and the Holy Roman Emperor will take months! But we're stuck with it, so all we can do is to make sure you're chosen as regent, and that will not be easy. You have very faithful enemies, Raymond, who'll be cursing you as long as they have breath in their bodies. If we are to thwart them, we must act quickly."

Raymond's dark eyes were fixed upon Joscelin's face, utterly inscrutable. "So, you are offering to take my side in the coming storm? May I ask why?"

"Can we speak candidly? If it were up to me alone, of course I'd rather see Sybilla on the throne than Isabella; Sybilla is my niece. But I do not think that is going to happen. Let's assume that this royal commission actually gets around to choosing our queen. The English king is not going to pick Sybilla. Yes, she is his cousin, but so is Isabella, and she is not married to Guy de Lusignan. Henry has good reason to loathe Guy; what king would ever forgive an attack upon his own queen? Even though he and Eleanor are now estranged, it is a matter of royal pride.

If he selects Sybilla, he'd be rewarding Guy for an unforgivable betrayal and, from what I've heard of the English king, he never forgets a wrong done him."

"So, you truly believe they would pick Isabella?"

Joscelin nodded. "I do. The Pope wants the English king's goodwill and the Emperor Frederick likes rebellious vassals no more than Henry does."

Joscelin could not tell if Raymond agreed with him; he continued to listen impassively.

"But whatever the royal commission decides, we will be facing a crisis of monumental proportions, Raymond. The problem is not with Sybilla or Isabella. It is that they are both married to men unacceptable to most of the Poulain lords. No one wants to see either one as king."

For the first time, he detected an emotion on Raymond's face, a glint of grim humor. "That seems to be the one thing we can all agree upon," he said dryly.

"The best we can say about Guy is that he is no coward. Humphrey may not be one, either, but many of the lords think he is. Whether it is because he is almost as beautiful as a lass or because he acts as meek as a novice nun or because Reynald has been mocking him since marrying his mother, I do not know. Fairly or not, many see him as a weakling, not man enough to defeat Saladin."

"If men think Humphrey is a coward, would they not see Guy as the lesser evil, then?"

"I thought about that, too," Joscelin admitted. "But there is one dramatic difference between the two sisters. We know that Sybilla will never leave Guy, not even if it costs her a crown. Whereas there is still hope that Isabella would prove more amenable to reason. She is very young, just fourteen, so she's not likely to be as stubborn as Sybilla. Moreover, we'd have the support of her family, for all know that Maria and Balian were never in favor of that marriage. And once Humphrey de Toron was sent back to Kerak to write poetry or play the lute, the High Court would be only too happy to crown Isabella . . . and her new husband."

"So, who do you see as the girl's new husband?"

"It has to be one of us, a Poulain, and he has to be highborn, well regarded by the other lords. There is only one man who meets those qualifications, your eldest stepson, Hugues." Joscelin paused then, keeping his eyes on Raymond's face. "We cannot be sure that will happen, of course. The best-laid plans can still go wrong. But what we can do is to make sure that you continue as regent, however long it takes until the succession is settled."

There, he thought, this was enough of a hint that, if Raymond was indeed lusting to be king as his enemies suspected, he'd have a valuable de Courtenay ally. "And I would want to continue as seneschal," he said, "whilst you hold power," again being deliberately ambiguous in his choice of words.

"Of course. You've served two kings ably in that post, and in this past year, I think we have worked well together." Raymond never slouched in public, his posture always so erect and upright that Gerard de Ridefort delighted in mocking it. But now Joscelin could see an easing of the tension in his shoulders, a relaxing of his muscles. "What do you have in mind, Joscelin?"

"I said you have enemies. Regrettably, they are all men in positions of power. You won Reynald de Chatillon's undying enmity by making that truce with Saladin, and Gerard de Ridefort is still nursing a lethal grudge because you let an Italian merchant outbid him for that heiress you'd promised him."

Raymond surprised him with a smile, one that was both chagrined and wry. "At the time it seemed like the sensible choice to make, for I still owed the Hospitallers a huge sum for putting up my ransom. I thought I could placate de Ridefort by offering him another heiress when one became available. I did not expect him to see it as such a grievous affront to his pride."

"He is thin-skinned for certes," Joscelin agreed quite sincerely, for he thought de Ridefort's hatred of Raymond was somewhat demented. "We know that he'll do all he can to keep you from continuing as regent, and so will de Chatillon. So . . . I've come up with a plan to keep them from meddling. We let the Templars escort the little king to Jerusalem for a royal funeral; that will keep Gerard occupied. Reynald will come to the city, too, for the funeral. In the meantime, you summon the other lords to Tiberias in your role as regent. I will join you there and we will hold a High Court session in which we reelect you as regent and choose men to travel to the West. By the time de Ridefort and de Chatillon find out what happened, it will be too late."

Raymond was quiet for so long that Joscelin began to worry. But then he rose to his feet, saying, "Between us, I think we might be able to save the kingdom. We owe it to Baldwin's memory to try, for we cannot let his legacy go up in flames. He deserves better than that."

To Joscelin's surprise, he felt no rush of triumph, and after Raymond had departed, he stayed in the solar, needing solitude to sort out his thinking. Raymond's last words had stirred up unwelcome memories of his nephew, for he knew Baldwin would hate what he was going to do. He felt a sudden heaviness settle over his chest, grief for the young man doomed to be known to history as the leper king and for the little boy who'd reigned so briefly and never got to rule.

He found himself wondering now if this was the right road to take. Raymond had spoken the truth when he said they'd worked well together for the past year. Was he letting Eraclius lead him astray? If he abandoned the patriarch's carefully crafted plot and threw in his lot with Raymond, might that be better for the kingdom and for his family? He mulled that over as daylight slowly ebbed away, so caught up in these unexpected doubts that he did not even notice the encroaching darkness. There was relief in finally concluding that he was doing what was right, what he must do to safeguard his own future and that of Outremer. He'd enjoyed considerable influence during Baldwin's reign and then as guardian of Sybilla's little son. But he would wield far more power as the uncle of the queen, the man who'd secured the throne for her. His loyalty must be to Sybilla, to their family. She was his niece, and blood was all.

Raymond and Eschiva said little on the ride back to their town house. They'd not eaten for hours, but neither had any appetite and they withdrew to their bedchamber. Servants had already lit oil lamps and several windows were open to combat the sweltering August heat. Eschiva sat down on the bed, saying, "I think you'd best tell me."

He did, giving her an almost verbatim account of his clandestine conversation with Joscelin. She blinked in astonishment a few times but held her questions until he was done. "Can you trust him, Raymond?"

"Much to my surprise, I think so. He seemed sincere and it makes sense that he should seek to befriend me now that the boy king is dead. He is well aware of the weakness of Sybilla's claim, and if she is not to be queen, he urgently needs allies. He pointed out that I have a multitude of enemies, yet that is also true for de Courtenay, most of them earned by Agnes. His sister was the family firebrand, shrewder and more vengeful than Joscelin. It was Agnes who secured the patriarchate for Eraclius, the constableship for Amaury de Lusignan, and the kingship for little Baldwin—not Joscelin, who has often seemed at a loss since her death. Agnes was quite capable of spinning spiderwebs in her sleep. But I cannot see Joscelin as the mastermind behind a coup to capture the crown. . . . Can you?"

Eschiva considered and then shook her head. "No, I suppose not. He's always struck me as more of a follower than a leader. And I agree that his offer is a logical one under the circumstances. He must feel very vulnerable now that he has no kin on the throne."

"But you still have doubts. Are they doubts about Joscelin himself or about the plan he has proposed?"

"I am not sure," she admitted. "It is just that the future suddenly seems so frightening now that the little king is dead. I was so hoping that it would never come to this. . . ."

"We all were." Crossing to the bed, he sat beside her and put his arm around her shoulders. She welcomed his comfort, for she'd been living in dread of this day for months, ever since they'd learned of little Baldwin's declining health. Despite what his enemies claimed, she was confident that Raymond would never have plotted against the boy he'd sworn to protect. But she knew he believed he should be king if it came to a choice between Sybilla and Isabella and their unpopular, inept husbands. He did not want to act unlawfully, wanted to be offered the crown. She did not doubt, though, that he'd seize the throne to keep Guy de Lusignan from becoming king, even at the risk of civil war, for he was convinced that Sybilla's husband would be the death of Outremer. Now Joscelin had shown them another way through the morass—end Isabella's marriage to Humphrey de Toron and wed the girl to her son Hugues.

The more she thought about it, the more appealing that road became. Hugues would be a capable king. He was no longer a lad, was twenty-five now, tested on the battlefield and as a prisoner of the Saracens. Men would rally around him and Isabella would not be the loser, for he'd treat her kindly. And Raymond loved him and his brothers as if they were his own blood.

So, when Raymond asked her what she thought he should do, she did not hesitate. "What choice do we have? We must trust in God and—as strange as it may sound—a de Courtenay."

Despite seven years in Outremer, Guy de Lusignan had still not adjusted to the heat of high summer in the Levant. He'd recently bought a new stallion and had wanted to take him out for a ride, but the day was so hot that he soon decided to return to Ascalon. As usual, its sight evoked contradictory emotions: pride that this prosperous city belonged to him and frustration that he'd had to settle for Ascalon and Jaffa when all of Outremer should be his and Sybilla's.

When he and his men reached the castle, he saw at once that something was wrong. People were milling around in confusion and so many of them wanted to tell him what had happened that he had to demand silence. Eventually, he learned that a man had ridden in with an urgent message for the countess, that after they'd exchanged only a few words, she'd burst into tears and fled the hall. Guy wanted very much to speak to that messenger. Concern for his wife overrode his curiosity, though, and he hastened from the hall.

He encountered one of Sybilla's attendants standing forlornly at the bottom of the stairwell. She could tell him only that the countess had dismissed her ladies. By now, he was very uneasy and took the stairs two at a time. He found his wife lying on the bed. At the sound of the opening door, she sharply ordered the intruder to get out. But when she realized who the interloper was, she sat up, and once she was in his arms, she began to sob again. All he could do was to hold her and wait until she was able to speak. He felt no real surprise when she told him that her son was dead. He could not imagine anything else giving her such grief.

"I am sorry, sweetheart, so sorry," he murmured. Although Baldwin had lived with them for three years, he'd never truly bonded with the boy. While he'd developed an offhand affection for his wife's son, he'd had to struggle with resentment that Baldwin would always take precedence over the sons he and Sybilla would have. He'd still done his best to comfort Sybilla when she missed him, and after Joscelin alerted them about the asthma attacks, he'd encouraged her to visit the lad at Acre even though he had to remain behind, unwilling to ask the Count of Tripoli for permission to see his own stepson. He'd lived in Outremer long enough to understand that sickly children did not thrive in this unforgiving land, so different from the lush French countryside. But because Sybilla wanted to believe that Baldwin would outgrow the asthma, he'd kept his dark doubts to himself.

By the time Sybilla stopped weeping, his tunic was sodden with her tears. Blotting her face with the edge of the sheet, she confided her greatest regret—that she'd not been with Baldwin when he died. Guy said nothing, for in the three years since her wretched brother had chosen the boy as his heir, she'd rarely seen Baldwin. She'd not seen him at all until the leper king was dead, for they'd feared that he'd try to end their marriage if she returned to court. Once he'd finally died, at least she'd had a few visits with the lad at Acre, though he'd not thought those visits gave her much joy. She'd return, fretting that he seemed like a stranger, jealous that her uncle's wife had assumed the role that should be hers—that of mother to the little king.

Even if he could not share her grieving, Guy's heart ached for her pain, and he yearned to comfort her. It occurred to him then that she might find solace in their two small daughters and when he suggested that they be brought to her, she tearfully agreed. But seeking solace would have to wait, at least long enough to learn the rest of the message that Joscelin had dispatched in such haste. When he explained that to her, he was relieved that she at once saw the sense in what he was saying, for they would have to act fast to outwit their enemies.

After he departed, Sybilla rose and crossed to a basin, where she splashed water on her face and pressed a wet cloth to her swollen eyes. She could feel anger beginning to stir, the simmering rage that she'd lived with for three years now, ever since her brother had forced her to choose between her son and her husband. It had been an indiscriminate fury, spilling over onto her mother, too, and all those hateful lords who'd turned on Guy, above all, the treacherous Count of Tripoli, the man who wanted her crown.

Guy was soon back, flushed with excitement, his hazel eyes glowing like amber. "I talked to Joscelin's man. There is no letter; the message was too dangerous to commit to parchment. Your uncle urges us to get to Jerusalem with all haste. The Templars are escorting Baldwin there for a state funeral. And then we will be crowned as King and Queen of Jerusalem."

Isabella was standing at the open window, gazing down into the palace courtyard. When Balian joined her there, she welcomed him with a smile, "Humphrey is playing camp-ball with Johnny and Thomasin. He is good with children, will be a loving father one day."

Not yet, dear God, not yet. Balian was not ready to see Isabella as a mother. It was hard enough accepting that she was a wife.

"It is not easy to be the father of daughters, is it?" Isabella murmured, surprising him by how easily she read his thoughts.

"It is sheer hell!" he said fervently, and they both laughed.

It was then that Maria entered the solar, accompanied by a servant bearing a tray of Isabella's favorite angel bread wafers. She paused to savor the sight of her husband and daughter together, sharing a laugh as if the past three years had never been. She was still marveling at Isabella's surprise visit, half expecting to awaken and find it had all been a dream.

"Angel bread? You remembered, Mother, how much I love them!"

"Of course I did." It seemed strange to be called "Mother" and not "Mama," yet more proof of the changes Isabella had undergone since Maria had last seen her. She'd left a child behind at Kerak and was reunited today with a lovely young woman, at once familiar and foreign. By now they'd joined her on the settle and she passed around napkins and warm wafers, then asked the question that had been hovering on her tongue since Isabella and Humphrey had ridden into the palace courtyard. "Do you know why they agreed to let you come to Nablus, *matakia mou?*"

That Greek endearment brought back to Isabella cherished childhood memories of being tucked into bed at night, sleepily sure that she was loved and safe. "I've given that much thought," she confided. "I think Reynald and Stephanie have realized that I am now much closer to the throne than I was at the time of my wedding. Then, no one knew how long my brother would live and we assumed Sybilla and Guy would be his heirs. But the past year has changed everything. Baldwin has finally found peace, most of the lords have rejected Guy, and my little nephew . . . Well, many wonder if he will reach manhood. For certes, Reynald and Stephanie do. I've heard them talking about him, and, yes, I do eavesdrop whenever I get the chance."

The smile that accompanied her confession was an impish one, but it faded almost at once. "Baldwin and I are strangers, even if we are blood kin," Isabella said sadly. "But I feel so sorry for him. He must be very lonely. And Reynald told Stephanie that he is quite sickly. He has an affliction of the lungs. . . . Asthma, I think it is called. Do you know what that is?"

They did and exchanged troubled looks. They'd been aware for some months that the young king's health was fragile, but it was more disturbing to give a name to his malady.

Isabella had curled up on the settle, tucking her feet under her like a kitten. But there was nothing childlike about the somber expression on her face. "Reynald and Stephanie are worried that this asthma might prove fatal. They know they've done nothing to endear themselves to me and I . . . well, I once warned them that queens have long memories. I think this is why they agreed to allow my visit. They are trying to regain my favor in case I should become queen."

She finished her wafer, licking the sugar from her fingers. "Our separation was mainly Stephanie's doing, Mother. She was trying to please Agnes, but there may have been another reason, too. Whilst she does not like me any more than I like her, it matters greatly to her that her son is married to a king's daughter and sister. She knows you and Pateras disapproved of the marriage and I suspect she feared that you'd find a way to get it annulled. That would have been much easier if it had not been consummated. She worries less about that now . . ." Isabella let her words trail off artfully, the hint of a smile hovering at the corners of her mouth, although she could not keep color from rising to highlight the elegant hollows of her cheekbones.

Balian looked from his stepdaughter to his wife. After a few hours of observing

Isabella interacting with Humphrey, Maria had pulled him aside and said simply, "He's bedded her." He still did not know why she'd been so sure of that. Nor was she happy to be proven right and for a moment, it showed on her face—just long enough for Isabella to catch it.

"He waited, Mother, as he promised he would," she said, sounding both defensive and defiant. "I am no longer a child. I celebrated my fourteenth birthday more than six months ago."

"I know your age," Maria said tersely. "I was present at your birth."

Isabella was frowning. "I want you both to like Humphrey, for he deserves it. He is quite clever; did you know he got one of Stephanie's dragomen to teach him Arabic? He plays the gittern and even composes songs for me. He has a way with horses and is an excellent rider. And he has been good to me, kind and generous. I admit I am not happy living at Kerak, but that is not his fault. I was ready to be his true wife and share his bed. He is very handsome, after all," she said, blushing more deeply this time and suddenly looking very young again.

Balian squeezed Maria's hand. She understood the message and after a long pause, she agreed that Humphrey was indeed quite handsome, adding almost plaintively, "All I want, Isabella, is for you to be happy."

Isabella's anger melted. Before she could respond, Humphrey burst into the solar. "A messenger has arrived from the Count of Tripoli. He told me—" He stopped then and stepped aside so the man behind him could enter, bearing the bad news that the boy king Baldwin's short, sad life and reign had ended.

Baudouin had ridden to Nablus as soon as he'd gotten Raymond's message. Even a bath and a good meal had not improved his mood any. Slouched in a chair in the solar, he gazed down into the dregs of his wine cup. "Does this make sense to you, Balian?"

Balian shrugged. They'd already discussed Raymond's letter at exhaustive length. In theory, the plan was a good one. Gerard de Ridefort and Reynald de Chatillon would do all in their power to thwart Raymond's reelection as regent, and the patriarch would speak out against it, too. Holding the High Court session whilst they were in Jerusalem for the little king's funeral would neatly thwart their opposition. The only weakness in this strategy was the involvement of Joscelin de Courtenay. Neither d'Ibelin brother found it easy to embrace Joscelin as an ally. Raymond was giving them no choice, though.

"I can see why Raymond believes Joscelin has decided their alliance is in his own self-interest," Baudouin said grudgingly. "It just seems unnatural to trust a de Courtenay." Glancing over at his sister-in-law, he asked her what would never have occurred to him to ask his own wife—what she thought of Raymond's actions.

Maria did not find that an easy question to answer. She had never warmed to Raymond, knowing he remained an enemy of the Greek empire. She thought he was an opportunist and had not forgiven him for his vengeful attack upon innocent Greek villagers and monks to avenge his wounded pride. Yet she could not deny that his interests and those of the other Poulain lords were in harmony, and she agreed that Raymond had shown he could rule and rule well as regent. He was also more likely to look favorably upon Isabella's claim to the crown, and she very much wanted her daughter to be Queen of Jerusalem, seeing that as her rightful heritage.

"I wish Raymond had told us more about his plans after he is reelected regent," she said. "Does he mean to honor his vow to submit Isabella's and Sybilla's queenship claims to the Pope and those western kings?"

Balian knew Maria thought that solution to the succession was both unwieldy and unworkable. He agreed with her and suspected that most of the Poulain lords did, too. It had been a compromise meant to satisfy both Raymond's allies and his foes and, like most compromises, it ended up satisfying no one. But since they'd all sworn holy oaths to adhere to its provisions, he did not see what choice they had. "Raymond's message was rather sparing with details," he acknowledged. "I suppose we'll have to go to Tiberias to get the answers we need."

"Isabella thinks she and Humphrey ought to attend Baldwin's funeral." While Maria understood her daughter's reasoning, she was loath to be parted from her so soon, and she had an almost superstitious reluctance to see Isabella ride away from Nablus again.

They considered that and soon agreed that Balian, Baudouin, and Humphrey would ride to Tiberias for the High Court session and Maria and Isabella would journey to Jerusalem for the little king's funeral. Since Isabella and Humphrey had already retired for the night, they withdrew to their own bedchambers, although no one slept well.

The following morning, their plan was quickly accepted by Isabella and Humphrey, for she was grateful to have her mother at her side for a funeral sure to be heartrending and Humphrey was always glad to avoid any encounters with his hated stepfather. They were finishing breakfast when they heard shouting. The noise did not subside and they headed outside to discover what was causing so much chaos.

A large group of horsemen had filled the courtyard, led by the Count of Trip-oli. He was accompanied by his wife and his four stepsons, all of whom looked very grim, even fearful. But it was Raymond who held their attention, for he seemed like a stranger. He'd always prided himself upon his public stoicism, his dispas-sionate response to setbacks or disappointments. This man's emotions were ex-posed for all to see: rage, shame, shock, and utter misery. His face burning with heat, he said hoarsely, "De Courtenay betrayed my trust. They are planning a coup, mean to crown Sybilla and Guy de Lusignan, and it may be too late to stop them."

CHAPTER 43

Upon learning of Joscelin de Courtenay's planned coup, Raymond had hastily sent out messages to the members of the High Court, urgently summoning them to Nablus rather than Tiberias. They soon began to arrive, horrified and angry, with some of their anger directed at Raymond for letting himself be duped like that. He was in no mood to accept reprimands, mortified that he'd fallen for Joscelin's ruse, and there were some tense exchanges, with Denys and Balian acting again as peacemakers. Before they could decide upon a course of action, they heard from Sybilla. Already assuming the authority of queenship, she invited them to come to Jerusalem for her coronation. After a hastily convened court session, they agreed to dispatch two Cistercian monks in response, forbidding Sybilla and her allies to proceed with the coronation, warning that would violate the holy oath they'd all sworn at the time of Baldwin's death.

Sybilla made sure that her son was given a regal burial; that was all she could do for him now. As his funeral cortege passed through the city streets on the way to the Church of the Holy Sepulchre, she wept again and was touched to see that some of the bystanders were crying, too, even though she sensed that their tears were as much for themselves as for the little dead king. The future, always precarious in Outremer, had never seemed so uncertain, so fraught with fear.

Guy had gone to consult with the man who would soon be their chancellor, Peter de Lydda, so Sybilla was alone when Patriarch Eraclius arrived at the palace and asked to see her. She would later realize that this had been deliberate on his part. But initially she had no suspicions, for he'd been very kind to her since their arrival in the city, and she escorted him up to the solar where, six years ago, it had been decided that she would wed Guy.

Once they'd been provided with chilled pomegranate juice, she hesitated before dismissing the servant, wondering if it would be proper for them to be alone. She reminded herself, then, that she was to be queen and no longer constrained by the foolish conventions that bound others of her sex. As soon as the door closed, she took a sip of her juice, regarding the patriarch pensively. She did not fully trust either Reynald de Chatillon or the grand master of the Templars and wished Joscelin had joined them in Jerusalem instead of remaining in Acre, which he'd now garrisoned with his own men. She did feel comfortable speaking candidly with Eraclius, though, for it was in the Church's interests to have a good working relationship with the new queen and king.

"Is it true, my lord, that the grand master of the Hospitallers has balked at taking part in my coronation?" She'd hoped that was just another of the wild rumors sweeping the city and felt a pang of disappointment when he said it was true, for Roger de Moulins had a reputation for probity and honor. "Why? How can he think Isabella has the better claim? I am the eldest!"

"He insists that since all the lords of the kingdom swore holy oaths to refer the succession to a royal commission, what we plan to do is lawless and offensive to God." Assuming she was unaware of it, he explained then that the coronation regalia was kept in the treasury, in a chest locked with three keys, entrusted to the patriarch and the grand masters of the Hospitallers and Templars. "De Moulins is refusing to surrender his key." Seeing how perturbed Sybilla was by that, Eraclius leaned over and patted her hand. "You need not fret, my lady. Reynald de Chatillon and Gerard de Ridefort have gone to the Hospitaller quarter to take the key from de Moulins. Then we can proceed as planned."

Sybilla was frowning. She'd been offended when the Count of Tripoli and the members of the High Court had sent those two Cistercian monks to deliver that insulting message, one that warned against holding her coronation. She'd taken it as a threat and she and Guy had approved when Reynald and Gerard ordered the city gates to be shut, keeping their enemies out. But she was troubled by the absence of so many highborn lords. She'd expected that they would rally around her once they realized her allies had outwitted them. So far, though, she could count only on the patriarch, her uncle, the grand master of the Templars, and just three of the barons—Reynald, Guy's brother Amaury, and her dead son's grandfather the Marquis of Montferrat. All the others were at Nablus, still defiant and determined to keep her from becoming queen.

"I do not want to rule over a divided kingdom. We need to unite against the infidels. Surely there must be a way to get the barons at Nablus to accept my queenship?"

Eraclius could not believe his luck. He'd not known how to ease into a conversation as dangerous as it would be difficult, and now she'd given him the perfect opening. "There is a way, my lady, but it will not be easy. It will mean putting the welfare of the kingdom first."

She nodded, thinking this was what Baldwin had always done. Despite her lack of experience, she had no illusions about ruling, had seen how heavily royal responsibilities had weighed upon her brother. Guy seemed to believe governing would be easy; she knew better. "What do you think I ought to do, my lord?"

Eraclius exhaled deeply and then went for it. "You need to end your marriage to Guy de Lusignan, my lady."

When she had time to think about it afterward, Sybilla would wonder why she'd not seen this coming. But she had been disarmed by his eloquent expressions of support and by the sympathy he'd offered for the death of her son. "I thought you were on my side!"

"I am, my lady, I am! You are our rightful queen. But you asked how you could conciliate the other lords and reconcile them to your rule. The only way to do that is to remove the reason for their opposition. They do not object to you; it is your lord husband they find unacceptable. Fairly or not, the great majority of the High Court members do not believe Guy can be a good king. They do not trust him, do not want to follow him into battle. If you agree to annul the marriage—and I can do that for you—their resistance will melt away and they will hasten to do homage to you as their queen, leaving the Count of Tripoli isolated and alone."

Sybilla got abruptly to her feet. Moving to the window, she gazed down into the courtyard below. He was encouraged by her silence, by the fact that she'd not rejected his proposal out of hand. "I know what grief this would give you, madame. But great sacrifices are sometimes required of the highborn. Your lord father was faced with just such a difficult decision, having to part from your mother ere the High Court would recognize his claim to the throne."

"Are you saying that you would refuse to crown me if I will not disavow my husband?"

"If it were just up to me, my lady, I would right gladly crown you, no matter what you might decide. Alas, I am compelled to speak on behalf of others. You need to understand the depths of the resistance to Lord Guy, even amongst those who have already declared in your favor. And as you already know, the barons at

Nablus are adamantly opposed to crowning your husband. This is your only hope of winning them over and avoiding a possible civil war."

When she remained silent, he quickly assured her that the legitimacy of her two young daughters would not be affected by an annulment. He was sure he could convince the others that Lord Guy should be permitted to retain the lordships of Ascalon or Jaffa. And of course she would have the final say when it came time to take another husband. "You have the blood right to the throne, madame, now that your brother and your son are dead. It would be a great pity if you forfeited it because of misguided loyalty."

He was pleased with that last sentence, feeling he'd conveyed clearly how much was at stake without stooping to threaten. When she turned away from the window, he found it hard to read her expression, but he was struck by her resemblance to her mother in that moment, for it was not always so noticeable.

"You have been candid with me, my lord, so I shall be candid with you. I will never agree to repudiate the man who is my husband, both by the laws of God and men. If I am to rule, it will be with Guy at my side. And if you balk at crowning me, your refusal will put you and your allies in a very awkward position. You and Gerard de Ridefort and Reynald de Chatillon will have to ride to Nablus and humble yourselves before the Count of Tripoli. Can you see them doing that?" She smiled then, again evoking memories of Agnes, for the smile held no mirth, only challenge and mockery.

His bluff called, Eraclius mustered up a mirthless smile of his own. "I hope you understand that I was not speaking for myself. It will be my honor to crown you as our queen."

Eraclius returned to the patriarch's palace in a foul mood. He was angry with Sybilla for being so stubborn and with himself for underestimating her. Whilst he'd realized he might be putting their relationship in jeopardy, the stakes were too high for timidity. He was not as sure as the Nablus barons that Guy was utterly unfit to be king. He did have doubts, though, about the man's ability to lead others, and he'd spoken the truth when he'd told Sybilla that the best way to unite the kingdom would be to annul her marriage. Yet if it came to a choice between Guy de Lusignan and the Count of Tripoli, he saw that as no choice at all.

He was still brooding later that afternoon when Reynald de Chatillon was announced. The other man was in good spirits, so Eraclius assumed his confrontation with Roger de Moulins had been successful. Reynald quickly confirmed this assumption by launching into a triumphant account of his clash of wills with the grand master of the Hospitallers.

"De Moulins is the worst sort of fool, an honorable one. He blathered on about the sanctity of holy oaths and the wishes of King Baldwin of blessed memory. He kept refusing to surrender his key to the treasury coffer until I thought Gerard was going to hit him. Our grand master is more bad-tempered than a badger."

"What happened? You look too pleased with yourself not to have the Hospitaller key."

Reynald grinned. "We kept at him until he'd had enough. By then he'd probably have given us the Holy Grail if that would shut Gerard up. He finally shouted, 'Enough!' and flung the key through the open window. We had only to head down to the courtyard to collect it. But I think we can safely say that none of the Hospitallers will be attending the coronation."

Reynald waited for the patriarch's response, got only a curt nod, and gave Eraclius a speculative look. "Why so downcast? Do not tell me you broached the subject of annulment with Sybilla? I warned you that was a fool's errand. You ought to have heeded me."

Eraclius wished he had. "It had to be done," he insisted. "Do not pretend that you think Guy has the makings of a good king. You'd have been relieved, too, had I been able to talk some sense into Sybilla."

Reynald shrugged. "But I knew you'd fail. No man would choose his wife over a crown. Women are irrational by their very nature, though, so it was only to be expected that Sybilla would cling to Guy like a limpet."

"Tell me the truth, Reynald. Are we about to make a mistake in crowning Guy de Lusignan?"

"I am a soldier, not a soothsayer. Whilst I cannot claim that de Lusignan has inspired confidence in anyone but his besotted wife so far, that is not to say that he cannot learn. And he is still the best of a bad lot. Would you rather have my craven milksop stepson on the throne? Or Raymond de St. Gilles, the man so eager to ally himself with infidel Saracens? If they are our choices, what else can we do?"

Eraclius had no answer for him. They were all in God's hands now.

Sybilla had been too young to recall her father's coronation, but she had vivid memories of the day her brother became king. He had not yet been told he was a leper, so it must have been a happy time for him. Her own emotions were conflicted, joy seasoned by unease, pride in her victory, sadness when she thought of her son, resentment that her coronation should be so poorly attended, and regret that her mother was not here to see the crown placed upon her head.

Gerard de Ridefort and Reynald de Chatillon had retrieved two crowns from the treasury; they glimmered on the high altar, their gems catching the candle-light, and she wondered if they'd be as heavy as they looked. When it came time for the patriarch to place one on her head, she discovered that it was. Once she was anointed with the sacred chrism, she rose to her feet and some in the church raised a cheer. What happened next took her by surprise, though.

Eraclius lifted the second crown, but instead of beckoning Guy forward, he held it out to Sybilla. "My lady queen, as a woman, you will need a man to rule at your side. Bestow this crown upon the one whom you most trust to govern your kingdom."

Sybilla's first reaction was anger, seeing this as the patriarch's sly way of de-flecting blame for Guy's controversial coronation. If his rule proved to be as inept as so many feared, Eraclius could then say he'd not been the one to crown Guy. But as their eyes met, she changed her mind, deciding this was meant as a gift, his at-tempt to make amends and regain her favor. If she crowned Guy, people would remember that, remember that Guy's claim to the kingship was utterly dependent upon her. Guy would remember it, too. And as much as she loved him, that was not a bad thing, either.

Turning toward him, she smiled. "I, Sybilla, choose as king my husband, Guy de Lusignan. I know he is worthy of this honor and that with the help of God, he and I will rule our people well." And when Guy knelt, she set the crown upon his bowed head.

At Nablus, the barons had chosen a serjeant to spy for them and, disguised as a monk, he'd ridden off to learn if their foes would dare to crown Sybilla and Guy. Now he was back and the barons filed into the palace great hall to hear his report. He began by explaining how he'd managed to get into the city. The main gates remained barred, but he'd been able to enter by a postern gate of the Jacobite church of St. Mary Magdalene. Although he was proud of his ingenuity, he knew better than to dwell upon it, and he wasted no time in confirming their worst fears, relating how he'd watched as the patriarch crowned Sybilla and she then crowned Guy.

"Many of the citizens came to watch and to cheer Queen Sybilla. All of the Hospitaller knights stayed away, though. But the grand master of the Templars acted as if the coronation was all his doing. When the new queen placed the crown on her husband's head, Master Gerard declared loudly that this was 'well worth the loss of Botron.' Most of the spectators did not know what he meant by that."

These men did, Count Raymond more than any of them. Botron was the fief of the heiress he'd promised to Gerard de Ridefort and had then given to a wealthy Pisan merchant.

Devastated by the realization that they had lost and Guy de Lusignan was now their king, the Poulain lords could only mourn the death of their hopes. The funereal mood in the hall was contagious, soon spreading throughout the palace and into the town. The leaders of the resistance withdrew to the solar to discuss their options. Since they did not think they had any, the silence was beyond oppressive; it was smothering.

Baudouin could not keep quiet for long, though, and his outrage soon broke free. "Those fools have driven a dagger through the heart of our homeland," he snarled. "Guy de Lusignan can no more rule the kingdom than my favorite hunting dog. It is only a question now of how long it will take ere he dooms us all. I'd rather leave Outremer than stand by helplessly and have to watch its death throes!"

That was such an extreme threat that none of them took it seriously. Balian poured his brother a cup of wine and carried it over to Baudouin. That seemed like a good idea to Denys and he did the same. His cousin Gautier, the Lord of Caesarea, was slouched on the settle, so weighed down with misery that his spine seemed to have compressed. Humphrey de Toron had found an inconspicuous corner. He was gazing off into space, his thoughts impossible to read.

Maria had moved to Balian's side. She looked as if she needed a hug, so he obliged, slipping his arm around her waist, still slender despite six trips to the birthing chamber. "I know Guy is not evil, not a monster like Andronicus," she said softly. "But I fear his weakness may do as much damage as Andronicus's cruelties."

So did Balian. "Sometimes men rise to meet a challenge, Marika. Mayhap that will be true for Guy, too." But she knew he did not believe that any more than she did.

Raymond had not spoken since they'd entered the solar, so lost in his own thoughts that he'd seemed oblivious of the others. But now he moved to the center of the chamber. "We need not despair just yet. There is another road we can take. Rather than letting them thrust Guy de Lusignan down our throats, we refuse to accept him as our king. Whilst Sybilla has a valid blood claim, she has disqualified herself by her stubborn refusal to disavow de Lusignan. So, we make her sister our queen. We crown Isabella and Humphrey."

There were exclamations from virtually everyone in the solar. The usually unflappable Denys spilled his wine. Hugues whirled to stare at his stepfather. Maria gasped "My God!" in Greek. Baudouin had just slumped down into a window seat, but Raymond's words jolted him to his feet. Balian, who'd turned instinctively toward Humphrey at the count's words, saw the young man's head come up sharply. He was still not in time to catch the initial horror on his son-in-law's face, for by then the lessons of a lifetime had come to Humphrey's rescue and his expression was blank, revealing nothing of his inner turmoil.

Denys was the first to point out the obvious. "Raymond, you are talking of a civil war."

"If need be, yes," Raymond said, managing to sound both matter-of-fact and defiant. "If we crown Isabella, she will have the support of the members of the High Court, virtually all of the lords of the realm, the Hospitallers, my Tripoli, the Prince of Antioch, and most of the people. I doubt that Sybilla could stand fast against them. But even if they refuse to abandon their coup, we must do this. We cannot allow Guy de Lusignan to assume power."

"Raymond is right." Baudouin strode over to stand at the count's side. "If we must weigh the risk of civil war against the fatal blunders Guy is sure to make, that is not a difficult decision—not when the very survival of the kingdom is at stake."

They were soon all talking at once, their voices agitated and then excited as they began to give serious consideration to Raymond's proposal. Humphrey watched in frozen silence as their fear and hatred of Guy's kingship overcame their caution, even their common sense—for that was how he saw it. He did not doubt their sincerity, nor did he disagree with their scathing assessment of their new king's abilities. But it was too late. Guy *was* their king now. This was a war they'd already lost.

Humphrey made no attempt to protest, knowing how futile that would be. Raymond and Baudouin had the persuasive passion of the newly converted, embracing Isabella's queenship as the salvation of the kingdom. They soon won over Gautier and Hugues and then Maria. Humphrey did not like his mother by marriage, believing her to be too quick to meddle in matters better left to men, too like his own mother in that regard, but also too Greek. He thought she took overweening pride in her royal blood and very much wanted her daughter to become a queen, too. So, he felt no surprise when she accepted the argument that a civil war was actually the lesser of evils. He lost all hope, though, when Denys and Balian eventually accepted it, too. They were greatly respected by the other Poulains, believed to be fair and reasonable men. If they argued for this, many of the lords would be influenced by them.

The events unfolded as he feared they would. Maria went to fetch Isabella, who understandably seemed somewhat dazed to have her life turned upside down like this. Humphrey was given no opportunity to speak privately to his young wife, although he did not think such a conversation would have changed anything. When the other lords were summoned back to the great hall, Raymond and Baudouin made a convincing case for crowning Isabella and her husband. The discussion that followed was loud and animated. To Humphrey, the outcome was inevitable, for he knew they desperately wanted a way to deny the kingship to Guy de Lusignan. Despite living seven years in their midst, he'd failed to win them over. They neither liked nor trusted him, some because they doubted his leadership abilities, others because he'd already begun to bring his own countrymen to Outremer to share in his good fortune and would lavish royal favors upon even more Poitevins at the expense of the native-born, the Poulains.

Humphrey did not care if their reasons were purely patriotic or utterly personal and petty, if they were moved by idealism or revenge, or if their motives were mixed. All that mattered to him was that they voted that afternoon to make Isabella their queen, for he dreaded what that would mean for him and for Bella, for their marriage, and for their homeland.

Isabella was lying on their bed, but she sat up when Humphrey entered. "Here I've been offered a crown and it gave me a throbbing headache."

He knew she was vulnerable to headaches in times of stress. Dipping a washcloth into a basin of water, he brought it to the bed. "Put this on your forehead. That sometimes helps."

She did as he bade and let him adjust pillows behind her back. "Ought we to have seen this coming, Humphrey? After Count Raymond was so badly outwitted by Sybilla's allies, I just assumed she'd be crowned and that would be that. I truly did not expect this. . . ." She gestured with her hand to encompass all of the day's remarkable happenings.

Reaching for that hand, he held it for a moment against his cheek. "We did not think they would be willing to fight a war to put you on the throne." Looking intently into the fair face upturned to his, he searched it for clues. What did she really think about this? "And there will be war, Bella. They are deluding themselves if they say otherwise. There will be a blood price for your crown. Can you accept that?"

"I hope it will not come to that," she said, although her words sounded hollow even to her ears. "I had not given a great deal of thought to becoming queen, since it seemed unlikely. For years, I expected Sybilla to reign after Baldwin and then her son or the children she had with Guy. I've not had enough time to adjust to this strange new world and I admit I find it rather overwhelming. But I think they are right about Guy. Not even his allies believe he is fit to be king. At least we know that your stepfather does not. It is Reynald's hatred of Count Raymond that has brought him to Jerusalem, not confidence in Guy's abilities."

She paused to give him time to respond. When he did not, she said softly, "All of the members of the High Court are in rare agreement on this. And my mother, my stepfather, and his brother . . . they want me to be queen. Baudouin can be reckless, but not Balian. He is the most levelheaded man I've ever known and if he believes this will be best for Outremer, I must believe it, too."

Humphrey had clung to a faint, foolish hope that she would share his sense of horror. He ought to have known better. How could he expect her to refuse a crown? To reject her own family's guidance? She was only fourteen.

Isabella was studying his face as closely as he'd been studying hers. "I know why you feel such unease. You hold yourself too cheaply, my love. You always have. Your mother and Reynald have made you doubt your own abilities, so much so that you fear you'd not make a good king. But you are wrong. I have no doubts at all and no one knows you better than I do." Leaning over, she kissed him, trying to convey her love and her faith in him.

They sat there for a time, holding on to each other as if that embrace could somehow keep the world at bay. Humphrey was the one to end it. "I will fetch Emma, tell her you need an herbal potion and a sleeping draught. Then you ought to go to bed, darling lass. I am not sleepy yet, so I think I'll take a walk."

Isabella promised that she would, surprised to realize how exhausted she was. "Tell Emma to hurry," she murmured, lying back against the pillows with a drowsy smile. He stood by the door for a while, looking at the bed and his girl wife, as if trying to burn the image and the moment into his memory, so deeply that it would never be forgotten.

CHAPTER 44

September 1186
Nablus, Outremer

N ormally the streets of Nablus were empty once darkness fell. Tonight, people were still out, for the town was filled with the High Court lords and their retinues. Humphrey soon noticed that passersby were turning to stare at him and he realized that word of the afternoon's dramatic developments had begun to circulate. How long ere it reached Sybilla and Guy?

When he got to the town stables, he was relieved to find a groom still on duty. The groom was openly puzzled why a lord—as his clothing, sword, and demeanor proclaimed him to be—would want to hire one of their nags. Humphrey could hardly explain that he dared not take his own stallion from the palace stables. Paying the man generously curbed his curiosity, and he even saddled the gelding for Humphrey, a courtesy not usually accorded their customers.

Humphrey had rarely traveled at night and never without squires or knights riding beside him. It was an odd feeling to be so alone in the dark like this, like being adrift on a vast, shadowy sea. He did not worry about encountering either outlaws or Saracen raiders on the watershed road, but he still checked to be sure his sword could slide smoothly from its scabbard if need be. A September harvest moon silvered the road ahead. The horse had no interest in setting a fast pace, and Humphrey did not push him, for he was in no hurry to reach his destination.

As the miles and the hours slipped by, he tried not to think of Bella's reaction once she learned of his disappearance. Instead, he focused upon the reasons he was so opposed to Count Raymond's plot to make Bella queen. He'd spoken the truth when he'd warned her that it would lead to civil war. Whilst the patriarch and even Joscelin might back off if it came to bloodshed, he doubted that Sybilla and Guy would. More to the point, he knew his stepfather and Gerard de Ridefort would hold fast even if it led to catastrophe for their kingdom.

Yet Bella had spoken the truth, too, when she'd said he feared being king. He had no illusions about his ability to exercise mastery over other men. He'd been taught how to fight and had fended off a Saracen ambush as he led reinforcements from Kerak to join the army at Saforie. Yet he had never learned how to command respect and he knew he would find it even harder than Guy to win the trust of his lords. He was one of them, not an outsider like Guy. But no one had cast aspersions on Guy's manhood, called him a coward or worse.

The unfairness of it forced him to face his third fear. Once he'd been judged and found wanting, the lords of the High Court would want to find a more worthy husband for Bella, a more worthy king for Outremer. If that happened, he was sure Maria and Balian would not speak up for him or defend the marriage. His only allies would be his own mother and Bella herself. But how could he expect a young girl to stand alone against so many highborn lords? How could she not be swayed by the mother and stepfather she loved? Again and again he went over these dark thoughts, yet by the time the sky had lightened and the walls of Jerusalem came into view, he still did not know which of these fears was the strongest, the one that had driven him to an act of such desperation.

St. Stephen's Gate was closed, manned by guards who were abusing their authority by smirking at the angry protests of people who wanted to enter. Humphrey supposed he could get in as their serjeant spy had done, through that church postern gate. But first he tried the easiest way, demanding entry as an impatient highborn lord would have done, with enough arrogance to do his stepfather proud. To his surprise, it worked, and he was allowed to ride his placid, swaybacked gelding into the city. It was soon obvious that a few of the men knew who he was, and when he said he wanted to see Queen Sybilla, they were delighted that they could deliver their prize catch without any awkwardness or resistance.

Not sure if Humphrey should be treated as a prisoner or an honored guest, his guards hovered nearby once they reached the palace. It was not long before Sybilla entered the great hall. Taking her seat on the dais, she beckoned for Humphrey to approach. She was scowling, making it clear that she saw him as the enemy, that she now saw her sister as a rival, not family.

When Humphrey knelt, even that did not appear to mollify her. He was puzzled by the level of her hostility, which seemed excessive since he was being deferential and had come of his own volition. That mystery was solved with her first words. "Have your traitorous friends set the date yet for Isabella's coronation?"

Humphrey was astonished that she already knew of their plans. Not only did she and Guy have a spy at Nablus, he'd gotten to Jerusalem first, must have raced along the same road Humphrey had followed hours later. Humphrey had often heard his mother and Reynald complain that Outremer was honeycombed with spies; now he believed it.

"Isabella and I had no part in that," he said firmly. "That I am here surely proves our innocence. We do not want blood to be spilled on our account and are quite willing to acknowledge you as our queen." He could see that Sybilla was conflicted, torn between her suspicions and her desire to believe that her sister had not conspired against her. "Isabella is just fourteen, Madame. We were pawns, not plotters."

Sybilla wanted to believe him and decided that she did. He was right; his presence here was indeed proof of innocence. Signaling for him to rise, she asked if he was willing to do homage to her and to her lord husband. When he assured her that he was, she favored him with a smile of sudden charm. "Then you and my sister will be very welcome at our court."

He thanked her, recognizing the irony in her words, for he doubted that he'd be welcomed again at Nablus, not after what he'd done, what the barons would see as an unforgivable betrayal. He could only pray that Bella would not agree with them.

When she awakened and saw that Humphrey's side of the bed was empty, Isabella felt an instinctive throb of alarm, for there were no signs that he'd ever returned to their bedchamber last night. Sitting alone in their bed, she had to admit that her husband may have been far more distraught than she'd realized.

She did not summon any of Humphrey's knights, for she trusted them no more than he did, knowing that his mother still maintained a stranglehold upon the life of her only son. She turned instead to Sir Fulcher de Hebron, who'd served her stepfather loyally for years. He rewarded her faith by asking no questions, merely listening as if it were part of his household duties to track down errant husbands, and some of Isabella's unease began to lessen. She'd almost convinced herself that she was overreacting by the time Sir Fulcher returned and reported that whilst Humphrey's stallion was still in the stables, no one had seen him since the night before.

Maria and Balian were still abed, for they'd begun their day by making love. They lay entangled in the sheets, perspiration drying on their bodies as their breathing slowed. "Have we really been married for nigh on nine years?" he murmured, leaning over to nuzzle her throat.

She opened an eye. "Are you saying the hearth fires ought to have cooled by now?"

"No. . . . I am much too good a lover for that."

"Modest, too."

He laughed softly. "I was actually marveling that I could have been so lucky for so long . . . my queen."

Propping herself on her elbow, she abandoned their banter for a question that was deadly serious. "Balian, are we making a great mistake in seeking to crown Isabella?"

"Christ Jesus, I hope not," he said, with such intensity that she felt a sudden chill. She'd not slept well, lying awake for hours as she found herself assailed by belated qualms, and it dismayed her now to realize he had misgivings of his own.

Reaching over, he brushed a raven strand of her hair away from her face. "If you are asking whether I have doubts, Marika, of course I do. I am sure that Isabella and Humphrey will be better rulers than Sybilla and Guy. What I fear is having to fight to put them on the throne."

She did, too. "Last night, when I could not get to sleep, I found myself trying to decide who deserves the most blame for this . . . this calamity we are now facing. There was no lack of candidates. Sybilla and Guy, obviously. Even more so, the men who hope to be kingmakers."

"The unholy trinity," he said, sounding too bitter for sarcasm. "Our unpriestly patriarch, that Templar hothead, and Reynald, of course; whenever there is trouble, he is in the midst of it."

She nodded. "Let's not forget the patriarch's puppet, Joscelin de Courtenay. But there is another kingmaker who ought to be mentioned, too. Raymond also bears some of the guilt; had he not colluded with his cousin to stage a coup, Baldwin would never have agreed to let Sybilla wed Guy." Shifting so she could see his face, she said, "Somewhere Lucifer must be laughing, Balian. Baldwin sacrificed so much to protect his kingdom. Yet he made two great blunders that contributed to our present peril. He married both of his sisters to men unfit to rule."

Balian could not judge Baldwin so dispassionately; he'd loved the leper king, and he hoped that Baldwin had never reached that same unsparing conclusion. Before he could respond, there was a knock on the door. When he heard Isabella's voice, he told her to wait and swung his legs over the side of the bed. Tossing Maria her bed robe, he grabbed a shirt off a wall hook, pulling it over his head and hips as he padded barefoot toward the door.

Isabella was very pale and she seemed to have dressed in haste, for her hair was not braided and her veil was slightly askew. When Balian hugged her, he could feel her trembling and shot Maria a silent message that something was gravely amiss. Maria had already deduced this. Patting the bed beside her, she invited her daughter to sit, prepared to be patient until Isabella was ready to reveal what had brought her to their bedchamber at such an early hour.

Isabella stayed on her feet. "Humphrey . . ." She swallowed before starting again. "He is missing." Seeing that they did not yet understand, she took a few steps closer to the bed. "When I awoke this morning, I saw that he'd never been to bed. I asked Sir Fulcher to look for him, but he is nowhere to be found."

Neither Balian nor Maria knew what to make of this. After exchanging glances with his wife, Balian said, choosing his words with care, "Bella, what do you think has happened?"

Isabella had been gazing down at her feet as she'd spoken. She looked up at that and he saw that her dark eyes shimmered with unshed tears. "I think that he has gone to Jerusalem to make peace with Sybilla and Guy," she confessed, and only then did her composure crack and the tears begin to flow, a slow, silent testimony to a heart badly bruised even if not broken.

None of the lords knew why they'd been summoned to Balian and Maria's bedchamber with such urgency. Few of them had slept well and they were already on edge as they entered the room. Isabella was standing as far from the door as she could get, flanked by her parents. She started to speak, but so softly that they could not catch all of her words, and Balian put a reassuring hand on her shoulder before telling them what she could not bring herself to do, that Humphrey de Toron had thwarted their plan to crown Isabella.

Their first reaction was disbelief, an unwillingness to accept that they'd been outmaneuvered yet again, followed by despairing rage. Isabella stood her ground even though she was unnerved by their shouting and tried to answer the barrage of questions as best she could. When the interrogation began to sound accusatory, Balian and Maria both intervened, she saying sharply that this was not Isabella's fault and Balian stepping protectively in front of his stepdaughter, making it clear by his body language that the cross-examination was over.

Baudouin had been one of the worst offenders, for he was prone to expressing himself loudly even in ordinary conversation. But as appalled as he was by Humphrey's flight, Isabella was his niece and family always came first. Moving to stand beside his brother, he said, "We are done here" in a tone that conveyed both a warning and a threat.

Raymond was still reeling from the blow Humphrey had delivered to his hopes and his family's future. He managed a grudging almost apology, muttering that they did not "blame the lass for de Toron's treason," then spun on his heel and left the chamber. After some uncertainty, the other men followed, only Denys and Baudouin remaining behind.

"We know none of this is your doing," Denys assured Isabella before addressing himself to the adults. "We must hold a court session, but it might be best to give them some time to come to terms with this. When a wound is so fresh, the pain is likely to overwhelm common sense."

"Do I have to be there?" Yet when they all assured Isabella that there was no need for her to attend the session, their support strengthened her resolve and she decided she did need to be present. It was a matter of pride and, she now realized, loyalty to Humphrey.

It turned out to be less of an ordeal than Isabella had expected. Fury had given way to fatalism and the men seemed unable to summon the energy for outrage, not when their defeat was so total. Balian spoke for Isabella again, tersely relating what they knew of Humphrey's disappearance, even summoning the stable groom, who told them of renting a horse to a young lord who'd taken the road toward Jerusalem. That was proof enough of Humphrey's treachery to his former allies. While some of them aimed threats and curses at his absent head, their hearts were not really in it, for all that mattered now was mending fences with the new king and queen.

Raymond and Baudouin made a last-ditch attempt to stave off surrender, arguing that Isabella could still be crowned. But no woman could rule without a man at her side and very few would be willing to follow a fourteen-year-old girl with a husband in the enemy camp. Many would decide that Guy no longer looked so bad if confronted with such a choice.

The session ended in disarray, for they all knew it was now every man for himself. Raymond remained rebellious, declaring that he would never do homage to Guy de Lusignan. The other barons were not impressed by his bravado, for he could better afford a grand gesture of defiance; even if he were rash enough to put Galilee at risk, he was still the Count of Tripoli. One by one, they thanked Balian and Maria for their hospitality, took care to bid a respectful farewell to Isabella, for she might still become their queen one day if Fortune's wheel took an unexpected spin, and returned to their own homes to lay plans for surviving this debacle.

Stephanie and Reynald had a town house in Jerusalem and Humphrey had been staying there since his arrival in the city. For once, he was in Reynald's favor; his stepfather had even congratulated him for "throwing the last shovel of dirt onto Raymond's coffin." His mother seemed more ambivalent. As Reynald's wife, she'd naturally given public support to the queen and king he'd done so much to make. She made a few ambiguous comments, though, that caused Humphrey to wonder if she entertained any regrets that her son had spurned a crown. He did not ask, doubting that she'd tell him the truth and not really caring if she did.

He'd written to Isabella, had yet to receive a response, and each day of silence inflicted another heart's wound. The rebel barons had begun to arrive in Jerusalem, seeking pardons from their new rulers. Humphrey watched a few of these submissions and was disgusted by the attempts to blame everything on Raymond, as if these lords had been forced at sword-point to repudiate their rightful king and queen. Much to his surprise, Guy and Sybilla had proven to be gracious winners. Apparently, they'd either realized or had been persuaded that they needed to unite the kingdom's rival factions, and Humphrey took what small comfort he could from that.

He'd still not heard from Isabella and as September ebbed away, he decided he had no choice but to return to Nablus and try to reclaim his wife. He'd been avoiding his mother and Reynald, so he was taken by surprise when Stephanie came to his bedchamber one evening and told him that Balian d'Ibelin and that Greek woman had appeared at the palace that afternoon, where they'd done homage to Sybilla and Guy and were received with more warmth and forgiveness than either of them deserved. She saw the question in his eyes and nodded.

"Yes, they brought your wife with them. I am pleased to report that Sybilla was very generous, making it clear that she does not blame Isabella for being led astray by bad counsel." Vexed by Humphrey's lack of response, she turned to go. She paused at the door, though, to try to prod him into action. "Do you plan to retrieve your wife yourself? Or should I ask Reynald to fetch her home for you?" This time her departure was real, so she was gone by the time he grabbed the closest item at hand, a book, and flung it at that closing door.

❖

Humphrey was kept waiting for so long in the great hall of his in-laws' town house that he wondered if he'd be turned away, denied even a glimpse of his wife. But then Balian entered the hall. "I am here to see Isabella," Humphrey said, seeing the futility of offering courtesy to a man who was making no attempt to camouflage his contempt. Humphrey was accustomed to Maria's coldness; it stung more now, coming from Balian, who'd always treated him amicably.

"I do not know if she wants to see you." Gesturing to the youthful squire who was glaring at Humphrey, Balian told Ernoul to deliver that message to his daughter. He was delivering a message of his own by stressing the word "daughter" and Humphrey understood; Bella would always be Balian and Maria's daughter, but she'd remain his wife only if that were her choice. He was not treated as a guest, offered neither wine nor a seat, and the very silence in the hall seemed hostile. When he could endure it no longer, he took several steps toward Balian, pitching his voice for the other man's ears alone. "I never meant to cause Bella any pain—"

"Do not say it." Balian's voice was low, too, yet it conveyed more menace than shouting could have done. Humphrey suddenly felt as if he were looking at a stranger, one whose anger was measured, deliberate, and dangerous. "If it were up to me, de Toron, you'd never lay eyes on my daughter again. But that is not my judgment to make. It is Bella's and we shall respect whatever she decides. So will you."

"I will," Humphrey said quickly. It was suddenly very important that he convince Balian he would never coerce Bella into doing anything she did not want to do. "I know you are not likely to believe me now that I've pledged my support to Sybilla and Guy, but I love Bella very much, enough to set her free if that be her wish."

"The reason I do not believe you is because you are a coward. You ran away and abandoned Bella to a storm of your making. If you truly loved my daughter, you'd have been honest with her, with us all. You'd have stood up and told us your reasons why you would not accept the crown. You'd have given Bella the chance either to agree with you or to decide she still wanted to be queen. Instead, you fled like a thief in the night, leaving her behind to face the fury that was meant for you."

Humphrey had no words, no defense, for only now did he truly understand just what he'd done to his wife. He'd feared that she would resent him for denying her the right to be queen. But that was just one of the wounds he'd inflicted and his shame and remorse were all the greater because he'd needed to have her stepfather point them out to him.

It was then that Ernoul returned. "I am sorry, my lord," he told Balian, sounding as if it were somehow his fault. "But Lady Isabella has agreed to see him."

Emma opened the bedchamber door. Humphrey knew she'd blamed him, as Maria had done, for not protesting when Bella was forbidden to see her family, but she'd become less judgmental once Bella had confided that she loved him. He saw now that he'd lost all the ground he'd gained and he was once more in enemy territory. "Just call if you need me, my lady," Emma said, and brushed by Humphrey without a word or glance.

He and Isabella regarded each other in silence for several moments. "Did you get my letters?" he asked at last, and her eyebrows shot upward in disbelief.

"Of course I did. What . . . you think my parents would have kept them from me? They would never do that."

"You answered none of the letters, though."

"Because we needed to *talk*, Humphrey."

"You did read them?" he persisted, for he'd poured out his heart in those letters, and he sighed in relief when she nodded. "Then you know how sorry I am for causing you any grief. . . ."

"I was hurt at first, but that soon passed. I am still angry with you, though." When he did not speak, some of that anger crept into her voice. "You do know why?"

"I cost you a crown. If not for what I did, you'd have been the queen."

She slowly shook her head. "No, Humphrey. I admit I was dazzled a bit at first; crowns seem to have that affect on people. But once I had time to think it over, I did not feel bereft that I would not be queen. I may even have felt some relief, for I would never want to go to war with my sister and that may well have happened. You were right about that."

During the weeks they'd been apart, he'd seen that crown as an insurmountable barrier between them, and he ought to have been very thankful to learn it was not so. But Balian's bitter words were still ringing in his ears. "Your stepfather called me a coward, Bella . . . and he was right. I was afraid to defy the Count of Tripoli and the High Court, so I took the easy way out. I ran away and left you to answer for my treachery, for that was how they would have seen it . . . as the worst sort of betrayal."

"Yes, they did. But I care more about the wrong you did me. You lied to me, Humphrey." Holding up her hand before he could protest. "Oh, yes, you did. A lie of omission is still a lie. You owed me better than that, should have told me the truth about how you felt. Had you only been honest with me that night, you'd have saved us both so much grief. Whether we'd run away to Jerusalem or stayed to confront them together the next day—"

"You would have done that? If I'd asked you, you'd have fled to Jerusalem with me?"

"Only if I'd not been able to talk you out of it. Of course, I'd have left a note for my parents if we had run away. That was another of your mistakes, Humphrey, riding off without a word. You must promise never to do that again."

He was not sure which of them was the one to take those first steps, but suddenly she was in his arms and his world was filled again with blazing sunlight, dazzling after so many weeks of darkness. After a time, he heard himself ask if she forgave him and she said she did, with a smile so bewitching it quite literally took his breath away.

"In many ways, my sister and I are as different as day and night. But Sybilla and I have one important quality in common. We are both very loyal to the men we married," she said, and laughed as he swept her up and carried her to the bed.

Eventually, the barons of the kingdom had made their peace with Guy, all but the Count of Tripoli and Baudouin d'Ibelin. In October, Guy summoned the lords of Outremer to attend a general assembly at Acre. To no one's surprise, Count Raymond ignored the summons. There was much more suspense as to whether or not Baudouin would appear, and when he was spotted riding into the city in the company of his brother and sister-in-law, people flocked to the cathedral of the Holy Cross, where the session was to be held, eager to witness the reckoning between the new king and one of the most powerful of his vassals.

As they entered the cathedral close, the d'Ibelins were greeted by the new bishop of Acre, Rufinus, for Joscius had recently been elevated to the archbishopric of Tyre, vacant since William's death. The king had chosen to hold the general assembly in their chapter house, he explained, and he would be pleased to escort them there, adding that he hoped they would be able to attend the feast that he was giving on the morrow, one of reconciliation. That was such a heavy hint that Baudouin chuckled. If he was amused by the bishop's overt curiosity, Balian was not, for he was one of the few who knew what Baudouin intended to do. He'd been hoping that Baudouin would change his mind at the eleventh hour, but there was no sign of that so far.

Isabella had been waiting in the cathedral cloisters and hastened toward them, trailed by Humphrey. Balian and Maria's meeting with their son-in-law was awkward for all three of them, but they'd resolved to be civil to him for Isabella's sake. Baudouin could only manage a grudging nod. He was very pleased, though, to see his eldest daughter, Esquiva, standing nearby. He greeted her affectionately, wishing he'd been able to warn her in advance, yet how could he confide in her when she was sleeping with the enemy? As he hugged his daughter, Balian and Maria exchanged the sort of mute message common in good marriages, one that communicated the same thought—sympathy for Esquiva, born a d'Ibelin and wed to a de Lusignan, and a determination to spare Isabella such torn loyalties if at all possible.

Upon their entrance into the chapter house, Baudouin was at once the focus of all eyes. Balian felt as if he were watching a rogue wave about to crash upon an unprotected beach, and anger began to stir, for he well knew Baudouin was relishing the attention, the speculation, and the coming confrontation with Guy de Lusignan.

The d'Ibelin women were not the only highborn wives present; so was Stephanie de Milly; her cousin Agneta; and, of course, Sybilla, who looked as if queenship agreed with her. Guy was in good spirits, too, for Baudouin's presence signified his surrender. While that had not really been in doubt, Guy was still pleased to have it finally over with.

After Bishop Rufinus opened the session by asking God's blessing upon their kingdom, Guy rose from the dais and approached the lectern. His speech was brief and to the point. He thanked the Almighty for showing him such favor and bestowing so great an honor upon him and he promised to prove worthy of it. He concluded by asking the assembled barons to again offer him the homage and fealty that vassals owed their liege lord. There was a smattering of polite applause when the audience saw that he was done, for most of the men were willing to acknowledge he could sound like a king when need be. He looked like a king, too, handsome and still in his prime. Whether he could act like a king remained to be proven.

Guy signaled then to Reynald de Chatillon, who was enjoying the humiliation of a man he'd long disliked, both because of the influence Baudouin d'Ibelin wielded and because he'd been impossible to intimidate. "Let the Lord of Ramlah be the first to come forward and bend the knee to his king, to do homage that is long overdue."

Guy had not wanted Baudouin's capitulation to be a public shaming, satisfied by the submission itself, and he tried to catch Reynald's eye. Reynald did not look in his direction, though, keeping his gaze locked challengingly on the Lord of Ramlah. Baudouin rose without haste and, ignoring Reynald altogether, gave his response to the man who would be his king.

"No, I will not do homage to you, my lord, not today, not ever."

There was a stunned silence, for none were expecting defiance, other than the few whom Baudouin had taken into his confidence. Guy seemed more bewildered than angry, pointing out that if Baudouin would not do homage to his king and liege lord, he would forfeit his fiefs of Ramlah and Mirabel, almost as if he thought that had somehow escaped Baudouin's attention.

"If doing homage to you is the price I must pay for holding those fiefs, it is too high. That is not an act I can live with. I am giving Ramlah and Mirabel to my heir, and I will commend those fiefs into the Crown's keeping until my son, Thomasin, comes of legal age. At that time, he can decide for himself if he wants to do homage to you. And until Thomasin reaches his majority, I entrust him to the care of my brother, Balian, the Lord of Nablus."

Baudouin had planned to elaborate upon the reasons why he could not accept Guy as his king, to indulge in the brutal candor of a man with nothing to lose. But as he gazed around the chapter house, he realized that there was no need for this. His dramatic repudiation spoke for itself. Looking back at the speechless king, he said calmly, "Well, I think we are done here. I will quit your kingdom within three days." And with that, he turned and walked out.

Balian was shocked by the number of Baudouin's knights who'd chosen to accompany him into exile. It was bad enough for the kingdom to lose a battle commander as experienced as his brother. Losing so many men, too, was a blow he'd not been expecting.

Baudouin was saying a final farewell to his younger daughter, Etiennette, her husband, and their small son while his wife fidgeted nearby, clearly eager to get on the road. Balian and Maria had wondered how Mary felt about starting life anew in Antioch, but apparently, she was fine with the move. It occurred to Balian that she shared his brother's belief that Outremer was doomed and was glad to escape the coming conflagration.

Catching movement from the corner of his eye, Balian saw his nephew had returned to the hall. Thomasin was distressed by his father's departure and so far, neither Baudouin nor Balian had been able to offer him much comfort. He did not understand and why should he? Balian was a man grown and he understood no better than the lad did.

Baudouin had noticed Thomasin's reappearance, too, and beckoned to him. The boy approached slowly, keeping his head down, and when his father attempted to give him another farewell hug, he stood rigid and unresponsive in the embrace. When he was released, he spun around and headed for the door; by the time he reached it, he was in full flight.

Baudouin took several steps after him, then gave up. Seeing Balian standing a few feet away, he turned to his brother, instead. "The lad is being so stubborn about this. It is not as if I've sent him off to strangers. He's been living with you and Maria for nigh on a year now."

While it was true that highborn sons were always placed in other noble households to learn the skills their rank would require, it was disingenuous to compare a separation like that with what Thomasin was facing now. Balian said impatiently, "You of all men ought to understand his unhappiness, Baudouin. You were about his age when our father died."

"God Almighty, I have not died! I will be seeing him again, will be seeing you all."

Hearing his defensive tone, Baudouin managed to rein in his temper. "Let's not quarrel, Balian. I do not want our last words to be accusations or recriminations."

"Nor do I." The temptation to make one final attempt to bring Baudouin to his senses was overwhelming, but Balian knew it was futile. They'd already said all there was to say.

Baudouin did not think so, though, and after they'd moved into the courtyard and his stallion had been brought over, he paused in the act of swinging up into the saddle. Turning around, he reached out and put both hands on his brother's shoulders. "Come with me, Balian. Bohemond was overjoyed that I was leaving Outremer for Antioch and he has already promised to give me lands equal in value to those I am relinquishing here. He'd welcome you just as warmly. If you settle in Antioch, you and Maria will not be the losers for it."

Balian shook his head. "You know we cannot do that, Baudouin."

Baudouin's hands fell to his sides. "No, I do not suppose you can," he conceded. "How could you abandon Bella?"

How can you abandon your homeland? The words hovered on Balian's lips; he bit them back. Baudouin believed his act was one of principle, defying a man not worthy to be king. Balian saw it as turning his back on Outremer in its time of greatest need. But an accusation like that would cast a shadow between them for the rest of their lives.

Once he was mounted, Baudouin gave the signal to depart. Balian walked beside him as they rode out of the courtyard and into the street. Baudouin looked back once and waved. His eyes burning with unshed tears, Balian did not return the wave. But he continued to watch until the riders were no longer in sight and even the dust had begun to settle.

CHAPTER 45

Gerard de Ridefort and Patriarch Eraclius had been expecting to be summoned to the palace, for Guy was facing the most serious crisis of his kingship since he'd been publicly repudiated by Baudouin d'Ibelin. To no one's surprise, it had been provoked by Reynald de Chatillon. Earlier in the year, he had again attacked a rich caravan passing through Outrejourdain on its way from Egypt to Damascus, seizing all the goods, slaying its guards, and taking the merchants off into captivity. This raid shattered the truce between the Franks and the Saracens and Saladin was outraged. He insisted upon the release of the prisoners and restitution for the stolen property. When Reynald had laughed at his demand, Saladin lodged a formal protest with the king. In hopes of salvaging the truce, Guy ordered Reynald to satisfy Saladin's claims. Since that was more than a fortnight ago, the Templar grand master and the patriarch assumed that Guy had gotten an answer from Kerak. They also assumed that they knew what the answer was.

They were ushered to the palace solar, where Guy and Sybilla awaited them. Guy's face was flushed with anger and he immediately launched into a diatribe against Kerak's lord. Reynald had refused to comply, as the other men had expected. But they soon learned that Reynald had done more than reject the compensation claim for the caravan's loss.

"Not only did he defy his king," Guy sputtered, "he dared to assert that he has the right to act as his pleases in his own lands. He said he did not make a truce with Saladin, so he was not bound by it. He even insisted that he is as sovereign in Outrejourdain as I am in Outremer!"

Gerard and Eraclius exchanged frowns at that. It served neither the interests of the Templars nor the Church if Outremer's barons felt free to act like crowned kings. But when Guy asked them how he should punish Reynald, they both agreed that there was nothing he could do.

That was not what Guy wanted to hear. Sybilla intervened before he could rebuke them for not offering useful advice. "Surely there must be some measures we can take. Reynald's defiance could be seen as a repudiation of my lord husband's authority."

Eraclius thought there was no doubt whatsoever of that. "Regrettably, madame, we have no means of compelling obedience from Lord Reynald. Even if Kerak were not such an impregnable fortress, we could not take military action against him. We need the man to defend our southern borders from the Saracens. That is why he was allowed to wed Stephanie de Milly."

Guy wanted to protest, but he reluctantly recognized the truth in what the patriarch had just said. "Well," he said at last, "should I call a High Court session?"

"No!" they said in unison, for why let the entire kingdom know that he'd been defied by de Chatillon? Seeing that Guy had resigned himself to reality, Eraclius made courteous conversation until his departure would not be too abrupt, and then rose to his feet. Sybilla did, too, saying that their youngest, Mary, was still teething and she wanted to check upon her.

Guy crossed to her side and gave her a quick kiss. "Let me know how the little lass is faring." He was pleased to see that Gerard remained seated, welcoming the company; not introspective by nature, he had never developed a taste for solitude.

They talked for a while about the Saracens. Guy was proud that the celebrated spy Bernard was now in his service and he told Gerard what Bernard had reported: that Saladin was increasingly suspicious of his nephew's ambitions. "So, Saladin ordered Taqī al-Dīn to join him in Syria and dispatched al-'Ādil to take command in Egypt again."

Gerard already knew about the shifting political sands in the sultan's empire; the Templars had an extensive spy network of their own. But he acted as if hearing Guy's revelations for the first time; he wanted to coax the king into better spirits before he broached his own plan. So, he flattered Guy with unwavering attention, interjecting the appropriate questions as they discussed the infidels and, then, the marital nets that Guy had been casting.

Guy was eager to share his good fortune with his kinsmen back in Poitou and he'd begun to arrange marriages for them with Outremer heiresses. This stirred up much resentment among the Poulain lords, who were furious to see royal patronage lavished on foreigners, and Gerard made sure that Guy knew of their discontent. The more isolated the king felt, the more he'd have to rely upon the few

allies he had left, and Gerard intended to convince Guy that he was the most steadfast ally of them all.

Guy remained a puzzle to Gerard. He did not understand why a man so blessed
by God should be so insecure, so easily wounded by what other men thought of
him. Why should a king care? But whilst he scorned Guy for such weakness, he
still realized that Guy was not as foolish as he sometimes sounded, and so he was
careful not to overstep his bounds, always according Guy the respect and deference he seemed so desperately to crave. So far, the strategy had worked well. It was
about to be truly tested now, though.

"May I ask you a question, sire? What mean you to do about the Count of
Tripoli?"

The mere mention of Count Raymond was enough to sour Guy's mood. Even
though there was no accusation in Gerard's tone or demeanor, Guy could not keep
a defensive note from creeping into his own voice. "I have demanded that he account for the expenditure of Crown funds during his tenure as the boy king's
regent."

"And I heard that he was greatly angered by that, which shows he has something to hide, for this was a reasonable request. But by not responding, he continues to defy you, just as he stubbornly refuses to do homage to you as our king. I
find it passing strange, too, that he has not returned to Tripoli. By remaining in
Galilee, it is almost as if he is deliberately taunting you."

Guy thought so, too. Raymond's continuing presence in his kingdom was like
a festering sore. Feeling cornered, he resorted to sarcasm, saying testily, "What
would you have me do, Gerard? Proclaim him a rebel and declare Galilee forfeit?"
He was startled when Gerard said that was indeed what he was suggesting. "You
cannot be serious?"

"I am very serious, my liege. The man is a rebel and deserves to be treated
like one."

"Yet you seemed untroubled by Reynald de Chatillon's defiance. You and the
patriarch insisted that his disobedience must be ignored."

"Reynald has not denied you his homage, sire. He is troublesome, but he does
not pose a threat to your throne. And we need him in the coming war against
Saladin. Raymond covets your crown, convinced that he has a blood claim stronger than Sybilla's. He cannot be trusted."

"Of course he cannot! That does not mean I ought to take up arms against him."

"Sire, may I speak freely? I have no doubts that Raymond de St. Gilles would
usurp your throne if the opportunity presented itself. But what I fear now is the

effect that his continued defiance may have upon the other lords of the realm. You know how stubborn these Poulains are, fancying themselves all to be kingmakers. Such lunacy would never be condoned back in your Poitou or my Flanders, yet in Outremer, they actually take pride in their intransigence."

Guy nodded; he found the bizarre beliefs of the Poulains to be as irrational as they were revolutionary. Who ever heard of electing a king? A kingship was divinely ordained. "You think they might see me as weak and, therefore, vulnerable if I overlook the count's defiance?"

"Unfortunately, sire, it is not just one lord refusing to heed you. Baudouin d'Ibelin left the kingdom rather than do homage to you. Raymond challenges your authority by remaining in Galilee. And it will not be long ere people learn that Reynald de Chatillon has also dared to defy you. My liege, it grieves me to speak so bluntly, but I do not believe you can permit three of your greatest lords to balk at obeying your commands. No king could allow that."

"Reynald de Chatillon defied Baldwin. For that matter, so did I. Yet his authority was not undermined."

"Baldwin saved the kingdom with his victory at Montgisard. Men respected him deeply for that miraculous triumph and for the courage he showed in fighting that loathsome disease."

"What are you saying? That they do not respect me?"

Gerard looked unutterably sad. "Respect is not a gift to be bestowed, my liege. It must be earned. I am not speaking for myself. You know how I fought to make you king. But Outremer has its share of fools, men who only understand glory won on the battlefield."

For a fleeting moment, Guy's guard dropped and he looked stricken. The Templar grand master said nothing, letting the silence speak for him.

Hugues of Galilee and his brothers had been shocked when a spy in Raymond's pay warned them that the king planned to muster the army of Outremer at Saforie and the target of their campaign was Tiberias. Even Raymond was deeply shaken. He'd been highly insulted by the demand for a financial accounting, but he'd never expected Guy to attack Galilee, to be willing to fight a civil war. He'd endured several days and sleepless nights weighing his options, and then announced that he would be gone for a time. Telling his family no more than that, he rode off with a handful of his most trusted knights, those who'd served him the longest in Tripoli.

He was gone over a week, returning after dark on the second Sunday in Lent. He'd offered no explanations for his absence, going straight to bed, and his family had to wait until the morrow for answers. Hugues and his brothers had talked it over, concluding that Raymond must return to Tripoli. But what were they to do? If Hugues made peace with Guy, that would be a betrayal of the man who'd acted as his father for more than twelve years. How could he abandon Raymond? Yet how could he abandon his family's principality of Galilee?

It was midmorning before they were summoned to Raymond and Eschiva's bedchamber. Raymond looked exhausted despite a full night's sleep; there was a gauntness to his face, evidence of a loss both of appetite and weight, and he even seemed to have gone greyer since they'd seen him last. Gesturing for them to sit, he remained on his feet, pacing restlessly about the chamber, and that, too, was unlike the man they thought they'd known so well.

"I will not yield," he said abruptly. "I will not surrender Tiberias. And I will never do homage to a man so unfit to rule."

Eschiva found herself in an impossible position, torn between her husband and her sons. "I will gladly go back with you to Tripoli, Raymond. But Galilee is Hugues's birthright and—"

Raymond swung around to face her. "I would never ask you to go into exile, Eschiva. This is your land, watered with the blood of past princes, and one day it will be Hugues's. When we wed, I swore to protect your principality and I will never break that vow."

His stepsons traded glances, impressed by Raymond's resolve but knowing they did not have enough men to defeat the king's army. They'd wondered if he had gone to talk with the Hospitallers; he was a good friend of their grand master, Roger de Moulins. Yet they knew the Hospitallers would not take up arms on Raymond's behalf. His cousin seemed a more likely ally. But he'd not been gone long enough to have sought out Bohemond in Antioch.

Hugues still asked, though. "Will Bohemond send men to fight for you, sir?"

"No." Raymond turned from his wife to face the young men he'd helped raise to manhood. "Bohemond is dealing with a threat of his own. Roving bands of Turkmen have been raiding Cilicia and were bold enough to cross into Antioch, too."

Raymond was dreading what came next, knowing how they were likely to react. It would be up to him to make them understand. Drawing a deep breath, he told them what he meant to do, what Guy de Lusignan had forced him to do. There was a frozen silence when he stopped speaking. He'd expected that, though. And so he set about convincing them that this was the only way to safeguard Galilee, relying upon their faith in him to overcome their resistance.

Jakelin received his usual warm welcome when he stopped at Nablus on his way to the commandery in Acre. Once his Templar companions had been made comfortable, Balian led him out into the pallid March sunlight toward the stables. Jakelin was soon leaning over a stall door, smitten with the occupants: a sleek Arabian mare and a suckling foal. "Khamsin's the sire?"

Balian nodded. "Baldwin bequeathed Asad and his mares to his stepfather, although he did specify that a few colts go to his little nephew, hoping they'd teach the lad that horses give men wings. But he remembered how much I love Arabians and he very generously gave me Star," he said, gesturing fondly toward the bay mare.

Jakelin had yet to take his eyes from the Arabians. "Have you named the colt yet?"

"I thought I'd leave that for you to do. He's yours, after all," Balian said and grinned at Jakelin's dumbfounded expression.

"Balian, are you serious?" Once he was sure that Balian was, Jakelin embraced him, thumping him exuberantly on the back. "How can I ever repay you for such a gift?"

"I'm sure I'll think of something," Balian assured him and they both laughed.

After a moment, though, Jakelin's smile ebbed away. "I cannot accept him, of course, but I will never forget your generous gesture."

"Why can you not keep him? I know about your vow of poverty, that Templars are not allowed to own any personal property. But Templar knights are permitted to have horses. Moreover, the marshal is in charge of the order's horses, the one who decides which ones the brothers get. So why would this colt pose a problem?"

"What you say is true. But there are other rules that govern our lives. One states that the grand master may take another brother's horse and keep it for himself or give it away. And the brother who loses his horse must accept its loss without becoming 'vexed or angry.'" For a few heartbeats, Jakelin let his gaze rest sadly upon the bay colt. "Can you honestly say that Master Gerard could resist the temptation to claim an Arabian, especially if he could take it from me?"

Balian wanted to argue with him. He could not, for he knew the nature of Gerard de Ridefort and knew, too, of the bad blood between him and Jakelin. "Well, as far as I am concerned, he is still yours and I am just boarding him for you. The colt will not be old enough to be ridden for a few years. Mayhap you'll have a new grand master by then."

Jakelin supposed he was violating the spirit if not the letter of his oath by taking such grim pleasure in that thought, for he and his brethren swore "to strictly obey their master, for nothing is dearer to Jesus Christ than obedience." He did not care, though, for he'd never known another man less deserving of such absolute authority than Gerard de Ridefort.

Hearing Khamsin's welcoming whicker, Balian moved toward his stall, leaving Jakelin to continue admiring the mare and her foal. He was feeding the stallion a lump of sugar when Jakelin finally joined him. "I've more sugar if you want to try giving it to Demon," he joked, and the Templar showed off his rudimentary Arabic with "*Ya ibn el kalb*," a Saracen curse that called Balian the son of a dog. Since they both liked dogs, that never failed to amuse them.

"I suppose you have gotten the summons from de Lusignan?"

Balian nodded. "We are to assemble at Saforie in a fortnight. I assume we are to ride to de Chatillon's rescue yet again, for I've heard that Saladin has left Damascus and is moving south. At least this time Maria and I need not fear for Bella's safety. We suggested to Humphrey that he and Bella celebrate Easter in Jerusalem, and he agreed. I'll be damned ere I let our daughter be caught up for a third time in Reynald's blood feud with Saladin."

Jakelin shared Balian's anger with Reynald for breaking the truce. He thought that sooner or later Saladin would have broken it himself, for their Templar spies had reported that the sultan seemed to be taking his pledge to wage jihad more seriously after almost dying of that quartan fever. But the timing could not have been worse for their kingdom. How could they hope to win without the Count of Tripoli, without Baudouin d'Ibelin, without aid from the West?

He said nothing, not wanting to burden Balian with his fears. His friend had enough fears of his own, for he had six hostages to fortune, and he would ride off to war haunted by the future of his wife and children. Jakelin had occasionally envied Balian for bedding a queen and siring sons, for a life so different from the lonely one he'd chosen for himself. Not now, though. On this blustery March afternoon, he was thankful that he fought only for Almighty God and the Lord Christ, that his family was to be found amongst his Templar brethren.

That evening, after a Lenten meal for the household and their Templar guests, Balian and Jakelin withdrew into the solar. Balian was teaching his nephew,

Thomasin, to play chess, and the board was still set up. Jakelin glanced at it wist-fully. He'd loved that challenging, strategic game, but it was another of the many activities forbidden to him as a Templar. One look was enough to show him the game's likely outcome and he shook his head in mock sorrow. "Whoever is playing red is sure to lose, so I assume it must be you."

Before Balian could riposte, Maria entered the solar, accompanied by a servant bearing wine and cups. "Are the children abed, Marika?"

"Abed, if not asleep." They exchanged the rueful look of longtime parents, and Balian explained to Jakelin that their children were all owls, not larks, making bedtime a war of wills.

Maria instructed the servant to put the wine on the table. "You have a visitor, Balian. He looks like a Saracen, dresses like one, too, but speaks fluent French. He gave me a cryptic message for you, saying you know him as Bernard." Balian's reaction to the name "Bernard" was so dramatic—he pushed away from the table, so abruptly that wine slopped over the top of the flagon—that it confirmed Maria's suspicions about the identity of this mysterious stranger. Telling the servant to escort their guest up to the solar, she then found a chair for herself, for this was clearly not a meeting to be missed.

Balian could not imagine why the kingdom's renowned spymaster would be seeking him out. Rising to his feet when Bernard was ushered into the solar, he invited the intelligencer to take a seat and passed around the cups of wine that had been poured by the servant. "You have already met my wife, Queen Maria, and this is the marshal of the Templars, Jakelin de Mailly."

Bernard acknowledged the introductions with grave courtesy, but his dark eyes held a gleam of dry humor. "I know you are too well-mannered, my lord, to ask me why I am here, so I will not keep you in suspense. I am on my way to An-tioch and decided to stop at Nablus and Sidon for there are things you and Lord Denys need to know."

Balian did his best to cover his surprise. "I take it you are not acting for the king."

"No, I am not. I've been aware for some time that you and Lord Denys are the only two lords left in the kingdom capable of recognizing the gravity of the danger facing Outremer. By now you will have been summoned to Saforie. Do you know what the king has in mind?"

"Brother Jakelin and I were discussing that earlier today. We assumed this would be yet another mad dash to Kerak to save de Chatillon from a reckoning he richly deserves. But your presence here raises doubts about that."

"De Chatillon is on his own," Bernard confirmed. "Fortunately for him, my sources tell me Saladin is not bringing siege engines, so Kerak Castle is likely safe enough. The same cannot be said, of course, for the surrounding villages or the town."

Balian studied the other man intently. "If we are not chasing after Saladin as he heads into Outrejourdain, who are we fighting?"

"King Guy plans to lead your army north into Galilee and lay siege to Tiberias."

"Christ Jesus," Balian whispered. Maria said nothing, but all the color had gone from her face. The table rocked again, this time as Jakelin leaped to his feet.

"I know who planted that malignant seed in Guy's brain!" he snarled. "This is Gerard de Ridefort's doing!"

"You are quite right, Brother Jakelin. Your grand master did indeed suggest this to Guy. At first, I thought Guy was susceptible because he feels he owes his crown in some measure to de Ridefort. But it is becoming obvious that our king is as malleable as wax, most likely to be influenced by whoever gets to him last."

That was a devastating judgment to pass upon a king, but it was not one they could refute. Balian glanced toward Jakelin, the same thought in both their minds: How could the Almighty have allowed Guy de Lusignan to rule over the Holy Land? And then Bernard said, "There is more. You've not heard the worst yet, my lords, madame."

While they could not imagine what would be worse than outright war between the King of Jerusalem and the Count of Tripoli, it did not occur to any of them to doubt Bernard. They were still not prepared for what he was about to tell them.

"Count Raymond has his own spy network, so it was not long ere he learned of the king's intentions. He still balks at doing homage to a man he believes is unworthy to rule, so he began looking for allies." Reading their thoughts, he shook his head. "No, not the Prince of Antioch; Bohemond has his own troubles this spring. Raymond reached out to Damascus and hastily negotiated a truce with Saladin."

His audience considered this news to be somewhat anticlimactic, for Antioch and Tripoli had occasionally made separate truces with the Saracens in the past; they considered themselves to be sovereign states. When Jakelin pointed that out, Bernard listened politely before saying, "This truce is not limited to Tripoli. It covers Galilee, too."

Balian's first impulse was to try to rationalize Raymond's action, for they'd been allies for years and both his brother and Archbishop William had believed the count to be a man of honor. But Galilee was an integral part of Outremer, and he sensed that Raymond had crossed a line. Maria and Jakelin shared his unease and they offered no defense of Raymond, either.

"There is more. Raymond also asked Saladin for military aid in repulsing an attack on Tiberias. The sultan was happy to oblige, dispatching troops to Bāniās, just a day's ride from Tiberias. And he is sending soldiers to reinforce Raymond's garrison in the town. So, when our army attacks Galilee, we'll be fighting the Saracens and the count's men."

A deathly quiet followed this revelation. It was true that Raymond was only trying to protect his lands and family and vassals. It was also true that what he'd done was treasonous. Maria was the first to break the stricken silence, saying she assumed he'd informed Guy de Lusignan of Raymond's alliance with Saladin.

"I did, madame. Guy was very angry, yet shaken, too, for he'd never expected that Tiberias would be defended by Saracens. But the Templar grand master assured him that Saladin's involvement would make no difference. He argued that the sultan would be occupied in besieging Kerak, so any help he provided to the count would be limited. And he bolstered Guy's resolve by reminding him how justified they'd been to suspect Raymond of treason."

Balian felt as if the ground were shifting under his feet, much like the earth tremors that occasionally rocked Outremer. "So, they still mean to besiege Raymond at Tiberias."

"They do," Bernard said. "Unless you can find a way to stop them, my lord."

Upon arriving at Saforie, Balian chose the two most important of his vassals to accompany him on the six-mile ride to Nazareth: Viscount Amand, Etiennette's husband, and Renier Rohard. He'd told them how much was at stake, so when they parted from Balian at the archbishop's palace, they headed to the closest tavern to drown their fears in wine.

Balian was admitted to Guy's presence without delay. He felt a stirring of hope when he saw that Guy was attended only by his brother. He'd been convinced for some time that the de Lusignan family's allotment of common sense had all gone to Amaury.

"I'm glad that you're here, d'Ibelin," Guy said with a smile that seemed sincere and actually was, for he respected Balian's proven prowess on the battlefield and he was willing to make a fresh start with the lords who'd done homage to him, letting bygones be bygones now that they'd accepted his kingship. "How many men did you bring with you?"

Amaury winced, for his brother should have known that Balian personally owed service for twenty-five knights, fifteen for Nablus and ten for Ibelin, while the total for Nablus was eighty-five knights and three hundred serjeants. He opened his mouth to ease the awkwardness of the moment. The words never left his lips, for Balian spoke first, saying in a low voice, "Not enough men, my liege, not nearly enough."

Guy was puzzled by the response. He glanced toward his brother to see what Amaury had made of it, in time to hear him say to Balian, "So you know."

"Yes, I know." Balian had given much thought to his strategy, deciding that Guy was more likely to be receptive to advice from an ally, not criticism from an adversary. "Sire, I understand your anger with the Count of Tripoli. My brother knew that he could not continue to hold Ramlah if he refused to do homage to our king. Count Raymond ought to have withdrawn to Tripoli after challenging your sovereignty in Outremer. But it would be a grave mistake to besiege Tiberias. We dare not fight one another, not when Saladin is gathering the largest army ever to threaten our kingdom, more men than we faced at Montgisard."

Guy appreciated Balian's admission that he had a legitimate grievance with the Count of Tripoli. Wanting to show he could be reasonable in return, he offered Gerard de Ridefort's rationale for their attack upon Tiberias. "Saladin will be too busy in Outrejourdain to pay much heed to what we do in Galilee."

"Sire, I would that were so. But Saladin has specific reasons for invading Outrejourdain: to protect Muslims returning from their hajj to Mecca and to take vengeance upon Reynald de Chatillon for his latest caravan raid. Once their pilgrims are safely past Kerak and Reynald's fields are wreathed in smoke, he will turn his attention again to jihad and to us."

Guy shook his head, saying they could not be sure of that. "And you do not know what Raymond has done," he said, pausing dramatically. "He has allied himself with Saladin!" Disconcerted when Balian said he *did* know that, he blurted out, "How?"

"A Devil's deal like that could not be kept secret for long, my liege."

"No, I suppose it could not," Guy conceded. "But if you know about Raymond's treachery, how can you argue we ought not to punish him for it? Surely you are not defending him?"

"No, sire, I am not. I expect that he will claim he never did homage to you, so his actions cannot be treasonous. Be that as it may, he *is* betraying our kingdom and his Christian brethren by making a military alliance with a man pledged to our destruction."

Disarmed by Balian's harsh judgment, Guy nodded approvingly. "I am glad that you see this so clearly. I still do not understand why you are so set against our laying siege to Tiberias. Would you have him escape the repercussions of such a despicable act?"

"Sire, I will never again look upon Raymond de St. Gilles in the same light," Balian said, and he was convincing because he meant every word of it. "But nothing matters more to me than the survival of our kingdom. I do not see how we can defeat Raymond and the Saracens, too. Tiberias would not be easy to besiege, for they could never be starved into submission, not when they can get supplies by way of the lake. And when Saladin returns from his raiding into Outrejourdain, we risk being caught between his army and the men defending the castle."

Amaury had been an intrigued witness to their surprisingly civil debate. Balian had made no argument that he'd not already made to Guy himself, but he was realizing that what was said did not matter as much as how it was said. "So, what do you think we ought to do about Raymond, Lord Balian?" he asked. He added mendaciously that a Poulain's viewpoint might be of special value. After fifteen years in Outremer, he thought he understood its peculiar politics as well as any of the native-born lords. He was quite willing, though, to endow the Poulains with a mystical wisdom if that would make it easier for Guy to embrace Balian d'Ibelin rather than Gerard de Ridefort as his military mentor.

"Sire, if you offer the count an olive branch instead of the sword thrust he expects and fears, I think he will reach for it." Balian looked searchingly into Guy's face. "If you succeed in luring him back into the fold, you will destroy a dangerous alliance without having to take the field. If he still balks, you lose nothing, for you will be able to tell your lords that you did all you could to effect a reconciliation. They will be more likely to rally around you then, especially if it seems that Raymond chose an alliance with the infidels over one with his fellow Christians."

Guy rose and moved to the window, where he gazed out at the soaring spires of the cathedral, a vast, impressive structure even though it was not yet completed; it reminded him that nothing was done overnight, that patience was needed both for masons and kings. Raymond deserved to be punished for his treachery. But at what cost? Could he forgive Raymond's treason if in doing so, he'd save his kingdom from being lost to the infidels? He decided that he could, and felt a touch of pride that he was capable of such magnanimity.

"It is worth trying," he declared. "I will disband the army and send envoys to

Tiberias, urging the count to discuss settling our differences and uniting against our common enemy."

Balian could only nod. The Almighty had not forsaken the Holy Land, after all.

Balian and Maria decided to attend Guy and Sybilla's first Easter court, for they agreed that if Balian was to exert any influence with the new king, they must forge an amicable relationship with him. Their presence in Jerusalem also enabled them to spend time with Isabella, for Humphrey had kept his promise and brought her to the Easter court. Guy had sent an envoy to Tiberias—his chancellor, Peter de Lydda—and the Easter revelries passed without incident.

After the festivities, Balian and Maria returned to Nablus, for they'd not taken their family with them and they did not feel comfortable being apart from their offspring for too long. Helvis and Johnny were now in their ninth and eighth years and Thomasin was almost eleven, but Margaret was just five and Philip still a few weeks from his second birthday; parents in Outremer never dared forget how vulnerable younger children were to fevers, miasmas, and mystery maladies in the land of the Lord Christ's birth. Balian had only been home a week, though, when a messenger arrived from Guy, summoning him back to Jerusalem.

"I've had an answer from Raymond de St. Gilles." Guy had not yet learned the royal skill of disguising his emotions and his face already revealed that answer. "Raymond refuses to reconcile our grievances unless he is indemnified for the losses he says he incurred as regent and he demands that Beirut be returned to his control. I cannot do that!"

"No," Balian agreed, suddenly feeling very tried, "of course you cannot."

Guy's first reaction to Raymond's message was to want someone to blame. Raymond was the obvious target, yet he'd been tempted to lash out at Balian, too, since this had been his idea. But he saw now that Balian's disappointment was as sharp as his own. His anger beginning to dissolve, he sank down in the closest chair. "So, what do we do now?"

Balian could not give in to despair. Taking some comfort from Guy's choice of pronouns, he sought to sound confident, as if he believed he were dealing with men of good faith, not with a floundering king in danger of drowning and a count who was proving Maria right. She'd often said Raymond de St. Gilles was always going to put his own interests before those of Outremer. "It does not sound as if the Count of Tripoli fully understands that the kingdom will be united against him unless he agrees to make peace with you. If we hope to disrupt his alliance with Saladin, he must be made to see that. But there is no need to take all of the burden upon your shoulders, sire. Let your lords bear some of it."

Guy considered this. "You mean call a High Court session?" The more he thought about that suggestion, the better he liked it. D'Ibelin was right; let the Poulains share the responsibility if it came to war. "Very well," he said, and Balian's relief was so great that words failed him.

Some of the members of the High Court were still in Jerusalem and others who'd already left hurried back in response to the urgent summons. Fortunately, Reynald remained at Kerak, making ready to fend off a Saracen army, for Balian was sure he'd have tried to scuttle any overture to Raymond. By now, the lords knew of Raymond's shocking pact with the Saracens. When Guy told them of Raymond's demand for Beirut and said he could not agree, he was relieved to see most of them nodding their heads. Since this crisis was of concern to them all, he concluded, he would hear what they thought. Sitting down, then, he prepared to do something that still did not seem very kingly to him: listening instead of commanding.

It was soon obvious that the members of the High Court did not want to commit themselves to a civil war unless there was no other option. They quickly concluded that one final effort ought to be made to bring the Count of Tripoli to his senses. And when Balian proposed they send another delegation to Tiberias, there was no disagreement. Not surprisingly, Balian was selected as one of these envoys. So was Denys. And it was decided that the Church would be represented by Joscius, the eloquent Archbishop of Tyre.

But when Guy demanded that the grand masters of the Hospitallers and Templars be included, that was not well received. While no one objected to Roger de Moulins, many of them felt that sending Gerard de Ridefort to negotiate with his mortal enemy would sabotage their mission ere it even began. Guy was insistent upon this, though, reminding them that the Templars wielded considerable power in the Holy Land and their grand master would be insulted if he were excluded. That was true enough and, since they suspected that Guy was loath to offend the fiery Templar, they reluctantly concurred. The other envoys were levelheaded, reasonable men, after all, and between them, they ought to be able to curb Gerard de Ridefort's more reckless impulses.

CHAPTER 46

April 1187
Nablus, Outremer

I t took a while to prepare for their diplomatic mission. A courier had to be sent to Tiberias to be sure Count Raymond was willing to receive them. Denys had agreed to participate, but he needed to make a quick trip to Sidon first. Since Sidon was much closer to Tiberias than to Jerusalem, it was decided that he would travel on his own to Galilee and meet the other envoys there. So, it was not until the evening of Wednesday, April 29, that Balian returned to Nablus. Maria had done her best to accommodate so many guests: the Archbishop of Tyre and several of his clerks; the grand masters of the Hospitallers and Templars, each man accompanied by ten knights of his order, plus three hundred brother serjeants. Few of the men were looking forward to the coming confrontation with Raymond, so they welcomed this overnight respite before resuming their journey on the morrow.

Balian and Maria had celebrated their brief reunion in their marriage bed, and were enjoying the erotic aftermath, sharing drowsy confidences, catching up on all that had happened during their time apart. When he shifted so they could cuddle together like spoons, she leaned back against him with a contented sigh. She was sliding into sleep when he said, "So . . . you want to tell me how Thomasin acquired that spectacularly bruised eye and swollen lip?"

Maria had hoped to avoid this conversation, wanting to spare him domestic drama until he'd dealt with Raymond. "He got into a fight with two boys from town. They claim he attacked them. They are older than Thomasin—fourteen or so—and at first, I thought their story unlikely. But they insisted that he started the trouble. As for Thomasin, he has stayed stubbornly mute."

"I'll talk to him in the morning ere we leave," Balian promised. Thomasin's behavior had changed for the worse since Baudouin's departure for Antioch. Normally a confident, cheerful child, he'd become withdrawn, even sullen at times. Knowing why he was acting so fretful had not helped them in easing his unhappiness. The boy was obviously angry with his father, and Balian did not think it fair to scold him for that; he was still angry with his brother, too.

Brushing Maria's hair aside, he kissed the nape of her neck, and soon after, they both slept.

Their horses were being saddled the next morning when Balian remembered his promise about Thomasin and sent Ernoul to fetch the boy. But Thomasin was nowhere to be found, and a stable groom had a troubling story to tell; he'd caught Thomasin trying to saddle Balian's palfrey, Smoke, and the boy had run off when he'd been challenged.

Maria assured Balian that she'd keep men hunting until they found the lad, but Balian could not bring himself to ride off as long as his nephew remained missing. Explaining the situation to the other envoys, he told them he'd catch up with them, if necessary riding through the night to rejoin them at the Templar castle of Le Fève. While none of them had experience with the demands of parenthood, Joscius and Roger de Moulins were too well-mannered to question Balian's decision. Gerard de Ridefort's grip on courtesy was a tenuous one at best. He liked Balian no more than Balian liked him, though, so he was glad to be rid of the Poulain lord's presence for the day. He even hoped Balian would fail to overtake them before they reached Tiberias, for he did not trust any of the Poulains to treat Raymond as severely as he deserved.

As soon as they departed, Balian resumed the search, this time with a posse of helpers. Fanning out, they swarmed through the palace grounds and then the town—to no avail. No one had seen Thomasin. As the hours passed, Balian's unease mounted. There were so many ways a child could come to grief and he could not keep his imagination from dwelling upon all of them. When he finally returned to the palace hall to consider their remaining options, Johnny came over to sit beside him, wanting to help hunt for Thomasin, and Thunder, one of Balian's favorite lymer hounds, lay down at his feet, resting his head on his master's boot. Balian was idly stroking the dog's floppy ears as he tried to reassure his son when an idea began to form in the back of his brain. It seemed dubious in the extreme. Yet what did he have to lose?

Whistling for Thunder, he and Johnny went abovestairs to the chamber that Thomasin shared with the other pages, where he had Johnny help him look for an item of the missing boy's clothing. A dirty pair of braies, crumpled on the floor by his bed, was perfect for Balian's purposes. Offering it to the dog to sniff, he said, "Find Thomasin," and held his breath, waiting to see what the hound would do. Thunder's sense of smell was superb and he excelled at tracking quarry on their hunts. But could he understand what was being asked of him now?

When the dog padded toward the door, they followed, trailing after him down the stairs and back into the great hall, then out into the courtyard. Balian felt hope quickening when Thunder turned in the direction of the stables, for Thomasin had been seen there by a groom; was that proof that the hound was indeed following the lad's scent?

Thunder had picked up the pace, heading toward the far end of the stables. Halting before the ladder that led up into the hayloft, he began to bark, the deep, stentorian baying that had earned him his name. Balian gazed up into the shadowed loft, ignoring the grooms who were insisting that the loft had been searched. Reaching for the ladder rungs, he began to climb.

"Thomasin?" His words were met with silence. "Thunder says you are up here, lad. You do not want to make a liar of him, do you?" This time he heard the squeak of floorboards. Before Johnny could climb up, too, Balian sent him to tell his mother that Thomasin was found. Then he swung up into the loft and sat down, waiting for his nephew to emerge from hiding.

It took a while for Thomasin to find the courage. He was so visibly scared that Balian's anger cooled. "How did you evade the search?" he asked, striving for a conversational tone.

Thomasin swiped at his face with the back of his hand, hoping his uncle would not notice the tear tracks. "After that groom caught me, I hid in the storage shed, waiting for another chance to saddle Smoke," he said almost inaudibly. "But ere I could try again, you and Aunt Maria discovered I was gone. I watched as they searched the stables. When they went outside to search other places, I sneaked back into the stable and up into the loft."

"Clever lad," Balian said, and Thomasin gulped, knowing it was no compliment.

"I am sorry, Uncle. I did not mean to cause so much trouble."

"We'll get to that, Thomasin. First, you owe me an apology for trying to steal my horse."

"I was just borrowing him. . . ." Thomasin saw that excuse was a bird with a broken wing, not going to fly. "I am sorry," he said again. "I truly am. . . ."

"I need more than that, lad. I need to know why you got into that fight and where you thought you were going after you'd stolen Smoke." In the silence that followed, Balian studied his nephew's profile, his eyes lingering on that blackened eye and cut lip. "Suppose we make a bargain. You answer those questions and I will convince your aunt Maria that you ought not to be punished for this escapade of yours."

Thomasin's eyes widened. "Truly?" he asked, and Balian nodded. Even though it took considerable patience on his part, the story slowly emerged. "Martin and his friend . . . I do not know his name, but Martin is the mercer's son. They were talking about my father, saying he'd abandoned us. They even dared to call him a coward!"

"I see . . . and that is when you took the two of them on."

Thomasin nodded. "They did not know I'd overheard them, so I caught them by surprise. I punched Martin in the stomach," he added, not without a touch of pride.

"And where were you going on Smoke, Thomasin?"

The boy ducked his head. "I was going to Antioch," he said, "to find my father. . . ."

"Ah, lad . . ." Balian reached over and drew his nephew toward him. "Your father is the bravest man I've ever known. We may not understand why he felt he had to leave, but you can be sure there was nothing cowardly about it. Or dishonorable. You are entitled to be wroth with him, Thomasin. You need not feel guilty about that. I was wroth with him, too. Never doubt, though, that he was doing what he thought was right."

"That was what I told those whoresons, that my father was no coward. . . ." Thomasin shot a quick glance toward his uncle, for "whoreson" was not a word he was supposed to know, much less use. Relieved to see Balian was prepared to overlook it, he slid closer, finding comfort in the bracing feel of the man's arm around his shoulders. "Will Papa ever come home?"

"I do not know, lad," Balian admitted. "Only time will tell. But your aunt and I will take you to Antioch to visit him, that I promise you." He was glad that his nephew did not ask when that would be, for he did not want to tell the boy that war was coming, as inexorably and inevitably as the Khamsin winds that swept up from Egypt every year.

Although the moon was waning, there was still more than half of it visible to illuminate their way as Balian and his men rode out of Nablus that night and headed north into the Samarian hills. But they'd not gone far when clouds blew in from the west, smothering the moon and stars. Because rain was not common in April and because the clouds appeared without warning, the more superstitious of Balian's companions gazed up uneasily at the suddenly overcast sky, hoping this was not an ill omen. Ernoul was one of those who felt a prickling of unease and he caught up with his lord to ask whose saint's day it was, thinking it would not hurt to offer up a prayer; all knew some saints were not always saintly if they felt slighted or ignored.

Balian had to think about it before recalling that it was St. Donatus. He entertained his squire by relating some of the legends about the saint, who was said to have defeated a dragon. He also assured Ernoul that St. Donatus would likely forgive them for not remembering him straightaway, for even amongst saints, some were more celebrated than others.

Ernoul nodded in agreement. "Like St. Thomas of Canterbury or St. George or St. Philip or St. Margaret . . . my lord?" His voice was raised questioningly as Balian muttered something that sounded suspiciously like a curse.

"That was not meant for you, lad. I just realized I'd forgotten that tomorrow is Philip the Apostle's saint's day." After a moment, Balian corrected that to "today," for it was already past midnight. He'd always had a special fondness for this saint, and it bothered him that he'd been so absentminded. They were not far from Sebaste and he made a spur-of-the-moment decision. St. Philip had been born in Galilee, so who better to ask for aid in making Raymond see reason?

"My squire has reminded me that May first is the saint's day of Philip the Apostle," he told his men, "so we are going to stop and hear Mass. We'll still be able to reach Le Fève in time."

Less than an hour later, Balian's men had settled down in the great hall of the bishop's palace. Bishop Ralph had soon appeared, awakened either by the noise or a zealous servant. He was a neighbor and friend, so if he was annoyed by the disruption of his sleep, he hid it well. After Balian explained that they would like to hear Mass in the morning, he'd been ushered into the bishop's private quarters, and Ralph subjected him to a scrutiny that seemed to see into the depths of his soul.

"Your devotion to St. Philip is praiseworthy, Balian. Yet failing to honor his holy day is surely a venial sin at most, if even that. I cannot help wondering if you've more on your mind."

Balian was not surprised by the bishop's insight; he read men as easily as he did his psalter. "I am anxious about this meeting with the Count of Tripoli. If prayers to St. Philip tilt the scales in our favor, it is worth delaying our journey for a few hours." He thought he was done, but then he heard himself admitting that he'd been praying more than usual in the last few months, adding, almost against his will, "I am not sure if the Almighty has heard them, though."

Ralph sat back in his chair, steepling his fingers. He regarded Balian in silence for several moments before saying, "In the past two years, you've had to bury two kings, then accept one few of us would have chosen. You've had to watch as Saladin grows more powerful by the day, as has the threat to our kingdom. And you've lost the two men closest to you—Archbishop William and your brother. So, it would not be surprising if you feel your faith is being tested. But is it more than that? Do you fear you are in danger of losing your faith, Balian?"

Balian's instinctive response was to deny it. Catching himself, he gave the question the respect it deserved. "No," he said, "not my faith. But I do fear that I am losing hope."

Another silence fell as Bishop Ralph contemplated Balian's response. "I think," he said at last, "that if you'd truly lost hope, you'd not be trying so hard to stave off civil war. You'd have followed Baudouin's example and taken your family into exile in Antioch."

Not only did that make sense to Balian, it even gave him a bit of comfort. "If you can absolve me of my sins as easily as you vanquish my cares, Ralph, I want you as my confessor."

The bishop chuckled. "I imagine your sins are rather on the tame side, at least since you married your queen." Leaning over, he put his hand upon the younger man's arm. "Remember," he said, "that when you ride away from Sebaste this morn, you will be going with its bishop's prayers—and surely with a saint's blessings, too."

Le Fève was one of the most important Templar castles, for it controlled the major crossroads in the Jezreel Valley. Balian had spent a few nights there over the years, so he was familiar with its layout. As its stone walls came into view, he told Ernoul about their large wheel that drew water from the nearby marsh into a cistern; he knew it would be of interest to the boy since it was pulled by a donkey.

They could see that a number of tents were set up around the castle walls, which surprised Balian, for he thought Le Fève was large enough to have accommodated the delegation. As they approached, they saw the ashes of campfires outside the tents, although the camp seemed empty. The castle gates stood open, but they'd not yet been hailed by sentries. Balian ordered one of his men to call out his identity. There was no response. By now they were close enough to see that the battlements were not manned.

They waited as one of Balian's serjeants shouted again. There was a foreboding silence enveloping the fortress and no signs of life. Balian's men were exchanging uneasy glances. It appeared that the castle had been abandoned, yet that made no sense. Even if the delegation had ridden on toward Nazareth, where was Le Fève's garrison? Where had they gone and why?

As they passed through the gates into the castle bailey, it was like riding into an opium-poppy dream, one in which reality was both familiar and distorted. The Templar citadel of Le Fève looked as it always did. But it was deserted. Their calls went unanswered and there were no footsteps on the wall ramparts, only an unnatural stillness that reminded some of the men of the eternal silence of the grave.

Dismounting, Balian chose several men to search the castle, allowing Ernoul to be one of them, for the boy's curiosity was on fire. Leading Smoke over to a horse trough, he let the stallion drink, all the while listening for sounds that could resolve the mysterious disappearance of the Templar garrison. His men soon returned, one confessing that he'd half expected to find uneaten food laid out on tables in the great hall, all reporting that the fortress was empty.

Ernoul had better luck, leaning out of an upper-story window to yell down into the bailey. When they joined him, he was glowing with pride as he led them into a small, shadowed chamber where two Templars lay on pallets against the wall. They were obviously ill, mumbling feverishly in response to all the questions directed at them, and that only deepened the mystery. Although Balian promised them that he'd send back help, he was not sure if they even heard him. Why had the garrison gone off and left behind invalids in need of care?

When they took the road north toward Nazareth, they kept glancing back over their shoulders at Le Fève, some thinking that it was rising against the sky like a tombstone. By now all of their imaginations were inflamed and they were as unsettled as they were mystified. They'd covered about three of the seven miles to

Nazareth when they saw the horse lying by the side of the road. Arrow shafts protruded from his withers and flank and his muzzle was stained with a bloody froth. Several ravens were fluttering about his head, pecking at his eyes, reluctantly retreating as the men rode up. The captain of Balian's household knights was the first to dismount. It took only a cursory examination of the dead animal for Fulcher to confirm their suspicions, that this was a knight's destrier and the arrows had been shot from a Saracen bow.

Swinging from the saddle, Balian joined Fulcher. As he started to speak, he glanced down, saw the footprints and bloodstains in the dirt. Touching the knight's arm, he pointed to the trail leading away from the stallion's body. The rider seemed to have been dragging a leg, and twice they found evidence that he'd fallen before staggering on. Ahead the ground seemed to dip and they followed the tracks down into a shallow wadi. There they found their man.

Unable to go any farther, he'd collapsed in a dried-up streambed. He wore the white mantle of a Templar knight, liberally splattered with blood. He was motionless, and at first they thought he was dead. As they approached him, though, he heard the rattle of pebbles kicked loose by their boots and made a panic-stricken lunge for the sword lying beside him in the dirt.

"You are amongst friends," Balian said quickly and when he saw that this was true, he slumped down again, tears squeezing through his lashes and trickling into his beard. Balian was close enough now to recognize him as one of the knights who'd accompanied Gerard de Ridefort from Jerusalem; he even remembered the man's name: Brother Andrew. Calling for a waterskin, he knelt beside the Templar and raised him up so he could drink.

Brother Andrew swallowed too much and choked. "Dead," he whispered, "all dead . . ."

The knights wanted to shout at him, to demand that he share his story at once. But he was obviously in shock, his eyes feverish; nor did they know how much of the blood soaking his mantle was his own. Balian heard their murmurings and raised a hand to quiet them. "Is that why Le Fève was deserted? The garrison went with you. But why? What happened?"

The Templar shuddered and they feared he was dying. After a few moments, though, he roused himself. "We'd reached Le Fève," he mumbled, "planning to stay the night. But then the messenger arrived from the Count of Tripoli. . . . We thought at first that it was a perverse joke, for it sounded quite mad. Yet the count's man swore it was true."

His eyes were roving around the wadi as if seeking an anchor, a way to hold on to reality. "He told us that Saladin's son had asked Count Raymond's permission to cross the Jordan into Galilee. He said the count did not want to agree, fearing they had a *razzia* in mind. But he claimed the count could not refuse them because of the pact he'd made with Saladin. So . . . so he laid down conditions, made them promise that they'd be back across the river by sundown and that they would harm none of the count's people nor do damage to any property in Galilee. He then sent out messengers to his towns and castles, warning them the Saracens would be passing through Galilee and telling them to stay indoors today from sunrise to sunset."

Gazing up at the incredulous faces encircling him, he said thickly, "You see . . . utterly mad. He sent a man to Le Fève, too. He knew we were on the way and he did not want us to run into the Saracens by chance. He ought to have known what Master Gerard would do. . . ."

He glanced toward the waterskin and Balian tilted it to his lips again. "Our master at once sent to the Templar castle at Khirbat Qara. It was just four miles away, so they got to Le Fève by nightfall, set up their tents. . . ." He seemed to lose his train of thought, had to be urged on by Balian. "We sent a man to Nazareth, too, telling their knights to be ready to ride with us on the morrow. Master Gerard gave a fiery speech, promising to send every infidel soul to hellfire everlasting. So did Roger de Moulins, speaking for his Hospitallers. We were not going to let them raid into Outremer, by God, we were not. . . ."

"Go on," Balian said through clenched teeth, not sure who he blamed more for this catastrophe, Raymond or Gerard. "What happened today?"

"We rode out at dawn, took every last man with us except a few too sick to ride. With the ten knights who'd escorted our grand master from Jerusalem and the garrisons of Le Fève and Khirbat Qara, we had ninety Templar knights. The Hospitallers had ten of their own, and when we got to Nazareth, we were joined by forty of their knights. One hundred and forty of the best fighting men in the kingdom, plus three hundred serjeants . . ."

Tears were freely streaking his face by now. "We found them at Cresson Springs, a few miles north of Nazareth. As we reached the crest of the hill and looked down upon them, we were stunned, for the Saracens had an army of thousands. We'd been willing—nay, eager—to do battle with them, all of my brothers and the Hospitaller knights, too. But this was self-slaughter, for we were hopelessly outnumbered. Roger de Moulins saw that straightaway and told our master that we ought to retreat, that we had no chance of winning. Others tried to persuade him, too. He would heed none of them. He said we had God on our side and reminded us that the Franks had been greatly outnumbered at Montgisard, that the infidels could never hold before a charge by armed, mounted knights. When they still argued, he called them cowards. . . ."

Balian was overcome by such hatred and rage that he felt as if he were choking. Fulcher sounded just as appalled when he asked, "Are you the only survivor, Brother Andrew?"

"No . . . there were four of us who got away. I did not leave the field until our banner had gone down and the banner of the Hospitallers, too. I swear it!" He fought back a sob. "But then I saw our master and two of my brothers break away, so I . . . I followed them. We got separated and I . . . I think I became lost. I was not thinking too clearly. And my poor Pilgrim . . . so gallant. He ran until his heart gave out. . . ."

Balian finally found his voice. "You are saying that Gerard de Ridefort is alive and the men who followed him are all dead?"

He was not the only one to feel a burning outrage at such an outcome, and some of his knights had begun to curse. But Ernoul was not thinking of the Templar grand master's miraculous escape. He was realizing how close they'd all come to dying on that battlefield at Cresson Springs. "My lord, if you'd not stopped at Sebaste to hear Mass, we'd have been doomed, too!"

"No," Balian said, and there was so much fury in his voice that his squire instinctively shrank back even though he knew he was not the target of his lord's rage. "I'd have stopped it. I'd not have let that madman murder so many of our own."

His knights did not doubt him, not after seeing the expression on his face. But Brother Andrew tried to shake his head. "He'd not have heeded you, Lord Balian. If he'd not listen to Roger de Moulins or our own marshal, there is nothing you could have said—"

"'Our marshal,'" Balian echoed, sure he'd misunderstood the wounded knight's words, for he was slurring them like a man deep in his cups. "What does Jakelin de Mailly have to do with this . . . this butchery?"

"He was there, my lord, with us. He did all he could to make the master see reason—"

"What are you talking about? Jakelin was not with us when we left Jerusalem!"

"He was at Khirbat Qara, my lord, brought their garrison in response to the master's summons. Like us, he wanted to confront the infidels. But when he saw how many there were, he said we'd be sorely crazed to attack them. The master refused to listen. He . . . he jeered that Brother Jakelin was too fond of that blond head of his to risk it, that he was a coward for not wanting to fight. Brother Jakelin . . . he said that he would die on the field like a man of courage and honor, that Gerard would be the one to flee. . . ."

Brother Andrew's words trailed off, for he was remembering that Brother Jakelin and the Lord of Nablus were friends. "He . . . he fought like a lion, my lord, died as he said he would, showing such courage that he'll surely have earned blessed martyrdom. . . ."

Ernoul and Balian's knights would have eased his anguish if only they could, but even the youngster knew there was no balm in Gilead for a wound so deep. They watched in a sorrowful silence as Balian rose and walked away, turning his back as he struggled to keep his pain at arm's length. There was no time for grieving, not yet. "Jake, you proud fool," he whispered, and in that moment, he truly felt as if his heart might break.

At Nazareth, they found a town in mourning. People wandered the streets, some wailing aloud in grief. Priests and canons seemed to be everywhere, but there were no vendors calling out to customers and the market square looked as abandoned as Le Fève. Balian's knights assumed the townspeople were terrified because of the defeat at Cresson Springs, fearing the kingdom would be crippled by the loss of so many skilled fighting men. A few questions revealed the troubling truth. Gerard de Ridefort had boasted that they would be winning a great victory and urged the residents to arm themselves and follow, promising spoils and booty. Many Nazarenes had heeded him. Arriving at Cresson Springs after the battle was over, these civilians were captured by the triumphant Saracens and dragged off as prisoners, leaving their families behind in Nazareth to grieve.

Brother Andrew had been riding with one of the knights, but he lost consciousness as they neared the Archbishop of Nazareth's palace and would have toppled into the street if another rider had not held him upright until he could be lowered to the ground. Two of the canons were soon there with a litter and carried the Templar into the cathedral close. Balian told his men to take their horses to the archbishop's stables and then meet him in the palace's great hall. As he turned away to find Archbishop Lethard, he heard his name called and saw the Archbishop of Tyre hurrying toward him.

"Balian, thank God!" Joscius came to an abrupt halt. He thought Balian looked like a man suffering from a grievous injury and was greatly relieved to find no blood on his hauberk. There was no need to ask if Balian knew. Stepping forward, he put a supportive hand on the other man's arm. "The man I saw being taken to the infirmary . . . was he another survivor from the battle?" Saying "Thank God" again when Balian nodded. "We have three others here, de Ridefort and two of his Templars. One is gravely wounded, the other's injuries seem minor, and Gerard has a head wound. He's said little about the battle, other than there was an ambush and the men are all dead."

He felt the contraction of the muscles in Balian's arm. "Not an ambush?" he guessed, feeling no surprise when Balian shook his head. "Come inside with me," he prompted, and they walked without talking across the close. Seeing Balian's footsteps flag as they passed the cathedral, he sent a questioning look toward his silent companion. "Do you want to go in and pray?"

"No. . . . I would like to sit for a while." This was the first time Balian had spoken, and Joscius did not think he'd have recognized the other man's voice, for it was utterly toneless, drained of all emotion or energy. Taking Balian's arm again, he headed toward the cloisters. Stopping at one of the carrels, they seated themselves on a stone bench.

"Roger de Moulins insisted that I remain here, pointing out that I had no hauberk, no helmet, no weapons, and no destrier. Whilst that was true enough, he was really saying that I am no warrior priest." Joscius felt as if his words had left his mouth of their own accord, yet he did not disavow them, acknowledging their confessional tenor with an abashed smile. "I knew he was right, that I'd be more of a hindrance than a help on the battlefield. But as soon as they left, I began to feel pangs of regret, even guilt—"

"No!" Balian said, so fiercely that Joscius stared at him. "There is no honor in dying for nothing. God does not ask that of us, nor does He want it."

Their gazes caught and held—until Joscius found he had to look away, thinking that he'd been right. Balian *was* one of the walking wounded. "What shall we do now?"

"I sent one of my serjeants back to Nablus with a message for my wife. I did not want her to fear for me when she hears of the slaughter at Cresson Springs. I also told her to summon as many of our knights as she could reach and have them join me at Nazareth. They ought to be here by the morrow, enough men to see us safely to Tiberias." It took an actual effort to get to his feet, almost as if his body was no longer allied with his brain. But when Joscius suggested he rest for a while in the archbishop's guest hall, Balian shook his head.

"My men are waiting for me. We have to requisition every packhorse and cart in the town, and that will take some time. We'll need help from the townsmen, too." He was looking at Joscius as he spoke, but the archbishop was not sure that Balian really saw him. "We must bring the bodies back to Nazareth. We must bury our dead."

They left Nazareth the next morning, soon after a dazzling sunrise that none even noticed. Balian and Joscius were accompanied by Archbishop Lethard, who'd volunteered to join them. They suspected he meant to threaten Raymond with excommunication if he still refused to make peace with Guy, but neither man cared. There was one conspicuous absence. Gerard de Ridefort had remained behind, telling them that he was in too much pain to ride. Balian had neither seen nor spoken to him yet, not trusting himself. He knew his decision to avoid the grand master had been the right one when Joscius reported Gerard's latest comment about their devastating defeat at Cresson Springs—that to die for the Lord Christ was to earn a martyr's crown of glory.

The two prelates rode at Balian's side, and he occasionally caught them casting worried glances in his direction, for he'd not slept and knew how he must look—like a man who'd spent hours on a battlefield strewn with bodies and blood, unable to identify them because they'd all been beheaded. He'd sent a messenger to Raymond, informing him that they were still coming, and they'd covered about half of the twenty miles between Nazareth and Tiberias when they were met by fifty knights, dispatched by the count to escort them safely through Galilee. The danger was over, though, for the sultan's army was gone. They'd kept their promise to the count and crossed the Jordan River at sunset, returning to their encampment at the site of another great Saracen victory, the skeletal, charred ruins of the castle that had once stood at Jacob's Ford.

When he saw the twin peaks known as the Horns of Ḥaṭṭīn in the distance, Balian knew they were less than five miles from Tiberias. They saw dust rising then, churned up by approaching riders. They were led by Raymond's stepson Hugues, and they were soon close enough for Balian to recognize Hugues's younger brothers, William, Odo, and Raoul. They hung back as Hugues spurred his stallion forward, riding out alone to meet the envoys.

"I have no words," he said in lieu of greetings. "We are all sick at heart. We never wanted this to happen."

Balian did not doubt Hugues's sincerity. He believed they did mourn the men who'd been slain at Cresson Springs. It was no consolation. "Are you speaking for your stepfather, too?" he said coolly, and when Hugues assured them that he was, the Archbishop of Nazareth inquired acidly why the count had not ridden out with them, then.

"My lord father is as grief-stricken as we are," Hugues insisted. "He did not want to let the sultan's men ride freely across Galilee, did all he could to keep blood from being spilled. He tried to warn his people to stay clear of the Saracens. If only he'd been heeded—" He stopped abruptly, for Balian had raised his hand and his knights were muttering angrily.

"You'll never hear me defend Gerard de Ridefort. But blaming the men who died is not the best way to exonerate Raymond. Whether you like it or not, Hugues, there will be many who see him as culpable, too, for what happened at Cresson Springs."

"I understand that," Hugues said softly. He'd known at once that he'd stumbled. Yet what could he say? Loyalty and love kept him and his brothers from admitting how horrified they'd been by the choices Raymond had made, first in allying with Saladin and then in allowing a Saracen army into Galilee. "So does my father. He knows that he contributed to this calamity. He was stunned when we saw the Saracens ride by with the heads on their lances—"

"You saw that?"

Hugues could not suppress a shudder. "We were so relieved when their army approached Tiberias on their way to cross the river. It was not yet sunset and we thought they'd honored their promise to do no harm in our lands. Then we saw the prisoners being herded along like cattle and then they were close enough for us to see the heads. My father and Roger de Moulins were friends. . . ." Hugues swallowed, then pleaded, "Tell us how to make amends and we will do it."

Again, Balian was sure that Hugues was speaking from the heart. He was still not convinced that he was also speaking for Raymond. Would the count's remorse be strong enough to prevail over his pride? "I cannot tell you that, Hugues, not until after I see your stepfather."

Hugues gave Balian a look of mute entreaty. He wanted to distance himself from Raymond's epic blunder but could not bring himself to abandon his stepfather in his hour of greatest need. He wanted to tell Balian how sorry he was for the death of his Templar friend, Jakelin de Mailly. He wanted to help his fellow Christians on their way to enslavement. He wanted to erase the images of those bloody heads from his mind and memory. Yet he knew that his family could overflow the Salt Sea with their tears and it would change nothing.

Eschiva and Raymond were awaiting them on the steps of the great hall. So was Denys, for he'd arrived from Sidon that afternoon, thinking he was to attend a peace conference and finding himself thrust into a maelstrom. As soon as very tense greetings had been exchanged, he pulled Balian aside and into an emotional embrace, for he'd heard of the disaster at Cresson Springs earlier in the day, but had only learned that Balian was not among the slain once he'd reached Tiberias.

"Hugues says the Saracen force numbered between six and seven thousand. Why did our men engage them when they were so greatly outnumbered, Balian?"

"Gerard de Ridefort."

Denys closed his eyes. "I ought to have guessed. . . ." Hugues had also told him that the Templar marshal, Jakelin de Mailly, had been slain, that they'd seen his head on a Saracen lance. Knowing that Jakelin had not been among the Templars escorting their grand master, he'd hoped that Hugues was wrong, for it would be easy to misidentify a man under such gruesome circumstances. Looking now at Balian's haunted eyes, Denys no longer doubted. They'd lost more than a hundred skilled fighters; they'd also lost two voices of reason and common sense in Roger de Moulins and Jakelin de Mailly. "In that message you sent to Raymond, you said de Ridefort was one of the few survivors. How could God have let that happen?"

Balian's jaw muscles tightened. "This was the Devil's doing, not God's."

They'd gathered in the castle solar, the four envoys on one side of the table, the count and his family on the other, for his wife and sons had insisted upon being included. Her eyes swollen and reddened, Eschiva took a seat beside her husband, proud of Hugues when he chose to sit on Raymond's right, for she knew how conflicted his loyalties had become. Reaching over to touch Raymond's arm, she tried to convey a silent message—that he must not seek to justify himself, for his reasons had become irrelevant as soon as the first knight had died at Cresson Springs.

At first, Raymond seemed to understand that, for he spoke with real emotion of his horror once they'd learned of the battle. He offered eloquent testimonials to the courage of the slain men, his voice thickening as he praised Roger de Moulins. The envoys listened in silence and that may have caused his expression of contrition to take on defensive undertones. He began to explain why he'd felt he had no choice but to do what he'd done, that all of his actions were reactions, prompted by his need to protect his family and lands. When he said that Cresson Springs need not have happened, that there would have been no bloodshed if the grand masters had only followed his instructions and remained at Le Fève, he found himself face-to-face with his new reality—that truth could not drown out the screams of dying men, not when those men were his fellow Christians.

The Archbishop of Nazareth was so enraged that he shoved his chair back, making ready to stalk out. Although Joscius was more restrained, it was clear that he, too, had been deeply offended. Denys simply looked away. And Balian discovered that his patience had been a casualty, too, of the battle at Cresson Springs.

"You can insist that Guy provoked you into rebellion, Raymond. You can blame Gerard de Ridefort for his recklessness and lunacy. You can argue that the Saracens did not seek this battle. You can defend yourself from now till doomsday. But it will not matter. Not anymore. Not after your countrymen were killed by an army you allowed to enter Galilee."

Raymond had not interrupted, although it was obvious that he was finding it difficult to keep silent until Balian had his say. He leaned forward then, his body language conveying not anger so much as the urgency of his need to make Balian and the others understand.

Hugues did not give him the chance. "He is right, Father. The townspeople were on the verge of rioting yesterday when they saw the Saracens ride by with their prisoners and those grisly trophies. You had to bring the sultan's men into the castle for their own protection. Some of your own knights are ready to rebel, to disavow their oaths if you hold to this alliance with Saladin. And whilst I cannot speak for my brothers, I cannot follow you on this road any longer. I cannot...."

Raymond opened his mouth, but no words emerged. Tearing his gaze from Hugues, he looked at his other stepsons, his eyes moving from face to face. He then glanced over at his wife. To those watching, he seemed to have aged in a matter of moments. His shoulders slumped and his fists unclenched, his chin sinking toward his chest. No one spoke for a time that seemed interminable to them all. When Raymond finally raised his head to meet Balian's eyes, saying, "What would you have me do?" they knew that they had won.

Upon hearing of the debacle at Cresson Springs, Guy de Lusignan hastily mustered an armed escort and headed north. He was on the road when he received a message from his envoys, telling him that the Count of Tripoli had agreed to all their demands. He'd ended the alliance with Saladin, banished all of the sultan's men from Tiberias, and promised to swear homage and fealty to Guy as his king. Guy sent back word that he would meet Raymond at the Hospitaller castle of St. Job, midway between Nazareth and Nablus.

When they reached Nazareth, the envoys were joined by Gerard de Ridefort, who'd recovered enough to bear witness to the public humiliation of the man he hated above all others. At first, Gerard had tried to justify his actions at Cresson Springs, but his protestations had goaded Balian into an eruption of volcanic rage. After that, Gerard displayed uncharacteristic discretion, staying away from Balian and keeping to himself, while Raymond ignored Gerard so completely it was as if the grand master were invisible to his eyes. It was not a journey any of them would want to remember.

Balian felt a weary sense of thankfulness as they saw the castle of St. Job come into view, for the Hospitaller citadel was only fifteen miles or so from Nablus and he desperately wanted to see his family, to embrace his wife and hear the laughter of his children. He was praying that the peace talks between Guy and Raymond did not veer off course at the last moment, for he trusted neither man to rise to the occasion and put the welfare of the kingdom first.

The castle gates were opening, and then riders emerged, galloping out to meet them. There was considerable surprise when they saw that Guy was in the lead, for they'd expected him to receive Raymond in the great hall, amid all the panoply of kingship. They were even more surprised when Guy halted his knights and then rode on alone. Raymond spurred his stallion forward and they met in the middle of the road. Dropping his horse's reins to anchor him, Raymond dismounted. So did Guy. As their audience watched nervously, the count sank to his knees before the man he'd refused to acknowledge as king. A collective sigh swept the ranks of the spectators, a wave of overwhelming relief that Raymond was doing his part as promised, humbling himself as his penance for Cresson Springs. But none of them had anticipated what happened next. Guy reached out and raised Raymond to his feet, then embraced him as if he were a former ally returning to the fold and not a man guilty of rebellion and possibly treason.

Balian had urged Smoke on, wanting to be closer to the two men in case Raymond's submission flared into yet another confrontation, and Denys and Joscius had followed after him. Drawing up alongside him, Denys said in astonishment, "Fiend take me, Guy's going to be a gracious winner! Who saw that coming?"

"Not me, for certes," the archbishop acknowledged, sounding suddenly cheerful. "And not Raymond, either. He looks poleaxed." Guy was speaking with animation, keeping his hand on Raymond's arm, and some of his words floated back toward them on the mild May breeze: "peace between us" and "Saladin the real enemy."

"Would I sound like an utter fool," Joscius asked, "if I dare to hope we can finally come together to unite against the Saracens?"

"They think so," Denys said, glancing over his shoulder toward the other men, who'd begun to cheer and clap. All but Gerard de Ridefort, whose face could have been carved from stone, so expressionless was it.

Balian said nothing, not wanting to rob his friends of this rare moment of hope. But even if the kingdom did unite behind Guy, it would not be for long. For their unity to last, Gerard de Ridefort would have had to die at Cresson Springs with the men he'd doomed. The snake was still in Eden.

CHAPTER 47

June 1187
Nablus, Outremer

Balian had mustered all of the knights and serjeants of Nablus in response to Guy's summons, and the palace courtyard was a tumultuous scene as men made ready to depart. Balian's children had seen him ride off to war before, but Thomasin and Helvis were old enough to understand that this time the danger was greater, for Saladin had gathered the largest army ever to threaten their kingdom. Balian had done his best to reassure his daughter and nephew, promising he'd return safely once the invasion had been thwarted. Did they realize this was a promise he might not be able to keep? He could only hope not.

Pained by the forlorn look on Helvis's face, he gave her one last hug. As he stepped back, his gaze rested for a moment upon Maria, standing in the doorway of the great hall. They'd said their farewells in the privacy of their bedchamber, with an unspoken urgency that left them both drained and shaken. But she seemed composed now, submerging the wife in the queenly persona she'd perfected in the twenty years since her marriage to Amalric had thrust her upon the public stage. As their eyes met, she even managed a smile.

Ernoul was holding the reins of Balian's palfrey, Smoke, for his war horses, Khamsin and Demon, would be led, not ridden. Balian started to swing up into the saddle, stopped in midmotion, and then strode across the courtyard toward his wife. Heedless of their audience, he gathered her into an embrace so tight that she felt as if all the air had been squeezed from her lungs. She did not complain, clung to him just as tightly. Neither one spoke, for they'd said what needed to be said during the night. When he returned to his stallion, she followed, beckoning to their daughter as he mounted and signaled to his men. He did not look back, but Maria continued to watch, an arm around Helvis's slender shoulders, until he was no longer in sight.

Just as Baldwin had done before Montgisard, Guy had issued the arrière-ban, requiring all able-bodied men to join the army. The kingdom could muster six hundred and seventy-five knights and over five thousand armed serjeants and turcopoles. The Templars could normally provide three hundred elite knights and close to a thousand serjeants, and the Hospitallers could supply three hundred knights and serjeants. But both orders had been weakened by their losses at Cresson Springs. Raymond had brought most of the two hundred knights of Tripoli, as well as one hundred knights from his wife's Galilee. Bohemond had signed a truce with the Saracens so he could drive the Turkman raiders out of Antioch; he'd still sent fifty knights under the command of his eldest son and Raymond's godson, Prince Raimond, in response to Guy's appeal. There was a contingent of Italian sailors, too, and the usual pilgrims eager to fight the infidel. When Guy boasted that this was the largest army ever to assemble in Outremer, few doubted him, for they had the evidence of their eyes. Their camp at Saforie had tents beyond counting, thousands of horses, and at night, the summer darkness was lit by hundreds of smoky fires.

Denys paused to watch as the sun sank below the western horizon, leaving a trail of flaming colors in its wake. He welcomed the coming of twilight, for that would mean a reprieve from the brutal July heat. He was starting back to his tent when his attention was drawn by a burst of laughter. A group of men were joking as they crowded around someone hidden from Denys's view. Their language was alien to him; he thought it was probably an Italian dialect. Most likely those sailors from Genoa, he thought. He was about to pass on by when their circle split and a familiar figure emerged from their midst.

Denys stopped at once, waiting for Balian to join him. "None of them speak any French," he explained, "so whenever a problem comes up, they ask me to interpret for them. I know some of my father's Piedmontese, and it is close enough to their Ligurian for us to communicate."

"How did you pick up any Piedmontese? Your father died the same year you were born."

"He'd wanted Hugh and Baudouin to learn some of his language, and they were happy to tutor their little brother." Balian smiled at the memory. "I've heard tales about how older brothers love to torment younger ones. Mine were more protective than not, mayhap because they were so much older than me."

As always when he spoke of his brothers, Balian's voice resonated with warmth. Denys thought he must have been shocked that Baudouin had not accompanied Prince Raimond and the knights from Antioch. He'd been startled, too, and he took this opportunity to learn more about Baudouin's puzzling absence. "I heard Raimond brought you a letter from Baudouin. How is he faring in Antioch?"

"I was taken aback that Baudouin did not come with Prince Raimond," Balian admitted. "His letter offered few answers. He mentioned campaigning against the Turkmen and spoke vaguely of coming when he could. But no matter how much he loathes Guy, he'd never be indifferent to the kingdom's survival. So, I questioned Bohemond's son and he finally confessed that Baudouin has been ailing and did not want me to know. He assured me that Baudouin is now on the mend, though."

Denys did not like the sound of that and he saw that Balian shared his concerns. Baudouin had once insisted upon going on a *chevauchée* despite being afire with fever and he'd continued on a boar hunt after he'd gashed his head when his horse stumbled and threw him. If he were truly "on the mend," he'd be at Saforie with them. But even if Baudouin was gravely ill, there was nothing Balian could do about it for now. Saladin had crossed the Jordan River five days ago, leading a vast army that was camped at Kafr Sabt, just ten miles from Saforie.

They walked in silence for a while. Balian invited Denys to share his supper and they were soon seated in Balian's tent, being served a mutton stew by his squires. After sending the youths off to eat, they relaxed over a flagon of wine. The tent flap was open, offering a glimpse of the darkening sky, but the lit oil lamps kept the shadows at bay. Aside from the ones lurking under Balian's eyes, Denys thought, for the younger man looked as though he'd gotten little sleep. Most likely he had not, for yesterday had been the two-month anniversary of the slaughter at Cresson Springs. The wound inflicted by Jakelin's needless death would take far longer than that to heal, assuming it ever did.

"I was skeptical at first," Denys confided, "when Guy bragged that no King of Jerusalem had ever led a larger army. But as I walked through the camp tonight, I thought he might well be right. We must have over fifteen thousand men here."

"Much more than that," Balian said, reaching over to pour them more wine. "I was curious, so I asked the constable. According to Amaury, we have twelve hundred knights, including the Templars and Hospitallers. We have four thousand mounted serjeants and turcopoles, and about fifteen thousand infantrymen. So, all in all, over twenty thousand men."

Denys grinned. "That many?"

"Unfortunately for us, Saladin's army is almost twice that number."

Denys's jaw dropped. He'd assumed that they'd be outnumbered by their Saracen foes, for that was almost always the case. He'd not realized the disparity was as dire as that, though. "Are you sure, Balian?"

"Ilyas and Dāwūd are," Balian said, naming two of their best turcopole scouts.

"Jesus wept," Denys said softly. "We ought to thank God fasting that Guy has actually begun to listen to us. Otherwise, he'd have taken the bait when Saladin tried to lure us out of Saforie on Monday."

"Let's hope he keeps heeding us," Balian said, knowing that Guy was getting more bellicose advice from Reynald de Chatillon and Gerard de Ridefort. "Reynald is nursing a new grudge for all the damage Saladin did on his spring raid into Outrejourdain. As for Gerard, that lunatic has never met a disastrous decision he did not run headlong to embrace."

Despite the bitterness in Balian's voice, Denys had to smile at that apt description of the Templar grand master. Before he could respond, Ernoul stumbled into the tent. "One of the king's men is seeking you, my lord," he panted, "and he says it is urgent."

He'd been followed into the tent by a knight Balian recognized as a member of Guy's household. "Thank Christ you are both here, my lords! The king wants you."

Even if the man were not so agitated, Balian would have known something was amiss; an urgent summons from the king was never a good thing. "What has happened, Sir Aubert?"

"A messenger has arrived from the Countess of Tripoli. She says Saladin has launched an attack upon Tiberias, taking the town in just an hour's time. The castle still holds out, but she entreats the king to send aid straightaway."

Guy's red command tent was already crowded by the time Balian and Denys reached it. Guy was flanked on one side by Reynald de Chatillon and on the other by Gerard de Ridefort, but that was not necessarily his doing; Balian knew both men were quite capable of shoving their way to the forefront, especially in a council of war. Denys's cousin from Caesarea was the last one to arrive and as soon as he moved into the circle of lords, Guy signaled for silence.

"The Countess of Tripoli has sent a message that she is under siege at Tiberias and the town has already been taken. Some of the townspeople were able to reach safety in the castle. Those who could not are dead or prisoners. She said Saladin himself is leading the attack, and she fears the citadel will fall to him if we do not come to the rescue."

Guy turned to the Count of Tripoli. "My lord count, since it is your wife in peril and your city under siege, it is only fair that you get to speak first. What would you advise we do?"

"Nothing, my liege." Raymond disregarded his stepsons' dismay, keeping his eyes upon Guy. "Saladin is setting a trap for us, with my wife as bait. If we leave Saforie and march to relieve his siege of Tiberias, we will be doing exactly what he wants us to do. He wants to force a battle and we must deny it to him, for it is not a battle we can win."

Guy was dumbfounded by Raymond's response. "If we do nothing, the castle is likely to fall to Saladin!"

"I expect that it will," Raymond agreed calmly. "But I would rather have that happen than we lose the kingdom." When two of his stepsons started to protest, he stopped them with a raised hand. "Saladin is not going to harm my wife. If she is captured, he will make sure she is treated with the utmost respect until a ransom can be arranged."

Hugues seemed willing to accept Raymond's reassurances. His brothers were less certain and the youngest, Raoul, asked plaintively, "How can you be sure of that?"

"Because I know Saladin, lad." Raymond glanced challengingly at the other men. "I know him better than any of you."

"I daresay you do," Gerard said with a sneer and Reynald laughed.

Raymond ignored them, turning back to face Guy. "Even if Saladin takes Tiberias, he cannot hold it for long. When he withdraws, I will reclaim it and repair the damage done. The loss is mine and I am willing to accept it if need be, for nothing matters more than the survival of Outremer."

Guy was still marveling at Raymond's sangfroid; he could not imagine himself reacting like that if Sybilla were the one trapped by a Saracen siege. Some of the other lords were regarding Raymond with grudging admiration, even those who blamed him for the disaster at Cresson Springs, for they realized this was not an easy choice for him. It was a natural instinct for a man to want to protect his own. Neither Reynald nor Gerard shared their approval, though, and the grand master was quick to make his feelings known.

"Your devotion to our kingdom would be easier to swallow if you and Saladin had not been such close friends just a few weeks ago," he jeered.

Raymond responded again with icy indifference, a weapon he could wield with peerless skill. Addressing Guy alone, he said gravely, "Sire, Saladin besieged Tiberias to lure us out of Saforie. He needs a decisive battle, needs a great victory. For years, he has been using jihad as the reason for his attacks upon other Muslims, claiming they must be united in order to drive the infidels from their land. Now that he controls Aleppo and Mosul, his people expect him to honor that holy vow. That is why so many thousands of volunteers flocked to his banners, why we are so vastly outnumbered. But he cannot keep them in the field for months. Crops will soon be ready for harvesting and men will start missing their women, their families. If we refuse to march into his trap, if we deny him his jihad, his army will soon break up as it has always done."

"If you fear facing Saladin's 'thousands of volunteers' on the field," Reynald taunted, "there is still time for you to skulk back to Tripoli. Most of them are civilian zealots, not real soldiers, eager to die for their false prophet and false faith. I say we oblige them. Hell's flames can always use more firewood."

Raymond did not find it as easy to shrug off the charge of cowardice as he had the accusation of disloyalty and he said sharply, "I will march if our army does."

Gerard gave a snort of disbelief. Before he could launch another attack upon Raymond's good faith, though, Denys spoke up. "I also think it would be madness to try to relieve the siege at Tiberias. Does that make me a coward, too?"

"Or me?" Balian pushed his way toward Guy. "I cannot believe we are actually considering this lunacy. Even if we were not so outnumbered, we'd never make it to Tiberias. That is over sixteen miles away as the crow flies, closer to twenty miles on these roads. Surely, I need not remind you that July is hellishly hot," he said, aiming a scathing look in Gerard's direction. "We could never cover a distance like that without enough water for thousands of men and horses, and every spring, every cistern, between Saforie and Tiberias will be guarded by Saladin's soldiers. All he'd have to do would be to wait for heat and thirst to do his work for him. And if we lose this battle, we lose the kingdom, too, for we have stripped our castles and towns of defenders."

Reynald and Gerard both started to object, but now that Denys and Balian had given voice to their own concerns, the other lords were quick to echo them. Guy found himself assailed by indignant voices as men emphasized the dangers of the heat, the lack of water, the distance, and the size of the Saracen army. When Balian pointed out the folly of doing exactly what Saladin wanted them to do, there was almost unanimous agreement with that. By the time that Humphrey, who rarely spoke up in councils of war, expressed his concern that they could be caught between Saladin's army at Kafr Sabt and his elite *askar* force at Tiberias, it was obvious that Reynald and Gerard were very much in the minority.

Guy had heard enough. Relieved that there was such a consensus among his lords, he announced that there was no need for further discussion. "It would be foolhardy to leave Saforie, where we are secure, have ample water, and are well situated to move against Saladin should he threaten other areas of the kingdom. Our very presence here will be a deterrent against an assault on Jerusalem. As long as he fears we could attack his rear, he will confine his aggression to Tiberias. And since Count Raymond is willing to absorb that loss and does not fear for the safety of his lady, we will adopt the strategy that our kings have employed so successfully in the past. If there is to be a battle, it will be at a time and place of our choosing, not Saladin's."

Gerard stood in the shadows, watching the king's tent. It was nearly midnight. Men had retreated to their tents or curled up in bedrolls before the fires; it could be surprisingly chilly at night in the hills. He could hear the snoring of nearby blanket-clad bodies, the snorting of a hobbled stallion, the crackling sounds of the closest fire, and an occasional burst of muffled laughter, followed by a few sleepy curses. Waiting did not come easily to him; as a youth, he'd often been told that he did not possess enough patience to fill a thimble. But he had no choice.

Finally, the tent flap opened and Amaury de Lusignan emerged, followed by the Bishop of Acre, who had the precious duty of safeguarding the True Cross. While it would normally have been in the custody of the patriarch, Eraclius had entrusted it to a surrogate caretaker, claiming that he was not well enough to join the campaign. Some of the men were skeptical of Eraclius's convenient illness, for his fondness for luxury was well known, and few thought he'd have enjoyed a sojourn in an army camp. Even though they were allies, Gerard was also suspicious of Eraclius's sudden ailment. But right now, he had no thoughts to spare for the patriarch, most likely tucked comfortably in bed with the mistress so notorious that Jerusalemites called her the patriarchess. All he cared about was the coming confrontation with Guy.

Once the bishop and Amaury had headed off toward their own tents, Gerard made his way around the sleeping men. He'd almost reached the royal tent when the flap was pulled back again and Guy's squire slipped through the opening. He jumped as Gerard suddenly materialized beside him, relaxing once he recognized the grand master. He answered Gerard's quiet query readily enough, explaining that the king was not sleepy yet and wanted some wine. He did not even blink when Gerard pressed a few coins into his hand and suggested he take his time with the errand, for he'd been secretly in the Templar's pay for months. He liked Guy, who'd proven to be a good master, but he rationalized his disloyalty by assuring himself that he was merely passing on gossip and rumors, nothing harmful to the king. Now he happily tucked the coins away in his scrip and ambled off toward the supply wagons, whistling under his breath.

"Back so soon, Julien?" Guy looked up in surprise from the letter he was reading, his smile waning at the sight of the Templar grand master. Whilst he knew Gerard was very unhappy about his decision to hold the army at Saforie, he was in no mood to rehash the argument. He could not dismiss the other man out of hand, though, for he owed Gerard better than that; he and Sybilla might not have been crowned if they'd not been backed by the powerful order of the Templars. "Come in, Gerard. I was about to go to bed, but I can spare some moments for you." He yawned then to make sure that Gerard took the hint.

"Sire, I regret having to disturb you at this hour. It is urgent that we talk, though, for I fear your kingship may be at stake."

Guy sighed softly. It was never easy with Gerard. "I know you disapprove of my decision not to go to the rescue of Tiberias. But almost all of my lords agreed with me, including the Hospitallers. I see no need to go over it again—"

"Sire, forgive me for speaking so bluntly. You are making a great mistake, for you are walking into a trap."

Guy frowned. "What do you mean?"

"My liege, Raymond de St. Gilles is utterly untrustworthy, as he has proved time and time again. He did all that he could to deny you and Lady Sybilla the crown, even if that meant civil war. Nor would he accept you as king as the other lords did. Instead, he formed a diabolic alliance with Saladin, showing himself to be a traitor as well as a would-be usurper. After his shameless scheming caused the death of so many good men at Cresson Springs, he realized he'd gone too far and he pretended to seek a reconciliation. But nothing has changed. He wants your crown. Frankly, I would not be surprised if he conspired with Saladin to set this trap. That would explain why he seems so unconcerned about his wife's safety, would it not?"

"I'll admit that his willingness to let his wife be taken prisoner is surprising. Yet I doubt that he is still plotting with Saladin. Raymond argued persuasively against the battle that Saladin supposedly wants. So how am I 'walking into a trap' by holding our army at Saforie? That makes no sense."

"The trap is one being set by Raymond, sire, not Saladin. Although if he succeeds, the Saracens would benefit, too. He is trying to discredit you with the Poulains, to raise doubts about your resolve and judgment, even your courage. You need only think back to what happened four years ago when you refused to do battle with the Saracens. Many of the lords advised you against fighting. Yet you were then severely criticized for that and your enemies were able to turn Baldwin against you. If it worked once, why would it not work again?"

"Raymond's voice was the loudest against going to the aid of Tiberias! How could he blame me for following his own advice?"

"I agree that is not fair, my liege. But that would not stop him. He knows the Poulain lords would rather have one of their own as king, that they are resentful of the favor you've shown your countrymen from Poitou. Whilst they may not be as treacherous as Raymond, that does not mean you can trust them, either. There is no such animal as a tame wolf, sire."

Guy was shaking his head. "I do not believe that would happen," he insisted, but Gerard caught the note of doubt in the king's voice.

"Sire, even if the lords at tonight's council truly believe it would be wiser to remain at Saforie, that is not a view shared by the rest of your army. A king's sworn duty is to protect his vassals and the Lady Eschiva, who holds Galilee in her own right, has sought your aid. If you ignore her plea, you risk losing the support of your liegemen. Many will be outraged that you'd let a highborn woman fall into the hands of infidel barbarians. And they will then question whether you'd come to their rescue if they were under Saracen attack. Some of them will even doubt your courage and that is fatal for a king, especially for one who has not yet proven himself on the battlefield."

"I am no coward!"

"I know that, my liege. But that is what your enemies will say about you if you fail to act, and there will be many to believe them, including some of my Templar brethren. Raymond and his allies will do all they can to fan the flames, spreading false rumors, denying that they advised you not to rescue the countess, pointing out that the kingdom can no longer rely upon aid from England now that you have grievously offended the English king."

"What mean you by that?"

"Sire, you have not thought of that? Of the money King Henry has been sending to the Holy Land for the last fifteen years? Nigh on sixty thousand marks, a vast amount from a man not known for his generosity. He was pressured by the Church to make amends for the murder of Thomas Becket in Canterbury Cathedral, and he avoided taking the cross by donating money."

"I know that already!"

"But do you know the stipulations that he placed upon the money, sire? It was to be held by the Templars and the Hospitallers and none of it was to be spent without Henry's express consent. Knowing how great your need was, I disregarded that restriction and gave you all of the money under the control of the Templars so you could hire soldiers. If we can tell the English king that his money made it possible for you to defeat Saladin and save the kingdom, I am sure he will pardon you for spending the funds without his permission. If we must tell him that the money is gone and we have nothing to show for it, I doubt that he will take it well. He is not renowned for his forgiving nature, as you know. Was it not his hostility toward the de Lusignans that compelled Amaury and then you to leave Poitou for the Holy Land?"

Guy could not hide his dismay. "You never told me that we needed Henry's consent!"

"You did not ask, sire. All that mattered to you was getting money to hire routiers and mercenaries. And you were quite right, for nothing is more important than protecting the kingdom from these godless heathens."

Guy had begun to pace as he tried to grasp the implications of what he'd just been told. "What am I supposed to do?" he demanded. "Lead our army to certain defeat to avoid the wrath of the English king? Even if Raymond is deliberately trying to sabotage my kingship, surely all the other Poulain lords are not lying, too? They seem convinced that we'd be doomed if we leave Saforie."

"Sire, do you think Reynald and I are lying when we say this is a battle we can win? Why would we put our lives and the fate of the kingdom at risk if we did not truly believe that? We have as much battlefield experience as these Poulain lords and we are confident that we can reach Tiberias in a day's march and raise the siege. Unlike the Count of Tripoli, we have no reason to lie to you and we want your kingship to succeed. We seek only to end the danger posed by this accursed infidel once and for all."

Gerard paused then, waiting for Guy to respond. When he did not, the grand master knew that he had won. Once again, he'd managed to pull this well-meaning but indecisive man back from the brink of disaster. After Saladin was defeated—and he would be defeated, for God was on their side—Guy would be acclaimed throughout Christendom as the savior of the Holy Land. And whatever his other faults, Guy was not ungrateful. Gerard knew he and he alone would have the king's ear, the king's favor, and the king's trust, enabling his Templars to exact retribution upon their enemies, be they Muslim or Christian, and to rule the Kingdom of Jerusalem by keeping a light hand on the royal reins.

The tent flap lifted again to admit Julien. "Here is your wine, sire. Shall I pour it?"

Guy nodded. He saw clearly now that he must take action, that he'd let the Count of Tripoli and the Poulain lords lead him astray again, just as they'd done four years ago. Commanding the largest army ever gathered in Outremer, how could he justify doing nothing as Saladin ravaged his kingdom? His knights would want to strike back at the Saracens and his subjects would want vengeance. So would the Holy Father in Rome, the hot-tempered English king, the rest of Christendom. They all expected him to defend the Holy Land. The Templar grand master had shown him that he had no other choice. But it was a great responsibility, having the power of life and death over other men. He wished he was as comfortable wielding it as Gerard de Ridefort seemed to be. Sybilla had assured him that this would come with time. He very much hoped she was right. So far, he'd not found as much pleasure in his kingship as he'd imagined he would.

Balian was not pleased to be torn from sleep so abruptly, for it felt like the middle of the night; the tent was still so dark that he could barely distinguish the forms of his squires, cocooned in blankets. Sitting up, he heard shouting and then, with a jolt, the sound of trumpets. Jesu, could they be under attack? Almost at once he dismissed that fear, for at Saforie, they had all the advantages and Saladin well knew that. Ernoul had burrowed out of his bedroll, while Brian seemed to be trying to ignore the bedlam outside, pulling his blanket up over his head. Although most people slept naked, no soldier did so on campaign, so they were all partially dressed. Saying he'd find out what was happening, Ernoul opened the tent flap, giving Balian a glimpse of a starlit sky. Telling Brian to wake up, Balian got to his feet, his eyes going instinctively to his scabbard and sword, always kept within reach.

Brian had managed to find flint and tinder to light a lantern by the time Ernoul rushed back into the tent. "The king has changed his mind," he gasped. "We are going to the aid of the Lady of Tiberias, after all!"

Staring at the shaken youngster, Balian experienced an eerie sensation, as if Jakelin's ghost were standing at his shoulder, for this was how he must have felt when he was told they were riding out to their deaths at Cresson Springs.

CHAPTER 48

July 1187
Saforie, Outremer

G uy had hoped to depart Saforie before dawn, thus escaping the worst of the coming day's heat. But his abrupt change of plans had caused so much chaos and confusion that they were still in camp by the time the sun had vanquished the most stubborn night shadows.

Amaury was convinced his brother was making a grave mistake, yet he'd had no more luck than the other barons in getting Guy to reconsider. Their protests had put him on the defensive and, as Amaury knew from past experience, Guy was never as stubborn as when he felt cornered. He'd refused even to discuss the reasons for his reversal, declaring that he need not explain himself to men sworn to obey him. The Poulain lords would have continued to argue, but not all in their army were displeased by the decision to ride to the relief of Tiberias. These knights and soldiers crowded around, loudly making their opinions known, while Reynald de Chatillon, the Marquis of Montferrat, and the Templars were already packing up their tents, ordering their squadrons to arm themselves. When the Hospitallers followed suit, the moment of incipient rebellion ebbed away and the lessons of a lifetime asserted themselves. Warfare was the vocation of men of high birth; to many of them, it would be dishonorable to desert their Christian brethren as they made ready to do battle against the infidels.

As constable, it was Amaury's responsibility to align the army for a fighting march and, calling for his horse, he and his knights set about doing that. He chose the Count of Tripoli to lead the vanguard, an ironic honor in light of Raymond's fierce opposition to the rescue mission, but that command was always given to the man whose lands were under attack. Guy and Reynald de Chatillon would take the center division, and for safety's sake, the True Cross and its caretakers, the bishops of Acre and Lydda, would ride with the king. The Templars would make up part of the rearguard, for that was always the most vulnerable position on marches like this, sure to bear the brunt of the Saracen attack.

When Balian heard his name called, he turned his stallion in a half circle, watching as Amaury rode toward him. "The Templars will be in the rear, for they fight like fiends. But de Ridefort proved at Cresson Springs that bravery alone is no virtue. I fear that if given a chance, he'll take on half of Saladin's army. So, I need another commander back there who has some common sense as well as courage. I want you in charge of the rest of the rearguard."

Getting a brief nod of acknowledgment from Balian, Amaury edged his destrier closer. "Joscelin de Courtenay and his knights will be riding with you." He paused, knowing he'd saddled d'Ibelin with the company of a man who was no friend of his, hoping he'd not protest.

Balian did not comment, merely nodded again. The expression on his face was a familiar one to Amaury, for he'd seen it on the faces of half the men in camp. Those who'd come to the Holy Land to fight the infidels; those who were unfamiliar with how war was waged in the Levant, like the Genoese sailors and newly arrived pilgrims; those who shared Gerard de Ridefort's certainty that victory was divinely foreordained—they were all eager to test themselves against the Saracen foe. The others, those who called Outremer their homeland and had grown to manhood fighting for its survival—they looked as Balian did now, their sun-browned faces gone ashen, jaws clenched to bite back curses, their eyes reflecting thwarted fury and the despair of men without hope, with only courage to sustain them.

Amaury knew what Balian was thinking without need of words, and he realized what a transformation his fifteen years in Outremer had wrought, making him one of the Poulains. He wanted to say he was sorry that it had come to this, that Guy was one of God's great fools. He could not, of course. But he could share a truth; surely d'Ibelin deserved that.

"I know why my brother changed his mind. I asked his squire if he had any visitors last night after I'd gone off to bed. He had one."

Balian felt no surprise. "Gerard de Ridefort." For a moment, his eyes and Amaury's caught and held, and he found himself responding with a truth of his own. "As much as I grieved for Jakelin de Mailly, I was angry with him, too, for throwing his life away for nothing. I could not understand why he did not just ride away."

"And now you do."

"Yes, now I do. He could not bring himself to abandon his men."

This was the first real battle for al-Afdal, the seventeen-year-old son of the sultan, and he was both excited and uneasy, some of his confidence undermined by his inexperience and his awareness that so much was at stake. Once they were sure that the Franks were actually going to attempt to cross that arid, exposed plateau between Saforie and the lake called the Sea of Galilee by the Christians, Salāh al-Dīn had been summoned from Tiberias. As soon as he returned to Kafr Sabt, he would take charge of their center and al-Afdal would ride proudly beside him. Until then, he could only wait while his cousin Taqī al-Dīn positioned their right wing along the ridge to the north of the Tiberias road, and his other kinsman Muzaffar al-Dīn led their left wing to harass the rearguard of the infidel army. As the morning dragged on, al-Afdal became more and more impatient to learn what was happening. He was delighted, therefore, when Muzaffar al-Dīn rode into their camp to see if the sultan had arrived from Tiberias yet.

Muzaffar al-Dīn was one of the sultan's most renowned amirs and al-Afdal's uncle by his marriage to Salāh al-Dīn's sister. He was better known as Gökböri, which was Turkish for "Blue Wolf," for men said he fought like a wolf on the battlefield, as he'd proven at Cresson Springs. Al-Afdal hoped that one day he'd earn such a colorful name for himself. He was intimidated by his brusque cousin Taqī al-Dīn, but he liked Gökböri very much, for the older man had a playful sense of humor and seemed to enjoy tutoring him in the ways of war.

Gökböri proved that now by laughing when al-Afdal began to pepper him with questions. The unbelievers were having a very bad day and it would soon get much worse, he predicted. He'd been sending his horse archers against their rearguard as soon as the fools left the safety of Saffūrīya. Al-Afdal had seen their horse archers in action, so he found it easy to imagine what the Franks were enduring. Their men would race in, aiming their arrows up into the sky in the hope that some would strike the knights' horses or the infantrymen trying to shield them. Before the infidel crossbowmen could retaliate, the Saracens would retreat, only to come back again . . . and again . . . and again.

"Where are they now, Uncle? How far have they gotten?"

"Well, they've passed the village at Tur'an, which is about six miles from Saffūrīya. I was hoping to be the one to tell the sultan that good news, for he feared they might try to make a stand at Tur'an, where they'd have water. But, Allah be praised, they did not even stop long enough for their men and horses to drink."

"Why would they do that?" al-Afdal marveled and Gökböri laughed again.

"I can only speculate, ʿAlī. I am guessing that they are trying to get to Tiberias by nightfall and decided they'd lose too much time if they halted at Turʿan, for the springs are away from the road, at the end of a narrow wadi. But it was a great mistake . . . as they'll soon discover."

The sky was barren of clouds and bleached of all traces of blue, such a washed-out white that when the wretched men glanced upward, they could think only of corpse candles, bones, and tombstones. They were surrounded by shimmering waves of heat, the road hot to the touch, and the air held so much dust that it stung their eyes, abraded any exposed skin, and sought to trickle down their parched throats. After marching for seven hours under a scorching sun, the infantrymen were so exhausted that they plodded along as if in a trance, soaked in sweat and focusing only upon putting one foot in front of the other. They were already desperately thirsty, for they'd long since drained their waterskins and their supply wagons had been left behind in Saforie, their leaders having decided that heavy water barrels would have slowed them down too much. The knights were somewhat better off, for at least they could ride, but the weight of their armor was pressing down upon them, and if a man carelessly touched any of the metal links not covered by his cloth surcote, he risked burning his fingers. The horses were suffering most of all, for they needed much more water than men, and no matter how stoic a knight was about his own ordeal, his destrier's obvious distress was harder to accept. The men under the king's command took what solace they could from the presence of the True Cross in their midst, a comfort denied those in the vanguard. And they all were thankful that they were not marching with the rearguard, for they well knew that those poor souls had been under attack for hours.

"Here they come again!" The cry ran through the ranks and the foot soldiers and crossbowmen braced themselves for another onslaught. The rearguard shuddered to a halt so their arbalesters could aim their bolts at their flying foes, for these nimble, speedy horses seemed to have wings, so swiftly could they attack and then retreat. The Saracens' strategy was always the same. They'd sprint toward the Franks, the archers launching their arrows in the span of seconds, then reaching into their quivers for more, all without slackening pace. Having dropped their reins to shoot, they controlled their mounts with their knees, wheeling and galloping away as soon as the Franks retaliated. While their arrows could not penetrate a knight's armor except at a close distance, they were killing foot soldiers and their primary targets, the stallions. A fighting march was always a great challenge to men whose natural instincts were to strike back, but none of these battle-seasoned soldiers had ever experienced one as terrible as this.

As the sky went dark with the flight of hundreds of arrows, Balian's men tried to deflect them with their shields. Most emerged unscathed from the assault, but not all. It was a war of attrition and Balian knew that the Saracens were winning. While Balian's arbalesters were doing their best, by the time their more powerful crossbows were cocked and fired, the enemy was already out of range. As soon as this last Saracen wave receded, Balian urged his men on, for they dared not stop; if they were cut off from the rest of their army, they were doomed.

Seeing a soldier sink to his knees, Balian yelled to the closest men to help, but several of his companions were already hauling him to his feet. He'd not been felled by a Saracen arrow, stricken by an even more formidable foe—the merciless sun. Although he was staggering like a drunkard, he kept moving and Balian turned his attention to another man in trouble, one of his knights, whose stallion had been hit by a Saracen arrow. While the horse was clearly in pain, the wound did not appear life-threatening. His master still chose to dismount and walk beside him, for that was all he could do. He was cursing under his breath and Balian reached down, briefly gripping his shoulder, for that was all *he* could do.

He was leading the first squadron, followed by Joscelin and his men, then the Templars with the infantry and spearmen forming a human barrier between the horsemen and the Saracens. While horses were still dying, it would have been far worse without the infantry's protection. Yet they also acted as an anchor. Their army needed to cross this barren sunbaked plain as swiftly as possible, but their pace had to be set by the foot soldiers, and at the rate they were going, Balian knew they'd never reach Tiberias before dark. How long could men and horses survive in such hellish heat without water? Christ help them all, they were going to find out.

The constant din of Saracen war drums was an added irritant. They used noise as a weapon in and of itself; any man who'd faced them on the battlefield would have his future sleep troubled by dreams of that cacophony of sound: drums, trumpets, cymbals. The sudden increase in the tempo of the drums alerted them that another attack was coming. Their column slowed, then came to a halt, despite the shouts of their commanders ordering them on.

Balian's knights had made several attempts to chase the invaders away, only to have them come back as soon as the Franks withdrew. But he made ready to try again. The infantrymen's ranks parted to allow the knights to pass through, and they charged the Saracen riders, who promptly spun around and fled. Balian's men knew better than to take the bait and wearily returned to their own lines, where one of the knights leaned from the saddle and vomited, another victim of the searing heat. And it was not long before their tormentors were on the attack again.

By noon, it was obvious to Raymond that they'd not be able to reach Tiberias that day. Even though the vanguard had so far been spared the attacks that were overwhelming the rearguard, they were slowed down by the growing fatigue of their infantry, some of whom were showing symptoms of heat prostration. The kingdom's army was spread out for over a mile and that would only get worse, making it easy for Saladin to separate and isolate the rear, and then the vanguard, from the center. When word finally came from Guy, telling him that the rear had been forced to halt, Raymond realized it was up to him if any of them were to survive this debacle. Summoning one of his knights, he gave him a desperate message for the king.

"Tell him that we will all die if we keep on toward Tiberias. We still have eight miles to go during the hottest hours of the day and we'll never make it. It is urgent that we find water for our men and horses, and there is only one source ere we reach the lake at Tiberias, the springs at the village of Ḥaṭṭīn. It has enough water for an army and is just three miles away. We can camp there for the night whilst our men recover and resume the march to Tiberias in the morning. But impress upon him the crucial need for speed. Once we leave the main road and turn north, Saladin will understand our intent and send his men to seize the springs. We must get there first."

To Raymond's vast relief and somewhat to his surprise, Guy agreed to follow his advice and head toward the springs at Ḥaṭṭīn. As word spread through the army, the men reacted with joy, and they summoned up their waning energy to follow the vanguard as it swung off the Tiberius road. The new route turned north past the village of Maskana, skirted the western side of the twin hilltops called the Horns of Ḥaṭṭīn, and then led down to the village of Kafr Ḥaṭṭīn and its life-giving springs. But the main road had been built by the Romans and was wide enough for six knights to ride abreast. The Ḥaṭṭīn path was narrower and a logjam soon developed as the men of the center surged toward this precious escape route.

Discipline broke down and confusion reigned. Gökböri was quick to seize his chance and moved to cut the rearguard off. Suddenly, the Franks found themselves fighting for their lives.

The village of Maskana, like those of Kafr Sabt and Kafr Hattīn, was deserted, the inhabitants long since fled. Raymond's knights had left their infantry behind, and they galloped past the ghost village as if it were not there, intent only upon securing the springs. It was a wild hell-for-leather dash; they were blinded by sweat, choking on the clouds of dust kicked up by their lathered horses, risking falls on the rocky, uneven ground. Despite their heroic exertions, they were too late. The way to Kafr Hattīn and its springs was blocked by Saracen soldiers, the right wing under the command of Taqī al-Dīn, dispatched by his uncle to deny the Franks their only chance of survival.

Raymond sent one of his stepsons back to Guy, urging him to join the vanguard, for he still felt confident that with reinforcements, they could break through the Saracen lines and reach water. The waiting was torture, but when Raoul finally returned, what followed was worse, for he bore a message that killed all hope.

The youth looked devastated. "He said . . . he said the center cannot come, that his men had to go back to help the Templars, who were sorely beset by the Blue Wolf. He said the rearguard is too bloodied and battered to continue on, that they need rest. So he has ordered us all to camp at Maskana for the night."

There was a stupefied silence, for they could not believe what they'd just heard. How could they last from midafternoon today until dawn without water? How would they be able to march and fight on the morrow after such a night? Struggling to fend off panic, they gathered around Raymond, as if expecting him to conjure up a miracle that would save them. But all the color had drained from his face. "God pity us—we are dead men and the land is lost."

Since they'd taken only what they could load onto packhorses, there were a limited number of tents, thus denying the men the shade they so desperately craved. And because Guy had expected that they'd reach Tiberias that day, there was not enough food for so many. At least for now, that presented no problem, for few had any appetite. The men with horses did what little they could for them, lacking what the animals most needed, water and grass for fodder. Most of the men merely collapsed onto the rock-strewn ground, their exhaustion prevailing over comfort. At nightfall, they would finally get some relief from the torrid heat, yet there were still four hours to endure till sunset. And all the while, they'd be envisioning the cold spring water at Kafr Ḥaṭṭīn—just three miles away—with the Saracen army between them and salvation.

❀

When Ernoul extracted the last of the arrows embedded in Balian's hauberk, they both sighed with relief. Raising his arms to assist the squire in pulling his hauberk over his head, Balian sank back on the ground once he was freed of its weight. His mail and padded gambeson had kept the arrow heads from penetrating his flesh, but not all of his men had been so lucky.

There were only two wounded knights; the others were serjeants and turco-poles. Balian had ordered the most seriously injured to be brought into his tent and they were displaying commendable fortitude, waiting without complaint to be treated by a Nablus apothecary who'd responded to the arrière-ban and was now pressed into service as a doctor. Several of the stricken men looked to Balian as if they'd not survive the night and he resolved to make sure a priest was on hand even if it meant waylaying one of the clerics protecting the True Cross.

Balian's squire had peeled off his sweat-soaked gambeson and replaced it with a cotton tunic; Balian had elected to retain his leg chausses in case he had to arm himself again in a hurry, although he did not expect Saladin to launch a surprise attack on their camp. Why should he, when the sun was proving to be such an effective ally? Getting to his feet with an effort, Balian braced himself to leave the heat of the tent for the even more sweltering temperatures outside.

The sight of his stallions caused him to clench his fists and bite his lip, torn be-tween outrage and anguish. Khamsin was pawing half-heartedly at the barren earth, seeking grass in vain, and Demon did not even raise his head at Balian's approach; never had he seen the high-strung destrier so lethargic. The horses of his knights and serjeants were in even worse shape, their eyes dull, the eyelids wrinkled, their breathing shallow and rapid. As he watched, one of the destriers began to urinate; instead of coming out in a golden stream, it was scant and dark brown in color.

Crossing to Khamsin, Balian stroked the stallion's neck, rubbed a favorite spot behind the Arabian's ear, murmured soothingly, all he could do. Lifting the horse's lip, he pressed his finger to the gum above the upper teeth. The gum turned white when he took his finger away and he waited tensely to see how long it would take for the natural color to return. Too long. "I am sorry, Khamsin," he said softly, "so sorry. . . ."

When he approached Demon, the stallion barely acknowledged his presence. Nor did he react when Balian reached for the halter to hold his head steady. Normally, Balian would have needed someone to assist him; now Demon did not protest even as his mouth was opened. There was no need to do the finger test, for the destrier's gums were a dark red.

"My lord."

Balian turned to see one of their turcopole scouts standing a few feet away. "May I speak with you, my lord?"

"Of course, Ilyas." Balian knew the scout had dared to venture from camp, gambling that from a distance Saracens might mistake him for one of their own. He did not look as if what he'd learned would be welcome news.

"I wanted to see if it would be possible to retreat to the waters at Tur'an if we are unable to force our way through to the springs at Kafr Haṭṭīn tomorrow. Tur'an has been taken by Gökböri's men, so there is no going back. With Taqī al-Dīn blocking the route to the Haṭṭīn springs and the sultan controlling the main road to Tiberias, there is no going forward, either."

"So, we are surrounded." Balian felt no surprise, for that was what he'd expected Saladin to do; it was what he would have done had their positions been reversed. For the moment, he felt oddly detached, almost as if he were watching a catastrophe that was happening to someone else.

Ilyas nodded. "If all goes as I fear it will on the morrow," he said, very low, "I cannot allow myself to be captured. The Saracens consider turcopoles to be renegades because we share some of their blood. I was raised a Christian, know nothing of the Muslim faith, but that will not save me if I am taken prisoner."

Balian did not hesitate. "Do what you must, Ilyas, and may God keep you safe."

The drums started beating at sundown. So did the triumphant cries of "*Allahu akbar!*" As the sultan had now moved his camp to Lubiya, just a mile from Maskana, their voices carried clearly to their enemies. So close were the two armies that Saracens could exchange taunts with the Franks who understood their language. Few slept well in either camp, but Salāh al-Dīn's men were eager for the morrow and the great victory it would bring, while their trapped foes dreaded the coming of the new day. It was Saturday, the fourth of July to the Christians and the twenty-fourth of Rabī al-Thānī to the Muslims, to both peoples a date never to be forgotten.

Two of Balian's men had died in the night. Several Templar serjeants had been slain during the march and three more of their brethren were dead by dawn. As hasty burials were arranged, camp morale plummeted even lower. Their foreboding briefly yielded to rage when Saracen soldiers boasted that caravans of camels had been bringing water from the lake all night long, proving it by dramatically pouring water onto the parched earth in sight of some of their thirst-maddened foes. But even that flare-up of fury did not last, for anger took energy.

Balian was tightening the peytrail, the breast strap securing Khamsin's saddle, when he was joined by Joscelin de Courtenay. "Did you hear? It has been decided that the Templars will be riding in the center today to protect the True Cross. So, we're on our own."

Balian merely shrugged, so exhausted that the only emotion he could summon up at the moment was indifference. But soon afterward, Denys came over to tell him that he and his knights had volunteered to take the place of the Templars. Unlike most of the men, Denys had somehow managed to hold on to his sense of humor and he explained dryly, "Whilst I am willing to die for God and kingdom, I'll be damned ere I die alongside Reynald de Chatillon and Gerard de Ridefort. That is asking for one sacrifice too many."

Balian stared at him and then surprised himself by laughing, laughter as bitter as it was brittle, but laughter nonetheless.

The Franks left Maskana at dawn. Guy had been urged by several knights who'd fought as mercenaries in Saracen armies to launch a surprise attack upon the sultan's camp at Lubiya, but he did not trust men who'd sold their swords to infidels. Moreover, he could see for himself the sad state of his army after a day and night without water. The infantrymen seemed to have abandoned all hope, stumbling along like men trapped in a bad dream, some of them no longer able to sweat or urinate. He'd been horrified to learn how many horses they'd lost on Friday to Saracen arrows and he realized that the sight of knights trudging beside crossbowmen was sure to erode what confidence his soldiers still had. Faced with nothing but bad choices, he decided to push ahead toward Kafr Ḥaṭṭin and its life-giving springs.

Some of the men were baffled that the Saracens did not attack at once, contenting themselves with harassing the rearguard again. These were the newcomers to Outremer. The Poulains knew Saladin wanted the sun and heat to continue to sap their strength. That the sultan was playing a waiting game was clear from the actions of Taqī al-Dīn, who retreated as Raymond and the vanguard advanced, yet always kept his men between the Franks and the springs. And they were about to discover that the Saracens had another nasty surprise in store for them.

The wind at this time of year always blew from the west and it soon carried to them the ominous smell of smoke. While they'd lain in wakeful misery in their camp at Maskana, the Saracens had sent their civilian volunteers to gather up brushwood and thistles, which had been piled along the route the Franks would take on the morrow and were now being set afire. To men already feverish, lightheaded, and weakened by thirst, this proved for some to be one trial too many. Five of Raymond's knights and several serjeants seized their first opportunity to flee, spurring their horses toward Taqī al-Dīn's soldiers and shouting that they wanted to surrender.

Their desertion sent shock waves through the vanguard, for they knew these men, they'd fought with them, trusted them. And as word slowly spread to the center, it raised fresh suspicions in the minds of those who still suspected the Count of Tripoli was colluding with Saladin. The men of the rearguard were spared this added burden, for they did not learn of the betrayal. Under constant pressure by Gökböri's horse archers, they were on their own, caught up in a harrowing, hellish ordeal of swirling smoke, choking dust, and foes who could not be defeated or even discouraged, who kept coming back.

During a brief lull in the attacks, Balian had sent a serjeant to warn Guy that they were falling farther and farther behind, but he did not know if the man ever got there. They did not have enough infantry to protect their horses and they left a trail of blood and slain stallions behind them, the crossbowmen marching backward at times as they bunched tightly together, for this was the only way they could stave off Death and the archers who swooped in like hungry hawks. Balian refused to let himself think of the inevitable outcome of their running battle, for he was no longer a husband and father with much to live for: his world had been reduced to this desolate stretch of road and his sworn duty to keep his men alive as long as he could.

When Salāh al-Dīn decided the fateful moment had arrived, he ordered Taqī al-Dīn to attack the Frank vanguard at the same time that he led an assault upon their center. The Templars launched a charge that pushed the Saracens back, but they could not break through the trap. Raymond's vanguard had also failed to clear the road to the springs. He knew that he had to keep trying, and he conferred with his stepsons, his godson, and their knights, declaring that he was not willing to wait for Death to find them. They agreed and he dispatched a messenger to tell Guy de Lusignan what he meant to do. He did not bother to wait for Guy's response, sure that they could not rely upon this inept, alien king for anything, much less leadership. Shielding his eyes to look up at the blazing sun, he saw it was nigh on noon. He supposed that another commander would have said a prayer first, yet his faith had never been a source of strength. He'd always preferred to depend upon himself rather than a God who'd never displayed a personal interest in his fate. Glancing around at his men, he gave the command they awaited.

Taqī al-Dīn was too good a commander to be taken by surprise. He'd been sure that sooner or later the Count of Tripoli would try to fight his way free, and he'd had time to devise a counterstrategy. Knowing they could not withstand a full-on, thunderous charge by so many armed knights galloping downhill, he'd given explicit orders to his most trustworthy men, and so they were ready when the ground began to shake and dust rose in billowing clouds and they heard the infidel battle cries of "Holy Savior, aid us!"

Even Taqī al-Dīn would admit that a charge by the unbelievers was an awe-inspiring sight, almost like an avalanche roaring toward them. But his men knew what to do and with perfect timing, they opened their ranks, their agile, cat-quick horses wheeling out of the way as the knights and destriers swept by. Carried along by their own momentum, the Franks were unable to halt until they reached the bottom of the wadi. By the time they'd regrouped, Taqī al-Dīn's men had closed ranks again, blocking the path.

The knights fell silent. Even the most inexperienced soldier, Raymond's young stepson Raoul, saw at once that there was no way they could charge back up that steep slope and fight their way onto the high ground held by the triumphant Saracens. And as they looked at one another, they shared the same emotion—an overwhelming sense of relief that they would not have to die on the Horns of Haṭṭīn after all, tinged with shame that they should feel such joy when so many of their Christian brethren would not be as fortunate.

Raymond was staring up at the Saracens massed at the top of the path. Glancing over at his stepsons, he saw they did not yet realize how much they'd lost—their principality of Galilee, their kingdom, their world. His own material losses would not be as great, for Saladin was unlikely to conquer Tripoli, too. God had given him back his life, but in such a way that his honor would be forever lost. "Never doubt," he said, "that the Almighty has a sense of humor."

Becoming aware of their danger, then, alone in a countryside soon to be occupied by an enemy army, they turned their horses and headed north. Hugues and his brothers occasionally glanced over their shoulders at the twin hills of Ḥaṭṭīn. Raymond never looked back.

"Now do you all believe me? I told you that treacherous hellspawn would betray us as soon as he had the chance!"

Not many of his listeners were paying much attention to Gerard de Rideforts rant. Even the men who shared Gerard's suspicions of Raymond were more concerned with finding a way out of Saladin's trap than in casting blame upon the count. Accusations and recriminations could come later, assuming there were any left alive to settle scores. The Poulains within earshot felt only envy, wishing they'd been riding in the vanguard with Raymond. It was a bitter fate, having to die for another man's mistakes.

Gerard was vexed that he was getting such a tepid response from his audience, for he felt thoroughly vindicated by the count's escape from the battlefield. Glaring at the closest Poulain lord, that milksop Humphrey de Toron, he thought none of these half-breeds were to be trusted, for they'd been corrupted by years of living side by side with the Saracens, seduced by the luxuries of life in the Levant. He'd heard rumors that Raymond had secretly embraced the unholy Muslim faith, and he found these stories easy to believe. Nor was the count the only counterfeit Christian in his eyes, for Denys de Grenier was said to have read the Qur'an, and why would any man of true faith show such curiosity in the Devil's work?

When he said as much to Brother Thierry, the grand preceptor of the Temple, the other man stared at him, unable to understand why the grand master was fuming about the Poulain lords when they were all likely to be dead by sunset. Easing his stallion's reins, Thierry let himself drop back, no longer riding at Gerard's side.

There had been a pause in the fighting; Thierry assumed that was because Saladin was conferring with Taqī al-Dīn, deciding upon their next move now that the Count of Tripoli, a seasoned battle commander, was no longer a threat. More fires had been set, and the wind was once again propelling smoke toward them. Thierry could hear strangled sounds as men tried not to inhale it. He imagined that the rearguard was getting the worst of it, for white clouds were rising into the sky to the west. Yet for all he knew, they could already have been overrun by the Blue Wolf, in a repeat of Cresson Springs.

Thierry was astride a white stallion named Roland and he was very worried about the destrier's heavy, labored breathing. He was thankful that so far Roland had not been hit by those showers of Saracen arrows and his anger was growing that their infantrymen had not yet come back to resume protecting the horses. They had broken ranks and run ahead when they heard that Count Raymond was trying to charge through the Saracen lines. Thierry did not approve of this breach of discipline, though he could understand it. Driven to desperation by their thirst and the unrelenting heat and their lack of confidence in their leaders, they'd tried to follow the vanguard, hoping they could somehow reach the springs. But they ought to have returned once they saw that the vanguard had failed and Taqī al-Dīn's men still blocked the path.

When Thierry saw Amaury de Lusignan spurring his horse from the king's squadron, he knew at once that they were about to get more bad news. Reining in before the Templar grand master, the constable said something too low for Thierry to catch. Gerard's reaction was so vehement that Thierry urged Roland forward to join them.

"The infantry has fled," Amaury said grimly. "They scrambled up the north horn and took refuge amid the ruins of an ancient hill fort. My brother ordered them to return and the Bishop of Acre pleaded with them to do their Christian duty, telling them the True Cross will be taken by the infidels if they do not come back. They would not listen, lay sprawled in the rocks, saying they were too thirsty and sick to fight."

Gerard was too enraged for words, sure that this disaster was all Guy de Lusignan's fault, that if he were not such a weak, indecisive king, the infantry would not have dared to defy him like that. Thierry asked what the king meant to do and Amaury said he'd ordered their tents to be pitched just west of the Horns as a rallying point for the rest of the army.

"What army?" Gerard jeered. "The vanguard knights have fled with that accursed apostate, seeking only to save their skins. The rearguard has been cut off, mayhap destroyed by now. Or they may have deserted us, too. D'Ibelin, de Grenier, and de Courtenay are all Poulains, after all. The craven infantry will soon be begging to surrender to the infidels. But all is not lost, for my Templars will make another charge, and we'll not be stopped until I can ram my lance down Saladin's throat!"

Amaury did not let his dislike of the grand master affect his military judgment. It was possible that the Templars could succeed this time; they had a better chance of breaking through than the knights with Guy did. Even if Guy objected, it would do no good. As de Ridefort often boasted, he answered only to God and the Pope. "I'll tell the king," he said tersely, and swung his mount about to return to his brother's shrinking circle of support.

Turning in the saddle, Gerard called to the gonfalonier, their standard-bearer. "Make ready, Brother John." As more and more of their brethren gathered around the grand master, he thrilled many of them by promising that victory was still within their grasp, concluding with a dramatic flourish that they were riding to glory or holy martyrdom.

Balian had felt no surprise when they got no response from Guy. As Joscelin had bleakly predicted, the rearguard was on its own. They'd fallen so far behind that they had no idea what was happening on the rest of the field. Balian been forced to call a halt when they saw smoke up ahead, not wanting to lead his men into that suffocating white cloud. Better to wait for it to clear whilst giving them a chance to rest. Some of the infantrymen simply sat down when they stopped, as did knights who'd lost their horses; others dismounted to spare their stallions their weight. Every moment of respite was precious, for they did not know when the Blue Wolf would launch his next attack.

Balian had stumbled as he slid from Khamsin's saddle, for his legs were cramping badly. He was trying to walk it off when Joscelin appeared at his side. "That fighting we heard a while back . . . you think it was their last stand?"

Balian could only shrug; his throat and mouth were so painfully dry that it hurt to talk. When they'd heard those muffled but familiar sounds of battle, the men of the rearguard assumed that Guy or the Templars had ordered a charge in a last-ditch attempt to break out of Saladin's trap. Few thought it had succeeded. They'd seen too many of their comrades die and too many of their horses go down for them to summon up any slivers of optimism. Some of them had even begun to wonder if they were already dead and in Purgatory, condemned to continue this accursed march to nowhere until they'd expiated all their earthly sins. That made as much sense to them as their doomed rescue mission did.

When horsemen suddenly materialized out of the smoke, there was a momentary panic. Fearing the Saracens were coming at them from a new direction, Balian's men scrambled to their feet and heaved themselves back onto their horses, their crossbowmen aiming their weapons at these intruders. They did not shoot, though, for there were fewer than a dozen of them and they wore the red cross of the Templars across their chests.

Balian was already in the saddle as they galloped toward him. The man in the lead looked familiar; Balian's tired brain finally summoned up a name to go with the face—Brother Thierry, the grand preceptor. Before he could speak, Thierry had reined in a white stallion splattered with blood. "Lord Balian! Thank God!"

Denys and Joscelin were at Balian's side now, and he let them interrogate the Templar, for he knew what the man would say—that they'd charged and failed. There was no other explanation for his presence here. Templars did not flee a battlefield until their banner fell.

Thierry was saying that now, expressing his relief that they'd run into the rearguard, for Templars had a duty to seek out the banners of other Christian lords if they could no longer fight under the black-and-white banner of the knights of the Temple. His story came out in breathless and sometimes incoherent bursts. They'd almost succeeded, he insisted. There had been a few golden moments when victory seemed to be theirs. Then the Saracens rallied and pushed them back, forcing them into some of the king's knights who'd been coming to join them.

"We lost so many good men." Thierry's voice thickened and his chest heaved, but his eyes remained dry; his body could no longer produce tears. "May God show them mercy."

He'd been joined by another Templar, his mantle as bloodstained as Thierry's. He resumed their story, explaining that they'd gotten separated from the others in the confusion of their retreat. "We tried to get back, but the Saracens were everywhere and they cut us off. We fought our way free, then blundered into those clouds of smoke and damned near choked to death." His reddened, swollen eyes and hoarse, raspy voice testified to the truth of that.

"We'd be honored to fight with you, my lords." Thierry's own bloodshot eyes moved from Balian to Denys to Joscelin. He shared the rest of the story then, telling them the Count of Tripoli and the vanguard were gone. Some of the other men had gathered to listen, too, and Thierry heard one voice say, "The lucky bastards," but he pretended not to hear. "In all honesty," he admitted, "I do not see how they could have gotten back up that hill. It is still hard not to suspect the worst of a man who'd been handfast with Saladin just two months ago."

None of the rearguard commanders wanted to waste their dwindling energy in a discussion of Count Raymond and his motives, so they said nothing. The sudden sound of drums spurred them all into action. As they made ready to face yet another attack, Thierry realized that he'd forgotten to tell them about the flight of the infantry. But the men of the rearguard looked as if they already knew the battle and the war were lost.

Despite watching the disintegration of his army, Guy did not think they were going to lose. The ramifications of such a loss would be so terrible, so catastrophic,
that he refused to consider it, assuring himself that the Almighty had not let him
become King of Jerusalem to preside over the death of the kingdom. Even if it took
a miracle to salvage a tattered victory from the jaws of defeat, it would happen. He
continued to believe this up until that moment in midafternoon when the Saracens
captured the most sacred relic in Christendom, the True Cross.

Guy's earlier attempt to set up their tents had failed and they'd been forced
onto the slope that lay between the Horns of Ḥaṭṭīn. Retreating to the south horn,
they succeeded in putting up the royal tent on the hill's flat top. Guy was in a state
of shock, as were most of the men, for the loss of the True Cross raised fears too
awful to contemplate, far worse than the dread of death—that the Almighty had
turned His face away from them, judging them unworthy to dwell in this land
where the Lord Christ had lived and died, died for them.

Guy still did not know the details of the loss. All he'd been told was that the
True Cross had been seized by the men of Taqī al-Dīn, that the Bishop of Acre had
died defending it, and that it had been carried triumphantly away by the infidels,
who knew full well its significance to their Christian adversaries. Its capture shook
Guy's soul to its very core, upending everything he'd been taught to believe. Even
if he got his miracle and his victory, the rest of Christendom would scorn him for
it, caring only that he'd failed to protect that precious fragment of wood, said to
have been stained with the very blood of the Savior.

It was Reynald de Chatillon who stopped him from surrendering uncondition-
ally to despair. He raged like a wild lion brought to bay, snarling that he was not
about to yield to these godless, loathsome, pox-ridden whoresons, that he would
gladly die today as long as Saladin died with him. His white-hot hatred acted as an
elixir for the knights, transforming their anguish into the holy anger of men given
one more chance to prove the purity of their faith. Guy felt it, too, and, grateful to
Reynald for his intervention, he gave the Lord of Kerak the honor of leading the
charge as they made ready to offer their lives up to the Almighty, to let Him decide
their fate.

Balian was never sure of the exact moment when he realized that the tide of battle
had shifted. They were still trapped only a few miles from Maskana, unable to

advance because of the steady stream of enemy horsemen heading north. These men showed no interest in detouring back to challenge the battered rearguard, clearly intent upon more important prey. Balian discussed this with Denys, Joscelin, and the Templar, Brother Thierry, and they agreed with him that these Saracens were hurrying to be in at the kill, just as hunters did once they knew their dogs had caught up with their quarry. It seemed obvious to them that their center would be the most tempting target. What soldier would not want to win lasting fame by capturing the infidel king, their cherished cross, or the man the sultan had sworn to kill with his own hand?

"But you may be sure they have not forgotten us," Joscelin said testily, for by now his nerves were shredded down to the bone and his frequent outbursts of anger kept him from having to admit the part he'd played in a tragedy of such epic proportions. "They know the Blue Wolf has us cornered, like ripe fruit waiting to be plucked."

Balian did not agree. "If I were Gökböri, I'd much rather be present when Saladin's jihad comes to a triumphant end. I doubt that he wants Taqī al-Dīn to claim all the glory. I think he's gone to join Saladin and the men he left behind are feeling cheated, losing interest in guarding us. How long has it been since their last attack?"

"You think we might be able to break through their lines, Balian?" Denys sounded dubious but willing to be convinced.

Thierry had no such doubts. "What do we have to lose?"

"For you, nothing," Joscelin snapped, "for you are sure to die whatever we choose to do. We all know Saladin would like nothing better than to rid himself of you Templars and the Hospitallers."

Thierry began to bristle; Balian was quicker. "You're right, Joscelin. You and Denys and I might well survive the battle, for the Saracens are accustomed to sparing highborn lords for ransom. Though I'm not sure how we raise ransoms if we're landless. But what of our men? If we're captured, they'll end up in shallow graves or the slave markets in Damascus and Cairo."

An odd expression crossed Joscelin's face; to Balian, it seemed almost like embarrassment. "I spoke without thinking," he mumbled. "It is a risk well worth taking." He hesitated, then offered an apology the only way he could, with stark honesty. "I spent twelve years as a prisoner of the Saracens. I'd rather die fighting than endure that again."

There was a moment of silence in acknowledgment of Joscelin's revealing candor, and then Thierry showed he held no grudges by uttering a heartfelt "Amen!" And with that, they turned back to tell their men what they meant to do.

Balian's gaze swept along the line of his knights. Most of them had reached the ends of their tethers and they understood this would be their last chance. They showed no eagerness but something better, a grim resolve. Balian looked back toward Ernoul, wishing again that he'd left the youth behind at Saforie with Brian and Smoke. Ernoul had pleaded to come, though, insisting that his lord needed him to take care of his weapons and stallions.

The unhorsed knights had lined up with the infantrymen and Balian could not help thinking of all the destriers they'd lost in these two days. One of them was Demon. He'd offered the stallion to Renier Rohard after the Nablus lord's horse was slain. Renier was grateful beyond words, for a knight afoot was like a crippled falcon. But a Saracen arrow had found Demon, too, and even in the midst of so much carnage, Balian still felt a pang for the stubborn black stallion that had borne him safely into so many battles.

Their plan was a simple one. The knights and Templars and serjeants still lucky enough to be mounted would strike the Saracen lines like a battering ram and, God willing, would scatter them like leaves on the wind, with the infantry and men like Renier following in their wake. Success would depend upon the element of surprise and Balian's reading of the Blue Wolf's troops. Balian raised his hand to signal his men and the other lords did the same, committing themselves to what Balian had heard one of his serjeants call a "try or die" sortie.

At first, they advanced slowly, keeping their stallions to a walk. They'd agreed that if they could somehow break free, they'd head toward the coast and Acre, for at Saforie or the lands north of Nazareth, they were sure to run into some of Saladin's army. Most of his elite *askar* and the Mamluks would be with him, but he had thousands of eager volunteers swarming these hills in search of Franks and booty.

Even after twenty years of fighting in Outremer, Balian was always surprised by how time slowed down once a charge began. Few civilians or clerics could understand the bond that formed between knights riding stirrup to stirrup into battle, and Balian had never had any luck trying to explain it to Maria. But he felt it now, a spiritual link forged by shared risk and reward, by the tumult of emotions men experienced only on the battlefield.

The first Saracen they encountered was a scout on a bay mare. The look of shock on his face was encouraging, for his surprise seemed to confirm Balian's hunch about the soldiers left behind to guard them. The scout whirled and sent the mare racing back the way he'd come, shouting in a language Balian did not understand, either Kurdish or Turkish. Alerted by his behavior that the Saracen camp must be close at hand, the Franks were ready when it came into view.

The Saracen soldiers were not ready. They'd been taking their ease between their lightning raids upon the stranded Franks, setting up a few tents for shade and even a fire for cooking. There was a string of camels, some still loaded with goat-skins of the water that was more precious than gold now to the Franks, and even more horses being held in reserve. Warned by the scout, men were sprinting for those horses, already gripping bows and quivers. But there were not that many left in camp and they were no match for the wave about to engulf them. The fighting was brutal and brief and when it was over, there were bodies sprawled on the ground, the survivors were in flight, and the unhorsed knights were running to-ward the Saracen horses, stopping only to untie reins or cut hobbles before vault-ing onto their backs. Most of the crossbowmen and spearmen had no familiarity with horses, neither liking nor trusting them, and some of them chose now to slip away on their own instead of following the knights.

Seeing several of his men homing in on the camels as if they were pearls be-yond price, Balian sympathized. Yet they dared not take the time to unpack the goatskins and he ordered them on. One of the more resourceful leaned from his saddle to cut the beasts loose, saying with a grin that they could chase them down once they got away. Balian did not share his optimism, for it had been too easy.

His instincts were soon proved right, for they'd just reached the Acre–Tiberias road when they saw a band of men coming toward them. Their saffron-colored tunics proclaimed they were members of the sultan's *askar*, as did their immediate response. Drawing their swords, they galloped toward the Franks. The knights of the rearguard quickly re-formed their line and spurred their own stallions forward. The Mamluks' pride had led them astray, for while they were indeed excellent soldiers, they still could not resist a charge of armed knights unless they had nu-merical superiority. When the Franks smashed into them, they gave ground and then peeled away, saving themselves by their fine horsemanship.

The Franks watched them ride off, soon disappearing over a nearby hill. But they'd be back and in greater numbers. Balian was sheathing his sword as Renier drew up beside him. His new Saracen mount was a mare and Khamsin's ears twitched as he reached out to touch noses with her. Balian was astonished to find a smile forming on his blistered lips when he noticed the stallion's interest; for most of the day, he'd doubted that he'd ever smile again.

"We're ready, my lord." Renier gestured behind him to Balian's knights and serjeants.

Balian refused to let his eyes linger on all the gaps in their ranks, to think of all the men who'd died in the two-day march that he imagined would become known as the Battle of Ḥaṭṭīn. These men were still alive and still in danger. "Go!" he said, and within moments, what was left of the army's rearguard was riding west, hoping to reach Acre before Saladin's army did.

Al-Afdal would have proclaimed his father's victory several times that afternoon; Salāh al-Dīn would have none of it. When al-Afdal expressed his excitement upon hearing that the Count of Tripoli had left the field, the sultan reminded him that if a man wanted to kill a snake, he must cut off its head. When al-Afdal exclaimed that the battle was surely won after the infidel infantry had fled and refused to fight anymore, his father's measured response was that a man did not have wheat until he harvested it. His rebukes were gently given, but al-Afdal saw them as rebukes nonetheless, and after that he tried to imitate his sire's impassive demeanor, for he took even his father's most casual comments as lessons in leadership.

Such control did not come easily to him, though, for he was very proud of the way his father had outwitted the Franks at every turn, luring them into this mad march to Tiberias, letting the sun and heat fight for him, sending his men to divide their army by cutting off the rearguard and the vanguard, isolating their king on the slopes of Ḥaṭṭīn. And now it was about to end in a glorious triumph. He felt truly blessed that he would be a witness to such a historic happening, the expulsion of the unbelievers from their land just as the sultan had promised.

And so, when the Franks launched a desperate charge toward the sultan, his son watched with more interest than alarm—until he realized that they might actually reach their target. Glancing quickly toward his father, he was shaken to see the older man's reaction; he'd paled noticeably and was tugging at his beard, a familiar habit in moments of stress. Drawing his sword, he spurred his stallion forward, crying out, "Give the lie to the Devil!" Following him, al-Afdal was greatly relieved to see their men rallying to the sultan, fighting so fiercely that they stopped the momentum of the infidel knights and then forced them back up the hill.

Reining in beside his father, al-Afdal could not stifle his joy. "We have routed them!"

His father shook his head, saying only, "Not yet."

Al-Afdal was unconvinced, but he lapsed into a dutiful silence as his father conferred with a messenger from Taqī al-Dīn, reporting that their infantry had climbed the northern hill and surrounded the infidel foot soldiers who'd taken refuge there, killing some and taking captive the ones who surrendered. The sultan sent word to his nephew to attack the knights who'd fled back to the southern hill, saying he would join in the assault, and al-Afdal kept close to his side, hoping that he'd at last get a chance to bloody his sword.

He soon saw that the Franks were not yet beaten, for they launched a second charge and this one, too, came dangerously close to the sultan. But Taqī al-Dīn had reached the slope between the two horns by now and the infidels were driven back again. Seeing them retreat, al-Afdal gave an exultant shout. "We have beaten them!"

His father turned on him with a rare flash of anger. "Be quiet, 'Alī! We have not beaten them until their tent falls!"

Al-Afdal subsided, startled by the realization that the sultan still feared victory might be denied them. His cousin's men were swarming up the hill now, and as they watched, a rider swung his sword at the guy ropes and the red tent collapsed into the dirt. All around al-Afdal, men were cheering and laughing, but when he turned toward his father, he saw that Salāh al-Dīn had dismounted. When he raised his face to the heavens, his son could see the tears spilling from his eyes. Then he did something that al-Afdal would never forget. Kneeling, he prostrated himself on the ground to give thanks to Allah for their triumph over the unbelievers.

Salāh al-Dīn had decided that on the morrow he would return to Tiberias to accept the Countess of Tripoli's surrender of her castle while sending their thousands of prisoners on their long, bleak journey to Damascus and the varying fates that awaited them—eventual freedom for those who could ransom themselves; slavery for those who could not; death for the captive Templars, Hospitallers, and turcopoles. The sultan believed the military knights were too dangerous to live and the turcopoles were traitors to their own blood. But tonight, the Saracens would camp at Haṭṭīn to treat their wounded, bury their dead, and rejoice in the overwhelming nature of their victory. Now all of the infidel kingdom lay undefended before them, including the city as sacred to their faith as it was to the Christians.

A large crowd of Salāh al-Dīn's soldiers had gathered outside his tent, eager to express their gratitude for his blessed victory against the unbelievers. For now, though, he was alone with al-Afdal, Taqī al-Dīn, Gökböri, his Mamluk bodyguard, and his chancellor, 'Imād al-Dīn, who was already composing the sultan's letter to al-'Ādil, sharing the news of Haṭṭīn and summoning him from Egypt to join them on their triumphant conquest of the lands of the Franks. There was also an honored guest, the amir of the holy city of Medina, fortunate enough to be an eyewitness to history. Cooks were busy preparing a celebratory feast. But first there would be a reckoning with their highborn prisoners and he sent men to have the most influential of the Franks brought before him.

When the captive lords were escorted into the tent, al-Afdal edged over to 'Imād al-Dīn's side, knowing the voluble chancellor would be the best source of information about these adversaries of Islam. 'Imād al-Dīn was happy to oblige, identifying them as they were prodded forward. The one who seemed dazed was their hapless king, and next to him was his brother, their constable. Behind them was the grand master of the Templars, may Allah curse them all. The old, white-haired one was the Marquis of Montferrat. The youth who looked more like a poet than a warrior was Humphrey de Toron, who was of interest because he spoke good Arabic. But the one who mattered the most to the sultan was the man on the other side of their king, Reynald de Chatillon, whose wickedness knew no bounds, their greatest enemy.

Al-Afdal stared with unabashed curiosity at the infidel lord they called Prince Arnat, for he'd heard stories since his childhood of Arnat's evil deeds. He broke truces with impunity, raided their caravans, even dared to threaten the holy cities of Mecca and Medina, supposedly with the intention to seize the body of the Prophet, the most blasphemous act al-Afdal could imagine. He'd been told Arnat was old, past sixty, and had wondered how he could still fight at an age that seemed so ancient to him. But the Frank appeared to be defying time as he'd often defied al-Afdal's father. His spine was straight, his shoulders squared, his step firm, with only the grey in his dark hair and the web of wrinkles around his eyes testifying to six decades of a life filled with adventures, risk-taking, and violence.

Arnat also seemed to be in better shape than the other lords. They looked drained and bleary-eyed, beaten down by thirst, heat, and fighting for two days under a burning sun. Al-Afdal felt a tingle of superstitious unease, for how could Arnat emerge unscathed from such an ordeal? Was he truly in league with the Devil, as his enemies claimed? But a closer look revealed the truth, that Arnat was sustained by arrogance and a rancor so malevolent it could overcome a man's natural fear of dying.

Salāh al-Dīn had met most of the Poulain lords at one time or another, but this was his first encounter with Guy de Lusignan. He studied Guy intently for a moment, marveling that a man so well-meaning could have wreaked such havoc. He'd never doubted the courage of the Franks and he knew that some of them were men of honor. He respected the d'Ibelin brothers and Denys de Grenier, whose Arabic was fluent enough to read Saracen poetry. He had never truly trusted the Count of Tripoli, although he thought Raymond was one of the most intelligent of the Franks. That could never be said of Guy. Yet he did not lack for courage, and the sultan bore him no grudge. He was amused now to realize that he even felt something oddly like gratitude to de Lusignan. After all, their victory at Haṭṭīn could never have happened without him.

A secret smile flitted across his mouth at the sheer incongruity of that thought. Turning to a servant, he told the man to offer a *jallab* to the king of the Franks, who looked very thirsty.

Guy spoke no Arabic and so was taken by surprise when a man approached with a tray and a golden goblet. During their hours on the Horns of Haṭṭīn, he and his knights had been able to catch tormenting glimpses of the Sea of Galilee in the distance, the lake shimmering like a mirage to the thirst-crazed men. Guy felt like that now as he stared at the goblet, almost afraid to reach for it in case it, too, was a mirage. Taking a deep breath, he lifted the cup from the tray, tilted it to his lips, and drank. He imagined this was how liquid gold must taste, and as the precious liquid trickled down his throat, he was sure no drink would ever be more delicious. With self-control that pleased him, he kept himself from draining the cup, turning and offering it to the man closest to him.

Watching as Reynald de Chatillon took several deep swallows, Guy hoped he'd leave enough for Amaury, belatedly regretting not having offered it first to his brother. Well, he could ask for more. But as he turned back toward the sultan, he saw that his benevolent host was gone, replaced by a man showing sudden anger, dark eyes as piercing as daggers. Guy stiffened before he saw that Salāh al-Dīn's daunting stare was aimed at Reynald de Chatillon.

After a very tense moment, the sultan gestured toward Humphrey de Toron. "Tell your king that I did not give him permission to share the drink with that accursed man. When he drank, it was none of my doing."

Humphrey hastily complied. He saw at once that Guy did not understand the significance of the sultan's words, knowing little of Saracen culture or their tradition of hospitality. He also saw that Reynald understood perfectly, for his mouth had twisted into a defiant smile. Moving closer to Guy, Humphrey did his best to warn the king what was about to happen.

"When the Saracens offer a man food or drink, sire, they are offering, too, a promise of his safety. If he is allowed to eat, he knows he will not be harmed as long as he remains under their roof."

Guy frowned, still slow to comprehend, for his brain felt as bruised as his body and all he wanted at that moment was to drink until he could not swallow another drop and then fall into a deep, dreamless sleep, waking up to find none of this had really happened. Seeing his confusion, Humphrey opened his mouth to try again. But time had run out.

Salāh al-Dīn rose to his feet, keeping his eyes upon Reynald. "You have broken oaths and truces, committed grave offenses against our faith, and proven again and again that you cannot be trusted. Have you any defense to offer?"

Reynald did not wait for Humphrey to translate the sultan's words. "I have done only what princes have always done," he shot back, in passable Arabic, making the words sound more offensive by his disdainful tone and the curl of his lip.

The sultan's hand had dropped to the hilt of his sword. Glancing toward Humphrey, he spoke too swiftly for Reynald to follow all of it. But he heard the word *Shahāda* and that was enough, for he knew what it meant—the testimony of faith. Under Muslim law, a man about to be executed must be given the chance to convert and thus save his life.

Humphrey turned from the sultan to Reynald. "Did you understand that? He'll spare your life if you say the testimony of faith." While the offer was grudgingly made, Humphrey felt sure that the sultan would honor it. To save himself, Reynald need only bear witness that there is no God but Allah and Muḥammad is the Messenger of Allah. But Humphrey knew what his hated stepfather would do; he'd never passed a bridge without wanting to burn it.

Reynald gave him a look of almost affectionate contempt. "No need to ask what you'd do in my place, is there? Tell him this for me, little lordling. No . . . I'll tell him myself." Raising his head, he stared challengingly at the sultan. "I would never embrace a vile, false faith like yours," he said with a sneer, wishing he had enough saliva to spit in the Saracen's face. That was to be his last coherent thought, for Salāh al-Dīn's sword was clearing its scabbard.

The blade sliced downward into Reynald's neck, nearly severing his arm at the shoulder and splashing blood over the closest men, Guy and Humphrey. As they recoiled, one of the sultan's Mamluk bodyguards came forward without haste, swung his sword, and beheaded the dying man. Grasping the body by the ankles, he dragged it toward the tent entrance, coming back a few moments later for the head.

To Humphrey, the strangest aspect of the execution was that it had been done in silence. Reynald had died too quickly to cry out. The other Franks were stunned, and the Saracens were only now beginning to talk among themselves in growing excitement, for they all shared the sultan's hatred of Reynald de Chatillon. A tall man with the sharp features of a hawk was complaining, half jokingly, that he ought to have been given the honor of slaying the infidel pig. Humphrey guessed that this was Taqī al-Dīn, just as he assumed that the youth with eyes as wide as moons was the sultan's son. Gazing down at the blood pooling on the tent rug, he thought, *My mother is now a widow for the third time, and two of the three died by violence. How unlucky is that? It will take a brave man to be willing to step into so many dead men's shoes. Or one so eager to be the Lord of Kerak that he'll risk it.* But he remembered then that the next Lord of Kerak was likely to be one of the sultan's kinsmen.

Salāh al-Dīn roused himself to nod and smile when the amir of Medina thanked him for the honor of witnessing the death of the devil, Arnat. He realized he was still holding his bloodied sword and delighted his son by saying, "Look after this for me, 'Alī." It was only then that his gaze fell upon Jerusalem's captive king.

Guy de Lusignan stood as if rooted to the spot. His eyes were glazed and unfocused and he appeared unaware that some of Reynald's blood had splattered his surcote, even matting his hair. When Salāh al-Dīn approached him, Guy seemed mesmerized by the red smear on the sultan's forehead, where he'd dipped his finger in Reynald's blood as a symbolic gesture to show he'd taken his revenge. Guy's hands had clenched into fists, not in aggression but in an attempt to conceal the involuntary tremors shaking his body. Salāh al-Dīn saw his fear, though he did not think less of the other man for it. In his ignorance of his enemy, Guy would naturally assume he'd be the next to die.

"Come and sit beside me," he said, taking Guy's arm and guiding him toward the cushions. Once they were seated, the sultan waited until his apprehensive prisoner had been given another *jallab* before calling Humphrey over to translate. "Tell him that I had sworn an oath to kill that man for his transgressions. But reassure him that he need not fear for his own life. Kings do not kill kings."

CHAPTER 49

August 1187
Jerusalem, Outremer

W hen Humphrey had suggested to Isabella that she remain in Jerusa-lem, she'd been delighted to escape Kerak. Sybilla invited her to stay at the palace and their relationship quickly changed. They'd been strangers, for they'd spent little time together and the thirteen-year gap between them had mattered much more during Isabella's childhood. Now that Sybilla saw her as grown since she'd been wedded and bedded and no longer considered her a rival for the crown, they were able to take their first tentative steps toward a genu-ine sisterhood. But then the world as they'd known it was forever changed on a sweltering July day in the barren hills of Galilee.

On this August afternoon seven weeks after the battle at Ḥaṭṭīn, Isabella had ventured out into the alien, chaotic city that Jerusalem had become, paying a duty call upon her husband's mother. She was now making her way along St. Stephen's Street toward her own mother's town house, but even with an escort—Maria's mainstay, her towering eunuch, Michael—it was like struggling against an oncom-ing tide. Jerusalem was overflowing with refugees and every day saw more arrive, the Holy City's population doubling from its normal thirty thousand to more than sixty thousand.

Her visit with Stephanie de Milly had been an awkward one. They had little to say to each other, yet they were bound by their shared fear for Humphrey, and despite her dislike for the older woman, Isabella pitied her, too. Many wives still did not know the fate of their husbands; Stephanie did. The story of Reynald's execution by Saladin's own hand had spread swiftly, growing more dramatic with each retelling, making him into a martyr who'd died for his faith. Isabella would never forgive him for scarring Humphrey's soul with his casual cruelties, but she knew Stephanie wept for him in the privacy of their marriage bed.

Isabella was tired, for it was a long walk from Stephanie's dwelling in the

Armenian Quarter to Maria's town house; the streets were so clogged with pedestrians that it was almost impossible to travel on horseback. She could not return to the palace, though, for her mother was expecting her. After Maria had reached Jerusalem with her children, household, and many of the citizens of Nablus, she had been hurt when her eldest daughter remained at the palace with Sybilla. Isabella explained that Sybilla had asked her to stay, but she'd not known how to explain that Sybilla needed her more than Maria did. Her mother was one of the strongest women she'd ever known, whereas Sybilla seemed like a lost wraith, tormented by fear for Guy and her young daughters, bewildered and dazed and still in denial, unable to admit that her husband's blunders at Hattin had doomed their kingdom.

When they finally reached Maria's town house, Isabella was waylaid by Dame Alicia. "You must hurry, my lady," she exclaimed. "He is abovestairs with the queen and she said you should join them as soon as you arrive." Although Isabella had no idea who "he" was, she hastened into the stairwell, already nervous. Since Hattin, the news had been nothing but bad.

Maria was sitting on the settle with a stranger, a man clad in Saracen garb who looked as if he could walk the streets of Damascus without attracting attention. He rose as Isabella entered, greeting her with the polished courtesy of a Poulain lord, and she suddenly knew who he must be—the legendary spymaster Bernard. Her knees going weak, she let him steer her toward the settle, where she closed her eyes in a swift, silent prayer that he had not come to tell her Humphrey or Pateras was dead. She knew Humphrey had survived the battle and was likely to be ransomed, yet men did sicken and die in captivity. Balian's fate was less certain. They'd heard rumors that he'd escaped the slaughter and had been seen in Tyre in mid-July, but his presence there had not been confirmed and until it was, she and her mother would know no peace of mind.

Maria had taken her hand, telling her that Bernard had come to share the news he'd brought to Sybilla and the patriarch earlier that day. "Sybilla will be summoning all of the highborn wives and widows to the palace to relay what she was told, but Bernard did not want us to have to wait." She turned to give Bernard a look of such gratitude that Isabella felt intense relief, sure then that her mother had not been widowed at Hattin or in its chaotic aftermath.

Bernard then repeated for Isabella what he'd already told her mother. The Lord Balian, together with Joscelin de Courtenay and Denys of Sidon, had been able to fight their way free and make it to Acre. Balian and Denys then took ship for Tyre. Lady Isabella had probably heard that Acre had yielded to Saladin? As Lord of

Acre, Joscelin had decided that a peaceful surrender would save thousands of lives and he entered into negotiations with Taqī al-Dīn. But after the citizens learned of this, some of them balked and rioting broke out in the town. When Saladin arrived, he told the burgesses they were free to leave if they put out the fires in the city. He even offered to let the merchants continue to live in Acre. They were too fearful or too bitter to accept the offer, though, and most of them headed for Tyre.

All of the prisoners had been taken to Damascus, where the highborn lords would eventually be able to ransom themselves and the less fortunate would be sold into slavery. The turcopoles were viewed as renegades by the Muslims and most of them were slain on the field rather than taken prisoner. The rumors of a mass execution of the Templar and Hospitaller knights were true. Sparing only their grand master, Gerard de Ridefort, Saladin had bought every knight for fifty dinars each from their captors, and then ordered them put to death. It had been brutally done; the sultan had turned the task over to the Sufis, Muslim holy men and scholars accustomed to wielding quill pens, not swords. Bernard saw no need to burden Isabella with that; instead, he told her that the doomed men could have saved themselves by converting to Islam, but the vast majority of them—two hundred and thirty or so—proudly refused, preferring to die as Christians. Brother Thierry was the acting grand master of the Templars until Gerard de Ridefort either regained his freedom or died in captivity, but the heart seemed to go out of the surviving Templars and Hospitallers after hearing of the massacre of their brethren in Damascus.

"What of the Count of Tripoli, Master Bernard? And his wife?"

"Count Raymond and his men got safely to Tyre. Fortunately for Lady Eschiva, Saladin's reputation for gallantry proved true. After accepting the surrender of her castle, he allowed her, her household, and the garrison to depart, even giving her an escort to Tripoli."

"Is the count still at Tyre with my stepfather and Denys? The city has not fallen?"

"No, it still holds out. But your stepfather's whereabouts are unknown at present. Count Raymond soon left Tyre, sailing with his stepsons and the Prince of Antioch's son for Tripoli. Lord Denys took command of Tyre and was negotiating with Taqī al-Dīn for a peaceful surrender. In mid-August, Lord Conrad of Montferrat arrived from Constantinople and he repudiated Denys's planned surrender, urging defiance. The citizens sided with him and Denys left for his own lands. After Sidon fell to Saladin, Denys was able to reach his castle at Beaufort."

Bernard paused to see if Isabella had questions; it had to be overwhelming to receive so much bad news all at once. For weeks, Jerusalem had been cocooned in silence, cut off from the rest of the kingdom by the Saracen soldiers roaming the countryside, exercising a soldier's right to claim booty. The survivors of Haṭṭīn had been forced to flee north, the only escape route open to them, so the citizens of Jerusalem had heard no firsthand accounts of the battle. All they knew came from what they'd been told by refugees, many of whom were only repeating rumors.

Glancing toward Maria, Bernard thought she'd made the right decision to flee Nablus. She'd shown no surprise when he'd told her that Nazareth, Bethlehem, Sebaste, and Saforie were all in Saracen hands; she'd understood the inevitability of that. She'd already heard that the d'Ibelin castle and village of Mirabel were lost, for after their surrender to Saladin's brother, al-ʿĀdil had provided an escort so the people could reach safety in Jerusalem. From them, she'd also learned of the tragic fate of Jaffa. Its citizens had refused to yield and al-ʿĀdil's men had taken Jaffa by storm, killing most of the men and enslaving the women and children. Bernard was not sure if she'd shared this with Isabella, so he made no mention of Jaffa.

Nothing he'd so far said was shocking to Isabella. She'd realized that their towns were doomed after the destruction of their army at Haṭṭīn. It was still devastating to lose the last shreds of hope. Her homeland was bleeding to death from a thousand cuts and nothing could be done to save it. "Are there any cities holding out besides Tyre?" she asked, the catch in her voice belying the calmness of her question. "What of Beirut? Or Ascalon? What of my mother-in-law's castles at Kerak and Montreal?"

"Beirut surrendered to Saladin in the first week of August, my lady. Ascalon has not fallen yet, but it will, for Saladin is marching south to join forces with al-ʿĀdil and lay siege to it. As for Lady Stephanie's strongholds, the garrisons of Kerak and Montreal remain defiant."

After waiting again for questions that did not come, Bernard rose to go and Maria rose, too. "Thank you, Master Bernard. We are in your debt and I hope that one day we will be able to repay it. What of you? What will you do now?"

"I've decided that Antioch has a healthier climate than Outremer," he said wryly, "at least for a man with a bounty upon his head."

Maria wished him Godspeed, but she did not doubt that he'd reach safety in Antioch. Chasing after the elusive spymaster would be like trying to catch hold of the morning mist.

Once he'd departed, she returned to the settle and sat down again, putting her arm around her daughter's shoulders. Isabella leaned into the embrace. "Mother . . . if Pateras is no longer in Tyre, where do you think he has gone? Could he be in Tripoli by now? Or even Antioch?"

Maria shook her head. "No. Balian will be trying to get to Jerusalem, to us." *Ere Saladin arrives to lay siege to the city.* She did not say the words aloud, but they seemed to echo in the air between them. They both knew that for Jerusalem, time was running out.

❧

Refugees from Beirut had been straggling into Tyre since their city had surrendered to Saladin on August 6. One of the last was Othon, the Bishop of Beirut. Unlike his fellow fugitives, he had influential friends in Tyre, and was soon comfortably installed at the archbishop's palace.

Seeing that his guest's wine cup was empty, Joscius signaled to a servant for a refill. His own cup was still full, for Othon had kept him busy answering questions. The bishop had been relieved to learn that the Hattīn casualties were not as horrific as rumor had it. Joscius believed that as many as three thousand men were able to escape the carnage on the field, although only two hundred of them were knights, those who'd ridden off with Count Raymond or had been with Balian d'Ibelin when his rearguard had fought their way free. Very few knights had been slain, protected by their armor and the Saracen desire for ransoms, but thousands of men had died in the course of those two terrible days, infantrymen and turcopoles and arbalesters. Even more had gotten through the battle only to face enslavement afterward.

Othon was encouraged by what he found in Tyre. The well-fortified seaport was crowded with the soldiers and knights who'd escaped Hattīn, and now that power was in the hands of a bold battle commander, Conrad of Montferrat, Tyre would not be easily taken. But Joscius reluctantly confirmed Othon's greatest fear—that the Holy City would soon fall to the infidels. Jerusalem was well-nigh defenseless, overwhelmed with panicked refugees and protected only by a young woman and a prince of the Church, neither of whom knew how to wage war.

Joscius shared then what he'd learned from Hattīn survivors and Franks seeking safety in Tyre. Saladin had so far shown surprising generosity in offering terms to the towns that surrendered, allowing citizens to depart with their possessions and sometimes even providing an escort, for the roads had never been so dangerous; the countryside was swarming with Saracen soldiers and bandits and Bedouins, all eager to take advantage of the chaos and lawlessness. The few towns that had refused to yield had suffered the usual fate of a city or castle taken by storm— no mercy. And with the king and grand master of the Templars held prisoner, the grand master of the Hospitallers dead at Cresson Springs, and the queen and patriarch trapped in Jerusalem, there were none to exercise authority, to rally their people, and offer resistance to the sultan's army.

"So this Conrad of Montferrat has taken power because there was no one else." While Joscius seemed impressed by Conrad, all Othon knew of the man was that he was the son of the Marquis of Montferrat, the brother of Sybilla's first husband. "Were there no others to take command here? What of Balian d'Ibelin? When Beirut learned of Ḥaṭṭīn, we heard that Balian saved the lives of many of the rear-guard by breaking through the Saracen lines. Is he not in Tyre?"

"He arrived from Acre soon after the battle, but he did not stay long. His wife had promised him that she'd flee if Nablus seemed in danger and after he heard that the Nablus garrison had surrendered, he set out for Jerusalem, where she would have gone. But on his first attempt, he ran into some of Taqī al-Dīn's men, barely escaping with his life. His second try was no luckier. On his third effort, he was wounded in an encounter with outlaws and retreated to Tyre whilst he recovered. He admitted that he'd have been captured or killed for certes if not for the speed of that magnificent Arabian of his, and I did my best to convince him that he'd do Maria no good by making her a widow."

"That sounds like a very desperate man," Othon said sympathetically. "I hope he is not still trying to reach Jerusalem?"

"He finally conceded that he'd never make it overland. He is now trying to find a ship that will take him to Ascalon so he can ask Saladin for a safe-conduct, allowing him to get his wife and children out of Jerusalem."

"By the rood!" Othon shook his head, for surely this was not a venture that would end well. "I will pray for him," he declared, and Joscius thanked him, thinking that Balian was likely to need all the prayers he could get.

Balian leaned against the gunwale of the *tarida* as it sliced through the waves. He'd noticed on the voyage that the westerly winds slackened as sunset neared, so he was not surprised to see the sailors hauling on the pulleys that controlled the halyard. Once the lateen sail was lowered, they pushed the oars through the oarlocks, settled on benches, and began to row.

The white banner with the red cross that flew from the mast, proud emblem of the city-state of Genoa, drooped as the wind continued to fall. A chance encounter with a Genoese sailor who'd fought at Ḥaṭṭīn had led Balian to the *San Giuan*, a merchant ship on its way to Alexandria, for in the Levant, trade had never been a casualty of war. The master of the *San Giuan* had been quite willing to take Balian and his companions with them if he paid for their passage, which the generosity of Archbishop Joscius had enabled him to do.

Balian turned as Renier Rohard joined him at the gunwale. He'd not wanted any of his knights to accompany him on this high-risk mission, but Renier had insisted, for his wife and elderly mother had taken refuge in Jerusalem, too. And Ernoul had overcome Balian's objections by arguing that he'd be better off with his lord than on his own in Tyre. He prevailed because Balian had left his other squire behind at Saforie; when the Saracens had taken it, they'd found it abandoned and Brian's whereabouts were unknown.

"Do you think Ascalon still holds out?"

Balian shook his head, for it was now September 5, which meant Ascalon had been under siege for more than two weeks. Renier did not disagree. Their homeland was in its death throes and they could only watch helplessly as it happened.

"There it is!" Ernoul cried. Whether the city had been captured or not, they'd not have attempted to land there; the offshore currents made Ascalon's harbor too dangerous to enter. They saw no signs of life on the seaward walls. But by then, they were close enough to catch sight of the banner flying from the castle— Saladin's eagle. None spoke, all sharing the same thought. Had the townspeople surrendered, sparing themselves Jaffa's fate?

Not long afterward, they were within sight of Tida, the ancient harbor that offered access to Gaza. A *tarida*'s flat bottom made it relatively easy to beach and after some skillful maneuvering by the Genoese oarsmen, the *San Giuan* was soon close enough to the shore for the passengers to disembark. As they splashed through the shallow water, the ship's master called out "Good luck!" in accented French, and then the *tarida* was on its way again.

Tida was deserted, no surprise since there was a Saracen army close by. Balian had been to Gaza before, so he knew they had a walk of nigh on two miles. *Taride* were often used to transport horses, but he'd had to leave Khamsin in Joscius's care, for the *San Giuan*'s hold was already filled with the cargo that its master expected to sell in Alexandria—silver, timber, and alum. Balian assumed the ship would winter in the Egyptian city since the sailing season ended in October, returning to Genoa in the spring with elegant silks and expensive spices. When the *San Giuan* next sailed for the Levant, would Outremer be only a memory?

The castle at Gaza had been given to the Templars by a king of Jerusalem and a town had grown up in its shadow. The sun was setting by the time the men gained admittance into the city. At once, they were surrounded by townspeople desperate to know what was occurring in the rest of the kingdom, so it took a while before they could approach the castle.

For Balian, it stirred up painful memories of his arrival at the abandoned citadel of Le Fève, for Gaza's stronghold was like a ghost ship manned by a skeletal crew, a few serjeants too old or too ill to have ridden off to war with their grand master. He was warmly welcomed, and felt obligated to relive the horrors he and his men had experienced at Ḥaṭṭīn, for his was the first eyewitness account of the battle that these elderly Templars had heard. He could not bring himself to tell them of the slaughter of their brethren in Damascus, but they obviously feared the worst, for they asked no questions about the fate of their brothers.

In the morning, the castle's guardians offered them the horses in their stables, saying they'd soon be claimed by the Saracens. The beasts were rejects, left behind and forgotten like their Templar masters, but Balian and his companions gratefully accepted, for it was eight miles or so to Ascalon.

Within a few miles, they ran into Saracen soldiers. The men seemed in high spirits, celebrating their latest victory, and Balian's flag of truce and his ability to speak Arabic were enough to secure him an escort to the Saracen camp. Upon their arrival at the sultan's tent, he was the only one allowed to enter, Renier and Ernoul forced to wait outside with their guards.

Salāh al-Dīn and several other men were seated cross-legged on cushions, sipping fruit juice and engaged in an animated conversation that stopped as Balian was shoved into the tent. His guard would have forced him to his knees had al-ʿĀdil not interceded, beckoning him forward as if he were a guest, not a prisoner. Salāh al-Dīn had recognized him, too, and gestured for a cushion to be provided, telling his companions that this was the Lord of Nablus. One of the younger men laughed at that; only later would Balian learn that this was Husām al-Dīn, the sultan's nephew, who was now the new lord of Nablus.

After a formal exchange of greetings, Balian could not keep himself from asking if Ascalon had surrendered. Nor did he try to hide his relief when the sultan said that the city had accepted his terms.

"They held out as long as they could." Al-ʿĀdil signaled for a servant to give Balian a cool drink. "We had your king brought from Damascus, offering him his freedom if he could get Asqalan to surrender. He had no luck, though. They jeered at him from the walls, calling him a coward. But after two weeks, they finally despaired and yesterday, they yielded."

"You have been extraordinarily generous in offering terms, my lord sultan."

Balian had no trouble in saying that, for he believed it to be true. Ḥaṭṭīn could easily have been followed by a bloodbath. In a land where the past was neither forgotten nor forgiven, all had heard stories of the tragic fate of Jerusalem's Muslims and Jews when the Holy City had been captured by the Franks in God's year 1099.

Salāh al-Dīn smiled. "I assume you are looking for terms, too, my lord Balian."

"I am, my lord. My wife and children have taken refuge in Jerusalem. It is my hope that you will issue me a safe-conduct so I can get them out of the city ere you lay siege to it."

The sultan was quiet for several moments, considering the plea. When he turned to the other men, they spoke in Kurdish, so Balian could only wait for the verdict. After what seemed like an eternity to him, Salāh al-Dīn's dark eyes shifted back to his face.

"Your request is granted—on two conditions. You may remain in the city for but one night and you must swear upon your holy relics not to take up arms against me."

It was only then that Balian realized he'd been holding his breath. "I will so swear. Thank you, my lord sultan."

There was something surreal about it—that they should find themselves made so welcome in the camp of their enemies. Renier and Ernoul had been allowed to enter the city so they could borrow a relic from one of its five churches, and when they returned, they were eager to tell Balian what they'd learned—that the Franks of Ascalon were going to be escorted by Saladin's men to the Egyptian port of Alexandria, where they would spend the winter at its governor's expense, and then take ship in the spring for countries in Christendom. Balian was not as amazed by this as they were, for he'd already heard of the remarkable clemency the sultan had so far shown. When he and Taqī al-Dīn had taken the stronghold of Toron, he'd even allowed the garrison to join the resistance being mounted at Tyre.

Balian was invited to dine that evening with al-ʿĀdil. Afterward, they strolled back to Balian's tent. He supposed they could not be considered friends, but they had enjoyed an easy rapport from their first meeting, and he had never felt so grateful to anyone as he did to al-ʿĀdil on this starlit September night. Realizing that Balian would need more than a safe-conduct to get to Jerusalem, al-ʿĀdil had arranged for an escort, even sending with them a young man named Adam ibn Ibrāhīm, the son of one of the Christian clerks working for his chancellor, al-Sanīʿa.

"Adam will accompany you into al-Quds. He is a Christian like you and he speaks some French. My men will camp outside the city whilst you go in to fetch your family. Send Adam out to them once you are ready to depart and they will see you safely to the Frankish lands in Tripoli." Shrugging off Balian's thanks, al-ʿĀdil added with a grin, "You'll need other horses, too. I saw that nag you rode in on, and I doubt that he could outrun a turtle with a broken leg."

"My money would be on the turtle, too," Balian conceded with a rueful laugh.

Al-ʿĀdil joined in and for a fleeting moment, they were not enemies by blood and birth, merely two men with enough imagination to realize that they were not as different as their world would have them believe. When Balian tried again to thank him, al-ʿĀdil joked that Balian could repay him by naming his next son Ahmad.

They stopped, then, for Balian's tent lay ahead. Al-ʿĀdil bade him good night, turned to go, and then came to a halt. Facing Balian again, he said with sudden gravity, "There is something you should know. My brother had summoned some of the Franks from al-Quds to discuss the terms of surrender. I doubt you'll be surprised to learn he was prepared to be very generous, more than fair. The Franks arrived on Friday, the same day of the sun's eclipse. They were shaken by the darkness at noon, for the eclipse occurred two months to the very day since their defeat at Ḥaṭṭīn. They said their God had punished them for being unworthy, false Christians."

Balian nodded bleakly. "They are not the only ones to believe that. But if God did indeed punish us, it was for crowning a fool, Gerard de Ridefort's puppet."

"Ah, I forgot to tell you. He is here, too, the Templar grand master. When my brother had your king brought from Damascus, he also sent for de Ridefort. He has been offered his freedom if he gets the Templars to surrender their castles at Gaza and Latrun and he has agreed."

Balian did not trust himself to speak, thinking of Jakelin and Roger de Moulins and the good men who'd died with them, thinking of the thousands of deaths on the Horns of Ḥaṭṭīn, and the Templars and Hospitallers who'd been executed in Damascus.

He did not need to respond, for his silent outrage was more eloquent than any words could have been. Al-ʿĀdil understood. "De Ridefort no longer matters. But this does. The men from al-Quds were foolish and arrogant. They spurned the sultan's offer, declaring that they would never agree to surrender their holy city to 'accursed infidels and heathens.' They said the son of their God had died for them, and they would die for him if need be. My brother was angered by their insolence and swore that he would take al-Quds by the sword."

"Jesu! Do you think he means it?"

"I am sure that he does. He takes a holy oath very seriously. And that is why you must get your woman and your children out of the city ere the siege begins."

With each mile that brought them closer to Jerusalem, Balian felt more and more grateful for their escort, realizing he'd never have made it on his own. He lost track of all the times they encountered soldiers in search of plunder. A few terse words from the man in command sent them on their way. The bandits kept their distance, looking for easier quarry than armed horsemen. Al-'Ādil's men seemed pleased with their assignment, and Balian soon understood why; they were eager for their first glimpse of the city they called al-Quds. The Holy City was so sacred to Christians that they sometimes forgot that it was revered, too, by Muslims and Jews. As Jerusalem's walls came into view, Balian's escort veered off to the northwest, telling him they'd await him at the village of al-Jīb. Once the Saracens were gone, Balian and his companions galloped toward the city. Men appeared on the walls, brandishing weapons. But as soon as Balian identified himself, they were permitted to approach the gatehouse and the outer portcullis was winched up, allowing them to enter the barbican. It was L-shaped, another obstacle for invaders, and as they eased their horses around the sharp turn, the portcullis slammed down behind them. After the inner gate rose, they rode into a city already under siege—assailed by fear. At once, Balian came under assault, too, being bombarded with questions from all sides as men scrambled down from the walls. He was surprised by their urgency, for with such a steady stream of refugees, surely they could not be that starved for news.

When they tried to make their way down David Street, it only got worse. People were surging toward them, hands outstretched, crying his name, sobbing, and thanking God. Balian was shocked by the hysteria and when he realized the reason for their bizarre behavior, he was horrified. These desperate, despairing people, most of them women and children and the elderly, apparently saw him as their savior.

"Madness," he whispered, "utter madness," for what could one man do against an army? The noise level was deafening. Not only was the city in a state of total panic, it was dangerously overcrowded. One glance at those congested, swarming streets told him that. It took them nigh on an hour to thread their way through the throngs to St. Stephen's Street. When they finally saw the town house up ahead, they felt as if they'd reached a refuge of their own, for people were still trailing after them, some even trying to follow when the gate was opened.

Word had obviously spread of their arrival in the city. As soon as Balian dismounted, his seven-year-old son was there, his nephew just a few steps behind John, both boys clinging to him as if they would never let go. Helvis was sobbing openly and Margaret was squealing "Papa!" as she tugged at his hauberk. For a few precious moments, the world beyond the courtyard receded and all that mattered was this, a father embracing his children, after almost giving up hope that it would ever happen again.

"Do not cry, lass," he entreated Helvis, shaking his head when she said he was crying, too. "Those are raindrops," he insisted, pointing toward the sun. "Look at those storm clouds." That made her smile and he gave her another hug. "Where is your mother, sugar?"

"I am here, Balian." At the sound of his wife's voice, he spun around to find her standing a few feet away, their youngest son, Philip, balancing on her hip, a blindingly bright smile upon her face, and the glimmer of tears on her lashes. Balian took them both into his arms, and they stood without speaking, for so long that Philip began to squirm impatiently and demanded that Papa make him fly, his favorite game. Once his father had boosted him up onto his shoulders, he whooped with delight, and for reasons he was too young to understand, that moment imprinted itself upon his memory. Long after he was grown, with sons of his own, he would recall very little of their flight from Nablus. But he would vividly remember the afternoon that his father came home and made him fly.

Balian managed to steal a few moments alone with Maria to tell her that he'd gotten permission from Saladin to take them from the city on the morrow. "I knew you would find a way," she said, no more than that, and he realized he'd never received a greater compliment than the one his wife had just given him, for she meant it. She had never doubted him.

A joyful pandemonium still reigned in their household several hours later. Isabella had arrived from the palace to join the celebration. As Renier had hoped, his womenfolk had taken shelter with Maria, and they'd had an emotional reunion. Balian's niece Etiennette wept with relief when he told her that her sister, Esquiva, was safe in Tyre, having accompanied Joscelin and his family from Acre after its surrender. He'd also been able to reassure her that her husband had been taken prisoner at Haṭṭīn and would be amongst the men ransomed. He did not tell her that he'd heard a rumor in Tyre that Baudouin was gravely ill; that must wait until they'd reached safety in Tripoli.

The tables in the great hall were being set for supper when there was a commotion out in the street and Patriarch Eraclius was ushered in, flanked by his usual entourage. He greeted Balian so warmly that strangers might have thought the two men were longtime friends and allies. Balian managed to be civil, all the while thinking of the Bishop of Acre, who'd died trying to protect the True Cross whilst the patriarch remained in Jerusalem. Eraclius soon revealed the reason for his unprecedented visit. "I've come to escort you to the palace. The queen is most eager to speak with you."

Balian had no desire to see Sybilla, but he knew that did not matter. She was still the queen and that *did* matter. Getting reluctantly to his feet, he said, "I cannot stay for long." He was about to insist that Maria come, too, but she was already at his side, silently daring the patriarch to object. He merely smiled graciously, which they did not find reassuring.

The ride to the palace was a repeat of Balian's entry into the city. The streets still teemed with people. Once again, they mobbed him, widows holding up children for his blessing, priests promising to pray for his victory against the infidels, youngsters eagerly offering to fight at his side if he could provide weapons, greybeards tearfully thanking him for coming back to save the Holy City. By the time they reached the palace, Balian felt as if he were bleeding from dozens of wounds. He saw that his wife was deeply shaken, too. He'd told her of the emotional frenzy he'd encountered, yet it was different to actually witness it for herself. But he noted uneasily that the patriarch did not seem to share Maria's shock. He even looked pleased by the uproar.

Sybilla was showing the strain of the past few months; her eyes were heavy lidded from lack of sleep, she was too pale, and she'd lost so much weight that she looked older than her twenty-eight years. But she brightened at the sight of Balian, crossing the chamber to greet him as warmly as the patriarch had done; only in her case, she seemed sincere.

"Lord Balian, I cannot begin to tell you how grateful I am to you for returning to Jerusalem. The patriarch and I have been in despair. We have more people in the

city than we can care for and most of them are women and children. The great
majority of the men now in Jerusalem are either elderly, priests, or green lads. We
desperately needed a seasoned soldier to take charge of our defenses, for without
such a commander, we are all doomed. So, you can imagine my joy when we heard
of your arrival. God has truly answered our prayers!"

Balian had listened in silence. Maria saw the tension in the set of his shoulders,
the tightening of the muscles in his jaw, and she reached over, unobtrusively resting her hand on his arm. He covered it with his own hand, but he kept his eyes on
Sybilla.

"No, madame," he said, quietly but firmly. "The Lord has not answered your
prayers. All the prayers in Christendom will not stop Jerusalem from falling to
Saladin. Its fate was writ in blood from the moment those fools sneered at the
sultan's offer. As I am sure they told you, he was greatly offended and swore that
he would take the city by the sword. I did not return to lead a doomed defense. I
am here to take my wife and children to safety, and for no other reason. We will
be leaving on the morrow—"

"No!" Sybilla was horrified by what she was hearing. It had never occurred to
her that he'd refuse the command. "You cannot go. I understand your concern for
your family. But there is more at stake than their lives. Once you think upon it, I
am sure you will see that."

Eraclius quickly spoke up before Balian could respond. "You've seen for yourself the panic of Jerusalem's citizens. If you abandon them, there is no hope, neither for them nor the Holy City. Promise us that you will not leave on the morrow.
Do not do something that you will regret for the rest of your life."

"I have no choice. I would not have been able to reach Jerusalem had Saladin
not given me a safe-conduct and an escort. But I had to swear an oath that I would
not spend more than one night in the city and that I would not take up arms
against him—"

"Is that all?" The patriarch gave an audible sigh of relief. "You are not bound
by such an oath. One given to an infidel counts for nothing. But if your conscience
is sore, I can absolve you of it. Right here and now if you wish."

"I gave him my word and I intend to keep it. I will not take command of the
city. Even if I were not bound by my oath, my first loyalty is to my family, and I
mean to get them to safety on the morrow."

Eraclius shook his head, as if in disbelief. "What of your loyalty to the
kingdom?"

Balian stared at the patriarch, incredulous at first, and then utterly outraged.

"I was loyal to that crowned fool you foisted upon us. We all were, and where did that blind loyalty lead us? To thousands of bodies still rotting unburied on the Horns of Haṭṭīn, to the dungeons of Damascus and the slave markets of Aleppo, and now the loss of the Holy City!"

Eraclius started to speak, then stopped, wise enough to realize that there were few emotions as raw or dangerous as fury indistinguishable from grief. Sybilla's first instinct was to defend her husband, to blame Gerard de Ridefort for their disastrous defeat at Haṭṭīn. But the images Balian had called up were so powerful that she shrank from them, for he'd breathed life into the victims of Haṭṭīn, forcing her to confront the men who'd been slain or enslaved because of Guy's mistakes. Seeing that Balian and Maria were about to leave, she cried out desperately, "You are our only hope, Balian!"

She saw him pause. But then he slowly shook his head and reached for the door latch. Sybilla sank down again in her chair, covered her face in her hands, and began to sob.

Maria slept poorly that night and she knew that Balian did, too. He'd insisted he was well, just too tired to sleep; she knew better. When she awakened again, it was not yet dawn and his side of the bed was empty. Finding her bed robe and felt slippers, she went in search of her husband.

He was not in the shadowed bedchamber. She went to check the rooms where their children slept, but she did not find him keeping vigil by any of their beds, as she'd half expected she would. Returning to their bedchamber, she sat down on the bed, at a loss. Then she thought of their balcony overlooking the courtyard.

He was there, sitting on the bench, gazing up at a sky still glittering with stars, lighting the heavens like the remote fires of an enemy camp. He was partially dressed in shirt and braies, with a mantle over his shoulders, for the night had been chilly. He turned as Maria stepped outside and when she sat beside him, he opened the mantle to envelop them both.

"Did you sleep at all?" she asked and he shook his head. There was such anguish in his eyes that she felt her heart begin to race. "What are you going to do, Balian?"

"Marika, I do not know," he confessed, sounding utterly defeated.

She felt no surprise. She'd seen how he'd reacted to the distraught and doomed people pleading for his help. It was nothing said by Sybilla or Eraclius that had stolen his sleep. It was the haunted faces of the women, the bewilderment of their children, the old men no longer able to play a man's part. Above all, it was his bitter understanding of what happened when a city was taken by storm. It mattered little whether the soldiers were Muslims or Christians. The looting, the raping, the killing were always the same.

"Whatever I do, it will be wrong," he said huskily. "If I get you and our children to safety and then come back, it will be too late by then. If I stay, all I can do is prolong the inevitable outcome by a few days, for Jerusalem is not Tyre. And even if I believed it was possible to defend the city, I could not take command without breaking my oath to Saladin. I have no choice but to hold to my vow and ride out to meet al-'Ādil's men, as agreed upon."

And yet if he did, she realized that he'd never forgive himself. Till he drew his last mortal breath, he would regret abandoning the helpless people of Jerusalem. He did not want to die in the ruins of the besieged city. His head told him that there was nothing he could do for these trapped civilians. His heart belonged to her and their children. But his sense of honor would be well-nigh impossible to silence, judging him for a chivalric sin that would shred his peace and might even poison their marriage if she insisted that he leave with her. He'd said none of this. He did not need to, for she knew him to the very core of his being, to the most shadowed corners of his soul, knew him even better than he knew himself.

She wanted him to hold her so tightly that she could barely breathe, wanted them to ride away from the horrors unloosed by Guy de Lusignan and Gerard de Ridefort, never to look back. "We agree that nothing is more important than saving our children," she said, somehow managing to sound as if they were in the midst of an ordinary marital discussion. "If their safety could be assured and you were not tethered by that oath to Saladin, what would you do, Balian?"

"I want to go with you, Marika," he said without hesitation. "I want to see our children grow up. I want us to grow old together. But I would stay here and do all I could to defend the city and its people."

She was quiet for a time, drawing upon the lessons learned long ago in her Constantinople childhood, that duty and honor were paramount, the cornerstones for the life of a Greek princess. "All you can do, then," she told him, "is to let Saladin know that you are faced with an impossible choice and ask him what he would do in your place."

CHAPTER 50

September 1187
Latrun, Outremer

When they reached the Templar castle at Latrun, Salāh al-Dīn instructed Gerard de Ridefort to order the stronghold to surrender. The Templars were appalled at the command, but they were sworn to obey their grand master without question, and they yielded, just as the elderly Templars at Gaza had done. The sultan was still at Latrun when Adam arrived with a letter from Balian d'Ibelin. There was a delay while it was translated into Arabic for Salāh al-Dīn, who then had it read aloud in council, to the amazement of his audience.

Gökböri was the first to respond. "Such crazed courage ought to be rewarded. Save this man from himself, my lord. Insist that he leave al-Quds whilst he still can."

After the laughter subsided, Taqī al-Dīn surprised them by offering rare praise for an infidel. "I agree that we do not want this Frank in al-Quds. He knows how to fight, as he proved at Ḥaṭṭīn." Adding with a sly glance toward Gökböri, "You can attest to that, I believe."

Gökböri scowled, for he'd endured more than his share of barbed humor over the failure of his men to keep the Franks' rearguard from escaping the battle. Before he could retaliate, the lawyer 'Īsā al-Hakkari smoothly interceded. "Will you be freeing the Templar grand master?"

They were united in their contempt for Gerard de Ridefort, scornful that he'd betrayed his brethren by buying his freedom with the order's strongholds, none believing he deserved to regain his liberty. The only opinion that mattered, however, was Salāh al-Dīn's, and he ended the discussion by reminding them that he'd given the Templar his word. Al-'Ādil evoked more laughter by observing that the Templar and the king of the Franks were the Muslims' secret weapons, sure to wreak more havoc amongst the Christians by their utter ineptitude. Soon

afterward, the council broke up, but al-ʿĀdil lingered, giving his brother a speculative look.

"I must admit that I admire Balian d'Ibelin for caring so much about his countrymen. He has integrity as well as courage, Yūsuf, and that is all too rare." He
waited but his brother merely nodded, so he tried again. "You have not yet told us
what you mean to do."

That earned him the shadow of a smile. "No," the sultan agreed, "I have not,
have I?"

Balian and Maria and their household were having their evening meal when Adam
burst into the great hall. "I have it, lord," he panted, "the sultan's answer!" Too
excited to remember his French, he blurted out his news in Arabic that only Balian
understood. But his presence was enough for Maria, who felt her knife slip through
suddenly numb fingers. Renier Rohard understood, too, for Balian had confided
in him when he'd questioned why they'd not left the city straightaway, and he half
rose from his seat. Balian sat frozen for a moment and then reached across the
table to take the letter that Adam was holding out.

As his eyes met Maria's, he mouthed the word "solar," and then he was gone,
so swiftly that the other diners noticed and began to murmur uneasily among
themselves. Maria forced herself to rise without haste, invited Adam to take a seat
at one of the tables, and signaled for servants to continue ladling out the food.
Only then did she follow her husband. When she reached the solar, she hesitated
for a moment before the door, dreading what she was about to learn. No matter
what Saladin decided, Balian would be the loser. And so would she.

Balian was standing by the window. He looked up as she entered, the expression on his face not easy for her to interpret. By the time she'd reached his side,
she'd decided that it was absolute astonishment. "He released me from my oath,
Marika. He said he understood why I felt compelled to stay. Not only is he not
wroth with me, he said that I am a man of honor and he will still provide an escort
for you, our children, and household."

They looked at each other in silence. "I'd best go to the palace and tell Sybilla
that I will take command," he said at last. She nodded mutely, determined to hold
herself together until he was gone. He halted at the door, gave her one final look
that communicated all they dared not say. As soon as the door closed, she stumbled
toward the closest chair. Her eyes were burning and she was finding it hard to

catch her breath. But she did not weep, for if she did, she feared she'd not be able to stop.

Isabella had rarely seen her stepfather angry in the ten years since he'd married her mother, but he was obviously angry now, and more disconcertingly, angry with her. "What you are doing is brave. It is also foolhardy, Bella. You have no idea what occurs when a city is taken by the sword. Yes, I know what you said, that you'd be safe if you stayed in the palace with Sybilla, that Saladin would not let the queen and her sister be harmed. But you do not know the madness that comes over some men at such times. Anything can happen—anything."

Balian paused, for she was still shaking her head stubbornly. "I cannot believe Sybilla would let you do this," he said, so sharply that she winced.

"She did not ask it of me, Pateras. I told you that. But when I said I'd stay with her, I could see her relief. She is overwhelmed, knowing she is responsible for the safety of her daughters and all the people in the city. She needs my support."

"And what of Maria? You think she will not need you? A widow with four young children?"

Isabella gasped, for until now, she'd not realized that he fully expected to die defending Jerusalem. She looked so stricken that Balian's anger ebbed away. Reminding himself that she was only fifteen, he took her in his arms and she dried her tears against his tunic. "There is more to it," she confided. "Humphrey's mother is not well. You know how she is, as prickly as a hedgehog, so she'd never admit she was needy. And I will not pretend that I like her. But she is still Humphrey's mother. How could I face him if she came to harm?"

Balian had no doubts that Humphrey's fears for his wife would be far greater than any fear for his difficult mother. He saw, though, that Isabella was trying to live up to the sort of high expectations the young too often demanded of themselves. She confirmed that now by another confession, that she did not want to desert the terrified people of Jerusalem, for the first time revealing that she shared some of her mother's pride of birth, the noblesse oblige of a king's daughter and an emperor's kinswoman.

"My mother is very distraught that I plan to stay," she admitted, "but in her heart, she understands. You do not think she'd ever have left you, Pateras, if not for your children?" She mustered up a small smile. "I promised her that I'd look after you since she cannot."

She seemed heartbreakingly vulnerable to Balian, innocent and obstinate, lost in that unexplored terrain between childhood and womanhood. "And you must promise me, Bella, that you will become Sybilla's shadow once the siege begins." Her only security would be found in the palace, for he was sure Saladin would send men to safeguard Sybilla as soon as the city fell.

He would have to stress that with Marika, the only comfort he'd be able to offer. Isabella promised that she would. Gazing up into his face, she wanted to tell him that she loved him as much as any daughter could love her father. But she saw that he already knew.

❖

They left the city at dawn. Al-'Ādil's men waited just out of arrow range. Adam waved to confirm that all was set and they would escort Maria, her children, and household members to the sultan's camp at Latrun, then on to safety in Tripoli. Renier's wife and mother were accompanying Maria and Balian had done his best to convince Renier to leave, too, arguing that they might need his protection on the journey. Renier had refused, saying Balian would have greater need of him. Balian had also failed to get Ernoul out of the city, despite ordering the youth to see his family safely through the war-ravaged countryside. Ernoul had not argued; he'd simply disappeared during the night, intent upon hiding until his lord's lady was gone.

Balian and Maria had rarely lied to their children, but they did now, assuring them that their father was remaining behind to take care of some important matters in the city and would join them as soon as he could. While the little ones did not question it, Helvis was old enough to harbor doubts and even John seemed uneasy. Eleven-year-old Thomasin understood all too well what his uncle was doing. He did his best, though, to reassure his cousins, and Balian was very grateful to him. He did not think he or Maria could have borne it otherwise.

He was astride the stallion al-'Ādil had given him, a bay palfrey that he'd named Bayard. His owner had probably died at Jaffa, but he'd trained the horse well and when Balian reined him in alongside Maria's mare, Bayard halted obediently, allowing his new master to lean over and kiss his wife. They did not speak. They'd said little during the night either, clinging to each other in a final farewell that held more pain than passion.

Isabella nudged her mare forward then, reaching out to clasp hands with her mother. "We will see you in Tripoli," she said, as convincingly as she could. Maria dredged up a smile from the depths of memory, squeezed her daughter's hand, and then urged her mount toward David's Gate. She did not look back, having promised Balian that she would not. The others followed slowly. Balian guided Bayard into the barbican, watching only long enough to see them greeted by their Saracen protectors. He turned the stallion around then and rode back into the city as the portcullis clanged shut behind him.

Balian spent the next few days in almost ceaseless activity. He began by meeting with Patriarch Eraclius, Sybilla, the master of the Hospitaller Hospital of St. John, the patriarch of the Armenian Church, the grand master of the leper knights, a few elderly Templar serjeants, and several of the most influential members of the burgesses' community. There he learned that their plight was even worse than he'd expected. Sybilla and Eraclius had done their best to shelter the thousands of refugees, housing some in the pilgrim hospices, others in the hospitals, calling upon churches to take them in, ordering bakeries to stoke their ovens from dawn till dusk to provide loafs of bread for the hungry. But they'd done little to bolster Jerusalem's defenses, had not even taken measures to identify the Muslim slaves and prisoners in the city.

Balian's first action was to find out the number of Saracens being held prisoner or enslaved by the Templars and Hospitallers, who used them for their building projects; he was troubled to learn there were five thousand of them. He and Renier inspected the city walls and gates, then assembled teams to shore up the most vulnerable areas. Balian next checked the city's water sources. Jerusalemites relied upon cisterns for drinking water, but there were also three reservoirs within the walls that could be used for animals and to extinguish fires. Unlike most of Christendom, Outremer did not have guilds. Some of the more affluent trades did have fraternities and he arranged to meet with the leaders of the goldsmiths, silversmiths, and mercers, telling them that he needed volunteers to man the walls and asking them to spread the word.

He used the town crier to summon carpenters to the palace, agreeing to buy all the lumber they had at hand. He and Renier sketched for them diagrams of mangonels, explaining that they would have to assemble them upon the roofs of David's Tower and Tancred's Tower. Renier took on the duty of finding men among the refugees and residents who'd ever operated mangonels and Balian put unskilled laborers to work lugging heavy stones up to the tower roofs.

One of the greatest challenges was supplying weapons. The need was far greater than the armories of the Templars and Hospitallers could provide. Jerusalem had a few bladesmiths, but swords were custom-made, so they had a limited number in stock, never mass-produced. Balian had to rely upon the blacksmiths for spears and axes and the bowyers for crossbows. The latter were fairly easy to learn, so he set up archery lessons in the open area between the grain market and Tancred's Tower.

He formed a squadron of gravediggers, too; in a city under siege, the dead needed to be buried quickly to ward off plague. When they pointed out that the charnel houses were located beyond the walls, he told them that the dead would have to be buried in the churchyards, even unhallowed ground if need be. After some of the priests heard this, they came to protest, insisting graves must be properly consecrated. Balian paid them little heed, for he was already on to the next problem—that many of the men he was conscripting expected to be paid for their labors. Apparently not even an impending Saracen attack was enough to suspend the normal laws of commerce.

It was then that a familiar figure appeared, hurrying toward him to volunteer. Balian had not seen Anselm since Baldwin's death and was very pleased by the sight of the older man. Anselm had two virtues worth their weight in gold—he was utterly reliable and almost impossible to fluster. Anselm proved it when given his first assignment, leading men to strip silver from the roofs of the richest churches and cart it over to the Royal Mint to be melted down into coins. A number of priests protested strenuously to that. But they found Balian had a strong ally in the patriarch, who had sharp words for any who came to complain about his orders.

Even with money to pay defenders, Balian knew that he could not muster enough of them. Eraclius had told him that they thought there were at least sixty thousand people in the city, and only about twenty thousand of them were males. It was his opinion that of this group, fewer than six thousand were capable of offering real resistance, the rest being too old or too ill or unwilling. For the specter of betrayal hung over the city, too. Eraclius admitted that he was not sure they could trust all of the Syrian Orthodox Christians.

"They'd lived under Muslim rule for centuries until the Kingdom of Jerusalem was carved from blood and bone and faith, and as much as it grieves me to say it, I think some of them might even welcome a Saracen victory. There are rumors that Saladin's spies have been trying since Ḥaṭṭīn to plant seeds of disloyalty amongst the Syrians."

Even at such a moment, Eraclius could not suppress his flair for oratory. Despite the ornate delivery, the warning was a credible one, but Balian could only deal with one threat at a time. He asked Eraclius for a list of the sons of knights and nobles, those who'd reached their legal majority of fifteen. Summoning these youths to the Church of the Holy Sepulchre, he awed and thrilled them by calling each one forward to kneel and be knighted. It was a solemn ceremony, conducted by candlelight in the most sacred church in Christendom, and their audience was moved to tears. Balian then shocked some of them by knighting forty more men. These new knights were well respected, pillars of the community. They were also burgesses, not of noble birth, and there were those who disapproved of Balian's action, viewing it as subversive, undermining the social order. Most of the trapped Jerusalemites were quite willing, though, to embrace whatever Balian did, seeing him as a gift from God, a man who knew warfare as they did not, the battle commander who would save them and their Holy City from an infidel army.

Balian had eaten little, slept even less, driven to get as much done as he could in the dwindling time they had left. By Sunday evening, he was so exhausted that he finally had to rest, and at Ernoul's urging, he agreed to sleep for an hour or so. Sprawling across the bed after pausing only to remove his boots, he fell asleep at once. When he was awakened by a hand on his shoulder, he felt as if he'd just closed his eyes. "Has Compline rung already?"

Renier shook his head. "No, not yet. But whilst you slept, Saladin's army arrived. They are setting up camp to the west. On the morrow . . ." He did not finish the sentence; there was no need. On the morrow, the Saracens would unleash hell upon Jerusalem.

The men of Jerusalem stood on the battlements, nervously clutching their weapons as they gazed upon the sultan's army. While many of them had convinced themselves that God would never let the Holy City fall to the infidels, their conviction wavered now that the day of judgment had actually arrived. Balian was one of the few who was encouraged by the sight meeting their eyes. Thousands of seasoned soldiers spread out below them, the victors of Ḥaṭṭīn. But Saladin had done what Balian had hoped he would do—he'd chosen to assault the city from the west, assuming that David's Tower had been built to bolster the walls where they were weakest. That was a mistake. Not only were these walls strongly buttressed, the terrain was very rough, choked with thorny underbrush and steep, rock-strewn slopes that would not make it easy for the Saracens to get close enough to fill in the fosse. The longer they could keep the sultan's men from reaching the walls, the more time they could buy for themselves.

Well aware that Jerusalem was a city without soldiers, Salāh al-Dīn and his amirs had not expected its defenders to put up much of a fight. But the assault did not go as planned. When they began to employ their siege engines, the Franks answered with their own mangonels, and it was soon apparent that theirs were more dangerous. Their height upon the tower roofs gave them a greater range and men scattered as rocks crashed down upon them. And when the Saracens launched their first attack, they found it was slow going. As they stumbled and lurched on the uneven ground, crossbow bolts and arrows found fleshy targets and stones were heaved from the walls, claiming victims, too. They were eventually forced to make a humiliating retreat.

The second day went no better for the Saracens. The mangonels of the Franks were operated in shifts so there was no respite, and several of their own siege engines were damaged by the lethal bombardment from the roof of David's Tower. The sultan and his amirs watched in frustrated fury as their men died without ever reaching the city walls.

On the third day of the siege, the Franks took the offensive, launching a sudden sortie as night fell. Salāh al-Dīn's men had withdrawn to their tents and their siege engines were not well guarded, for none of them thought civilians would dare to venture beyond their protective walls. So they were taken utterly by surprise when they found themselves confronted by charging horsemen. As they ran for safety, the Franks threw torches at several of their siege engines, then wheeled about and galloped off. By the time the chaos in the Saracen camp had settled down, it was too late. One of their mangonels was in flames and their foes were safely back in the city.

By the fifth day of the siege, nothing had changed. The Saracens had been unable to cross the fosse and their casualties were much heavier than they'd anticipated, while they knew the Franks' losses had been minimal. Another assault had failed to reach the walls and more men had been killed by the aerial onslaught from Tancred's and David's Towers; when the Franks ran out of rocks, Balian had sent men to dig up paving stones. Salāh al-Dīn met with his amirs and soon afterward, the Saracens' own mangonels fell silent. In late afternoon, men up on the walls began to shout and cheer, and people rushed from their houses and shops to be told that the sultan and his men were dismantling their mangonels and packing up. As the citizens watched in awe, the Saracen army moved off, eventually disappearing over the hills to the north of the city. Jerusalem erupted in joyful celebration, its citizens dazed by their sudden deliverance.

Later that night, Balian was summoned to the palace. The streets were still thronged with people on their way to churches to thank God or to taverns to savor their reprieve and he was cheered and applauded by all who recognized him. When he did not respond, they were not offended, agreeing that the poor man was simply exhausted, looking as if he'd not slept in days.

Upon Balian's arrival at the palace, Sybilla had the same reaction as the citizens in the streets, for he was unshaven, eyes swollen and bloodshot, clearly starved for sleep. "Balian, you are not ailing? Do you even remember when you last ate? Or slept?"

The patriarch did not share her solicitude, for he put a more ominous interpretation upon Balian's haggard appearance. D'Ibelin had accomplished a miracle, saved the Holy City from the infidels. So why was he not happier about it? "Although the siege is over," he said, "we may be still in danger. The people are dazzled, even besotted, by the sweetness of salvation, and who can blame them? But our future remains imperiled. Saladin can always come back—"

"He *will* be back."

Sybilla seemed genuinely surprised by Balian's words and he found himself thinking that she and Guy were well matched, both happily dwelling in a fool's paradise in which the only facts that mattered were the ones they chose to believe. At least the patriarch had a better grasp of reality, for he interrupted when Sybilla started to protest.

"How much time do you think we have ere he lays siege to Jerusalem again?"

"The siege is not over. When he broke camp today, he was not giving up. He was admitting he'd made a tactical mistake. Their army will return on the morrow and this time they will attack the most vulnerable sections of the wall, east of St. Stephen's Gate."

Balian paused, for he'd almost lost his train of thought. Until now, he'd not realized that fatigue can affect a man like too much wine. He'd pushed himself to the brink, but he did not see that he had a choice. Besides, there was a mercy in being too tired to think. He found one final truth for them, then, answering the question they feared to ask.

"No . . . we will not be able to keep them from breaking into the city." *Or from taking vengeance for all the blood spilled by the Franks when they took Jerusalem in God's year 1099.* For Sybilla's sake, he left that truth unspoken.

The city awoke the next morning to discover that the Saracens had returned. As Balian had predicted, they were now aiming their assault at the northern wall, following the trail blazed by the men of the first crusade, ironically aided by the large stone cross the crusaders had erected above the spot where they'd breached the wall.

Because they'd deluded themselves into believing that the threat was over, at least for now, the shock was shattering for the Jerusalemites. And they soon saw that they'd no longer be able to keep the enemy at a distance. It was now too risky to employ the siege engine on David's Tower, for if the arc fell short, the stones would slam down into the streets, killing their own citizens. While the mangonel on Tancred's Tower did not have to shoot over the city, they'd have to aim it at an angle and none of the novice operators had the requisite skill for that. Balian ordered the mangonels dismantled and reassembled atop St. Stephen's Gate, but without the height advantage, they'd forfeited the greater range that had proven so effective during the first part of the siege.

The Saracens were benefiting, too, from a sudden shift in the wind, blowing from the north instead of the usual westerlies at that time of year. They hastily loaded dirt into their mangonel buckets and sent it swirling up into the sky, creating dust storms that enveloped much of the city. These dust clouds drove coughing defenders from the walls and sent people scurrying for shelter. While the visibility was so dramatically diminished for the Franks, the sultan's soldiers advanced to the fore wall that fronted the city's northern wall. By now their mangonels were being rolled up and were soon in action. By day's end, they had already done more damage than they had during their five days' assault from the west.

The next two days were harrowing for the trapped civilians. The Saracens continued to assemble more and more siege engines. So many archers were shooting up at the defenders that it seemed to be raining arrows. On Saturday afternoon, Balian was summoned to the roof of St. Stephen's Gate, where he found Renier staring toward the east. "Look at that siege engine they're setting up," he said, "the one so much bigger than the others. Is that what I think it is?"

Balian studied it, then confirmed Renier's fears by muttering an obscenity. The trebuchet was still uncommon, too heavy to be wheeled like the mangonels, relying upon a counterweight to launch its load. It did not have the range of a mangonel, but it was more powerful and could propel boulders airborne, doing much more damage when they hit its target. It was also more accurate, and as they watched helplessly, the Saracen engineers initiated its maiden run. Winching down the verge, a long beam that pivoted on an axle, they loaded huge rocks into its sling. When the hook was released, the counterweight plunged downward and the beam shot up, the sling cracking like a whip as the rocks hurtled toward the city. They'd been aimed at the wall by the postern gate of St. Mary Magdalene, and they struck with a thunderous sound that reverberated throughout the Syrian Quarter.

As long as daylight lingered, the trebuchet continued to wreak havoc upon the walls, the rocks sometimes sailing over the battlements into the city, invariably followed by screams. With so many mangonels in action, the men up on the walls spent more time ducking for cover than shooting at the enemy army below them. Their own mangonels were still functioning, until a boulder roared down upon one, smashing the frame into kindling and killing all its operators.

On Sunday, the Saracens unleashed a new and even more terrifying weapon, using their trebuchet to launch a clay pot of the flammable liquid known as Greek fire. A panic broke out when it flew over the wall, a tail of fire trailing behind it. Balian dove for the battlement stairs, following its fiery descent until it disappeared from view. He could hear shouting coming from Jehoshaphat Street and headed in that direction. It had barely missed two shrines, the chapel of St. Savior and the house of Pontius Pilate. A nearby hospice for pilgrims was not as fortunate and when the clay pot shattered against the wooden door, it burst into flames.

Bystanders were kept away by the intensity of the heat, but a few men were running toward the bathhouse by Jehoshaphat's Gate, yelling that they'd fetch water. As Balian reached the scene, the hospice's shutters were jerked open and several of its panicky residents scrambled out onto the street. Balian and a priest hastened over to help them escape. Smoke and flames were spreading when two Templars emerged from the Templar compound, rolling a large barrel.

Balian yelled that they must not pour water on the fire. They ignored him, lifted the barrel, and dumped sand onto the burning door. Clad in the brown mantles of Templar serjeants, they were men long past their prime, judged too old to fight at Hattīn by Gerard de Ridefort, and they watched now with satisfaction as the fire slowly suffocated. Glancing toward Balian, one said, "We are not green lads. We learned long ago that Greek fire burns even brighter in water. Only sand can snuff it out, though vinegar helps, too." He paused, his grin belying his age. "Well, there is one other way. If the sand did not work, we were going to piss on it."

Both serjeants laughed at that, and after a moment, Balian joined in, for any opportunity to laugh was not to be spurned, not in the middle of a siege that could have only one ending.

Vespers had sounded, the churches filled to overflowing as people entreated the Almighty to protect them from their enemies and from the temptation to sin.

Many were convinced that Ḥaṭṭīn had been a test of faith and they'd failed it. Balian was offended by this increasingly popular explanation for the disaster that had befallen their kingdom, for it implied that the men who'd suffered and died on the Horns of Ḥaṭṭīn deserved their fate. He did not believe that their defeat was divine retribution for the sins of the Poulains and he thought few soldiers believed it, either. This argument was always made by priests. To his relief, he was spared this sort of harangue during the evening's sermon, and afterward he headed for the palace and a meeting with the queen and patriarch. He sought Isabella out first, though.

She looked so fragile to him that he silently cursed himself for not forcing her to leave the city with Maria. If she'd had moments, too, when she regretted her gallant impulsiveness, she was not willing to admit it, and they did not speak of regrets. Instead, she told him that her mother by marriage was still ailing and Sybilla had agreed to let Stephanie stay in the palace. She confided that she'd offered to help at the women's hospital run by the Hospitallers, which was housing hundreds of female refugees, but they did not think it seemly work for a king's daughter. And she asked him numerous questions about the mysterious Greek fire.

Balian was willing to indulge her curiosity, for that kept him from having to dwell upon the ordeal that lay ahead for her. Greek fire had been employed by the Greek emperors for centuries, mainly in sea battles, for it would burn upon the surface of the water. Its ingredients were a closely guarded secret, but the Saracens had eventually come up with a variation of their own. He was not sure about its elements; an alchemist had once told him it likely contained quicklime, sulfur, resin, naphtha, and pitch. He told her about the Templar serjeants and confirmed that they were right: whilst Greek fire could best be extinguished by sand, urine could also be used to fight it. So if they ran out of sand, he supposed they could always form squads of men ready, willing, and able to piss upon any future fires.

As he'd hoped, that made her smile. It lost its luster, though, when he rose to go, and she asked plaintively if he could not stay awhile longer. Shaking his head, he reached out and took her hands in his. "Remember what you promised me, Bella, that you will stay closer to Sybilla than her own shadow. Do not leave the palace again."

Wide-eyed, she agreed solemnly, and he had to content himself with that.

Sybilla and Eraclius listened as Balian told them that he'd ordered barrels of sand to be placed at strategic locations throughout the city in case the Saracens continued to make use of Greek fire. Sybilla was struggling with a severe headache and merely nodded. Eraclius pondered what he'd just heard. "You sound as if you do not expect the Saracens to keep hurling Greek fire at us. Why would they not do so? They frightened the people half out of their wits."

"If one of the fires got out of control, it could destroy much of the city. Saladin does not want to claim a smoldering, charred ruin." Balian could see that his honesty did not please them, but the time was long past for polite dissembling. "I fear the Saracens used the Greek fire as a distraction, a way of keeping us from recognizing the real danger. Soon after their return on Friday, they started to build cats—wooden structures to shelter their soldiers as they worked to fill in the moat. I think the cats were also meant for another purpose. Saladin has hundreds of men from Aleppo in his army."

They did not seem to understand the significance of that, so he said, "Aleppo is famed for its sappers, engineers skilled in mining. The Saracens are digging a tunnel."

That they did understand, for even noncombatants had heard stories of sieges in which castles or towns were taken when the attackers tunneled under the walls. Sybilla leaned back in her chair, rubbing her fingers against her throbbing temples. Eraclius had long ago mastered the requisite political skills that had enabled him to rise so high in the Church, one of which was his ability to conceal his thoughts from others. It failed him now, though; he paled visibly and his shoulders sagged like a man who'd just been blindsided. "Can we stop them?"

"No," Balian said wearily, "we cannot."

By Monday morning, the Saracen sappers had done what the sultan had required of them, excavating a tunnel of more than one hundred feet that burrowed under the foundation of the wall east of the postern gate of St. Mary Magdalene. They'd shored up the tunnel with wooden struts, and now set fire to them before hastily racing back to the surface. Their commanders had gathered to watch from a safe distance. After the props burned, the tunnel caved in and took down the section of wall above it. There was a loud rumble when it collapsed, so much dust kicked up that the wall was temporarily hidden from view. As it settled, they saw rubble strewn over a wide area and a breach in the wall, as if Allah had carved out a gate for the sultan's army to reclaim al-Quds. What happened next was even more dramatic and so symbolic that they burst into wild cheering. The large stone cross erected by the Franks to commemorate their victory eighty-eight years ago began to sway and then it came crashing down, shattering as it hit the ground. Their triumph was made all the sweeter by the wailing and screaming coming from the city as the unbelievers saw their cross brought low and realized that all was lost.

The patriarch rose to his feet as Balian entered. They both were exhausted, Balian having spent the day protecting the breach in the north wall and Eraclius trying to find men to defend it once night fell. Despite offering a generous bonus to anyone who'd guard the breach from dusk till dawn, he'd been unsuccessful. Gesturing toward a table with a wine flagon, he told Balian to help himself. "So how can we keep the Saracens from streaming into the city after dark? Have you any thoughts on that?"

"Build bonfires in the gap. The Templars did that when Saladin was besieging their castle at Jacob's Ford."

"A good idea," the prelate said approvingly. "Who can we get to tend the fires through the night?" Neither man mentioned that the bonfires had only delayed the inevitable. The fortress at Jacob's Ford had still fallen to the Saracens, with a great loss of life.

Balian said the Templar serjeants would be willing to guard the fires. He dispatched Ernoul to the Templar commandery and then accepted Eraclius's invitation to share the evening meal when he realized he'd not eaten all day. Eraclius did not think it was appropriate—or convenient—to use the patriarchal palace as a shelter for refugees. But he did not feel he could turn his fellow clerics away and some of the fugitives who'd flooded into Jerusalem were priests or monks. Feeding so many men was a logistical challenge and the great hall was so crowded that Eraclius had begun taking his own meals in his private quarters. He'd gone to the door to tell a servant that the Lord of Nablus would be his guest that evening when he saw one of the canons hastening across the cloisters toward him. After a brief exchange, he turned back to Balian, his expression that of a man pushed to the limits of his patience.

"Ere we can dine, I must talk with Father Jerome and some of his more fervid acolytes. Since you are in the wrong place at the wrong time, you will have that privilege, too."

Balian understood the patriarch's sardonic tone, for he'd also had several encounters with Father Jerome, the parish priest of St. John the Evangelist, and those whom Eraclius dryly dubbed his acolytes. Theirs were the loudest voices insisting that Hattin was God's punishment and Balian had found them to be more harmful than helpful as he'd organized Jerusalem's defenses. Their dire proclamations and street-corner sermons kept the populace in a state of frenzy. Instead of volunteering to man the walls, Father Jerome led processions of priests and nuns through the city, and fearful citizens soon swelled their ranks, seeking to show the Almighty the depths of their remorse. Balian said nothing, but he was no more pleased than Eraclius. *What now?*

When Father Jerome was ushered into the chamber, his followers crowded in behind him. Some were priests. Some were too old to fight, others too young. Among them were pilgrims unlucky enough to have taken the cross in a year of jihad. Affluent merchants stood beside men who'd sometimes had to beg for bread. A few looked as if they'd spilled their share of blood, if only in tavern brawls or dark alleys. All they had in common was that they were male and they were drunk on despair.

Balian and the patriarch were not long kept in suspense, for Father Jerome was eager to reveal his overwrought vision. The city was doomed now that the wall had been breached, he declared, but they need not cower in their homes and churches awaiting slaughter like sheep. No, they could ride out to confront the accursed infidels and die like men, killing as many heathens as they could in the name of the Lord of Hosts and His Beloved Son, and by their sacrifice earning holy martyrdom.

"We come for your blessings, my lord patriarch, and to invite you to join us as we ride to glory everlasting. You, too, lord." Father Jerome included Balian with obvious reluctance. He believed those who'd fought at Haṭṭīn were tainted by their defeat, having been judged and found wanting by the Almighty, all save Reynald de Chatillon, who'd died for Christ in Saladin's tent.

This was to be one of the rare times when Balian and Eraclius were in complete harmony. Exchanging a quick glance to confirm that they had the same opinion of this vainglorious suicide mission, they shocked the men by rejecting it out of hand. Balian thought the patriarch's objections would carry more weight with them, so he confined himself to just one question. "What of the thousands left behind as you ride out to seek martyrdom?"

Eraclius was even blunter. "I could never bless such a selfish undertaking," he said coolly, evoking a chorus of gasps and indrawn breaths. "For every able-bodied man in the city, there are more than ten women and children, as well as the elderly and the ailing. If we could save them by offering up our own lives, I would approve. But once we are dead, they will be at the mercy of the Saracens. Whilst we embrace salvation, they will be slain or enslaved and, worst of all, many will be forced to renounce the faith of Jesus Christ, especially the children, and their souls will be lost to God."

Not all of the men were willing to give up the intoxicating appeal of martyrdom and they continued to argue for dramatic battlefield deaths. But in reminding them of the most vulnerable, many of them their own families, Eraclius had forced them to see their intended action in a harsher, less heroic light. Eventually a blacksmith posed the question that signified the patriarch had prevailed. "I'll die defending my woman if it comes to that. But is there no longer any chance of avoiding a massacre?"

Eraclius and Balian had asked themselves that, too, in the four days since the siege resumed. Neither man had much hope, for they could think of no way to persuade Saladin to disavow his oath to take the city by the sword. But if there was even the faintest chance, they had to try. As all eyes turned toward Balian, he got to his feet. "On the morrow," he said, "I will ride out to Saladin's camp and do my best to convince him to accept our surrender."

Soon after sunrise, Balian rode out of Jehoshaphat's Gate. He was alone, protected only by a flag of truce, and had no idea what to expect from the Saracen soldiers. Saladin's command tent was pitched on the Mount of Olives, so he guided Bayard in that direction.

Some of the most popular pilgrimages were to sites on or near the Mount of Olives: the cave of Gethsemane, where the Lord Christ has been betrayed by Judas, the chapel built around the rock where Jesus had prayed before his arrest, the tomb of the Blessed Virgin in the church of St. Mary, now enclosed within a Benedictine monastery. Balian assumed that Saladin would destroy the abbey, but he hoped the sultan would spare Mary's crypt, for she was beloved by many Muslims, the only woman to be mentioned by name in the Qur'an. The True Cross had been lost because of the blunders of their rulers, yet surely their ancient holy sites would survive the death of their kingdom? As he rode toward the Saracen camp, Balian sought to keep his thoughts upon the fate of these sacred shrines, for then he could avoid thinking of the thousands of men, women, and children under sentence of death and dependent upon him to save them.

To his relief, he encountered no open enmity. The Saracens merely glanced at his flag of truce and then moved aside to let him pass. He wondered if they'd been told to expect an overture from the Franks; if so, did that mean Saladin was willing to listen to what he had to say? He was nearing the sultan's camp when a man rode out to meet him. Mounted on a chestnut stallion that reminded Balian of Kham-sin, al-'Ādil reined in beside him. "I was hoping you'd come."

As they rode toward the camp, Balian was greatly encouraged by what al-'Ādil told him. He wanted Balian to convince his brother to accept the surrender of the city. Many of their amirs did, too. Their reasons were pragmatic ones. If al-Quds was taken by storm, it would be plundered by their soldiers. If it surrendered, the city's riches would go into the sultan's treasury. He needed the money, al-'Ādil admitted, for his generosity was as lavish as it was legendary.

This made sense to Balian and he decided to stress the practical benefits of allowing the city to yield. "It gladdens me that you and I are in agreement about the wisdom of a peaceful surrender," he said, and the sultan's brother shrugged.

"We'd rather avoid any more deaths." He paused before adding very dryly, "Had the sultan known you'd be so good at commanding their defenses, I think he'd have insisted that you honor your vow to depart the city with your family."

"We want to avoid any more deaths, too," Balian said, so fervently that the other man gave him a searching glance and then an unexpected smile, one that held something almost like sympathy.

"It cannot have been easy, being acclaimed as a savior by a city of terrified people."

Impressed by his insight, Balian confessed that it was an experience he could have done without. As their eyes met, he offered a heartfelt thank-you, a bit em-barrassed by the emotion suddenly surging into his voice.

Al-'Ādil seemed to understand, for he responded with surprising candor. "You owe me no thanks. I want this for my brother. If he insists upon honoring his oath to take al-Quds by the sword, I fear that he'll come to regret it. He does not like to shed blood unless he deems it absolutely necessary, as with the Templars." When he smiled again, this one was more familiar to Balian, for it was flavored with ironic amusement. "Nor would history treat him kindly for a slaughter of thou-sands of women and children, and like all great men, he cares how posterity will judge him."

By now they'd reached the sultan's command tent. After they dismounted, al-'Ādil handed his reins to Balian, telling him he should wait there until summoned. Once he disappeared into the tent, Balian found himself the focus of hundreds of eyes, some angry, others challenging, all curious. Studying the faces of these Sara-cen soldiers, he decided that many of them wanted a peaceful resolution to the siege, too, and for the first time, he allowed himself the luxury of hope, allowed himself to believe that Jerusalem would be spared the carnage promised by Saladin.

He was not sure how much time had elapsed since al-'Ādil had entered the tent, but it seemed a long while. He was mentally rehearsing what he would say when the sultan's brother finally reemerged. One glance at his face and Balian went cold, an icy shiver shooting up his spine as if it were the dead of winter, not a day of summery September warmth.

"I am sorry," al-'Ādil said softly. "He refuses to see you. He says there is nothing to be said."

CHAPTER 51

September 1187
Jerusalem, Outremer

B alian had become the most recognizable man in the city and as soon as he rode through Jehoshaphat's Gate, people flocked to him, begging for salvation. He could only shake his head and had to watch as understanding dawned on their upturned faces, as hope died. By the time he reached the palace, word had spread, and when he was ushered into the queen and patriarch's presence, they remained seated, staring at him in shock. Trying not to sound defensive, he told them of the sultan's rebuff. It was not easy, for he felt that they were blaming him for his failure. And why not? He had failed them, after all.

"He would not even see you?" Sybilla's chin trembled as she sought to keep her voice level. Never had she felt so overwhelmed, so utterly alone. She knew she should address the people; that was what queens did. But what could she say to them? Baldwin would have known. That thought was both unexpected and insidious, for it led her dangerously close to a conclusion she could not live with—that although her brother had been stricken with the most loathsome of all diseases, he had held their kingdom together and kept the Saracens at bay for nigh on eleven years, whilst her husband's kingship had not even lasted a twelvemonth.

As Balian turned to go, Eraclius found his voice. "What are you going to do now?"

Balian glanced back at the patriarch. Eraclius had done his share to bring them to this. But what did it matter now? "I will try to keep them out of the city as long as possible."

By day's end, they still controlled the breach in the wall, gaining one more night's reprieve. As the sky darkened, Renier came over and put his hand on Balian's arm. "Go home. Try to get some sleep. I'll make sure we keep the fires burning."

Balian was too tired to argue. As he started for home, he was not surprised that the streets were still so crowded. All day long, priests had led penitential processions around the city, most of the people barefoot and some in sackcloth and ashes to show the Almighty the depths of their remorse for past sins. Looking at the bloodied footprints left by women unaccustomed to going without shoes, Balian felt an overpowering weariness, both of the body and soul. But when he approached his town house, he paused only briefly before continuing along St. Stephen's Street. Despite his exhaustion, he was sure he'd not be able to sleep, and he did not want to lie awake in the bed he'd shared with Maria as time ran out for the Holy City.

He'd not realized he had a destination in mind, not until he turned right when he reached the Street of the Holy Sepulchre and began to walk beside the wall bordering the church. He attracted glances from passersby, some of them hostile, for they'd anointed him with their trust, to no avail. One woman with a baby in her arms and a toddler clinging to her skirts cried out when she recognized him, asking why Saladin would not show mercy. He had no answer for her.

The main entrance into the Holy Sepulchre was through two bronze-covered double doors on its south side. There was a closer entrance from the Street of the Patriarch and Balian headed toward it. When he descended the stairs into the rotunda, he was not surprised to find the church packed with people wanting to feel closer to God in the hours they had left.

As always, there was a long line waiting to get into the Lord Christ's tomb. Only five at a time could fit into the small space, so the priory usually had porters there to keep the crowd from becoming unruly. There were none in sight now, and there was some pushing and shoving as people waited their turn. Balian detoured around the sacred sepulchre and into the southern transept, where their kings were buried. Baldwin's tomb was flanked on one side by his father's sarcophagus, on the other by the pitifully small tomb of his nephew. Reaching out, Balian rested his hand upon the smooth marble. In a life of great suffering, at least Baldwin had been spared this. Yet Ḥaṭṭīn would never have happened if Baldwin could only have lived a few more years.

Acceptance was so much more difficult without understanding. How often had Baldwin asked why? Had he finally realized that all he could do was to echo the anguished words of the Lord Christ in the garden of Gethsemane? The words came unbidden to Balian's lips, for he'd often heard William quote them, the only answer the archbishop could offer when despairing men and women came to him for spiritual comfort. "'Father, if Thou be willing, remove this cup from me: nevertheless not my will, but Thine, be done.'"

"Forgive me, my lord. I . . . I did not know that you were praying."

Balian spun around at the sound of a female voice. A woman was standing beside him, a stranger clad in black, her clothes threadbare, her hands so reddened and rough that she was likely a laundress. "Forgive me," she said again. "When I saw you, I . . . just had to ask. This is my daughter." Only then did Balian notice the girl. She was easily overlooked, reed thin and sallow, as timid as a fawn. Balian guessed her to be about nine, the same age as his Helvis, and was surprised when her mother said that she was twelve before saying softly, "If I cut her hair short and dress her as a lad, would . . . would that spare her from shame when the city falls?"

Balian looked at the trembling girl and for a dreadful moment, she *was* Helvis. Knowing that the only comfort he could offer was a lie, he said, "It might," and winced as he saw her smile. She was still stammering her thanks when one of the priory canons strode over. Paying her no heed whatsoever, he urged Balian to follow him, saying his help was greatly needed.

Balian was irked by the man's officious attitude. He recognized him as one of the church porters, though, so he asked what was amiss. The canon was steering him toward the stairs leading up to the chapel of Mount Calvary and when he glanced back, the woman and her daughter had vanished. As they climbed the stairs, they heard the muffled sound of wailing and the cleric launched into a bizarre rant about women carrying cauldrons into the chapel and setting them up before the rock where the Lord's cross once stood.

"I tried to stop them, my lord, but they would not listen. They lured me away from the vestibule so they could bring the cauldrons up the outdoor stairs into the Chapel of the Crucifixion. They insist they are doing penance. It is most inappropriate, though, to have female nudity in so holy a site." Flinging open the door to Mount Calvary, he said indignantly, "There, see for yourself that I spoke the truth!"

The sight that met Balian's eyes was one that he knew he'd never forget, however long the Almighty allowed him to live. Large iron cauldrons had been dragged toward the altar of the Lord's Suffering and filled with cold water. Frantic women had then forced their daughters to strip and climb into the tubs, where they crouched, shivering, their teeth chattering, some weeping, others enduring the ordeal in silence, their faces streaking with tears. A few tried to protest as their mothers hacked away at their hair, cutting it down to the scalp and then flinging the shorn hair onto the floor in front of the altar as if it were an offering to placate their wrathful God. It was a scene that sickened Balian, for the girls were obviously terrified. If they survived the city's fall, their last memories of their mothers would be the madness of fear. He would have stopped it if he could, but he knew his interference would only make it worse.

"See their shame!" the canon hissed. "Naked in God's house as if it were a bordel, exposing their daughters to the eyes of strange men. And look what they have done to this holy chapel. They have scratched the marble floor with those cauldrons and soaked it with water! Can you not halt this sacrilege, my lord?"

There were screams from a few girls as they saw the two men standing in the doorway, although most were too numb to react. Balian jerked his arm away when the canon grabbed the sleeve of his hauberk. "You'd do better to worry about the blood soon to be soaking these floors," he snapped. He at once regretted it, for the cleric's face turned a sickly shade of grey. Balian did not apologize, though, turning toward the stairs. But if he could no longer see those quaking girls, he imagined he could still hear their sobbing even after he'd gotten out of earshot.

Moving into the canons' choir, he stood, irresolute, not knowing where to go. The Holy Sepulchre might be the most sacred church in Christendom, but it was no place to pray, not tonight, not when it was more crowded than the busiest market, not when it had become a flooded receptacle for the city's fears. He supposed he could go in search of another church—if he had the energy. Before he could decide, he heard a familiar voice call out, "Lord Balian!"

Anselm was hurrying across the choir toward him. "You came, too, to bid farewell to our king," he said gratefully, then confided that he'd just sprinkled holy water over King Baldwin's tomb. Seeing Balian's puzzlement, he smiled. "I wanted to give him one last gift. I usually bring flowers, but all I could find were some wilted Michaelmas daisies."

Anselm actually sounded cheerful and Balian found himself returning the other man's smile. "I wish I knew your secret," he confessed. "You may be the only one in the city who seems at peace tonight."

"I am an old man, am ready to be reunited with my young king after my stint in Purgatory." Glancing around, Anselm lowered his voice when he saw several children close by. "I do not fear dying, have been shriven of my sins. But I do dread having to kill Cairo. I cannot leave him to fend for himself, though, for all know the Saracens have no liking for dogs. I'd not have him starve. Am I doing right by him, you think, giving him a quick death?"

Balian nodded, and his gaze rested for a moment on those nearby youngsters. Were there parents in the city who'd want to spare their children suffering, like Anselm and his dog? Could any of them commit so grievous a sin, one that would deny them salvation? Horrified by his own thoughts, he shook his head as if that might somehow banish them to the back of his brain, and bade Anselm good night, saying he needed to find a quiet place in which to pray.

"I know one, my lord." Anselm beckoned for Balian to follow. The chapel was tucked away in the far northeast corner of the church and Balian stumbled as they entered, for it was a few steps below ground level. It was very small and dark. It was also deserted, which seemed almost miraculous when every nook and cranny of the church was filled with repentant sinners and fearful supplicants.

"Wait here, my lord. I'll be right back," Anselm promised, returning with a lit candle. As he set the candle upon the small altar, Balian realized where he was, in the Prison of Christ. It was here that the Savior had been held with the two thieves as their crosses were being prepared for their crucifixion. It was usually a popular pilgrimage site, but Balian understood why it would now be shunned. Tonight of all nights, desperate Jerusalemites would not want to be reminded of their Lord's suffering as he awaited one of the most agonizing deaths known to the Roman world. They needed hope, preferring to flock to the tomb where the weeping women had been told, "Why seek ye the living amongst the dead? He is not here. He has risen!"

❀

Balian had lost track of time. He could have been kneeling before the small altar for an hour or for several hours. He'd pleaded for the citizens of Jerusalem, entreating God to show them mercy even if Saladin would not. And he'd prayed for divine guidance. Eventually, he'd prayed, too, for acceptance, to be able to embrace God's will, no matter what it might be.

When he finally rose to his feet, he moved around the little chapel until moving no longer hurt, hunching his shoulders so his head would not scrape the low ceiling. On one wall hung a length of chain, said to be the very one that had bound the Son of God. Balian touched his fingers to the links even though he doubted their authenticity. Like many people, he was skeptical of some of the holy relics that churches so proudly displayed to pilgrims. Hay from the Christ Child's manger? A long-dead saint's fingernail clippings? He'd heard that when the devout came to Canterbury Cathedral to honor the martyred Thomas Becket, they could buy small vials of the saint's blood. Becket must have bled enough to flood the cathedral, for he'd been dead for nigh on seventeen years and the monks were still selling those vials to pilgrims.

But relics in his homeland were different, far more likely to be real, not a hoax or a fraud. The Lord Christ had walked the streets of Jerusalem. Balian could think of dozens of sites intimately associated with the Savior. He'd watered the Mount of Olives with his tears and Golgotha with his blood. Four of the fourteen stations of the cross were to be found in this very church. How could the Almighty allow the Holy Land to be lost to the Saracens?

Coming back to the altar, he leaned against it, watching as the candle's flame flickered and the wick burned down. He'd been going over his meeting that morning with the sultan's brother, searching his memory for clues. Al-'Ādil had been surprisingly candid, acknowledging that he and many of Saladin's amirs preferred a peaceful surrender of the city. Only Saladin had balked. Why? Balian doubted that he truly wanted a bloodbath. The only towns that had suffered after Ḥaṭṭīn were those that had refused to yield. He'd even allowed Ascalon and Beirut to surrender after holding out for a week or two. And according to al-'Ādil, he'd been willing to offer Jerusalem generous terms, too, swearing to take the city by the sword only after he'd been provoked by those fools in the Jerusalem delegation.

Standing there in the quiet, darkened chapel, Balian could hear al-'Ādil's voice again, sounding both amused and affectionate. "Nor would history treat him kindly for a slaughter of thousands of women and children, and like all great men, he cares how posterity will judge him." Saladin had valid reasons to want to avoid a massacre. What he needed then was a valid reason to disavow his oath. But surely al-'Ādil and the other amirs had made all of the arguments in favor of surrender. What could he say that they had not?

The next morning, the sky was marbled with clouds, an unusual occurrence for the first day of October. But the citizens of Jerusalem had no thoughts for the weather. Soon after dawn, the sultan's siege engines were in action again, pounding the walls and clearing the streets. So there were few witnesses as Balian rode through the city toward Jehoshaphat's Gate.

The guards opened the gate for him, but they were clearly skeptical of his chances for success. He ignored them, concerned with getting safely to the sultan's camp on the Mount of Olives. The Saracens had just launched another assault upon the breach that had gashed the city's defenses like a bleeding wound. Once again, though, he found that he had either a perpetual safe-conduct or a guardian angel, for he was allowed to pass through their ranks, waved on when he claimed that the sultan's brother was expecting him.

Escorted by a sentry to al-'Ādil's command tent, he was dismounting from

Bayard when al-ʿĀdil emerged. After a quick scrutiny of Balian's face, he said, "I've seen men looking better than you as they were about to be sewn into their burial shrouds." Telling one of his guards to see to Balian's stallion, he pulled back the tent flap so Balian could enter. "Stay here," he said, "and I will do my best to persuade my brother to talk with you."

Balian nodded and murmured, "*Insha'Allah,*" Arabic for "God willing." The phrase was a subtle reminder that they shared a belief in one God and that the Muslims viewed Christians as "people of the book." He thought he caught a gleam of amused understanding in al-ʿĀdil's dark eyes, but before Balian could be sure, the other man had gone. Left alone, he sank down upon a cushion to ease his aching muscles. After another sleepless night, his body was punishing him for it, and this morning he felt as if he were decades older than his thirty-seven years. He tried not to dwell upon his coming confrontation with Saladin. His brain would not cooperate, though; it kept stirring up doubts. Could he be convincing enough? Could he carry this off?

He was expecting a summons to the sultan's tent—if al-ʿĀdil was successful. So, he was startled when the canvas flap was pulled aside and the sultan himself entered. Giving Balian no chance to rise, he strode forward and sat down on one of the cushions. He was followed by al-ʿĀdil, but the latter's face was expressionless, offering Balian no hints or guidance.

Salāh al-Dīn did not keep him in suspense. "I agreed to see you as a courtesy to my brother. But there is nothing you can say to change my mind. I offered your people a chance to save themselves. They scorned my mercy. So, let them pay the blood debt the Franks owe for their massacre of the innocent."

He seemed genuinely angry; Balian did not think it was assumed. Was he the object of the sultan's anger? He might well have repented of his generosity to the d'Ibelin family, for it had cost Muslim lives. Or was he angry at being compelled to act against his own nature, regretting an oath given impulsively? "I do not defend the slaughter that took place when Jerusalem fell to the Franks, my lord sultan. Even at the time, their brutality was not approved by all Christians. But the men who accrued that blood debt are long dead. There is no one in the city who was even alive in July of God's year 1099."

"The voices of our dead cry out for justice," the sultan shot back. Before Balian could respond, they heard sudden shouting. Al-ʿĀdil opened the tent flap, a moment later calling for his brother to join him. When Salāh al-Dīn rose, Balian did, too, and followed them outside.

There was considerable excitement in the camp. At the sight of the sultan, several of his men pointed toward Jerusalem. "Look, my lord, look!"

All eyes were on the city walls, where fighting had broken out upon the battlements. When the sultan's banner was hoisted aloft, the men began to cheer and laugh. Salāh al-Dīn turned upon Balian, fiercely triumphant. "You are too late, d'Ibelin. The city is mine."

Balian was speechless, unable to take his despairing gaze from those distant ramparts. But as he watched, the Franks launched a desperate counterattack and drove the Saracens back. Several were pushed from the wall and the sultan's banner was flung down after them, the others retreating through the breach. The camp was suddenly silent. Salāh al-Dīn's mouth hardened. Glaring at Balian, he said, "Go back to the city. I've nothing more to say to you."

Balian stood his ground. "Listen to me, my lord. You need to hear what I have to say."

Salāh al-Dīn scowled. But his brother was also frowning, urging him to hear Balian out, so he nodded curtly and they returned to al-'Ādil's tent in a tense silence. Once they were sitting again, the sultan gestured, indicating that Balian could speak.

Now that the moment had come, Balian found that time seemed to slow down, as it did whenever he'd taken part in a battlefield charge. "We both know that the city will soon be yours. I entreat you not to stain a great victory with the blood of the defenseless. You are a man of clemency and mercy, my lord, as you've often proven. Show that mercy to the women and children sheltering in al-Quds."

Al-'Ādil flashed Balian an approving grin for the use of *al-Quds* rather than *Jerusalem*. Salāh al-Dīn no longer seemed angry; he suddenly looked weary, as weary as Balian. "I cannot grant your plea, Lord Balian," he said somberly. "I have sworn a holy oath to take the city by the sword, to avenge the deaths of the thousands who were slain by the unbelievers."

Balian had been expecting this reply. "My lord sultan, understand that there is no enmity in my heart. I am grateful for the kindness you showed my family. I came only to rescue my wife and children. I never meant to stay or to take command of the city's defenses."

"You have acted in good faith," the sultan agreed. "But I do not see what that has to do with the fate of al-Quds."

"I wanted to be sure that you remember I have been honest with you from the first, for I am being honest with you now, too. You need to know what it will cost you if you insist upon taking the city by storm. We want to live. But if we are denied your mercy, we shall sell our lives dearly. If we see that death is inevitable, we shall slay our women and our sons, leaving none alive for you to enslave. We will burn all our property and goods and kill our livestock, so you will not benefit by so much as a single denier. There are over five thousand Muslim prisoners in the city and we shall put them all to death. Then we will destroy the shrines you hold most sacred, the Dome of the Rock and the al-Aqsa mosque, and come forth to do battle with your army. We know we will be riding out to die, but there are none so dangerous as men with nothing to lose. Ere you kill us, we will kill many of you. And when the battle is done and you can lay claim to the city, you will find only ashes and cinders and rubble and bodies."

Balian had spoken in measured, matter-of-fact tones, knowing there was no need for drama or hyperbole, not when he was describing an apocalypse. When he was done, he leaned back, seeking to judge the impact of his ultimatum upon them. Al-'Ādil's eyes had widened slightly when Balian had begun to speak and a muscle was twitching in the sultan's cheek. Otherwise, their faces gave away no secrets, their thoughts hidden.

They exchanged a look he could not read, then both men rose to their feet without haste. "You were right, Lord Balian," the sultan said coolly. "I did need to hear what you had to say." For a moment, he regarded Balian impassively, his eyes utterly inscrutable. "You are a man of surprises. You may wait here whilst we discuss what you have said with my amirs."

Balian would have thought waiting would be intolerable with so much at stake. It was not. He was aware only of an eerie sense of calm, knowing he'd done all that he could. He'd even begun to doze, jerking awake when the tent flap was pulled aside and al-'Ādil entered.

"Napping, were you? What do you have in your veins, ice water?"

Balian explained that he'd not slept in days, his eyes searching al-'Ādil's face all the while. "What did the sultan decide?"

A corner of al-'Ādil's mouth was curving. "I think you know. He has taken the counsel of his amirs and he has decided to accept the peaceful surrender of al-Quds."

Balian exhaled his breath as a prayer, a whispered "Thank God."

As he started to rise, al-'Ādil reached down to help him to his feet. "I've come to take you to the sultan's tent to discuss the terms of surrender." He made no move to go, though. "That was a most memorable threat. Did you mean it?"

"What do you think?" Balian parried, and al-'Ādil laughed, then reached for the tent flap.

'Imād al-Dīn had taken ill after Ḥaṭṭīn and was convalescing in Damascus, so al-'Ādil's chancellor, al-Sanī'a, was chosen to record the surrender terms. Balian recognized two of the men he'd met at Ascalon: the sultan's nephew Ḥusām al-Dīn and the lawyer 'Īsā al-Hakkari. He recognized, too, a man he'd not seen for twelve years, for Taqī al-Dīn had not changed at all; he still had the hawklike features and a smoldering intensity that never seemed to burn itself out. Also present was the amir Balian had faced at Ḥaṭṭīn, Gökböri, the Blue Wolf. They greeted him amicably, clearly pleased that he'd been able to convince the sultan to accept the city's surrender; even Taqī al-Dīn was civil. Two of Salāh al-Dīn's young sons were there, too, visibly excited that they were to reclaim the city so holy to Muslims. They were being careful, though, not to gloat, seeking to emulate their father's composed demeanor. There was an unreality about the scene for Balian, yet that had often been true since Ḥaṭṭīn. There were times when he'd felt that he was trapped in the mother of all bad dreams. But reality came crashing down upon him when the sultan named a ransom figure far beyond their ability to pay.

"Thirty dinars for every man, ten for every woman, and five for every child?" Balian echoed, hoping he'd heard wrong. When Salāh al-Dīn calmly confirmed it, Balian shook his head slowly. "My lord sultan, we could never raise such a high ransom. There are about sixty thousand people in the city, mayhap more, and I would guess that for every one who could pay their own ransom, there are one hundred who could not scrape together even two dinars."

"How many poor are there?"

Balian paused to consider. "I would say at least twenty thousand, not including all the refugees who lost everything when they fled their homes."

Now it was Salāh al-Dīn's turn to consider. "I am willing, then, to free them all for the sum of one hundred thousand dinars."

"We could never come up with so great an amount." Balian could not hide his dismay, for once again the fate of thousands of Jerusalemites was resting upon his shoulders; he may have saved their lives, but any who could not ransom themselves would be sold as slaves.

The sultan asked how much the Franks *could* pay to ransom their poor. Before Balian could reply, 'Īsā al-Hakkari interceded. Experienced in negotiations and a good judge of character, he did not think the Frankish lord was dissembling, and that meant they had a long and arduous bargaining session ahead of them. "May I suggest that we have food sent in?" he murmured. "It seems that we will be at this for quite a while."

When the Saracens suddenly pulled back, the city's residents were thankful, but they saw it as only a brief respite, sure that their foes would soon launch the final, fatal attack. But then the sultan's siege engines fell silent. Venturing cautiously from their houses and shops, the Jerusalemites clustered in the streets to discuss this unexpected lull. A rumor soon spread—that Balian d'Ibelin had been seen riding out to the Saracen camp that morning. And as the hours passed without a resumption of hostilities, people dared to hope that he had somehow managed to save Jerusalem. A crowd gathered by the palace, an even larger crowd by Jehoshaphat's Gate, and when Balian finally returned, he was welcomed with excitement that bordered on euphoria. While he was touched by their rejoicing, his own spirits were unable to soar with theirs, tethered by the bleak knowledge that there would not be a good outcome for them all.

Balian's welcome at the palace was only a little less frenzied. So many people were waiting that they had to meet in the great hall. Flanked by the patriarch and queen, Balian gave them the details of the deal he'd struck with Salāh al-Dīn. They would formally surrender the city on the morrow, handing over the keys to David's Tower. The sultan would then station guards in each street to make sure both the Saracens and Franks would keep the peace. The ransom had been set at ten dinars for every man, five for every woman, and two for every child, and they would be allowed to take with them all of their movable goods. Those able to pay their ransoms would be escorted to safety in Christian territory by the sultan's men.

Balian was bracing himself to tell them the rest—the worst—when his stepdaughter asked what would befall those who were too poor to pay the ransom. Isabella's dark eyes were so sorrowful that it was obvious she suspected what the answer would be.

"They will have their lives spared, but they will be sold as slaves. Some will be freed, though. The sultan has agreed to ransom seven thousand of the poor for a single payment of thirty thousand dinars. And I am sure that the Church, the Templars, the Hospitallers, and the more prosperous of our citizens will also assist those unable to pay."

Balian did not get the wholehearted response he'd hoped for from his audience, despite being the ones most able to aid their indigent countrymen. It grew quiet as they absorbed what they'd just been told, a silence finally broken when the patriarch of the Armenian Orthodox Church asked Balian how he could come up with the vast sum of thirty thousand dinars.

"The Hospitallers are still holding thirty thousand dinars for the English king," Balian said, reminding them that whilst the grand master of the Templars had used their share to finance the Ḥaṭṭīn campaign, the Hospitallers had refused to release their funds without King Henry's prior approval. He'd had no luck getting them to offer any of it for the city's defenses, either. But he was not going to be thwarted again, not when that money could buy freedom for seven thousand Jerusalemites.

Eraclius at once backed Balian up, saying that it was the duty of all Christians to come to the aid of their less fortunate brethren. Sybilla echoed the sentiment and urged them to open their hearts and empty their coffers for the city's needy. Only the most cynical among them noted that the patriarch had said nothing of spending the Church's wealth on behalf of the poor.

On the following day, the city of Jerusalem was formally turned over to Salāh al-Dīn, to the great jubilation of his amirs and soldiers. They watched as the banners of the Kingdom of Jerusalem were lowered and replaced by the sultan's eagle, and many of the Franks wept. Now that the initial joy of their reprieve had passed, they faced a brutal truth, that they would be abandoning their homes, their shops, their churches, the only lives they'd known, for a future obscured by uncertainty and peril. Nothing would ever be the same. And throughout Christendom, they would be blamed and reviled as the ones who'd lost the Holy City to the infidels.

The Hospitallers left behind in Jerusalem were accustomed to obeying orders, not to acting on their own initiative. So Balian and Eraclius found that they were still reluctant to release the money in their custody, insisting they needed the authorization of the English king or their acting grand master in Tyre. They yielded, though, after the patriarch gave them a scathing lecture about Christian charity and Balian pointed out that the Saracens were not going to let them depart the city with thirty thousand dinars in their saddlebags. After turning the funds over to Salāh al-Dīn, Balian began trying to raise more money for the rest of the city's poor, and the Saracens set up a collection plan for the ransoms.

In theory, it sounded feasible. People could leave Jerusalem only after displaying a receipt given by the sultan's clerks as proof of payment, and once they exited the city, they were to camp outside its walls while arrangements were being made to convey them to Tyre, Tripoli, and Antioch. But when 'Imād al-Dīn arrived from Damascus, he discovered to his dismay that in practice, the system was easily abused. Some of the Saracen guards were willing to be bribed. Desperate Franks climbed over the walls at night; others were caught sneaking out of the city in Saracen garb. And the collection process was repeatedly sabotaged by the generosity of 'Imād al-Dīn's master, for Salāh al-Dīn rarely turned away a supplicant. When his amirs asked to share the ransoms, he agreed at once, for money mattered little to him. He rewarded their soldiers with a lavish hand. And he was equally magnanimous when appealed to by the women of Jerusalem.

'Imād al-Dīn was baffled that his sultan had allowed the unbelievers' queen to depart with all of her possessions, charging no ransom for her or her household and giving her permission to join her husband, who was now being held captive in Nablus. Saladin did not even demand a ransom from Stephanie de Milly, the widow of their great enemy, Prince Arnat. And when some of the Frankish women came to him after paying their ransoms, weeping that they had nowhere to go, for their husbands were either slain at Hattīn or held prisoner in Damascus, he told 'Imād al-Dīn to free the husbands and to give money from his own coffers to the widows. 'Imād al-Dīn did as the sultan bade him, but he was not happy about it.

What upset the chancellor the most, however, was the duplicity of some of the Franks. Their patriarch had paid the ransoms for his household, which included a veiled woman said to be his concubine, the notorious Pasque de Rivieri, and their daughter. He'd then packed up the treasures of their Church, filling carts with the gold and silver plate, the costly fabrics, and the gem-encrusted chalices and reliquaries that had adorned the Holy Sepulchre. 'Imād al-Dīn had been indignant enough to go to the sultan about this blatant breach of the terms of surrender. He'd argued that the Franks were to take only their own goods, that nothing had been said about the property of their churches. Their patriarch ought not to be allowed to enrich himself at their expense, especially since he could have ransomed many more of their poor with those relics.

Salāh al-Dīn had agreed it was not honorable, calling the patriarch "an unholy man." But he'd refused to interfere, saying, "I'd not give the unbelievers any grounds for accusing the People of the Faith of breaking faith." So 'Imād al-Dīn could only fume in private, torn between frustration at his lord's impracticality and admiration for his indifference to the material trappings of their world.

Many of the poorer Franks were forced to sell their belongings to raise their ransoms; their goods were bought at bargain prices by the Saracen merchants of the *suq al 'askar*, which traveled with their armies and supplied food for their soldiers. The Syrian Christians still had to pay their ransoms, but they were spared exile and allowed to stay in the city as dhimmis, reverting to their former status as "protected people." They, too, purchased goods very cheaply from their banished neighbors, which increased the rancor and resentment between the Christians of Constantinople and Rome. There was no violence, though; Salāh al-Dīn's soldiers saw to that.

Since over forty-five thousand Franks would be departing the city, they were split into three groups of fifteen thousand each, to be led by the Templars, the Hospitallers, and lastly Balian and the patriarch. Sybilla and her daughters had been the first to leave, eager to join Guy at Nablus. The Templars and their charges were the next to go, followed by the Hospitallers' party. Those who would be leaving with Balian and Eraclius were still camped outside the walls, preparing for their departure. But fifteen thousand wretched Franks remained in the city, those intended for the slave markets in Damascus and Aleppo.

Once most of the Franks had left the city, Salāh al-Dīn set up his headquarters in the priory next to the Holy Sepulchre. But on this mild October afternoon, he had summoned Balian and the patriarch to David's Tower. They found him attended by his brother and al-Sani'a; his second son, Uthman; 'Īsā the lawyer; Gökböri; 'Imād al-Dīn; and Joseph Batit, a Greek Orthodox scholar who stood high in the sultan's favor. His eldest son and Taqī al-Dīn were already gone, and the sultan would soon be leaving to lay siege to Tyre, the only city not yet under Saracen control. On the morrow, Balian and Eraclius would be departing, so this was their final meeting.

Salāh al-Dīn introduced them to Falak al-Dīn Sulaimān, the man who'd be leading their escort. As he'd done with the earlier refugees, the sultan was sending fifty of his best *fursan*, the Saracen equivalent of knights, to see them safely into Christian territory. While they were being served iced *jallabs*, almonds, and oranges. Salāh al-Dīn told them that he'd made a decision about the fate of the Holy Sepulchre. Even though some of his amirs had urged him to destroy it, he'd decided to spare it, and Christian pilgrims would eventually be permitted to visit it again.

Balian and Eraclius expressed their great relief at hearing that, and al-'Ādil could not resist observing that it was a pity future pilgrims would find it stripped bare of its finery. At that, all of the men turned to stare at Eraclius, who carried on with his usual aplomb. He did not meet Balian's eyes, though, for they'd had a heated quarrel over the patriarch's treasure-laden carts. He'd insisted that he had a duty to keep Church reliquaries and relics out of infidel hands. That explanation had not placated Balian, who could not reconcile it with the teachings of Scriptures, which declared that "He that hath mercy on the poor, happy is he," nor with the fate of the seven thousand men and eight thousand women and children who'd been unable to pay their ransoms.

The sultan had been relying upon Joseph Batit to translate since the patriarch spoke no Arabic, having chosen the Orthodox Christian because he knew that would vex Eraclius. He supposed he ought not to take pleasure in such pettiness. But he still had to suppress a smile, for what he was about to reveal would be sure to outrage the patriarch. "I recently received a letter from the emperor of the Greeks, congratulating us upon our great victory at Ḥaṭṭīn and asking us to return the control of its Christian shrines to the Greek Church, as it was ere the coming of the Franks. I think that is a reasonable request, one I shall probably grant."

Eraclius was indeed outraged. "It grieves me," he said coldly, "that one who calls himself a Christian should rejoice in our sorrows. The Greeks are an unprincipled people, guileful and corrupt." He paused, then turned toward Balian as if remembering Maria was Greek. "I hope I have not offended you by my candor. Naturally I was not speaking of your lady wife."

"You need not worry," Balian said, just as coldly. "My wife and I know what weight to give to your words."

Joseph Batit gleefully translated that icy exchange and Salāh al-Dīn decided he would indeed turn the city's Christian shrines over to the Orthodox Church. He rose, signifying that their meeting was done, when a high-pitched shriek turned them all toward an open window.

Al-'Ādil was closest to the window. Looking out, he saw a group of Franks being led down David Street toward the open space between the grain market and Tancred's Tower, where those who could not pay their ransoms were being assembled for their journey to Damascus. A woman no longer young had begun to scream and rend her garments, paying no heed to the attempts by her companions to comfort her. Their Saracen guards did not seem to know what to do either, obviously reluctant to lay hands upon a woman old enough to be their mother. Balian lost color as she continued to wail, giving the patriarch a look that was murderous.

Eraclius did not notice, for he was visibly shaken, too, pushing away from the table and snapping, "For the love of God, close the window!"

Not needing a translation of that, al-'Ādil reached out to latch the shutters. That did not completely muffle the sounds of her anguish, which eventually gave way to broken sobs. The silence that followed was a lengthy one, fraught with all that was being left unsaid. Balian suddenly slammed his fist down upon the table, hard enough to bruise his hand, causing the patriarch to jump and grab for his *jallab* before it spilled into his lap. Taking their cue from the sultan, the other men had gotten to their feet, belatedly followed by Eraclius and Balian.

Al-'Ādil had yet to move from the window. "Yūsuf, I would seek a boon from you. Will you give me a thousand of the Franks who are to be enslaved?"

Salāh al-Dīn was surprised, not so much by the request as that al-'Ādil had spoken in Arabic; they usually switched to Kurdish for family conversations. "Of course, Ahmad. What mean you to do with them?"

"What I think best." Al-'Ādil's eyes swept the chamber before settling upon al-Sanī'a. "Send men to choose a thousand of the Franks and arrange to free them."

Salāh al-Dīn said nothing, merely nodding to acquiesce to al-'Ādil's generous gesture. The other Saracens nodded approvingly, too, for the Qur'an viewed the manumission of slaves as a praiseworthy act of benevolence and piety. Only 'Imād al-Dīn showed displeasure, for this was yet more money that would never reach his lord's chancellery. He was quite exasperated, therefore, when Balian then stepped forward, asking earnestly, "My lord sultan, may I request the gift of slaves, too, to honor God as your brother has done?"

Salāh al-Dīn looked amused. "I suppose the patriarch wants to make a similar request?"

"Indeed, he does, my lord," Balian assured him, before offering Eraclius a terse explanation of what was occurring. While the patriarch did not find it easy to ask for favors from men he saw as God's enemies, it would ease his conscience if he could assist in the freeing of some of those miserable souls, and he hastily added his voice to Balian's, both men falling silent, then, as they awaited the sultan's verdict.

"Very well. I shall give you each a thousand of the slaves, too." Telling his unhappy chancellor to see to it, Salāh al-Dīn waited until al-'Ādil and the two Franks had thanked him before making 'Imād al-Dīn even unhappier. "Now that my brother and Lord Balian and the patriarch have performed their acts of charity, I shall do my own almsgiving. The elderly amongst the poor Franks no longer need pay their ransoms and are free to leave the city."

"I will be sure that the other Franks know of your clemency and generosity, my lord sultan." Balian was grateful to Salāh al-Dīn for sparing so many and was even more grateful to al-'Ādil. He wondered if the other man had acted impulsively, moved by the misery of the enslaved Franks. Or had he always intended to make this request, confident that his brother would welcome an opportunity to display mercy again?

Becoming aware of his speculative gaze, al-'Ādil glanced in Balian's direction and winked. Balian smiled, realizing he'd never have the answer to that question. He could answer another question, though, one that he'd pondered since their first meeting in Salāh al-Dīn's tent at Marj al-Sufar. They shared neither the same faith nor the same blood. But al-Malik al-'Ādil Saif al-Dīn Abū Bakr Ahmad bin Ayyūb was his friend.

CHAPTER 52

I
t would prove to be a hellish journey. Balian had often traveled with an army
on the march, but never with thousands of women and children and the elderly slowing them down. Emotions were raw, tempers quick to flare, for
they were mourning their yesterdays and dreading their tomorrows. They were
fearful, too, for their safety, knowing the countryside was swarming with bandits
and Bedouins and not sure at first if they could trust their Saracen escort.

Some of that anxiety eased after the *fursan* chased away horsemen who'd begun shadowing them, showing a sinister interest in stragglers. These young Muslim soldiers were also displaying remarkable patience with their heartsick charges,
keeping an eye out for those who fell behind, ordering their servants to dismount
so the elderly and exhausted could ride for a while, and taking weary children up
onto their own horses, turning the grueling trek into a game for the youngsters
perched in front of their saddles.

Their commander, Falak al-Dīn Sulaimān, soon won their confidence, too, for
he maintained discipline, commended his men for showing kindness to the
Franks, and remained vigilant, rotating the vanguard and rearguard so that there
were always sentries to watch over them when they camped at night. Balian was
aware how much more difficult their odyssey could have been had the sultan not
chosen so wisely. But because Falak al-Dīn was not given to idle conversation, it
was not until they'd been on the road for over a week that Balian learned he was
al-'Ādil's maternal half brother.

Yet even such competent shepherds could not protect their flock from the
haunting memories and bitter regrets that trailed after them as they left Jerusalem
behind. For Balian, seeing the milestone pointing toward Nablus was a low point,
and even worse lay ahead. As they turned onto the road to Acre, a road Balian and
his rearguard had ridden not so long ago, he and Renier and Ernoul tried to keep

their eyes away from the twin hills rising to the north. The Horns of Haṭṭīn, where their kingdom had breathed its last, was now a cemetery for their unburied dead, and they were thankful they did not have to look upon its gruesome graveyard.

They halted at Acre for supplies and some of the people wept again to see Saracen banners flying from its castle and battlements. Others took heart, for they were now only twenty-six miles from Tyre, where many of them expected to end their journey. Upon reaching that formidable seacoast city, they found a Saracen camp already set up, awaiting the arrival of the sultan with the bulk of his army. The Saracens had been alerted that refugees would be arriving, though, and with Falak al-Dīn to speak for them, they encountered no trouble from the Muslims. That came from their Christian brethren. Before they could approach the triple walls guarding the landward entrance, it was shouted down from the battlements that only men of fighting age would be admitted and the rest of them would have to continue on to Tripoli.

Balian had entered the city to try to change Conrad of Montferrat's mind about admitting only men able to fight. A fair-haired man in his early forties, with a resemblance to his dead brother, Conrad received him cordially and willingly heard him out. He then shook his head. "Of course I have pity for the Jerusalem refugees. That does not mean I will accept them. We are already overcrowded, and food is getting scarce. We can afford no more useless mouths, people who cannot aid in the city's defense."

Balian could see the cold logic in Conrad's position. But the refugees were not just "useless mouths" to him; they were people who'd suffered through the siege of Jerusalem. "As you will," he said reluctantly. "I shall ask the younger men how many want to join you."

"I suppose you'll not be one of them? More's the pity, for it would embolden our citizens to have Jerusalem's savior fighting with us." Conrad grinned when Balian grimaced at "Jerusalem's savior." "The refugees we did accept made you sound like a cross between the legendary King Arthur and the Archangel Michael. I know you're set on joining your wife in Tripoli, but you're always welcome to return to Tyre. I've need of a reliable second-in-command."

Balian's eyebrows rose, for Conrad's authority in Tyre was based more upon expediency than legality—being in the right place at the right time. But his cockiness was contagious, his bold confidence sure to appeal to the fearful townspeople. Balian understood how he'd won the citizens over to his side, convincing them that defiance made more sense than surrender.

Declining an invitation to spend the night at the castle, Balian explained that he'd assured the refugees he'd not be gone for long, which seemed to amuse Conrad. "They do not trust the patriarch to act in your stead? Tell Eraclius he is welcome in Tyre, provided those carts of his come with him."

Balian was not surprised that Conrad knew about the treasure-laden carts, for it was no secret to the Jerusalem exiles. He just hoped the gossip had not spread beyond the city walls, or they'd be attracting bandits like carrion drew vultures. "I suspect the patriarch will decline," he said dryly, adding that he wanted to see Archbishop Joscius ere he returned to the camp.

"Alas, you're too late. As soon as we learned that you'd persuaded Saladin to accept Jerusalem's surrender, the archbishop sailed for the West. The sailing season was past, but he said he had to risk it, for Christendom must know that Jerusalem is lost." Conrad had risen when Balian did, and as they walked, he dramatically described Joscius's ship leaving the city's outer harbor for the open sea, its sails dyed black to mourn the Holy City's fall.

"I've a surprise for you," he said as they crossed the great hall, "although I am loath to let him go. But I promised the archbishop I'd see that you got him back, so consider this proof of the goodwill I bear you."

Balian had already quickened his pace and Conrad had to lengthen his own stride to catch up. By the time he emerged into the castle bailey, Balian was standing by a chestnut stallion, rubbing his ears as the horse nuzzled him affectionately. Conrad sighed regretfully and offered to buy the Arabian if Balian ever wanted to sell him. As he expected, Balian paid him no heed.

Swinging up into the saddle and luxuriating in the familiar feel of Khamsin's surging power, Balian reined in before the new lord of Tyre. "Good luck and God keep you all safe during the siege." Conrad wished him "Godspeed" in return, adding that he did not need luck. Oddly enough, Balian almost believed him.

On the following day, they resumed their journey. While some were disappointed at being turned away from Tyre, they soon had new worries. When they halted at Beirut for more supplies, Falak al-Dīn was warned by the castle's Saracen garrison that the refugees led by the Hospitallers had been attacked and robbed after they'd crossed into Tripoli. Falak al-Dīn had intended to leave them once they reached the kingdom's border. What he'd learned in Beirut changed his mind and he told Balian he'd escort them as far as Jubyal before turning back.

Jubyal had been in Muslim hands since August; its lord, Hugh Embriaco, had been taken prisoner at Hattīn and ordered the castle garrison to surrender in return for his freedom. The Franks spent the night there and set out again before dawn the next morning, feeling suddenly vulnerable without their Saracen protectors. They still had about twenty-seven miles to go before they reached the city of Tripoli and Balian decided it was safer to press on even though that would mean continuing to travel once night fell. He sent Ernoul ahead to alert Count Raymond that he and the patriarch would be arriving long after dark with the last of the refugees and ordered all the men with horses and weapons to ride with him so they'd be ready if bandits struck. While he did not know the identity of those who'd attacked the earlier group of refugees, the Lord of Nephin had a foul reputation, so Balian made a wide detour around that seacoast stronghold despite adding more miles to their journey. He missed their Saracen escort even more than the weary refugees did, for he had a better understanding of the dangers they still faced.

Time had little meaning on the road. Balian knew it was November and guessed that it was past Martinmas, for the temperature dropped once night enveloped them. The moon was almost full, but the countryside still seemed fearfully dark to people who'd lived all of their lives in cities. Spotting lights in the distance, some thought the illumination must be coming from Tripoli. Balian knew better, knew they were looking at torches, held aloft by horsemen. What he did not know was if the approaching riders were friendly—not until he recognized the rider spurring ahead of the others. Ernoul was within shouting distance now, calling out that the lords with him had come to escort them to Tripoli, and only then did Balian ease his grip on the hilt of his sword, letting the weapon slide back into its scabbard.

Ernoul's use of the word "lords" was not just a courtesy, for the approaching knights were led by two of Count Raymond's stepsons, Odo and Raoul. They at once wanted to know if he'd had any trouble getting past Nephin. Balian was very glad he'd bypassed it when they told him that its lord, Routared, was the one who'd ambushed those unfortunate refugees as soon as their Saracen escort had turned back.

Eraclius and Renier had ridden up to join Balian and expressed their anger that Christians should prey upon Christians. Balian was somewhat surprised that the Lord of Nephin would have dared to defy Count Raymond so openly even if he was ill; Conrad had heard he'd sickened soon after returning to Tripoli. When he said as much, the count's stepsons exchanged a quick glance before Odo spoke for them both. "You have not heard, then? The count is dead." He sketched a quick cross, adding an almost perfunctory "May God assoil him. He was stricken with pleurisy, dying after hearing that Jerusalem had fallen."

The patriarch did not doubt that God had justly punished the count for his many mortal sins. He would not show his satisfaction before the count's stepsons, of course, so he confined himself to a polite platitude, saying he hoped Count Raymond had been shriven ere he died. Balian expressed his condolences, but the political implications of the count's death were too important to ignore. "May I ask whom he chose as his heir?" he queried, half expecting them to name Hugues since the count had died without children of his own.

"He wanted to leave Tripoli to his godson, the Prince of Antioch's eldest son, Raimond," Odo said, and though his words were neutral, his tone was not, sharp enough to slice bread in Balian's opinion. He could understand their disappointment, for Hattīn had changed everything. Now that the principality of Galilee was lost to their family, how could they not have hoped Raymond would leave Tripoli to the young man he'd raised as a son?

"You say he 'wanted' to make his godson his heir. Did he change his mind, then?"

"No such luck," Odo muttered, and Raoul shook his head, saying that Prince Bohemond was the one to object, for Raimond would inherit Antioch after his death and he thought ruling over both realms would be too much of a burden. So, he sent his younger son and namesake, Bohemond, to Tripoli instead.

"Whilst Count Raymond was not pleased, he was on his deathbed, so there was little he could do about it. He ordered the lords of Tripoli to swear allegiance to Bohemond."

Neither Balian nor Eraclius could remember how old Prince Bohemond's younger son was, but they did not need to ask, for Odo volunteered that information, saying disapprovingly, "He is just sixteen. At least his brother had bloodied his sword."

Turmoil in Tripoli could be disastrous for the refugees and indeed, for their kingdom, or what was left of it—Tyre and a few beleaguered strongholds like Kerak. Balian refused to let himself dwell upon that now, not with his wife and children just a few miles away. Al-'Ādil had assured him that his family had been safely escorted to Tripoli, but he yearned for details and once they were on the road again, he interrogated Odo and Raoul at length. They were able to reassure him that Maria and the children had been received warmly and Eschiva had invited them to stay at the count's palace in the city. Nor had Raymond's death changed that. Odo grudgingly admitted that young Bohemond seemed pleased to have them there, even finding them a town house of their own.

Balian was relieved to hear that, but he realized that his family's future was going to be even more complicated than he'd first thought, with Conrad laying claim to Tyre and a young stranger ruling in Tripoli.

✤

The stronghold of the Counts of Tripoli had been built on Mount Pilgrim, a steep hill overlooking the city and the sea. It was to the castle, not the town, that they were heading, for Odo and Raoul said the new count was staying there until their mother was ready to move out of the palace into her dower fief. They were less than a mile from the citadel when they saw riders galloping toward them, led by none other than Count Bohemond. "I could not wait," he said, reining in beside Balian. "Welcome to Tripoli. It is an honor to meet the man who saved the Holy City. I cannot wait to hear all about it!"

Bohemond had inherited his father's dark coloring. He was taller, though, with broad shoulders that made him look older than sixteen. But his enthusiasm and exuberance demonstrated both his youth and his privileged upbringing as a prince's son. Utterly unlike the late Count Raymond, who'd measured his words as if they were coins to be counted before being spent, Bohemond chattered on cheerfully as he rode beside Balian toward the citadel.

The Jerusalem refugees would have to camp outside the walls, but he'd make sure that they were guarded and fed. On the morrow, he'd have to determine how many of them could stay in Tripoli. He'd had to turn away most of the earlier refugees, for the city could not accommodate so many new residents. He'd sent them on to Antioch, for his lord father had agreed to take them all in since Antioch had far greater resources than Tripoli.

Balian listened without interrupting, needing time to observe Bohemond before forming any impressions about his character or his understanding of a ruler's responsibilities. He seemed surprisingly self-confident for a sixteen-year-old, which could be either a blessing or a curse, depending upon how amenable he was to taking advice. Bohemond had seemed at ease with the count's stepsons, apparently willing to overlook their resentment. Odo had told him Hugues was no longer in Tripoli, having joined Conrad at Tyre, and Balian suspected Hugues's brothers would eventually join him there, too. He and Maria would have to make decisions of their own about the future. Not yet, though, God willing, not yet. For now, he wanted only to rejoice in his reunion with his family.

As the castle came into view, casting an impressive silhouette against the night sky, the barbican's portcullis was winched up and Bohemond gestured for Balian to enter with him. "I know it is too late for supper and too early for breaking our fasts. But I assumed you must be hungry after being on the road for so many hours, so I ordered a meal to be prepared for us."

"That is most kind of you, my lord, but I would rather see my lady first. Or is she at the castle awaiting us?" Balian frowned at the startled expression on Bohemond's face, for he'd entrusted Ernoul with two tasks; the lad was to ask for an escort to be sent out to meet them and he was to request that they let Maria know of their imminent arrival. He glanced over his shoulder at his squire, who insisted that he'd done as his lord bade, telling Count Bohemond himself.

Bohemond looked uncomfortable, or as uncomfortable as princes ever got. "He is right. He did tell me and I meant to send a message down into the town to Queen Maria. But in all the excitement, it must have slipped my mind."

Balian shrugged. "No matter. It will be better this way, for I'll get to surprise her."

"But what of the meal we have waiting for you? I want to hear about the siege and how you bluffed Saladin into backing down—you were bluffing? And I need your advice about how to punish that bandit lord at Nephin. I want to talk to you, too, about staying in Tripoli. I know you'll be going to Antioch to visit your ailing brother and my father will be sure to try to gain your allegiance for himself. I want to make my argument ere he does!"

At that moment, Bohemond sounded very much like a young lordling accustomed to getting his own way. Balian had no intention of indulging him, not if it kept him from his family for a few more hours. "It will be my pleasure to spend time with you later, my lord count. But I am bone weary and in desperate need of a bath and a bed and there is a beautiful woman below in the city who means the world to me. With all due respect, you cannot compete with that."

Balian had tried to keep his tone light, hoping that would mollify Bohemond. The new count did summon up a brief smile, but it was obvious he was not happy about having his plans disrupted—not until a melodious female voice entered the conversation. Isabella had unobtrusively nudged her mare closer and she gave Bohemond one of her most captivating smiles. "I do not believe we've met, my lord count. I am Lord Balian's stepdaughter, the Lady Isabella."

Bohemond suddenly had eyes only for Isabella, dismounting hastily so he could approach and gallantly kiss her hand. When she murmured that she would be pleased to accept his invitation to dine, he beamed and declared magnanimously that of course Lord Balian would want to see his wife first. Isabella glanced triumphantly toward Balian, amused to see he was scowling, his protective paternal instincts triggered by Bohemond's behavior. He would have to understand that beauty was a woman's weapon, one she was learning to wield with some skill. Favoring Bohemond with another dazzling smile, she asked him to send a knight with her stepfather so he'd be able to enter the city and find her mother's town house. He would indeed do that, he assured her, and while he beckoned to one of his men, she took advantage of his distraction to urge her mare over to Balian's side.

"Do not fret, Pateras," she said softly. "This will not be a cozy meal for two. The patriarch and your friend Renier must be famished and I know all of my household are, especially Stephanie. Can you imagine a better guardian than Humphrey's crocodile of a mother?" The enchanting smile she'd used on Bohemond gave way to a grin of pure mischief. "Go to my mother. Let us worry about getting those poor, weary souls settled in. You've earned this."

Balian was realizing belatedly that he was looking at a composed, clever young woman, one who would have made a far better queen than her sister. What had happened to the little girl whom he'd called "kitten" and comforted after her pet lark died and taught to speak some of his father's Piedmontese dialect? "Daughters grow up much too quickly."

She laughed. "Tell my mother that I am eager to see her and that I am very proud of her husband. But then, I am sure she is, too."

Balian and Ernoul followed Prince Bohemond's knight down a street not far from Tripoli's cathedral, which was still being rebuilt after having been destroyed in the great earthquake of 1170. Balian was impressed by what he could see of the city, which, like Tyre, was protected on three sides by the sea. He knew Maria had missed living by the seacoast and he wondered if she'd like to make their home here in Tripoli rather than Antioch. He did want to visit Antioch as soon as he could, although Maria may have news of Baudouin's illness, for Conrad had told him that his niece Esquiva had sailed for Antioch whilst he'd been in Jerusalem.

"There it is, my lord." As the knight rode off, they approached the gate. Dismounting, Ernoul pounded on the door until a sleepy porter peered down at them. He was opening his mouth to complain about the early hour when he recognized

Balian and let out an excited shout. With surprising speed, the door swung open and Balian got his first look at his family's new home. Like many houses in the Levant, its center was the courtyard, surrounded by the two-story living quarters, the windows overlooking the court rather than the street. The porter was hovering beside them as they dismounted and volunteered to show Ernoul the gate leading out to their stables. Their voices carried to Balian as they led the horses away, the porter peppering Ernoul with questions about the siege and Ernoul happy to respond. Balian wished that he could delegate the youth to answer all of the questions he was sure to get for the foreseeable future. He had some healing to do ere he wanted to discuss what had happened in Jerusalem.

He was about to head toward the closest door when a window opened overhead and he found himself gazing up at his wife. "Wait there!" Maria disappeared before he could reply. In what seemed like the blink of an eye, she was in the doorway and then she was in his arms.

Her hair was loose, flowing down her back like a midnight river, and she wore only a woolen mantle, having been in too much of a hurry to look for her bed robe. Exploring the soft curves and warm skin underneath the cloak, he pulled her even closer. "You are cruel to tempt me like this, Marika, for I will be of no good to you until I can get some sleep first."

"A bath might help, too," she suggested, and he agreed with a grin, knowing full well how much he needed to soak away the grime of the road. Noticing that she'd not even taken the time to find her bed slippers, he guided her toward the closest seat, a marble bench by the fountain, and she tucked her bare feet up under her, becoming aware how chilly the paving stones were. The sky was still starlit, but to the east, a silvery glow was visible; it would not be long until the last of the night shadows would be banished by the splendors of another Levant sunrise.

After assuring her that Isabella was fine and would be with them soon, he shifted so he could gather her onto his lap. "Passing strange how little we seem to need words anymore. If more couples followed our example, marriages might be much happier."

"It helps, too, that we keep having these dramatic reunions," she pointed out, and he pressed a kiss into the palm of her hand.

"There is so much we need to discuss, Marika—our future, the future of Outremer, what life will be like for our children. But not yet. For now, I just want to sit here, holding you and letting our silence speak for us."

"You know I've always been one for planning ahead, Balian." Reaching up, she touched her fingers to his unfamiliar new beard, thinking it almost made him look like a Greek. "That was the old me, the other me. Now I am quite content just to savor my miracle."

"Miracle?"

"That I am not a widow." He kissed her again, very tenderly, for that seemed like a miracle to him, too, and they remained there in the garden courtyard until the peace was shattered by the joyous sound of young voices, as their children awakened and came flying out to welcome their father home.

TELL THE WORLD THIS BOOK WAS

GOOD	BAD	SO-SO

AFTERWORD

Sybilla remained loyal to Guy and that loyalty would lead to her death at age thirty-one. After he was freed by Saladin, Guy and Sybilla headed for Tyre, but Conrad of Montferrat refused them entry. In desperation, Guy and his small band of followers then lay siege to Acre. To the amazement of most people, probably including Guy himself, the siege became a symbol of resistance to the Saracens. The fight for Acre continued for several years, not falling to the Franks until after the arrival of Richard the Lionheart in the summer of 1191. By then, Sybilla and her two young daughters were dead, dying when a plague swept the siege encampment in the summer of 1190. Guy still claimed the crown, but the Poulains rallied around Conrad and only the misguided support of the Lionheart allowed Guy to make his tenuous claim. Richard had conquered Cyprus on his way to the Holy Land and eventually he arranged for Guy to take control of that wealthy island; Guy moved to Cyprus in 1192 but did not enjoy his new possession for long, dying in 1194.

Amaury de Lusignan would prove to be much more successful than his younger brother. Assuming power in Cyprus after Guy's death, he managed to get the Holy Roman Emperor Heinrich to recognize him as King of Cyprus in 1197. He eventually became King of Jerusalem, dying of food poisoning in April 1205, but the de Lusignan dynasty would continue to rule Cyprus for almost three hundred years.

After Sybilla's death, the crown should have passed to Isabella, but no one wanted to see Humphrey de Toron crowned and Conrad took full advantage of that reluctance. Great pressure was put upon Isabella to disavow her marriage to Humphrey. This eighteen-year-old girl showed considerable courage, insisting that she loved her husband and did not want to be separated from him although she faced opposition from her mother, Maria, and stepfather, Balian, virtually all of the Poulain lords, and the princes of the Church. They believed that Conrad would be a far better king than Humphrey, and they finally convinced Isabella that this was a sacrifice she must make for her beleaguered kingdom. The papal legate and the Bishop of Beauvais dissolved her marriage and she was wed to Conrad of Montferrat in November of 1190.

As readers of my novel *Lionheart* know, this marriage lasted less than two years. In April of 1192, Conrad was elected king by the Poulain lords, but he was soon murdered by two members of the Assassin sect. Isabella, then pregnant, thwarted an attempt by the French to take control of Tyre, and when Henri, the young Count of Champagne, arrived in Tyre, he found himself acclaimed as the kingdom's savior, implored by the citizens, lords, and churchmen to marry their newly widowed queen. Henri had misgivings, for like most crusaders, he had never planned to remain in the Holy Land. But Isabella was willing, so he agreed to wed her and was soon smitten with his beautiful bride. Henri and Isabella had what seems to have been a happy marriage before his unexpected death in a bizarre fall in September 1197. Isabella had little time to grieve, for Outremer needed a king, and so she wed Amaury de Lusignan. Isabella died at thirty-three, not long after Amaury, in April 1205. Maria, her daughter by Conrad, then became queen. Isabella and Henri had three daughters, one of whom became Queen of Cyprus. She and Amaury had two daughters and a son, who died very young. Humphrey de Toron, Isabella's unfortunate first husband, moved to Cyprus with Guy de Lusignan and died soon afterward; he never remarried.

After the surrender of Jerusalem, Balian d'Ibelin and Maria Comnena lived in Tripoli, although they eventually joined Guy and the other Poulain lords at the siege of Acre. Balian and Maria allied with Conrad, who would become their son-in-law after his marriage to Isabella. Balian appears occasionally in my novel *Lionheart*; he helped to negotiate the peace treaty between Saladin and Richard I. He was dead by the end of 1193, for he disappeared from historical accounts after that. Even though Maria was only thirty-nine at his death, she never remarried; she apparently died in 1217. Their two sons, John and Philip, rose to prominence during the reigns of Isabella and her daughter, Maria; John, in particular, became a trusted adviser, serving as constable and regent of the kingdom. Their daughters, Helvis and Margaret, made prestigious marriages. Helvis first married Renaud de Sidon (Denys in my novel), who was much older than she. They had three children before Renaud's death in 1202. Helvis then wed one of the de Montforts—yes, a kinsman of my Simon de Montfort in *Falls the Shadow*. During the thirteenth century, the d'Ibelins became one of the most influential families in the Levant, Balian and Maria's children and grandchildren benefiting from their blood bond to the queens of Jerusalem.

Balian's elder brother, Baudouin, seems to have died in 1187; the last reference to him occurs in June of that year, before the battle at Haṭṭīn. I could find no date of death for his third wife, Mary de Brisebarre, or for his daughter, Etiennette.

Esquiva died in 1196, her son by Amaury becoming King of Cyprus. Baudouin's only son, Thomasin, seems to have died very young, probably in 1188.

Women often slip through history's cracks, so we do not know for sure when Stephanie de Milly or Joscelin de Courtenay's wife, Agneta de Milly, died. There is some confusion about Joscelin's death, but it seems likely that he was dead by 1200; he apparently played no role in politics after the battle of Ḥaṭṭīn. The death date of the Princess of Galilee and Countess of Tripoli, Eschiva de Bures, was not noted, either. Her sons had important roles in the politics of the kingdom.

Patriarch Eraclius died at the siege of Acre in the winter of 1190–1191. Joscius, Archbishop of Tyre, served as chancellor to Henri of Champagne and Isabella and died circa 1202.

Upon regaining his freedom, Gerard de Ridefort assumed command of the Templars and took part in the siege of Acre. He died at the siege in October 1189, and there are two different accounts of his death. One claims that he died fighting, refusing to retreat. The more credible one by the Saracen chronicler al-Athīr reports that he was captured by Saladin, who had him beheaded, for he'd sworn a holy oath that he'd not fight against the Saracens after being freed.

We know nothing of the family or fate of Balian's squire, Ernoul, but he deserves to be mentioned here, for he wrote a history of the last years of their kingdom, a continuation of the history written by William of Tyre. Sadly, his history was lost, but we have several garbled versions of it in other continuations. These chronicles have a fascinating and confusing history of their own, which I discuss in the author's note.

Bohemond, the Prince of Antioch, died in 1201. His second son and namesake, who became the Count of Tripoli, outmaneuvered his older brother and eventually ruled both Antioch and Tripoli. Bohemond's wife, Theodora, may have wed a Poulain lord after their divorce.

The Third Crusade helped to confer immortality upon both Saladin and Richard the Lionheart. Saladin and Richard signed a peace treaty in September 1192; see my novel *Lionheart* for these events. Saladin died in March of 1193, at age fifty-five. His eldest son, al-Afdal, became the amir of Damascus and another son became the sultan of Egypt, but none of the sultan's sons inherited their father's abilities and the brothers were soon fighting among themselves. Not surprisingly, the far more capable al-'Ādil eventually took power in 1200 and had a very successful reign, dying in 1218 at age seventy-three. His eldest son, known to history as al-Kamil, also had a long and successful reign. There are no death dates for the wives of the sultans; even their names are not known, with only a few exceptions.

Taqī al-Dīn died while besieging a Syrian castle in October of 1191. 'Imād al-Dīn wrote several biographies of Saladin and died in 1201.

After Balian convinced Saladin to accept the peaceful surrender of Jerusalem, their kingdom consisted only of Tyre and several defiant castles. This would change with the Third Crusade. Richard I's enemies dismissed the crusade as a failure because he'd not recaptured the Holy City, and Richard himself saw it that way. But by the time he left Outremer in October 1192, the kingdom stretched down the coast from Tyre to Acre and Ascalon was no longer in Saladin's control. While he'd not retaken Jerusalem, Richard did buy the kingdom one hundred more years of life, for it existed in its truncated form until May of 1291, when Acre and then Tyre were captured by the Mamluk sultan of Egypt. The kingdom still survived longer than Antioch, which was taken by Sultan Baibars in 1268, and Tripoli, which fell in 1289.

AUTHOR'S NOTE

Researching *The Land Beyond the Sea* was one of the easiest and yet most challenging tasks I've faced. It was easy because I'd been collecting books about the Holy Land and the Crusades for years, preparing to write *Lionheart*. So by the time I was ready to write about the Kingdom of Jerusalem, I already had an extensive library. It was still challenging because both the medieval chroniclers and subsequent historians all had their very own sharp axes to grind. There is something about the Levant that seems to make it impossible for people to be objective or dispassionate, and so I had to sort through a fair amount of propaganda in order to find a plausible version of what really happened.

There is one very reliable account of the history of the kingdom, written by the man considered to be one of the greatest historians of the Middle Ages: William, the Archbishop of Tyre. His *A History of Deeds Done Beyond the Sea* offers us a riveting glimpse into a bygone world, and it is filled with personal details that historical novelists rarely encounter: William's graphic description of Amalric's obesity, Guillaume of Montferrat's fondness for wine, and William's heartbreaking story of discovering that Baldwin might be a leper. Unfortunately, his chronicle ends in 1184; it is such a loss to history that we were denied William's perspective on the events leading up to the fateful battle at Ḥaṭṭīn.

William's history was widely read during the Middle Ages and beyond. For a long time, historians tended to take his chronicle as gospel; today it is recognized that he was writing to convince the rest of Christendom that they had a vested interest in the survival of Outremer. With that aim in mind, he sometimes gave a spin to known facts; for example, he made it seem as if young Baldwin was the one solely responsible for their remarkable victory over Saladin at Montgisard, whereas the Saracen chroniclers all identified Reynald de Chatillon as the battle commander. Yet William never lied; any sins he committed were sins of omission. *A History of Deeds Done Beyond the Sea* was translated into English in 1943, and for years it was very difficult to obtain. But, as I mentioned in the acknowledgments, it is now available from Amazon as an ebook.

After William's death, a continuation of his history was written by a man named Ernoul; he is believed to have been Balian d'Ibelin's squire, although nothing else is known about him. Unfortunately, Ernoul's history was subsequently lost, and here is where the confusion set in. Later chroniclers wrote their own histories of the period, making use of Ernoul's book with their own embellishments and additions. There are several of these "continuations" of William's work, and we have no way of knowing how much was drawn from Ernoul's history. They were written in the thirteenth century, too, and so it was inevitable that mistakes would be made. For example, we know that the number of the Acre garrison executed by Richard I after the fall of Acre was twenty-six hundred, as Richard himself mentioned that number in a letter to the Abbot of Clairvaux, and it was confirmed by a contemporary Saracen chronicler. Yet one of these continuations reports that sixteen thousand were slain at Richard's order! So these accounts have to be approached with caution.

We do have several valuable Saracen chronicles of the period, which I relied upon for *Lionheart* and again for this novel. They offer a fascinating portrayal of Saladin written by men who actually knew him; details are given in the acknowledgments.

Mark Twain observed that "The very ink with which all history is written is merely fluid prejudice." That is so true of the medieval accounts written after William's death and true, too, of many of the modern histories of this period. I've been writing for more than thirty years and I cannot recall ever encountering so many biased sources. Let's start with the portrayals of Agnes de Courtenay. William loathed her and delivered a devastating verdict, describing her as "a woman detestable to God." He thought that she was power hungry, greedy, and ruthless. But he never even implied that she was sexually promiscuous. That was not the case with the thirteenth century "continuations" of his work, for they transformed her into the Whore of Babylon, claiming that she flaunted her lovers—among them Amaury de Lusignan and Patriarch Eraclius—and rewarded them with high offices.

There is no evidence for these claims, but subsequent historians accepted them without hesitation, including some of the most respected scholars of the era. Eventually, Bernard Hamilton took a hard look at these accusations; and in *The Leper King and His Heirs*, he argues convincingly that Agnes has been maligned. One reason historians accepted this view of Agnes is due to a misreading of a paragraph in William's history. He was discussing the annulment of Amalric's marriage to Agnes, but some historians erroneously thought that he was saying Agnes had been disavowed by her fourth husband, Renaud de Grenier, called Denys in my novel. This is not so; they were wed circa 1170 and were still married at the time of Agnes's death in 1184. Had historians realized this, they would not have been so quick to believe that Agnes openly took lovers and lavished favors upon them. A medieval lord like Renaud would never have allowed himself to be publicly cuckolded like that. Agnes certainly had her flaws, but sexual sins were not among them. Other historians, Peter Edbury in particular, provide a more balanced analysis of the power struggle that would eventually doom the kingdom; I cite Edbury's work at greater length in the acknowledgments. But earlier historians, such as Steven Runciman, offer an outdated and inaccurate image of Agnes.

Another historical figure whose reputation has fluctuated as much as Agnes's is Raymond, the Count of Tripoli. Historians like Runciman and Marshall Whithed Baldwin saw the civil strife in the kingdom as a struggle between hawks and doves, and cast Raymond as the hero. The hawks were Agnes and her brother, Joscelin; Reynald de Chatillon; Gerard de Ridefort; and Guy de Lusignan, seen as aggressive newcomers who scorned the Saracens as evil infidels. The doves were the native-born barons, the Poulains like the d'Ibelins and the lords of Sidon and Galilee and Caesarea, led by the Count of Tripoli, men more knowledgeable about life in the Levant, understanding that survival was possible only through accommodation. In this reading, the doves were the good guys and the hawks were the villains. And Baldwin? He was more or less overlooked, dismissed as the invalid king whose mortal illness made him vulnerable to manipulation by his mother and her allies.

Reality is never this simple, of course. The pendulum may swing widely in its historical arc, but eventually it swings back; and in recent years, historians have followed the lead of Bernard Hamilton and Peter Edbury, recognizing Baldwin's remarkable courage and arguing that the court factions were not so clearly drawn. Raymond's actions were stripped of that heroic haze and he was viewed in a less-admiring light. I personally think he was a man motivated mainly by self-interest; and his credibility was so damaged by his past actions that his enemies were not willing to listen when he did act selflessly, trying desperately to convince them that it would be madness to take Saladin's bait at Hattīn. They saw his charge with the vanguard as an act of treason, many sure that he was still conspiring with Saladin. It would have been impossible for Raymond and his men to fight their way back up that steep slope to rejoin the battle; any doubts I may have had were dispelled as soon as I looked upon that rocky terrain for myself. There is confusion, too, as to whether he was acting on his own or at Guy's behest when he led the vanguard in that final charge, as the chroniclers tell differing stories. Whatever the truth, I do not see it as treachery; had he succeeded in scattering Taqī al-Dīn's men, the rest of the Franks could have followed him as the infantry tried to do.

While researching the history of Outremer, it struck me that there were few villains, that most of them were flawed people doing what they thought was best for their homeland and for themselves. That cannot be said of the Templar grand master Gerard de Ridefort, whose vengefulness and arrogance did so much to bring about the kingdom's downfall. As king, Guy de Lusignan must bear the ultimate responsibility for riding right into Saladin's trap, but their fatal march was Gerard's doing. A few of the historians who have rejected the hawks-versus-doves scenario have gone even further and attempted to rehabilitate Guy's reputation, arguing that his decision to venture into an arid wasteland without water was not as mad as it seems. For example, one of them sought to excuse Guy's refusal to halt at Tur'an by citing modern statistics to argue that the spring at Tur'an would not have had enough water for such a large army. But Saladin thought otherwise; we know that he was greatly relieved when he heard that the Franks had bypassed Tur'an and were marching on to their doom. The most scathing verdicts come from fellow soldiers, from the military historians I cited in my acknowledgments. The battle of Ḥaṭṭīn is considered to be one of the great battlefield blunders of all time, right up there with the Little Big Horn and Napoleon's invasion of Russia.

Readers will be interested to know that my description of the end of the battle comes from an eyewitness, Saladin's son al-Afdal, who later related the day's events to the Saracen chronicler al-Athīr. I was able to use some of the actual dialogue in the confrontation between Reynald de Chatillon and Saladin in the latter's tent and again at other times during the battle. We do not know how Balian managed to break free with the survivors of his rearguard, but the suggestion of the historian David Nicolle made the most sense to me—that he took advantage of the distraction of the Blue Wolf's men.

As always, historical novelists must fill in some of the blanks. We do not know the exact death dates for many of the major characters, including Balian, Baudouin, Maria, William, Agnes, and even Baldwin. Nor do we know the year of Balian's birth, with historians estimating it at between 1143 and 1150. I thought the German scholar Hans Mayer made the most convincing argument for 1150 and adopted that one. We do not know the name of Amalric and Maria's second daughter, who died very young, so I gave her the name of Amalric's mother. And we do not know the cause of death for many of the characters, which is a common problem for historical novelists. William reported only that Sybilla's first husband, Guillaume of Montferrat, sickened and died within two months. Nor do we know the ailment that claimed Baldwin's life. Because kidney failure was so common among lepers, I chose that as a likely cause of his death. And we do not know what killed Baldwin's nephew, the young king. After learning that Saladin's eldest son suffered from asthma, I selected this as the fatal malady for that unlucky little boy.

I faced a greater challenge when it came to William of Tyre's last years. According to the later continuations of his history, he fell victim to the machinations of his political rival, Patriarch Eraclius. William was supposedly excommunicated by Eraclius and was poisoned at the patriarch's orders as he traveled to Rome to appeal to the Pope. But no source contemporary with William made any mention of this rather lurid tale, neither the Saracen chroniclers nor any of the English or French chroniclers who had a keen interest in the Holy Land. While most historians have dismissed the entire story out of hand, Peter Edbury and John Gordon Rowe, authors of William's only biography, think that it is possible he was excommunicated by Eraclius, for it was often used as a political weapon in the Middle Ages. I've found no historians who believe the claim that William was murdered. Nor was I convinced that he was excommunicated, finding it unlikely that no one would have reported the disgrace of so prominent a churchman, who was both an archbishop and a highly regarded historian. There is confusion, too, about the exact year of William's death. We know it occurred on Michaelmas, September 29, but we cannot be sure if it happened in 1184, 1185, or 1186. I thought 1185 was the most likely year under the circumstances.

Now a word about Jakelin de Mailly. He was identified as the marshal of the Templars in contemporary sources and none thought to question it. But a letter eventually surfaced, written by Gerard de Ridefort to the Pope, reporting the death of his Templar brethren and the grand master of the Hospitallers at Cresson Springs; he mentions several men, Jakelin being one of them, but the title of marshal appears behind the name of another Templar. So in recent years, some historians have concluded that the medieval sources must have been in error. I do not agree. Obedience was the cornerstone of the Templar order and its members were pledged to follow their grand master without question; this is why the Templars surrendered their castles at Gaza and Latrun to Saladin after being commanded to do so by Gerard de Ridefort. We have a vivid account of the bitter quarrel before the battle at Cresson Springs, when Jakelin argued against making an attack because they were so outnumbered and Gerard impugned his courage. I cannot imagine an ordinary knight daring to challenge his grand master like that. It makes sense only if Jakelin was indeed their marshal, for he'd then have been in charge of military matters. So if a mistake was made, I think it is more likely that it was made by a papal clerk when he copied de Ridefort's letter for the papal archives, putting the title of marshal after the wrong man's name.

Balian and Maria's marriage is a remarkable one because of the disparity between her rank and his. By medieval standards, he was definitely not a worthy husband for a former queen, the kinswoman of the Emperor Manuel. We know nothing of the circumstances leading up to this unlikely pairing, only that their marriage seems to have been a happy one. There are only two logical explanations for the marriage. Either it was a love match in which Maria was prepared to defy her own kinsman, King Baldwin, and the social mores of the time in order to wed Balian. Or the marriage was meant to be a disparaging one for Maria. I think it was a punitive act that boomeranged badly, a suggestion that Peter Edbury also made in his biography of Maria and Balian's eldest son, John, Lord of Beirut.

I always clear my conscience in my author's notes, alerting my readers if I have taken any liberties with known historical facts. Because I am obsessive-compulsive about historical accuracy (one reason my family and friends will no longer go with me to see historical films, tired of hearing me muttering into my popcorn from the first scene to the last), I try to keep these liberties to the bare minimum. In this novel, I twice allowed al-'Ādil to venture from Egypt to visit his brother Saladin when I needed to bring him to the reader's attention. Since he certainly did visit Saladin from time to time, I did not have any conscience pangs about this. I took another small liberty in letting Baldwin learn of the results of Reynald's audacious raid into the Red Sea. We cannot be sure if even Reynald knew what happened to the men who were captured and subsequently executed.

I occasionally have to alter the names of minor characters, given the lamentable medieval tradition of recycling the same family names over and over; I can assure you no author wants to have to keep track of half a dozen Edwards or Eleanors or Henrys in the course of one book. To make it easier for my readers, I was asked to change the name of Agnes's husband and Baldwin's stepfather, Renaud de Grenier, because there were two other major characters named Reynald and Raymond. So he became Denys for this book. I often resort to variants of a name in different languages, like Henry and Heinrich. This time I let the young king Baldwin lay claim to that name, and went with the French version for Baudouin. The same was true for Eschiva and Esquiva, Hugh and Hugues, Agnes and Agneta. I called Taqī al-Dīn's son Khālid because he shared the name Ahmad with al-'Ādil, and I slightly altered the name of the elderly Patriarch of Jerusalem to Emeric. I also referred to Hugues by his title, calling him Hugues of Galilee rather than Hugues de St. Omer, his family name.

We know Baldwin had a spymaster; all medieval kings did. We do not know his identity, since secrecy was an essential element of his job description. I gave Baldwin's chief spy the name of one of the Lionheart's agents who was famed for his ability to spy on the Saracens and avoid detection. While Anselm is my creation, the real Baldwin must have had an Anselm of his own as his health deteriorated.

For readers who guessed that Saladin's favorite game of mall is today known as polo, you are quite right. And al-'Ādil's children really did have a pet giraffe, which they brought with them from Egypt to Syria.

The cover of *The Land Beyond the Sea* is a depiction of a painting by the nineteenth-century French artist Charles-Philippe Larivière, celebrating Baldwin's victory over a much larger Saracen army at Montgisard. Sharp-eyed readers may notice that there are two archers in the foreground and that Baldwin has a beard. The artist did not know that the Frankish army used crossbowmen, their only archers being mounted turcopoles, or that noblemen in the kingdom were clean-shaven. We decided, though, that the dramatic impact of the scene far outweighed these minor anachronisms.

Finally, a few comments about the last chapters. It is usually said that Conrad of Montferrat reached Tyre on July 15, 1187, but he actually arrived in mid-August. Some historians say that Prince Bohemond's eldest son briefly became Count of Tripoli after the death of Count Raymond, but Jochen Burgtorf, author of "The Antiochene War of Succession," a chapter in *The Crusader World*, edited by Adrian J. Boas, effectively refutes that. Because it was reported that Stephanie de Milly and Isabella entreated Saladin to free Humphrey, I assumed this occurred right after the surrender of Jerusalem to the sultan. I'd already written the final chapters when I discovered a passage in 'Imād al-Dīn's chronicle that said the women came to see the sultan on Humphrey's behalf in November of that year. So we cannot say with certainty whether Isabella remained in the city during the siege or if she departed with Maria and the younger children.

Sometimes the most credible information comes from hostile sources. For example, I'd have been skeptical if Christian chroniclers had been the ones to report that Richard had ridden in front of the Saracen army after the battle of Jaffa and none had dared to accept his challenge; it sounds too Hollywoodish, doesn't it? But that story came from several Saracen chroniclers, who were mortified that no one had been willing to take on the Lionheart in single combat. In the same vein, I'd probably have been hesitant about accepting stories of the kind treatment of the Jerusalem refugees by Saladin's men had they come from Saracen sources. They were reported, though, by Christian chroniclers, who also spoke admiringly of the generosity and magnanimity of al-ʿĀdil and the sultan to their defeated foes. And Balian's desperate ultimatum to Saladin was quoted by all the Saracen chroniclers, so I was able to draw upon his actual words in that dramatic scene.

I'd like to end by saying a few words about Balian d'Ibelin. For more than thirty years, I've been blessed, able to research and then to write about some of the most remarkable men and women of the Middle Ages. Most of them are better known than Balian, who was slandered by the chroniclers of the Third Crusade because he was allied with Conrad and hostile to Guy. History then seems to have forgotten about him. His one brush with fame came in *Kingdom of Heaven*, where he was magically transformed into an illegitimate French blacksmith who still managed to bedazzle a queen, only she was Sybilla, not Maria. The filmmakers did get one thing right: Balian truly was the savior of Jerusalem, rescuing thousands of civilians who faced death or slavery. I've written about men of great courage in past books, but I do not think any of them showed the courage of Balian d'Ibelin, who could not turn away from the terrified citizens of the Holy City, even if it meant sacrificing his own life in an attempt to save them.

SKP

January 2019

www.sharonkaypenman.com

ACKNOWLEDGMENTS

When I did the acknowledgments for *Lionheart*, I quoted one of my favorite lines from *Casablanca*: "Round up the usual suspects." That quip applies equally well to the acknowledgments for *The Land Beyond the Sea*, for I've enjoyed remarkable stability with my editors and agents. I've been blessed to work with an editor extraordinaire, Marian Wood, since the very start of my writing career, and in the course of our long partnership, she has truly been a godsend—teacher, critic, guide, and occasionally guardian angel. I am so grateful to her. Good editors are hard to find, yet I've managed to strike gold time and time again. Marian is, of course, the mother lode, but I've been so fortunate, too, in being able to work with Jeremy Trevathan, my British editor at Macmillan, and now with Gabriella Mongelli at G. P. Putnam. If we consider editors to be literary midwives, *The Land Beyond the Sea* could not have gotten off to a better start in life.

I have been equally blessed with my agents, both of whom have been with me since the publication of *The Sunne in Splendour*. There is not a better agent in the United States than mine, Molly Friedrich of the Friedrich Agency, and my British agent, Mic Cheetham of the Mic Cheetham Agency, shines just as brightly on her side of the pond. They navigate the stormy publishing seas with impressive ease as they steer their writers toward a safe harbor. I also benefit from their insights and instincts, for they both would have made excellent editors had they chosen another career path. So . . . to my wonderful editors and my amazing agents—this is a heartfelt thank-you.

Thanks are due, too, to the friends who made my research trip to Israel possible. In a time of turmoil, Enda Junkins and Paula Mildenhall were willing to accompany me in pursuit of my ghosts—the remarkable men and women who lived and died in the twelfth-century Kingdom of Jerusalem. Not only was I able to visit the sites so crucial to the novel, I collected a treasure trove of memories—wandering the ancient streets of the Old City, discovering that Jerusalem has almost as many outdoor cafés as Paris, marveling as Paula proved to be a magnet for the countless stray cats of Jerusalem; we'd not realized that she is a Cat Whisperer. It was one of the most memorable trips of my life.

I owe a debt of gratitude, too, to our Israeli friends, Koby Itzhak and Valerie ben David, and to our American friend Elke Weiss, who was living in Jerusalem at the time of our visit. Elke gave us an insider's tour of the city, explained local customs, showed us sites we might otherwise have missed, and was able to get me in to see Christ's Tomb in the Church of the Holy Sepulchre. She was also delightful company, and whenever I think of Jerusalem now, I think, too, of Elke. Koby and I had corresponded for years, never imagining we might meet face-to-face one day, much less that he'd be our guide at Jaffa and Acre or that we'd get to meet his family, too. I will never forget our discussions about the battle of Ḥaṭṭīn as we explored the ruins of Sepphoris (called Saforie in my novel), while our friends teased us that we sounded as if the battle had been fought yesterday. Valerie ben David was a Facebook friend who generously offered to drive us out to the battlefield at the Horns of Ḥaṭṭīn; it was not well marked and I doubt that we could have found it on our own. I feel so lucky to have been able to see Israel through the eyes of my Israeli friends.

I have always attempted to visit all the sites I've written about, failing to do so only with *Lionheart*. It is true that modern life has often swept away the medieval past, and it is possible nowadays to find videos online of many of these historical ruins. I still like to see the stark silhouette of an ancient castle and to walk across a battlefield where armies once clashed. And every now and then, a place will resonate in a way I'd not expected. I had an emotional, visceral reaction to Welsh castles like Dolwyddelan and Criccieth. Standing in the piazza outside the church in Viterbo that had been the scene of one of the most shocking murders of the Middle Ages, I experienced an eerie sense of timelessness, half expecting to see the cobblestones stained with the blood of the de Montforts' cousin. And I had a similar reaction at Ḥaṭṭīn.

Valerie gave me such a gift by making it possible for us to see the Ḥaṭṭīn battlefield for ourselves. When I began to write about it, I still had vivid mental images of the rough, rock-strewn terrain, the barren hills, the utter desolation. From the summit of one of the Horns, I could glimpse the shimmering blue of the Sea of Galilee, and found it all too easy to imagine how that view must have tormented the thirst-maddened men. The utter insanity of Guy de Lusignan's decision to march across this waterless wasteland proved yet again that truth is stranger than fiction. If he'd not actually embarked on this mad trek, I'd not have dared to have him take such a risk, fearing readers would not believe it.

I would like to thank my writer friend Priscilla Royal for her unflagging support and willingness to share her impressive knowledge of the Middle Ages. Another writer friend, Stephanie Churchill, has been there for me whenever I was in need of encouragement; she was also kind enough to set up my Facebook author page. And special thanks to my friend Rania Melhem for vetting my use of Arabic phrases in the novel. I would like to thank a family friend, Haralambos Haranis, for answering my questions about the Greek language. I would like to mention my Facebook allies, too, those brave souls who volunteered to manage my Facebook fan clubs: Jo Nelson, May Liang, Fiona Scott-Doran, Lesley West, Celia Jelbart, and Stephen Gilligan.

In my past acknowledgments, I have always given credit to my friend Valerie LaMont and her husband, Lowell LaMont, for their invaluable aid. Valerie shared my passion for the past and I drew often upon her medieval lore and insights while writing these novels. Lowell was my computer guru, able to exorcise the most stubborn computer demon. But we lost Lowell and then Valerie in the years since *A King's Ransom* was published, and the world is a sadder, bleaker place without them. There truly are people who are irreplaceable.

I cannot mention all of the books I consulted while researching this novel; my readers know how obsessive-compulsive I am about this! I hope to add a bibliography section to my website, but it is still in the planning stage. So I am listing here the histories that I found most helpful. For those who are interested in the culture and society of the kingdom, I recommend *The Crusaders in the Holy Land*, by Meron Benvenisti; *The World of the Crusaders*, by Joshua Prawer; *The Crusader World*, edited by Adrian J. Boas; and *Crusader Archaeology: The Material Culture of the Latin East*, by Adrian J. Boas.

Sadly, with one exception, there are few biographies of the major characters in my novel; that exception is, of course, Saladin. For the d'Ibelin family, the closest we come is a biography of Balian and Maria's eldest son, *John of Ibelin and the Kingdom of Jerusalem*, by Peter W. Edbury. The German historian H. E. Mayer has a fascinating article called "Carving Up Crusaders: The Early Ibelins and Ramlas," in *Outremer: Studies in the History of the Crusading Kingdom of Jerusalem Presented to Joshua Prawer*, edited by B. Z. Kedar, H. E, Mayer, and R. C. Smail. Bernard Hamilton's *The Leper King and His Heirs: Baldwin IV and the Crusader Kingdom of Jerusalem* offers an overview of the royal family and major lords. Peter W. Edbury and John Gordon Rowe have written *William of Tyre: Historian of the Latin East*. A few articles have been written about the Queens of Jerusalem, with the focus on Sybilla, including *"La Roine Preude Femme et Bonne Dame*: Queen Sybil of Jerusalem (1186–1190) in History and Legend, 1186–1300," in *The Haskins Society Journal* 15 (2004); "Queen or Consort: Rulership and Politics in the Latin East (1118–1228)," by Sarah Lambert, in *Queens and Queenship in Medieval Europe*, edited by Anne Duggan; *Gendering the Crusades*, edited by Susan B. Edgington and Sarah Lambert; and "Women in the Crusader States: The Queens of Jerusalem (1100–1190)," by Bernard Hamilton, in *Medieval Women*, edited by Derek Baker.

These books cover Baldwin's reign and life in Outremer. "Propaganda and Faction in the Kingdom of Jerusalem: The Background to Haṭṭīn," by Peter W. Edbury, in *Crusaders and Muslims in Twelfth-Century Syria*, edited by Maya Shatzmiller; *The Crusader States*, by Malcolm Barber; *The Crusades and Their Sources: Essays Presented to Bernard Hamilton*, edited by John France and William G. Zajac; *Franks, Muslims, and Oriental Christians in the Latin Levant*, by Benjamin Z. Kedar; *The Latin Church in the Crusader States: The Secular Church*, by Bernard Hamilton; *The Latin Kingdom of Jerusalem: European Colonialism in the Middle Ages* and *Crusader Institutions*, both by Joshua Prawer; *Crusade and Settlement*, edited by Peter W. Edbury; *Alliances and Treaties Between Frankish and Muslim Rulers in the Middle East: Cross-Cultural Diplomacy in the Period of the Crusades*, by Michael A. Köhler; *The Experience of Crusading, volume 2: Defining the Crusader Kingdom*, edited by Peter Edbury and Jonathan Phillips; *Kings and Lords in the Latin Kingdom of Jerusalem*, by Hans Eberhard Mayer; *The Road to Armageddon: The Last Years of the Crusader Kingdom of Jerusalem*, by W. B. Bartlett; *A History of the Crusades, volume 2: The Kingdom of Jerusalem and the Frankish East, 1100–1187*, by Steven Runciman; *Montjoie: Studies in Crusade History in Honour of Hans Eberhard Mayer*, edited by Benjamin Z. Kedar, Jonathan Riley-Smith, and Rudolf Hiestand; *Tolerance and Intolerance: Social Conflict in the Age of the Crusades*, edited by Michael Gervers and James M. Powell; *Autour de la Première Croisade: Actes du Colloque de la Society for the Study of the Crusades and the Latin East: Clermont-Ferrand, 22–25 Juin 1995*, edited by Michel Balard (excellent essays in English about the Holy Cross and messenger pigeons in the Levant).

Saladin: The Politics of the Holy War, by Malcolm Cameron Lyons and D. E. P. Jackson, remains the best history of Saladin's rise to power and his reign. There are numerous biographies of Saladin, but I would recommend the following books: *Saladin*, by Anne-Marie Eddé, translated by Jane Marie Todd; *Saladin: Empire and Holy War*, by Peter Gubser; *Saladin*, by Andrew S. Ehrenkreutz; and *Saladin and the Fall of the Kingdom of Jerusalem*, by Stanley Lane-Poole. There are no biographies of al-'Ādil, but his reign is covered by R. Stephen Humphreys in *From Saladin to the Mongols: The Ayyūbids of Damascus, 1193–1260*. I also recommend *The Crusades: Islamic Perspectives*, by Carole Hillenbrand. There are many books about medieval Islam and the role of women in Islamic society; others dealing with medieval medicine, slavery in their world, even Muslim cookbooks, which were very useful in chapter eight. There are too many to include here, but I promise to list them on my website.

Now . . . the battle of Ḥaṭṭīn. Let me begin with the best, two accounts by military historians: *Piercing the Fog of War: Recognizing Change on the Battlefield: Lessons from Military History, 216 BC Through Today*, by Brian L. Steed, and *The Battle of Ḥaṭṭīn, 1187*, a master's thesis by Eric W. Olson, presented to the faculty of the US Army Command and General Staff College. Steed and Olson have studied the battle with a soldier's eye, and the results are well worth reading. Another excellent account is *God's Warriors: Knights Templar, Saracens, and the Battle for Jerusalem*, by Helen Nicholson and David Nicolle. So are *Ḥaṭṭīn*, by John France; and *Ḥaṭṭīn, 1187: Saladin's Greatest Victory* and *Saladin: Leadership, Strategy, Conflict*, both by David Nicolle; "The Battle of Ḥaṭṭīn: A Chronicle of a Defeat Foretold?" by Michael Ehrlich, in *Journal of Medieval Military History*, volume 5, edited by Clifford J. Rogers, Kelly DeVries, and John France; *Crusading Warfare, 1097–1193*, by R. C. Smail; and *Lionhearts: Richard I, Saladin, and the Era of the Third Crusade*, by Geoffrey Regan, which has a detailed description of the siege of Jerusalem and Balian's efforts to save the city.

Other recommended books include *Encounter Between Enemies: Captivity and Ransom in the Latin Kingdom of Jerusalem*, by Yvonne Friedman; *Noble Ideals and Bloody Realities: Warfare in the Middle Ages*, edited by Niall Christie and Maya Yazigi; *Crusader Warfare*, volume I: *Byzantium, Western Europe, and the Battle for the Holy Land*, by David Nicolle; *Western Warfare in the Age of the Crusades, 1000–1300*, by John France; and Malcolm Barber's *The New Knighthood: A History of the Order of the Temple*.

Lastly, the chronicles. We are fortunate to have three contemporary accounts of Saladin's reign, written by men who knew him, two of whom were members of his inner circle. Bahā' al-Dīn ibn Shaddād wrote *The Rare and Excellent History of Saladin*, translated by D. S. Richards; he did not join Saladin's service until 1188, so he never appears in this novel, but his chronicle does touch upon events prior to that date. *The Chronicle of Ibn al-Athīr for the Crusading Period from "al-Kamil fi'l-Ta'rikh,"* Part 2, *The Years 542–589/1146–1193: The Age of Nūr al-Dīn and Saladin*, translated by D. S. Richards, is a compelling account of history in the Levant written by a man who had a more balanced view of Saladin than Bahā al-Dīn or 'Imād al-Dīn, who idolized him. 'Imād al-Dīn's history of the sultan is available only in French, *Conquête de la Syrie et de la Palestine par Saladin*, translated from Arabic by Henri Massé. However, you can find excerpts in *Arab Historians of the*

Crusades, edited by Francesco Gabrieli, and in *Jerusalem: The City of Herod and Saladin*, by Walter Besant. Some of the events in the novel are also covered in a later chronicle, *A History of the Ayyūbid Sultans of Egypt*, by Ahmad ibn' al-Maqrizi, translated from Arabic by R. J. C. Broadhurst.

William of Tyre's history is perhaps the most famous chronicle of the Middle Ages, but it ends in 1184. Balian d'Ibelin's squire Ernoul wrote a continuation of William's history, but it has not survived. All we have are versions of it, sometimes garbled, that appear in chronicles written in the thirteenth century. I discuss this at greater length in the author's note. You can find portions of these continuations in Peter W. Edbury's *The Conquest of Jerusalem and the Third Crusade*.

William's history of the Saracens was lost after his death. His chronicle about the Kingdom of Jerusalem, *A History of Deeds Done Beyond the Sea*, has long been out of print. I was fortunate, for my friend Valerie LaMont was able to secure a copy for me when I was researching *Lionheart*. But I have good news for those of you interested in reading William's history. It is available now from Amazon and Amazon.UK as an ebook, very reasonably priced. There are two huge volumes and not all of it will be relevant to readers. But I'm sure you'll find William's personal account of the last years of the kingdom to be as fascinating as I did.